EROTICA ITALIAN STYLE

'*Amore*,' he said, squeezing her solid left breast through her shiny black frock to make sure she understood his requirement.

She smiled and then surprised him by turning to bend over and grip the side of the big bathtub. The position was new to him and he seized the opportunity. He lifted her frock at the back to her waist, revealing a round bottom clad in white cotton knickers that extended down her plump thighs to just above her knees.

She was grinning at him over her shoulder while he slipped her underwear down her legs. She waggled her bare bottom at him.

'This is not the first time you've been had this way,' he exclaimed, thrilling at the sight of her big white cheeks and the dark-haired split between.

*Omnibus editions of erotica
available from Headline Delta*:

The Eros Collection
The Ultimate Eros
The Complete Eveline
Follies of the Flesh
Forbidden Escapades
Hidden Pleasures, Secret Vices
Lascivious Ladies
The Power of Lust
Wanton Excesses
Habits of the Flesh

Erotica Italian Style

Anonymous

Copyright © 1991, 1992 Richard Arlen

The right of Richard Arlen to be identified as the Author of the Work has been asserted by him in accordance with the Copyright, Designs and Patents Act 1988.

This omnibus edition first published in 1994
by HEADLINE BOOK PUBLISHING

A HEADLINE DELTA paperback

10 9 8 7 6 5 4 3 2 1

All rights reserved. No part of this publication may be reproduced, stored in a retrieval system or transmitted, in any form or by any means without the prior written permission of the publisher, nor be otherwise circulated in any form of binding or cover other than that in which it is published and without a similar condition being imposed on the subsequent purchaser.

All characters in this publication are fictitious and any resemblance to real persons, living or dead, is purely coincidental.

ISBN 0 7472 4323 9

Phototypeset by Intype, London

Printed and bound in Great Britain by
Harper Collins Manufacturing, Glasgow

HEADLINE BOOK PUBLISHING
A division of Hodder Headline PLC
Headline House
79 Great Titchfield Street
London W1P 7FN

CONTENTS

Love Italian Style   1
Ecstasy Italian Style   235
Rapture Italian Style   437

Love Italian Style

In the evening there generally is on St Mark's Place such a mixed multitude of Jews, Turks and Christians, lawyers, knaves and pick-pockets, mountebanks, old women and physicians, women of quality with masks, strumpets bare-faced, and in short, such a jumble of Senators, citizens, gondoliers and people of every character and condition, that your ideas are broken, bruised and dislocated in the crowd...

John Moore, 1781

ONE

'Fantastic!' Adrian gasped.

'*Si, fantastico*,' the Italian girl agreed, bouncing up and down astride his lap so energetically that her naked and chubby breasts were flip-flopping against his shirt, as if she were performing some remarkable kind of body massage.

From the mainland a railway bridge all of two miles long runs out in a straight line across the lagoon to Venice and here the express train from Milan slows down to cross it at little more than a walking-pace. Alongside the bridge the safe channel for shipping is marked out with triangular pilings, and all sorts and sizes of craft ply back and forth at a leisurely maritime pace – small fishing boats with patched sails, short-funnelled passenger ferries, elderly red-rust streaked coasters.

It was a little after midday on a clear, hot and sunny day in June, when the glitter and promise of the early Italian summer could be observed on all sides. But although the window blind of his sleeping-compartment in the Wagon-Lit was only half-down Adrian Thrale saw nothing of the busy sea-traffic to the side of the moving train and nothing at all of the ancient domes and towers and spires of Venice that seemed to rise ever higher – like a fairy-tale city set in the sea – as the train rolled sedately towards it.

'*Fantastico!*' he sighed, using her word, his hands gripping the cheeks of her bare backside to assist her fast up and down movements.

He had been looking forward to his first glimpse of Venice for over a week, since his visit was decided. He had bought an illustrated guide-book and studied it diligently, and he had sought out books with illustrations of Canaletto's paintings of Venetian scenes. Although he had never been there, he felt that he knew the city well from these pictures – he could see in his mind's eye the entrance to the Grand Canal, with the Customs House and the church of Santa Maria with its white steps and green dome. Or the red-brick church of San Giovanni and San Paolo, facing a little canal across a cobbled square. And above all, the view down the length of the Piazza San Marco to the many-domed church that reminded him of a more magnificent version of the Prince Regent's Pavilion at Brighton.

And now the moment was here – in another minute or two he would arrive in Venice – and Adrian's attention was directed elsewhere. While the train rolled across the long bridge, he was most intimately involved with a dark-haired and half-naked young woman who had told him her name was Gina – he was fast approaching the culminating moments of this overwhelming encounter, and the only word he could utter was *Fantastic!*

He had boarded the train in Paris the day before, at the Gare de Lyon, after two enjoyable days of looking at paintings in museums and galleries, art being his business, and two evenings spent in cultural pursuits of a less elevated nature, at the Moulin Rouge and the Folies Bergère. Just where Gina had got on the train was a mystery to him – he had first become aware of her presence halfway through the morning. He was standing in the corridor to watch the agreeable Italian countryside through which the train was passing at what was acceptable hereabouts as express speed, but which would have been laughed to scorn on the Night Flyer from London to Scotland.

He had seen it reported with approval some months ago in *The Times* that Italy's new Prime Minister, Signor Mussolini, had made the trains run on time. That might well be true, Adrian considered, though Italian time-table schedules seemed so easy-going that it could hardly have been difficult to enforce them. On the other hand, this was the land of lemon trees and myrtle and grapes and figs – what could be the point of hurtling about in express trains in so fascinating a country?

It was at some point after the train pulled out of Verona station that Adrian had discarded the guide-book to Venice he had brought with him and went to stand out in the corridor to see as much as he could of the Venetian plain and the palatial villas built by Andrea Palladio for long-dead noblemen. He put his elbows comfortably on the window ledge, and stared out at the commendably green plain. He could hear the engine puffing rhythmically up front somewhere, and the smell of smoke drifted back through the half-open window from time to time, the wheels were making an almost hypnotic clackety-clack on the rails and the day was as pleasing as any Adrian had ever known.

If at that moment he had remembered Browning's poem, he would without the least hesitation have agreed that all was very much right with the world. Here he was on a beautiful day, travelling abroad at the expense of his very respectable employers, having been entrusted with an important mission – not to dirty old Birmingham or dreary old Exeter but to *Venice*. The Most Serene Republic, *Venice* – of all the wonderful and exotic places! The landscape no longer held his attention – he was staring instead at his own reflection in the window.

What the glass showed him was a long and handsome face that narrowed from the cheek-bones to a pointed chin, chestnut-brown hair worn longer than the brilliantined straight-back style that most men affected, and parted in the middle, so that soft wings curved over his ears. His eyes were large and bright with intelligence, but his mouth was the full-lipped mark of a sensualist. In bodily form he was a tall and willowy young man, well-dressed and with a look of importance about him.

By degrees and slowly into this reverie of self-satisfaction and self-congratulation there insinuated itself a perfume – and it was one that made his pulses beat a little quicker. He became aware that someone – a woman, of course – was standing next to him in the carriage corridor. Her perfume was sweet and strong and suggestive – not at all the sort that a lady would wear – and most emphatically not an English lady. He turned his head to the right and found himself staring into a pair of shining dark-brown eyes set in a round and smiling face.

Altogether she was a very pretty girl, in the dark and full-fleshed Latin way, Adrian decided. Her hair was thick and very nearly black, and she wore it longer than the fashionable Eton crops and shingled styles of London – and with a fringe combed forward to her eyebrows. Observing his interest in her, and his favourable assessment of her, for no woman is ever in doubt of a man's feelings towards her, even if he has not yet recognised them himself, she smiled again and yet more pleasantly at him, with full lips that were painted a dark red.

She could hardly be more than twenty, he thought, five or six years younger than himself. He returned her smile and bravely tried out his non-existent Italian by wishing her *Buon giorno*. Her acquaintance with the English language proved to be as minimal as his with hers, but she acknowledged his greeting gracefully and at once launched into an animated conversation which owed everything to smiles, raised eyebrows, hand gestures and shrugged shoulders – and almost nothing at all to mere words. Adrian joined in with a will, highly delighted to have someone to talk to – and especially a girl as pretty as this one – after travelling alone in enforced silence.

His efforts to make himself understood to her were received with a lively enthusiasm that flattered him. She greeted his confirmation that he was English with smiles and exclamations of admiration and pleasure. Ten minutes of this flattery and Adrian was congratulating himself on having become acquainted – however informally – with so charming a companion for the final stretch of his long journey.

Like every sensible and decent Englishman travelling abroad on the Continent of Europe, he was dressed very practically in a navy-blue double-breasted blazer and grey flannel trousers. The young lady excused herself politely and begged his permission before she touched his sleeve with her ungloved hand and then exclaimed in wonder at the quality of the wool.

She asked him by signs what the badge on the blazer pocket signified and seemed to understand in part his explanation of cricket clubs. More than that, she gave every indication of real interest in the subject. And, if that were not enough to enchant Adrian completely, she wiggled her body slightly but continuously the whole time, when she was speaking and when she was listening, so that her plump breasts moved visibly under her clothes. Though from good manners he tried to keep himself from staring at them, Adrian found his gaze drawn back again and again to those deliciously jiggling prominences.

She was wearing a light summer costume of jacket and skirt in mustard-yellow, the skirt with a broad pleat down the front and the jacket buttoned low to display the white blouse beneath. To Adrian's not very expert eye her clothes seemed to be of middling quality, though stylish. There were no signs of rings on her fingers and she was very obviously travelling alone – if he had met an English girl on a train he would have been able to place her socially, of course, by her clothes and the way she spoke. But here all was exotic and different, and he had not the least idea of who she might be.

He was sure that she had not been on the train overnight from Paris, or he would have seen her before now in the dining-car. She wore no hat or gloves, and no stockings, he realised when he glanced down as nonchalantly as he could to look at her legs. She had good legs – well-shaped calves and although the hem of her yellow skirt descended below the knees, the way she stood with one hip pressed against the side of the carriage to steady her against the rocking of the train caused the thin material to outline a rounded thigh in a way that was extremely provocative.

She had a large and shiny black patent leather handbag hanging on her arm, with gilded metal initials set on it – GL – and by pointing to these and looking his question with lifted eyebrows, Adrian managed to extract the interesting information that her name was Gina Luzzi. He introduced himself and tried to ascertain her point of embarking on the train. Whatever she said by way of reply was beyond his understanding, although he did make out that she was born in Venice and lived there.

So far, so very good, he thought, and taking the absence of a gold ring to mean that she was unmarried, the hope that grew in his mind was that it might be possible to meet her in Venice during his short stay and let her show him the main sights. And after he took her to dinner, with lots of delicious food and wine and music – there must be music, he would insist – who could say what fascinating and rewarding acts of friendliness might follow after such entertainment?

With much linguistic difficulty, but with all the charm at his command, he set out to suggest that they meet that evening – or if that was not convenient for her, then the next day for lunch, for he very much wanted to see her again, he told her. To his surprise she took hold of his hand and turned it over to see the time by his wrist-watch. And apparently then satisfied by what she saw, she announced with a pretty smile that she would go with him in his *compartimento* for five hundred lire.

'I don't understand,' he said, puzzled by her words and sure that he had misunderstood her, 'why do you ask for five hundred lire?'

'For *amore*,' she answered with a broad smile and a shrug.

This was undoubtedly not the sort of thing that happened on the London Midland and Scottish Railway, or even the Great Western. While Adrian's mind was grappling with the unthinkable – that a pretty young woman was offering him her personal services on a train, she took him firmly by the elbow and urged him across the sideways swaying corridor and into the sleeper she deduced was his. The Wagon-Lit attendant had long ago stripped the bed and made up the compartment for day use, while Adrian had been in the dining-car for a meagre Continental breakfast of rolls and apricot jam, but until the train reached Venice the sleeper was still his.

There were no windows to the corridor side of the compartment and the blind on the window to the other side was pulled halfdown. Gina flicked the door-bolt across with the assurance of long familiarity and before Adrian had got over his surprise, she laughed and pushed him down lightly to sit on the dark-blue upholstered seat. She stood in front of him, balanced on spread feet and bent knees against the roll of the carriage, while she unfastened the two buttons of her mustard yellow jacket and took it right off.

The situation was so very un-English that even now he was at this point of no return Adrian was not truly convinced that what was happening was happening in reality. He half-believed that he was asleep in bed and having an exciting dream – but his incredulity vanished when Gina unbuttoned her blouse and pulled it open to show him her big soft breasts.

'I say!' he exclaimed, struck by the fact that she wore no slip underneath her blouse, as he would have expected. 'What a marvellous pair of melons you have!'

'Si, *melone*,' she said with her broad smile, giving the word its three syllables in Italian. '*Melone grande* – you like?'

'Si, si!' he answered eagerly.

She leaned forward to rest her hands on his shoulders and let her well-developed charms dangle loosely where he could reach them and gorge himself on the sensation of their warm weight in his hands. She leaned closer to him still, with pouting red lips which he met with his own, and a moment later she had his blazer open and her hand was down in his lap, to unbutton his trousers and delve under his shirt.

In the ordinary course of events Adrian did not avail himself of professional services, although he found nothing unusual or distasteful in the thought of pretty women offering for money access to the pleasures of their bodies. His London place of work was in Curzon Street, Mayfair, and as a convenient short cut, morning and evening, he strolled through Shepherd Market – a beat patrolled by some of the best-looking trollops in the West End. The regular girls had got used to seeing him pass by every weekday in his neat black jacket and pin-stripe trousers – and well-brushed bowler hat set at a jaunty angle – and while they knew he was not a client, most of them smiled at him when he passed, for he was a well-set and good-looking young man.

Only once had he been tempted, and that was five years ago and very soon after he had started work at Mallards, the fine-art auction house. He had been strolling about restlessly one lunchtime, pondering the reasons for his very limited success with the girl he had taken out the evening before. On the corner of Hertford Street he was accosted by a girl he had seen many times before and, five minutes later, his jacket, waistcoat and trousers off and strewn across the floor, he was on top of her with his shirt tucked up around his waist, pumping away for dear life.

She had taken him up to a tiny flat above a hardware shop, had her clothes off in an instant and spread herself naked on a day-bed for his attention. She was a thinnish fair-haired woman in her late twenties, and on the way up the stairs he had learned that she called herself Viv. Her breasts seen bare were rather flat and disappointing and her belly was narrow, with a wispy tuft of mouse-brown hair between her parted legs. But the moment she had Adrian inserted, she started to wiggle and heave her hips upwards, urging him on with enthusiastic sighs and moans. Her ecstasy was so blatantly fake that it struck him as comic and he almost burst out laughing. Her determined writhing under him kept him keen enough to jolt away until he unburdened himself of his desire into her.

The entire process, from the moment Viv slid out of her pink knickers to his final twitch inside her clasping flesh, took no more than three minutes. Afterwards, when he was dressed again, she decided to make him a cup of tea, evidently disinclined to resume work immediately. She wrapped her thin body in a frilly pink negligee and sat with her feet up while they chatted for ten minutes, as if this were an ordinary social visit. When he left she went to the door with him to kiss him on the cheek in a sisterly manner, and let him have a last feel of her breasts before she pushed him out of the flat.

She was a pleasant sort of woman, Adrian concluded on his walk back to work but, all-in-all, the experience was not one that he particularly wished to repeat. Therapeutic it no doubt was, and even slightly ridiculous, but it was neither romantic nor memorable. From then on, when he passed Viv on her street-corner he smiled politely and raised his bowler-hat to her, but to her unspoken invitation to enjoy her facilities again, he responded with a courteous shake of the head and the murmured excuse that he was late for an appointment and in a tearing hurry.

Very fortunately for him, his social life took a turn for the better not long after the encounter with squirming Viv on her day-bed. A colleague of his own age at Mallards introduced him to his sister, and although she proved to be a tease, it was through her that he met a long succession of very decent girls who were willing to accommodate him in various interesting ways – just so long as he was *careful*, as they euphemistically put it. From that time on, his main evening and weekend pursuit was the investigation of their responses to his kisses and increasingly bold caresses, to find out how far they would let him go. And however matters developed between him and the girl of the moment, he found these sensual explorations unfailingly fascinating, almost always memorably exciting, and sometimes even romantic.

What was happening to him now with Gina was very romantic, to his way of looking at it. Well, what could be more fabulous and exciting than to have an unknown foreign girl bare her breasts for you in a First Class sleeping-compartment? And such lovely big soft breasts at that, not the skimpy little bumps that he so often had to make do with in London. The sight of them was enough to arouse him – to feel them made his heart race – and added to that, Gina's manipulating hand in his open trousers – and he was as stiff as a poker.

In Adrian's enthusiastic view a woman's supreme glory was not her hair, as some idiot had maintained, but her bosom. It was utterly astonishing to him that English women went to extremes to flatten their chests and conceal their natural endowment – especially when so many of them had little enough to begin with. A woman's twin softnesses were intended to be felt and handled by a boyfriend until he became intoxicated with the sensuous delight of her flesh in his palms. Pointed little prominences with pink tips might be considered stylish and even sophisticated, but what every man wanted at heart, whether he admitted it or not, was a pair of powerful and heavy breasts to fondle – a pair such as Gina was presenting to him now.

The friend's sister who had turned out to be a tease – Pansy Butterfield – had handsomely rounded breasts. After Adrian and she had known each other for almost three weeks of outings and parties and theatres and exchanges of kisses that grew warmer and longer with each session, she let him slip a hand inside her clothes to feel her considerable charms. But that was as far is it ever went with her. She would never allow him to remove any of her clothing to see the bosom that fascinated him – his knowledge of it was gained entirely by touch.

And needless to say, every time he tried – almost frantic with the urgency of the desire that had been built up in him by feeling her unseen breasts – to put his hand under her skirt and slide it up between her thighs to her knickers, she pulled away from him at once and brought matters to an instant close. But through her he had become acquainted with a friend of hers who revelled in baring her breasts – she did it without being asked, whenever the opportunity served, whether in the privacy of his digs in Chelsea or on a weekend ramble out at Hampton Court by the river.

Jennifer, her name was, and she adored having her breasts felt. On the sofa in his tiny sitting-room or sprawled on the grass after a picnic in a secluded spot, she would pull up her jumper to her armpits or if she was wearing a blouse she would open the buttons. While Adrian watched with bated breath, she would drop the shoulder-straps of her slip to reveal her charms and invite him to take them in his hands. And after they had been fondled and admired to her satisfaction, she had no objection to spreading her legs and letting him feel how wet he had made her. And from that it was a short and easy step to having her knickers off and mounting her properly. But even Jennifer withheld the ultimate pleasure – she had no faith whatsoever in protective devices and lay tense and ever more nervous as his excitement grew. When she felt the short sharp thrusts begin, she pushed him off her quickly, so that his thwarted part had no choice but to splurge its passion on to her bare belly.

This curious state of affairs continued for nearly three months before Adrian came to realise why Jennifer never became so carried away by desire that she wanted him to complete the sexual act inside her. The reason for her control was that her breasts were so sensitive that she always reached her climax in secret before he got his stiffness into her. Well might she lie on her back gauging the intensity of his arousal and poised to evict him from his comfortable billet before the critical moment arrived!

When he eventually became certain enough to confront her with his suspicions, she calmly told him that he was right and took the wind right out of his sails by informing him that usually she climaxed three or four times while he was playing with her, before she let him put his hand between her legs. And what added insult to injury for Adrian was the breasts to which he had devoted such lavish attention as a preliminary to getting Jennifer on her back, were small and spiky and widely separated. Taken together – which was not remotely possible – the pair would hardly have made a handful.

Of course, in the years since then he had fared better with other women. But this was his first encounter with so bountiful a pair of breasts as had fallen forward into his hands out of Gina's blouse when she undid it. So much warm and pliable flesh to knead and roll in his palms, such firm-standing red-brown tips to stroke between his fingers! *Melons* he had called them in his delight when she had unbuttoned her blouse and she had been amused by the word and accepted it as a compliment. Oh, to have his hands on a pair like these every day!

It went without saying that Gina was acutely aware of his breathless interest in her bared beauties, it being her business to interpret men's emotions. She waggled them heavily in his hands while she pressed her advantage.

'You a rich English gentleman,' she informed him with her welcoming smile as she strained her resources of language to the limit, 'five hundred lire is nothing. You like me, yes?'

'Si, si,' he murmured back, kneading her paired plumpnesses while he did the arithmetic in his head and concluded that she was asking well over three pounds – a lot compared with the two pounds that Viv charged in Shepherd Market. But whatever he gave Gina would be Mallard's money, not his own, and on that basis he was quite prepared to be thought a rich English gentleman.

Taking his squeeze of her melons to signify acceptance, Gina at once demonstrated her permanent state of readiness for the business of *amore*. She hoisted her yellow skirt up her legs and over her well-upholstered bottom – to let him see that, just as she wore no slip to cover up her big breasts when her blouse was opened, neither were her other charms hidden in knickers, for she had none on.

She was not very tall, but she did not give the impression of being dumpy, even though her body was generously proportioned, for the heaviness of her breasts was matched by a broad and gently out-curving belly with a deep-set button. Her skin was not white but a pale and subtle olive tint that held all the warmth of Italian sun and temperament, and the prominent tips of her breasts were a rich reddish-brown. Between her sturdy thighs she sported a thick bush of curly black hair, and to this Adrian's hand went at once, to feel its crinkly texture.

'Money first,' she said, her hand squeezing his throbbing part vigorously.

He flipped his wallet from an inside blazer pocket and found a five hundred lire note for her. She nodded and put it into the black handbag that lay on the seat beside him, and when the cash was safely tucked away, she bent her knees outward and let him feel her as much as he wished. The touch of smooth and warm lips under his fingers caused his upright part to twitch in her hand, and when he opened them and pressed slowly inside to find her hidden button, the twitching became a furious leaping.

'*Fa presto, fa presto!*' she murmured, but her exhortation to speedy action meant nothing to Adrian.

He took her by the hips with both hands to pull her down on the blue-cushioned seat beside him, intending to stretch her out on her back and climb on top to make his grand entrance. But she resisted him, shaking her head so firmly that her soft breasts wobbled deliciously from side to side.

'No time,' she said, shaking her head again and tapping his wrist-watch with a finger-nail, 'Venezia two minutes.'

And indeed, Adrian realised with unpleasant suddenness that the noise of the train had changed to a hollow rumbling that could only mean it was crossing a bridge. He glanced out of the window under the half-drawn blind and there was the sea with the sun glittering on it. *Oh, no!* he moaned in disappointment, but before he had time to consider the position further, Gina had straddled his lap and was feeding his stiffness into the place meant for it between her parted thighs. Adrian smiled up at her round face and put his arms round her while she rode him hard and fast, her red mouth set in a grin of concentration.

'*Fantastico!*' he said with a grin, using her word.

A comic image had come into his mind – one of the many bawdy pictures the Prince Regent had bought from Thomas Rowlandson, now the property of His Majesty King George the Fifth, and well out of sight in the Royal Collection at Windsor Castle. A set of prints of the originals had come up for sale at Mallards and had been bought by a foreign collector. The print that most resembled Adrian's own present happy position depicted a fat-bottomed woman with her frock up round her neck, perched astride a man on a green chair. There were some ludicrous verses underneath the picture, of which Adrian remembered a line or two . . .

> Across his legs the nymph he takes,
> And with St George a motion makes,
> She ever ready in her way,
> His pike of pleasure keeps in play,
> Rises and falls with gentle ease,
> And tries her best his mind to please . . .

To think of himself now as a character in a Rowlandson scene caused Adrian to chuckle so much that he almost lost sight of what he was about. Luckily for him, there was nothing of *gentle ease* in the way Gina was bouncing on his lap, sliding herself up and down his embedded part with ferocious energy, clearly determined to uphold the honour of her profession by giving him his money's worth. So lively was her attack that in a remarkably short time Adrian gasped out loud and delivered his spurting tribute into her hot depths.

'Si, si, si!' she exclaimed, carried away by the pride she evidently took in her professional skills, and with her hands clamped tightly on his shoulders, she rode him to a standstill. Outside in the corridor the sleeping-car attendant tapped discreetly on the locked door and announced that they had arrived in Venice. With a last shudder of pleasure Adrian came to a halt as the braked carriage-wheels screeched on the steel of the rails and the train stopped in a long exhalation of steam. Adrian let himself slump against the seat-back, his arms about Gina and his fingers slowly unclenched their grip on the flesh of her bare bottom.

TWO

Outside the railway station Adrian found himself bustled along by a crowd of travellers on a broad quay-side. He stopped in his tracks to stare – his guide-book had given him no idea of how wide the Grand Canal was – there were sixty yards of opaque water between him and the far bank, where half a dozen gondolas were moored under the classical white portico of San Simeon. The porter trailing behind him with his heavy suitcase put it down and waited patiently, well accustomed to the quirks of foreign tourists who stop to stare with big eyes at churches as if they'd never seen one before.

When he considered that Adrian had wasted enough of his time he picked up the suitcase and gestured toward a landing-stage where a disorderly crowd were boarding a waiting water-bus and enquired, *Vaporetto Signor?* But Adrian shook his head at once – he had no intention of making his first voyage down the Grand Canal crammed into a little steamer as if he were on a bus along Piccadilly in the rush hour. He looked along the quay to where two or three gondolas were tied up between long poles sticking out of the water and pointed. *Si, Signor*, the porter responded at once, scenting a good tip.

And so it was that Adrian made his entrance into the city of Venice in style, lolling on the faded cushions of a slender black gondola. Behind him the straw-hatted gondolier balanced upright on the swaying craft and leaned into his long oar with the rhythm of a lifetime of practice. Past the Scalzi church, which looked like an elaborate wedding-cake with two tiers of white columns, and there ahead on the left bank stood the Palazzo Vendramin, its white facade gleaming in the sun. As the gondola progressed downstream, Adrian dropped his guide-book and used his eyes instead.

The Grand Canal, as he knew from his reading, winds its way through Venice from west to east in the shape of a backward S. But the small illustrations in his book had not prepared him for the impact of the two hundred palaces in different styles pressed close together along the banks of the two-mile stretch of water. He stared in wonder at every architectural style from the simple proportions of thirteenth century Byzantine, the elaborate stone tracery of Venetian-Gothic, the splendour of seventeenth-century Baroque and the dignity of eighteenth-century Classical.

Above all, this was a city of the sun – from a clear blue and cloudless sky the light was reflected from the restless surface of the water to the facades of the buildings, gleaming white and pink and ochre and burnt umber and sienna and every shade between. To someone accustomed all his life to the drab overall greyness of London streets, the effect was little short of overpowering – and eventually his overloaded mind switched off – there was too much to take in!

He sprawled back on the cushions, his eyes half-closed as the slow sway of the gondola lulled him into an almost incredulous reverie of his arrival in this stupendous city. His frolic with Gina on the train seemed to him so preposterous that he almost doubted that it had ever happened. Surely he had dozed off in his sleeper and the rocking of the train had induced a fantasy, an erotic dream . . . but no, when he slid two fingers down into the breast pocket of his blazer, there was the piece of paper torn from his guide book on which she had scribbled her address for him.

It had really happened, this heroic and comical welcome to Venice, he told himself with a sigh of pleasure, and the best of it was when Gina opened the buttons of her white blouse to show him her soft and chubby breasts. Until then he might have shied away from her direct approach, but he was lost when she put her hands on his shoulders and leaned forward to make her breasts dangle where he could get at them. What followed then was a foregone conclusion – but even so, she had shown herself to be extraordinarily good at fitting these soul-stirring events into the time available.

The pleasing memory of his *ride* on the express train brought about a gradual and inconvenient stiffening in Adrian's grey flannels. It was not practical on the gondola's very low seat to contain this ill-timed swelling by crossing his legs, and so he spread his guide-book, open and face-down, over his bulge. Not that there was anyone close enough to observe his condition except the gondolier standing behind him, and he was probably too occupied with his balance as the narrow craft dipped and rolled in the wash of the water-buses to pay any attention to his passenger. That being so . . . Adrian slipped a hand under the book and held his unruly part fondly through his trousers.

The encounter with Gina on the train had opened his eyes to the possibilities of finding other locations for love-making. Specifically, would it be practical to do it in a gondola? he asked himself. There was plenty of room to stretch out full length, and the rocking of the boat would be conducive to the mood . . . *was* conducive, he corrected himself, for he could feel the effects on himself now. To be rowed slowly along the Grand Canal by night, with lights glowing golden in the window of the palaces . . . a pretty girl lying beside him, her mouth on his in a long kiss, his hand up her skirt and inside her knickers to caress smooth warm lips under a mop of curls and feel them becoming slippery as her excitement grew . . . and then her hand at his trousers to open them and feel inside for his hard-swollen part . . .

He was certain that Venice's greatest son, Giacomo Casanova, had contrived to enjoy plenty of girls on gondola rides. It had to be admitted that the only version of Casanova's *Memoirs* in English – for reasons too complicated to follow – was a pirated translation of a pirated French translation of the authorised German translation of the original French that Casanova had chosen to write in, but even so, it was clear enough about his exploits. An evening, for instance, when he had been drinking in a tavern and a gondola arrived with a hooded girl. She was a young contessa looking for the lover who had deserted her, but Casanova soon had her on her back and consoled her.

Or there was the day when the dashing Venetian had been rowed a mile across the lagoon to Murano, the small island where glass-blowers had their workshops, but not to buy their wares. His interest was in a fifteen-year-old girl named Caterina he had enjoyed in the Guidecca gardens in Venice, and whose father had sent her to a convent to keep her safe from further dishonour. Only by attending the Sunday Mass could Casanova catch a glimpse of her, and she of him, and as Fate would have it, another lady present at the Mass, not a nun, saw him and sent a secret invitation to meet her in a house on the island. She proved to be a blue-eyed blonde named Maria-Eleonora, and by Casanova's own account, he had her seven times that night and forgot all about his little fifteen-year-old.

A man of Casanova's accomplishments must undoubtedly have made frequent use of gondolas to pleasure young women when the blood ran hot and no other accommodation was instantly at hand, though Adrian could not remember an exact instance from the *Memoirs*. In those days ladies wore no knickers under their full skirts and petticoats – when Casanova slipped his hand up their clothes, the soft and furry mound was bare to his touch. And when he rolled the girl on her back and flipped up her skirts, there was nothing to hinder him from sliding straight into her . . .

Adrian's gondola took a long turn to the right where the Grand Canal curves back on itself, and there was the Rialto Bridge to arouse him from his erotic fancies. He stared in delight at the single slender span of white stone, so familiar to him from Canaletto's many paintings of it, and like millions of others before him he marvelled at its gracefulness, even though it was wide enough to carry two inward-facing rows of shops. And the reason that Antonio Canaletto had produced so many painting of the Rialto bridge was that the scene was a favourite souvenir for young English gentlemen on the Grand Tour in the eighteenth century – no stately home in the shires could be considered complete without a view by Canaletto, to prove that the young master had whored and drunk his way round Europe.

But architectural appreciation did not hold Adrian for long – he was too engrossed in his fantasia of making love to a girl in a gondola – it had become so vivid to him that it was like a film playing on a screen. He summoned up a cherished memory of Rudolph Valentino pressing beautiful Agnes Ayres close to him in a passionate embrace that bent her over backwards – and so forced her belly and thighs hard against him! Now that was an ideal moment to reach round and feel her bottom, and press a finger between the cheeks . . . but they couldn't show you that on the screen, of course. Whatever the scene, it always faded out when the time was exactly right for the hero to slip his hand in between the girl's legs.

But of course, everyone knew what came next in real life, after a kiss like that. It was because the secret thought of being ravished by a film star aroused girls that they would let their breasts be felt in the picture-house, and sit with their knees apart for their boyfriend to take advantage of the dark.

Some girls became so deeply aroused that they could easily be persuaded to squeeze a hand down the front of the boyfriend's trousers, to confirm that he was similarly affected – and once or twice Adrian had gone out into the street at the end of the show with a grin on his face and a wet sticky patch on his underwear, because the girl of the moment had played with him just a second or two longer than was prudent.

A voice broke into these fond memories – the voice of the gondolier announcing, *Ca' Malvolio, Signor*. That was why love in a gondola was a non-starter, thought Adrian crossly – there was a confounded rower standing right behind you all the time with an uninterrupted view of what you were doing to your girl, even on a dark night. *Thank you*, he responded, and sat a little more upright to see his destination coming into sight. He knew from his guide-book that the Venetians had the odd custom of calling a palace a house – a *Casa*, and shortening that to *Ca'* as if modestly downgrading the glories of their city. The Palazzo Malvolio was where Adrian was going, and his map placed it on the left bank, just about where the Grand Canal sweeps round to the left in its final curve.

The word palace has a greater significance in England than in Italy. For the English it never fails to conjure up thoughts of Buckingham Palace and of royalty, whereas ever since the tenth century or thereabouts every Italian nobleman and landowner has built himself a grand house and called it a palace. Even so, it is almost impossible to conceive of a city where there are two hundred palaces along a single street – that is if a waterway can be called a street – each given the name of the wealthy family that built it in the distant past and whose descendents often still live in it. Adrian stared almost open-mouthed as the gondola rowed steadily on towards the Palazzo Malvolio, where he would be staying for the next day or two as a guest.

It was not one of the oldest palaces of Venice, for the style said very clearly that it had been built in the eighteenth century – and by Venetian standards that was fairly recent. The imposing facade was of white stone, turning sadly grey by the years and neglect, three storeys high, though Adrian guessed that there was another floor under the red-tiled roof, for the servants' quarters. In the centre of the ground floor was a tall arched doorway, flanked by Corinthian columns supporting a line of stone balconies the width of the building, and above them rose another tier of columns in pairs, and a double tier again above that. He counted seven large double windows on each of the two upper floors, and guessing that Canal frontage was so expensive to buy that this would be the short side of the palace, he knew that it must be a very large building.

Along the front of the palace ran a broad stone landing-stage and in front of that a line of wooden pillars rose out of the water – striped like so many barber's poles, but cracked and split and half-rotted through from years of water and sun. According to Adrian's guide-book they were used in the good old days to moor the nobleman's own gondolas and were painted in the colours of the house. Sure enough, as the gondola slid alongside the landing-stage, out from the huge central entrance of the Palazzo trotted a footman dressed in threadbare livery – white stockings and knee-breeches and a long velvet jacket that had once been purple and yellow before the colours faded. And looking from him to the mooring posts, Adrian dimly discerned that those had been the original colours.

The stone-flagged entrance hall was dominated by an elaborate marble staircase. At its foot waited an imposing figure in an ancient black swallow-tail coat and striped waistcoat – silver-haired and with a chest like a pouter-pigeon. He bowed slightly and introduced himself as the major-domo, which Adrian took to be the equivalent of butler. In very passable English he said that Signora Tandy was not at home, nor were any members of the family, but that instructions had been left that Signor Tralee was to be welcomed in every way. He added that lunch was ready in the Small Dining Room, if the Signor would follow him.

After his genial exertions on the train Adrian had a ravenous appetite and accepted at once. Another footman in the Malvolio livery emerged from somewhere and took the suit-case, and Adrian observed that the one who had conducted him from the gondola to the entrance hall was merely in charge of the door and nothing else, which made him wonder how many footmen there were in the household. He followed the major-domo up the broad staircase at a sedate pace, looking with interest at the life-size statues set in niches in the walls on either side. On the left was a Venus, bare-breasted, of course, but draped modestly from hips to feet.

Her hair was drawn back from a centre parting and tied in a pig-tail, her right arm was raised and she held an apple in her hand.

The white plaster of the niche behind the goddess showed long stains, as if there had been a water leak from the floor above at some time. Quite evidently a pigeon or two had got in from outside, for there was a streak of droppings down the perfection of her shoulder to her right breast. Facing her across the marble stairs stood a round-bearded and naked Hercules with a massive club in his hand and a lion skin thrown over his shoulder. Muscled like a heavyweight boxer he might be, but the equipment that hung between his legs was smaller than could reasonably be expected of a hero, Adrian considered. Certainly Venus would have found it disappointing – even when it was at full stretch. And this observation had evidently been made before – some past Malvolio seemed to have fired a pistol shot at Hercules' little dangler, missed it, and left the equivalent of a long scar on his marble thigh.

These evidences of neglect were distressing to a connoisseur of fine art, but not surprising in view of Adrian's mission. At the head of the stairs a large stone plaque set on the wall displayed the Malvolio coat of arms, elaborate, ancient and, of course, irrelevant in the twentieth century. The footman with the suitcase went off one way and the major-domo led Adrian the other way, along a wide and high-ceilinged corridor hung with old paintings and through suites of reception rooms that opened into each other, and through sitting-rooms and music rooms and rooms which had no obvious purpose at all except to house marble statues of naked gods and goddesses, busts of bearded Greek philosophers and smooth-shaven Roman emperors. In spite of Adrian's professional interest in art, there was too much to take in while walking, and besides, he was hungry – he simply ignored the art about him.

The Small Dining Room, so called, was large enough to hold a polished mahogany table with chairs for eight round it, two long matching sideboards on each of which stood half a dozen heavy silver serving dishes, a glass-fronted rosewood cabinet to display thirty or so large porcelain plates with exquisitely hand-painted rural scenes, two waist-high Sevres jardinieres, a massive mottled-yellow marble fireplace on which stood five half-size bronze busts with a Baroque look about them. The walls were painted a pleasing pinkish ochre, what could be seen of them, for there were several painting on each – mostly portraits and family groups, but with a few landscapes as well.

Adrian ignored them resolutely and advanced to the table, where a short fat priest in a rusty black cassock was already seated, with a glass of white wine in his hand. He got up to shake hands and introduce himself as Padre Pio, confessor to the Malvolio. Evidently he had found it prudent to learn to speak English, though with a profound accent, now there were no more Malvolio and his patron was an English lady. He conveyed the apologies of Signora Tandy for not being present to greet her guest.

The meal was simple but good. Luigi the major-domo stood like an imposing statue between the two sideboards and under his stern gaze the two footmen – one for Padre Pio and one for Adrian, served the food and wine. They started with a mountain of risotto flavoured with tiny clams, spaghetti being no great favourite in Venice; then came a thick slice of white fish Adrian did not recognise, cooked in white wine and served with French beans, and then the main dish – thin slices of veal and courgettes baked in the oven with butter and cheese. Adrian's glass was never empty – each time he took a drink to wash down another mouthful of delicious food the footman at his elbow filled it again. After the veal a huge antique silver bowl of peaches and figs was placed on the table and coffee was served.

Throughout the meal Padre Pio chatted away amiably – clearly his position in the household called for him to be a companion as much as a priest, and he was well versed in the art of light conversation. All that Adrian learned from two hours of amusing and interesting talk was that the good father was nearly seventy and that he had joined the Malvolio household in 1879, in the time of the 'Old Count' whoever he had been. And indeed, after the excitement of his entry into Venice, the heat of the day and the amount of food and wine he had consumed, Adrian was feeling decidedly sleepy. Padre Pio noted his drooping eyelids and suggested it was time for the siesta – and asked Luigi to have the Signor shown to his room.

For this purpose yet another footman was sent for, the two in the dining-room being, it seemed, specialised in the serving of meals only. The new one was as old as all the others – in his fifties by Adrian's reckoning – and his purple and yellow livery was just as threadbare. He led Adrian back to the marble stairs and up another flight, between large facing oil-paintings of battles fought with muskets and cavalry, and down yet another endless gallery hung with more paintings that would be found in the average English provincial museum, and finally into the room allotted to him. The shutters were closed against the heat, but he could see it was a large room with a faded but good Oriental carpet on the tiled floor.

There was a broad and high old-fashioned bed, and that was what took his interest just then. It was placed sideways on against the wall, with curtains flouncing out to enclose its head and foot. Adrian saw his suitcase had been placed ready for unpacking on a carved wooden chest, but he was too tired to trouble with it just then. Almost before the footman was out of the door he had his blazer and shoes off, loosened his tie and climbed on to the bed, spread himself out on the shiny satin coverlet and went to sleep instantly. He intended to indulge in no more than an hour's doze, but when he woke up and raised his arm over his face to glance at his wrist-watch, he was astonished to see that it was already after six o'clock.

With returning consciousness came the realisation that he was very hard inside his underwear. He put a hand down to touch the long bulge in his grey flannels and impressed himself by its rigidity. He flipped open his buttons and pulled up his shirt to let this pleasant evidence of his resurgent virility rear up proudly, intending to admire it a little – when a sound in the room shocked him. He turned his head and to his horror there stood a maidservant in a black calf-length frock and a white apron. She was busy with his suitcase on the chest – she was trying to open it and shaking her head to find it locked.

The window-shutters were wide open – it was the noise of them being pushed back that had woken Adrian. The maid stared across the room at his red-blushing face and the straining part in his hand, smiled broadly and then burst into loud giggles. Adrian's relief that she had not run screaming from the room brought a grin to his face. Now that he was over his shock, the situation seemed laughable – to be discovered by a chambermaid with his stiff six inches out and feeling it! He sat up on the bed and made himself decent, thankful at least for the girl's sense of humour. When her giggles came to an end she went through a complicated pantomime of hand gestures and Italian explanations until he understood that her name was Teresa, that she had been assigned to look after him, that the hour for dinner was approaching, that he must wash and dress, and that his bathroom was next door.

She threw open a once white-painted door in the wall opposite the foot of the bed, to reveal a cavernous bathroom with a floor tiled in black and white hexagons. While she was turning on the taps Adrian slid from the bed, checked that his trousers were properly buttoned over his ill-disciplined part and went to the windows. Outside was a stone-balustraded balcony and he saw that his room was on a side of the Palazzo away from the Grand Canal. He overlooked a cobbled square that had a brick church for one side and a small restaurant on another, with tables set out in the fresh air. A black-haired waiter in a white jacket leaned against the restaurant wall and waited for the first customers.

Teresa came to the balcony and let him know that the bath was ready, and indicated with a twisting motion of her fingers that he should give her the key to his suitcase so that she could hang up his clothes. That done, he went into the bathroom, closed the door carefully and stripped. The bath was an enormous white tub on lion's-paw metal feet that had once been gilded but now were sadly tarnished. The water was not really hot, but pleasantly warm for a summer evening, and Adrian lay soaking, staring with mixed emotions at his inconveniently rearing stiffness and willing it to go soft. He sat up and soaped himself thoroughly from face to toes, certain all would be well if he could turn his attention elsewhere.

Perhaps it would have worked, given enough time – but he had no opportunity to find out. The bathroom door opened briskly to admit Teresa, and without a word she knelt to wash his back, as if that were part of her everyday duties. Whether she glanced down at the fleshy column between his thighs or not, he did not know, for in his embarrassment he was staring straight ahead and pretending that nothing unusual was happening at all. Such nonchalance was not easy to preserve when Teresa stood up again and held a large white towel with a frayed M embroidered in one corner. Evidently she meant him to stand up and be wrapped in the towel – and perhaps rubbed dry!

He took a deep breath and stared up into her face, hoping to catch a hint of a smile on her lips or perhaps the faintest of gleams in her dark eyes. This was the first time he had looked properly at her – in the bedroom his embarrassment had been so acute to be found by her with his proudest possession in his hand that he had kept his eyes away from hers. Now that he looked, he saw that she was a fairly plump-bodied woman in her twenties, her hair of so dark a brown that it was almost black, and worn pinned up into a bun on top of her head. He smiled at her, determined not to be embarrassed any longer, and stood up in the bath, his projection nodding up and down to his sudden movement. The maid took no notice of it – she waited for him to step out of the water on to the tiles and then swathed him from shoulders to knees in the big towel.

As he had guessed she might, she started to rub him dry. She worked her way down his back from the nape of his neck to his thighs, and it seemed to him that her hands lingered over the cheeks of his bottom, giving them a good strong squeeze after she had dried them. It was somewhat infuriating not to be able to make himself understood by her, and not to understand what she was saying to him, for she chattered away non-stop while she rubbed at his body. When she had finished his back she moved round to stand in front of him and her capable hands were soon moving down from his chest to his belly . . . the bath towel was hanging loosely from his shoulders like a cloak and there was no attempt by him, or by the maid, to hide his six inches of impressive stiffness.

In fact, Adrian saw that she was looking down at it – and in another moment she had it in her hand, wrapped in a fold of the towel, and was rubbing it slowly dry – that at least was one possible interpretation of what she was doing to him! Into his mind came one of the few words of Italian he knew – one that he had learned that morning – he stroked the maid's hair and said, *Amore?* In a questioning tone. *Ma no – impossibile!* she said in reply, and it was hardly necessary to speak Italian to know what she meant. But under the pleasing stimulus of her hand continuing to smooth the towel up and down his hardness, Adrian was persistent.

'*Si*,' he told her, '*amore*,' and he put his hand on her solid left breast and felt it through her shiny black frock. At once she began to speak very quickly, her face stern and her black eyes flashing – presumably with indignation – though she kept a firm hold of Adrian. Whatever it was she was saying, it was totally lost on him, of course, and it was only when he reached down to get his hand under her clothes and bring it up between her legs, until he was clasping her warm mound through the thin material of her underwear, that she fell silent and looked at him open-mouthed.

'*Amore,*' he said again, making his stiff length jerk in her hand and squeezing between her legs at the same time, to make absolutely sure that she understood his requirement. Not that she had been in any doubt, of course. She smiled at him at last and nodded her head vigorously, and then surprised him when she turned to bend over and grip the side of the big bathtub. The position was one he had never before had the pleasure of trying out, and he seized the opportunity. He lifted Teresa's frock at the back up to her waist, revealing a round fat bottom clad in white cotton knickers that extended down her plump thighs to just above her knees.

She was grinning at him over her shoulder while he fumbled under her clothes to slip her underwear down her legs and round her ankles. She stepped out of them and waggled her bare bottom at him.

'This is not the first time you've been had this way,' Adrian exclaimed, smiling to view the big bare cheeks that she thrust towards him, and the dark-haired split below them. Trusting to what he had seen in illustrations, he moved in close behind her with as much confidence as if he had enjoyed dozens of girls in this position before, and opened her with his thumbs.

'*Ah!*' she gasped, when she felt the head of his insatiable part touch her pink-fleshed petals, '*pieta, Signor!*'

Adrian pushed right in, until his belly was pressed against her bottom. He reached forward and under her, to take hold of her chubby breasts through her frock and squeeze them while he rode her.

'That's absolutely *fantastico*!' he sighed, remembering the word from his adventure on the train. 'You're the sort of chambermaid every man dreams of meeting when he stays in a country house or a hotel – except that they always turn out to be forty and sour-faced. I'm delighted with you, Teresa,' and I hope that you will make my stay here very happy.'

Perhaps his heroic stiffness when he woke from his siesta was caused by a forgotten dream – some returning memory of Gina sitting astride his lap as the train rattled across the long bridge into Venice. Whatever had brought it about, the truth was that he had been so highly aroused before he set eyes on the maid, and even before she had taken him in hand in the bathroom, that the need for relief was an urgent necessity if he was to present himself decently for dinner. He slid happily in and out of Teresa's increasingly wet warmth and felt himself on the brink of his crisis after no more than fifteen or twenty strokes. His grip tightened on her breasts and the pace of his stabbing accelerated to short fast digs.

Three seconds later he was babbling an incoherent *Ah,ah*, his hands clenched in her soft flesh and his back arching, while he squirted his hot desire into her.

'*Madonna mia!*' Teresa cried out, and her body shook heavily against him as climactic sensations overwhelmed her.

THREE

Mrs Delphine Tandy was a woman of magnificent appearance, her long oval face discreetly made-up, her chestnut-brown hair worn up on top of her head, her green-grey eyes bright and very clear. Her evening frock was of black velvet, strapless, and cut straight across her considerable bosom, revealing a pair of well-shaped shoulders and nicely rounded arms – and because it reached no lower than mid-calf, it also revealed a pair of fine ankles. Her jewellery was very simple – a long looping pearl necklace and a pair of diamond earrings. Sitting in the anteroom on an Empire chair beautifully inlaid, she was every inch the great lady – not even a clod could have been in any doubt of that.

When Adrian had been instructed by the head of Mallards to go to Venice and meet her, he had been briefed carefully about the lady's past. As a debutante, Miss Illington-Darby had enchanted the whole of fashionable London with her looks and charm, and she had made a brilliant marriage to the Hon. Frederick Tandy, who had just entered Parliament and was expected to become Prime Minister one day. But a few years of playing the society hostess to boring politicians in London, and riding to hounds three days a week in the country, were enough to persuade her that this was not entirely the life she wanted.

In consequence, she had abandoned her husband without a word of explanation, to run away with Count Rinaldo Malvolio, who was attached to the Italian Embassy in London. That would be about 1906, said Adrian's informant, and although Malvolio had been killed in the War, Mrs Tandy had not been seen again in London. Tandy, who had failed to become Prime Minister and was now Lord Brangton, had revenged himself by refusing to divorce her until he knew that her lover was dead, and so had made it impossible for her to become Countess Malvolio.

Delphine's younger sister Marina, also a good-looking girl by all accounts, had travelled abroad to visit her sister before the War and damned if she hadn't fallen for an Italian too and married him! 'But there you are,' said Adrian's boss, 'there's no accounting for taste, and women are easily taken in by all that bowing and hand-kissing nonsense the Continentals go in for. And between you and me, my boy, young fillies can sometimes be very flighty when it comes to a question of bedtime matters.' He tapped the side of his nose and fixed Adrian with a piercing look that caused him to square his shoulders and declare that there was no trusting a nation that didn't play cricket.

But damn the cricket, he said to himself when Delphine held out her hand to him, palm down, and he realised that he was expected to kiss it rather than shake it. And kiss it he did, and caught an exhilarating trace of her perfume – he looked up into her eyes while he was bowing and decided that she was easily the most elegant and interesting woman he had ever met in his life. Even though she was forty-four, he calculated, and getting on for twenty years older than himself! That notwithstanding, it was easy to see why the late lamented Count Malvolio had found her attractive enough to run away with, in spite of the scandal that must have descended on him. In his shoes I'd have done the same thing myself, Adrian thought gallantly, and he smiled at Delphine Tandy with all the charm he could muster.

In dinner-jacket and black bowtie Adrian stood by her chair while she talked to him graciously. She was solicitous in her enquiries into whether his long journey had been tolerable, and he kept a straight face while he assured her that it had been most interesting, in particular the last stretch between Padua and Venice, which he had found inspirational. *Yes, very pretty countryside*, she said, *there's a Malvolio villa on the banks of the Brenta that the Count left to me, but you can't see it from the train.*

The ante-room, where the family were assembled for a drink before dinner was a high and square room with walls papered in striped grey and hung with portraits of dead and gone Malvolios – men and women in a variety of eighteenth and nineteenth century clothes. A dozen Empire-style chairs stood about, and two settees, each long enough to seat four people. The chairs had a scuffed and worn look about them, and the once-superb red-and-gold carpet underfoot was worn through in places to the backing.

A pleasant half-hour was passed in talk before Luigi appeared and bowed low before Mrs Tandy while he announced that dinner was served. He had changed the swallow-tail coat Adrian had seen him in at lunch for a slightly less elderly one and round his neck he wore a chain of heavy silver links that carried an elaborate plaque engraved with the Malvolio arms. Delphine took Adrian's arm and graciously let him lead her into the dining-room. They strolled through white and gold double doors, a footman in livery bowing on either side, and Adrian's eyes opened wide at what he saw. He now understood why the room where he had enjoyed lunch with Padre Pio was called the Small Dining Room and sat only eight. This one had a table for twenty down the middle of the honey-coloured wooden floor. One look at the chairs told him they were from the workshop of an eighteenth century master and, if they ever came up at Mallards for sale, worth a great deal of money.

Furniture apart, it was the murals that had made him stare on entering the room. The walls were painted in arched panels from waist-high up to the ceiling, ten panels altogether, each with a mythological scene of life-size figures. The scenes were of ancient Roman gods and goddesses, either feasting or engaged in the preliminaries to feasting. Needless to say, they were all nude, or very nearly so. A barebreasted and long-thighed Diana accompanied by hounds hunted a stag with bow and arrow through a countryside of trees and streams. A blonde-haired Venus lying on her side on an ivory couch stretched out an arm to take a bunch of black grapes from a Cupid – so that the twist of her body threw her breasts into prominence and revealed her belly down to her groins, where the merest wisp of almost transparent tulle concealed her treasure.

Elsewhere round the walls could be seen Mars, Mercury, Juno, Minerva and the other Roman divinities, all busy with eating or drinking, and on the high ceiling overhead was a banquet scene – all the deities together round a table loaded with food and wine. And perhaps it was only a first impression, but Adrian noted that although the goddesses were all satisfactorily full-breasted, the gods seemed to have undersized parts. He wondered if the artist were revealing a national characteristic, and he thought it would be interesting to make enquiries when, and if, he went to visit Gina Luzzi – for who more able than she to speak with authority on the adequacy of the natural equipment of her countrymen?

Leaving aside questions of merely biological interest, Adrian intended, when opportunity served, to examine the murals thoroughly – for though their colours had been dimmed by the accumulated grime of centuries, there was no doubt in his mind that they were the work of a most important artist – perhaps even Tiepolo himself. But then, he thought, everywhere you look in this Palazzo there are masterpieces – pictures, furniture, statues – collected over centuries by generations of rich Malvolios. Neglected and decaying it may all be, but it is magnificent – and a palace ought to be magnificent... well then, I refuse to be impressed any longer. From this moment on I shall regard it as a home and no more than that.

Indeed, the family were more interesting than works of art, now that his attention was turned to them. Altogether there were seven for dinner, and places had been laid at one end of the vast table, Delphine at the head of it, Adrian on her right and a strongly-built man in his fifties on her left. She had introduced him as Herr Adalbert Gmund, and had said he was an Austrian, her tone of voice indicating that he was no casual visitor but a long-term and intimate friend. From that Adrian concluded that Gmund was her lover, and this surprised him a little, since the Italians had fought the Austrians bitterly during the War, not that many years before.

Delphine's sister was a few years younger and much like her in appearance, though she tried to look different by having her dark-brunette hair cut straight across her forehead and flicked forward in points on her cheeks. Her face was a little rounder and less oval, and her expression a little less composed than Delphine's. By marriage Marina had become the Contessa di Torrenegra and clearly the title pleased her, for she almost purred when Adrian imitated what he had seen on stage in the theatres of Shaftesbury Avenue and Drury Lane and murmured respectfully, *Contessa*, when he bowed over her hand to touch his lips to it. The little smile with which she rewarded him was so stunningly gracious that he almost felt himself in the presence of royalty!

The Contessa was placed on Adrian's right at the table, and while it was true that her poppy-red evening-frock, unlike her sister's, had shoulder-straps, it was equally true and far more interesting to a connoisseur of high fashion that it was cut in a V that plunged deep down between her breasts. Adrian took an interest in everything that concerned pretty women – or so he prided himself – and his delight was keen each time that Marina leaned towards him a little in their conversation, and even touched his sleeve to emphasise a point or two – for this gave him an excellent view of her full breasts.

Her jewellery was somewhat more impressive than Delphine's – she had a broad choker round her neck of emeralds and rubies, and long matching earrings that swung to the movements of her head. A closer inspection showed Adrian that the settings were old-fashioned, and he made a guess that the set had belonged to her husband's family for the last seventy or eighty years. Her daughter Bianca sat across the table from her and, if anyone had offered a choice, Adrian would have chosen her to sit beside him. She was seventeen or eighteen, he estimated, and by far the most beautiful girl he had ever seen in his life. She had her Aunt Delphine's calm oval face and her mother's dark-brunette hair, very dark eyes and a creamy complexion that was all her own. She was in a white frock that covered her to the throat, but left her arms bare – and they were long and slender and had the most fascinating elbows. Her only jewellery was a string of white coral beads, from which hung a small and plain gold cross.

Bianca's father was seated on her left, Count Massimo Enrico Francesco Vittorio Giambattista Scaloto Lombardini Manzetta di Torrenegra himself, looking as splendid as a Prince and handsome as a film star. His smooth face owed much to daily massage, thought Adrian, for the Count was well into his fifties and must be fifteen years older than his wife. His hair was shiny-silver, worn longer than was usual for men, and arranged in waves over his ears. His thin moustache was perfection – as if each hair had been trimmed separately to contribute to the final result. And his evening clothes! His jacket was broad in the shoulders and nipped-in at the waist, the lapels of black watered silk, the buttons covered to match – and the white handkerchief that showed from his breast pocket was of impossibly fine lawn linen. Count Massimo is a foppish fashion-plate, thought Adrian, a tinge of wonder in his mind – but his daughter quite obviously adored him.

Facing the Count, on the other side of Marina from Adrian, sat Padre Pio, the fat little priest. He had on the same worn black cossack, and maybe that was the only one he possessed, Adrian speculated. Whether the Malvolio paid, or had ever paid, a salary for the spiritual services he rendered them was one of those mysterious religious questions that were never asked or answered. Perhaps he was a sort of feudal retainer, given bed and board and no more. With Marina's whole attention fixed on Adrian and the Count chatting away to his beautiful daughter, the good Father had no one to talk to and devoted himself to the food and wine, which was delicious – and overwhelming in quantity. The liveried footmen skipped silently about the table with their silver serving-dishes and bottle, anticipating every wish, while the major-domo stood behind Mrs Tandy's chair like a statue and directed the staff with looks that no Emperor could have bettered.

It was only towards the end of the meal, when appetites were satisfied and the good-humour of repletion was everywhere to be discerned, that Delphine made her announcement. She waited for the Venetian glass goblets to be cleared away from which they had eaten their desert – a rich mixture of cream cheese with chocolate and candied fruits, over which Maraschino had been poured – and large bowls of fresh fruit put on the table with the coffee. Then with a glance round the table that silenced the English and Italian conversations in progress, she gained everyone's attention.

'Perhaps you have been wondering who Mr Thrale is,' she said, speaking in English for his benefit. 'He works for Mallards in London and he's here because I'm thinking about sending some of the pictures to auction.'

She paused while her announcement sank in and the Count burst into indignant-sounding Italian. She let his outburst run its course and answered him in English.

'I understand all that, Massimo, but you know very well there's nothing else for it. We need money urgently and that's the end of it. That is not for discussion in front of our visitor.'

'Well I think you're doing the right thing,' said Marina in support of her sister. 'Nobody ever wants to sell off family heirlooms and all that, but we know the position we're in – I haven't had a new frock for two years. Be sensible, Massimo – be brave, *carissimo* – it's not as if you were a Malvolio.'

'Yes, be brave, Babbo,' said Bianca, leaning sideways to kiss Daddy on the cheek, 'if Delphine gets a fortune for a few dusty old pictures she'll give some of it to you and you can buy more beautiful clothes for yourself and a solid gold cigarette-case and all sorts of lovely things.'

Adrian was very pleased to hear that Bianca had been taught to speak good English, for he wanted most fervently to make her aquaintance during his stay in the Palazzo and he had feared that communication might be impossible. At the same time, the conversation he was hearing was, to say the least, astonishing.

The Count folded his arms, raised his chin and stared coldly down the table at Adrian, as if he were a a burglar come to steal the priceless Malvolio treasures.

'You are a dealer?' he asked and though his accent was soft, his tone was insulting.

A person who had never heard of Mallards! Was it possible? Adrian met the icy stare and returned it in good measure while he deigned to explain that the English aristocracy disposed of unwanted pictures and antique furniture by sending it to be auctioned and bought by the wealthy middle-class.

'*Businessmen*, you mean?' the Count demanded, making them sound much less respectable than brothel-keepers. 'Adalbert – I appeal to you! I beg you to make use of your influence to stop Delphine from committing this monstrous act!'

The Austrian shook his head sadly and said that Delphine had consulted him before writing to London for an expert, and sadly he had been compelled against his will to accept her judgement of the gravity of the family situation. He had urged her, with all possible appeals to tradition, to dispose only of treasures which could be regarded as slightly outside the mainstream of Malvolio history.

Finding no support there, the Count addressed himself to the priest, who was peeling a peach and trying to be invisible.

'I insist that the Church forbids my sister-in-law from this sacrilege!' the Count said in a fiery tone, staying in English to intimidate Adrian. 'Put her under an ecclesiastical ban of some sort – threaten to call down a malediction on her head if she defies you and goes ahead with this selling of family treasures to boot-polish factory owners! Speak now!'

Padre Pio dropped his peach and crossed himself in acute embarrassment at thus being involved.

'These are terrible times, my son,' he said, also in English, 'we must all pray to God for patience to sustain us through the trials and tribulations of this world. Signora Tandy, on whose name I invoke a blessing, has the responsibility for all of us – a very great responsibility for a lady to bear on her own! I cannot approve of what she will do, but I must acknowledge her difficulties and I pray for her on my knees before the altar.'

Disappointed by his last possible supporter, the Count threw his hands dramatically in the air, his flashing eyes turned up to Heaven in silent appeal, and he said no more. But his sharp and unexpected response to Delphine's little announcement put a stop to any further discussion of the matter that evening. The silver bowls of fruits were left untouched as Delphine rose from the table and the entire family, and Adrian, trooped after her out of the dining-room and into the Yellow Drawing Room. It was so named because of the colour of the faded paper on the walls, and a magnificent carpet that had once been gold and scarlet.

A footman brought fresh coffee and Adrian was questioned by all three ladies about what was was being worn in London this year. He did his best to entertain them with what he could remember seeing in the windows of Marshall and Snelgrove and other shops, and he related the gossip he thought would amuse them, rather over-stating the extent of his own participation in the more fashionable social events of the capital. At about ten-thirty Count Massimo made his excuses to Delphine, saying that there was an engagement of some importance he must attend. He bid his wife goodnight with a kiss on the cheek, hugged his beautiful daughter, bowed very slightly to Adrian and left. Marina's face flushed a faint pink for a moment or two, as if her husband's departure embarrassed her, and Bianca seemed to be suppressing a giggle. From these reactions Adrian assumed that the Count kept a young mistress somewhere in Venice, of whom the family was aware, and he had gone to visit her.

Soon after eleven o'clock Delphine rose from her chair and wished Adrian goodnight, saying that they would meet and talk further of paintings for auction in the morning. Marina offered her hand to him to be kissed again, and he obliged with a smile into which he crammed all the charm he could. He was hoping that Bianca might stay with him in the Yellow Drawing Room for a while after the other ladies had retired, but things were not done that way in the Palazzo Malvolio.

'Come along, Bianca,' said her mother, cutting short a silent exchange of looks and smiles Adrian had managed to institute with the delightful young girl in white. He was permitted to touch her hand briefly – he would have preferred to press a lingering kiss to it, but thought it unwise under the watchful eyes of her elegant Mamma.

Naturally, he had very little idea at all of how to find his way back to his room, but a footman was waiting to show him. He undressed and got into bed wearing only pyjama trousers, for it was a hot night. His long sleep in the afternoon had refreshed him so much that he was unable to fall asleep. But he had a book to read – bought in Paris during his stay there, the book that literary London had been talking about for the last year or two. It was the book of an Irish writer, a Mr James Joyce, entitled *Ulysses*, and reputed to be so obscene that no English publisher dare bring it out. The curious who wanted to read it must make the trip to an oddly-named book-shop, *Shakespeare and Company*, on the Left Bank.

Comfortably settled against big square pillows, Adrian opened the book in pleasant anticipation. Ten minutes later he put it down with a puzzled frown – it was not in the least amusing and what he had read so far seemed uninteresting and pointless. Fortunately he had another English-language book he had bought in Paris, in a less intellectual book shop on the Place Pigalle in Montmartre – *Madame Birchini's Revels* – and this had a more promising look about it. But he had turned only to page one when the door of his room opened quietly and he thrust the shameful volume under his pillows as Contessa Marina came into the room.

Before he had time to rise to receive his unexpected visitor, she had crossed the room swiftly and silently on bare feet and was sitting on the side of the bed, facing him. The little lamp by which he had been reading cast a golden glow that made Marina seem even more glamorous than at dinner, now that her poppy-red frock had been changed for a full-length black *frou-frou* negligee so flimsy that the flesh-tones of her arms showed clearly through its sleeves.

'I know you must think me awfully impolite to barge into your room like this,' she said, her hand resting on his shoulder for a moment or two to indicate that he was not to get up, 'but of course after what happened at dinner I felt that I simply had to come and warn you.'

Adrian assured her that he knew her to be a lady of excellent breeding and exquisite manners, and her entrance into his room was in no way resented – far from it, she was most welcome at any time. He said it was very good of her to come so late to warn him. His understanding of the situation was that Mrs Tandy had the right to dispose of whatever part she chose of her inheritance from the late Count Malvolio, but perhaps he had missed something?

'It's not the pictures,' said Marina, 'she can sell the lot for all that anyone can do to stop her.'

'Then I am at a loss,' he said untruthfully.

'Oh, silly boy – my husband is terribly jealous – he saw the way you were trying to look down my frock at dinner. I'm sure he'll arrange to have something very unpleasant done to you.'

Adrian tried to visualise the matinee-idol Count as a jealous and possessive husband, but he failed utterly. The departure to an *important engagement* after dinner put paid to that concept.

'Was I looking down your frock?' he asked, smiling a little. 'How very *gauche* of me! I must apologise for that.'

'I didn't think you rude,' said Marina, 'it wasn't that. In fact, I was flattered to think that a beautiful young man like you could be interested in a married woman with a grown-up daughter. But, you see, my husband is so unreasonable. He imagines things, and gets himself into a foul temper. You must take great care while you are here. Don't be alone when you go out of the Palazzo.'

While she was giving Adrian this excellent advice, stressing the importance of it with rapid little hand gestures in the Italian way, it seemed that her black lace-edged negligee came unfastened at the waist. In the intensity of her concentration on her warnings not to stand too near the water's edge or to climb up to the top of tall bell towers, naturally she did not notice that her flimsy robe had fallen open, to reveal the top of her black lace nightgown, cut straight across her bosom.

When she did become aware of the sight disarray she fumbled at it briefly without looking, while continuing her discourse, and made matters worse. Not only had she not covered her bosom, but one of the narrow straps of her black lace nightgown had slipped right off her shoulder, to half-expose a good-sized and admirably pointed breast. Adrian told himself that so delicious a sight merited the very fullest attention, and he reached up to tug the Contessa's nightgown down further, until he had bared her right breast completely.

He took its pink point between his forefinger and thumb and rolled it gently.

'No, no, you must not distract me from what I have come to tell you!' Marina exclaimed.

'I am all attention, I assure you,' said Adrian. 'Please go on, Contessa.'

She sighed softly and put her hand on his chest. Her touch was cool and gentle, and very arousing – especially when her palm slid down to his belly and rested there.

'How exquisite is this moment,' he told her – a commonplace thing to say in the circumstances, but the best he could think of on the spur of the moment.

'Am I?' she whispered, not listening closely to his words. 'Am I exquisite?' and her hand slipped down his belly and inside his pyjama trousers, until her fingers could entwine themselves in the curls there. He had been sitting with his knees up to read and now he let his right leg sink down flat along the bed, to facilitate Marina's explorations. A moment later she touched the hot hardness that reared up under the sheet.

'Adrian,' she sighed, 'in spite of all I have told you, I am afraid that you still do not believe me.'

Her long fingers wrapped themselves round his stiffness and began to stroke it up and down. He let his other leg fall flat and parted his thighs.

'My dear Contessa,' he said, 'I shall not be diverted from what you are saying – whatever you do to me. I feel that I must grasp the situation completely, if I am to have faith in you.'

'Yes, you are right,' Marina exclaimed in agitation. 'Unless you have a complete grasp you will never understand me,' and so saying, she used her free hand to throw her negligee off her shoulders, so that she could slip the other shoulder-strap down. While Adrian watched in growing delight, she pulled her lace-edged nightdress down to her waist to bare both breasts.

'If there is a danger of violence from the Count for glancing down your frock,' said Adrian, fondling her bounties with a swelling heart, 'then what would he do if he knew you were here with me now, almost naked?'

'He would have your life,' she murmured.

Adrian leaned forward to put his face between her breasts and licked her delicate skin with the tip of his tongue. She gave a charming little sigh, he kissed her pink points to make them stand up and sighed himself at the almost intolerably delightful sensation of her fingers sliding gently up and down his stiffness. He sucked at the engorged tips of her breasts and felt so intense a throbbing through his body that he thought the climactic moment had arrived, and he groped blindly under her nightgown, wanting to open her to him. Her thighs parted and he touched curls, and then fleshy petals that seemed to blossom open of themselves to his caressing fingers.

In one long sinuous movement Marina was on her feet to strip off her negligee and nightgown, and an instant later she had thrown aside the sheet that covered Adrian's hard-straining part and stretched out full-length beside him, murmuring *Adrian . . . carissimo . . .* He knelt between her spread thighs, his hand at the little patch of dark-brunette curls that she was offering him, then he opened her wide with careful fingers and rolled her wet little button until she trembled and held out her arms to him in welcome. He rid himself of his pyjama trousers and put his belly on hers – and one strong push took him all the way into her slippery softness.

'Ah, ah . . . *Adriano mio!*' she exclaimed.

Her shuddering legs rose up off the bed to wrap themselves tightly round his waist, while she pressed her lips to his and breathed jerkily into his open mouth, spasms shaking her belly.

'This is madness, my beautiful darling!' she gasped. 'What you are doing to me . . . Massimo will have you killed . . . faster, faster!'

Adrian was aroused beyond belief by the theatricality of her words, her little cries, her sighs, gasps and moans. This was the most exciting day of his life – he had made love to three women – three women in one day! One for money, one for duty, one for pleasure – each wonderful in her own particular way. Was ever a man so bountifully treated by a benevolent Destiny? He thrust into Marina with short sharp strokes, feeling himself growing harder and thicker all the time. Marina had passed with amazing rapidity beyond coherent words and was making exciting, gurgling sounds as she bounced beneath him. At the first throb of his climax he called out her name, and rammed furiously into her. Marina's climactic shriek was satisfactorily piercing and prolonged – her heels drummed on Adrian's bare backside as it thumped up and down between her spread thighs, and he spouted his frantic desire into her.

FOUR

After the agreeable exertions of his first day in Venice Adrian slept soundly. Marina had not been content with one climactic release of her marital grievances – she had stayed in Adrian's bed and whispered and caressed him with teasing hands until he had recovered sufficiently to mount her again and ride – not at a gallop this time, but at a steady trot – to a satisfactory conclusion. After that, though she held on to his soft wet part in hope, he fell fast asleep, pleasantly fatigued by his fourth performance of the day. At some time in the night she went back to her own room, though Adrian knew nothing of that.

What woke him was, yet again, the noise of the shutters being opened. He rolled over and saw the maid standing at the windows and when she had let bright sunlight into the room, she picked up a tray and brought it over to the bed. It was only when she was beaming down at him and saying, *Buon giorno, Signor* that he realised he was lying naked on top of the crumpled coverlet. On the other hand, he said to himself, it seems hardly likely that Teresa will complain at the sight of what she became intimately acquainted with yesterday.

And indeed, beyond a glance or two and a grin at his limpness she paid no attention to it. She plumped the pillows up behind him, set the large oval antique silver tray on the bed beside him and poured coffee for him. While he was drinking it and spreading butter and quince jam on a soft roll, she picked up the evening clothes he had thrown over a chair when he went to bed, brushed the trousers and jacket and hung them in an ornately carved wardrobe. Through the open windows Adrian could hear the bustle and chatter of people in the sunny little square below and a feeling of contentment surged gently through him.

Venice was without any doubt the most wonderful city in

the world, he decided, though all he had seen of it yet was the Grand Canal. But the rest would be equally beautiful, he was certain of it, for any city whose pretty women were so very obliging had to be beautiful. He was, of course, falling into the error of tourists in Italy since the Renaissance – he was falling in love with a make-believe country of his own devising – an open-air museum of masterpieces of architecture crammed with wonderful paintings, all under cloudless blue skies, where the people sang from morning to night, the food was invariably delicious and everyone did their utmost to make him happy.

When Teresa took the finished tray from the bed he put his hand on her chubby bottom and gave it a good squeeze through her black skirt. She grinned and shook her head and pointed to his wrist-watch lying on the beside table. He picked it up to look at the time – about eight, he thought – and then shook it in disbelief to see the hands showing five to ten. But it was ticking properly, and he had to acknowledge that he had slept late. In fact, if Teresa hadn't taken it upon herself to wake him with his breakfast, he might be sleeping yet. He tried to convey his thanks, and she with many words and even more hand gestures, shrugs and facial expressions, made him understand that Signora Tandy wanted to see him that morning.

'Good,' he said, reaching out to where she stood beside the bed so that he could put his hand under her frock and run it up the back of her leg to feel her bottom. She let him do what he liked, a grin on her face, and soon his hand was between her thighs, and he was stroking her plump mound through her knickers – and his ever-ready part started to grow longer and thicker on his bare belly. Nothing like a tumble before getting out of bed to set you up for the day, he thought, and nothing could surely be more aristocratic than being serviced by the chambermaid who brought in the breakfast.

But Teresa stepped away from his probing fingers and tapped his stiffness lightly in reproof, treating him to a lengthy explanation in urgent Italian. At the look of incomprehension on his face she took his watch and pointed to numbers on the dial, saying *Signora Tandy*.

'What do you mean?' Adrian demanded. 'She wants to see me at ten-thirty? But that's out of the question – it's past ten now! Surely you mean eleven-thirty?'

By dint of repetition the maid conveyed to him that the hour at which he was expected was indeed ten-thirty. With a bellow of dismay he leaped from the bed and ran to the bathroom to shave and wash. Teresa had suitable clothes laid out on the bed by the time he came back, and with admirable skill assisted him into clean underwear and socks. While he was pulling a shirt over his head she was on her knees to slide his trousers up his legs and fasten the buttons – at any other time he would have found that arousing, but his anxiety at the thought of being late for his appointment was so great that he hardly noticed it when she gave his dangling part a friendly little squeeze.

He had no idea of where he was supposed to go, and even if he had he would not have known the way. As soon as he was ready, Teresa led him along the interminable picture-hung rooms and corridors of the Palazzo, past the Roman marble busts and the Greek busts and the Renaissance bronzes and all the array of priceless bric-a-brac. Delphine Tandy was waiting for him in a large room that had bookshelves round three sides, packed with works bound in leather, with the Malvolio coat of arms embossed in gold on the spine. She was sitting at a huge desk of dark walnut that must have been older than the palace itself, and Adalbert Gmund was with her, perched on a window-seat.

She was looking informally regal this morning, in a creamy-white silk blouse with a little stand-up collar. It was tucked into a pastel grey skirt. Adrian noted, with a tight belt round her waist – soft black leather fastened with a large circular silver buckle set with coloured stones. Gmund looked absurdly foreign in a tubular white linen suit and a stiffly starched collar with rounded corners.

There were the usual morning greetings and polite enquiries into whether Adrian had slept well – before Delphine turned to the business of the day. She apologised for the outburst by her brother-in-law and repeated what she had said in her letter to Mallards – that she was of a mind to dispose of a painting or two, if she could be assured of an appropriate price for them.

'There can never be any guarantees,' said Adrian instantly, trying to soften his words with a winning smile, 'everything depends on the quality of the pictures themselves, the buoyancy of the market and the interest of collectors and institutions. Your letter mentioned works by Cranach the Elder.'

'Do you mean there is more than one Cranach?' she asked with a certain vagueness he had not expected. 'I didn't know that. I am no expert on art, Mr Thrale, as I'm sure you realise, but I am advised that we have two paintings here by someone named Cranach. Is his work in demand? Or should I say *their* work?'

'Yes, and no,' said Adrian cautiously. 'The German Renaissance masters are always of great interest, but on the other hand, Cranach's output was prodigious – I assume that we are talking about Lucas Cranach the Elder?'

'Are we, Adalbert?' Delphine appealed to the Austrian on the window-seat, and he nodded.

'That is correct,' he said solemnly, 'The same Lucas Cranach who was the Court painter to Friederich of Saxony.'

'Good,' said Adrian, slightly reassured by Gmund's words. 'He became Court painter in 1505 or thereabouts, which means he was at work in Germany at the same time as Michelangelo in Rome and Raphael in Florence.'

'And Titian here in Venice,' said Gmund, determined to yield nothing in the way of expert knowledge.

'Quite so,' Adrian conceded. 'Is there anything of Titian's in the Malvolio collection?'

'Only one painting,' Gmund replied at once, 'there is a Saint Renata by him in the chapel. You must see it while you are here, but there is no question of disposing of it, nor of any of the other Italian masters – only the German pictures.'

'May I see your Cranachs before we continue our discussion?' Adrian asked Delphine direct, not very pleased to find himself dealing with her Austrian friend.

'They are in the Small Music Room,' she answered, 'I must go out now, but Mr Gmund will take you to see them and tell you as much as we know about them.'

She stood up to signify that the interview was over, and left the room. Adrian turned to Adalbert Gmund with a cheerful smile in the hope of getting on good working terms with him. Gmund returned his smile, though there was a touch of cynicism about his expression. At a leisurely pace he led the way back through the maze of the Palazzo to one of the many rooms Adrian had rushed through earlier that morning, in the wake of Teresa. Its name might have been the Small Music Room, but it proved to be large enough to contain a grand piano at one end, a harpsichord at the other, a gilt harp with naked cherubs painted on it, and spindly-legged chairs for twelve. Adrian wondered what the Large Music Room was like and asked Gmund, who told him that it was not called that – it was the Ballroom.

One side of the Small Music Rooms was all windows, with a view over the Grand Canal. Around the other walls were fourteen or fifteen pictures, but at a glance Adrian picked out the two he wanted, hanging above the white marble mantelpiece. They were small – about eighteen inches high and twelve inches wide – and each was of a naked girl, standing and full-length. Gmund stood back, his arms folded, half-smiling to himself as he watched Adrian stare intently at the paintings.

'First impression – a pair of Venuses painted in the 1530s or a little later,' said Adrian. 'As Cranach got older, his models got younger – neither of these girls can be more than seventeen or eighteen, and he was over sixty when he painted them.'

'A dirty old man, I think you English say,' Gmund commented.

'Oh yes,' said Adrian, 'a dirty old man of genius.'

He went close to the mantelpiece to scrutinise the pictures in more detail. The young Venus on the left stood half in front of a stone arch that set off her naked pink flesh to great effect. Her hair was red-gold, hanging in long ringlets down below her shoulders, and around her neck was a double-stranded gold necklace. She was tall, slender and long-legged, with pink-tipped little breasts like apples and a gracefully curving belly with a deep-set button. In one hand she held a gauze scarf with which she was pretending to cover her loins, but it was totally transparent and through it could be seen the hairless little treasure between her long thighs.

The girl in the other picture stood against a background of dark-green foliage and wore a bright red hat with a cartwheel brim. Her body was turned slightly more to the side than the first girl, throwing her round little breasts and almost plump belly into prominence. She held her strip of gauze with both hands, in the same pretence of hiding her loins. Her mound was fuller and boasted a feathering of almost blonde down, though she was obviously a year or two younger than the other girl.

After a while the sheer sensuality of the two painted figures seduced Adrian away from his objective contemplation. His mind drifted into thoughts of how delicious it would be to touch the smooth pink flesh of these young girls – to kiss their round little breasts and lick the inside of their long slim thighs. It was the expression on their faces that made them so utterly desirable – in piquant contrast to the virginal innocence of their naked bodies they both had the same knowing look in their heavy-lidded eyes and a secret little grin at the corners of their mouths.

'You like to look at naked girls, Mr Thrale?' asked Gmund, breaking into Adrian's train of thought.

'Little bosoms and big feet – had you noticed that?' Adrian countered. 'See their size? Pretty German girls had big feet in Cranach's day. Do they still?'

'*Ach, Gott*!' Gmund exclaimed, moving in to stand alongside Adrian and peer more closely at the paintings. 'What you say is correct – I had not noticed that before. Venus with big feet!'

'If we can authenticate them, the pictures may well fetch a lot of money at auction,' said Adrian, 'but if they belonged to me, I would never let them go. Last night at dinner I gathered it was your recommendation that they should be sold.'

'It is true,' said Gmund shaking his head sadly, 'and I hate and despise myself for it. But you have seen our situation, for you are an intelligent man. The Palazzo is crumbling, there is no money to pay for anything – and so Mrs Tandy has no choice.'

'Why these two paintings?'

'Because they are the only non-Italian works of art here. All the others – the pictures, the statues, the busts, the bronzes – everything is Italian and part of the Malvolio past. If a sacrifice must be made – as it must now – then with regret I suggested that the least harm would be done by choosing the German pictures. Do you agree?'

'I suppose so, but it does seem a shame. Did Count Malvolio leave no money at all to Mrs Tandy?'

'Come up to my quarters and we'll have a drink and a chat – I have a bottle or two of excellent *grappa*,' said Gmund in a most hospitable way.

'Thank you,' Adrian accepted, wondering what grappa was, and pleased to have a chance of finding out more about this odd household. 'I shall need the pictures taking down so that I can examine them closely in a good light. Can you arrange that for this afternoon?'

'*Mein Gott*, you English!' said Gmund with a grin. 'In Italy we take the siesta after lunch – nothing can be done between two o'clock and five o'clock. But I will give instructions to have Cranach's naked young girls taken down from the wall and put in the Biblioteca – the Library where Mrs Tandy talked to you – is that satisfactory?'

Adrian agreed that it was, Gmund summoned the majordomo and relayed the orders to move the two pictures, and led the way to what he had called his quarters. As Adrian had guessed, he was a permanent guest, judging by the suite of rooms he occupied. His sitting-room was furnished grandly, but also comfortably, though everything looked worn and in need of some attention. He fetched a bottle of clear spirit from an ornate cupboard, and two glasses. They drank cheerfully to each other and Adrian found out that grappa was a sharp, strong liquor. For eleven in the morning it seemed a little overmuch, but the opportunity to ask questions of an insider was not to be missed.

'Have you lived here long?' he asked, phrasing his question in as neutral a way as he could. He was to discover that Gmund, who asked to be called Adalbert, was completely open about his position – and everybody else's.

'Since the War ended,' he answered, 'seven years. Rinaldo Malvolio was my friend before the disastrous war that destroyed the Austrian Empire and deprived me of my estates, where he and I often went shooting the wild boar together. It was in those years that I became acquainted with Mrs Tandy, when Rinaldo brought her to Venice from England.'

'I say – being on opposite sides in the War, you and he might have killed each other!' said Adrian. 'That would have been most irksome for you both.'

'Fortunately, Rinaldo was flying his airplane against my countrymen in the mountains near Trieste. My regiment was with the German Kaiser's army on the Western Front, defeating the French. So Rinaldo and I were not required to harm each other personally. You are thinking that I came here as soon as the War ended and he was dead, to seize possession of my poor friend's palace and his beautiful English mistress – but that is not correct. Let me fill your glass again – do you like this drink?'

'Very potent,' said Adrian, 'though unsophisticated. I assure you it never crossed my mind for a moment that you had moved in here to . . .' and he let the sentence tail off, for some things are better left unsaid.

'I like you,' said Adalbert expansively, swallowing down his third glassful, 'I have always liked the English. Before the War I had my clothes made in London. I shall be frank with you – my mistress in those days was the beautiful Marina.'

'What!' Adrian exclaimed. 'But that's impossible!'

'And why do you think that? Fifteen years ago I was a good-looking fellow. Why shouldn't Marina love me?'

'But she couldn't have been married to the Count more than a couple of years, if I've got my dates right?' Adrian objected.

'*Mein Gott* – her marriage to Massimo! What a catastrophe! They married in 1907, and she was twenty-two and so beautiful that any man's heart would be melted. Bianca was born the next year – a beautiful child who has grown to be a greater beauty than even her mother was. But Massimo by then had decided that his true preference lay with pretty young men, not with his beautiful young wife. The relations between them have been purely formal ever since.'

'Good Lord – are you telling me that he's a . . .?' and again the sentence faded away incomplete. Adrian being unable to think of a polite way of saying what he meant. Adalbert nodded and said it was not at all unusual among the Roman aristocracy.

'I took him to be Venetian, like the Malvolios,' said Adrian.

'No, his family is from Rome. Marina made his acquaintance when Rinaldo took her and Delphine to meet the Holy Father and see the other sights of Rome. The Torrenegra family have been paupers for two generations – when Massimo met Marina he had nothing but his good looks and a lot of fine clothes that were never paid for. He had no income of any sort and the thought of employment has never crossed his mind in his entire life. It was natural that he leapt at the chance of marrying Marina and bringing her to live here, as Rinaldo's permanent guests. You can judge how penniless he was – Marina had to pay their train fare to Venice from Rome.'

'You said *in those days*,' Adrian observed cautiously, 'does that mean that you and the Contessa are no longer such close friends?'

'That is so,' Adalbert confirmed, nodding his head solemnly while he refilled both their glasses, 'about a year after

49

I was invited to live here when the War had ended Delphine and I fell in love, and my long liaison with my darling Marina ended. To be truthful, I have to say that I was relieved that it did.'

'But why?' asked Adrian. 'Your affection for her is still great even now – that's obvious enough.'

'But you see, Massimo was becoming suspicious of me, and that was very dangerous, however discreet and careful we were,' the Austrian explained. 'He has killed two men already for paying too much attention to his wife.'

'I find that hard to believe,' Adrian said, and thought to himself, *Pull the other one!* 'Not five minutes ago you told me that his interest is in pretty young men – why should he be jealous of the Contessa?'

'My dear young friend – you do not understand the Italian minor aristocracy,' Adalbert answered genially. 'Massimo may be a pauper, and dependent on his sister-in-law for every mouthful of food he eats, but he is consumed with the pride of race and breeding. Marina is his wife and bears his ancient family name, she is the Contessa Scaloto Lombardini Manzetta di Torrenegra – and if another man entertains designs on her, that touches the family honour – or so Massimo believes. He has not shared a bed with his wife – or even slept in the same room – for seventeen years or more. But no one else is permitted to do so.'

'Has he really killed two men?' Adrian asked uneasily.

'There was one before the War and one since,' said Adalbert, 'their admiration for Marina was a little too obvious and they let it be seen that they wanted to become her lover. Nothing was said by Massimo, of course, but one was found floating face-down off the island of San Giorgio. It was said that he must have fallen into the Grand Canal and drowned. The other man vanished without any trace and has never been heard of again – I assume his body was carried out to sea. Do you suppose this is coincidence?'

'Good Lord,' said Adrian, who assumed Marina was fantasising when she had told him of her husband's jealousy, 'do you know if either got as far as making love to the Contessa?'

'Of course not!' Adalbert exclaimed. 'She was faithful at all times to me. The two admirers died for their intentions, not for their achievements.'

'But how truly terrible!' said Adrian, feeling his face turn pale as he wondered what dreadful fate would overtake him if Massimo ever found out that he had enjoyed his wife twice.

'It is life,' said Adalbert, getting up to fetch another bottle of grappa, the first being empty, 'Let me advise you to be extremely careful in the way you converse with Marina and especially the way you look at her when her husband is present. Now that reminds me...'

He filled the glasses and went to a tall bookcase of polished walnut and brought out a cardboard portfolio tied with a green ribbon. He opened it and laid it carefully cross Adrian's knees to display the single unmounted picture inside. Adrian stared at a very curious antique work of art – an engraving of a well-muscled naked man sitting on the side of a low ornate bed, his legs together and his feet on the floor. Across his lap, her back to him, sat a naked woman, with a hand down between her parted thighs to hold his stiff part and steer it into her. The man's face was hidden by the woman's shoulder, and she was looking down to observe what she was doing, but her face in profile bore a striking resemblance to Marina.

'Is this a copy of a Raimondi print?' asked Adrian.

'It is not a copy – it is an original! It is one of a set of sixteen engravings of positions of love that Pope Leo the Tenth commissioned from Marcantonio Raimondi. That was about the same time that Cranach was painting young girls naked in Germany.'

'An original! Then it's valuable,' said Adrian, 'is it part of the Malvolio collection?'

'No, no – it belongs to me. In a modest way I am a collector of antique erotica. Some day I will show you more of my little treasures. But you have noticed the resemblance of the woman in the engraving to Marina? I bought it for that, of course.'

'I shall be honoured to see your collection, Adalbert,' said Adrian, beginning to feel very drunk. The second bottle seemed half-empty already, though he couldn't recall if he'd had any of it or not. It must be Adalbert soaking it down, he said to himself, but to speak truthfully, he felt that he ought to lie down for a little while before lunch.

He got to his feet not very steadily and said he must be on his way, there being much to do in so short a stay. Adalbert nodded and shook his hand.

'Stay here longer,' he advised, 'why should you hurry back? Venice has much to offer. In case you are wondering about it, I am not Mrs Tandy's lover any longer.'

'You seem to switch your affections about with remarkable ease,' said Adrian, struggling against his rising drunkenness to remain coherent, 'but you are a foreigner, though a charming one, and that may account for it. Why did you give her up?'

'*Ach, ja*,' Adalbert said, his speech also a trifle affected, 'but you see, my dear Adrian, I am like Lucas Cranach in this. As I become older, the girls must be younger. I shall be sixty soon and I need girls under twenty to stir my affections now.'

'That must make your life very complicated,' said Adrian, shaking his head sadly.

'Not at all – this is Italy, not your cold and rainy England. I have a good friend I visit twice a week, and she arranges all these matters for me – for only a few lira. *Auf wiedersehen*.'

'*Auf wiedersehen* and thank you for the grappa,' Adrian said, feeling very cosmopolitan. Outside Adalbert's sitting-room he weaved his way along a statue-flanked corridor which led into a room lined with gold-framed mirrors tarnished by age, and he kept going until he was completely lost. Surely there ought to be a servant on hand to guide him – his new chum Adalbert had told him that the staff of the Palazzo numbered forty-six – though their wages hadn't been paid for the last four years. Maybe that explained why there was not one of them in sight!

He was thinking of opening a window and putting his head out to shout for help when fifty yards up ahead of him a white and gold door opened and out came Marina. Hearing her name called, she glanced over her shoulder and waited for him. Her frock was white and sleeveless, showing off her finely-shaped arms, and it had a broad Greek key pattern in crimson round the neck and down the front of the bodice. Without a thought, Adrian put an arm round her and kissed her, fondling her breasts through thin silk. She gave a gasp of surprise, and then he felt the tip of her tongue slide between his lips.

At once he reached under her frock and put his hand flat on her bare belly. She sighed into his mouth, her tongue flicking over his. Under his hand the warm flesh of her belly was smooth as satin and in his half-drunk condition he would have fallen to his knees to kiss it. But Marina had her arms tightly round his waist to keep him standing upright, and so he slid his hand down inside her knickers until he touched her short and springy curls.

'*Dio mio!*' she murmured, her mouth pressed hotly to his.

Her feet moved apart to open her thighs. Adrian's hand slid a little deeper into her silk underwear and caressed the fleshy lips he found. Marina responded by groping for the hard shaft inside his grey flannel trousers.

'I want you now,' he announced when the kiss ended at last, his fingers busy down below.

'Adrian – this is insane!' she breathed ardently. 'My husband is in his room, dressing for lunch – just along there! He will see us when he comes out!'

Despite Adalbert Gmund's blood-curdling tales of revenge and assassination in the dark, the grappa had made Adrian bold to the point of foolhardiness. He pushed Marina back into the room she had come out of and kicked the door shut. It was a sitting-room, furnished in faded gold and yellowing white, and it was empty. In another moment he had her standing with her back to the wall and was kissing her hard while he reached under the hem of her frock to get his hand into her knickers again.

'*Adriano mio,*' she murmured, reaching up to stroke his face, 'there is a settee over there that would be more comfortable.'

'Later,' he said thickly, feeling the soft split between her legs becoming wet to his touch and her legs start to tremble just a little. He knew that he had won her over when her fingers grasped at the long bulge in his trousers.

'This is the most absolute madness – Massimo will have you killed,' she gasped, forcing her hand down the front of his trousers and into his underwear.

She grasped his headstrong part and jerked it up and down so very furiously that Adrian was afraid she would rip it from his body. Her head was lolling against the wall and she was shaking and moaning as her crisis of sensation approached, and rubbing her wetness against his fingers. His mouth found her open mouth and they exchanged gasps of delight while he tore open his trousers to let his quivering pride jut out – then with a quick bend of his knees and a strong push upwards, he was in her. Ten savage stabs and for Adrian the moment had come – he cried out loudly as a torrent of passion spurted into Marina's wet warmth.

She squealed and bumped her belly against him fast, each

hard forward thrust forcing him to slither deeper – until screams of delight proclaimed that her climactic sensations had arrived. Adrian was too far carried away to even care whether she was heard or not, or even whether the Count stood outside the door with a pistol in his hand. Eventually both were quiet again – Adrian leaning helplessly on her, and she leaning back against the wall sighing in satisfaction.

When his dearest possession dwindled and slipped out of her, she put an arm round his waist and led him across the room and into her bedroom. He lay on his back on a broad four-poster bed wondering why the room was rotating about him like a merry-go-round, unaware that the Contessa had pulled her pretty frock over her head and discarded her knickers and was kneeling above him, rubbing his wet part with eager fingers in the hope of stiffening it. But nothing would avail – the grappa had done for him and he was unconscious. Sighing in exasperation and in disappointment, she put her clothes on again and went down to lunch, leaving him to sleep it off on her bed, flat on his back and with his trousers down round his knees.

FIVE

Adrian woke up with a dull headache on Marina's bed. The watch on his wrist showed ten past three and lunch was long over – she evidently did not intend to come back to her room until he had gone. With an effort he eased himself up off his back and sat on the edge of the high four-poster bed, his feet dangling, and his trousers down round his ankles. He raised his shirt to look in wonder at his limp part and consider the dangers it had led him into since he arrived at the Palazzo Malvolio. If it was risky for Marina to visit his room by night, then it was sheer blind folly to stand her against the wall of her own sitting-room in broad daylight, and her husband only two doors away!

His small pink betrayer – as innocent and harmless to look at as those of the Roman gods in the dining-room murals – gave a brief twitch, as if disclaiming responsibility for whatever stupid adventures its owner involved himself in. And an instant later Adrian's blood ran cold in his veins – from the next room came the murmur of voices, and one was a man's. And not just any man's – it was impossible not to recognise the cultivated drawl of Count Massimo! He was with Marina in her sitting-room, and there was no more than a door between him and the besmircher of his honour, bare-bottomed in his wife's bedroom!

In total silence Adrian slid off the bed and pulled up his trousers. He tiptoed to the door and listened, hoping to hear the Count leaving. But not a bit of it! The conversation went on and on and on between the Count and his wife, good-tempered and calmly unhurried. A sexually jealous husband he might be, a sexually frustrated wife she might be, but they were on good terms. They were talking in Italian, which meant nothing to Adrian, but after a while he guessed from the number of times that Bianca's name was spoken that she was the subject of their careful interest.

He heard his own name mentioned by the Count, who pronounced it Trull, and with marked distaste. The tone of Marina's response seemed to Adrian to indicate that she was discounting the suspicion her husband had voiced, whatever it was. With a heart heavy as lead, Adrian contemplated the strong possibility that the Count had noticed his admiring glances at his daughter and was expressing his deep resentment that an untitled Englishman had the insolence to desire her. All in all, thought Adrian, a bad situation to be in – if I touch his daughter he'll have my pompoms cut off, and if he finds me here in his wife's bedroom he'll have my throat cut!

He heard the Count raise his voice to emphasise some point or other – and sudden panic gripped him. He darted silently across the room and slid under the broad bed. The floor was wooden and dusty and for thirty heart-stopping seconds he thought he would sneeze and give the game away. But the maddening urge died away at last and in the heat of the afternoon and the stuffiness beneath Marina's bed, he dozed off. It was twenty past four when he woke again, and hearing nothing, he slid out from under the bed and stood up to stretch his aching back. He was not, as he had believed, alone in the room – the Contessa Marina lay asleep on the bed.

She had taken off her white frock with the Greek key pattern and had lain down for her belated siesta in a pale grey *crêpe-de-Chine* slip. She lay on her side, facing towards Adrian, one hand under her cheek, her beautiful face tranquil. She had also removed her silk stockings and her well-shaped legs lay bent at the knee. Adrian knelt at the bedside to gaze in silent rapture at her breasts, almost out of the top of her slip because of the way she was lying. He reached out a careful hand to pull the slip down just a little, and the sight of her soft red buds made him want to lick them.

By now his innocent little tassel had stiffened to a six-inch length of throbbing readiness in his trousers. With a hand that shook, he raised Marina's slip in front just enough to give him a view of her thighs, round, smooth and maddeningly desirable. She slept on peacefully, knowing nothing of Adrian's raging passions and of his hand so close to the tuft of dark-brunette curls that showed through her *crêpe-de-Chine* knickers. But just as he was about to pull them down and press his face to the soft flesh of her belly, cold fear stopped him.

The Count was not likely to be in Marina's sitting-room on his own – he had surely gone back to his own suite before she part-undressed for her siesta. But how far away was that? *Just along there* was how Marina had described it when he had her up against the wall. Did that mean out of ear-shot? – for Marina's climax was accompanied by shrieks of delight. He had got away with it this morning – he had her against the wall almost under the Count's nose – but he'd been full of strong drink then and hardly knew what he was doing – and didn't care. But if he took Marina's knickers off now, would his luck hold out?

Thus conscience, as William Shakespeare wrote, makes cowards of us all. Except that Adrian's change of heart had nothing at all to do with conscience. It was self-preservation that pulled him reluctantly to his feet and away from Marina's uncovered breasts and thighs – and forced him from the bed where she lay in gentle slumber like a sun-ripened peach waiting to be picked and tasted. He rambled along through passages and rooms until finally he came across a footman bound on some errand with a tray on which he balanced a bottle of champagne and one glass.

Earlier that day Adrian had ascertained from Teresa that for some strange reason of their own Italians called a room a *camera* – what they called a camera he had no idea. By repeating the word several times and tapping himself on the chest, he conveyed his meaning to the footman, who showed him the way to his room. Perhaps it was as well, he thought, that he had not woken Marina – his headache had come back and he felt sweaty from hiding under her bed. He stripped naked and got into his own bed, and fell asleep again.

It was with some pride that he made his own way that evening to the ante-room, where the family assembled for drinks before dinner. Mrs Tandy was in olive-green – a shade that perfectly set off her dark chestnut hair. It was a high-waisted evening frock, cut low across the bosom but rising to a point, and held up by a halter of gold chains about her neck. Her dangling earrings were large pink pearls, and that was the only jewellery she was wearing. Bianca was looking very young-girlish and very desirable in a pastel-pink frock, with half-sleeves and crystal buttons from throat to waist.

During the chatter Adrian learnt that the Count and his lady were dining out with friends, and that Padre Pio had gone to visit his married sister. *You won't mind if we are terribly informal tonight, Mr Thrale, and eat in the Small Dinning Room?* asked Delphine. It was not a question that required an answer, thought Adrian, just a pleasant smile and a brief bow. He was determined not to drink too much this evening – in the day and a half he had been here he had been drunk twice. Both times he had behaved foolishly – for he now thought that it had been a mistake to have the chambermaid, since there was no telling how the news would be received if it got out.

He was sure that the regal Mrs Tandy would be very displeased to hear of her female staff being made casual use of by a guest – he thought it probable she would send him away instantly and write a nasty note to Mallards that would put paid to his prospects. And it had been the height of idiocy to back Marina up against a wall within ear-shot of her husband – aristocrats always had sporting guns and pistols handy – even impoverished ones. All in all, it was too easy and far too dangerous to get drunk in the Palazzo Malvolio.

With this in mind he drank sparingly of the crisp white wine and the full-flavoured red wine that accompanied five delicious courses of food. He had the pleasure of Bianca sitting next to him and she chattered away as if they were old friends. He told her that he had seen nothing of Venice yet and she immediately asked her aunt if they might visit the Piazza after dinner. And when that was readily agreed, Adrian informed Mrs Tandy that he needed longer than he at first thought to reach a conclusion on her paintings and that he would telephone London next morning to advise Mallards – if that was convenient to her.

'Take all the time you wish,' she said generously. 'Stay for a month if you can. But there is no *telefono* in the palace – I cannot bear the dreadful things. You can call London from the Post Office, but not tomorrow. It is closed on Sunday.'

'I've lost track of the days,' said he. 'I shall telephone on Monday, then.'

'What do you think of the paintings?' Mrs Tandy asked.

'Fine examples of the work of Cranach's studio,' he answered cautiously. 'I have not had time yet to go into the question of provenance – that's very important.'

'Our good Padre Pio is the keeper of the Malvolio archive,' Adalbert told him. 'He will show you the documents you need.'

'Which pictures are you selling for thousands of millions

of lire, Aunt Delphine?' Bianca enquired, 'I hope it's those ugly murder scenes in the chapel. They terrify me.'

'You wouldn't dare speak like that if Padre Pio were here,' said Delphine with a brief smile, 'the martyrdom of saints is a sanctified subject in his eyes, though I must agree that our pictures are so dreadfully gory that they are in bad taste. Mr Thrale is here to give an opinion on the German paintings in the Small Music Room.'

'The nudes over the mantelpiece,' said Adrian helpfully, and Bianca grinned at him.

'Oh, do you mean the two girls with the long legs and little bosoms?' she asked. 'I never knew they were Germans. The one in the big round hat looks exactly like my friend Maria-Luisa.'

'Does she indeed?' said Adrian, enchanted by what he heard, 'Then your friend is a very pretty girl.'

'But not as pretty as me,' she answered at once.

'You said examples of the work of Cranach's studio,' Adalbert said, wrinkling his face in a frown. 'Does that mean you think they may not be the work of Lucas Cranach himself?'

'No, no, I am not ready to express a final opinion yet,' said Adrian hastily, knowing how very touchy owners could be about their possessions – and even if Gmund was not an owner, he had an interest, 'I need more time.'

'You must take all the time you want,' Delphine Tandy said, 'take all summer, if you like. The paintings have been here for two hundred years – what are a few more months?'

After dinner she sent for a wrap for her bare shoulders and they set out on their little expedition to the Piazza. She led the party down the white marble staircase and out to the Grand Canal, and it was with pleasure that Adrian learned they were going by water – and more pleasing yet, by Malvolio gondola.

'My sister and her husband have taken the motor-launch,' said Delphine, the slightest trace of apology in her voice, 'I hope you won't mind travelling in a gondola, Mr Thrale. I've never cared for them myself, but we have two in service.'

The gondolier was the first and only young male retainer that Adrian had seen in the Malvolio household. Rowing a boat up and down the canals was evidently no job for an old man – this one was strongly built and looked to be in his middle twenties, the face under his flat-brimmed hat handsome but unintelligent. He handed the ladies into his swaying black craft and stood by to assist the gentlemen, if they needed him. A private gondola, Adrian saw, was better than the public ones plying for hire. For one thing it had a low and open-ended little cabin where two could take shelter from winter rain – or pleasure each other without being seen. This was more like the gondolas in which the inexhaustible Casanova had seduced pretty girls and young nuns by the score! Adrian found himself seated next to Mrs Tandy, facing forward, while Bianca and Adalbert sat side by side opposite them. As soon as they were under way, Delphine gestured towards a large building a little way further downstream.

'That is the Palazzo Mocenigo,' she said. 'Lord Byron lived there when he came to Venice. They say it was because he made his sister Augusta pregnant, but I've never believed that. Her husband was too stupid to notice what was going on, and the prosaic truth is that Byron was head over heels in debt and the bailiffs seized his furniture. He rented the Mocenigo palace cheaply and moved a baker's wife in to keep himself amused.'

'A man of vigorous passions,' Adrian commented carefully.

Water lapped over the lowest of the broad steps leading up to an unimposing doorway, above which was an ornate stone balcony. The gondola mooring posts were well-rotted through, the colour too faded to be distinguishable.

'And of low tastes,' said Delphine, thus confirming Adrian's belief that if she was ever told that he'd had one of her maids she'd send him packing. 'But we must not be too hard on him,' she continued, 'most men have low tastes, if they give way to them. He was famous for swimming in the Grand Canal, you know – he'd dive in stark naked from the Palazzo here and swim all the way up to the Rialto Bridge and back again – no doubt to get away from his baker's woman when she got on his nerves.'

'I know very little about him,' said Adrian, fascinated to hear Delphine speaking of a man dead for a hundred years as if he had been a neighbour of hers last week. 'I tried to read *Don Juan* at school, because it was said to be racy, but it was too long for me and I gave up. Did he live in Venice a long time?'

'Five or six years. He got rid of his bakery woman when he fell in love with someone more suitable – Contessa Teresa Giuccioli. She was nineteen and her husband was sixty – an Italian marriage custom that always led to problems. After she became Byron's mistress he invited himself to stay with her and the Count at their home in Ravenna. That's about seventy miles down the coast.'

'Ravenna... then that explains something that puzzled me once,' said Adrian. 'In Harriette Wilson's memoirs she includes a letter she wrote to Byron in Venice asking him for money, and he answered from Ravenna, but without explaining why he'd moved there.'

'Who was she – another light-of-love?' asked Delphine. 'Did he send her anything?'

'Fifty pounds. She was a very fashionable London courtesan in Regency days – Beau Brummell and the Duke of Wellington were among those who contributed towards her upkeep. When she lost her looks she let it be known that she was writing her life-story for publication, and was inundated with cash and bankers' drafts from titled gentlemen who wished not to be mentioned.'

'I cannot imagine that Lord Byron was so concerned about his reputation that he would pay to protect it.'

'Nor I,' Adrian agreed, 'he probably sent Harriette the money for old times' sake. Did he move back to Venice eventually?'

'No, The Holy Father was persuaded to annul the Contessa's marriage after this extraordinary *ménage à trois* at Ravenna had gone on for a couple of years. Byron took her to Pisa, but this domesticity was too much for him, and he left her and went off to Greece. And, of course, never came back. It was at Pisa that he wrote *Don Juan*.'

'Then he must have found his Contessa inspiring, to write a poem with all those hundreds and hundreds of verses,' said Adrian. 'But perhaps he might have written it just as easily in Kensington, if he'd met a Contessa or two there. Didn't Wagner come to Venice to compose *Tristan and Isolde*?'

'He rented a floor of the Palazzo Giustinian,' Delphine said. 'We passed it some way back on the right. He found it necessary to drape the inside of his rooms in dark red cloth to hide the frescoes before he could compose – a curious proceeding indeed. Are you an admirer of German music, Mr Thrale?'

Her tone was so disapproving that Adrian denied all interest in Wagnerian opera. Soon the gondola swooped in to the side – and they disembarked on a broad quay between two tall marble pillars surmounted by bronze lions. At this time on a Saturday evening there were a great many people strolling in the warm night air, and Adrian took Delphine's arm to steer her gently through the crowd. Adalbert and Bianca were in front, ambling across the *piazzetta* that leads into the Piazza itself. Adrian stared enthralled at the graceful stone arches of the Doge's Palace on his right and Delphine said he must take a morning off from his work to go and see round it.

They turned into the Piazza, the vast square in front of the church of San Marco. Adrian had an idea of what it looked like from the illustration in his guide-book, but the magnificence of the reality impressed him. The Piazza was about perhaps two hundred yards long, he estimated, and about sixty yards across, with three of its sides enclosed by grandiose buildings with arcades. He could hear music playing, and he saw that halfway down each side of the Piazza stood rows of tables and chairs of the two cafes that faced each other.

'We always come to this cafe,' said Delphine as they strolled towards the one on their left. 'It's called Florian's and it's been here for over two hundred years. I like things to last.'

The four of them sat down at a table under the velvet black sky and an attentive waiter took their order for coffee and cognac, and pistachio ice-cream for Bianca. The string orchestra up on its platform played a Viennese waltz, which brought a pleased smile to Adalbert's face.

'When Venice belonged to we Austrians,' he said, 'Italians came to this cafe and the Austrian officers of the garrison sat in the one opposite – Quadri's, it is called. But nowadays I am a Venetian by adoption, and I sit on this side of the Piazza.'

'Venice has never belonged to anyone except the Venetians, whoever may have occupied it by force,' said Delphine Tandy in reproof. 'That French charlatan, Napoleon, and your muddle-headed Austrians – they were no more than passing tourists who stayed too long. Even now, sixty years after Venice chose to become part of the Kingdom of Italy, it does not belong to Italy, whatever they think in Rome. It is still secretly the separate Republic it has always been.'

Adrian's attention drifted away from what seemed to him no more than meaningless debate to a contemplation of the golden arches and domes of the church of San Marco across the end of the Piazza. Stunning though it was, it was almost dwarfed by an immensely tall bell-tower standing alone to one side of it. And before he had time to ask about that, Bianca started to talk to him, and in competition with the fascination of a beautiful young girl, the appreciation of old church buildings comes a poor second.

Not that she had anything in particular to say or to ask, but he was delighted by this show of goodwill and asked her about herself. He learned that she had never been out of Italy and hardly even out of Venice, except for the family's annual stay at the Malvolio villa a few miles inland along the Brenta, and one visit to Rome with her parents, to be introduced to thirty or forty of her father's close relatives. Adrian found her to be more charming than any girl he had ever known, in addition to being more beautiful. Evidently she found him of interest, for when Mrs Tandy decided to walk back to the Palazzo, Bianca offered to take him back by gondola and show him where Wagner composed his romantically tragic opera.

'Very well,' said Delphine, 'and on another day you can show him where the man died.'

'Where was that?' Adrian enquired.

'The Vendramin-Calergi palace,' she said, 'it's up past the Rialto Bridge, not very far from the railway station. One of the Vendramins died of plague soon after being elected Doge, but that was a long time ago. I don't know what Herr Wagner died of.'

So it came about that Adrian found himself in a gondola in the moonlight with beautiful Bianca. And what was more – in a gondola with a little varnished wooden roof to conceal them from the gondolier in Malvolio colours. In spite of all the forebodings Adrian had experienced that afternoon when he heard – but did not understand – the conversation between the Count and Marina, forebodings for his own life if Count Massimo ever found out about his active interest in the Contessa, all that was forgotten now in the warm summer night and the rocking of the gondola in the wash of a passing vaporetto. So far was it forgotten, in fact, that he was unashamedly stiff inside his underwear.

They were hardly under way and heading for the entrance to the Grand Canal when Bianca turned her head to look at him and murmur, *You can kiss me if you want to*. Needless to say, he put an arm round her at once and pressed his lips to her – judging the kiss expertly to aim at conveying his keen interest, but no menace. She returned his kiss warmly, and he realised with a start that her hand was resting on his out-stretched thigh – and stroking it very gently.

At once he cupped her right breast in his hand. With no break in the kiss, she acknowledged his interest by sliding her hand up his thigh to pinch the bulge between his legs. The unseen gondolier standing on the poop behind the little cabin began to sing softly, his Venetian dialect so impenetrable that Adrian could make out not a single word – not that he cared much about folk music just then. He turned towards Bianca on the low seat and unbuttoned the crystal buttons down the bodice of her pink frock. Inside it he found a thin silk camisole, loose enough for him to put his hand down the top and feel her bare breasts. Their warm fleshiness was very exciting under his hand, though their tips were still soft.

Still the kiss continued, while Bianca flipped his trousers open and slipped a hand inside. Adrian was taken aback by the casual way she did this. If she had been a London girlfriend with him at the flicks, he would have expected this response to having her breasts felt – but she was the daughter of a foreign Count and lived in a palace and was only seventeen! And that raised in his mind the question of how far Bianca had gone in her exploration of the pleasures of sensuality. With what sort of lads of her own age did her mother and her mad and conceited father allow her to associate?

However much they might try to chaperone and shelter her, she was no innocent – this was not the first time her breasts had been felt, Adrian was sure of that. He was equally sure that some young Venetian had initiated her into the pleasures of stroking a male part. And since one thing leads naturally to another, it was more than possible that she had been fingered between the legs, although Adrian would have taken a reasonable bet that she was still a virgin. Being taken aback by her ready response was one thing, but to let his surprise get in the way of the pleasures offered by her obliging nature was quite another. He played with her breasts until their buds were firm and prominent under his fingers and his excitement grew almost frenetic at her casual handling of him. There was no possibility of getting on top of her in the gondola, he guessed, and so he was content to enjoy what was offered and let matters take their course.

Inside his open trousers Bianca's fingers moved very slowly

along his hardness and over its sensitive head. With delicacy, so as not to disturb the dreamy mood, he reached down to slide his hand under her pale pink evening frock and caress slowly up between her legs. His fingers traced lightly over her stockings until he reached her knees, when she pulled away at last from the long kiss and rested her head on his shoulder. Adrian had paused in his upward caress at the ending of the kiss, thinking that she meant him to go no further, but after a pause of two or three heartbeats, her knees moved apart and his hand was allowed higher, up between her satin-skinned thighs and into her flimsy knickers.

For Adrian this had always been one of the most enchanting moments that life could offer – the sweet belly-twisting agony of giddy-making anticipation in that instant or two before his fingers touched the curls between a girl's legs. How many times had his whole body throbbed in the grip of this pleasure – and how very many times it would again! Yet there were one or two experiences that fixed themselves in the memory and assumed the status of cherished souvenirs. There was, for example, a Sunday outing once with Jennifer Turner – a hot afternoon when they lay together in a clump of bushes, the picnic basket emptied. She had unbuttoned her blouse for him to take her breasts in his hands, and when he had fondled them enough to satisfy her, she let him put his hand up her skirt and he discovered he had made her so wet that he could feel her excitement right through her thin knickers, before he took them off.

And there was a night when he took black-haired Dulcie Morgan home to Kensington from somebody's dance. He kissed her in the taxi and felt her breasts through her clothes and stroked her thighs under her frock. They'd both become so aroused that they stood pressed together in the dark entrance-hall of the block of flats where she lived with her family, while he insinuated an eager hand up her clothes and laid it flat against her warm thigh, pausing for long moments of unbelievable excitement before feeling up into her knickers ... Dulcie was murmuring, *No, you mustn't* – but he did!

Another cherished memory was of Pamela Benson, tall and thin and long-faced, but with a plump bosom. It was autumn and she kept her coat on in the cinema – the Haymarket Plaza it was, he seemed to recall – but he unbuttoned it to give her soft and fat breasts an unsatisfactory squeeze through a thick woollen frock – before putting his hand up it. When his hand reached above her stocking-tops she clamped her thin thighs together to stop him going any higher. The struggle was delicious beyond anything words could tell – until at last she surrendered and released her grip. The arousal caused by eager anticipation was so intense by then that, when he touched bare flesh between her legs and realised that she was wearing no knickers, it was like being struck by a bolt of lightning. She knew that he would want to feel her and had come to their meeting ready for him – and her little struggle had only been for show! The thought was so provocative that Adrian's belly clenched involuntarily, and to his amazement, he squirted his pent-up desire into his own underwear.

An especially memorable afternoon was the first time that his girlfriend of the moment, blonde-haired Barbara Chetwynd, with whom he was at least half in love, came to his Chelsea digs for tea. Sitting in an armchair by the gas fire, he pulled her down onto his lap to hug her and kiss her – and ease his hand up between her thighs under her frock – gunmetal grey with a white collar, he recalled. She let his hand lie on the smooth flesh above her silk stocking, her body trembling against him, and the moment was so perfect that dusk crept through the room before he felt down the front of her knickers and touched the moist and pouting lips inside them.

All these treasured memories were as nothing to him now, in a gondola on the Grand Canal with Bianca Manzetta di Torrenegra. His hand was trembling as he felt delicately between her legs. He touched thick soft curls and guessed them to be as very dark as the hair of her head. He stroked thick fleshy petals and they parted readily to allow his middle finger to slide in. He caressed her hidden nub deftly and soon she was murmuring his name. Adrian was half out of his mind with the delight of feeling her body squirming against him, and her thighs opening and closing rhythmically on his wrist.

'We are at the Palazzo' he exclaimed in dismay, glancing out at the building that loomed up above them as the gondola slid in towards the side of the Canal.

At once she raised her head from his shoulder and called out in Italian to the gondolier behind them. He answered her in a deferential tone and the long slender craft turned away from the landing-stage and headed upstream again.

'I've told Mario we want to see the Palazzo Vendramin,' said Bianca, settling back against Adrian's shoulder, 'but if you dare look away from me to see a mouldy old building where some dismal musician died, I'll never forgive you!'

His fingers resumed their slow ravishing of her, and before they reached the bridge she gave a convulsive jolt, her body taut and arching away from the backrest. The effect on Adrian of her little climax of pleasure was swift and dramatic – his belly tightened and, through a haze of dizziness that engulfed all his senses, he gasped to feel his ecstasy pouring out into Bianca's palm.

'*Santo cielo!*' she murmured. 'Give me your handkerchief.'

He was too lost in sensation to do what she asked, his loins bucking upward in convulsive release. She plucked the white handkerchief from his breast pocket and wrapped it round his jumping part to soak up the warm flood of his desire, and then chuckled. Adrian opened his eyes to look at her – she was doing up the buttons of her bodice.

'Make yourself decent,' she said with a smile, 'Aunt Delphine will be waiting for us.'

'Bianca – I think you're adorable,' he said, 'may I come to your room tonight? I want to hold you naked, and kiss you, and make love to you for hours and hours.'

'No,' she said, kissing his cheek lightly.

'Then when?' he asked eagerly. 'Tomorrow?'

'Maybe sometime, maybe never,' she answered, and with that he had to be content.

SIX

On Sunday morning Adrian was woken by church bells – not just the bells of one church, but at least a dozen different chimes that he could distinguish. Some were close, some further off, deep-toned peals, high-pitched ringing, and most possibilities on the scale between. After a while Teresa brought his tray and threw wide the shutters to reveal a glorious sunny day.

While he was drinking a cup of *caffe-latte* the maid went into a long explanation of something or other which baffled him. He smiled and shook his head, and after a few moments thought, she started again, this time miming without words. She knelt beside the bed, her hands clasped together as if in prayer, she stood up and imitated a priest giving a blessing – she pointed to his watch, she conveyed with her fingers the idea of walking down the stairs – and her performance eventually made Adrian understand what she was trying to tell him. The family would assemble for Mass in the private chapel at nine o'clock and then have breakfast together in the Small Dining Room.

Adrian wondered if he was expected to attend the Mass. It had not occurred to him before, but Delphine Tandy and the Contessa must have converted to the Roman Catholic faith, and Bianca was automatically brought up in it. He enquired whether he ought to attend the Mass by tapping himself on the chest and looking the question at Teresa.

'No, no,' she said, and pointing at him, added with a smile, '*Protestante. Eretico.*'

That sounded enough like heretic for him to understand. He grinned and nodded, and the maid crossed herself and grinned back. She chattered on cheerfully while she brushed his evening clothes and hung them up in the huge wardrobe, and Adrian half-listened, wishing that he could speak Italian.

His complacency was shattered by a word that he thought he understood.

'*Confessionale?*' he repeated. 'What do you mean, Teresa?'

Her previous success at acting out her meaning encouraged her to fling herself into another pantomime of kneeling with eyes downcast and hands together, and whispering to someone. There could be no doubt of the significance of what she was telling them – Padre Pio heard confession before the Mass.

'Who confesses?' Adrian demanded nervously, and hoping that it was the right word, '*chi?*'

Teresa made all-embracing gestures with her arms, confirming his worst fears.

'Signora Tandy?' he asked. 'La Contessa, Signorina Bianca?'

'Si, si,' said the maid.

This was bad news for Adrian. The next time he saw Padre Pio the priest would know all about his adventures with Marina, and his little venture last night with Bianca in the gondola. As he understood the rules, priests never revealed the secrets of the confessional – but suppose the situation was slightly different for a family chaplain? Suppose that Padre Pio was so concerned about the family he served that he dropped a hint or two to the Count that the foreign visitor had played havoc with the honour of his wife and daughter! Without realising what he was doing, Adrian slid a hand under the bed-sheet to clasp his treasured parts defensively, as if the Count's paid assassin was already in the room with a stiletto in his hand.

Teresa saw how he was clutching himself and giggled. Another horrible thought came into his head – did the family retainers also confess to Padre Pio? His heart was in his mouth as he pointed to the maid and in pidgin English asked her, 'Teresa confession Padre Pio?'

She laughed and nodded and said, *Si, si*, and by means of his watch indicated that she and other servants went to confess at ten o'clock on Sunday mornings, when the family had finished their breakfast.

'My god!' Adrian exclaimed, 'when the priest hears I've had one of the maids as well as two of the family he'll think I'm a sex-maniac! He's bound to say something!'

He wanted to ask Teresa if it was absolutely necessary to her moral well-being to reveal their negligibly important escapade to Padre Pio, but it was too complicated. He got out of bed to act out his meaning, pointing to himself and to her, and then to the bathroom where the pleasant little encounter had taken place. And to remove any possibility of being misunderstood, he flicked his tassel out through the slit of his pyjama trousers and touched her white apron low down on her belly. She looked at his soft part, looked towards the bathroom door, and shook her head in vigorous denial. Adrian breathed a sigh of relief to know that at least one of his secrets would be preserved from the disapproval of Mother Church.

But he was making a mistake. This became very obvious to him when Teresa put her hand flat against his bare chest and pushed him over backwards on the canopied bed. *But* . . . he stammered, and fell silent as she reached under her black frock to take down her long-legged knickers, before gathering apron and frock round her waist and kneeling over him over his thighs. She had understood the mime to mean that he wanted to make love to her in the bathroom again, and her only objection was to standing up while he did it! By the time he had this clear in his mind, his pyjama trousers were gaping wide and his over-indulged part was clasped in her hand and she was shaking it briskly to rouse it to life.

This was quickly done, the sight of her dark fur muff enough by itself to stiffen his resolve. With her belly laid bare, she held his swollen six inches tightly between her short fingers and manoeuvred it and herself until she had brought his head up to the mark. She sat down on him to force his hard length up into her and he shivered with pleasure to feel the slow slide of her velvety folds of warm flesh along his captured part.

'Now you'll really have something to tell the priest, my dear,' he said. 'I did not expect this first thing on a Sunday morning.'

'*Ehi! Ehi! Cavallo! Trotta!*' said Teresa, and it required no knowledge of the Italian language to guess she was calling him her horse and telling him to start trotting. And with that, she bounced up and down on his embedded stiffness in a strong rhythm that made the ancient bedstead creak under him.

Through the sensations of delight that flooded through his body, Adrian marvelled at how casual love-making with the chambermaid was. She asked for no persuading, no kisses, no caresses or foreplay – he had only to indicate that he wanted her and she bared her hairy mound for him. Had he considered the implications further he might well have become anxious, but there was no time for reservations when a well-fleshed young woman was impaled on his stake.

'*Su! Su!*' Teresa encouraged him, as if she were galloping him round the Palio course in Siena.

There was no possibility that her ride could last more than a minute or two – she was ramming herself so fast and hard on him that his loins jerked up in uncontrollable spasms between her wide-spread thighs and he moaned at the feel of his desire pouring into her hot and clinging depths. Teresa gasped noisily ten or a dozen times, heaving herself up and down on him. Then she was still, and she slumped forward in the sweet lethargy of satisfaction. Adrian saw beads of perspiration on her forehead and under her chin, and he hooked a finger in the neck of her frock and pulled it down, to see the little drops that were running down the crease between her plump breasts.

She was not one to neglect her duties – in another moment she had unplugged him from herself and stood between his dangling feet while she put on her knickers. When that was done, she bent over him to dry his softening shaft on her clean white apron. Adrian lay still and let her attend to him, slightly dazed by the speed and dexterity with which she had aroused him and then relieved him of his desire. She's some sort of love-machine, he thought, you wind her up and press the switch and two minutes later it's over – you've been drained and purged of all carnal emotion. And when you are excited again, you simply repeat the process. It was very convenient, but he could see it would become unsatisfactory after a while.

He shaved and dressed without hurry, having decided against going to Sunday breakfast with the family. Every other day of the week breakfast was served in bed, and this Sunday gathering had the sound of a family ritual he would be happier to avoid. Apart from which, he was reluctant to face Padre Pio across the table so soon after letting Teresa service him. He asked her by signs how to get down to the little square beneath his bedroom window and she mimicked going down a flight of steps, along and round a corner to the left, down more steps and to the right.

When he was dressed he went out on the balcony, where

there was a square wooden chair bleached by the sun. He made himself comfortable and read while he waited for the cafe down in the *campo* to open for business. *Campo* was another word Teresa had taught him – the Venetian word for every square in the city except the big one by San Marco, which alone had the name of *Piazza*. It was not Mr Joyce's unintelligible novel he took out to read in the morning sun, but the other book he had bought in Paris – the anonymous *Madame Birchini's Revels*. This literary gem appeared to be set in Paris in the Naughty Nineties and was mainly concerned with pretty young ladies of good family being made to bare their bottoms for chastisement, for the entertainment of gentlemen who came to call on Madame Birchini, a jolly-sounding woman, in Adrian's estimation.

'Now Lavinia,' she said, 'you are in my charge and you may not interrupt me. I demand absolute submission and I shall exact the most meticulous obedience. Bend over the divan and pull your nightgown up to your hips and spread your feet apart.' Lavinia flushed scarlet with fear and shame, but dare not for her life disobey her instructions.

She lay on the edge of the divan and stretched her legs out straight backwards, so that the tips of her toes were touching the floor, and with a trembling hand she raised the hem of her nightgown level with her knees.

'What – you dare to defy me!' Madame Birchini exclaimed. 'I shall make you suffer dearly for this! Pull your nightclothes up at once – I despise this absurd coyness!'

While Lavinia still hesitated to expose her person so openly, Madame Birchini herself reached under the girl's nightgown and outraged her modesty by pulling it up so far that the whole lower portion of Lavinia's body lay bare.

'There's a pretty sight,' she cried out, 'a fine pair of legs and thighs and two plump white cheeks!' She stepped up close to the trembling girl and pressed down with both hands on the small of her back, giving Monsieur Raoul a signal to begin the chastisement.

His hand fell smack, smack, smack on Lavinia's bare behind, and she cried out in desperation, writhing in her attempt to get away from her tormentors. It was in vain, Madam's hands on her back kept her down. In her dire distress, Lavinia kicked out backwards, lifting her legs high up, while spreading them far apart, so that Monsieur Raoul had the opportunity to enjoy an unhampered view of her most intimate parts.

His burning eyes stared right into the deep cleft between her *thighs and Lavinia sobbed with shame to know that a man was staring at her most intimate secret with lust in his heart. Yet try as she might, she was unable to control the kicking of her legs and close her thighs together . . .*

Adrian stopped reading and gave himself up to a consideration of whether it would be exciting or not to smack a girl's bare bottom. The opportunity had never come his way, and he doubted if it ever would. It was possible to pay someone like Viv in Shepherd Market to let him smack her bottom – but that was not really a fair test – the knowledge of collusion would prevent any proper enjoyment of whatever pleasure there was in it. What was needed was a girlfriend of equable temperament and a sense of fun who would take a brisk bottom-slapping in good part. No chance of that with Barbara, desperately fond of him though she claimed to be. She was too gentle-natured for any robust form of sexual play – a smack across her bottom and she would burst into tears.

Soon after ten o'clock the little cafe in the square below was ready for customers – the waiter had set out the tables and the sun-umbrellas and was serving a middle-aged couple whose casual clothes suggested they were tourists. With Teresa's wordless directions in his mind, Adrian threaded his uncertain way through the Palazzo until he came at last to a door of dark wood, ten feet high and four feet wide, heavily reinforced by black metal straps with *fleur-de-lis* ends. A footman in livery appeared from nowhere to turn a foot-long key in a vast iron lock and pull the creaking door open for him. Adrian went down two broad stone steps and stood blinking in the bright sunshine of the square.

When the waiter – a man of fifty with long side whiskers – saw him emerge from the Palazzo Malvolio and stroll across to the cafe, he rushed diligently forward to pull out a chair for him and, in a frenzy of politeness, bow deeply, wish him *Buon giorno, Signor*, flick at invisible crumbs on the spotless white table-cloth, and enquire what he might have the pleasure of bringing for the Signor – and all this without a pause to draw breath! Adrian ordered coffee and settled himself to enjoy the sights of the square – the locals in dark Sunday clothes entering and leaving the battered brick church which formed one side of the *campo*, as if the Mass was a continuous performance, and the tourists who wandered past, guide-book in hand, on the trail of the next Titian or Veronese or Bellini or Tiepolo.

At lunch everyone was present – Mrs Tandy, the Count and Countess and their daughter, Adalbert Gmund – and Padre Pio in a slightly less worn-out cassock than his shiny black weekday outfit. To his embarrassment, Adrian found that the priest had taken the chair next to him and was contemplating him with an expression of active interest on his round face. By now he knew well enough that the Torrenegra mother and daughter had been defiled, Adrian suspected, and it was not at all easy to answer him calmly when he enquired if Adrian was enjoying his visit to Venice and had he yet found time to see the collection of Old Masters in the Accademia Galleries?

Soon or later he'll slip a trick question into the chit-chat, thought Adrian, gulping down his wine – some fiendishly subtle Jesuit question that will trip me up and make me reveal unwittingly that I've had two of his little flock – no, three, since by now he's heard Teresa's confession as well and knows about this morning's little hanky-panky. But the conversation remained on a polite level and Adrian was beginning to believe that his fears were groundless when, right at the end of lunch, Padre Pio asked him to come and see him at ten the next morning.

When the family dispersed to their rooms for the siesta – or whatever alternative pleased them – Adrian decided to spend an hour or two doing the job Mallards had sent him to do. In the two days he had been in Venice, only ten minutes had been given so far to looking at the German paintings. If he had been sent to an English country house to inspect pictures, by now he would be suffering pangs of conscience at neglecting his duties – but here in Venice matters seemed to move at a different and more comfortable pace. Nevertheless, he felt that he ought to make a gesture, at least.

Without a guide, and losing his way only twice, he sauntered through the maze of fading splendour of interconnecting rooms and galleries until he found himself in the Biblioteca with the leather-bound books. The two small paintings had been brought there, as he had requested, and were lying on the huge antique desk of dark walnut. Adrian opened the window-shutters to let the light into the room and then, his notebook and fountain-pen ready, he took up each painting in turn and made a very thorough examination. The elaborately carved and gilded frames were Italian, he decided, and made a century or so later than the pictures were painted. The paintings themselves were on wooden panels, as was to be expected of Cranach. They were dirty – the flesh tints of the girls and the colours of the background were dimmed by the accumulated dust of years.

He put the pictures side by side on the floor beneath an open window, propped against the wall, and pulled a chair to where he could sit and view them comfortably, the girl with red-gold hair on the right and the girl in the cartwheel hat on the left. As was usual with this painter, the two Venuses were looking at the viewer – not quite directly, but in a slightly oblique way that was part of the knowing look on their faces. *I'm standing here naked for you to look at,* they seemed to be saying, *I'm very pretty – see how round my breasts are! And my bare belly – you'd like to touch that! And you can look at the smooth little Schatz between my legs, which I'm pretending to hide with this gauze scarf – I'm sure you'd get down on your knees and kiss me there if I were to let you . . .*

Not for the first time, Adrian asked himself how the old devil had done it. These were not imaginary women – they were real girls of flesh, with fully developed personalities, young as they were. How had the elderly German Court painter with the forked grey beard persuaded these elegant eighteen-year-olds of good family to strip naked for him? And how had he conveyed that marvellously exciting sensuality – not only in the expressions on their faces but with their whole bodies – the way in which they stood with their feet apart and their bellies thrust out a little . . . and when Cranach had captured the sexuality of these enchanting young girls in paint, did he lead them to a couch in the studio and have them?

'You like to look at young girls naked, Adrian?' asked a voice behind him, and there was Adalbert Gmund, smiling.

'If they're as pretty as these two,' he answered, slipping his note-book and pen into his inside pocket.

'It is four o'clock,' said Adalbert, 'you have worked enough for today. Come with me for a little promenade and I will show you a real girl with no clothes.'

That was an invitation not to be missed. Adrian was on his feet at once, to put the paintings back on the desk where they were safe and follow the Austrian out of the library and to the great door on the landward side of the Palazzo, that opened into the square with the cafe. Adalbert was oddly attired, in a suit of Tyrolean green with a belted jacket and a green felt hat with a pheasant tail-feather rising from the band. Adrian was grateful that his companion was not wearing leather shorts at least, and was convinced that his own white linen jacket and well-pressed trousers were very much more stylish.

By narrow and deep-shaded alleys between buildings and across sun-beaten squares, and by stone bridges over back canals, they came after a few minutes back to the Grand Canal. To Adrian's surprise Adalbert led him down to the water's edge and into the public ferry waiting at a jetty for enough passengers to make the crossing worth the ferryman's while. Adrian sat down on a bench running along the gunwales, but the Venetians who joined them on board stood casually upright, while gondoliers fore and aft rowed the boat across, rocking and dipping in the wash of busy water-buses.

'You are asking yourself why we did not take one of our own boats at the Palazzo,' said Adalbert in a confidential tone of voice. 'I will tell you – the servants gossip. Our destination would be known by everyone in the Palazzo by dinner time.'

'Including Mrs Tandy?'

'I have no doubt of it. The gondolier tells the porter, who tells every footman who passes him. From them it reaches the maids, and eventually Signora Tandy's personal maid whispers it to her. The Palazzo Malvolio is like a village, where everyone knows the affairs of everyone else.'

'I find that very disconcerting,' said Adrian.

'So you should, my young friend. It is already common gossip that you enjoyed the favours of Contessa Marina in her sitting-room yesterday morning. You were seen by a chambermaid. I did warn you of the dangers.'

'Good Lord – does the Count know that?' Adrian asked, ashen-faced at the implications.

'He is one of the very few who has not been told. Giorgio, his valet, is a discreet man who protects the Count as much as possible from the little unpleasantnesses of life. You should be grateful to him.'

'But I am!' said Adrian. 'How far should my gratitude go?'

'To about fifteen hundred lires worth,' said Adalbert. 'More than that would spoil the man.'

Adrian did the calculation in his head and found it came to eleven pounds. When he got back to London he would have to invest several plausible explanations for spending Mallards' cash on girls and bribes. Even so, eleven pounds seemed a small enough sum to preserve his life from the Count's jealousy.

The ferry deposited its passengers on the right bank of the Grand Canal at the paved area in front of the fabulous Baroque glories of Santa Maria della Salute, a church built, as Adrian knew from his guide-book, to thank God for taking the plague away from Venice. Adalbet put a few coins on the bench when he and Adrian stepped ashore. *That is the custom*, he said, shrugging, *the fare is put on the seat, not in the gondolier's hand.*

He led the way through narrow streets and by a bridge over a small canal, turning left and right at little squares and between buildings until Adrian had lost his bearings. They came to another back canal, with a broad paved walk on both sides in front of three-storey buildings of crumbling brick, and halfway along, Adalbert turned into a narrow entry. Adrian followed him up two flights of broken stone steps to a small landing with a wooden door from which the paint had long since flaked away. It opened instantly to Adalbert's knock and the two men entered a square room with a tiled floor and windows that looked out over the narrow canal below. The room served a double purpose, being furnished with half a dozen wooden armchairs near the window, and a dining-table with four different chairs at the other end.

The woman who had admitted them was, in spite of the heat of summer, swathed from her thin neck down to her skinny wrists and almost to her ankles in a frock of shiny black satin that to Adrian had an old-fashioned look about it. He put her age in the late thirties. Adalbert introduced him in Italian as Signor Adrian, with no mention of a surname, and her as Signora Fosca, with no suggestion of a Christian name. She fussed about him in a flattering sort of way, smiling and chattering to herself in the Venetian dialect. When she had the two men seated, she went to a cupboard behind the dining-table.

'Signora Fosca is in mourning,' said Adalbert. 'The Italian word for it is *lutto*. I have know her for five years and all that time she has been in mourning, though it is impossible to find out for whom. She ignores questions on the subject and I think that she has herself forgotten the reason.'

Signora Fosca bought them each a long glass of a greenish liqueur and took a chair facing them. While she and Adalbert conversed in Italian, Adrian gave her a closer look, wondering how to place her. She was long-faced with thick black eyebrows arched in enduring surprise. She had a bean-pole look, lacking any observable breasts, hips or belly, so that her black frock clung closely to her body. Her hair was even blacker than her eyebrows, in tight natural curls and cut short. She smiled at Adrian, noticing his interest in her, and he raised his glass in salute to her, wondering if the curls between her skinny thighs were equally black.

Whatever assurances were required of Adalbert as to the good-will and trustworthiness of his friend were soon given. Signora Fosca nodded and smiled and left the room, and Adalbert leaned towards Adrian to explain what was happening, a foolish smile of happiness on his face.

'Signora Fosca has gone to wake her niece up,' he said. 'She was taking a long siesta. The Signora has many nieces, and she permits me to meet all of them when they come to stay with her. In return I demonstrate my appreciation and gratitude by making regular donations to her housekeeping expenses. She has a niece named Emmelina visiting her at present – a charming girl of sixteen! As I told you, my friend, my tastes are those of Lucas Cranach.'

Adrian nodded in pretended sympathy and asked himself why he had been brought here. He guessed the answer when Signora Fosca returned from the bedroom with her *niece*, as they had agreed to call her. Emmelina wore very little more than Cranach's young Venuses with their strip of gauze held across their loins – she had evidently come to the sitting-room straight from her bed, where she had been taking a siesta in chemise and stockings, or so her *aunt* would have it believed. The chemise was short, barely reaching her knees, ivory in colour and hemmed top and bottom by a broad band of machine-made lace. Her stockings were flesh coloured, gartered just above her knees, and she had neither slippers nor shoes on.

At the sight of Adalbert Gmund she uttered little cries of girlish delight and threw herself into his arms, sitting on his lap to kiss his bony forehead where his sandy hair had receded. From where he sat and watched this welcoming performance, Adrian was in no doubt that Emmelina was in no way the innocent sixteen-year-old that she purported to be. She was shorter than Signora Fosca, but inside the flimsy chemise was hidden a sturdy body with fair-sized breasts and solid hips. Her face was pretty, in an unrefined way, and her hair was the shade of gingery-auburn seen in Old Master paintings of Venetian women – Titian-red, to be polite about it.

Her effusive greeting to Adalbert completed, she pretended to notice Adrian at last and blushed in convincing confusion. Eyes bashfully downcast, she got to her feet and held out her hand – and Adrian, playing along with the comedy, stood up and kissed her hand with exaggerated courtesy. Signora Fosca made the introductions, and Emmeline apologised with becoming modesty – or seemed to, in Italian – for appearing before a stranger in so informal a manner. Adrian smiled and brushed aside her trembling words, squeezed her hand while he kissed her lightly on the cheek, and sat down again.

Certain now that she had a second admirer, Emmelina returned to Adalbert. With smiles and rapid little words to soothe him, she pushed his knees apart and stood between them, leaning over him to put her arms round his neck and tickle his ear with her warm breath. Her posture was calculated to let Adalbert glance down the front of her chemise as it hung loosely away from her bosom, and he availed himself of the opportunity with a broad smile. More than that – he slid his hands up the girl's legs inside her chemise, to stroke her bottom.

'She is a sweet child,' he said, turning his head to smile at Adrian while he handled her with no sign of embarrassment on either side. 'With her I can always do it twice.'

'My congratulations,' Adrian commented dryly.

'Look,' said Adalbert, 'see how young and pretty she is!'

He raised Emmelina's chemise up to her waist to show him her round belly. His interest caught at last, Adrian stared at the bare place between the girl's thighs where, he guessed, a tuft of thick and gingery curls had been shaved off to assist her young-girl appearance. Adalbert ran his hand over the plump cheeks of her bottom, while she smiled down at him, then felt between her thighs and fingered the bare and pouting lips she was offering him. She giggled as he pressed a gentle fingertip between them, and Adrian decided that she was twenty at the very least, with a juvenile appearance that was evidently of great commercial value to her.

In another moment she had seated herself astride Adalbert's lap, her chubby thighs immodestly wide. While Adalbert played with her, she reached down to unbutton his trousers and pull out his immodest part. She closed both hands about the shaft, so that only the purple head was visible, and whispered into Adalbert's ear. Adrian rose to his feet to leave, not amused by this unexpected display. At once Signora Fosca spoke rapidly to her *niece*, who sprang from Adalbert's lap and, holding on to his swollen part, tugged him to his feet and led him out of the room. Adrian nodded briefly to Signora Fosca and said goodbye.

She jumped to her feet to stand between him and the door, her hands plucking at his sleeves, while she spoke to him in a most conciliatory way. There was no need to understand her language – her manner and tone indicated that she was most anxious for Adrian not to leave so abruptly. She even managed to make him understand that he was welcome to have Emmelina, after Signor Gmund had finished with her. The offer displeased Adrian all the more, and when he felt her hand groping between his legs to encourage him to stay, he became angry and indignant. That this black-clad creature should think her crude persuasions enough to overcome his natural distaste! She must be taught a lesson.

He put his hands on her thin shoulders and gripped very hard while he forced her downwards, his face stern, until she fell to her knees and stared up at him in astonishment. His fingers were so tightly clamped into her shoulders that they must be causing her pain. He ignored her little cries of outrage and thrust his loins forward at her, telling her to *Take it out!* The English words meant nothing to her, but his gesture showed what he wanted, and she plucked at his buttons until she had them undone and his fast-growing part uncovered.

'No, no no . . .' Signora Fosca protested in implausible alarm, but he sank his fingers even harder into her skinny shoulders, forcing his will on her. She gave a last sob of protest and then sucked his pride into her mouth as if she were swallowing a long strand of spaghetti. Her calling might well be that of professional *aunt* these days, thought Adrian, but she had not forgotten what *nieces* did to entertain gentleman visitors. With ten or a dozen passes of her wet tongue, she had him up at full stretch and put her head back to stare into his face. Her thick black eyebrows were arched in a plain enough question – had he now changed his mind about staying until Emmelina was unoccupied?

The crudity of the enquiry, silent though it was, made Adrian even more determined to make his displeasure felt. He released one shoulder to twine his fingers in her hair and drag her long face towards his belly. *Do it!* he said in a tone that brooked no contradiction. Signora Fosca uttered a low moan of protest before she surrendered, and took at least half of his impatient length into her mouth again. He slid his feet apart on the tiled floor, and gave himself up to the thrills rippling through him from the Venetian woman's lapping tongue, staring down at the length of throbbing flesh that jutted out of his trousers. He smiled triumphantly to see Signora Fosca's dark head bobbing up and down as she ministered to him.

Total submission! he was thinking. *I've beaten her! That'll teach her!* But his sense of triumph was illusory, for Signora Fosca's experience of the potential for sensation of the human body was far greater than his. While her mouth coaxed his male pride to swell thicker and longer yet upon her tongue, she slipped a wily hand into his trousers and between his legs, to take hold of his hairy pompoms and tug at them.

Adrian gasped in spasms of delight, his hips jerking to slide his hardness in and out of the wet mouth that engulfed it. The hand in his trousers reached suddenly further, and then a thin and stiff finger probed the little knot of muscle between the cheeks of his bottom. *Ah!* he gasped in apprehension, at the very instant that the finger was thrust deep into him. A blaze of sensation like a dynamite explosion roared through his body – his legs shook under him and, with a grin on her long face, Signora Fosca sucked his passion from him in hard throbs.

SEVEN

On Monday morning Adrian kept his appointment at ten with Padre Pio. A footman showed him where the priest worked – a large and square room lined with broad shelves stacked up to the high ceiling with ancient leather boxes on which the Malvolio arms were fading into indecipherability. Padre Pio stood at an elbow-high writing desk which Adrian recognised as a fine eighteenth century piece which would fetch a good price at auction if the dilapidation were expertly restored. The priest looked up from the document-strewn surface, pushed his gold-rimmed spectacles up his forehead, and came forward to offer Adrian his hand.

'*Buon giorno*, Signor Trell,' said the fat little priest with a beaming smile on his round face, 'please to sit down while we have the discussion together. I have much of importance to say to you.'

With apprehension in his heart, Adrian sat down on a leather-seated and uncomfortable Renaissance cross-legged chair that was only held together by string. He assumed as demure an expression as he could manage, and waited to be denounced for his mortal sins of lust and debauchery with three female members of the household. What his response would be, he was still undecided – there was no point in a denial if all three had confessed to the priest – and the choice seemed to lie between shrugging indifference or an apology and a promise not to do it again. Not that there would be the slightest intention of keeping a promise like that – it was Adrian's intention to avail himself of Contessa Marina's charms and of the chambermaid's obliging nature every time the opportunity arose – and to lure Bianca as soon as possible into a convenient place to get his hand up her skirt again and see how far she could be persuaded to go.

It was fortunate, he considered, that confession was required only once a week, otherwise Padre Pio would have something else to bemoan – late last night, when the Palazzo was silent and only the rats moved in its faded magnificence, Marina had come to Adrian's room. The light was out and he was half-asleep, but it was not pitch dark in his room, for he was unable to bear the local custom of sleeping with wooden shutters closed over the windows. He was lying on his side on the antique canopied bed by the wall, and he watched her disrobe in the moonlight, first her frilly negligee and then her nightgown rustling down her legs to the floor, and it was like a scene from a fantastic fairy-tale! Her body had the luminescence of alabaster, and he stared enthralled at her well-shaped breasts, at her round flat belly, and then at the shadowy darkness between her thighs.

They lay naked and entwined, kissing and caressing each other's warm flesh, until Marina turned on her back and tugged at him to lie on her and penetrate her softness. And afterwards he had licked her body from the high arches of her little feet right up to the hollows of her throat, missing nothing in between, and then she was lying on top and making love to him with slow deliberation. They slept, and when Teresa woke him with his coffee and sweet rolls, Marina was long gone, but her expensive perfume clung to the pillows and sheets. The maid was aware of it at once, and stared at him curiously – especially at his limp tassel, for he had fallen asleep naked.

But the denunciation Adrian expected was not forthcoming from Padre Pio. The purpose of the invitation to his work-room was business, not social or moral. He waved a hand at the old boxes stacked all around the walls and explained that these were the archives of the Malvolio family, but only back to the building of the present palace in 1736, all previous records being lost in the fire that had destroyed the earlier Malvolio palace.

While Adrian digested that item of information Padre Pio shuffled the documents on his desk and selected one. He held it up and pulled his spectacles down over his eyes, read aloud a few words from it that meant nothing to Adrian, and then told him it was a bill of sale for two paintings on wood by Lucas Cranach, and it was dated 1766.

'Let me see that,' said Adrian, up on his feet at once to take the creased and almost disintegrating sheet of paper with great care from the priest's hand. The date in ink faded almost yellow was clearly enough made out – *22 Settembre*

1766. As for the rest – he asked the priest to translate.

'The pictures were bought by Jacopo Malvolio for five hundred ducats from Domenico Barbaro,' said Padre Pio, 'Barbaro is known to be a dealer who had a house near the church of San Zaccaria.'

'How much is that?' Adrian asked.

'It is difficult to calculate what these old prices meant,' said Padre Pio with a shrug, 'but five hundred silver ducats might be as much as eleven thousand lire now.'

Adrian did the arithmetic in his head and concluded that Jacopo had paid about forty pounds each for his two Cranachs – although eighty pounds in Venice then was perhaps a large sum of money. He looked at the document closely, in search of anything that would bring its authenticity into doubt, but decided that it was genuine.

'How do we know that the paintings Mrs Tandy intends to sell are the two mentioned in this bill of sale?' he asked, and the priest tapped the papers on his high desk.

'Here in the archive are catalogues of furniture and pictures and statues and books and everything else in the palace,' he answered. 'There is a catalogue of 1736, when the palace was first built and furnished, and there is a catalogue of 1769, by when much had been added to the original collection. Next is a catalogue of 1780, made after Napoleon's troops had looted Venice and much was stolen. But after Napoleon was defeated by your General Wellington and the Prussians there is a catalogue of 1816, listing all the precious objects that had been hidden from the French that were now brought back into the palace. The catalogue of 1879 was made by myself at the request of the old Count, in the first year I came here to live here. From 1775 on, the catalogues list *two small paintings on wood of young girls by Lucas Cranach* as part of the decorations of the Small Music Room, except for 1780, when most of the paintings were hidden. What more proof could there be, Signor Trail?'

'That's very impressive,' said Adrian, wishing that Italians might sometimes get his name right, 'and probably as conclusive as we can ever hope to be.'

He gave the eighteenth century bill of sale back to Padre Pio and sat down. The priest remained standing at his tall desk.

'Everything is so completely documented,' said Adrian with a genial smile, 'my congratulations to you, Father – you are an admirable keeper of the Malvolio chronicles and secrets.'

The priest stared at him thoughtfully.

'Secrets, Signor? All great families have those. Has it ever occurred to you that if confidential matters become known while those involved are alive, that is scandal? After they are dead for ten or fifteen years, it becomes amusing gossip, and when they are dead for a century or more, what was once scandal is suddenly history and is written about by scholars. This is what you call the irony, I think.'

'I've never considered things in that light,' said Adrian. 'Do you have an example of what you mean?'

'Many,' said Padre Pio. 'Are you acquainted with the history of Italy and our great families?'

'Not in detail.' Adrian confessed.

'Then I shall give you examples from your own country. Now if I were to tell you that your charming Prince of Wales – Edward – goes every afternoon at five o'clock to the home of a lady who is the wife of a Member of your Parliament, and passes two hours with her alone – that would be a scandal, and therefore I shall not say it. Instead, we may consider his grandfather, your King Edward VII. It was well known in the capitals of Europe that Mrs Lillie Langtry was his mistress, and after her the Countess of Warwick, and then Mrs Alice Keppel. It was also known that on his visits to Paris he committed the fornications often with many famous actresses and courtesans – for example, with Madame Hortense Schneider, with Madame Sarah Bernhardt, with Miss Cora Pearl, who was English-born, with Madame Giulia Barucci and La Belle Otero, to name a very few of them. But the point is that he has been dead just long enough for his sins to be an amusing topic for conversation.'

'I never knew all that,' said Adrian, 'only about Mrs Langtry and Mrs Keppel. I've read Cora Pearl's memoirs – she was a real goer, if the book's genuine.'

'If I may continue,' said Padre Pio, pushing his spectacles up above his eyebrows and wagging his head in disapproval of Adrian's enthusiasm, 'I shall show you how scandal and gossip eventually turn themselves into history and engage the earnest attention of solemn professors in universities. Consider your King George I, who died two hundred years ago. His fornications with Madame von Schulenberg, and with Madame Kielmannsegge who was also his sister, though illegitimate, were a scandal while he was alive, then amusing gossip in the reign of his son – and are now investigated with great seriousness by historians, to find out what influence these German ladies had on English policies towards the rest of Europe.'

'You are better acquainted with English history than I am,' said Adrian, amazed by what he had heard. 'Why is that?'

'I have never studied history,' said the fat priest. 'In this I find that I am compelled to agree with the notorious atheist Voltaire, who said that history is no more than the record of the crimes and misfortunes of mankind. My interest lies in the genealogy of the great families of Europe, and my position here gives me access to the Malvolio documents and Library.'

'But how does that include the English Royal Family?' Adrian asked in surprise. 'How do you know that King George committed incest with his sister?'

'The Royal Families of all Europe are related to each other, Signor Trail, and if we had enough time I could tell you many things. You have heard of Giacomo Casanova, I am sure, who was born here in Venice in the year 1725 and grew up to be a cheat, a seducer of women, a heretic and a Freemason?'

'I have read *his* memoirs too,' Adrian said proudly.

Padre Pio shook his head sadly at this further evidence of depravity and continued 'Then you will know that his mother was Zanetta Ferussi, an actress seventeen years old when Giacomo was born, and that he was not the child of her husband, Gaetano Casanova, but an illegitimate son of the owner of the San Samuele theatre where she appeared on stage.'

'Yes,' Adrian answered doubtfully, not clearly recalling much apart from the accounts of Casanova's seductions.

'But what you cannot know from the Memoirs is that Casanova's younger brother Francesco was an illegitimate son of your English King George II.'

'How is that possible?' Adrian enquired, sceptically.

'Zanetta toured many of the capitals of Europe and was loved by rich men wherever she went. The Prince of Wales found her very interesting when he saw her on the London stage and made her his *petite amie*, as the French say. Her son Francesco was born in London in 1727, the year in which your Prince of Wales became your King George II.

The details appear in letters and journals – and it is far enough back in time to be a subject of importance to historians, not merely gossip any more, and not scandal.'

'That's fascinating,' said Adrian. 'Do you suppose that I may in the remote future become a tiny footnote in the long history of the Malvolio family, as the Englishman who made it possible to restore the Palazzo by a sale of some of its contents?'

'There is no Malvolio family, Signor,' the priest answered. 'It ended when Count Rinaldo's airplane was shot down in 1917. It is possible that you may become a footnote in the history of the Torrenegra family, if it is ever written.'

That remark removed any lingering doubt that Adrian might have had whether the Contessa and Bianca had mentioned him in their confessions. Padre Pio was obviously aware of his frolics with them, and with the chambermaid.

'It may be difficult for a priest devoted to God and celibacy to understand the strength of the carnal desires that a man of my age feels,' said Adrian in some embarrassment.

'Not in the least,' Padre Pio replied suavely. 'I am almost seventy and I have been confessor to the Malvolio since 1879. In the great days before 1914 every possible expression of sexuality was confessed to me in the chapel here – and some that I found difficult to believe. We are all weak and sinful, Signor Trell, but God forgives us, even a Protestant like yourself.'

Adrian was relieved to know that he was not condemned for his adventures. If he had understood the priest correctly, scandal had a way of turning into chit-chat if kept secret long enough – but he could expect there to be ructions if his depredations amongst the females of the Palazzo came to the attention of the Count. Partly reassured by this, he turned the subject back to paintings, on which Padre Pio proved more knowledgeable than Adalbert Gmund. When a degree of professional understanding had been established, Adrian probed delicately into the history of the Malvolio family in recent times, especially into the doings of the Old Count – Rinaldo's father – and the priest told him something of Count Paolo's dashing reputation around European capitals in the Naughty Nineties.

They talked on until after midday, Padre Pio standing at his desk the whole time and showing no sign of weariness, in spite of his age. Eventually Adrian remembered he had to telephone London to explain the delay in his return. He asked how best to go about it, certain that a long distance call to an overseas number would prove to be complicated.

He was dismayed to learn that it was very nearly impossible. If he presented himself at the main Venice Post Office, Padre Pio explained, an operator would try to connect him with London through a chain of cities all the way across Europe. This might take hours, according to how busy they were in Verona or Milan or Turin or Lyon or Dijon or Paris or Dover . . . and naturally Post Offices in Italy closed in the afternoon to allow their employees to go home for siesta . . .

Asked for his advice, the priest suggested it would be easier and very much faster to send a telegram. He even produced from the litter on his desk a proper Post Office telegram form, and after a moment or two's thought Adrian composed a few words for his chief in London:

++++MR LUCIUS BOSQUET MVO MALLARDS CURZON STREET LONDON STOP GERMAN PAINTINGS HOLD GREAT PROMISE BUT MORE TIME REQUIRED TO INVESTIGATE PROVENANCE STOP WILL COMMUNICATE PROGRESS AS SOON AS POSSIBLE STOP ADRIAN THRALE PALAZZO MALVOLIO VENICE++++

Without looking at what was written, Padre Pio folded the form, put it into an envelope and rang a little brass bell that stood on his desk. After a minute or two's delay there appeared a liveried footman, to whom the envelope was handed with long and detailed directions in Italian that Adrian did not understand.

'There – it is on its way to London, your message,' said the priest with a beaming smile, 'and it is almost time to eat.'

Lunch was served in the Small Dining Room, and Delphine Tandy and Bianca were the only others present beside Adrian and Padre Pio. Count Massimo and Marina were out for lunch, though not together, as Bianca told it, and Adalbert had gone out for the day. As Adrian enjoyed his first course of good thick soup of *pasta e fagioli*, he asked himself what the residents of this most illustrious city of Venice did all day long? Naturally they would have friends – the Count would surely go wherever pretty young men of his own persuasion congregated. And Marina would have women-friends to meet in the fashionable cafes and restaurants of the city.

And in view of the Contessa's keen interest in the exercises of love, it seemed very unlikely to Adrian that she had lived in absolute chastity before he arrived in Venice. Surely there was a lover or two she dropped in on, away from the palace and the eyes of her husband. Adrian summoned up delicious memories of the night, when Marina's smooth naked body writhed under him in the moonlight, her hands cupping his face as she kissed him hotly. And then a different image entered his mind uninvited – Marina on her back with her slim legs spread wide while a dark-haired Venetian plunged his stiffness into her and made her cry out in ecstasy.

I am not jealous, Adrian told himself firmly. The thought was ridiculous – that emotion was reserved for her husband. All the same, the prospect of another man taking his pleasure with the Contessa was not comfortable to linger on, and to banish it Adrian speculated on the whereabouts of Adalbert Gmund. Now *his* friends in Venice were very hard to imagine, apart from Signora Fosca. Adrian was fairly certain he recalled Adalbert telling him that he went to see her twice a week, so he would hardly be there again today. It was mysterious to Adrian why Adalbert had taken him to meet Signora Fosca and Emmelina, but as the visit had not been a success, maybe there were other *aunts* with young *nieces* to be visited to find a menage with more chance of captivating Adrian.

Mrs Tandy broke in on his thoughts by asking what progress he had made in his examination of the pictures and he answered her not wholly truthfully that he had not yet reached a conclusion as to their possible price of sale at auction. He had informed his superior in London that he would require more time – at least that much was true. Mrs Tandy nodded and smiled graciously and said he must be sure to see the Guardi frescoes and the Tiepolo ceilings in the palace – and he mustn't miss the collection of drawings by Longhi.

The truth was that Adrian had never had so marvellous a time in his life as these past few days in Venice. He meant to stay on at least until the next weekend, although strictly speaking his mission was at an end and he could catch the next train for London. But duty had lost its hold on him – and who could blame him for that? In an amazingly short period of time he had pleasured himself on a beautiful Contessa and a homely chambermaid and an excitingly well-endowed rider on express trains – and he had been pleasured by the hand of a Contessa's daughter and the mouth of a professional aunt. Small wonder that he proposed to prolong his stay in this Wonderland. His hostess had urged him to remain for as long as he liked, so it was only a question of stringing Mallards along for a while by sending important-sounding telegrams.

Bianca was looking very young and pretty in a short-sleeved ivory silk blouse, tucked into a taffeta skirt checked in black and white, that just covered her knees. Adrian chattered away cheerfully to her, making her smile and blossom like a delicate flower beneath a gentle summer sun. After a while she asked him questions about his work, and he contrived to amuse her with a tale or two of comic dramas fought out in Mallard's sale-rooms.

'I don't know much about painters and their paintings,' said she, 'they look well on the walls as decorations – at least, the ones that are pretty, not the horrid subjects – but otherwise I walk past them without hardly even seeing them.'

'But the Lucas Cranach pictures caught your eye,' Adrian said with a slow smile, 'you said that one of the girls resembled a friend of yours – I'm afraid I've forgotten her name.'

'Maria-Luisa Dandolo. It's just like her.'

After that it required very little to persuade Bianca to show him the resemblance, and when the excellent lunch was finally completed they sauntered together through the gold and marble splendours of rooms and galleries to the Library, to which the Cranach pictures had been taken for Adrian's convenience. The window-shutters were closed to keep the sun out and the Library was in semi-darkness. Adrian opened one set of shutters and the soft light reflected upwards from the waters of the Grand Canal danced on the ceiling.

He took the paintings from the dark walnut desk and leaned them against the wall below the bookshelves, in the light, and drew Bianca gently by the hand across the room, to sit with him on the board window-seat.

'Which of them is like your friend Maria-Luisa?' he asked.

'The girl in the big round hat,' she answered at once.

'A facial resemblance, you mean, of course.'

The naked Venus in the cartwheel hat had the round little

breasts that Cranach sought out in his models, and the way she stood threw her belly into a prominence that was almost plump. The modest strip of gauze between her hands was transparent and did nothing to conceal her mound and the blonde down on it.

'No,' said Bianca thoughtfully, her head turned a little to one side as she studied the painting, 'it's not really the face so much – this girl has a more innocent look than Maria-Luisa – it's her figure and the way she's standing. I've seen her stand like that a million times.'

'Naked?' Adrian asked lightly.

'Why not?' she replied, turning on the window-seat to stare at him boldly. 'We practically grew up together. We learned how to make love by playing with each other.'

Adrian slipped an arm about the beautiful seventeen-year-old so close to him on the thin-cushioned seat and touched his lips to hers. Bianca leaned towards him and returned his kiss with enthusiasm. And while they kissed, he undid the buttons of her ivory-white blouse and put his hand down inside her chemise to feel her soft breasts – and she opened his trouser buttons and felt inside until she had hold of his fast-lengthening part.

'I knew this was going to happen as soon as you started to talk about paintings,' she whispered, her breath hot against his ear. 'Wait while I lock the door.'

She skipped across the Library and turned the key of the tall double doors by which they had entered.

'No one will try to come in,' she said, 'but if they do we'll hear the handle rattle and do a quick vanishing act through the servants' door.'

'Where's that?' Adrian asked, looking doubtfully round the book-lined walls, 'I see no door.'

'Over there on the right,' she answered, sitting down beside him again, 'it's hidden behind fake books – it swings out when you pull, if you pull at the right place.'

Her warm hand was back in his trousers, stroking briskly.

'Just like you, really,' she said with a giggle, 'you'll soon swing out if I pull the right place.'

Little thrills were rippling through Adrian's belly and with a sigh of unalloyed delight he put his hand between her thighs, where the skin was like satin, and felt up into her loose silk knickers. The moment was here – that soul-shaking moment before he touched her most secret place. His breath was rasping in his throat and his hard-standing six inches leaped so strongly in Bianca's hand that she breathed *Oh!* And then his finger-tips encountered thick curls and soft warm flesh.

He caressed her very gently, using only the tip of his middle finger, and making no attempt to part her petals yet. Her oval face was turned up towards him and through a long passionate kiss her eyes remained open, large and dark-brown, and so close to his own, their expression sensual and curious at the same time. He felt his head spinning with excitement as her fingers traced patterns of bewitchment along his pleasure-loving part that made him shiver with sensation.

'I want to see you naked,' he murmured, 'come to my room with me now, and we can undress completely.'

'No,' she said at once, 'that's not safe in the daytime with servants wandering about. Stay here!'

And she skipped away from him again, this time to the hidden door in the shelves of books. She dragged a heavy wooden chair across to it and jammed the door by tilting the chair back and wedging its top under a convenient shelf. She came back smiling to the window-seat and started to take off her clothes.

'If we hear anyone at either door, we'll vanish through the other,' she said.

In delight he watched her remove her blouse and taffeta skirt and then her chemise, baring her breasts for his approval. She took off her shoes and stockings and paused for effect, pushing out her young-girl belly a little to emphasise the rich curves of her body, as did the painted Venuses staring at her. Adrian thought she was the most exciting girl he had ever seen naked – young as she was, she had the full breasts of her mother and her figure already held a hint of Italian sumptuousness.

'Kiss me, Adrian,' she murmured, kneeling at his feet, her slender arms about his waist. His hands trembled with desire as he cupped her bare breasts, and his high opinion of Venice went soaring into sublimity. What more perfect way could there be to pass an afternoon than to play with a beautiful naked girl in the magnificent Library of a palace overlooking the Grand Canal? The famous old definition of Heaven being the place where *pâté de foie gras* was served to the sound of golden trumpets faded into total insignificance in comparison with Bianca's offering.

'*Carissimo*,' she whispered, while he kissed the pink buds of her breasts, 'could you love me? No don't answer yet.'

She pressed her mouth delicately to his and had him lie on his back along the worn green cushions of the window-seat. The initiative for the moment was hers, he recognised, and he was content to let it be so for now. She unbuttoned his trousers and slid them down to his knees, bared his swollen and shaking part and ran her finger-nails along its length.

'You're very beautiful, Adrian,' she murmured, 'I'm going to make you fall in love with me.'

The exquisite sensations that rippled through Adrian's body amplified in his thoughts a comparison that engaged his rapt attention – the comparison of Bianca with her mother. They were so very similar, he thought, in that both displayed a delicacy of approach that concealed the same sexual rapacity.

'I'm a little in love with you already,' he sighed, pleased to join in her game.

'That's a start,' she said softly, 'but before I've finished you'll be so head over heels that you'll be on your knees at my door every night begging to be let in!'

She wriggled out of his grasp and lay on her back beside him on the broad window-seat, her hand clasping his leaping part. She pressed her lips to the corner of his mouth and asked why he didn't touch her – and immediately he twisted himself about to slide his hands along her slim legs and kiss her warm belly. He stared in delicious anticipation at the silky brown tuft of curls between her thighs, his self-willed part bounding so very furiously in her hand that she could hardly restrain it. And here it was again – this enchanted moment before he touched a girl between the legs – this moment that sent an intense *frisson* down his spine to make his six inches vibrate in a rhythm of its own!

His finger-tips slid lightly over the warm pink lips beneath the curls and then he leaned over her to kiss them. Bianca lay trembling slightly, her satiny thighs well parted, waiting for the moment when his wet tongue pressed between her secret lips to find the centre and source of her sensations. She drew in a long gasping breath.

'Come to me, Adrian,' she said softly, raising her knees and parting them widely in invitation to him to lie on her.

She held his impatient part and guided it till he felt its hot swollen head enveloped by soft moist lips. His entire body was shaking with passion as he pushed slowly up into her warm wetness, the ease of his penetration disabusing him of the idea that she was a virgin. The pleasure of entering her was so tremendous that he knew he was on the brink of climactic release. Down below on the Grand Canal, a tourist on a passing water-bus stared up amazed at the unshuttered window and hurriedly pointed his Kodak at the scene.

'Kiss me, kiss me!' Bianca sighed.

Her long slender legs opened wider, her bare feet rising off the seat and up into the air, then her ankles crossed behind his back to hold him. She moaned softly in ecstasy to feel his stiffness slither into her depths, and Adrian thrust fast and hard, so aroused that he was unable to control his actions. Her belly jerked up rhythmically to receive him, and she began to cry out in staccato little shrieks. Perfection on this sublime scale was more than the human nervous system could bear for any longer than four or five seconds – Adrian gasped in triumph and poured his throbbing desire into her belly.

Long after he had finished she held him prisoner in her soft body, her legs entwined over his waist, her arms tightly round his neck. And while she held him there, she told him that she was *stufa di Venezia* – fed up with Venice, and she wanted to go away. He listened amazed while she told him of her plan to run away to London with *him*, which was why she wanted him to fall in love with her. For a while Adrian thought she was joking, but soon it was apparent that she was in solemn earnest.

His victorious part shrank in dismay and he summoned all his tact to attempt to dissuade her from what she planned. However delightful the prospect of constant access to her charms, there was little doubt in his mind that her parents would blame him if she ran off, and that would surely be fatal to his future at Mallards, and perhaps even to his life, if her father fell into a fit of snobbish rage.

EIGHT

After his love-making with Bianca in the Library, Adrian went that same night to her bedroom, by invitation. In between their pleasures she again begged him to take her to London with him when he left Venice. He played for time, being very naturally unwilling to commit himself to so dangerous an enterprise. Yet he was reluctant to refuse outright, for fear she might clamp her legs together and tell him to go. In this way they passed most of the night together, in alternating satisfactions and dissatisfactions, and the question remained unresolved when he crept back to his own room in the gathering light of dawn.

The maid Teresa gave him a strange look when she came with his breakfast an hour or two later. Evidently she thought that Contessa Marina had spent another night with him, though there was no trace of her perfume about the bed. While he drank his coffee she tidied the room and hung up his clothes, and when he put the tray aside she came to his bedside to smile at him and touch his shoulder while she asked, *Amore?* But after his long night with the delectable Bianca Adrian had no immediate desire to make use of the maid's readily-available facilities, and he did the most difficult thing in the world – or attempted it – to refuse a woman's offer of her body without giving offence.

Teresa sniffed when he smiled and shook his head, and turned away from him to get on with her work.

Adrian shut himself in the bathroom and stayed a long time, shaving and soaking in the tub, hoping that she would finish and go away before he emerged again. Needless to say, she did no such thing. She waited him out, and when she became too impatient to wait any longer, she bustled into the bathroom, without even a *scusi, Signor* and put herself with her back to him while she cleaned the wash-basin and polished the mirror above it.

Her sullen face warned Adrian that he had made an enemy of a friend. Supposing that she hinted to the Count her suspicion that the Contessa had visited Signor Trill's room? With a sigh of resignation, Adrian climbed out of the bath and said, *Teresa* in as affectionate a tone as he could manage. She turned slowly and unwillingly to face him, her face impassive as she stared at his wet nakedness. He pointed to the big towel and smiled at her most winningly, and when she brought it to him, he raised his arms and stood still, his pose inviting her to dry him. She grumbled in Italian, and he guessed she was telling him she had to get on with her work and had no time for his nonsense.

All the same, she wrapped him in the thin towel and rubbed at his back and chest. *Si, bene,* he said, hoping his words would indicate approval to her, and her hands descended to his belly – and then his bottom, giving it a brisk rub through the towel. He grinned at her and moved his feet apart on the tiled floor, and when she did not respond, he took her hand and pressed it to his dangler. She shrugged her shoulders and did nothing – and her nothing showed him very clearly that she was not easily to be got round. A demonstration of his eagerness was required to efface the memory of his earlier refusal.

Gritting his teeth – though only metaphorically – he took her by the waist and walked her slowly backwards until the large white wash-basin was pressed to the back of her thighs and she could go no further. She stared impassively into his face, her brown eyes close to his, and he reached down to get his hands under her skirt and between her plump legs. This seemed to him not to be an appropriate occasion to indulge his anticipatory delight in delay before touching her – too much was at stake to bother with his own pleasure just then. Without hesitation, his hands were in her loose knickers and between her thighs. His thumbs split her fig and probed the soft pulp inside.

'*Delicatamente, Signor,*' she sighed, and her cheeks flushed a pale pink. The big towel had slipped from his shoulders and lay on the floor behind him, and his licentious part had grown to full length in her hand. She said things to him in her soft Venetian Italian, incomprehensible, though the general drift was clear – she was rebuking him for his indifference earlier on and forgiving him now that he had changed his mind. Not that she was content to let it go at that – her words went on and on, seemingly without end, and Adrian concluded that she would make some unlucky man a nagging wife one day.

To put a stop to the continuing flood of words, he shut her mouth by kissing it, and said, *'I've got to have you, Teresa – rest your bottom on the basin!'*

His words meant as little to her as hers to him, but there was no mistaking their import. While Adrian hitched her skirt into her apron-strings to keep it up out of the way, and dragged her knickers down her chubby thighs, she spread her feet well apart and lifted her bottom onto the basin. Adrian gave a silent sigh of relief and pushed straight into the slot he had prepared with busy fingers.

'*Dio, Dio!*' she moaned as he gripped her by the waist and stabbed hard and fast into her.

Adrian did not intend to waste his strength by squirting it into the maid. His thought was to go at her briskly until he rode her over the edge and, while she was lost in her cataclysm of sensation, to pretend by means of a few short stabs and some plausible gasps that he had done the deed. He had heard of many an instance when women had faked a climax to please a partner – why shouldn't he play the same trick on Teresa?

He reckoned, of course, without the sensuality of his nature. With his cheek against the maid's cheek, he thrust manfully to hasten her release, and to sustain his stiffness he closed his eyes and imagined that he was making love to beautiful Bianca. In the cinema of his thoughts he called up images of being in her bed only a few hours before, and projected these entrancing pictures onto the screen of his mind. It was Bianca pressed against him, her bare belly on his, her warm softness embracing his shaft and welcoming it deeper and deeper.

The film ran on in his brain, sixteen frames a second of the most fervid fantasy – Bianca's little hands on his shoulders to hold him close to her, Bianca's breasts squashed against his chest . . . and his ruse worked, and worked better then he thought it would, for of a sudden he found himself stabbing into the belly against him with a frenzied determination that did not spring from his conscious will, but from his own desire. Before he could check himself and play out his original scheme, the crucial moment had arrived and was past – and his legs were shaking and his breath gasping as he poured his ecstasy into Teresa's heaving belly.

For the time being the situation was saved, but later on that morning he almost collapsed with fright when Count Massimo came looking for him. Adrian put his hands in his pockets so that their trembling would not be noticed, and claimed to have much to do. The Count refused to be put off, and with the reluctance of a man being led to the foot of the gallows, Adrian went with him to the landing-stage on the Grand Canal. They got into the speed-boat, the Count explaining that he had no time for slow and old-fashioned gondolas.

Without being told, the boatman in faded purple and yellow Malvolio livery moved into the stern and sat down, while Count Massimo took the wheel. Adrian's bottom landed with a thump on the front seat as the Count opened the throttle wide and the long slender boat roared away from the Palazzo, and out in a sharp turn into the water-traffic of the Grand Canal. The Count did not deign to sit down, he stood with one hand on the top of the windscreen and the other on the wheel, sliding the boat in tight and dangerous turns between heavy barges loaded with crates and boxes and all manner of goods.

They were going very much faster than the regulations allowed or commonsense suggested. Gondoliers lurched and waved their arms to keep their balance as their craft pitched in the white wash of the speed-boat, some flung curses that were drowned by the roar of the engine. The Count created maximum havoc with a thin smile on his handsome face, his silver-grey Borsalino hat on the side of his head, and Adrian asked himself seriously if the man could be deranged in his mind. Adalbert Gmund's words came back to him vividly – how an admirer of the Contessa had been found floating face-down in the lagoon off the island of San Giorgio. What about an admirer of the Contessa who had been in bed with the Count's daughter the night before – where would he be found floating?

The boatman was present, and perhaps a witness would hamper the Count's thirst for revenge. On the other hand, the boatman was an old family retainer, and probably believed as firmly as the Count himself that besmirchers of the family honour ought to come to an unpleasant end. The only redeeming point Adrian could think of was that the boat was racing *up* the Grand Canal, in the direction of the Rialto

Bridge. Eventually they would reach the top end, by the railway station. San Giorgio was the other way. Not that one stretch of water had much advantage over another as a place for a drowning. Between the station and the mainland lay two miles of open lagoon, crossed by the long bridge on which Adrian had been given a warm welcome to Venice by Gina Luzzi. If he was dumped over the side of the boat with a crack on the head half way across and well away from the bridge, that would do for him as well as anywhere else.

He very nearly went over the side when the speed-boat shot under the Rialto Bridge on a collision course with a water-bus that came chugging unexpectedly towards it round the sharp bend. The Count whirled the wheel over hard and slammed the throttle open to the limit – the speed-boat lay far over on its side and Adrian clutched at the seat with a cry of alarm as he was almost thrown into the churning water. The water-bus went by so close that the abuse of its helmsman was very audible, even over the scream of the speed-boat engine. Not that the Count was put out of face for a moment – he made an extensive gesture with the hand that should be holding the wheel – a gesture that no one could interpret as other than grossly offensive.

The speed-boat came upright again, still at full throttle, and sliced through the gondola traffic like a knife through soft cheese, drenching the goggling tourists with their cameras and straw hats. Adrian held on for grim life, and through the water-streaked windscreen he saw coming into view up ahead on the right the palace Bianca had taken him to see by gondola – the one where Wagner died. That outing was when he kissed her for the first time – and more than that – it was the first time he had put his hand up her clothes. Could it be that the Count had somehow discovered that his daughter had been interfered with on this stretch of the Grand Canal and had brought the man responsible back to the scene of his misdeed to drown him?

Adrian's heart pounded and he closed his eyes tight in horror as the Count wrenched the wheel over hard left and pointed the prow of the speed-boat at the buildings on the canal side, only twenty yards away. The boat and its passengers would be smashed to matchwood and bloody pulp against the stones of an ancient palace – and then the engine was cut and Adrian opened his eyes as the boat shot into a narrow side canal between high walls, its speed falling off rapidly. The walls were of crumbling red brick, with close-shuttered windows and a heavy door or two at the top of steps leading out of the water. Further along the boat glided beneath a footbridge connecting alleys on either side, and the Count slid it expertly alongside a small quay and sprang ashore.

With thanksgiving in his heart that he was still alive after so eventful a boat ride, Adrian climbed up on to the stone quay and looked about. They had come to a small square, with houses along two sides and a tall brick church forming the side facing the canal. Without a pause, the Count strode towards the chairs and tables of a small cafe on the right, and Adrian trotted after him. The waiter evidently knew his distinguished customer and bowed almost to the ground, addressing Massimo by his title half a dozen times in one sentence. He also knew his tastes, it seemed, for without any order being given, the drinks appeared in less than two minutes.

Adrian looked doubtfully at the violet liquid set before him, but the Count was already raising his and wishing him *chin-chin* – a greeting supposedly English, though Adrian had never heard it spoken before. He repeated the words politely and took a tentative sip of his ice-filled drink. It proved to be *crème-de-menthe frappé*, which on reflection seemed not inappropriate to one of the Count's preferences.

'Look here,' said Massimo in his competent though accented English, 'I have been wanting to talk to you in confidence. You are a man of the world, I believe, a man of intelligence.'

Oh dear, thought Adrian with a sinking heart, *an introduction like that means trouble anywhere in the world. I'm about to be warned off. But off what? His wife or his daughter?*

Fortunately, it was neither. The Count wanted to explain that it was unthinkable for Delphine to sell any of the treasures of the Palazzo Malvolio. When Adrian asked why not, if she owned them by the bequest of the last of the Malvolios, he was told a tale of confusion and uncertainty. Perhaps there were no more Malvolios, but there were distant connections who had a claim, said Massimo, and an action at law was in progress. When Adrian asked for how long the law-suit had been proceeding, and when it was thought it might be settled, the Count said eight years so far, and as to how long it would continue – he shrugged and thought that so complicated a process could not be brought to a conclusion before another ten or fifteen years.

Adrian imitated the shrug and said he saw no reason to advise Mrs Tandy not to sell. Massimo tried another approach, saying a dear friend of his had very valuable art-objects to dispose of, and if Adrian undertook the business, there would naturally be a percentage for him personally, that his company would not know about, apart from whatever official commission his company took on the deal. This was, of course, on the understanding that he would drop Mrs Tandy's business completely. The entire affair sounded suspicious, but Adrian decided to play along for a time until he found out more.

'May I know the name of your friend?' he asked, beckoning the waiter to bring two more of the ice-cold violet drinks.

'Certainly, Mr Troll,' said Massimo, his words and manner breathing integrity and good faith, 'my friend is no less an international personage than the Princess Zita.'

The name meant nothing to Adrian, and he enquired if it was possible to meet the lady and talk about her *art-objects*.

'Naturally,' said Massimo, 'that is where we are going now – to her palazzo for lunch. One more drink while I tell you about this great lady.'

The waiter came scurrying at his casual gesture, and this time he brought doubles.

'The Princess is not Venetian,' said Adrian, trying to show off with an item of information gleaned from his guide-book, 'for a Republic can have no Princes or Princesses. The Venetian ruling classes only became Counts and Countesses when the city was handed over to the Austrian Emperor, after the defeat of Napoleon.'

'But she *is* Venetian,' Massimo replied, not at all impressed by Adrian's knowledge. 'She has been married several times, and her last husband was Prince Ivan of Bulgaria. When he died most tragically she came back to her ancestral home. You will find her charming.'

'Tragically? He was killed in the War, you mean?'

'In a manner of speaking, yes, he was a casualty of the War. He was massacred by the wretched peasants on his country estate for some grievance they thought they had – they were particularly hungry, perhaps, or a village girl had been handled more roughly than usual in the chateau – who can say what goes on in the minds of peasants? Zita was able to save some of the better art-objects before the soldiers were sent to put down the rioting.'

After yet another of the violet drinks *for the road* Adrian's cheerfulness had returned and he was pleased by the prospect of meeting an international personage, as the Count described her. In his elevated state of mind he asked the Count to call him Adrian, and even went so far as to address him as Massimo. The Count's brief and sour smile testified to his feelings, but he let it pass, and Adrian's intake of alcohol blinded him to his gaffe. The waiter hovered about them with a scrap of paper in his hand, and Massimo very graciously allowed Adrian to pay the bill. They strolled across the little square in the sunshine, through a narrow and shadowed alley alongside the church, over a footbridge above a green-scummed and empty canal, and so to a square of small shops and houses.

One whole side of the square was dominated by a four-storey palazzo in a style that Adrian had learned to classify as Venetian-Gothic – an edifice of brick that the centuries had weathered to dusty pink, tall and narrow windows with pointed arches like an English church, balconies of enlaced stonework across the frontage. One side of a huge dark wooden double door was thrown open by a servant and in they went, Massimo swaggering in his tight-waisted suit and the two-tone shoes, Adrian looking about him with interest, a happy smile on his face. Another man-servant conducted them up the statutory grand staircase and to a large salon where Princess Zita was holding court to a dozen or more of her friends and acquaintances.

She and Massimo advanced on each other with little soprano cries of delight. He bowed to kiss her hand, then they touched cheeks and repeated their little cries of joy, almost like two exotic birds in a mating ritual. Adrian was introduced – he too kissed the heavily-jewelled hand extended to him – and was rewarded by being drawn into the light hubbub of conversation around the Princess. The company consisted almost exclusively of men, he saw, his hand shaken by Roberto and Giulio and Nino and Emilio and Sandro and Attilio and others whose names passed him by hazily. Mainly they were very young men, he noted, not one above twenty, apart from Massimo and another silver-haired Count in his fifties.

Besides the Princess there were only two other women,

and the family resemblance of their features made him think of them as sisters. Both were in their thirties, very fashionably dressed, with scarlet-painted finger-nails and bright predatory eyes. It stuck Adrian that they were in the wrong place to be hunting prey, unless some of the young men were ambidextrous.

As for the Princess Zita, he hardly knew what to make of her. She was older than he had expected – fifty at least – but well-preserved, as they say. She had kept her figure well – her bottom and belly had not been allowed to spread, and her bosom was impressively prominent under her Paris-made clothes. What she wore was simple, but elegant and unmistakably expensive – a mid-length smock in emerald-green shantung, over a skirt of the same that fell to an inch below her knees.

Her mouth was painted a bright flame red, her eyebrows were plucked to a thin line and darkened, the lines on her face were well concealed by expensive make-up. Most spectacular was her hair – it was the rich Venetian golden red that Titian favoured in his paintings of women – and she wore it piled high on her head. Her throat showed her age, but around it was a string of large matched pearls. Not being a complete fool, Adrian assumed that henna played a major role in holding the years and grey hair at bay.

Without considering what he was doing, he kept drinking from the glasses put into his hand by attentive servants – they were not in livery, as at the Palazzo Malvolio, but in black suits. The glasses contained what he took to be sweet champagne at first, but then recognised as Asti Spumante. By the time the Princess led the way into the dining-room, he was in a very joyful mood. The room was large and beautiful, a treasure-trove of paintings and sculpture, the food was delicious and the wines excellent, and he was seated next to the Princess herself.

She chattered to him about London and the many friends she had there, about the state of opera in Venice, about the couture-houses of Paris, about winter cruises to South America, and many another of her interests. Adrian chattered back, borne along on a tide of alcohol, and eventually he found that she was talking to him about icons. It was an effort to switch his brain back to paintings, but he recalled that was why Massimo had brought him here. She had a small collection of icons, she said, which she might consider disposing of, if she could be assured of a proper price for them. Not Greek icons, she explained, but Slav icons, in the Bulgarian Orthodox style. They had belonged to her late husband, Prince Ivan.

Adrian had never to his knowledge seen a Bulgarian icon, but he assumed them to be much like Russian Orthodox icons. Warily he said that he would have to see them before offering a view of their sale value. The Princess nodded and smiled incessantly and promised he should see them before he left, and the meal continued through its five courses until fruit and coffee were on the long table. The time by Adrian's wrist-watch was twenty minutes to four, but he didn't believe it. Princess Zita said she would take him to see the icons, and he rose unsteadily to his feet and followed her out of the dining-room.

They were climbing a staircase which seemed to become steeper and steeper, so that he was grateful for Zita's arm round him to help him upwards. Even that was not enough when they got to the top, and he had to lean against the wall.

'I think you need to rest, Adriano *caro*,' said the Princess, 'and then you will feel better. I will show you where you may lie down for a little while, then you shall see my icons.'

His arm over her shoulders to support him and steer him, she got him through the nearest door. He found himself sitting on the side of a canopied bed, in a large room made cool and dark by the shuttered windows.

'Take off the *cravatta*, Adriano, you will be more comfortable without it,' she said in a soothing tone, and she was at his side, her fingers busy with the knot of his tie. 'Yes, you will be so much more comfortable without it, and your English jacket – let me help you with it,' and she slid it over his shoulders and down his arms and away.

'Isn't that better?' she asked, 'Yes, much, much better dear Adrian. Lie down and rest for a little – I will help you.'

She lifted his legs up on the bed and assisted him to stretch himself out at full length on his back. The palm of her hand rested lightly on his forehead.

'There! Now you can rest. But your face is so flushed – are you too hot, *caro*? Yes, I see that you are – it is the wine you have drunk that makes you hot. Be still and I shall help you to be cooler.'

Adrian lay somnolent and uncomprehending while she undid the buttons of his white shirt all the way down and pulled it open, to let the air cool him a little. He felt her fingers trailing lightly over his bare chest.

'So smooth and tender,' she said appreciatively, 'not black and hairy like a monkey. You are very beautiful, *Adriano mio.*'

'I shall be all right in a little while,' he said, making an effort to return her courtesy. 'Please forgive me for spoiling your luncheon party – I think the heat and the wine were too much for me.'

'The party is not spoiled,' said she, her long thin fingers brushing back his chestnut hair from his forehead in a calming way, 'everyone is still talking and drinking and telling indiscreet stories about you and me. They enjoy that very much. I must take care of you, until you are strong enough to see my treasures.'

'If I rest for twenty minutes I shall be fine,' said he.

'Excellent! I shall let nothing disturb you,' she answered, her finger-tips still stroking his chest. 'I think your belt is too tight and constricts you. You will feel easier if you loosen it – let me do it for you.'

He felt her fingers struggling with the buckle of his belt and then she was undoing his trouser-buttons. In his befuddled state it took a little time to realise what she was at, and by then she was running her hands slowly along the insides of his thighs, in his underwear.

'Magnificent,' she said, 'such long strong thighs! I admire the tall men like you.'

Quite casually, she took his lifeless part in her hand and looked at it.

'But this is so soft and weak,' she exclaimed, 'this is very impolite towards a lady!'

Her scarlet-nailed fingers tugged at his tassel and rolled it between them, displaying a certain familiarity with male parts and their ways. Adrian sighed in frustration when nothing happened, and his legs twitched irritably.

'It's as I thought,' Zita observed, 'men are brave and hard enough when they are with silly young girls who know nothing and can be seduced. But with a woman of experience, you are all like little boys – and I fear that you may burst into tears.'

'Please accept my most sincere apologies,' said Adrian, his voice faint, 'this is a rare and unfortunate occurrence.'

'Why, of course – but on the condition that you allow me to know best,' Zita retorted at once.

She leaned over him, and he felt her hot breath on his belly as her lips wandered downwards towards the join of his thighs.

Confused though he was, there came into his mind the thought that the initiative was certainly not his in this encounter. If he had been given a choice, he was far from sure that he would have made any advances to the Princess Zita. To say she was old enough to be his mother was a truism – she might even be old enough to be his grandmother! It was just as well that nothing could happen in his drunken condition, or when he slept it off he might have a feeling of self-hate, besides a headache!

Zita was very well versed in the ways of men, and undoubtedly had some suspicion of what was passed through his fuddled mind. She erased his awkward reservations by nuzzling her face into the curls on his belly, and then kissing his thickening part – for he was surprised to see that it was responding to her! Her wet tongue darted out to flick over the head she had unhooded and shudders of pleasure ran up his spine.

For a moment or two she slipped the whole purple head into her mouth, to let him feel the warmth and softness, then pushed it out slowly with her tongue and stood up by the bed. Adrian turned his head on the pillows to watch her pull her expensive Paris smock over her head and throw it carelessly aside. Off came her skirt and her silk chemise, to reveal a heavily-boned bust-bodice with ribbon shoulder-straps. When she removed that, her soft and massive breasts hung down slackly halfway to her belly button. She smiled encouragingly at Adrian while she bent over to slide lace-trimmed knickers down her thin legs. And in spite of all, his stiffness jerked when he saw her in only her stockings and a narrow white suspender belt.

The thick tuft of curls between her legs had been dyed to the same rich dark red as the hair of her head. Adrian reached out in wonder to touch this unexpected work of art, and she moved her feet apart on the floor, and he stroked the long soft lips between her thighs. Anticipation had aroused her, and without a murmur she let him slide three of his fingers joined into her. Her hips wriggled with pleasure, and she supported her sagging breasts on her hands, while she tickled their russet tips with her thumbs.

'I've never seen a woman with one that colour before,' said

Adrian, drunk enough to preserve the polite formalities.

Zita began to breathe loudly and jerk her belly backwards and forwards in the motions of love-making, her red-haired split so hot and slippery that Adrian thought she was in the throes of a climax already. That idea excited him greatly and with fingers hooked inside her he dragged her onto the bed with him.

'Lie on your back,' he said, 'I must have you.'

'But no, you are too tired, my poor Adrian,' she murmured as she stroked his face with curved and feline fingers. 'It is you who must lie on your back while I do it to you.'

'No, that's out of the question,' he said, utterly confused, 'that would be no way to repay your hospitality, Princess.'

By then she was on her knees beside him. She held his wrist and rubbed the palm of his hand over her creased belly and down between her thighs to her golden-red thicket, murmuring that he must feel how wet he had made her. He made an attempt to assert his manhood by sitting up to get his arms about her and force her to lie on her back – but effort on that scale was beyond him. Instead, it was Zita, a toothy smile on her painted face, who pushed him down flat and, her unhitched stockings hanging loosely about her knees, straddled him with wide-splayed thighs.

Her scarlet-nailed fingers combed through her thick fleece, holding his rapt attention for as long as she chose – then she opened her fleshy petals with one hand while the other held his now rampant part at the right angle to spike herself on. Her knees moved outwards while she lowered herself and forced him in deep – and at once she began to ride him, panting loudly in her eagerness. Her huge unsupported breasts flopped up and down before Adrian's glazed eyes, their swollen buds puce against her pale skin.

'Zita, your hospitality is overwhelming,' Adrian gasped.

'I like my guests to go away satisfied,' she replied, and she leaned forward to dangle the tip of a long slack breast to his mouth. He sucked it in and used his tongue on it while she bounced on him. Soon she was murmuring continuously, and as her excitement grew keener, she lapsed from English into her own language. The endearing tone of her voice suggested to Adrian that she was telling him he would be welcome in her Palazzo at any time. He giggled drunkenly and her wet breast slid from his mouth. He looked down the length of his body and sighed with a strange pleasure to see himself entrenched in her henna-red nest, his hands clenched in the flesh of her thighs.

'*Si, Si,*' she said, her voice jerky. '*Si, caro!*'

He stared up into her face, and saw her red-painted mouth was drawn back in a fixed smile – and happily for his ease of mind he failed to recognise triumph and mockery in her expression. He lifted his head from the pillow to catch her dangling breast again, but his drunkenness confused his sight so close-to, and instead of two red-tipped comforters swinging over his face, he could see four. He giggled again to feel how her slippery flesh was gripping and milking him with ruthless skill.

'This is the most . . .' he began, then couldn't remember what it was he was going to tell her.

'*Caro!*' she moaned back, heaving up and down on his belly, '*ah, che bello!*'

She groaned and cried and sobbed loudly, sucking in her breath and blowing it out like a porpoise, while she rode him with an unexpected spryness. The enthusiasm of her movements kept her spongy breasts flopping in an hypnotic rhythm, smacking on her belly on the down-stroke and soaring almost to her shoulders on the up-stroke. So much soft female flesh on the move – Adrian was entranced by the sight and sound of it!

'Give me!' he moaned.

Her hand shaking with passion, Zita stuffed the whole end of her left breast into his open mouth and he sucked at it as if he were a baby. *Carissimo!* she gasped and the furious speed of her ride advised him of a fast-approaching climax. There was no time to rack his brain to recall what it was he wanted to tell her, for she reached the peak of arousal and announced it with a long cat-like shriek. For some seconds her body was rigid and motionless, as if turned instantly to stone by her extremity of sensation, then she fell forward. Her breast was dragged out of his mouth, and her pair of flabby monsters smacked his cheeks in her fall. She lay heavily on him, her sweating flesh pinning him down on the bed. Her mouth was wide open and pressed on his and she was making rasping noises in her throat.

Trapped underneath her squirming body, a violent shuddering overcame Adrian. A full awareness of his situation dawned for a moment in his fuzzy brain – this Princess worn-out and used-up in thousands of beds had amused herself casually with him as an after-lunch entertainment! And he had let her, being too drunk to refuse! He gurgled incoherently and tried to slide away from under her stifling weight. But matters had gone too far to be checked now, and his body betrayed him. Zita held him in a long sucking kiss that dragged his tongue into her mouth – and at that moment his belly clenched and squirted his elixir into her. Her body rolled on him, and while his breath fled, the sucking grasp of her belly on his embedded part drained him in spurting jolts.

NINE

On the morning after his misadventure at the hands of Princess Zita, Adrian awoke with a headache and a sense of humiliation. He had never got to see her Bulgarian icons, and in retrospect he thought it possible she had no such works of art. The offer to show them was her equivalent of a man promising to show his etchings to a timid girl, to lure her up to his flat.

The shutters of his room in the Palazzo Malvolio were closed, for which he was grateful, his head being too uncertain to take the full light of a sunny Venetian morning. He lay with closed eyes, trying to ignore the voices and sounds of people walking across the little square below his window. He wore only pyjama trousers, and had thrown aside the bedsheets in the night, but he was hot and sweating. And worst of all, Zita's perfume still clung about his skin – a sweet and heavy attar of roses scent, with which she evidently drenched herself. The more aware of it he became, the more oppressive it seemed, until he gagged and feared he would be sick. But the nausea abated, and he lay in a half-doze, waiting to feel better before making any decisions.

In this distressed condition of mind and body, it was all too easy for him to recall the feel of Zita's naked flesh pinning him to the bed and squirming in ecstasy on him. She had sucked his tongue into her mouth at the very instant she had forced an unwanted climax upon him – the memory of those seconds churned his stomach in his body. Suddenly his mind was made up – Venice had allowed the Carnival mask to slip and he had seen the other face of the city. Not the clear shining face that had so easily seduced his senses, but a face worn-out with the exploits and escapades of long-ago. A city with long flopping breasts and a tuft of grey hair dyed red between flabby thighs.

The job he had been sent to do for Mallards was finished,

and had been for days. Sending the telegram to London was an excuse to stay on and enjoy himself. But the enjoyment had gone stone cold on him at Zita's lunch party and what he most wanted to do now was return to London and the comforting arms of his regular girlfriend. He decided that he would say goodbye to Mrs Tandy that very morning and catch the evening train for home. Making the decision brought a sense of peace to his troubled emotions, and he sank into a light doze almost at once.

The noise of the shutters being opened to let in the sunshine woke him. He rolled over and saw Teresa standing at the windows in her plain black frock and long white apron. She wished him, *Buon giorno, Signor*, in an irritatingly cheerful tone and brought her antique silver tray to the bed, plumped up his pillows and poured coffee for him. She was beaming at him and casting sly glances down his body – and a bleary glance showed him that his useless part was lolling out in plain sight through the slit of his pyjama trousers.

If the maid was hoping for any joy of it on that morning, she was sadly mistaken, Adrian thought. He swallowed half a cup of coffee and conveyed to her in mime that he had drunk too much the day before and had a hangover. It took some time, but she at last understood what he meant, removed the heavy tray from the bed, settled him down again, indicated midday on the dial of his wrist-watch, closed the shutters to darken the room, and went away to let him sleep it off.

Princess Zita had not been content to violate him once, for that was how he categorised their encounter to himself. In the dire drunkenness that made him her captive, it had seemed to him that hardly more than a few moments had passed since she straddled him and drained him of his virtue before her naked, sweating flesh was on him again, flattening him on the bed. She had reversed position, to bring her mouth into action on his wet and shrunken part, in order to raise it to full strength again. Her red-dyed tuft was near his face, presenting him with a close view. He wondered fuzzily how many thousands of men – tens of thousands – perhaps hundreds of thousands – had pierced that voracious split and gratified it.

Then Zita was sitting astride his thighs, facing him again, and rubbing his useless dangler against her henna-tinted tuft, cooing like a dove and trying all she knew to resurrect it. But to no avail – Adrian slid into unconsciousness. When he came to it was early evening and he was alone on the bed. He dressed as best he could, his headache thunderous and his stomach churning like a tub of boiling tar, and staggered on unsteady legs down empty passages and stairs. Eventually a manservant found him wandering about and in reply to his question informed him that the Princess had gone out to dinner. With a sense of relief at that, Adrian asked to be shown to the door, and was soon out in the square where Massimo had initiated his downfall with strong and evil violet drinks.

He wandered about in a daze until he found the Grand Canal and a gondola to take him back to the Palazzo Malvolio. He went straight to his room, threw off his clothes and collapsed into bed, waking with a vile headache at dawn. But by eleven he was feeling better and stood under the shower for twenty minutes to wash away his lingering malaise. He dressed quickly, determined to be out of the room before Teresa returned at midday. Seeing him so well recovered, she might very well expect him to avail himself of her facilities, and for that he had no appetite. His mind was made up – he was leaving Venice that day, and what he had to do was find Mrs Tandy and say goodbye to her.

He made his way to the Library where the Cranach paintings had been taken for his examination – the Library which became memorable for another reason entirely – it was here on one of the window-seats that he had made love to beautiful Bianca. No one was there, so he took the paintings, one under each arm, and went to find a servant. A passing footman said that he knew where Signora Tandy was to be found and led him through suites of rooms decorated in tarnished gold and yellowing white, their double doors folded back to present long views of threadbare magnificence. They came to a place Adrian had not seen before, the liveried footman bowed and withdrew, leaving him to knock briskly on a tall gilded door and go in.

As if he were in a Hall of Mirrors, he found himself in yet another suite of connecting rooms, their doors open to give a long vista. By Malvolio standards the room he had entered was small, but beyond it, through double doors, he saw a dressing-room with vast polished wardrobes, a huge dressing-table with an oval Baroque mirror, adorned with carved wooden cherubs whose gold leaf was peeling away. Beyond the square dressing-room lay the largest bedroom he had seen outside the Palais de Versailles, with a gigantic canopied bed that stood on raised steps in the centre.

Before he had time to scrutinise this further, a maid working in the distant bedroom saw him and hurried to close the doors.

'Mr Thrale,' said Delphine Tandy's voice, 'I didn't expect to see you until lunchtime, if then. Are you better?'

This evidently was her private suite of rooms, thought Adrian in some dismay, silently cursing the footman who had brought him here. He was in the sitting-room, where Delphine sat on a faded pink velvet chaise-longue, wearing glasses and holding a copy of the Venetian daily newspaper.

'Do forgive me for bursting in on you like this,' he said. 'I can never get your servants to understand what I am saying. 'Yes I am feeling much better, thank you.'

He had forgotten about the efficiency and speed of the Palace grapevine — naturally she knew that he had rambled back drunk yesterday evening, and almost fallen into the Grand Canal when he tried to climb ashore from the swaying gondola. Only one leg had gone in to the knee before the gondolier grabbed him, and the Palazzo porter came trotting to the rescue and helped him inside.

'Your brother-in-law took me to lunch with Princess Zita,' he said, knowing it was pointless to dissemble, 'and I'm afraid I rather disgraced myself.'

Delphine laughed, put her newspaper down and took off her tortoise-shell reading glasses.

'Do sit down,' she said solicitously, 'you look a little pale still. Would you like coffee, or something stronger, to aid your recovery?'

'A cup of coffee would be very welcome,' Adrian said, very grateful for her suggestion. The orange wooden chair facing her looked more valuable than comfortable, but he sat on it.

Delphine rang a little silver bell that stood on a red-lacquered table beside her. The black-frocked maid bustled in from the dressing-room and was despatched to the distant kitchens to fetch coffee.

'If it is any comfort to you,' said Delphine, 'you are not by a long way the first young man to drink too much at Zita's and make an ass of himself. It's by way of being her speciality.'

'I guessed something of the sort,' Adrian replied, trying to sound unconcerned, miserably uncomfortable though he was with the shameful thought that Delphine Tandy knew what fate befell drunken young men in Princess's Zita's palace. Her next words did nothing to ease his mind.

'Did she show you her collection of icons, Mr Thrale?'

'There was some talk of it at lunch, but that's as far as it went,' he answered evasively.

The expression on Delphine's face was one of kindly interest, but she was mocking him, he was sure of that. To be laughed at was not a thing that happened to him often, and especially not by so superb a woman. And without any doubt, Delphine Tandy was superb, casually dressed though she was in a sleeveless red and yellow silk blouse over a white pleated skirt. It was obvious she had expected no visitors that morning, for her face was innocent of make-up, except for a discreet touch of lip-rouge. Her chestnut-brown hair was piled neatly on top of her head and held by a pair of dark tortoise-shell combs.

Adrian stared into her grey-green eyes and saw the mockery in them. He took a deep breath to dispel his embarrassment, then shrugged and grinned at her.

'Are there really any icons?' he asked.

Delphine laughed again and assured him that the late Prince Ivan's collection was very fine indeed. Before Adrian could ask any more questions, the maid returned. She set a large silver tray with a pie-crust edge on the low table near Delphine and served the coffee. When she turned to leave, Delphine spoke to her in rapid Italian, and Adrian thought he heard a phrase much like *not disturb*. In the circumstances, that was just as well, for he feared that the next twenty minutes were going to prove difficult for both of them.

'I see that you've brought my paintings with you,' Delphine said nonchalantly, as if she had only just noticed them, 'have you come to talk to me about them?'

Adrian had put them on the parquet floor when he sat down, leaning them against a leg of his chair. He drank his coffee and frowned slightly while he considered his words.

'Do you know very much about these pictures, Mrs Tandy?'

'Only what others have told me. Padre Pio has shown me the catalogue entries all the way back to when they were bought in the eighteenth century. Mr Gmund assures me that paintings by Cranach fetch a lot of money at sales. What else is there to know?'

'Paintings by Lucas Cranach are very valuable, that much is true,' said Adrian somewhat awkwardly, now that the moment had come for plain speaking, 'but these two pictures I came here to look at are not the ones listed in the 1769 catalogue. They are not the pictures referred to in the bill of sale of 1766.'

'But that's utterly absurd. These are the only two paintings by Cranach in the palace. They must be the ones listed.'

'These two paintings are not by Lucas Cranach,' said Adrian. 'They are forgeries, made no more than fifty years ago.'

'What nonsense!' Delphine exclaimed, her cheeks blushing a pretty pink in her emotion. 'How can you make so extraordinary an assertion – where's your proof?'

'You asked Mallards to send an expert,' he answered, hoping to prevent the temperature of the discussion from rising. 'I'm the expert. These pictures are expertly and beautifully painted in Cranach's style. They're not copies of actual paintings by him – or none that I know about. The subjects are perfect, the colours and the treatment is correct. They're not Cranach – but they are originals.'

'I really don't see how you can be so very sure of that, Mr Thrale,' said Delphine, a tiny frown-line making its appearance between her eyebrows. 'I have documentary proof that they are by Cranach. What do you have?'

'A pair of eyes. And these two Venuses are so good that they deceived me at first. Then I saw the difference, though it took some time. The reason I know these Venuses are not Cranach's is that they are lifeless – the man who painted them was compelled to concentrate so tightly on reproducing Cranach's technique that there was no creative energy left over to put life in them – assuming that he was capable of that in the first place.'

'I'm afraid I don't understand what you are saying,' Delphine said slowly. 'Can you be more precise?'

Her request presented problems. Doubt of the authenticity of the pictures had first invaded Adrian's mind when he was making love to Bianca in the Library. The two paintings were leaning against the panelling beneath a bookcase and he was staring at them across the room while Bianca explained why she thought one of them bodily resembled her friend Maria-Luisa – whom she had seen naked many times. And with his mind ablaze with lubricious images of the two pretty seventeen-year-old girls naked in each other's arms, he had put his hand up between Bianca's thighs, where the skin was like satin.

The moment of enchantment had arrived – he felt up into her loose silk knickers, his breath rasping in his throat, making himself wait to savour the spell to the full before he touched Bianca's warm and secret place. *Oh!* she breathed gently, and his finger-tips brushed lightly against curly hair and soft flesh. Her face was turned up towards him, her dark-brown eyes open and very near his, their expression sensual and curious at the same time. The impact was so tremendous that the falsity of the paintings revealed itself, and while he was kissing Bianca passionately, his glance slid sideways towards the pictures, to compare the painted look in the eyes of the two Venuses with the look he had just experienced in reality.

Naturally, it was out of the question to tell Delphine that in credible detail, and so Adrian tried to explain as best he could that Cranach's models had a livelier expression on their pretty faces than was here depicted. Delphine said she had no idea what he was talking about and suggested he showed her what he meant on the pictures themselves. So it came about that he found himself sitting next to her on the faded pink velvet of the chaise-longue, holding up a painting in one hand and using the other to indicate the details of what he was struggling to put into inoffensive words.

The painting he held was of the naked Venus in the cartwheel hat – the one Bianca said resembled her friend. He pointed out to Delphine the provocative posture of the model, standing so as to throw her little belly into prominence and push her round little breasts out further than Nature had intended. Delphine said she could see what he meant, and that the girl who modelled for the artist had obviously been a minx, young as she was. Adrian nodded in complete agreement and drew her attention to the girl's sly smile and the knowing look in her eyes. Delphine looked hard, looked twice, looked doubtful, and said that must be in his own imagination, for she could see nothing of the sort.

'Exactly!' said Adrian. 'You can't see it because it's not there – and it would be if Cranach had painted these pictures. He looked at his young models with eyes of sexual desire, and he painted it into the picture. These are not his work.'

Delphine refused to accept his verdict and there developed

a long wrangling discussion. Eventually she took the painting out of his hand and put it on the red-lacquered table, joined her hands in her lap and turned to him with a smile.

'What am I to do with you?' she asked.

Adrian took the question to be rhetorical and said nothing. A moment later Delphine answered her own question by taking his face between her hands and kissing him. Her lips were full and warm and soft, and their touch on his instantly obliterated any final lurking trace of self-contempt occasioned by the Princess Zita's abuse of him. His arms went round Delphine at once and he returned her kiss with the greatest of pleasure. Her mouth opened to let his tongue in, and in another moment he had her silk blouse out of her waist-band, and an eager hand up inside it, to feel her plump breasts through her brassiere.

For five agonising heartbeats he was mortally afraid that her breasts would, like Zita's, sag down towards her belly if deprived of support. That would cool his ardour faster than a bucket of water over him, and bring to a sudden and dismaying end the warm friendship that seemed to be developing. But all was well – he undid the brassiere and with his hand ascertained that Delphine's breasts were only a little slack – no more than her sister Marina's. Not that a comparison was required, but it was proposed by his imagination anyway.

Perhaps she guessed something of his mood, for she did not touch him after that first kiss of encouragement. She lay back against the sloping end of the chaise-longue, her eyes closed, and let him do whatever he liked. He undid the buttons of her red and yellow blouse and pulled the open brassiere up her chest out of the way, so that he could see her full breasts while he handled them, and then while he kissed them, until their russet buds stood firmly under his tongue. She surprised him by saying that she had wondered since the first time she saw him what it would be like to be made love to by him.

She turned and put her legs up on the chaise-longue, and then stretched herself at full-length on the faded pink velvet, her hands joined under her head in surrender, her bountiful breasts offered for his pleasure. He kissed them and stroked them again and again, breathlessly deferring any greater delight, until Delphine unfastened the placket of her white skirt and asked him to take if off for her. He slid it down her legs and away, and kissed her round belly and prominent mound through the thin *eau-de-nil* silk of her knickers.

The silk was so thin that through it he could see the dark shadow of her curls. For a little longer he denied himself the supreme pleasure of feeling inside the flimsy knickers, and was content to let his trembling hands lie on the smooth skin above her silk stockings. But her legs were shaking and her closed eyelids were tremulous, he saw, and he eased her knickers down her thighs and over her knees, and then to her ankles and off altogether, gripped by the intensity of emotion that he was experiencing.

He gasped aloud as Delphine drew up her knees and parted them with deliberate slowness, spreading her long thighs and opening herself to him. He stared down, hardly able to breathe, as he saw that the tuft of chestnut-brown hair between her legs had been trimmed to a small neat triangle. He stared mesmerised at it and then at the pale and tender hollows of her groins, and the fleshy lips that seemed to pout at him. Still postponing the enchanted moment when he touched her there, he stood up and removed his jacket and tie. Delphine's eyes opened and she smiled affectionately at him and whispered, *Show me*. At once he ripped open his trousers and let his stiff and twitching part leap out into sight.

She looked at it, and smiled up at him again, the adoring and welcoming smile of a woman whose lover is ready to mount her and carry her up to the topmost peak of ecstasy. Adrian sank to his knees on the wooden floor, aroused almost to delirium by the sight of the long lips between her thighs, put his mouth there and kissed her in wonder. The thought of making love to her had been far from his mind when he came to see her that morning, but his revived self-esteem urged him to seize his luck with both hands. He dropped his trousers to his knees, lay on Delphine's bare belly, and guided himself into her with an eager hand.

'Oh, Adrian, my dear man!' she exclaimed as he thrust slowly home to the hilt. Her feet rose up off the chaise-longue as if her slender legs were about to cross over his back and hold him tight, but second thoughts seemed to prevail, and only her knees gripped his hips, and that lightly and in a way that was comforting. He was already sliding in and out of her, not furiously but with a strong and stately motion that heightened his self-esteem with every stroke. Delphine was still offering herself passively for his pleasure, her only movement being a small thrusting of her loins up against him with fast and nervous little twitches.

It was all happening so marvellously that Adrian could hardly believe it. The comparison forcing itself into his mind was not with Contessa Marina any more – it was with Bianca. Making love to her in the Library had been a superbly sensual treat, and in her bed that same night he had repeated the experience twice. But for all the delight her youth and beauty had given him, she was outmatched now by her Aunt Delphine, almost thirty years older than her niece, but endowed with a body that seemed a perfect instrument for love-making.

As his emotions rose in a throbbing crescendo towards their summit, Adrian stared down in wonder at the face below him. Delphine's green-grey eyes were staring at him with gleaming desire, her mouth was open a little to her rapid breathing. The climax of her passion came quickly and easily while he watched – her arms tightened about him to hold him close to her body, while her mouth stretched wide in a long silent moan. Her back arched up off the chaise-longue, so that Adrian was drawn into the depths of her soft belly – a sensation so thrilling that he gushed his desire into her instantly.

Afterwards, while they lay side by side in each other's arms, Delphine broke into his pleasant languor with a question about the paintings.

'What?' he asked, collecting his thoughts.

'You said my paintings are copies and only fifty years old – I asked how anyone could know a thing like that?'

'Not copies, forgeries, and I told you how I know that. When they were painted is a trickier question. Whoever produced them is a master of his trade, and I'm sure that a close scientific inspection would not give much away. But I've had the advantage of talking to Padre Pio about the Malvolio family, especially the old Count, as he calls him – Count Paolo – who died a year or two before his son Rinaldo brought you here to the palace.'

Delphine looked at him thoughtfully.

'Count Paolo's way of life was spectacular,' Adrian went on. 'He moved between Paris and London for twenty years and more, leaving his wife and son in Venice, while he enjoyed himself on a scale that can only be called magnificent. Your Padre Pio is a discreet man, but his pride in the Malvolio archives he keeps makes it possible to find out some interesting things about the old Count.'

'What things?' Delphine asked. 'That he was a *bon viveur*? That was never a secret.'

'How could it be, given his ostentation?' said Adrian with a smile that betrayed a distinct envy of Count Paolo Malvolio's advantages in life. 'He loved expensive women, and he showed his gratitude most generously. From the pictures, billets-doux, letters, notes, bills, newspaper cuttings and other souvenirs, it is clear that his more celebrated mistresses included the Princess de Sagan, Lady Mordaunt before and after her divorce, the Duchess de Mouchy, Mrs Lillie Langtry, after she ceased to be the Prince of Wales' *petite amie*, Catherine Walters, who was known in London Society as Skittles, several of the dancers at the *Moulin Rouge*, a couple of world-famous ballerinas from the Paris Opera, Madame Adelina Patti, the prima donna ... I can't remember all the others names at the moment.'

'I was presented to the Prince of Wales as a girl,' Delphine said, 'at a Ball at Londonberry House, if I remember correctly. He was a most charming old gentleman, but even then I wondered how he managed his lady-friends with the paunch he had on him. It would be like having a thick cushion between, and I couldn't think how he'd be able to put anything inside them, unless he had one a foot long. I was a virgin then, and the prospect of finding myself in bed one day with a man with a foot-long part terrified me.'

'And have you ever met a man so monstrously endowed?' Adrian asked, conscious that at six inches he could offer no more than the average man.

Delphine's hand slipped down his belly, tickling him in a way that sent shivers of pleasure through him, and gave his limp dangler an affectionate squeeze.

'No, never,' she said with a deep chuckle. 'I've always found your size perfectly satisfactory for its purpose. As you have demonstrated.'

'Thank you, Delphine,' he said, using her name for the first time. 'I'm delighted you found me to your liking – I thought you were absolutely wonderful.'

'Not too fat and middle-aged for you, then?'

'You? But like Cleopatra, age cannot wither you, nor custom stale your infinite variety,' he answered, adapting what little he remembered of Shakespeare's words to his purpose. 'But you know, until you mentioned it I'd never thought of the problems a fat man must encounter in bed. And if his partner also has a paunch sticking out in front, love-making becomes difficult to the verge of impossibility! The missionary position is clearly out of the question – they must tackle things another way.'

'How?' Delphine asked, sounding innocent of all such arcane matters, as if lying on her back were the only posture she had ever tried. 'Standing? Impossible! Sitting? Nothing changes for them. Then what?'

'Am I to believe that you have lived twenty years in Italy and never once seen Raimondi's famous Love Position pictures? Why, Adalbert Gmund has one he claims is an original.'

'Oh, that print of the woman who looks like Marina, sitting across a man's lap with her back to him, you mean? That's not a very comfortable position for the woman. And anyway, it would be useless with a very fat man, because she wouldn't be able to get her bottom close enough in for him to put it inside her.'

'I daresay, but what I had in mind was another position – the man lying flat on his back and the woman sitting across his thighs. Then the two bellies could rest against each other and neither would be in the way.'

'Yes, I see what you mean,' she said, 'but what has this to do with my German paintings?'

'Very little, unless Count Paolo grew fat with good living. The only portrait of him I have seen in the palace shows him in his prime, at about thirty, very elegant in evening-dress.'

'I don't know what he was like in his later years,' Delphine said. 'As you say, he died in Paris before Rinaldo brought me here.'

'Aged fifty-eight, in an expensive brothel,' said Adrian. 'I have seen a copy of the French police report in Padre Pio's archives. The point I am making is this – for hundreds of years the Malvolio were very rich. They built palaces, bought great works of art, and generally lived like Lords. Since the time of Count Paolo they have been poor. Forgive me if I sound presumptuous, but it is obvious that Count Rinaldo had little to leave you but this decaying palace.'

He was afraid that Delphine might take umbrage at his plain speaking and that would be the end of it. But she said nothing, only stared pensively at him and waited for him to continue.

'From these well-established facts,' he said, 'I deduce that

Count Paolo was forced to start selling off works of art from the Malvolio collection to finance his expensive pleasures. And to keep what he was doing secret, he had good forgeries made to put in their place. It would take me ages to go round the whole palace and decide what genuine works you still have – if any.'

'You have a vivid imagination,' said Delphine. 'Have you ever thought of writing novels? I'm sure you've read Elinor Glyn's *succès de scandale* – you obviously have a taste for tales of torrid passion.'

'The famous *Three Weeks*, you mean?'

'Three weeks of love-making on a tiger-skin rug. You'd enjoy that – the tiger-skin, I mean, not just the book.'

'That I would! Is there one in the Palazzo? Was Count Paolo ever a big-game hunter?' Adrian asked.

'All his life, as you've seen from the archives. But his prey was more dangerous and far more fascinating than wild animals.'

'You say nothing to my conclusions about the dispersal of the art collection – does that mean you accept I am right?'

'I say nothing because your conclusions are too ridiculously romantic to take seriously,' said Delphine, with a fond squeeze of his awakening part. 'I can't offer you a tiger-skin, but my bed-cover is a Gobelins tapestry brought from France when the Palazzo was built and furnished. It's faded a little, but you can see that it's authentic. Would you like to make love to me on that?'

What red-blooded man, what adorer of women, what connoisseur of art could turn down such an invitation? In less than five minutes Delphine lay naked on her huge canopied bed, and Adrian on the steps beside it was stripping his own clothes off fast. The tapestry was, as she had promised, large and fine and only a little faded. It showed a musical party in a garden landscape, with elegantly silk-clad ladies and gentlemen talking as they half-listened to the player. Adrian smiled at the little shock of recognition he felt when he realised that the scene was based closely on a well-known painting by Antoine Watteau of a Venetian Festival. That seemed apt, considering the use made by the Malvolios of the tapestry for the last two hundred years.

Delphine lay on her back on this precious and irreplaceable work of art, her long hair freed from the carved combs that had pinned it up, and spread around her head like a giant chestnut-brown halo, though no pictured Saint in any church Adrian had seen offered her sumptuous body so openly to the sight as she, or folded her arms beneath her head in just that way, to throw her breasts into greater prominence. Her body was too elegant and well-proportioned to be thought *plump*, but in the Edwardian style she was enchantingly well-fleshed. Her belly held a pleasing roundness, her hips swelled out from a narrow waist and curved gracefully down to long full thighs. Nature had made her for sensuality and comfort, thought Adrian, to give a man pleasure and to take it in return.

Naked, he set a knee on the priceless tapestry and gave it a last look.

'We are committing a terrible act of vandalism, to make love on this,' he said slowly, his fingers running over the richness of the wool and silk weave.

'What nonsense,' said Delphine, 'things are made to be used, not put in glass cases and stared at.'

Stifling his last artistic pang, Adrian mounted the great bed and in a daze of delight kissed Delphine's sumptuous body from forehead to toe, and back again. His hands ranged over her warm and springy flesh, over those superb breasts, across her belly and between her legs, where her neatly-trimmed little tuft of dark-brown curls excited his fantasies. There was so much of Delphine to kiss and fondle, so much to enjoy, that to be given the freedom of her generous body was like being at an orgy.

Adrian's hot-blooded part had been standing stiffly from when they had entered the bedroom together, from even before she had undressed to let him admire her fully. When his caresses had brought her to a level of arousal that threatened to overpower her senses, she took Adrian by his stiff handle and pulled him onto her. With a slow push he sank deep between her splayed thighs, and began the same stately thrusting that had delighted them both when they lay together on the chaise-longue.

'Not like that,' said Delphine breathlessly, 'be strong with me now, be forceful! Ravage me and conquer me if you hope ever to have me again!'

With this exhortation burning in his brain, Adrian lunged faster and harder into her smooth wetness. She moaned in her gratification and wriggled her soft belly against him, driving him wild with desire. Very soon she was wailing to the spasms of delight that shook her, and her back came arching up off the marvellous tapestry to push her hot belly at him.

'Oh, Delphine!' he cried out, feeling the golden moment fast approaching and unstoppable. 'Yes, now, now!'

Her arms were round his neck and her mouth pressed tightly to his. Adrian had forgotten all about forged works of art – he was obsessed by Nature's work of art underneath him, and with a long gasp into her open mouth, he spurted strongly up into her belly. The convulsions of his climax carried her to the peak of sensation and she panted, *Yes!* and squirmed wildly under him.

TEN

Adrian's morning visit to Delphine changed his mind for him – he decided to stay in Venice at least until the weekend, with suitable excuses sent by telegram to Mallards. The true reason for this was that he wanted to repeat the experience as often as possible – but with all too human self-deception, he told himself that he needed a few days to persuade her to accept that her two Cranachs were forgeries.

She had refused outright to believe him, insisting that the documentation proved them genuine. How many original Cranach paintings had he actually seen? she asked. When he told her he had seen four altogether – two in London and two more in Paris in the Louvre, she smiled and shrugged gracefully and asked him to consider carefully whether he might not be mistaken about her pictures. To him it might only be an intellectual exercise, she reminded him, but to her and the future of the Palazzo and the family it was a matter of the utmost importance.

He promised her to give further serious consideration to the paintings before setting his final recommendation to Mallards whether or not to accept them for auction as genuine Cranachs, but he was doubtful that his assessment could be reversed, no matter what further documentation Padre Pio produced. And on that note of polite disagreement, he left her lying enticingly on her magnificent bed and its Gobelins tapestry – though not without regret.

So many days in Venice already, and he had not been to visit the Accademia Galleries on the Grand Canal, the most celebrated collection of Venetian paintings in Europe! He decided he must go there that very afternoon – apart from the obvious pleasure there was a possibility there might be a German Renaissance picture or two to set his mind working on the question of the disputed Cranachs. But as he left the Palazzo Malvolio by the landward door, he met Adalbert

Gmund, also going out, and still dressed in his comically old-fashioned stiff collar. Adalbert shook his head when he heard Adrian's destination, and told him the Accademia was closed.

Disappointed in that hope, Adrian accepted an invitation to accompany Adalbert on his outing – having checked that he was not about to call upon Signora Fosca and her niece. Not at all, Adalbert protested with a grin, he was going to see a dealer in unusual *objets d'art*. Adrian's interest was captured, and they strolled through narrow streets and little squares, crossed footbridges over back canals, passed the church of San Fantin and the Fenice Theatre, and came at last to a tiny shop in an alley, with a reproduction seventeenth century map of the world in the window. The door was closed and locked, but when Adalbert had knocked long enough, a man appeared behind the glass and opened it to let them in.

He was a thin man in his fifties, his receding hair dyed jet black. His shoulders were stooped and he wore a garment Adrian described to himself as a grey dust-jacket. He led them into a small room behind the shop, and found chairs for them amidst a waist-high litter of old and tattered books, papers and printed pictures. Adrian stared thoughtfully at the junk and wondered what purpose it could possibly serve, other than establishing a false facade of mouldy and trivial antiquarianism. There were introductions and hand-shakings, and Signor Corradini claimed, through Adalbert as interpreter, to be greatly honoured to have so distinguished a representative of the internationally famous Mallards in his humble premises.

Adrian waited patiently through the preliminary chatter. He took note that Corradini addressed Adalbert as Signor Gmund, while Adalbert addressed Corradini as Niccolo. This presumably reflected the relation between buyer and seller, though Adrian doubted if Adalbert ever got the better of a bargain. The eyes behind Niccolo's gold-rimmed spectacles gleamed with bright and vigilant cleverness, and his permanently gesticulating hands had an artist's long fingers.

When at last the polite preliminaries were completed, Niccolo produced from somewhere amongst the debris of his back room a cardboard folder and opened it to reveal half a dozen black and white prints. Adalbert looked through them with a fond smile before passing the folder to Adrian. The top print showed a man in eighteenth century wig and knee-breeches, sitting on an armchair. Between his spread knees he held a naked woman with her back to him, she down on one knee. On the floor before her lay an open musical score, and the man had his arms about her – one hand on her left breast, the other down between her thighs, so that he seemed to be playing a tune on her, as if she were a cello.

The rest of the prints had interesting subjects too – pretty girls closely examining each other's charms, impossibly elegant women being enfiladed delicately by gentlemen, lonely ladies in canopied beds giving themselves the solace of their fingers. With a grin Adrian handed the folder back to Adalbert.

'I find them charming,' he said, 'though modern, of course.'

'You do not know this artist?' Adalbert asked, raising his eyebrows. 'He is Franz von Bayros, and some think him a better artist than your English Aubrey Beardsley. I met him in Vienna several times before the War. His work was often commissioned for private editions of special books – I have some of them.'

'Then you will hardly buy these prints,' said Adrian. 'They must be over-runs by the printer, sold off separately.'

'I asked Niccolo to let you see them because I thought they would interest you,' Adalbert answered, 'but what I have come to see today is a small collection of wax replicas Niccolo sent word he has acquired. Perhaps I may buy them for my collection of rare and amusing artefacts, if I can negotiate the price.'

'Replicas?' said Adrian. 'Of what?'

Adalbert spoke to Niccolo, who burrowed under the litter on a side table until he found a flat and circular mahogany case. He opened it to reveal a blue velvet-lined interior, on which there lay in slots, like the spokes of a wheel, six fully-erect male parts in pink wax. The largest was about eight inches long, the shortest about four, in Adrian's estimate.

While he was pondering what the significance of the exhibit might be, Niccolo began what was very clearly a sales pitch of some eloquence, even though not a word could Adrian understand. Adalbert was nodding wisely and smiling, and throwing in a word or two now and then. When at last Niccolo finally stopped talking, Adalbert turned to Adrian to enlighten him.

'These are exact life-size replicas of very famous men,' he said, 'made when they were in Venice. They were made by pouring melted coloured wax into plaster moulds taken from life. Do you see the little brass plates fitted at the base of each one – the name of the man! What do you think of that?'

'Astounding!' said Adrian, grinning at the thought of famous men of the past having the vanity to want the size and shape of their choicest parts recorded for posterity. 'I assume that the moulds were made by pretty girls, to keep the sitter stiff long enough for the plaster to set. But who are they?'

Adalbert reached for the longest replica, to take it from the case, but Niccolo stopped him at once and spoke quickly.

'He says they are irreplaceable, and far too precious to be touched,' Adalbert translated. 'He has a list of names copied from the little plates.'

Niccolo's finger moved round the wax erections, never quite touching them, as he reeled of the names.

'Giacomo Casanova... Lord Byron... Count Cagliostro...'

'Cagliostro?' Adrian interrupted. 'The famous conman who had a hand in stealing Marie Antoinette's diamond necklace? I thought he was a Sicilian – when was he in Venice?'

'In 1789,' said Niccolo at once, letting Adrian see that he understood English better than he had let on earlier, 'after he was forced to leave Paris because of the scandal. He came here to sell his celebrated Elixir of Youth to the rich middle-aged ladies. He fell in love with one of them – her name was Cecilia Tron, an aristocratic married lady, who returned his passion. The love letters they exchanged were found and published only fifty years ago. That was how *his* looked, Signor,' and Niccolo pointed to an average-sized but thick pink exhibit.

Adrian envisaged a dull afternoon ahead of him, waiting while Adalbert discussed the price of this collection of what might be almost considered relics, albeit profane ones. He extricated himself politely, leaving the two of them to haggle with each other, and set off alone in the direction of San Marco to enjoy an ice-cream and a cup of coffee in the square. Before he got that far, another thought came into his head – why not make his deferred call on Gina Luzzi? It was not easy to explain even to himself why he was experiencing this sudden urge to have her so soon after Delphine. Gina had been his welcome to Venice, and Delphine's generous charms had restored his high opinion of the city. It seemed perfectly logical to find her again and celebrate this renaissance with her.

The scrap of paper with her address was in his pocket still. His guide-book showed him where the street was to be found, and he waited near the Doge's Palace for the next water-bus to go up the Grand Canal. It took him past the Palazzo Malvolio and under the Rialto Bridge, and dropped him off on a jetty by the *Ca'd'Oro* – the Golden House – which proved to be a five-hundred-year-old palace of pinkish-grey stone in the Venetian-Gothic style. Across the frontage at water level an arcaded gallery gave on to the Grand Canal, and above that were two long galleries of stone lace-work and pointed windows. So elaborate was the facade that it looked more like a stage set than the front of a family home – a stage set for an impossibly romantic tragicomedy with music.

Not that it was a family home any more; the ever-handy guide-book informed him that it had been given by Baron Franchetti to Venice in 1916. Perhaps he couldn't afford to pay the rates, Adrian thought, with a touch of cynicism. But his professional interest awoke when he read that the Baron had also left his picture collection in the palazzo. The guide-book noted works by Titian and Mantegna, among others.

With a great sense of virtue, Adrian decided to postpone his visit to Gina Luzzi and look at the Baron's pictures instead, for an hour or two. But his good intentions were thwarted when he found that the Palazzo was closed, and he strolled on inland away from the Grand Canal, not knowing whether to be pleased or sorry. The map in his guide-book showed him where the church of Santa Maria Valverde stood, beside a canal that opened out into the lagoon to the north, and from there it was easy enough to find the street he was looking for. After the palaces of the Grand Canal, it was with a sense of shock that he realised that he had found the poor backstreets of Venice.

He walked along a stone-flagged quayside that bordered a long straight canal. There were no sleek gondolas carrying British honeymooners and sight-seeing tourists with their Kodaks. The traffic along this canal was heavy black barges – the lorries of Venice – delivering their loads of food and goods to shops and traders, and hauling away the city's rubbish. The tenements were old and peeled and patched, plaster that was once ochre now flaked away by time and weather, to lay bare red crumbling brick. Here and there on the brickwork were yard-long patches of dirty cement, like giant sticking-plasters on a bad graze. The Venetians who lived here knew much less about palaces than Adrian himself, and nothing at all about paintings and statues.

The side streets off this workaday canal were no more than alleys, twelve or fourteen feet wide. Clotheslines ran across from window to window, all four stories up the buildings, with rough overalls, worn bed-sheets, fraying underwear, mended shirts, and less identifiable garments hanging out to dry in the sun. The doors of the buildings were made of short horizontal planks, any paint they ever had long since worn off. Very few people were about – it was, after all, the siesta hour – and those who were gave Adrian a look of curiosity as he passed by. In general the prospect was not inviting, and he begun to feel regret that the *Ca'd'Oro* had been closed. Slums could be seen in any city anywhere.

From his breast-pocket he pulled the scrap of paper on which he had scribbled Gina's address, and compared it with the name of the alley he had come to. It was deserted, and he made his way into it under the hanging washing overhead, looking at numbers. The door he wanted stood half-open, and when he pushed it he saw a stone-flagged passage leading to a stone staircase. On the left of the passage stood the door to the ground-floor apartment and, not without trepidation, he knocked and waited.

In a minute or two he heard shuffling footsteps, and then the door was opened by a woman of about thirty, with a short fringe of frizzy dark hair.

'*Signor?*' she said, stifling a sleepy yawn with a hand on which Adrian saw a narrow gold wedding-ring.

'I am looking for Signorina Luzzi,' he said slowly, 'does she live in this building?'

'Signorina Luzzi? Si, si! She live with me,' answered the woman in recognisable English. Her dark-brown eyes weighed him up – his elegant grey and black striped blazer, his tie and shoes, the hat in his hand, and other indications of financial standing. What she saw was evidently acceptable, for she smiled and took a step backwards and said, 'You come in, please.'

The combined sitting- and dining-room was much like that of Signora Fosca on the other side of the Grand Canal, though not so well furnished. The woman of the house introduced herself as Signora Zula while she shooed Adrian to a chair and brought him a tiny but hospitable glass of a yellowish liqueur, telling him that it was *Strega*. She had very obviously been sleeping when he knocked, and had come to the door in a wrap-around garment like a kimono, though with no embroidery on its plain brown material. It was knee-length, with a darker strip round the hem, below which her legs and feet were bare. She had a round face, cheerful and plump-cheeked, and when she smiled she displayed a gold tooth. Her best feature was surely her eyes, thought Adrian, very dark pupils that shone brightly on the white.

'Are you related to Signorina Luzzi?' he enquired, to which Signora Zula shook her head and said that they were friends and that Signorina Gina rented a room here in her *casa*.

Adrian complimented her on her English, and she explained how she used to be employed in the office of a travel company near the railway station, where she had learned a little of English, French and German, to be able to deal with foreign tourists. Adrian looked round for somewhere to put down his empty little glass, but she immediately filled it again from the long-necked bottle. In doing so she bent forwards, and he had a view down the front of her loose wrap to the deep separation between plump breasts. It did not escape her where his interest lay, nor that she had given away that she was wearing next to nothing under her wrap.

With her free hand she pulled it close at the neck, smiling as she did so. Her modest gesture strained the thin cotton over her breasts, so that the dark buds showed prominently through. Adrian was not certain how to proceed. It was hardly possible that Signora Zula was ignorant of her lodger's mode of life, even if the carnalities were conducted elsewhere. But courtesy and caution were needed, for the merest suggestion that this was a *disorderly house*, as the legal phrase was in England, was sure to give offence. He asked with a very friendly smile if Signorina Luzzi would be back soon.

'Where you meet Gina?' Signora Zula countered, not answering his question.

'On the train coming to Venice,' he said, with perfect truth.

'On the express train,' said Signora Zula, and she nodded and smiled in a knowing way that indicated her familiarity with what Gina did in railway carriages. 'I remember now, she told me she met a nice English gentleman – that was you, yes?'

'Yes,' he agreed, flattered that he had been mentioned, and

reassured that over-much caution was no longer necessary.

'What is your name, Signor?' she asked, and he told her. But when she enquired at which hotel he was staying, he thought it sensible to say the Hotel Danieli, rather than to mention the Palazzo Malvolio. Even so, the Signora was suitably impressed, it being the premier hotel of Venice, and once a palace itself. She told him Gina would not come back before midday tomorrow, and he guessed that she must be working the overnight train.

'*Mi dispiace*,' said Signora Zula, *I'm sorry* – a phrase Adrian had learned from the chambermaid Teresa.

'*Che peccato!*' he answered, trotting out another phrase he had learned, *what a pity!*

Perhaps it was his pronunciation of the Italian that made his hostess laugh, but perhaps not – for she joined the thumb and forefinger of her left hand to make a circle, through which she slid her right forefinger in a rapid movement of unmistakable meaning, repeating *che peccato* several times, laughing heartily enough to make her loose breasts shake inside her thin wrapper.

'Is your husband at home?' Adrian asked, his interest awake.

'He is working,' she said, her fingers still performing their little in-and-out movement. 'He is a gondolier. Perhaps you see him when you arrive in Venice – he waits at the station.'

'Perhaps,' said Adrian, shrugging and grinning at her. 'To me all gondoliers look alike – men with flat hats and long poles.'

That set her off laughing again. On a sudden impulse, Adrian reached out his hand, and she took it. He pulled her to him and sat her on his lap. She pressed her warm body against him, put an arm round his neck, and nuzzled his cheek.

'If my Beppo come home and find me with you – *ahi*!' she said, smiling broadly while she undid the knot of Adrian's tie.

'Is that likely to happen?' he asked carefully.

'No, he never come back until he wants to eat – about eight in the evening.'

His fears allayed, Adrian slid his hand inside her loose wrap to feel her bare breasts. And as he had hoped, they were full and bountiful and seemed to drop naturally into his hands. With joy in his heart, he felt and rolled, squeezed and kneaded the wealth of soft and pliable flesh Signora Zula was offering him, until he was half-drunk with delight. Not even the sudden and menacing entrance of the gondoliering Beppo himself could have dragged his hand away. She opened all the front of her wrapper down to the waist, and he played with the red-brown tips of her fat breasts until they stood firm between his fingers.

It was almost an afterthought to ask Signora Zula her name at this advanced stage of the proceedings, but he learned that it was Clara. She was smiling and beaming at him, her round face almost moonlike in radiance, as she showed him her pleasure in being handled so thoroughly. When he was ready to move to the next delight, he slipped a hand under the hem of her wrap to stroke her bare thigh. Clara opened her wrap completely and let him see that she was wearing open-legged knickers of thin white cotton. If he could get them off, he reflected pleasantly, she would be naked for his further attentions. So far she had been extremely obliging – with any luck at all she would continue to be so until he had her on her back.

An instant before his hand up the leg of her knickers touched the curls between her legs, she pressed her thighs together – and at this point he learned that it was not a question of luck holding out. She told him plainly that she was a poor woman and that *amore* was not free for the asking – at least, not from a married woman. But for the same as he had given to her friend Gina on the train, she would let him do the same to her. There was no question by then of Adrian refusing her offer – the weight of her breasts in his hands had convinced him that he must have her. With a grin he asked her what her husband would say if he knew she made *amore* with another man.

'He is responsible,' she replied, her dark eyes flashing with momentary anger. 'He must give me more money, then I don't do it. You understand me, Signor Adrian?'

'Perfectly,' said Adrian, long past caring how he was going to explain away in London the expenditure of another five hundred lire of Mallard's money. On a woman endowed with a pair of melons like Clara's, it was cash well spent!

While he paused to savour this thought, she parted her thighs and let his hand slip higher. His groping fingers touched the warm flesh between her legs, and if she had asked him for twice as much, he would have given it without hesitation. He removed his hand from between her thighs for long enough to extract a bank-note from his wallet, and she got up from his lap and led him by the hand from the sitting-room into a small bedroom. The shutters were closed, and the room was cool and dim, the floor tiled and the walls white-washed. Over the single bed hung, in garish tints, a religious picture of depressing incompetence, showing two female saints with halos and sentimental smiles.

'This Gina's room,' Clara announced. 'Nice, yes? We do it in here, Signor Adrian?'

She rolled the 500-lire note into a cylinder and tucked it into an ugly red Murano glass vase that stood on the bedside table. A moment later Adrian helped her out of her knickers and she was grinning and pulling his trousers down. They lay naked on the bed together, his hands roaming over her warm skin in sensuous delight, while she held his wilful part and jerked at it encouragingly.

Seen without clothes, she was narrow in the waist, and by contrast her breasts seemed bigger than they were. Her belly was broad and round, the dark-brown hair between her legs was a veritable thicket that spread into her groins. Adrian combed his fingers through it, his mind occupied with the unoriginal but permanently fascinating reflection that no two women were the same in this respect.

Clara lay at ease on her back, smiling through his lengthy and pleasant investigation of her body by hands and mouth. She began to sigh after a while, when he pushed her legs wider open and parted the now-moist lips under her bush of brown hair. Her eyes closed and her heavy breasts rose and fell quickly to the touch of two fingers inside her.

'*Ah, Signor Adrian – che gentilezza*,' she murmured, wriggling in delight, and though he did not understand her, he knew that she intended a compliment. *Si, si!* he murmured, and continued to flutter his fingers as lightly as a butterfly's wings in her slippery warmth. Her plump thighs strained wider apart and she gasped, *Aspetta!*. He was not to know that she meant him to stop and he speeded up his attentions and Clara came to an instant climax. He watched in delight the quaking of her belly and the drumming of her heels on the bedcover, but it was over quickly and she opened her eyes to stare at him with a lop-sided smile on her face.

'*Fantastico!*' he said, remembering the word from Gina.

Clara's grin spread wider and she dragged him closer by his protruding handle. He had reached a high pitch of arousal in observing her climax that made his response as enthusiastic as any woman could have wished – he threw himself on her belly and pushed into her wet depths with one long straight thrust of his hips.

'*Si, fantastico!*' she gasped as he penetrated her to the limit, and she squirmed beneath him to his pounding and dug her finger-nails into his bottom. The sharp little pain spurred him on, and only moments later he cried out and discharged his surging emotions into her belly.

When he recovered his breath he was pleased to find that she did not want to leave right away. But then, why should she? he thought, lying on his back beside her, cooling down slowly. After all, this might be the back streets of Venice, but what he had come across was nothing less than the archetypal bored housewife with nothing to do until her husband came home for dinner. The situation was one he might as easily have fallen into in any London suburb on a dull afternoon – Bedford Park or Chiswick. A handsome, well-dressed man knocks at the door and is invited in for a moment's conversation – and the housewife routs her boredom by letting her chance visitor understand that he can have her if he wants.

In Bedford Park or in Chiswick, it was unlikely the visitor would be asked three pounds for the pleasure of removing the housewife's knickers, thought Adrian, who had done exactly that on more than one memorable occasion. But it had to be accepted that Clara's claim that she was poor was truthful – and there was no reason in the world why she shouldn't obtain cash, as well as pleasure, from the unexpected encounter. She already found it necessary to supplement the family income by letting a room ... and at this moment he asked himself why she had a spare room to let, and saw the answer.

'You have no children, Clara?' he asked lazily, lying with his ankles crossed and one arm under his head. She rolled on her side to face him.

'No children,' she said. 'Five years married with Beppo, but nothing from him. Maybe you make me a baby with this,' and she prodded his limp morsel with her forefinger.

'Beppo would be angry if I did,' said Adrian.

'He never know who did it,' said Clara, her voice thoughtful. 'You make this stand up, Signor Adrian, for *amore* again.'

Not for the first time since he came to Venice, he made the interesting and useful discovery that a change of partner is an aphrodisiac more powerful than any drug. In London he had never made love to a girl more than three times in an evening, and he had been completely without appetite the next day. But on his first day in Venice he had made love to three different women without hesitation – Gina, the maid, and the Contessa Marina. And he had been ready for more the next day! His romp in bed with Delphine before lunch would normally have been enough for the day, but he had gone looking for Gina Luzzi afterwards. Not finding her, he had jumped at the chance of having her friend – and now that Clara wanted him to do it to her again, he found himslf ready and able. And if Marina comes to my room tonight, he thought with a smile, I shall attend to her with pleasure.

'But why like that?' he asked Clara, when she indicated that she wanted him to have her on hands and knees this time.

'Good for making, baby, like goat,' she said with a grin.

Why not? Adrian thought – in London he had never dreamed of asking a girlfriend to let him do it in that position, and he couldn't imagine one agreeing to it. Certainly not Barbara, the girl he was half in love with – it had taken him some time to get her to cross her legs over his back when he was in her, she thinking the woman's role was to lie still with her legs open and look beautiful. But as he stared at Clara's bottom, turned up towards him, he began to have second thoughts about Barbara Chetwynd. Venice had shown him a more imaginative and lively approach to love-making, and he had no intention of reverting to the prosaic on his return.

But that was only a passing thought, for there were immediate pleasures to occupy him. Clara was on her hands and knees on the bed, her plump breasts swinging loosely under her, and there was no way of resisting an invitation like that. He knelt behind her, both hands feeling the generously fleshy cheeks of her bottom that she presented for his admiration. He kissed them, he put out his tongue and licked them, which made her giggle, he nipped at them with his teeth, and she gave a little shriek. Despite his recent attentions to her, his ever-handy part had risen again to an impressive length and thickness, poking out from between his thighs and nodding its swollen head at the moist and split fig beneath Clara's bottom. He put his hands on her broad hips and pulled himself close to her, his belly pressed against her warm bottom.

Unfamiliar though the sight of a naked woman on all fours

was to him, Adrian found it extremely arousing. She seemed to be giving herself to him more fully than when she was on her back – all her body was at his disposal, her bare rump, her dangling breasts, her strong back. He pressed closer yet against her and felt beneath to run his hands over the curve of her belly, and she sighed in noisy pleasure and jerked her bottom backwards at him to urge him to pierce her. But Adrian never liked to rush his pleasures – he sat back on his heels to examine her plump fig. Seen from behind, it was a long and fleshy split festooned with dark curls he had himself made wet, and he played with it for a while, sliding his fingers inside until Clara turned her head to stare at him over her bare shoulder, a pleading look on her plump-cheeked face. At that, ever courteous, he grasped her by the hips, presented the purple head of his stiff length to the lips he had so well prepared, and pushed strongly into her.

'*Ah, si!*' she exclaimed. '*Di piu, di piu, Signor Adrian!*'

That she was asking for more was lost on him, but it did not matter. He was well mounted on her rump, and he swung his loins back and forth in a steady rhythm that soon had her gasping to the thrills he was sending through her. She responded to his efforts by bumping her bottom against him. Thus urged on, he moved faster and harder into her slippery depths, while she moaned and slammed her rump frantically at his belly. The little silver cross round her neck swung wildly from side to side on its chain, and Adrian lay forward over her back to feel beneath her and get hold of her jiggling breasts. Shudders of delight were running through his entire body, Clara was already panting in the bliss of incipient ecstasy, and in five seconds more his torrent of desire would be unleashed into her – when the sound of a door banging shut inside the apartment brought them to a twitching and startled halt.

'*Madonna mia* – Beppo!' Clara exclaimed in great agitation. 'He is back too soon – he will kill you! What is to do?'

While she was speaking, she had already pulled away from Adrian and was off the bed and scrambling into her knickers. He followed her example and grabbed for his shirt and trousers. In the sitting-room a man's heavy voice was calling for Clara, and she, standing on one bare foot to pull up her knickers, called back – the Italian words incomprehensible to Adrian but not the meaning – she was telling her husband that she'd be with him in a minute. In an access of blind panic, Adrian snatched up his jacket, crammed socks and shoes into the pockets, and made a dash for the shuttered window.

The man's voice called again – the deep-chested tones of a heavy-set and no doubt burly-muscled rower – and from somewhere closer than before.

'He's coming in!' Clara gasped, staring in desperation at Adrian by the window. 'He wants to make love to me!'

Adrian moaned to himself at this unwanted information, pushed the battered green wooden shutters outwards and, without even a glance, he leaped through the open window to escape. He dropped six feet into the stagnant water of a narrow back canal, and as his bare feet touched the sticky mud of the bottom, he pushed sharply upwards. He came up spluttering just in time to see the window-shutters above him being pulled to, to the accompaniment of a laugh as, presumably, Beppo got his hands on Clara to rip off the knickers she'd just put on, before flinging her on her back on the bed.

Adrian's predicament down in the canal was quite as awkward in its way as hers up on the bed. On both sides of him there rose crumbling red-brick tenement walls sheer from the turbid water, with no hand-hold or possibility of climbing out. There was nothing for it but to swim for a hundred yards or so to where the buildings ended and the canal ran into a broader one. His water-logged jacket slung over one shoulder, he set out in a steady breast-stroke for the corner – and emerged from the back canal to find himself about to be run down by a large black-painted barge.

With a gurgling shout that gave him a mouthful of dirty water to swallow, he twisted sideways, just saving himself from being over-run. The barge slid past so close to him that he was able to reach up and grab the gunwale. He was carried along through the water until the boatman heard his shouts for help over the chugging engine and throttled it back. The barge lost way only slowly, gliding on with no one at the helm, and threatening to mash Adrian against yet another brick wall, while the boatman came forward to look at him in unwarranted amusement. When he had finished his guffaw, he pulled Adrian aboard by the wrists.

Slumped on stained and dirty boards, his back propped against crates of mineral water, Adrian coughed up a pint of canal. The boatman was back at the helm and the barge chugged along on its delivery run again. When he felt better, Adrian started a long and complicated discussion with a man whose acquaintance with English was even more rudimentary than Adrian's with Italian. But the universal language of commerce and social dealings came into its own eventually – Adrian's wallet was still inside his jacket pocket, and by brandishing a sodden five hundred lire note at the boatman and repeating *Palazzo Malvolio* enough times, agreement was reached. The barge eased round the next turn to the right, slid between two palaces, and came out on the Grand Canal, not far from the *Ca' d'Oro*.

The hot sun was drying out Adrian's clothes, but his shoes and socks were too uncomfortably squishy to put on. He hoped that his beautiful blazer had not been ruined by immersion, and he was reflecting on his adventure and promising himself a hot bath and dry clothes at the Palazzo Malvolio, when he heard women's voices calling his name – or something as near it as he had heard from a Venetian – *Signor Trill, Signor Trill!* To his right a speed-boat had cut in close to the barge and was running alongside. In it were the two ladies he had seen at Princess Zita's lunch party, one of them steering, the other waving, and both calling to him. He had been introduced to them by Massimo, but he couldn't recollect their names.

'You fall in the canal, Signor Trill?' said one of them, and when he grinned and nodded, she instructed the boatman in rapid Italian to stop the barge, the other woman skilfully laid the speed-boat alongside, and Adrian transferred himself from one craft to the other.

He gave the boatman a wave of thanks, which was returned very cheerfully, the five hundred lires earned without the need to prolong the journey for another mile along the Grand Canal. Watching the barge turn away, Adrian was unaware that the speed-boat had also turned off the Grand Canal, until he looked forward again and saw that they were entering a narrow canal on the right bank – heading in the general direction of Zita's palace.

'Where are we going?' he asked, unable to remember how well or otherwise these two ladies understood English. 'Is this a short cut to the Palazzo Malvolio?'

One of his rescuers was too preoccupied with steering the boat to give him her attention, but the other half-turned to smile at him as he sat dripping on the back seat.

'It is very unhealthy for you to wear your clothes wet,' said she, showing off her grasp of the language. 'You must take them off and be dried. Our house is much nearer than Palazzo Malvolio – you will see.'

ELEVEN

Adrian had forgotten the names of the two sisters he had met at Princess Zita's, but as the speed-boat slid slowly and carefully between the high walls of narrow, back canals, they reminded him that they were Carlotta and Gabriella, with different surnames of their husbands. Both were in their thirties, with a distinct facial resemblance, and both stylishly dressed. The older by a couple of years, Carlotta, was at the wheel of the boat, and she glanced frequently over her shoulder to speak to Adrian and smile at him. The other sister had slewed round in her seat and with sharp-nailed fingers was unbuttoning Adrian's shirt to let the warm afternoon air reach his chest, and telling him he must not wear wet clothes a moment longer than necessary, for the sake of his health.

She smiled in his face while her fingers found and tugged at his trouser buttons – those that he had time to fasten while Beppo was on his way into the bedroom. Finding so many undone, she laughed and asked what he had been doing when he fell into the canal, and she looked sideways at her sister and explained her interesting discovery in Italian. Adrian smiled and said nothing while she opened his trousers to the groin and tugged his shirt out of them. In no time she had it up over his head and flung it down on the seat beside him. Her fingers ran over his hairless chest as if in pleasurable surprise, and Carlotta beside her broke into rapid Italian, giving the impression that they were discussing him.

The mention of husbands curtailed Adrian's interest in the sisters – he felt that for one day he'd had enough of husbands appearing at the instant he was about to unleash his passion into an obligingly errant wife. Seeing the look of caution that spread over his face, Gabriella laughed and told him that she was separated from Signor Mosta, who lived in Milano, and that her sister's husband had been in Argentina looking after his investments for the past five years. While she imparted this reassuring information, her restless fingers seemed to flicker lightly in and out of Adrian's trouser-front, perhaps to check how uncomfortably clammy his underwear was.

Whatever her reason, her caring gesture focused Adrian's attention on the plight of his watery limpness, and he blushed almost to realise how far from impressive a figure he cut just then. Gabriella obviously thought so too, for she laughed and made a comment that he did not understand to Carlotta at the wheel. There was no doubt in his mind that he had been rescued by a playful pair of ladies. And why not? he asked himself. He had pitched neck and crop out of Clara's window almost at the critical moment itself – and been forced to flee in horrible frustration. Now this benign and delightful city of Venice was consoling him by letting two good-looking ladies pop up from nowhere, to replace the one of whose accommodating nature he had been deprived!

Carlotta brought the speed-boat in to a short quay with stone steps and before Adrian had time to stand up and climb out, the sisters were ashore and had the boat tied up. They were at the side of a little cobbled square, the other three sides of which were buildings. The largest was of brick with white stone balconies, and had a look of antiquity about it. As he learned, it was an old palace converted into apartments, and the sisters had the best floor – one flight up a marble staircase. He had very little time to see anything as he was rushed bare-chested and bare-foot past a surprised-looking maid, and into a pink-tiled bathroom.

In the dash through the apartment the sisters discarded their hats, and Adrian was reminded of something that had amused him at Zita's. Both women were brunette, probably a nondescript middle-brown if the truth were known. Each had improved on nature in her own way – Carlotta had turned blonde, or as blonde as she thought acceptable, without flaunting a film-star platinum shade, while Gabriella had darkened her hair to a near-black. But their eyebrows were identical thin arcs of black, their mouths similarly shaped and painted the same scarlet. Carlotta's frock was brown – a rich copper tone, while Gabriella's was emerald green – and Adrian realised that the clothes were interchangeable – each would have looked just as well on the other.

Over the huge bathtub hung a brass shower-head the size of a dinner plate. It was Carlotta who turned on the taps and then adjusted the temperature of the water, she seemingly the more practical-minded of the two. Not that Gabriella was idle – she pulled Adrian's soaking-wet trousers and underwear down his legs and off, and was running a hand tentatively over the taut cheeks of his bottom, while staring at his shrunken part with a grin on her face. She called Carlotta's attention to it, and there was a conference in Italian that might have embarrassed another man in Adrian's plight. But he stood fast and let them look and comment all they wished, certain that his time would come eventually.

Carlotta motioned him to get under the shower, and he climbed into the old-fashioned high-sided bath and positioned himself beneath the hot downpour. She had gauged it exactly, and it was very pleasant – he had not realised how chilled he had become in his clinging wet clothes, even though it was a hot day. The sisters stood back and watched him standing and soaking in the grateful warmth – and exchanging casual remarks between them on his physique, now that it was fully revealed to their critical gaze. He was very surprised – and disappointed – when they left the bathroom, and he wondered if he had failed to meet their expectations. With Niccolo Corradini's case of wax replicas in his mind, he had a dismaying thought that perhaps only the very largest would be up to their standards. He had to admit that, even at full stretch, he would qualify for the middle range, and at present not even for that.

But he was wrong in his conclusions – in minutes the sisters were back, and without most of their clothes. The stylish and expensive brown and green frocks were gone, and so were shoes, stockings and almost everything else. Carlotta and Gabriella in only flimsy lace-trimmed knickers – one pair a pale coffee and the other *eau-de-nil* – were at the bathside to wash him down with gardenia-scented soap. It was a game, a giggling, splashy, exciting game of warm and soapy hands sliding smoothly over his body, under his arms, over his chest, across his belly, down in his groins, between his thighs, and up again between the cheeks of his bottom.

The chattering ladies touched him and felt him and caressed him everywhere, with the single exception of his enthusiastic part. That they left completely alone, as if to tease him – but it very soon became stiff enough and long enough to please any woman. Apart from the sensual pleasure of being washed all over in this charming way, for Adrian the fascination was to see two pairs of round bare breasts lolloping about him, as the sisters handled him with a vigour that made his blood flow briskly and his skin glow. He thought, after prolonged and pleasant visual inspection, that Carlotta's were somewhat more pointed that Gabriella's, though there was little to choose between them.

When the thick creamy lather was all washed off, they helped him climb out of the bathtub so that they could dry him. Teresa had performed this service for him, he remembered very well, on his first day in Venice. But while that was acceptable enough at the time – he then being an unenlightened newcomer – it sank into insignificance in comparison with the drying Carlotta and Gabriella gave him. The bath-towels were six feet long and four feet wide, whatever that might be in their absurd Continental system of measurement – and two were draped about him, so that he stood like an ancient Roman in his toga, with two handmaids to caress him gently dry while they exchanged giggling comments he could not understand – though from the tone he guessed them to be favourable.

When at last the towels were allowed to slide to the floor, they checked all over him with their palms to make sure he was dry, then smothered his body in gardenia-scented talcum powder. Naked and with his excitable part sticking out in front of him like the bowsprit of a ship, he was led out of the bathroom and to a bedroom. The door was closed, the key turned in the lock, and he was pressed to sit down on the side of an old-fashioned bed with carved panels in dark wood at head and foot. Carlotta in pale coffee silk knickers sat close on one side of him, and Gabriella in *eau-de-nil* silk knickers on the other, both gazing down at the jaunty part.

Tweedledum and Tweedledee, thought Adrian, and smiled at each in turn. He was wondering which to have first – blonde Carlotta with the just slightly more pointed breasts, or black-haired Gabriella with the very slightly more prominent buds to hers. The sisters saw his hesitation and Gabriella burst out laughing at something Carlotta said on the subject.

'My dear ladies,' said Adrian with a broad grin, 'you are so delectable that I don't know where to begin. Is there protocol for these happy occasions – or do you know of any etiquette to guide me?'

'*Etichetta?*' Gabriella asked blankly, her thin black-drawn eyebrows rising.

'Oh, you pair of hussies!' said Adrian. 'The problem is left to me to solve, is it?'

He wasn't expecting an answer, having forgotten for a moment that the sisters spoke English adequately.

'You are the man here,' said Carlotta. 'You decide. Which of us do you want most? And what is a hussy?'

'I want you both,' he answered instantly, 'and I mean to have you both.'

They were sitting close to him on the bed again, each with an arm around his waist, each with her face turned towards him with an expectant smile. He put his hand flat on Carlotta's belly, and slid it down inside her knickers, to feel her.

'A hussy is a beautiful woman who lets me do this to her,' he said with a grin, his busy fingers exploring her curls and the fleshy lips under them. On his other side, Gabriella's face was pink with emotion to see what he was doing to her sister, but before she could say anything, he slipped his other hand down the front of her knickers. Her thighs parted, and Adrian's mind was a blaze for delight as he told himself that, for the first time in his life, he was simultaneously feeling two women. Few men ever experienced that pleasure, he thought, and none at all of his friends in London.

There was a hand on his right thigh, and a hand on his left thigh, both caressing slowly upwards. He was in a fever of high expectation which of his playful women would first take hold of his hard and bobbing part. But neither did – they sat close to him, with their legs apart and his hands down inside their knickers, and waited for him to make the next move. He saw that Carlotta's words were intended literally – he was the man here and it was for him to take what he wanted.

'You are both utterly adorable,' he said, finger-tips moving gently inside their slippery softness. 'And since there is no obvious way to choose who shall be first, we must resort to a guessing-game. I am thinking of a number between one and twenty – whoever gets closest to it is the winner. Ready? Go!'

In the same instant Carlotta said seventeen and Gabriella seven. He smiled at each in turn and announced that his number had been eleven, and that Gabriella was therefore the closest. She stood up at once, to pull her knickers down her legs and off and Adrian stared happily at the expanse of bare and ivory-tinted belly she had uncovered. Below it grew a thick tuft of hair of what could only be called a middle-brown. Carlotta gave a whoop of laughter at her sister's unveiling, and stood up herself to do the same. The identical colour of her tuft of curls proved the validity of Adrian's speculations on the original shade of the two women's hair, before they diverged into blonde and black.

There was to be nothing commonplace in this rare adventure of having two women at his disposal at the same time, Adrian had decided. The simplest thing would be to lay Gabriella on her back on the bed and leap on top of her – but that was precisely how he had made love to darling Barbara, on the evening before he left for Venice. Except that it had taken him the best part of an hour to get her clothes off her, for she had clung round his neck and wanted to kiss him interminably, and had kept her legs together for the longest time, even after his hand was up her frock . . . whereas the enthusiastic Venetian sisters had stripped off their clothes before the game was hardly begun.

He arranged a very willing Gabriella on the side of the bed, with her back on it and her bottom protruding over the edge. She was smiling broadly and her big brown eyes were shiny with desire – her thighs stretched wide open for him to stand between them. He took her under the knees and picked up her legs to rest on his shoulders – a love position he had observed in a Rowlandson print and never had the boldness to try until now. Gabriella reached down between her thighs with both hands to open herself for him, and he drove his stiffness into her with a long *Ah* of pleasure.

Carlotta had moved round on the bed to seat herself alongside her sister and take the opportunity to enjoy a full view of the love-making. Adrian rocked back and forth in a stately and, he hoped, long-sustainable tempo, leaning well forward above her to penetrate to the full. For a few moments he thought that the sight of Carlotta's face, observing the proceedings with a look of complete fascination, would throw him off his stroke, and he stared downwards to where his shiny wet part was sliding in and out of Gabriella's hairy split. A gasp of surprise burst from him when Carlotta and Gabriella began a staccato conversation in Italian – very obviously exchanging comments on his bedside technique and the effect it was producing.

Fortunately this unexpected commentary did not put him off – on the contrary, the growing breathlessness of it aroused him, and he felt the impulse to join in, while his strokes became faster and harder into Gabriella.

'You are beautiful, beautiful,' he babbled, 'and when I have had you I am going to have your sister ... and then I'm going to have you again ... and then her again ...'

Gabriella's gasping report to Carlotta broke off. She moaned and her belly bounded upward to meet his thrusts. He observed the exact moment when her climax began, and he responded to it at once by flooding her belly with hot passion.

'Bravo!' Carlotta's voice reached him over Gabriella's ecstatic gasps. *'Molto bene, Adriano!'*

When he was calm again, he lay on his back beside Gabriella to rest for a little while. She sat up and leaned over him, her breasts lying on his chest while she kissed him and stroked his face and told him how very good it had felt. Carlotta sat close on the other side, her fingers trailing lightly over his belly and slipping down between his thighs, reminding him that he had a commitment to her. He put a hand on her thigh to reassure her that he had not lost interest, and stroked the smooth skin with tender fingers. She pulled his hand between her thighs to let him feel how wet and ready she was, and with a grin he heaved Gabriella off his chest and turned his attention to Carlotta.

He twined a hand in her blonde hair to pull her face to him and kiss her ardently – or as ardently as he could manage just then. She stroked his hairless chest for a while, and without being prompted, took up the very same position on the edge of the bed as she had seen Gabriella serviced in. But Adrian felt it sensible to be a little less athletic this time, to conserve his strength for later, and pushed her further onto the bed, so that her soft round bottom was firmly on it and only her legs hanging over the side. He stood between her parted knees, his well-used part only half-stiff, Carlotta staring up at it with an expression of dismay on her face. She said something to her sister, and with a grin Gabriella came to the rescue.

She slid off the bed to stand behind Adrian, her warm belly pressed to his bottom, and her chin resting on his shoulder. He felt her arms reach round his waist and then she had hold of his lazy part in one hand and his pompoms in the other.

'Ah,' he sighed as she handled him briskly.

'I will make this stand up strong and hard,' she said over

his shoulder, 'then you make Carlotta happy with it.'

Adrian was quite happy to take her at her word and he leaned forward, his feet apart, and his hands resting on Carlotta's open thighs. He stared in anticipatory pleasure at the moist pink split in her thicket of brown curls, relishing the spasms of sensation Gabriella's manipulation was sending through him.

'Cosi va meglio!' she murmured in his ear, 'that's better!'

Indeed, her attentions had already brought him up to full stretch, and she further speeded up the pace of her massaging, until his shameless part started to jerk and thrust in her hand. Carlotta was staring up from the bed with shining eyes at this gallant achievement, her wet tongue appeared and licked round her red-painted mouth, while she opened her legs even wider to welcome Adrian into her. What followed next made him laugh, aroused as he was, for Gabriella began to taunt her sister. The words were meaningless to him, for they spoke to each other in their own language, but it was impossible not to understand the gist of their exchange.

Gabriella, her hand sliding firmly up and down, told Carlotta she was going to make Adriano do it all over her belly – and what did big sister think of that? Carlotta went red-faced and demanded to have it put up her at once. Back and forth they batted the joke – if it was a joke – between them, and Adrian laughed to think of his thrill-seeking part being squabbled over by two naked women. At the same time, while the issue was being settled without his intervention, that same part of his was jumping for joy and rearing itself up even higher.

And yes, it was a joke between the two women. When Carlotta had been reduced to useless threats, Gabriella let go of Adrian and slipped round to the side of him. As if to make up for her teasing, she guided the purple swollen head of his arrogant part to the Carlotta's moist petals and pressed it in. Carlotta had become so excited by being made to wait that her loins rose up to meet Adrian's push, and he was at once as deeply embedded in her hot belly as he ever could wish. He would have liked to lie on her without moving for a while, just to enjoy the squeeze of her voluptuously clasping flesh, but she and Gabriella were of another mind.

His feet were planted firmly on the floor, his hands rested on the bed, taking his weight, with only his belly resting on Carlotta, because of the heat of the afternoon. Carlotta raised her arms to pull his mouth down on hers, and as her tongue slid into his mouth, he felt Gabriella join in the embrace. She put her hands on his hips, as if they were playing at leapfrog, and sprang up on his back. Her knees gripped his waist and her hands were on his shoulders – she was perched like a jockey on a racehorse, and she jolted up and down, her weight adding to the force with which he was ramming into her sister.

'*Ah, si!*' Carlotta gasped into his open mouth. 'Give me!'

'*Si* – give, give, give!' Gabriella cried out above him.

Held between the two women's hot and naked bodies, almost as if he were the salami in a long sandwich, Adrian's excitement erupted immediately. With an outcry that was almost a scream of delight, he sent a furious torrent spurting into the depths of Carlotta's shuddering belly, and her eyes rolled up in her head until only the whites were showing.

While they were cooling off, Gabriella wrapped herself in a thin silk dressing-gown and went to the kitchen to fetch a jug of iced lemonade, spiked with gin. She relocked the bedroom door when she came back, and the three of them sat naked and cross-legged on the wide bed and chatted while they drank to refresh themselves. To Adrian's chagrin, the ladies told him that when they met him at Zita's with Count Massimo, they thought he was one of Massimo's boys – a *finocchio*. They found it interesting that he was not the black-haired and liquid-eyed adolescent type that the Count usually favoured.

'Me?' Adrian exclaimed, red-faced and indignant. 'Why? Do I look like a . . . whatever you said?'

Gabriella tittered and Carlotta said you could never tell by appreances, especially in Venice. They had realised the error when Zita took him away from the table after lunch and returned an hour later without him.

'Did she give you anything?' Gabriella asked, trying to make her question sound innocent.

'Certainly not!' said Adrian. 'Whatever you may think, I'm not a gigolo either – at least that's one Italian word we all understand.'

'Gigolo is not an Italian word,' Carlotta retorted. 'Everyone makes that mistake. It is French. But why do you not answer my sister's question? Are you ashamed?'

Adrian explained, a little huffily perhaps, that he was in the honourable business of selling works of art, and not his abilities in bed – Zita had lured him away to show him a collection of icons, or so she said. But then he was too drunk to make any sensible resistance when she jumped on him. Both women laughed at that, and Gabriella said that the Princess had come back to the table with a contented look, from which all present assumed that she had got what she wanted from him.

'She violated me,' said Adrian, and the moment he said it he knew how foolish it sounded. Carlotta and Gabriella burst into hearty laughter.

Their mirth was vaguely insulting, he thought, but it had one merit – it made their bare breasts swing and leap in a way that was absolutely fascinating. He thought it might be worthwhile to persuade one of them – or better still, both of them – to do callisthenics while he watched. Just simple exercises, skipping up and down, swinging the arms forward and back, bending over to touch the toes . . . those full breasts of theirs would bounce up and down, swing sideways and forwards, dangle and sway under them when they reached down! The possibilities were dizzying.

When the laughter had run its course, Gabriella asked him if, when Zita jumped on him, his *cazzo* had been stiff or not – and he admitted sheepishly that it had been. That caused more laughing and an unanswerable statement that he must have wanted to do it as much as Zita, or he would have been small and soft. He saw there was no point in disputing with them and smiled and shrugged.

'Although I am English, I have an Italian temperament where women are concerned,' he told them.

'*Ah, si?*' said Gabriella.

'*Ah, si?*' Carlotta echoed.

'If a woman lays her hand on *this*,' he said, taking his soft little part in his hand, 'it swells up, even for a woman I dislike. And once it is stiff, I cannot help myself – I have to slide it between whichever pair of legs is open for me. The Princess guessed this and took advantage of me. She is a detestable woman.'

'No, no, no' said Carlotta, 'she is a sad woman. Her life has brought her many sorrows. When she was young she was beautiful, and many men wanted her. She had bad husbands, and she suffered much. Now she is too old to attract the pretty young men, and so she does as best she can.'

'But the young men at her lunch party were all . . . what was the word you used?'

Si – but some of these boys are very complaisant – do you understand me? They may prefer to go with a Count, but when a woman offers five hundred lire, some will close their eyes and do their best for her. With you Zita was fortunate – you wanted no money from her.'

'Why do you say she married bad husbands?' asked Adrian.

'When she was very young and very, very beautiful, her father married her to a banker from Milano. He was more than twice as old as Zita, and he made a great scandal when he found her with a young cavalry officer. They separated, and when he died she did not get much of his money. She was still young and still beautiful, and she married a German Baron who was very rich and wanted sons. Poor Zita could not oblige him – there is only a daughter. The Baron became involved in a great scandal with little boys and shot himself in his hunting-lodge in the forest. That was twenty years ago. Zita was then rich and she married a Bulgarian Prince she met in Vienna. But he was a monster, and when the peasants killed him during the War, she came back to Venice, to her family palace, and she will not marry again, I think.'

'This Prince – in what way was he a monster?' Adrian asked, interested in the misfortunes of the lady who had violated his male pride, apart from his body.

Carlotta and Gabriella looked at each other doubtfully, as if wondering whether the confidences of the Princess ought to be revealed to an outsider. The doubt was short-lived, the human desire to spread gossip vanquishing scruples.

'After the wedding, when Prince Ivan took Zita to his castle in Bulgaria,' Gabriella took up the story from her sister, 'she discovered that he was addicted to the – how do you say it in English – the *sadismo?*'

'Sadism, do you mean? He was cruel to her?'

'She told us about it when she came back to live in Venice,' said Gabriella, nodding vigorously. 'Her Bulgarian Prince had all the works of the Marquis de Sade in his library, bound in skin – the skin of young virgins, he told Zita. he made her read these books to him, an hour every day.'

'In Bulgarian? Surely not – how could she know that?'

'In French, of course,' said Carlotta. 'Zita has travelled much in Europe with her banker and with her German. She speaks the languages, just as we do, Gabriella and I.'

'I can see that the Princess had a boring married life, out in the countryside in an old castle, with a slightly deranged husband and servants speaking only Bulgarian,' Adrian said with a shrug. 'At least the Prince did not find her in bed with any cavalry officers, as her first husband did.'

'For two years he kept her locked up in a bedroom,' Gabriella continued, frowning at Adrian. 'She had no clothes and no shoes – all day and night she was naked. All day Prince Ivan was out hunting with his friends, but after dinner he came drunk to her room and made her read to him from his terrible books.'

'But this is ridiculous,' said Adrian. 'We live in the twentieth century, not the Middle Ages – how can a Prince keep his wife a prisoner like that? Zita was romancing to you, surely.'

'Do you think that the Balkans are like England?' Carlotta asked. 'The Bulgarians were set free from five hundred years of Turkish oppression by the Russians only fifty years ago. Much can happen there that would not be believed.'

'How little we know about the history of other countries!' said Adrian. 'In England we pay little attention to the doings of foreigners. But please go on – I am agog to hear what followed Zita's nightly readings to her lunatic husband.'

'Prince Ivan was not a lunatic,' said Carlotta. 'He believed that his destiny was to continue the work of the French Marquis in his own life. After Zita had read enough to him each night, he seized her and bound her hand and foot to a post of the bed, with her arms high up over her head. Then he taunted her and handled her body roughly, and when he had excited himself like this, he took a whip and flogged her back and bottom and thighs until she screamed for mercy.'

'Good God!' said Adrian, appalled by the account of Zita's domestic trials. 'She must have learned early on in her married life to start screaming after the first cut or two!'

'Perhaps,' Carlotta said with a shrug, 'but when the whipping stopped, there was worse. Ivan had no appetite for making love in the way men normally do to women. While Zita was still tied to the bedpost, he seized the cheeks of her bottom with brutal hands and pulled them open. She could scream as loud and long as she wished, but no one ever came to save her.'

'He penetrated her bottom and did it to her there?' asked Adrian, his eyebrows shooting up his forehead. 'How curious!'

'In England, maybe,' said Gabriella with a grin, 'but many men make love in their women's *culo* – Greek men, Bulgarian men, Egyptian men, Syrian men, Turkey men.'

'Italian men?' Adrian asked, fascinated by the information.

'Si, sometimes,' Carlotta answered for her sister, shrugging and setting her bare breasts jiggling, 'if the woman says yes. But Prince Ivan did not ask – he just did.'

'How long did this go on?' asked Adrian, astounded by what he had been told of the marital habits of foreign nobility.

'For two years almost,' said Gabriella, taking over again. 'Every night poor Zita was the victim of her savage husband and suffered as a martyr. Then he wanted to make other experiments that she had read to him from the books, and so he left her in peace while he did things to young girls from the village.'

'A welcome respite, I've no doubt, though hard on the village girls. What did he do to them?'

'Zita was never told, but it must have been even worse than what he had been doing to her. He did not neglect her entirely – when he remembered her locked in her bedroom, he sent one of his friends to tie her up and violate her – in the front or the back, whichever he preferred.'

'Always the same friend?'

'No, no – many different friends, many, many, she says. Then the War began, when all the world was mad – as mad as Prince Ivan – the peasants came one day and invaded the castle and cut Ivan's head off. They found Zita naked and tied down on a bed, with her arms and legs apart. They all had a good look at her, and they felt her all over before they set her free. That was after their leader got on the bed and had her, to find out what it was like with a Princess.'

'That is the most dreadful story I have ever heard,' Adrian said, 'I have misjudged the Princess Zita.'

'Perhaps,' said Carlotta with a sly smile, 'but now at least you understand why she takes a little revenge on young men when she can get them in her hands.'

'Why young men particularly?' Adrian asked. 'Prince Ivan was surely her own age when they married?'

'He was only eighteen,' said Carlotta, 'and Zita was almost forty. She thought he would be very strong for *amore* – and so he was, but in his own way.'

'Carlotta – look!' Gabriella exclaimed, pointing.

While listening to the story of Princess Zita and her marital records, Adrian had forgotten that he held his cherished part in his hand, having taken hold of it by way of emphasis or demonstration – he wasn't sure which – while he was telling the sisters about his lascivious temperament. It was limp no more – in the hot palm of his hand it had grown long and thick.

'*Aha!*' said Carlotta. 'Our English friend is hard again! It has excited him to hear of Zita being whipped and ravaged in her bottom! I think he enjoys the *sadismo* too.'

'I remember what he said to us,' Gabriella said with a grin, 'he said when it is stiff he is compelled to put it in between any legs that are open. We must guard ourselves, or perhaps he will throw one of us down and push it in!'

'It's time he learned what we do to men who try to rape us,' said Carlotta, shaking her blonde head.

Adrian had no time to protect himself before the two women hurled themselves bodily at him. he collapsed on the bed in a welter of arms and breasts and bellies and legs and he grinned and struggled in vain. They had him down on his back and were nipping at the flesh of his belly and thighs with their teeth, their hands all over him. Carlotta rolled over on to his chest and then Gabriella was across his thighs, and their combined weight pinned him to the bed. Then in a flurry of movement the sisters shifted their positions, so that Gabriella sat astride his loins and had his upright part in her hand, while Carlotta was squatting over his head, her wet and hairy fig poised above his face.

He stared at short range at her brown thatch and the fleshy pink lips beneath it, and he could not resist poking out his tongue to touch their moist softness.

'I think you liked it a lot when Zita violated you, Adrian,' she said, 'so we are going to violate you now – both of us!'

He looked down the length of his body to where Gabriella held his rearing part in her hand, and separated the pouting lips between her thighs with its distended head. *Santamaria*, he heard her sigh as she sank down slowly to impale herself on it, *Santamaria!*

Carlotta, kneeling astride his head, also lowered herself, until she rested on his face, his mouth under her warm split. Delicious thrills were flickering through his belly from Gabriella's ride on his embedded part, and without a pause he pushed his tongue into Carlotta to find her nub and lap at it. Evidently he had touched the right spot, for she began a little movement of her loins that slid her wet lips over his wet lips, in a tantalisingly slow tempo. By now his body was ablaze with sensation, and his mind was equally ablaze with thoughts he had never before thought. *Venice, Venice!* he cried in silent and passionate delight, *every time I think I have reached the limit of possibility, you give me more! To have two beautiful women at the same time is utterly fantastic – but to be had by them at the same time – there are no words for it! Life can never be the same again! Oh, my gorgeous Tweedledee and Tweedledum – you can ride me to a total standstill and I shall adore you forever for it!*

The wet slide of Gabriella's soft flesh up and down his stiff part was getting faster and more frantic, and he knew she was near the crucial moment. And so was he – his belly was quaking and his legs trembling. To what state Carlotta had come, he had no way to tell – she was rubbing herself against his mouth at the same steady pace. He forced more of his tongue between the wet lips that were kissing him with an unimaginable kiss and jerked his loins up and down to increase the soft sliding sensations inside Gabriella. It felt so good that he rammed up as high as he could reach and pumped furiously.

'Oh yes!' he gasped into Carlotta's slippery split, while his whole body convulsed and his frenzied desire exploded into her. Then Carlotta's soft thighs clamped his head between them tightly and the felt her quick little spasms against his panting mouth and his throes of ecstasy redoubled themselves.

When they were finished, the sisters rolled sideways off him and lay sighing and trembling for a few minutes. Carlotta was the first to recover – she slid round on the bed to take his face between her hands and kiss him on the mouth and lick his lips, testing the flavour of her own excitement. She moved down until her head lay on his belly, and she stuck out her tongue and lapped the head of his dwindled part, comparing the taste of her sister's excitement. But then Gabriella had her breath back and was leaning over him to rub her soft breasts against his face.

'Five minutes of repose, *carissimo*,' she said with a smile, 'then Carlotta and I change places and we have you again, *sì*?'

TWELVE

It was a measure of Adrian's growing confidence and familiarity with the interminable galleries, salons and marble statue-lined passages of the Palazzo Malvolio that he found his own way to the room where he had talked with Padre Pio. The stout little priest was leaning over his elbow-high desk, examining a faded document through a magnifying-glass when Adrian knocked at the door and went in. He glanced up, his gold-rimmed glasses up on his forehead, and beamed at his visitor.

'*Buon giorno*, Signor Trill,' he said, putting the glass down, 'is there something I can do for you?'

Adrian grinned at that, the irreverent thought crossing his mind that perhaps he might ask the priest to use whatever spiritual authority he had over the palace staff to tell Teresa to behave chastely towards him for the rest of his stay. *Amore* had become for her the first consideration of the day when she brought his morning coffee, and Adrian could think of no way to avoid it without offending her. In order to conserve his energies for whatever adventures Venice might offer him each day, he had instructed the maid to bring the coffee earlier – at seven – so that he could go back to sleep for another hour or so, after a quick tumble on the bed with her.

But it was not to complain about an over-obliging servant that he had come to talk to Padre Pio. In any case, the priest heard of the services Teresa gave him from her regular appearance in the confessional. Besides, thought Adrian, suppressing his desire to keep grinning, what sort of man complained because a young woman pulled off her knickers for him first thing every day? This morning she had been persuaded to do the work herself, by sitting over him and making the antique bed creak and groan to her bouncing up and down on him. She seemed to enjoy it – at least there was a broad smile on her face throughout the frolic. When she had finished him off she wiped him dry with a corner of the sheet, retied the cord of his pyjamas and left him to doze off.

'Forgive me for disturbing your work, Padre Pio,' said Adrian as he sat down very cautiously on the rickety and uncomfortable leather-seated chair. 'An interesting thought came into my mind this morning before I got up.'

'Strange thoughts come into men's minds before they get up in the morning,' Padre Pio commented, his head nodding up and down in resignation or agreement – it was impossible to tell which. 'They can be banished by getting out of the bed immediately on waking and kneeling to give thanks to God for preserving your soul through the perils and temptations of the night.'

'Yes,' Adrian agreed vaguely, wondering what the priest would advise in instances where the temptations of the night had been freely indulged. An act of penitence, perhaps?

The inadmissible truth was that Contessa Marina had come to his room in the night, after a long absence. Adrian had been in a deep sleep and did not wake until she was naked in bed beside him, her hand seeking inside his pyjama trousers. The room was dark, but he knew his companion by her perfume.

'What time is it?' he asked foolishly while he struggled up towards full consciousness.

'Almost two,' she whispered, her lips against his cheek. 'I dared not leave my room until I was certain Massimo was asleep. He suspects you, Adrian, which is why I could not come to you these last nights. Have you missed me, *carissimo?*'

'Tremendously,' he answered, wide awake as the impact of her words struck him. 'How do you know he suspects us – has he said anything about me?'

'No, that's not his way. But he comes into my room every day to have breakfast with me, before I am up. He sits on the bed and kisses my cheek while he wishes me *buon giorno*. But this is a ruse – he's looking for marks on my shoulders and neck. You must be very careful not to bite me, darling Adrian.'

'I think you're reading too much into simple affection,' said Adrian. 'What more natural than a husband wanting to breakfast with his wife?'

'Yes, but Massimo's affection has always been strange,' said Marina. 'While we are drinking our coffee together, he tells me to pull down my nightdress to uncover my breasts. I sit half-naked while he stares at me as if I were a marble statue! His desire has never been anywhere but in his eyes.'

'Not entirely,' said Adrian, wondering why he was embroiled in someone else's tiresome domestic grievances in the middle of the night, 'you have a daughter – that required more than the use of eyes.'

'When we were first married and he wanted a son, he used to come to my room in pitch darkness and stay no more than fifteen minutes. His mother had special nightdresses made for me as a wedding present – made of thick linen, that came up to my chin and were tight round the wrists and reached to my feet. It was like going to bed in a bag!'

'But if you were bundled up like that,' Adrian asked, amazed by what she had told him, 'how on earth did he manage to . . .?'

'There was a discreet little slit in the front, just about big enough to let him enter. No part of his body touched mine, except the few centimetres needed for his purpose. But when he was fully dressed in the mornings, he wanted me to sit naked to the waist while he drank coffee and told me I was as beautiful as a bust by Canova. But I've always believed he's looking for another man's love-bites.'

'At least you've given up wearing the comedy nightdresses with the slit in front,' said Adrian, grinning in the dark at the thought.

'When I told him I was pregnant, he never came to my room at night again. He was very disappointed with me when Bianca was born, instead of a boy, and to spite him I started to wear the tiniest and flimsiest nightdresses I could find in the shops.'

'I think you're right, he does suspect me,' Adrian said, his arms round her and his hands lying idle on her bare and warm bottom. 'You should not be here – suppose he checks your room in the middle of the night to see if you're there?'

At first he had dismissed Marina's anxieties as make-believe, whether deliberate or unconscious. But her reminiscences of married life cast a new light on the Count's frame of mind. And on reflection, the lunch Massimo had taken him to at Princess Zita's took on a more sinister appearance. Massimo had got him drunk and thrown him to Zita as if he were a juicy Christian fed to a ravenously hungry lioness in the arena. This must have been some sort of warning to stay away from Marina.

'In fact,' Adrian went on, 'it is too dangerous for you to be here, dearest Marina – I would never forgive myself if anything unpleasant happened to you because of me. I think you should go straight back to your room – it's a foregone conclusion he'll look in during the night to make sure you're there.'

'You are so sweet to worry about me,' Marina murmured, little kisses showering on his face while her hands opened his pyjamas from neck to groin, and caressed his chest and belly, 'I can't possibly leave you to another night of loneliness – that would be too frightful. You know I adore you too much to deny you the satisfaction I can give you – but in case Massimo does go into my room to see if I'm there, you must be quick.'

After Charlotta and Gabriella, not to mention Clara and a swim taken involuntarily in a sour-smelling canal, Adrian wanted to sleep, not to make love to a beautiful but neurotic Contessa. He tried all he could to convince her of the danger and of the prudence of returning to her own room, but she was too aroused to listen to such trifles, and by then the proximity of her naked body and the stroking of her hands had brought Adrian's disobedient part to the condition of stiffness she desired. And confident that he would now assume the initiative, she turned on her back and stretched her arms above her head, offering herself fully.

'Since Massimo thinks the worst of me,' she said, 'let's make his suspicions come true. Lie on me, darling – I want to feel your weight crushing me!'

Adrian half-sat up to strip off his undone pyjamas and throw them to the foot of the bed. Enough starlight came in through the open shutters to show him the alabaster sheen of her body, the dark hair cut in a bang across her forehead and the equally dark triangle between her strong thighs. It was sensible, he thought, to postpone his grand entrance a while, to give his lukewarm desire time to hot up and burst into flame, and so he bent over her to kiss her again and again, and feel the breasts which were being thrust up into his hands. Their buds were firm already to his touch, and he ran the balls of his thumbs over them while the palms cupped a breast each, squeezing and slowly kneading them.

His tongue left Marina's hot mouth, to lick at each breast in turn, and to lap at each bud. She sighed without a stop, and he drew a bud into his mouth and sucked at it strongly. *Adrian, oh Adrian*, she whispered, and his hand separated her legs so that he could finger the silky hair of her mound. When she started to gasp eagerly for more, he drew the tip of his middle finger up the soft lips, opening them and pressing in, until he could touch her secret nub. Under his teasing finger it felt hot and firm – and slippery with desire.

'Oh, darling...' she murmured, flinging her legs wide apart. 'I'm ready for you!'

And so she was, but he was not ready for her. A pleasingly hard part was one thing, and easily achieved lying in bed with a beautiful naked woman, but from that to climactic release was a long stride after the day he'd had. Before he took the stride he wanted to be quite sure he was strong enough not to fall down flat. His finger-tip moved deftly over Marina's hidden nub and she writhed in delicious spasms and murmured that she would go out of her mind with sensation. *Yes, enjoy it, darling*, said Adrian, speaking with a forked tongue, *it's been so long for us both!* He was delighted by the way her body shook and wondered how many times he should diddle her off before slipping inside to finish her.

'You're making me do it!' Marina gasped urgently. 'Put it in me quick or you will be too late!'

Without troubling to reply, he ravished her with his fingers until she went into convulsive shudders. her body arched upward on the bed and she gave a long loud cry of ecstatic pleasure as she reached the peak of sensation.

'Why are you doing this to me?' she said faintly when she was able to speak coherently. 'Don't you want me, Adrian?'

'I want you frantically,' he said, 'and I mean to have you – but first I mean to assist you to revenge yourself on Massimo in pleasure he could never imagine. Pleasure after pleasure, my *carissima*, pleasure piled up on pleasure, pleasure to rack your body and burn out your mind!'

He had touched the right note – Marina sighed and opened her legs wider.

'And also for me,' he continued, 'because it has been so long since we made love, I feel this enormous urge to play with you, so that the feel of your body will always be with me, however long it may be till next time.'

'Darling – what a beautiful thing to say,' she murmured. 'You can do anything you want with me!'

Adrian had become more aroused by the smooth wet open feel of her fig, and the words were hardly out of her mouth before his hand was between her legs again and his diligent finger at work on her secret button.

'And I must play with *you*,' Marina whispered, 'so that I can remember the feel of *this* when we are apart from each other.'

She held *this* in the hot clasp of her hand to squeeze it and massage it while she let him have his way with her, teasing her soft wetness with two finger-tips together. She drew her knees up and held them well apart, her pale belly twitching in the faint starlight, and he fingered her and stroked her expertly, kissed her eyes and her mouth and whispered endearments to her. He thought the second time would take longer than the first, on the analogy of his own sexual responses, but he was wrong about that. Her womanly nature was stirred as much by his words and his kisses as by the direct manipulation of her body, and long before he expected it, her bottom lifted off the bed and she wailed softly in climactic delight.

That was not at all what he intended – he wanted to bring her near to exhaustion before he gave her the one shot he knew was his limit that night. As soon as her throes ended and her legs lay slackly stretched out along the bed, he half-lay over her belly, to use his mouth on her breasts while again his fingers flickered inside her very slippery entrance.

'You mustn't tire me out, *carissimo*,' Marina murmured, her fingers running through his hair. 'I don't want to fall asleep when you are lying on top of me.'

'You won't, I promise you,' he said, and drove on forcefully, stimulating her with three joined fingers. In a very short time she moaned loudly and her belly shuddered in long spasms as she reached her peak yet again. Her repeated climaxes were causing his disorderly part to throb in her tight grasp, and he decided the time was right to give her what she had come to him for. He knelt between her parted legs and she stared as if hypnotised by the long and hard projection pointing towards her. She held out her arms in welcome, and a moment later Adrian's belly was on hers, and he was pushing deep inside her. She gave a lengthy sigh of satisfaction to feel herself penetrated at last, and threw her arms round him to hold him close.

Adrian's mouth fastened on hers and his hands slid under her bottom to grip her by the cheeks while he rode briskly in and out with short strokes. Her hot belly rose up to meet his push, and she amazed him by going instantly into a climax of heaving and squirming and crying out, which lasted for all the time he was plunging in and out. The sudden spurt of his desire seemed to throw her into ever stronger convulsions of delight, and he had long finished and was lying calmly on her belly recovering before she finally became still under him.

Which was all very well, except that the intensity of delight Marina had enjoyed made her want to do it all over again. But Adrian talked of the dreadful outcome if Count Massimo looked in her room to make sure she was there – there would be no more love-making by night for either of them then! At last she was persuaded of the good sense of Adrian's argument and slipped on her long silk dressing-gown to leave. Even then she sat on the side of the bed for another ten minutes, to rain kisses on him and hold his limp and slippery part in the palm of her hand, no doubt hoping it would grow strong again and give her a reason to stay with him for another half-hour. But it didn't, and off she went at last.

Adrian's wrist-watch showed twenty past three. He turned over and fell into the sleep of the just – or perhaps the sleep of the over-satisfied. Whichever it was, the duration was not long – at five minutes past seven white-aproned and smiling Teresa was at his bedside, pouring him a cup of coffee. No sooner had he drunk that than she asked her usual morning question, *Amore?* He would have preferred to say, *Non, grazie Teresa*, but that would have brought on a fit of the sulks and who knew what else by way of retaliation. So he smiled back at her and threw the sheet aside, to let her see he was naked. He gestured with both hands to indicate that she should bestride him, and she grinned and took down her knickers of pink artificial silk.

None of which concerned Padro Pio, thought Adrian, although his advice on getting out of bed immediately on waking to pray left no doubt that he was well aware of the thoughts that came into Adrian's head in the mornings. Though not perhaps what had been in Teresa's head when she spiked herself on his gluttonous part – and then recognised the perfume that lingered on the bed and on his body. *Madonna mia*, she moaned in dismay, *la Contessa! O Signor Adriano.* All the same, the knowledge that she was trespassing on the territory of a member of the family had not inhibited the chambermaid from servicing Adrian vigorously.

'The thought that came to me,' said he to the fat priest,

'is to do with the Malvolio patronage of art.'

He was telling the truth, and it seemed unnecessary to add that the thought had sprung into his head just after Teresa had ridden him to a pleasant, though unwanted climax.

'*Si Signor?*' said Padre Pio, his smile beaming out. 'How can I assist your interest? My instructions from Signora Tandy are to put the archive at your disposal.'

'The abiding Malvolio interest in painting is self-evident,' Adrian began carefully. 'Merely to look about oneself at the treasures displayed here in the palace is to see how deep and enduring this interest was.'

The little fat priest was looking at him quizzically.

'Count Paolo must surely have shared this family passion for art,' Adrian went on. 'You told me that he lived many years in England and France – and in Paris these were the great years of the Impressionist and the Post-Impressionist painters. Perhaps he bought some of their work, but if so it is not here.'

Padre Pio shook his head sadly in agreement.

'The Old Count inherited his ancestors' love of fine art,' he said, 'but unlike them he did not buy. The income of the estate was much diminished over the years, and he chose to spend what he had on other interests. This you know from our talk before.'

'The Count's interests were those of a gentlemen of the Belle Epoque,' said Adrian judiciously, 'and for that very reason it occurred to me to wonder if during his years in Paris he made the acquaintance of a French gentleman whose tastes were partly similar – I mean Count Henri de Toulouse-Lautrec.'

'Yes,' said Padre Pio, after a pause, 'they were acquainted. The Count de Toulouse-Lautrec gained a reputation of sorts as a painter of posters to advertise places of entertainment.'

'He did more than that,' Adrian said, certain that the priest knew more than he was saying, 'he was a painter of great talent and skill. His pictures are not valued very highly, but this is often the case for the first twenty or so years after an artist's death. Eventually his work will be reassessed and will become very valuable. There is not much of it, because he died before he was forty, and that too will enhance the price.'

'You are an expert in these matters and I must defer to you judgement,' said the priest, 'but how does this affect me?'

'Toulouse-Lautrec was as incessant sketcher,' Adrian said,

'wherever he was, even in a cafe getting drunk on absinthe, he would pull out a pad and sketch the people at other tables, if they looked interesting to him. He would have sketched Count Paolo, if they knew each other. Do you know of any sketches?'

Padro Pio nodded and smiled and explained that there was a book of sketches bound up together, and that Signor Treel was very welcome to look at it, for no art expert had ever examined it before. So saying, he pulled down one of the leather boxes that were stacked about the walls and opened it to produce a fairly thin book bound in red leather, with the Malvolio arms gold-stamped on the front. He laid it on the desk and opened it with great care, and Adrian stood beside him to look through it with him. The book contained about thirty sheets of paper torn from a sketch-pad, each with a characteristic drawing – mainly women in big-brimmed and feathered hats, sitting at small round tables on cafe terraces or in bars, a drink in front of them.

Several of the little drawings were of a man in frock coat and top hat, also sitting at a cafe table, but with a bottle of champagne and a glass before him. His face was known to Adrian from the portrait of Count Paolo that hung in the Small Salon. Unlike the unsmiling or blank expression of all the women, he looked to be in the best of humours – as well he might be, for the Count was rich enough to have any and all of these women by snapping his fingers. Adrian advised Padre Pio to look after the little book well, for one day it might be elevated from the archives to the art collection. He spent some time pointing out to the priest, who seemed very interested, the idiosyncrasies of Henri de Toulouse-Lautrec's style, and the easy mastery of line.

Before he returned the book to its box, the fat little priest paused as if in deep and solemn thought. Eventually he produced a leather folder from the box and told Adrian that as an expert it was permitted for him to see more of the records of Count Paolo's years in Paris, though a promise was required never to divulge what he had seen to anyone else. Adrian agreed at once, guessing that some aspect of the Count's life was about to be revealed of which a priest could not approve – and it did not need much guessing to know what that was likely to be!

The folder held three small water-colours, each about twelve inches by eight, and there was no need to look for the little TL signature in the corner to know who had painted the top one. It showed a scene in a high-ceilinged room with mirrors and white and gilt panelling, and a long red-plush sofa on which sat two women and a man. Unmistakably it was the salon of a good-class Paris brothel in about 1890. The women wore black stockings and knee-length white chemises, one was blondish and the other was ginger-haired. The gentleman who sat between them was Count Paolo, in white tie and tails.

'This is wonderful!' said Adrian, studying it closely. 'It must have been painted in the celebrated bordello in the Rue des Moulins where Toulouse-Lautrec lived for a time.'

'It was my fear that it was in some such sinful place,' Padre Pio said, shaking his head sadly, 'but how are you able to say where it was so certainly?'

'The facts of the artist's life are well-known,' Adrian told him. 'He painted this salon more than once – the red sofas and the women are immediately recognisable.'

The next picture in the folder was astonishing.

'Well!' said Adrian, marshalling his words carefully. 'Two things are apparent – this is *not* by Toulouse-Lautrec, but some lesser artist, and it is *not* set in the same establishment.'

'I know little of artistic matters,' said Padre Pio, 'but I guessed that another painter was at work. Only the first one of them has the signature TL – the others are signed PZ. Do you know who that was, Signor?'

'Not off-hand,' Adrian answered, leaning over the tall desk to look very closely at the signature. 'I know an MZ – he was a court painter to Czar Alexander in St Petersburg. He produced a marvellous series of etchings on erotic themes when he was living in Paris for some years.'

'And his name?' asked the priest, his pencil poised over a note-book to write it down.

'Mihaly Zichy – he was a Hungarian by birth. But these water-colours are not by him. The style is wrong – and they're not good enough to be Zichy's work.'

Adrian's interest was less in the artist than in the scene. The water-colour depicted Count Paolo Malvolio with three male friends in a salon of gilded furniture, swagged curtains and a great circular crystal chandelier. The men were in immaculate evening attire, as were the ladies with them, and it was almost a genre picture – a social gathering, a *soirée*. What made it unlike the many similar groups Adrian had seen was that one of the ladies was bending over with a smile on her pretty face and her arms resting on a yellow plush chaise-longue. Her stylish cerise frock was turned up over her back to bare a plump round bottom. Behind her stood Count Paolo, his evening trousers open and an impressively rigid part jutting out. He held it in his hand and was about to plunge it into the smiling young lady in cerise. The other members of the party stood together in pairs, chatting casually, while they watched the Count demonstrate his Italian virility.

'You understand, Signor Troll, why these are always kept in the secret archive,' said Padre Pio. 'They cannot be destroyed, for they are records of the Malvolio, however deplorable they may be. They have a true historic significance.'

'They do,' Adrian agreed, keeping his face straight with some difficulty. 'Do you know who the other gentlemen in the picture were?'

'The one standing on the left with an arm about the female in blue was a close friend of the Count's,' said the priest, 'a Venetian nobleman whose name I will not mention. As for the others, they were most probably acquaintances the Count made in Paris, but I do not know them. The women were . . . well, the picture speaks for them.'

'How interesting that an artist was invited along to record the *conversazione*,' said Adrian. 'He had a sense of humour, your Old Count.'

'But a misplaced one, I regret to say,' the priest replied.

In the other water-colour the Count was shown sitting on the side of a gilded four-poster bed with crimson curtains, wearing only his shirt. Beside him lay a buxom young woman, naked and stretched out on her back, one arm bent under her head and the other arm across her body so that her open hand rested over the thatch of dark curls between her parted thighs. Her eyes were closed and she was clearly in the last stages of fatigue, while Count Paolo looked extremely cheerful and was pouring himself a glass of champagne. Five empty bottles lay on the floor, which Adrian took to be a symbol for the Count's performance with the woman, rather than the amount they had both drunk. Again, the initials P.Z could be discerned in the bottom right corner.

'As you say, a priceless record, Padre Pio,' said Adrian with the merest hint of amusement in his voice. He left the pictures on the desk and returned to his hard-seated chair.

'When I get back to London I shall do a little research to find out who the artist PZ was – shall I write to inform you if I succeed?'

'I will be most grateful,' said the priest, his beaming smile again visible, 'these are questions of historical fact and must be established if the Malvolio archive is to be complete. You are very kind, Signor Trill, to take the trouble to help me. It was once a matter of family honour to keep archives, so that in a hundred years, or two hundred, or however long passed, it was possible to say what had been bought and how much was paid, and who the artist was. But since the Malvolio line came to an end when Count Rinaldo died, no one cares any more. But I came here more than forty years ago to maintain the archive, and I shall do so until I am summoned by God to account for my shortcomings.'

The fat little priest crossed himself three times, perhaps as a pious plea to the Almighty to postpone the summons Above for as long as possible. Adrian decided to tease him a little.

'It is regrettable that these pictures of Count Paolo cannot be framed and hung with those recording the doings of some of his ancestors,' he said. 'I much admired the large painting in the gallery beyond the salon of Cosimo Malvolio taking ship to defeat the Turks at Lepanto. And at the tip of the staircase there is an even more heroic painting of Lodovico Malvolio in top hat and sash, fighting to free Venice from Austrian rule. There is another painting over a door in the Library showing a Malvolio dressed like a bandit with rifle and cartridge-belt slung round him, posed with the great Garibaldi in front of a ruined building, helping to create the Kingdom of Italy.'

'The Malvolio have played an important part in the history of Venice and of Italy,' said Padro Pio, shaking his head slowly in regret. 'There were no great patriotic causes left for Count Paolo, and he followed the path of indulgence instead of duty. Not every man can be a hero, Signor Trill.'

'But Count Paolo's son was a hero – he lost his life fighting against the Austrians in the Great War.'

'That is true,' said Padre Pio with a sigh. 'Count Rinaldo redeemed the irregularities of his early life by dying nobly in his airplane.'

'By irregularities I take it you mean his friendship with Mrs Tandy?' said Adrian, amused by the success of his teasing.

'What else, Signor? To abscond with the wife of another

man is a serious matter. At least she accepted instruction from me and was received into the True Faith when she came to live here with Count Rinaldo.'

'And would have been married to him, I suppose,' said Adrian, 'but for the unfortunate circumstance of the Count dying before Mr Tandy, who is now Lord Brangton and has never done anything worthwhile. At least you have the memory of Count Rinaldo dying a hero for his country.'

'Much against my will, my regard for the truth forces me to the painful necessity of informing you that Count Rinaldo died only semi-heroically,' said Padre Pio reluctantly.

'But he *was* shot down flying against the Austrians?'

'Not precisely, Signor. The Count was on his way to fight the Austrians when his airplane crashed. An enquiry revealed that a mechanic had forgotten to put *benzina* in the tank.'

'A tragic death!' said Adrian, struggling to sound suitably solemn. 'In the years since then Mrs Tandy has been left alone to cope with the Palazzo and the Malvolio inheritance. Not easy for a lady, that. It is not for me to pry into personal affairs and finance, but the fact that I am here to look at the German paintings is proof enough that Count Rinaldo had very little to bequeath to Mrs Tandy. And the reason for that is not hard to deduce – his father Count Paolo spent the Malvolio fortune on enjoying himself in London and Paris.'

'What you say is true, I cannot deny it,' said the priest.

'A familiar story,' said Adrian. 'The same sort of thing was happening in England right through the eighteenth and nineteenth centuries – the new heir dissipates the family capital on wine, women and song – and gambling, of course. Was Count Paolo a gambler?'

'To folly, Signor! He lost hundreds of thousands at roulette at Baden-Baden and Monte Carlo. And as much again at cards with his self-styled friends in Paris and in London.'

'Perhaps it is surprising that the Malvolio fortune lasted as long as it did,' said Adrian, steering the conversation in the way he wanted it to go. 'At least the money held out to the end and he was able to die in style in the arms of a pretty woman in an expensive bordello. How miserable it would have been for him if his last years had been spent penniless here in Venice.'

'But you are wrong,' Padre Pio objected. 'The money was spent years before the Count died in a state of mortal sin. I pray for his soul daily, and say Requiem Mass for him on the anniversary of his death each year, to shorten his stay in Purgatory.'

'Your loyalty is commendable,' Adrian said. 'So he went to the money-lenders to finance his fun after the fortune ran out, did he? I'm sorry to hear it. At least not everything was sold to repay the debts after his death – the palace and the art collection remained for Count Rinaldo.'

'If you knew, Signor Trall!' the little priest exclaimed, throwing up his hands towards Heaven. 'But I have already said too much.'

'Please don't think I'm asking you to betray the secrets of the Malvolio family,' said Adrian carefully. 'That would be despicable! But there are certain things I can guess from what I see around me in the Palazzo. Not everything here is what it seems to be. As a man with a regard for the truth you will not deny that?'

Padre Pio shook his head and looked woebegone.

'My reading of the situation is that Count Paolo financed his playboy life by selling off masterpieces in secret, and putting good copies on the walls in their place,' said Adrian, risking offending the priest by stating his beliefs bluntly. 'I cannot be certain that there is one genuine painting or statue left in the entire palace. Count Rinaldo must have guessed this when he inherited from his father, or he would have raised cash to keep things going by a judicious sale or two.'

Padre Pio stared at him silently.

'I do not expect you to confirm this,' Adrian flattered him, 'not after a lifetime of loyalty to the Old Count, whatever he got up to abroad. But somewhere in your archive there will be a record of money paid for copies – someone here in Venice is my guess. Naturally, it will be in the secret archive.'

'Your hypothesis is most interesting, Signor, though it is no more than that. If I allow myself to accept your speculation as an amusing game, then what train of thought gives you to think that a local person was used to copy works of art, if any were ever copied?'

'Occam's Razor,' Adrian answered, 'a principle of economy formulated by an English Franciscan monk named William Occam. He said you shouldn't multiply entities if you don't need them – or words to that effect.'

'Did your terrible King Henry Eight kill this Franciscan?'

'No, he lived a couple of hundred years before Henry

closed down the monasteries and waved goodbye to the Pope.'

'I see. And how do you apply this principle of his to your hypothetical consideration of Count Paolo?'

'Easily,' said Adrian, with his most charming smile. 'Italy is the mother of European civilisation, whatever the French may claim. Painting, sculpture, drawing, architecture, music – all had their origin here. Where the best painters are to be found, there also are the best copyists and forgers. How could it be otherwise? The bulk of the Malvolio collection is by Venetian artists – who better to make copies? The little pictures I am here to look at are German, that I concede, but the Count would stay with the same copyists who had served him before – that is a matter of simple commonsense.'

'Your theory is fascinating,' said Padre Pio. 'Fascinating! Now if you will excuse me, I have much to do this morning.'

'Of course,' said Adrian, rising to his feet. 'You have been most kind in tolerating my idle chatter for so long. Just one small point – if there were any truth at all in my ridiculous theory, do you know the names of any copyists thirty or forty years ago capable of so excellent a standard of work?'

Padre Pio looked at him thoughtfully.

'Do I know the names of nineteenth century copyists?' he repeated. 'In the course of my work I have come across the restorers and other experts whose skills have been used here in the Palazzo. Dust and moisture in the air from the canals, summer heat and winter cold, even the passing of time itself, steal the colour and brightness from pictures and eat into marble statues like a disease of the skin. Much work has always been necessary, when the money was available to pay for it.'

'Yes,' said Adrian, 'but if there was one name in particular that would interest me . . . the name of the most talented of the Venetian picture restorers of forty years ago . . . then with all proper regard for the truth, Padre, what would that name be?'

'Antonio Bassini,' said Padre Pio, pulling his gold-rimmed spectacles down over his eyes to stare pensively at Adrian. 'He was a highly talented man, but a great sinner with young boys, may God rest his soul.'

THIRTEEN

Adrian had been greatly encouraged by what Carlotta and her sister Gabriella had told him about Princess Zita – so much so that when he went to the Post Office before lunch to send a telegram to Mallards saying he was making progress and would be returning to London in a day or two, he also made a telephone call to Zita's ancestral palace on the other side of the Grand Canal. A man-servant answered and kept him waiting a long time while he ascertained first if the Princess was at home and, secondly, if she was at home, whether or not she wished to speak to Signor Trale.

Patience was ultimately rewarded and Adrian was informed that the Princess would receive his call – and in no more than another three or four minutes her voice came on the line with little expressions of delight at hearing from him. She claimed to be overjoyed that he was still in Venice, for not having had any message from him she had assumed that he had gone back to London, or so she said, though Adrian was certain that Massimo would have kept her informed. He thanked her courteously for her kindness and hospitality when he had visited her, and took the opportunity to remind her that he had not yet seen the icon collection she had promised to show him. She suggested that he came round for lunch right away, and afterwards she would show him her collection. With a total disregard for truth. Adrian told her he had a lunch appointment already, but it would be an honour to call on her at about three o'clock, if that would not cause any inconvenience.

Not the least inconvenience, said Princes Zita breathlessly, he would be most welcome – she would look forward to seeing him and did he remember where she lived? He answered, aiming at a gallantry that would flatter her, that he would come by water and he was sure that every gondolier in Venice knew where to find the Palazzo of the celebrated and beautiful Princess Zita, and only when she chuckled and said, *Only the young ones*, did he understand the unintended *double-entendre* of his words. He had no arrangements for lunch, but he was determined not to fall once more into the trap of getting accidentally drunk – that gave Zita the advantage over him.

He found his way to the Rialto Bridge and chose a restaurant beside it, and ate alone. He ordered *fritto misto*, a deep-fried mix of bits of white fish, scampi, chopped octopus tentacles, sardine and squid, garnished with slices of lemon. A salad of thinly-sliced tomatoes and onion complemented it, and a carafe of cool white Soave wine from Verona washed it down. He followed that with soft Bel Paese cheese, a handful of green figs, and a cup of coffee with a tiny glass of French Cognac to set him up for the afternoon.

He had taken a table just inside the long open front of the restaurant, so that he could watch the boats along the Grand Canal, the broad slow water-buses chugging from stop to stop, stately gondolas dipping and swaying under the curving stone arch of the bridge, grimy work-barges with high-piled loads, darting water-taxis speeding by – the endless traffic of the great waterway – and while he watched he thought about his adventures in Venice and how little time he had left before Mallards and London reclaimed him.

Slow and gentle love-making with Barbara Chetwynd would seem a very tame affair after his frolics with the Contessa, and with Clara on all fours, and Bianca in the Biblioteca on the long window-seat, and Teresa straddling him in his pyjamas in the mornings, and Gabriella and Carlotta both having him together, and Delphine Tandy in her Sun-King Bed, and Gina in a railway carriage . . .

Dear sweet Barbara, he thought sadly, we are fated to part, I fear. So much had happened to him in his short time in Venice – could she learn to meet his new aspirations? It did not seem at all likely – when they first met he had taken her out for a week before she let him do more than kiss her. Then one evening after a concert at the Royal Albert Hall he had taken her home in a taxi, and going up Kensington Church Street he had forced the pace by cupping a breast in his hand while he pressed his mouth to hers. Two evenings later they went to a cinema early in the evening and held hands while they watched Gloria Swanson in the screen.

There was a scene in which she was only half-dressed,

wearing a close-fitting petticoat that reached less than halfway down her silk-stockinged thighs. A collective sigh arose from the audience in the cinema, and Adrian put his arm round Barbara's slim waist and in almost imperceptible stages moved his hand up to her breast. She wore a thin white jumper that evening, under which he would have liked to slip his hand, but a broad leather belt round her waist barred the way. He put her hand on his own thigh and parted his legs to encourage her, but she gasped faintly and snatched her hand away.

After the picture show she came back to his rooms and he made coffee. They sat together on the sofa to drink it, both knowing what he was going to do next. While he kissed her, he opened her belt-buckle with one hand and felt her breasts under her jumper and through her slip. She showed some reluctance at first, but he persevered until he succeeded in getting the jumper off, so that he could get a good look down her slip at her high-set, firm and pink-tipped breasts. He was sure that she was not a virgin, but she needed a great deal of persuading before he got a hand up her skirt and between her bare thighs. His fingers touched soft curls and warm lips, and that was the extent of his explorations for the evening – she let him caress her for a few minutes, then pulled his hand away and closed her legs and said it was time to go.

At their next two outings she declined to go back to his digs with him, and he was about to give her up as a lost cause when she arrived unexpectedly on a Saturday afternoon. They had an arrangement to go dancing that evening and he was surprised to see her. She said she had been shopping not far away and had called in on the off-chance. It sounded unconvincing, he thought, and she seemed nervous. He gave her a cup of tea and put an arm round her shoulders – and she pressed her mouth to his in an uncharacteristically hot kiss. Five minutes later he had her stripped to the waist and kissed her breasts until she was sighing and shaking.

He put his hand inside her thin silk knickers and played with her until she was wet and ready, but even then she did not want to go all the way. *Wait*, she whispered, *wait, Adrian*, and she fumbled his buttons open and got hold of his unruly part with a hand that was trembling. For all her reluctance, she knew well enough what to do with it – her long fingers slid up and down and, before he had fully realised her intention, she had milked him in hot spurts that wet her thighs and knickers. When he recovered from the shock, he was indignant at her duplicity and demanded to know why she had come to see him if she didn't want to make love properly.

He got no satisfactory answer, of course, her motives being as obscure to herself as to him. But when the confused emotions had settled a little on both sides, she took her knickers off and let him hang them from the mantelpiece to dry off before she left, and when he started to kiss and hug her again, she showed more warmth than before. He was able to feel her breasts without hindrance, and she held his softened part between her fingers, more interested in it since coaxing its strength from it. Evidently she felt more secure now, believing it harmless and spent, her experience of men limited to cooler natures than Adrian's. She let him stroke her between the legs, and press a finger-tip between the soft lips to touch her hidden nub. But not for long.

'No, you mustn't do that, darling,' she whispered when he began to tease it and arouse her in earnest.

'Only for a second or two,' he agreed but, with the skill of long practice on more willing girls, he soon had her excited to the point where she let her legs fall open and pushed her loins up at him. In a moment he was lying on her belly, and his newly sprung-up part was inside her. She sobbed and pleaded with him to get off, but her body told a different story, jerking under him to push her belly at his. He closed her mouth with his own and in short fast strokes forced her to the climax of sensation and gushed his desire into her quaking belly. After that he had no more trouble with her – it was understood that whenever they went out together she would accompany him to his rooms afterwards to make love.

Which was all very well, Adrian thought, staring out of the restaurant at the sun-shimmer on the opaque water of the Grand Canal, but Barbara's love-making was always half-hearted. He must woo her at some length each time, almost as if she were a self-renewing virgin. He accepted her listlessness because she was so beautiful and he adored taking her out and showing her off to his acquaintances. But it was impossible to imagine her on her hands and knees with her bottom bare and waiting for him to climb aboard. Or to think of her getting astride him in the mornings for a quick thrill before he went to work. Venice had worked its spell on him, he knew, and the old ways had become unsatisfactory.

He crossed the Grand Canal by the hump-backed Rialto

Bridge, looking into the display windows of the little shops that lined both sides. No Venetian came here to buy – the shops were for tourists with money to spend on high-priced souvenirs – gold and silver jewellery, cameo rings and brooches, bracelets and necklaces of polished red and white coral, tall goblets and long-stemmed drinking-glasses, candlesticks and chandeliers of gaudy red Murano glass. Adrian's guide-book had an odd item of information that amused him – long ago, it said, some of these small business premises on the bridge had been moneylender's booths and some brothels. Perhaps, thought Adrian, the idiotic merchant of Venice that Shakespeare wrote about came here for a loan from Shylock, and treated himself to a pretty whore with some of the cash.

He walked down the far side of the bridge into the street-market beyond. It was a narrow street, and with stalls on both sides there was not much room left for shoppers. The high-piled fruit was a delight to see – oranges and gleaming red cherries, yellowy-green melons, downy-skinned peaches, green figs, apples of every hue from pale green to dark red, long golden pears. But for the fact that he'd just finished lunch, he would have been tempted to gorge himself as he moved slowly along between the stalls. He bought a slice of crunchy white coconut, cooled under running water, and nibbled it as he strolled on towards the landmark he had noted in the guide-book, the Frari church.

This proved to be an enormous red-brick Gothic structure with a separate bell-tower, surprisingly grandiose for the mendicant and barefoot Order of Franciscans who had it built in the long ago. There were paintings inside by Titian and Bellini, said Adrian's book, but he had no time for religious art just then, and besides, this being the siesta hour, he was quite certain that all the doors would be locked tight. Between here and the church of San Giacomo, in a warren of old buildings, narrow streets and canals, lay the square dominated by Princess Zita's palace, if he could find it.

Like an uneasy conscience, the guide-book reminded him that San Giacomo had paintings by Veronese that he ought to see, but he comforted himself with the assurance that he could come back another day for that. There were Veronese pictures enough and to spare in Venice, but there was only one lewd Princess with a fine collection of antique Bulgarian icons.

With the aid of the map in the back of the guide-book he

175

came at last to the little square he wanted and tugged a bell-pull by the massive door of the Palazzo. The walls were too thick to hear any ringing, and some minutes passed before the door was hauled open slowly by a black-suited man-servant with a polite sneer on his face. Without troubling to ask Adrian's name he let him in and conducted him to a room furnished in the modern style, the furniture upholstered in peach-coloured satin and a few Cubist-style paintings on the walls. This was a side of the Princess he had not seen before, and he wondered what it meant. But before that line of thought could go further, Zita rose to greet him and offer her hand to be kissed.

She was in a stylish frock of royal blue crepe, with a little turn-down collar and no sleeves. It had a ribbon-like belt of the same fine material tied low under her hips, with trailing ends almost to her knees. Her Titian-red hair was brushed back in two wings and fastened behind her head, her wedge-shaped face was carefully made-up, her finger-nails gleamed as red as fresh-spilled blood – in short, Princess Zita was in fighting fettle and ready for active service at the drop of a hat. Not that Adrian had a hat to drop – the man-servant had taken it to hang up somewhere – but he was conscious of presenting a fine appearance, suitably informal for an afternoon call.

His elegant grey and black striped blazer had survived its immersion in the canal very well. It had been rinsed through by the laundry-women of the Palazzo Malvolio, dried care-fully and expertly pressed, as had the dove-grey trousers he had worn at the time of the *accident*. Zita drew him down to sit beside her on the peach-coloured sofa scattered with soft cushions, and they chatted as casually as if neither of them knew what he was here to do to her. And only when the proprieties had been adequately acknowledged in this way did Zita's scarlet-nailed hand rest on Adrian's thigh. He laughed and put his hand over it to stop her sliding it up into his groin, and said that he had come at her invitation to see the icons *first*.

Zita laughed too and took him to a square room not far from the large salon with a honey-coloured parquet floor and walls painted white. Around the walls hung the celebrated collection of her late and unlamented Bulgarian husband, more pictures of Saints in glory than Adrian had ever seen in his life before or was ever likely to see again. They were all painted on wooden tablets, the largest perhaps twelve inches deep by nine inches wide, the smallest a miniature of about four by three. Only the head and shoulders of the Saints were shown, the space around them covered in dully gleaming gold sheet. Some icons had gold frames, studded with gemstones of red and blue and green, some had frames of black wood, adorned with white stones and ivory.

'*Stupendo!*' said Adrian, a word he had learned from Carlotta and Gabriella, who had used it to compliment him when they were having him the third or fourth time.

Zita was very knowledgeable about her collection, and pleased him by giving the dates of many of the icons and the workshops and monasteries where they were painted. Many were recognisable at once as St Mary, Mother of God, and the convention was to show her with a long face and a bright blue wimple. The child she cuddled was aged, according to the painter's preference, anywhere from a week to six years. The four Evangelists could be seen many times on the walls, and the Apostles under golden haloes the size of cartwheels. Adrian asked if there were any specifically Bulgarian Saints, and Zita nodded in confirmation and pointed some of them out to him.

'This is St Slovensky,' she said, indicating a solemn-faced man with a fringe of black beard, 'an early missionary who went to Bulgaria to help convert the people to Christianity. But his head was cut off by a nobleman who disagreed with the doctrine that he must have only one woman.'

'Not a tactful man, Slovensky,' said Adrian. 'He should have left that bit of the teaching for later. Aristocrats with lots of women in the castle to take to bed are bound to get touchy when someone says they are doing wrong.'

'But, according to the legend, it was the noblewomen who asked for him to be killed,' said Zita. 'Perhaps the Count would have been happy to get rid of them if he was old and worn-out, but for the women it would be losing their position. If the Saint said they could stay as ladies of the castle, but not lie down any more for the nobleman, they would not have hated him.'

'On the other hand,' Adrian suggested, 'a man in the prime of life would have taken very sharply against any Saint who told his women-folk to keep their legs together.'

'*Si* – over here is St Irene of Plovdiv – she was a martyr for keeping her legs together, as you say.'

'She looks very young,' Adrian said, his head on one side to study the pale round face with big black eyes.'

'*Tredici* – how do you say it? Thirteen. Her husband had her thrown in a river to drown when she stopped going to bed with him because of his sins.'

'Her husband?' said Adrian, raising his eyebrows. 'They must have married young in the old days in Bulgaria.'

'The peasants still did when I lived there,' Zita informed him. 'In the towns the girls are not married before fifteen or sixteen years of age, but in the country villages they think it better to give them a husband as soon as they can have babies.'

'How did this unfortunate child become a Saint after she was drowned in the river?' Adrian enquired.

'She made miracles after she was dead and in heaven, so they knew she was a Saint,' said Zita, surprised at his question.

'Miracles at her tomb, you mean?'

'No, she was not buried anywhere. The Maritsa river carried her away. But at the place on the river-side where her husband had her thrown in, if women prayed to her when they were pregnant but did not have a husband, she made them not pregnant again so nobody knew they had been with a boyfriend.'

'But that's outrageous!' said Adrian. 'A Saint who performs abortions – I've never heard of such a thing!'

'People must live,' said Zita, 'and the best Saints are those who help with the important things, not who expect everyone to be holy all the time. This one over here – he was a much too holy man – he is called St Vaclav the Pure.'

'He has a most unhappy look,' Adrian said thoughtfully. 'Why was he nicknamed *the Pure*? He had nothing to do with women, I suppose?'

The face was that of a man in his twenties, round but stern, black-bearded, and completely bald under his halo.

'The story says that he went with women all the time when he was young and was the papa of eighteen children by many women. One day in church he heard a bishop preaching about sin between men and women and he went home and took a knife and cut off his *coglioni* – you understand *coglioni*?'

To make sure that he did understand, she put a hand between Adrian's legs and clasped his pompoms.

'These,' she said, smiling at him, 'he cut them right off

and then went to live with the monks in the forest.'

'The man must have been demented,' said Adrian in amazement, while he shuffled his feet apart a little way on the parquet to accommodate Zita's clasp.

'Come and see this one,' she said, leading him by the grasp she had on him, 'he had a different idea to stop himself sinning with women – there, St Elias. Perhaps you will like him.'

'Tell me about him,' said Adrian, feeling his reckless part starting to grow long and thick in his trousers.

'He was a young priest and the people of the town where he lived believed he was very holy. Each night a different woman was sent by her husband to sleep in the priest's bed, to prove he was a Saint. He was naked and she was naked, and all night they lay like that in the bed, saying prayers, and outside the door sat two or three old women to make sure Elias did nothing to the woman.'

'How long did this go on?' Adrian asked, thinking that the wily priest sounded like a character from Chaucer's *Canterbury Tales*. One of the disreputable characters who were passed over in silence by school-masters.

'Years and years and years,' said Zita, chuckling with him, her other hand sliding down the top of his trousers to feel how stiff he had become, 'until he was a very old man with a grey beard and it wouldn't stand up, not even when the woman with him held it in her hand to make a test of his celibacy. But I know these Bulgarian people and how they think, and all those years when Elias had a naked woman in his arms every night to prove his holiness, I think he had the silent *orgasmo*. What do you say?'

'I think so too,' he agreed, his stiff six inches leaping in Zita's hand. 'Why don't we go up to your bedroom before I have the not-so-silent *orgasmo* standing here?'

The first time he climbed the staircase, Adrian had needed an arm round his waist to help him up, but not this time – his arm was around the Princess and he was almost dragging her up the wide marble stairs.

'You are very hot for me today, *caro*,' said Zita with a lewd smile, still caressing him slowly through his trousers. 'I knew you would come back to me.'

In the dim cool of her shuttered bedroom, she led him to the canopied bed and pushed him to sit down on it while she leaned over him and used both hands to unbutton his trousers and pull out his impatiently jerking part. Adrian threw off his blazer and striped tie while she was feeling him, then put his hands on her shoulders and forced her to her knees. Zita stared up at his face with a happy smile – she expected him to stay passive while she made use of his body to amuse herself. But he had come with a different programme of activities in mind, and the time was not far off when she would find out what he intended. He stretched out his legs and parted them, leaned back on his hands and let her think she had him at her command.

'There is one icon you haven't shown me yet,' he said with a grin, 'you have a Titian-red one that performs its own miracles when it's displayed. Take your clothes off and let me see it.'

Zita stared at his erect part and licked her lips greedily, before rising to her feet. She undid the low-slung belt of her elegant blue frock, put her hands behind her head to open buttons, and pulled the frock over her head. She was wearing no chemise over her strongly boned bust-bodice, and that came off to let her long flabby breasts dangle down almost to her belly. Her silk stockings were gartered above the knee, and when they were removed, only think white satin knickers covered her secret work of art. She hooked her thumbs in them and slid them down her legs and away, then stood up straight to let Adrian look.

'*Ecco*!' she said, smiling, 'the most precious icon of all. I call it St Zita in Triumph.'

'*Fantastico!*' said Adrian, staring at the bright red dyed curls between her legs. 'Will it perform a miracle for me?'

'For the faithful it performs miracles every day,' she said, 'five or six times, if their faith is strong enough. But first you must do what believers always do with icons – kiss it.'

Very nimbly for a woman of her fifty years or more, Zita took two steps forward and knelt on the bed, her legs straddled over Adrian's lap and his face pressed between her dangling breasts. He grasped the slack cheeks of her bottom to steady her, bowed his head to her creased belly and kissed the big loose lips under the red-gold tuft. And then, to maintain her sense of half-contemptuous superiority until he had her where he wanted, he ran his tongue slowly up and down.

'That's good!' she said. 'That's the sort of devotion I like to see. St Zita will make a special miracle for you.'

She pressed her hands on his shoulders to make him lie

back, meaning to impale herself on his rampant part.

'Just like old times,' said Adrian cynically, resisting her.

'*Si?*' she asked, not understanding why he didn't lie down on his back for her to mount and ravage. She put her hands under her long slack breasts and lifted them towards him, and he took hold of them and stood up quickly, so that she slipped off him to the floor. Down on her knees, she stared up at him with a startled expression, and still holding on tightly to her loose breasts, he sat down again on the bed. Zita grinned uncertainly when he wrapped her softly pendulous flesh about his hardness, then murmured, *Ah, si, cosi!* and took over from him, squeezing the warm slackness about his male pride.

'That's the idea!' said Adrian, jerking rhythmically between them, and together he and the Princess stared down fascinated at the purple head that popped out from its pale-skinned burrow and vanished back down again. The sight was as stimulating to her as to him, for she let go of her breasts, bent her neck and opened her painted mouth to suck in the head of his fully distended part. Her wet tongue lapped slowly, setting up the most delicious thrills of sensation and, looking down at her head bobbing up between his thighs, Adrian smiled mockingly – Princess Zita's delusions of superiority were about to be put to a severe test.

He seized the dyed hair above her ears to hold her fast and pushed his stiffness deep into her mouth, almost choking her. Her dark eyes rolled up to stare at him in surprise, and then anger when the speed and strength of his strokes between her lips made her think he was going to do it in her mouth instead of in her red haired split. Her clenched fists thumped heavily on his thighs, but Adrian squeezed her body between his knees to keep her still and gripped her hair so fiercely that the ivory comb holding it pulled loose and fell to the floor behind her. The moment had come for him to put his theory to the test.

'Since the firm hand of your last husband was removed,' said he outrageously, 'you have got above yourself, dear Princess – and the result is deplorable! Without regular beatings to keep you in your proper place, you have slipped into an attitude of sneering contempt for men.'

Whether her knowledge of English was good enough for her to understand all he was saying did not much concern him. His tone was deliberately domineering to convey his meaning. Before she had time to rebel, he loosened his hard knee-grip and jerked her shrieking upwards by the hair. As soon as he had her half-upright and off-balance, he twisted her sideways across his lap, face-down. She was huffing and puffing and kicking out behind her, but he steeled himself to be implacable. He held her head down near the floor with a hand on the nape of her neck, while he stroked the large and flabby cheeks of her rump and ran his fingers up and down the deep furrow.

'Are you by any chance acquainted with a French lady named Madame Birchini?' he asked, to which the only reply was a flow of furious Italian, which he took to be profane. Some of it was so abusive-sounding that it might even have been Bulgarian.

'No?' he asked, trying hard not to laugh at the ludicrous situation he had created. 'Madam is unknown to you? Then let me quote her words, as nearly as I can remember them: *you are in my power and I must have total submission. Do not dare to defy me, or it will be the worse for you!*'

His inspiration was the book he had bought in a shop on the Place Pigalle in Paris. A little experimentation soon showed him that, preferable to the back-of-the-neck grip, was his left forearm pressed heavily down across the small of Zita's back to stop her bucking. Nothing would stop her noisy abuse, short of a gag . . . and no sooner had the idea occurred to him than he snatched her white satin knickers from the pile of her clothes beside him on the bed and reached down left-handed to stuff them in her mouth. She tried to bite his fingers off and, when he took his hand away, she used her own to extract the wad of thin material from her mouth. Undaunted, Adrian fondled her bottom and felt between her legs and underneath her to pinch her soft and hairy folds, while she heaved and wriggled to free herself.

'*What? You hesitate to expose your person to me?*' Adrian said loudly, almost giggling as he tried to remember the old-fashioned words of the book, '*then your modesty shall be further outraged!*'

He raised his hand and brought it down hard across her bare backside. She cried out in indignation while he smacked again and again, chanting the words as he recalled them.

'*Smack, smack, smack fell his hand on her bare behind, and she cried out in desperation, writhing in her attempt to get away from her tormentor. It was all in vain, the strong hand on her back kept her down!" In her dire distress, she kicked and lifted her legs and spread them apart, giving Monsieur Raoul an opportunity to enjoy the view of her intimate parts!'*

'Stop this! Stop it, I tell you!' Zita cried, struggling to be understood in English. 'Are you insane, to treat me so?'

Adrian was enjoying himself hugely. His male pride swelled thicker and thicker, trapped under her belly and rubbed against her soft skin by her squirming. The feeling was sheer delight, and he knew this to be one of life's unrepeatable moments. For the rest of his days he would remember with joy and pride the smacking of Princess Zita's bare bottom! And, as he slapped at those wobbling cheeks, he recited from *Madame Birchini's Revels* in a theatrical manner, as if declaiming words of purest poetry from Nobel Prize-winner W. B. Yeats' own pen:

> *Raoul's burning eyes*
> *stared into the cleft*
> *between her thighs*
> *and she sobbed with shame*
> *to know a man was looking*
> *at her most secret parts*
> *with hot lust in his heart*
> *but try as she might*
> *she could not control*
> *her kicking legs*
> *or close her thighs.*

Through his wildly soaring euphoria, Adrian was aware that if he went on like this much longer he would saturate Zita's belly with a flood of his own lust. That would be a sad waste of a never-to-be-repeated opportunity! He knew he must move fast – he stood up quickly, pitching Zita off his lap, and while she flailed about with her arms and cursed him to hell and back in various languages, he grabbed her shoulders, swivelled her about on her knees and threw her forward on the bed. She landed as he intended, spread-eagled and face-down, her legs trailing on the floor.

At once he was on his knees knees her, and his wanton part was nodding as he pushed his trousers down and stripped his shirt over his head. It was quickly done, and before Zita had recovered from the shock of landing face-down like a sack of flour, he had his hands on her back and his weight on them, to immobilise her. Seen from where he knelt, and in his state of extreme arousal, her soft-cheeked bottom had become a vision of sensuality with the angry red patches his hand had imprinted on white skin, and he stared entranced.

Zita had fallen with her legs apart, the way a sensible woman did in such circumstances. There, where the crease between her cheeks ended, there below it lay exposed to him her bright red-dyed mound. Adrian pressed his longest finger will into the slack-lipped slit and Zita said, *Ah*! and twitched once or twice and stopped trying to break free. She knew where she was now and what he was going to do, and she lay still and waited for him to slide into her. he shuffled in close between her splayed legs and put his proud part to her split. She sighed and said *Finalmente!* and felt under her own belly to prise herself open for him.

Adrian slid in with great ease – the indignity of having her bare bottom smacked had evidently excited her, in spite of all her obstinate resistance. And that proved his case – her body and her mind wanted different things, perhaps, but the body was the winner every time. Guessing this about her had given him the upper hand this time, as it had given her the advantage the last time. It was Zita's turn to lie under him to be used, not the other way round as when he was drunk.

His ever-eager part slid between her fingers and deep inside her, and almost at once she began to tremble feverishly. There was no call to hold her down now – he rested his hands on her hips to support himself while he see-sawed to and fro. Smacking her bare bottom had made him very excited and it would take little more to tip him over the brink into climactic release. Zita was moaning lightly, her big flabby breasts sliding back and forth along the bed as her body jerked to his sturdy push, and the rub of her engorged buds on the satin bed-cover seemed to delight her. Indeed, any residual anger she felt from her humiliation was being fast transformed into a more pleasurable emotion – her moans and heavy sighs became high-pitched little squeals.

Adrian rode her fast, delighted by the sound of the rhythmic slap-slap his belly made against her bare behind. The moment of truth came rushing towards him, and into his whirling mind came an inappropriate thought – who was having who now? He had been very firmly in command when he turned Zita over his knees and paddled her bottom, and the proof was that she responded with gratifying fury and verbal abuse. But how could it be true now that she was so obviously enjoying being ravished, face-down though she was? Adrian had the uncomfortable feeling that he was doing what Zita wanted him to do. Whether he was on top or she was on top, he was giving her the thrill she expected.

He had to regain the initiative or his second encounter with her would be as gross a defeat as his drunken first. He pulled his wet six inches out of her at once and sat back on his heels to consider, his mind in a turmoil. Zita began to moan and sigh, *No, no, no! Put it back! Put it back, caro!* and he reached a decision which bewildered him. He put the head of his slippery length to the puckered knot of muscle in the crease between her slack cheeks and pushed! He felt himself sliding straight in, without obstacle or excessive tightness, and Zita exclaimed in astonishment.

For that matter, Adrian had also astonished himself by what he had done, he had never in his life – not even in the wildest of his erotic fantasies – dreamed of making use of this orifice of a woman's body for his pleasure. Nor even imagined any woman wanting it used for that purpose – and yet if Gabriella was to be believed, Bulgarians, Turks, Greeks, Egyptians – to name but a few – made love in the women's *culo!* And Prince Ivan had done this to Zita nightly! How little he knew of sensuality, Adrian thought deliriously, and how much he had learned here in Venice!

He thrust with short and cautious strokes into this unknown aperture, trying to come to terms with the sensations coursing through him. It seemed that Zita was stirred to new heights of pleasure by what he was doing to her, for her little shrieks of pleasure were more forceful, and her squirming was rubbing the soft flesh of her bare cheeks against his belly in a way that brought him to mind the gyrations of an accomplished Arabian harem belly-dancer.

'Zita you trollop!' he sighed. 'This is *fantastico!*'

She heaved her back up under him and pushed hard against his furious strokes. Adrian passed beyond the familiar ecstasy of love-making to a plane of mental and physical disorientation where pleasure and pain could no longer be told apart. With a loud shuddering wail, he squirted his fiery passion into Zita's ravished bottom, at which she screamed and writhed frantically under him. The very complex emotions that surged and boiled in him blanked out his mind for a moment or two, and when he next was aware of his surroundings he was lying on his back on the bed. Zita hovered over him, he long sagging breasts trailing on his chest as she licked his mouth and eyelids. When she saw his eyes flicker open, she held his face between her hands and kissed his mouth and babbled, *Amore, amore!*

FOURTEEN

After a restful night during which Contessa Marina did not come to his room, Adrian woke early in the sunlight streaming through his unshuttered windows. He had been dreaming, and he lay still trying to catch the fading wisps before they vanished forever. A phrase lurked in his mind – *lady of the house* – and his irrepressible part was at full stretch in his pyjamas. There was a half-glimpsed fantasm of a naked and dark-haired woman and, as Adrian's mind began to function consciously, he put a name to her – Cynthia Parker – a housewife he had met briefly a year or so before.

He had gone on a grey and drizzly autumn afternoon to a dull suburb to look at a picture. A letter signed K. Parker had been delivered to Mallards informing them that the writer owned a painting by Thomas Gainsborough which had been the property of his late father, Mr P. Parker. It was a large portrait of a lady in pink, with a straw hat. The size made it difficult to bring in to Mallards, but if someone could be sent to look at it and give a rough estimate of its value, K. Parker was inclined to put it for auction in their esteemed hands.

'A Gainsborough in Bedford Park, wherever that may be?' said Adrian scornfully to his superior when he was shown the letter. 'But stranger things have happened. I'll go there after lunch and have a look at Mr Parker's treasure.'

The Wisterias proved to be a dull semi-detached house in a dull street of semi-detached houses in the dullest of suburbs between Shepherds Bush and Acton Green. Adrian stood in the entrance porch and banged the knocker, pleased to be out of the drizzle after his uncomfortable walk along the street. He took off his bowler hat to shake the rain from it, and was bare-headed when the door opened. The lady of the house, for so he thought of her, was a slender woman of about thirty with curly dark-brown hair parted at the side and swept off her ears. She was not pretty, nor was she plain – and she had a marvellously clean pink complexion, innocent of powder, rouge, or any other cosmetic aid.

Adrian introduced himself and she asked him in. The entrance was small and cluttered with a hall-stand for umbrellas, hats, mackintoshes, walking-sticks and other outdoor equipment. Mrs Parker found a hook for Adrian's hat and coat and eased past to show him into the front parlour, as she called it, to view the painting. She turned half-sideways to pass him in the narrow space, and the back of her hand accidentally brushed against his thigh. The touch was light and fleeting – but it flashed a message through Adrian's body that brought a smile to his lips.

The passing contact of her hand had not been done with any conscious intent, he knew that, but some secret aspect of her mind wanted to convey a possibility that Mrs Parker might be shocked to admit. Like others of an enquiring mind, Adrian had taken an interest in the theories of Dr Freud, and he agreed with the Viennese sage that sexuality permeated every aspect of life – and directed it. He had read about *Freudian slips* – the unintended words and acts that gave away people's hidden urges and undermined their defences. This was one, he was certain – and for proof he had the fact that Mrs Parker was trembling slightly and looked bemused. She had realised the significance of her *accidental* touch on his thigh, and knew herself to be vulnerable to him!

'You can see it in here,' she said, her hand on the brass knob of the parlour door, and although she meant the picture he had come to value she *might* have been thinking of something else. Adrian decided he would enliven a dull afternoon with a little genuine experimentation. He reached past her to put his hand over hers on the door-knob, so stopping her turning it.

'It will be a pleasure to see it,' he said, 'but before you show it to me, how long has your husband had it? Not long?'

'No, it hasn't been all that long,' she agreed, her voice faint and a pale pink blush on her cheeks. 'We've been married eight years and it was soon after that.'

'Is he very fond of it?' Adrian asked, noting that she did not move her hand away from under his. 'I mean, does he get a *lot* of pleasure out of it?'

Mrs Parker's wonderfully clear complexion was bright red now.

'You'd have to ask him that,' she whispered, her voice almost inaudible.

During this short interrogation, Adrian had inched himself closer and she had responded imperceptibly by turning to face him, her back to the parlour door. He was so close that he had only to sway forward slightly for his belly to press on hers and his thighs to touch her thighs. Mrs Parker sighed and let herself slump back against the door, and he put his hands on her hips and kissed her. She shook and trembled against him, and he pressed harder against her to make her aware of how hard his ready part was. Her arms slipped round his waist and she pulled him closer still, and while he kissed her breathlessly he put his hands on her bottom to knead the cheeks through her green tweed skirt.

Without a word spoken, she led him up stairs carpeted in blue and with polished brass stair-rods into the front bedroom. Net curtains screened the bay window from inquisitive eyes, and she stood by the matrimonial bed and let him undress her. Her name was Cynthia, he learned, and she was thinner than he considered becoming in a woman. Off came her home-knitted jumper to show a vest of ribbed white cotton, and down came her tweed skirt to surprise him by revealing bright red knickers, into which the vest was tucked, and a white suspender belt that supported her beige stockings. In the nick of time Adrian recognised a look of near-panic in her eyes and he put both arms round her and pressed her close while he kissed her, forcing his tongue into her mouth until pleasure overrode fidelity and she responded.

Her belly was tight to his, while his hands were behind her, tugging the thin white vest out of her knickers and squeezing the cheeks of her bottom. When he was sure her qualms had been banished, he pulled her gently down to sit with him on the side of the double bed – on which her husband claimed his conjugal rights when he was in the mood, but if that thought was also in Cynthia's mind she was unperturbed by it. Her arms were round Adrian's neck and she wanted to kiss and be kissed endlessly.

His hand crept up her warm thigh and then into the leg of her artificial silk knickers. She was very hairy between the legs, he found, and when his finger-tips brushed over the soft lips there he found them closed and not easily separated. She was not used to taking handsome callers upstairs in the middle of the day, he guessed, and she needed encouragement to go all the way. He unbuttoned his trousers and guided her hand inside, and though she hesitated at first her desire got the better of her and she grasped his gallant part. After that it was easy to pull her vest over her head, get her knickers off and lay her on her back.

Before there was time for her to cool off, he had his clothes off and was beside her, caressing her small soft breasts.

'I can't believe I'm letting you do this,' she whispered, but before second thoughts could change her mind, he put his mouth to her breast and his fingers between her legs, and stimulated her to moistness and acceptance of what he was going to do to her. Her legs opened a little, though not enough to signify any wild enthusiasm and Adrian wondered if she was like this with her husband, the absent K. Parker. To consolidate his position he put his belly on hers and pushed his boisterous part inside her. Her eyes closed at once and she lay still while he trust away – and perhaps it was only nervousness, but she came to no climax when he squirted his passion into her belly.

She didn't seem to mind her own inadequate response – she lay beside him afterwards, stroking his face and hair and pecking at his mouth with little kisses. *Not good enough*, Adrian said to himself, *I'm not letting you off that lightly, Cynthia*. He let the kissing go on while he stroked her belly and between her thighs until he regained his strength. And then, greatly to her surprise, he rolled on top of her again. To show her how to go about making love, he reached down with both hands and gripped her thighs, pulled her legs right up until her bent knees touched her belly and she was wide open.

Her face turned scarlet, her eyes stared at him in surprise, and he plunged in and out of her, his hands kneading her small breasts. This time he made her so wet and hot that she began to whimper and he kept her hanging over the brink of ecstasy for at least five minutes. Only when she became almost hysterical with overwhelming sensation did he finish her off with short hard strokes. She screamed at the instant of climax, her back arching up off the bed in frantic spasm.

When she could speak again she spent at least five minutes in red-faced apologies for making so much noise and, when he had persuaded her that he loved her ecstatic outcry, her wonder and gratitude were so immense that she showered kisses on his face and eyes and murmured incoherently. But at last she was calm again, and they dressed and went downstairs to see the picture. With all the tact he could muster, Adrian told her it was sadly not a Gainsborough, not a painting at all, but an oleograph. At that she looked puzzled, until he explained that it was a copy of a well-known Gainsborough portrait, printed in oil colours, worth nothing.

Cynthia looked disappointed and relieved at the same time, in about equal measure. She went to the kitchen to make a pot of tea, the standard English response to all life's vicissitudes. She and Adrian sat side by side to drink it, on a bottle-green moquette settee under the fake picture, and he decided to have her again. The intensity of the climactic pleasure she had felt upstairs seemed to have cured her of nervousness. She let him kiss her and put his hand up her jumper to squeeze her breasts and, when he took her knickers off, she leaned back with her thighs open as far apart as her green tweed skirt let her.

Adrian played with her delicately, delighted to know that she surrendered to his greater experience of sensual pleasures. His fingers were in her wet folds, teasing her bud, arousing her so furiously that she let herself be stimulated to climax twice, a look of bewildered delight on her face as her own potential for ecstasy was revealed to her. She lay back with her skirt round her waist, her adoring eyes on his face, beyond speech or even rational thought. He spread her on her back on the settee and lay on her, making her sigh and babble and clutch at his neck. With a gasp of victory, he penetrated her slippery depths, and did it to her once more for luck, and when her climactic release came she almost passed out.

Lady of the house, he thought with a wry affection as he lay in bed in the Palazzo Malvolio, smiling fondly over the memory of Cynthia Parker. She was unlike Zita in every way – or was she? The upshot had been much the same with both of them – Cynthia had cried at his leaving and begged him to come back any afternoon he could and, although Zita was less sentimental, she too had sighed and implored him to return to her soon. Can it be true, he asked himself, that old Rudyard Kipling got it right – *the Colonel's lady and Judy O'Grady are sisters under the skin*? Ultimately, it was a question of style and custom, and soon he would have to reconcile himself to the English way again.

With all this reminiscing and philosophising about the sexual nature of women, home and foreign, Adrian greeted with a warm smile the arrival of Teresa with his breakfast tray. *Amore*, he said before she had time to pour the coffee, flinging away the sheet to show her his impudently swaying part. Teresa shrugged and took down her knickers, hoisted her clothes and would have mounted him in the manner of their recent morning exercises. But with ardent and triumphant memories of Cynthia and Zita in his mind, he was not in the mood to be passive – he rolled the maid under him and was in her like a rabbit darting down its burrow.

By mid-morning he was sitting with a cup of coffee and a soft bread roll outside Florian's cafe in the Piazza San Marco and mulling over his next move. In effect his mission for Mallards had been over for days, and it would be impossible to justify staying more than another day. True, he had not managed to get to the Accademia Galleries to see the world's finest collection of Venetian painting, as the guide-book had it, but he could do that next time he came, for one thing was certain in his mind – he would be back at the earliest possible moment. For that he would need money, and much more money than the salary he was paid by Mallards.

With that in mind, he paid the waiter and strolled out of the Piazza towards San Moise, the only truly ugly church he had seen in Venice. How the Venetians had transmogrified the Jewish Patriarch Moses into a saint of the Catholic Church, the guide-book gave him no clue. But an alley to the right led, as Adrian recalled, to the narrow street where Signor Niccolo Corradini, dealer in unusual *objets-d'art*, had his premises. The same dusty and unwanted map of the world as the sixteenth century knew it was on show in the window – and obviously had been there for many a year.

Signor Corradini was behind the counter of his tiny shop, in his hand a cracked leather-bound book from shelves of musty old books behind him. All part of the scenery, thought Adrian with a knowing smile – nobody in his right mind would every buy them. The dealer greeted him effusively, remembering his name and addressing him as Signor Trall. Adrian shook hands and accepted an invitation into the backroom for a glass of wine. Corradini had dyed his hair again since he last saw him and it was glossy raven black. Perhaps the grey had been growing though, Adrian speculated, and wondered why it looked so totally unconvincing.

They sat in the litter of the backroom and chatted over a glass of two of pleasant Bardolino, and when cordial relations seemed established, Adrian enquired if Signor Gmund had bought the interesting case of replicas. *Certainly*, said Corradini, as if it were a foregone conclusion, nodding his head and waving his arms emphatically. By slow and careful stages Adrian turned the conversation towards picture restorers of notable ability, and Corradini caught on very quickly. When he let fall casually the name of Antonio Bassini, the dealer's eyes gleamed.

'I knew him well,' he said proudly. 'Some of his finest work passed through my hands.'

'He was an amazing artist,' said Adrian with feeling. 'I have had the pleasure of examining some of his achievements in the Palazzo Malvolio.'

'*Davvero?*' said Corradini. 'There were rumours in the trade that he had been commissioned by the very highest in Venice to do special work for them, but I have not seen for myself.'

'Do you have anything of his at present, Niccolo?' Adrian asked. 'There is a special reason for my question.'

The dealer looked at him thoughtfully for some seconds before making up his mind.

'Because you understand these things,' he said, 'I will show you something of great interest – a Faenza plate of the seventeenth century – a masterpiece!'

He went to one of the tall cupboards, unlocked it with a key from his pocket, and came back holding a flat object wrapped in a green cloth. He put it on the book-littered desk in front of Adrian and undid it to reveal a painted and glazed faience plate, of about eighteen inches diameter. The design had a border of four rows of half-circles in golden-brown, and in the middle two figures were painted.

'It is Ganymede with a satyr,' Niccolo explained, 'an unusual subject for the seventeenth century, and that makes it more valuable.'

Ganymede was the central figure of the design – a slender naked youth of sixteen or so. He stood under a spreading tree, poised as if to run away, and held his right hand over his face to cover his eyes, as if in shame. Beside him knelt a satyr, a creature with a man's body and hairy goat-legs. Curving horns jutted from his forehead, and from between his thighs jutted an over-sized male part that reached as high as his belly-button. His hands were laid on Ganymede's thighs, close to the slender part he had teased upright.

'The satyr tempts Ganymede,' said Niccolo, 'see how well the artist has caught the expressions of their faces – one has the grin of knowledge, and the other is shocked and yet fascinated. What will happen here, we ask – will Ganymede run away, as he half-does already? Or will he surrender himself to the promise of pleasure the satyr offers – the pleasure that we can say he is beginning to experience, for his *erezione* betrays him.'

'You sound like a damned art-critic,' Adrian said with a grin of his own. 'May I see?'

He took the thick plate gingerly and examined it front and back, turning it this way and that to catch the light on the shiny surface.

'It's very good,' he pronounced at last, 'the slight cracks in the glaze are totally authentic, and the colours are dulled exactly enough for three centuries. The crazing on the back is precisely what one would expect. It's a wonderful work of art and worth a great deal of money to a collector. Now you mean to tell me it's a fake?'

'That is Antonio Bassini,' said the dealer, pointing to the satyr's grinning face. 'It is a self-portrait, this plate.'

'I was told that his interests were unorthodox,' said Adrian, amused by the loving detail of the satyr's rumbustious part, 'I'm sure he enjoyed creating an antique work of art displaying his true nature. I heard a priest pray for the repose of his soul quite recently.'

'Bassini would not wish to be in Heaven with sexless angels and the purified souls of the Blessed,' said Niccolo, shaking his head. 'Your religious friend wastes his time in praying for that. I am certain he is elsewhere, with all the beautiful young boys of history.'

'How well did he paint beautiful young girls?' Adrian asked. 'Could he have copied a Cranach Venus convincingly enough to deceive an expert?'

'*Deceive!*' said Niccolo, pursing his lips in disapproval. 'A harsh northern word for one of your English moral certainties. In Italy all is done for show, Signor, you should remember that – *un mondo di favole*, we say – a world of make-believe, in your language. If we ask ourselves which is the real and which is the almost-real, and which the better-than-real, there is never an answer to these questions. You must read what one of our great Italian philosophers of the past wrote – Giambattista Vico – and also what our greatest living philosopher, Benedetto Croce, writes about it.'

'Spare me the university lecture, Niccolo,' said Adrian with a smile. 'In a word, why is nothing as it seems in Italy?'

'*Dio*!' You ask me to summarise twenty-five centuries of our history in one word? Impossible! But I will answer you in one phrase – poverty, injustice, fear. That has been the experience of life of all the generations. We shield ourselves as best we can from these oppressions, we compensate for the brutalities and inequalities of existence. Do you understand now?'

'No, I don't suppose so, but I sympathise with you. Perhaps moral rectitude is an over-rated virtue. I've never found much pleasure in it.'

'If I may ask, Signor Adrian, have you come to buy or sell?'

'To learn by asking – and perhaps to suggest a venture that might be very profitable for both of us.'

'I am at your service,' said Niccolo, turning his hands palms up in an expressive gesture.

'Those Viennese pictures you showed me when I came here with Signor Gmund were all very well,' Adrian began, 'but in London I could get a very fine price for a portfolio of etchings by Felicien Rops. I'm sure you know his work well.'

'The Belgian? I met him in Paris when I was a very young man – that would be in 1895 or 1896. A great artist in his field.'

'Yes – suppose you came across a portfolio of ten etchings – a plump naked Belgian woman playing with herself before a long mirror, or on her back with her legs wide apart while her young cousin kisses her *fica*, or two women pleasuring each other – you know Rops' favourite subjects.'

'Her *fica*,' said Niccolo with a thin smile, 'you are learning to speak Italian, Signor Adrian, and I see you are starting with the important words. But this superb portfolio of etchings by Felicien Rops would be impossible to dispose of through the sales rooms of the internationally esteemed Mallards. As soon as the catalogue appeared the police would seize the etchings and arrest you.'

'The threat of that puts the price up even higher. There are many rich collectors of erotica in London to whom I could offer the portfolio privately.'

'Without knowledge of Mallards, you mean?'

Adrian nodded, and Niccolo was silent for a while in thought.

'To obtain a portfolio like that is very difficult,' he said at last. 'It would be expensive.'

'It's not at all difficult,' Adrian retorted. 'You must know four or five artists good enough to do it. The difficult bit is the documentary proof that the etchings are genuinely Rops' own – straight from the master's own hand. His autograph signature on the cover might do. That's what makes it expensive.'

Niccolo nodded and laughed and refilled their glasses.

'I think I could lay my hands on what you want,' he said. 'It will take a month or six weeks. How could I get it to London? It would be seized by Customs and burnt if it went by post.'

'I shall be back here in Venice in less than three months,' said Adrian. 'You can give me the first portfolio then and I will smuggle it past Customs.'

'The *first*? Bravo, Signor – I see we shall be good partners in business? How many rich collectors will you deal with?'

'That depends on the price I get for the first portfolio. Ten or twelve, eventually, if it goes as I expect. We shall need a plausible source for this sudden treasure-trove and I am not at all sure who inherited Rops' estate, his wife in Belgium or his mistress in Paris. I shall make enquiries.'

'Have you done any business of this type before?' Niccolo asked him.

'Not precisely. I have catalogued paintings for Mallards that have sold for fifty or a hundred times their value as a result of an attribution I have suggested – which others older and far more experienced than I have been willing to accept because of the amount of money involved.'

'In the business of buying and selling fine art there always are areas of uncertainty,' said Niccolo with a cynical smile, 'areas where only judgement can guide us.'

'That is true,' Adrian agreed with an answering smile. 'You will naturally give me a solemn assurance as a respected dealer that the portfolios are authentic Rops' etchings.'

'Naturally,' said Niccolo. 'But will you have the money to pay me when I have the first portfolio?'

'Yes, by means of another proposal I have for you, Niccolo. Have you ever dealt in photographs?'

'Photographs of naked women? No – the pedlars in the Piazza do that business. For two hundred and fifty lire you buy two or three, or perhaps four if you are good at bargaining. What are you thinking?'

'I was talking the other day to a man who studies the royal families of Europe. He told me about the many mistresses of our King Edward the Seventh, who died about fifteen years ago. It gave me an interesting idea.'

'A king's mistresses and photographs?' Niccolo said with a broad grin. 'I believe I know what you want to do. Let me show you some pictures to see what you think of them.'

From another of his locked cupboards he extracted a green cardboard box and took off the lid to show it was half-full of postcard-size photographs. Adrian dipped in and skimmed through a handful, discarding them rapidly until he had chosen six.

'This is the style I'm after,' he said.

Niccolo took the first one and studied it carefully. A naked woman knelt on an ornate brocade armchair, her back towards the camera, but half-turning to look over her shoulder, so that one full breast was shown in profile. But the point of focus of the picture was her big and beautiful bottom, the cheeks displayed to the viewer as if he were being offered some wonderful treat – as perhaps he was. The second picture had a different woman, spread out naked on a velvet chaise-longue. She let one arm hang gracefully down over the side, and the other was raised to rest her hand under her head. The knee nearest the camera was raised and turned inwards, concealing in consciously teasing fashion the tuft between her thighs.

'I understand,' said Niccolo. 'Discretion and good taste.'

'*Ma non troppo*,' said Adrian, showing off his few words of Italian, 'don't overdo it.'

Niccolo looked with interest at a photograph of a woman who sat on a divan before a large gilt-framed mirror. Her face was sideways to the camera, as she looked at her reflection, but her naked body was full on to the viewer, her thighs together so that only a wisp or two of hair showed. The expression on her pretty face invited the beholder to put his hands on her knees and pull them apart. A variation of the pose appeared in another picture, where a woman with her hair in a fringe half-lay on a leather armchair, wearing only black stockings and high-heeled shoes. Both hands were behind her head to push her breasts out, and her long thighs were crossed to minimise the area of dark fur on show between them. Her mouth was half-open in a smile that clearly said, *Uncross my legs and feel me* . . .

'The ladies in whom you are interested,' said Niccolo, 'who are they – how many?'

'I've scribbled them down for you,' Adrian said, handing him a sheet of writing paper on which was embossed the Malvolio coat of arms. 'The most important are Lillie Langtry, Alice Keppel, the Countess of Warwick, Cora Pearl, Sarah Bernhardt, and Hortense Schneider. What I want is an oldish leather-bound photograph album with the royal cipher ER in gold on the front, and photos of twelve naked mistresses – the numbers can be made up with French duchesses and countesses and a few Paris music-hall stars of fifty years ago.'

Niccolo looked up from the sheet of paper on which he was jotting notes to look with respect at his new collaborator.

'I assume that women can be found who look like the important ladies and who will pose with no clothes on,' said Adrian. 'I will send you newspaper and magazine pictures of the English mistresses as a guide. I leave it to you to select the French ones. All we need is a good facial resemblance, but the models must have pretty bodies.'

'I salute you!' said Niccolo. 'This is a plot of genius! If you are discovered they will call it treason and your head will be cut off in a dungeon in your terrible Tower of London for insulting the King and his ladies! How much will you ask for the royal photograph album?'

'I thought two thousand guineas about right for so very extraordinary a royal souvenir,' Adrian answered. 'A third of it to be yours, for finding the women and a photographer who can be trusted to keep his mouth shut, and two-thirds mine for having the idea and finding the buyer.'

'What is guineas?' asked Niccolo.

'It means two thousand two hundred pounds sterling, and your third of that will be about one hundred thousand lire,' said Adrian, calculating rapidly.

'Excellent,' Niccolo said. 'I will begin as soon as I receive the cuttings from you. How shall I convey the album to you? Not by post.'

'We'll meet in Paris,' Adrian suggested. 'I'll give you a hundred pounds in sterling then, and the rest when I've sold it. Have two or three albums made, because there is an American collector who visits England twice a year and he is fanatical about our royal family. He'll fall over himself to buy one at any price to show them back home in St Louis.

And I know of someone in Paris who may be interested.'

'*Dio!*' Niccolo exclaimed. 'I am a dealer in rare and unusual *objets-d'art* – and you want me to set up mass-production!'

'Why not?' said Adrian with a grin. 'You need the money.'

They shook hands on the deal and Adrian slipped a handful of the naughty photographs into his pocket. They went to lunch at a restaurant of Niccolo's choosing – it had five pink-ginghamed tables outside, overlooking a narrow canal where gondolas were moored while their owners ate. The food was delicious – melon with thin-sliced ham, followed by a risotto of rice and cuttlefish, then *fegato alla Veneziana* – sliced calf's liver in rich cream with fried shredded onion. They drank two bottles of wine with the meal by way of celebration, and Adrian couldn't resist trying something he'd seen on the menu – *zuppa inglese* – which translated as *English soup*, but turned out to be trifle soaked in sweet-tasting and highly intoxicating liqueur of some sort.

At three o'clock Niccolo left, saying he would put matters in hand at once and write to Adrian of the progress being made. He proposed to send head-and-shoulder photographs of the intended models for Adrian's approval, before paying them to bare all. The two men shook hands enthusiastically and Adrian sat on, to drink one more cup of fragrant coffee and one more little glass of *Sambuca*. He was drunk enough to bring out the handful of photographs he had taken from Niccolo's box, and spread them on the tablecloth for study.

The message he had been trying to get through to Niccolo had to do with the expressions on the women's faces. There were no insuperable difficulties in finding women with pretty breasts and nice legs who would pose in the nude, but in order to make the pictures live a photographer was required who knew enough to get a provocative look into their eyes and on their lips. It interested Adrian to see that the local convention was to hide the hair between the thighs. It seemed an oddly genteel thing to do in postcards for shifty sale to tourists, but it had a certain rightness for the portraits Niccolo was going to fake for King Teddy's Personal Photograph Album.

After looking at his pictures for five minutes, Adrian swept them up and into his pocket, and paid the waiter, who had stood staring and grinning. Down below on the narrow canal some of the gondoliers had returned from their lunch break and siesta, and he climbed unsteadily into one of their craft. *Santa Maria della Salute*, he said. Niccolo's photographs had put an unsettling thought in his head – he had never in his life had a woman who was shaved bare between the legs and he'd only ever seen one. Signora Fosca's *niece*, Emmelina – Adalbert Gmund's regular girl. If he was leaving Venice tomorrow or the day after, now was the time to make good this deficiency in his experience.

The gondola made its way by back canals and under low bridges until it slid out into the Grand Canal, opposite the Customs House, where *carabiniere* armed with pistols guarded boxes and bales. The gondolier weaved across the Grand Canal, through afternoon traffic of barges and water-buses that threatened to run him down and sink him, and dropped Adrian off near the white-domed church he had asked for. The route from here to where Signora Fosca lived had disappeared from Adrian's conscious memory, but he ambled along by canal-sides and across squares with stone wells in the centre, letting his steps be guided by luck or accident or coincidence or hidden recall, and before long he found himself at the foot of a flight of broken stone steps in an old and uncared-for building.

Signora Fosca was very surprised to see him, but she hid it well and clucked over him affectionately. She gave him the best chair and a tiny glass of *Strega*, her dark brown eyes alert and weighing him up. Emmelina was nowhere in sight, and when Adrian asked he was told she was asleep. Signora Fosca wore her black mourning still – rustling satin from neck to ankles, of a shade of darkness that matched her thick eyebrows. She observed her unexpected visitor and waited for her opportunity to unburden him of some of his money.

Adrian was expansive with drink and in no mood for niceties. He put the tip of a forefinger to his lips and slid it in and out, grinning at Signora Fosca as he reminded her of what she had done for him on his last visit. She threw up her hands and directed a spate of rapid Italian at him, presumably to let him know that there would be no second performance of that little game. And while she was expostulating, she drifted within reach and he grabbed her wrist and pulled her down to sit on his lap. She looked at him warily, but did not try to escape.

'Emmelina, *si*?' he said pleasantly as he stroked her thigh through her frock, 'Emmelina, *amore*?'

haps the words were intended for her more than for him, for she moaned and sighed and jerked upwards to receive Adrian's short sharp thrusts. He felt her legs winding themselves over his own to hold him close, and he flooded her hairless split with his passionate offering.

Signora Fosca fussed over the pair of them when they lay side by side to cool off for a little while. Her understanding was that he had contracted for twice with Emmelina, and she seemed very surprised when he pulled her down on his other side and put a hand up her long black frock and between her thighs. Then it was his turn to be surprised, for she wore no knickers, and his questing hand touched springy curls and moist flesh.

'*Non deve fare questo*,' she said, trying to catch his hand through her frock, and he took that to mean that she objected.

'*Si*,' he told her, racking his brains. '*Due* for one thousand lire.'

'*Ma non!*' she retorted. '*Due volte Emmelina.*'

'You've got it all wrong,' said Adrian, giving up the fight to make himself understood in Italian. 'What I came for is her and you. I've had her, so now it's you. Lie on your back.'

He pulled up her long frock to her waist, and though she let him, she stayed on her side facing him. He had a close look at her dark brown patch of curls and was fascinated to see how the thin inner lips of her *fica* pushed out through the thicker and darker-skinned outer ones, as if permanently begging to be stroked. Why he wanted her he had no idea, and the drink was beginning to catch up with him. Soon he would be incapable and Signora Fosca, who was guiding his half-ready part, guessed his condition. She was a woman of her word – or in this case, where no word had been given – a woman of principle, for she slid her belly closer to his and pressed the tip of his wayward part just between the protruding inner lips of her split.

'*Sta tranquillo*,' she said softly, which sounded soothing.

Her hand slid up and down, coaxing him to full stiffness, and rubbing the sensitive head against her hidden bud. Adrian found it very pleasant and lay at ease, letting her manipulate him as she pleased. As his excitement grew, he began to murmur to her, *Si Assunta, si*, having picked up her name from Emmelina's wild babbling. *Si, Signor Adriano*, she agreed, and her cunning hand milked him to throbbing completion. *Siiii*, he sighed in ecstasy, and Signora Fosca reached a sobbing and shaking climax of her own at the feel of his warm squirting on her bud.

FIFTEEN

On Adrian's last evening before leaving Venice he found all the family assembled for drinks before dinner in the anteroom with the portraits of important Malvolios dating back to Piero in 1314. He was shown in the height of fourteenth century fashion – a blood-red tunic, a squashy black hat with a long scarf dangling from the side to drape over his shoulder, and a gold chain like the Lord Mayor of Clacton-on-Sea. There were Malvolios before him, right back to when Venice was established in 600 and something, but Piero was the first of them to have his portrait painted and his sharp-nosed features could be made out in all subsequent portraits – even Count Paolo in his Naughty Nineties evening rig, ready for dinner at Maxims with a duchess or a ballerina, or to crack a bottle of champagne or two with his chums in any good-class bordello. The facial set declared him unmistakably of Piero's blood, though perhaps it had become a little diluted over the centuries.

Here was Count Rinaldo, who had been the greatest lover of Delphine Tandy's life, portrayed in comic opera uniform, eleven medals, crosses and stars on his chest, and golden epaulettes heavy enough to make a lesser man round-shouldered. Yet, for all that, Rinaldo retained the sharp-nosed Malvolio look about him and was self-evidently a descendant of Piero's – even if it had to be said that the glint of high intelligence in the eyes was dulled by the intervening generations.

The Last of the Malvolio, thought Adrian, comparing that for pathos with The Last Days of Pompeii, The Last Supper, The Last Chronicle of Barset, The Last of the Mohicans – They all had a gloomy ring. He recited in his head some lines of Shakespeare's moralising that he had learned at school: *Time hath, my lord, a wallet at his back, wherein he puts alms for oblivion, a great-sized monster of ingratitude; those scraps are good deeds past, which are devoured as fast as they are made, forgot as soon as done.*

Delphine in an innocently cut evening frock of pearl-white satin and a ruby choker looked like a queen in exile. She held court from the best of the Empire-style chairs, Adalbert Gmund hovering to one side, his head bent attentively to her words, and Padre Pio in his scruffy black cassock on her other side. Bianca and her father were standing near a long window, their heads together and laughing, her hand tapping his arm. It went without saying that Count Massimo Enrico Francesco Vittorio Giambattista Scaloto Lombardini Manzetta di Torrenegra appeared immaculate, and more than immaculate, in his impossibly white shirt-front and impossibly black tails.

Bianca had kept out of Adrian's way since their encounter in the library and his night in her bed afterwards, when she had given him everything and asked for the impossible in return – to be helped to run away. Her tangerine short frock made her bare arms and shoulders glow with youthful well-being and vitality – not that she needed the help of any dressmaker to achieve that. Her glossy dark hair was arranged to hang straight to her shoulders, framing her face like a work of art. She glanced away from her father to Adrian, as he came into the anteroom, and then back to the Count. He circled the room, as was expected, to greet everyone individually with a polite *buona sera* and kiss Delphine's hand, but Bianca gave him only the curtest of nods, and the Count's response was a brief and ironic bow.

Contessa Marina was nowhere in sight and Adrian thought it less than prudent to enquire after her, the state of Massimo's jealousy being so uncertain. He took a tall crystal glass from a tray offered by a footman in the primrose and purple livery of the Malvolio and sipped. It was champagne, he found, or more precisely it was a well-chilled best-quality sparkling Italian wine that doubled for French champagne. Before he had time to attach himself to Delphine's little group of courtiers, the Count came across the room, treading softly on the worn-out red-and-gold Aubusson carpet, took his arm and led him to a corner where the portrait of an eighteenth century Malvolio in long white wig and and red velvet breeches stared down from the wall.

'A word in your ear, *Adriano*,' said Count Massimo, who seemed to be enjoying a huge private joke. 'It is being whispered that a certain international celebrity rewarded your services to her by the gift of a valuable religious painting.'

'How every interesting, Massimo,' said Adrian, pleased to see the flicker of annoyance on the Count's face at the use of his Christian name by an inferior, 'who is whispering this?'

'People,' said Massimo vaguely, before resuming the attack. 'Naturally, I find it almost impossible to believe this story can be true – it is my impression until now that Englishmen do not sell sexual favours. Am I wrong in this?'

'I can't claim to be as expert as you on buying and selling sexual favours,' Adrian said in the friendliest possible way, 'but in this case, you're quite right – I was given a leaving present by the Princess, to remind me of her until I come back to Venice. Not an antique from the famous collection of icons, but a pretty little portrait of St Dimitar of Lom.'

'*Che stupidita!*' Massimo said, which sounded very rude.

'An interesting person, St Dimitar,' said Adrian, unabashed, 'his relics were preserved in a monastery at Lom until fairly recently, I've been told. Apparently he had a *cazzo* as long and as thick as an ordinary man's forearm! During his lifetime people came from miles around to touch it for good luck. When he died they cut it off and embalmed it, and kept it in a big gold cylinder in the chapel. Do you think the Princess intended a compliment of some sort by her gift?'

Massimo spat out a word Adrian did not understand, though it sounded insulting – and dangerous, like the sound of a stiletto plunging into someone's back. He turned on his heel and strode away, his jaw set in a snarl that showed his ivory-white teeth. Adrian chuckled, then saw that Delphine and her entourage had watched the encounter with keen interest. Before matters could go any further, a late entrance by the Contessa Marina diverted everyone's attention. If Delphine looked like an exiled queen that evening, Marina looked like a prince's mistress. She wore a short evening frock of flimsy mauve *crêpe-de-Chine*, with wide bishop-style sleeves and a scooped neckline so low that to all intents and purposes her breasts were in full view. Just to see her made Adrian's rash part quiver in his trousers, and when it was his turn to kiss her hand, it rose to full stretch.

The monumentally dignified major-domo in black graciously allowed Contessa Marina five minutes to twitter her apologies to her sister and down a glass of Asti before announcing that dinner was served. Delphine beckoned Adrian to her and took his arm to let him escort her into the great dining-room, while the others followed in pairs, except Padre Pio who brought up the rear alone.

'I am glad you have agreed to see things my way,' Delphine said softly to Adrian as they led the way. 'I knew when I first saw you that you are *simpatico*.'

'I've prepared the necessary papers,' said he, inclining his head in acknowledgement of her compliment. 'If I may see you for an hour tomorrow morning to obtain your signature?'

'An hour?' she said, her beautifully trimmed eyebrows rising up her forehead. 'What a lot of papers to sign!'

'Only two,' he answered with a smile, 'but in fairness I must explain the implications to you. And sometimes it takes a long time to *explain* satisfactorily.'

'Yes,' she agreed. 'Come to my sitting-room at eleven and you can do all the explaining you like – or I can bear.'

At the long silver-laden table Adrian was on Delphine's right and Adalbert Gmund on her left. On Adrian's right was Bianca, and beyond her sat the Count. Marina was on Adalbert's left, facing her daughter across the table, and on her left was Padre Pio, his countenance beaming at the prospect of food and wine. The other diners, so to speak, the gods and goddesses painted round the walls and on the ceiling above, were old friends now, Adrian thought, giving them a grin of acknowledgement as a manservant in velvet livery filled his glass for the first of many times that evening.

They were there in force at the feast, those superannuated immortals of the Romans – bare-breasted and long-thighed Diana and her hounds, bare-breasted and yellow-haired Venus ready for instant love-making on an ivory couch, bared-breasted Minerva wearing a golden military helmet with a red horse-hair crest, bare-breasted Juno – big-breasted Juno, in fact, hers being notably fuller than the others! With them were their consorts, Mars in a war helmet, Mercury wearing winged sandals, two-faced Janus and heavy-muscled Vulcan – all of them displaying their undersized parts, except Jupiter, their celestial boss, and he had the sense to be shown with a sort of sheet round his waist, as if he'd just got out of the bath.

Signora Fosca had been so understanding towards Adrian, or so he thought when he woke up on the bed between her and Emmelina, that he had raised with her this difficult question of whether small parts were an Italian characteristic. That is to say, he tried with hand gestures and the use of his own body as a model to get the question across to her. It was not easy, and in the absence of a common language she had taken it to be a request to help lengthen his dwindled part, ready for another bout with her or Emmelina. Persistence had eventually made her understand that the reference was not to his own now-satisfied part but to men's parts in general – at least, he thought that was what she understood.

Her answer came complete with expansive and elaborate hand signals, rolling of eyes, measurements indicated with opposed palms drawing away from each other, curved fingers together to signify thickness – and all this with constant interruptions, commentaries and corrections from Emmelina, who seemed to hold complementary though not entirely similar views on the subject. The Italian word for big he knew – *grande* – and the word for little – *piccolo* – but the discussion was sadly hampered by not knowing the Italian word for – *average*. It was complicated even further for him by Signora Fosca rattling away in centimetres.

Despite past efforts by schoolmasters to teach him rudiments of the foolish Continental system of weights and measures, none of this had any significance for Adrian. A giggling Emmelina stroked his awakening part to full length and told him that was *quindici* – and interpreted that by holding up fingers to total fifteen for him. Even so, he lacked all notion of whether she or her Auntie regarded that as above or below average. This was a rare and baffling situation, he realised – he had been given a reply he did not understand, with no certainty that the question had been the one he had asked. It would take a trained philosopher to make anything of that, and since by definition philosophy was either lies or twaddle there was nothing to be gained by pursuing that line any further.

With the procession of courses and wines, Bianca's attitude thawed towards Adrian. After a risotto of rice, peas and ham, a thick fish soup, and chicken breasts with yellow corn polenta, the main course proved to be slices of veal cooked in Marsala wine, and by then Bianca was markedly friendly. She offered her apologies for not seeing him more in the past day or two, and he told her how happy he was that they were friends again. The Count on her far side intervened to break up their increasingly affectionate conversation, his eyes flashing with jealous anger. Adrian gave him a brief smile of derision, and turned his attention to the others at the table.

It seemed to him, glancing round, that in the space of only a week and a half it was not only Bianca's attitude towards him that had changed. They had all changed, some for better, some for worse, but all of them entertainingly. Take her mad dandy of a father – he had started by despising Adrian as an inferior, and had gone so far as to devise a contemptuous trick to play on him, by casting him to Princess Zita to be ravished. Now his scorn had turned to outright hatred and he was twitchy to let his beautiful daughter even speak to Adrian! That had to be rated success. Or take the Contessa – she had seen him at first as a useful playmate at bedtime. Now she was frantic because he was going away, and had wept a few tears at their last encounter and claimed that she would be lonely beyond words without him.

Adalbert Gmund, the ageing Austrian playboy sitting across the table – he had been patronising toward Adrian when he arrived at the Palazzo. He had bragged of his past exploits with the Contessa and her sister Delphine. He had taken Adrian with him on a visit to Signora Fosca's, to demonstrate his prowess with self-styled sixteen-year-old Emmelina. There was a shock in store for him when he learned that Adrian had gone back alone to sample Emmelina's smooth-shaven split – and Signora Fosca's furry one. As the women were not likely to tell him themselves, Adrian intended to, after dinner.

When it came to Delphine, it was harder to judge because he was not at all sure what her attitude had been at the beginning or what it was now. Obviously she had seen him as a handy fool to be used in salvaging her finances. At the first resistance from him, when he had denied the authenticity of her pictures, her knickers were off as a bribe. Naturally, he had taken her bribe – only a gibbering idiot would turn away from a woman so voluptuous. He had decided to go along with her fraud over the so-called Cranach paintings, and Delphine probably still rated him a handy fool. Except that for this compliance he was going to insist on having her knickers off again, many times, and a reasonable slice of the profit – a secret commission Mallards would never know about. That might change her opinion of him.

When dinner was finally finished, Delphine led the way to the Yellow Drawing Room and fresh coffee was brought – all part of the family evening ritual. Before long Count Massimo consulted his watch and made his excuses. With sardonic amusement Adrian watched Massimo kiss the Contessa's cheek and bid her goodnight – and her response could only be described as cool. Bianca said, *Goodnight, Babbo* and giggled, as aware as the rest of them that he was off to meet Nino or Sandro or Emilio or Roberto or some other beautiful young man. In the slight hush that followed his departure, Adalbert proposed a game of bridge.

Bianca came to Adrian's rescue by insisting it was impossible to sit playing cards on his last evening in Venice, when he ought to be in the Piazza enjoying a drink. Delphine and Marina both agreed with that, and off Bianca took him, leaving Padre Pio to make the fourth for bridge. Adrian was delighted by the escape from a tedious hour or two and decided to leave the deflation of Adalbert for the next day. He waited at the top of the long marble staircase while Bianca went to her room for a stole – a wisp of chiffon for her bare shoulders.

A speed-boat was moored at the Grand Canal landing-stage, and when Adrian said he thought her father always took that, Bianca laughed and told him she had asked Toto the boatman to say that it was broken down. The Count had gone off, grumbling, by gondola to his rendezvous. The point of this was lost on Adrian, though not for long. Bianca told the boatman he was not required, took the wheel and demonstrated whose daughter she was by skimming the boat out with roaring engine into the middle of the Grand Canal. She laid it over on its side in a tight turn toward San Marco and raced down the Canal at full throttle, weaving round other craft as if they were standing still.

Needless to say, the destination she had in mind was not the Piazza San Marco and Florian's Cafe. Adrian clung on tightly as the boat hurtled past the Accademia Galleries he had failed to visit, past the dome of Santa Maria della Salute, his landmark for finding his way to Emmelina's hairless plaything, and out into the basin, leaving the Doge's Palace and the Byzantine glories of San Marco off to the left. When they were well out into the lagoon, away from the lights of Venice, away from the ferry routes to other islands, Bianca asked him to hold the wheel, and he grabbed at it as she let go. He was terrifyingly aware of the wooden pilings that stuck up out of the black water at regular intervals, and knew it must have a vital significance to mariners, but had no idea what.

Beside him, Bianca stood upright in the racketing boat and

to his amazement pulled her short tangerine evening frock over her head and threw it behind her carelessly. Off came her underwear and her stockings, and she balanced herself with a hand on the windscreen, her other arm raised high in the air and her long dark hair streaming out behind her in the slipstream, almost a handsomely carved figurehead on an old sailing ship! Adrian stared up at her, open-mouthed in admiration. Seen against the dark sky her body had a pearly luminescence like fine marble, a setting for the patch of darkness between her thighs. Her full breasts jutted out into the hot wind of the boat's wild career across the lagoon in the enchanted Venetian night.

'Faster!' she shouted over the roar of the engine. 'Faster, Adrian!' But the hand throttle was wide open already and the engine flat out – yet he caught her elation and flung the boat into continuous left and right turns so abrupt that it lay over until rushing water came in above the sides. Bianca was shrieking in exhilaration and Adrian joined in with a throaty howl until, after ten or fifteen minutes of this reckless ride, they had both shouted themselves hoarse. Adrian cut the engine and let the boat glide to a stop, the bows dropping back into the water as the way came off.

Wherever he looked it was dark – not a light, not an island, not another vessel – only black empty water under a starry sky. He ripped off his evening jacket and black bowtie and flung them in the back with Bianca's clothes. She dropped suddenly into his arms, kissing him and holding him tightly, her tongue sliding into his mouth, making his heart pound while his hands caressed the bare warm skin of her back. If she had the Count's temperament in driving boats, she had the Contessa's style in more intimate matters – while Adrian was stroking her smooth back, her hand felt inside his trousers and took possession of his hard-swelling part.

Adrian sighed and felt for her breasts, and she plunged both hands into his underwear and had his throbbing stiffness out in the open. Not to be outdone, he put a hand between her legs and stroked her warm *fica* until she sighed that there was more room in the back of the boat. They climbed over the seat-back and lay on the clothes on the rear cushions. Adrian cupped her soft breasts in his hands and kissed them. The light was dim, but it was enough for him to see her beautiful face.

'I want you to fall in love with me,' she said. 'Why won't

you? Have you got a girl in London?'

'Several,' he answered tactfully, 'but none half as pretty or enchanting as you are.'

'Then why won't you?' she asked, her hands fluttering on his rampaging part to send spasms of delight through him.

He was very clear that it would be exceptionally simple to fall in love with Bianca – and ridiculously dangerous, with a demented father like hers. *Why* she wanted him to fall in love with her didn't matter a damn – if he let himself succumb, then he would carry her off to England like Lochinvar in the ballad. Which was neither here nor there – love needs must take second place to love-making just then, and while he murmured that she was adorable, he smoothed his fingertips delicately over the buds of her breasts until he felt them stiffening.

'I could fall in love with *you*!' she sighed, 'if you wanted me to. Do you want me to, Adrian?'

His head was dizzy with pleasure and he paid no attention to her words. His face was at her breasts, sucking their firm tips one after the other, and he heard little gasps of delight. The beat of her clasped hand on his bounding part quickened and her legs opened wider, to let his fingers play between them. There was no more to be said, only to be done. He turned her on to her back on the boat-seat and with one quick movement rolled on her belly and pushed in deep. And then it was all action and energy, bouncing up and down, gasping and panting together, his eyes and her eyes wide open and bright with excitement as they stared at each other.

The speed-boat drifted on the current and rocked under them to the rhythm of their furious love-making. Faster and stronger it grew, until they passed beyond sensation into the nothingness of total release. His strength poured into Bianca in jolting spurts, and she responded with spasms of her belly that carried him further and further into ecstasy, and herself with him.

When their wild climax was over and they lay recovering, she told him she understood how impossible it was for him to assist her to run away and begged him to come back to Venice soon. He promised most faithfully that he would be back in three months and she gazed down at him with a thoughtful smile on her face as he sprawled on the boat-cushions, his trousers gaping wide to reveal his wet part against his belly.

'If I run away on my own when I'm older and arrive in London, will you look after me?' she asked.

'With all the pleasure in the world,' he said, and meant it. 'But why not leave that until you're twenty-one?'

'Will you come back to Venice often?' she asked, 'so we can fall in love with each other?'

This talk of falling in love was a joke and not a joke, as he well understood. Bianca wanted to achieve an ascendancy over him, and against that he must guard himself.

'If we make love often enough, perhaps we may fall in love,' he said lightly.

With that she seemed satisfied, and changed the subject. She told him that she found his love-making very Italian, and when he asked what that meant, she said he was always very *ardente – molto appassionato* – and therefore it was over too soon. She had been told that Englishmen were calmer than Italian men and naturally she had expected to be loved for a long time. While she was explaining it to him, her hand stroked his shrunken part with soft little touches.

Adrian arranged her on her back with her legs hooked over his shoulders as he knelt on the seat. He stroked her belly until she trembled and sighed, and reached forward to roll and fondle her plump breasts. By nature she was extremely *Italian* herself, as she had called it, and when his fingers had played over and inside her slippery fig for a short while, she had very nearly reached the moment of climax. He dropped his evening trousers round his knees and leaned right forward to penetrate her pink flower with his stiff part.

'*Dio mio!*' she gasped. 'Oh, Adrian, yes!'

Her moment had come, with no realisation that he was playing with her. He slid half of his six inches into her and waited – his fingers deep-kneading her soft belly, and arousing her till her bare bottom writhed on the cushions and her legs drummed on his shoulders. She jibbed her loins up at him, trying to force his lodged part deeper, but he moved with her, keeping just the top of himself inside her. Her climax came, and through the gasping convulsions he plucked at her breasts, sending her soaring into heights of pleasure, he remaining unaffected by the ecstatic turmoil of her belly.

When her throes subsided at last he grinned down at her and put his tongue out.

'Was I too quick for you that time?' he asked. 'Or were you too quick for me?'

'You are cold-blooded,' she complained.

Adrian had other ideas about that. He rolled the softening tips of her breasts between his fingers and pinched them lightly to make her gasp. When they were firm again, he inserted a finger into her wetness, just above his half-sheathed part, and rubbed her tiny pink pearl. He had learned this from a married woman named Marjorie Foster, on evening visits to Chiswick when her husband was at his Lodge meetings. She was an enthusiast for the pleasures of the flesh, and fantasised of an impossibly endowed man who could make use of all her openings at the same. Adrian had never tried on his girlfriend Barbara the pleasures that Marjorie had invented, but they seemed right for Venice.

'Ah no!' Bianca exclaimed, shuddering violently as his finger moved alongside his embedded part. 'It is too much!'

'Darling Bianca,' Adrian murmured, demonstrating the next stage of Marjorie Foster's teaching. His other hand was behind Bianca's raised thighs, spreading the cheeks until his fingertip found the little node between them and pressed against it for admittance. Bianca stared up at him incredulously, her legs thumping on his shoulders and spasms shaking her belly.

'It's too much!' she gasped. 'No more!'

He paid no attention to her little cries, her moans and her gasps, certain that she was enjoying being forced against her will. He pushed forward abruptly to sink his jerking part in to the limit – all the way to his hairy pompoms! She shrieked and rolled from side to side on the cushions, making the boat rock wildly. *This is it*, he told her, launching into a strong steady stroke, feeling himself growing harder and thicker and longer. Bianca made gurgling sounds as she squirmed and bounced beneath him, and he loved every moment of it.

I'm having Bianca, the Count's beautiful young daughter! the exultant thought ran through his whirling mind. *She's naked for me out here on the Venetian lagoon, under the stars!*

He felt the first throb of his climax and said, *Now, Bianca!* stabbing hard into her quivering belly. Her ecstatic squeal was piercing and prolonged, to his great satisfaction. They were in the after-throes, he trembling on her with his mouth pressed to hers and her arms tight round him, when a hoot from a passing steamer brought them back to reality. Bianca laughed shakily and pushed him off her, still half-stupefied by the sensations of what he had done to her. She stared at the lighted boat over to their right and said it was the water-bus service from Murano to San Marco. She gave Adrian a final kiss, then put on her clothes and tied his bowtie skilfully for him.

'Then this is goodbye, Bianca?' he asked.

'No, this is *arrivederci*,' she said. 'Until we see each other again, we say in Italian. When will you come back to Venice?'

She drove the speed-boat back to the Palazzo Malvolio at a sedate pace – sedate for her, that was – while he explained he had prospects of a lot of very profitable business in pictures and other works of art in Venice and intended to come here on a regular basis. When they reached the Palazzo landing-stage the boatman was waiting, and inside the liveried porter sat dozing. Adrian took Bianca's hand while they went up the marble stairs and kissed her *arrivederci* one more time under the Malvolio coat of arms.

The bridge party had broken up, and only Adalbert was left in the Yellow Drawing Room, slumped in an armchair with a bottle of cognac. He waved Adrian to a chair and poured him a glass.

'Did you have a nice time in the Piazza?' he asked, and when Adrian said he'd had a nice time, Adalbert asked slyly if he'd kissed Bianca on the way back. Adrian ignored the question and smiled thoughtfully at the half-drunk Austrian.

'I saw a dear friend of yours yesterday,' he said casually.

'Niccolo Corradini, you mean? Did he tell you that I bought the case of replicas – at my own price, naturally, not his.'

'I went to call on a lady with a young niece,' said Adrian. 'They were both in excellent form, I thought.'

Adalbert's sandy eyebrows met in a sudden frown.

'Why did you go there?' he asked.

'For the same reason that you do, Adalbert my dear old chum – to have the pleasure of Emmelina's bare-skinned plaything. How could I possibly leave Venice before I'd tried out this rare delight for myself?'

'*Ach Gott!*' said Adalbert, scowling at him. 'Why did you do this – to insult me?'

'Heavens no! I thought that was what you took me there for – to sample something different. Don't tell me you never meant me to have Emmelina? I say, I am sorry if I've upset you!'

His pretence of regret cut no ice with Adalbert, whose

angry face grew red, then dark red, then almost purple.

'Naturally,' said Adrian innocently, 'for a proper comparison of smooth with hairy I had the *aunt*, too. Did you know she wears no knickers? If you feel up her skirts you get a handful of soft warm *fica*. You should have her sometime – in her way she's as enjoyable as her niece. Well, I'm off to bed, Adalbert. I'll say goodbye now in case we don't run across each other tomorrow before I leave.'

He held out his hand and Adalbert glared at him. But good manners prevailed and they shook hands, though grudgingly on one side. At the door Adrian turned and smiled serenely

'I almost forget to tell you, Adalbert – Signora Fosca asked me to mention to you that she had another *niece* arriving next week. She told me her name but I can't remember it now – was it Tina? Or Gilda? Something like that. She particularly asked me to say that the new niece is thirteen years old, which I suppose means an underdeveloped sixteen or seventeen. Still, it takes all sorts. Chin chin, old sport, and keep up the good work!'

He left Adalbert in the grip of complicated emotions and went to bed. Though not to sleep – for he would have bet any amount of money that the Contessa would slip into his room for a last fling. And he would have won his bet. He turned off the light and lay waiting, and at the dramatic hour of midnight his door opened and she glided in, her hour-glass figure well displayed by an oyster-silk negligee trimmed down the front with delicate white marabou feathers. He thought she would strip naked and get into bed with him, but instead she sat on the bedside and took his hands in hers.

'My darling, I am so afraid,' she whispered in the half-dark. 'Massimo isn't back yet, but I couldn't stay away from you on your last night here. If he goes into my room and finds me gone he will come straight here and kill you.'

'Does he know about us?' Adrian asked, not believing her.

'He knows! He has guessed! You saw my bruise at dinner – I wore that frock to shame Massimo by letting everyone see the evidence of his brutality.'

'Bruise? Show me,' said Adrian.

The Contessa wanted nothing better than to open the front of her silk negligee and let him see she was not wearing a nightdress. She raised her full breasts on her palms and said, *Look*!

'Where?' he asked sceptically, seeing no mark on her pearly white skin.

She showed him with her fingers – a small pinkish smudge the size of a thumb-print on the inside of her right breast, not far from the bud.

'What happened?' Adrian enquired, suppressing his amusement at the prospect of another instalment in the unending story of the catastrophic connubials of the Torrenegras.

'You know how Massimo comes into my room every day while I am still in bed and makes me pull down my nightdress to uncover my breasts. This morning he found a love-bite, or said he did.'

'But we weren't together last night,' said Adrian. 'I waited for you, but you never came.'

Strictly speaking, that was not the truth. After having aunt and niece twice apiece in the afternoon, and a heavy dinner, he had fallen asleep as soon as his head touched the pillow.

'I was too afraid to leave my room last night,' said Marina. 'Did you miss me, darling?'

'Terribly,' he assured her.

'And did *this* miss me?' she asked, slipping a hand into the bed to lay hold of his standing part.

'I could hardly sleep for the frustration it suffered,' he said. 'But what happened with Massimo this morning?'

'He sat on the bedside staring at my naked breasts, shaking his head and saying, *troppo, troppo, troppo!*'

'What does that mean – *troppo*?'

'It means *too much*,' Marina answered, her voice quavering in humiliation. Instantly Adrian put his arms round her and kissed her bare breasts lovingly.

'What a ridiculous thing to say!' he comforted her. 'Your breasts are beautiful, Marina. I could kiss them for hours.'

She pressed his face into the deep and perfumed cleft between them while she went on with her tale of woe.

'Suddenly Massimo started as if he had been struck, stared at me and said furiously that there was a bite mark! He took hold with thumb and finger and pinched my breast very hard. Then he got up and walked out, and we have not spoken since. At dinner he refused to look at me, knowing everyone was staring at the mark he'd made on me.'

'Poor darling,' said Adrian, his hand probing gently between her thighs to stroke her. In her hand his cherished part stood bolt upright and quivering, its blind desire urging him to have her, even if the Count should return and find him lying on her and at the very moment of spurting into her belly. He eased her down to lie beside him, her thighs parted and his hand busy in between them.

'Did you miss *me* last night?' he asked.

'I dreamed about you,' she said, 'I dreamed that Massimo was inspecting my breasts for love marks, then you were standing at the bedside. You pulled back the sheets and made me lie down – and pushed my nightdress up to my waist, and ran your hands up my thighs and into the hair between them . . . and Massimo sat silent and watched us.'

'Was it exciting, this dream?' Adrian asked, suspecting that she was making it up, but not sure.

'Oh yes,' Marina murmured, trembling to the stimulation of his fingers. 'I was completely aroused when you touched me and opened me with your fingers . . . you stood leaning over me, and I knew you were going to make me do it . . . I tried to close my legs, but Massimo held my ankles to stop me. He kept saying, *troppo, troppo* and I was terrified of what he'd do to me when he saw my climax.'

'Ah,' Adrian sighed, his urgent part twitching in the clasp of her massaging hand.

'You sat down on the opposite side of the bed to Massimo and leaned over me to kiss my breasts while you were teasing inside me – and I stared at Massimo to try to make him understand that it wasn't my fault, what you were doing to me – I hadn't asked you to my room. He stood up and walked away, and I woke up all hot and sticky . . .'

By this time she and Adrian were so highly excited that their need was ferocious. He leaped on her and drove in deep and hard and thrust so strongly that she moaned in ecstasy and wrapped her legs round him. He was in Heaven – not two hours ago he was enjoying her beautiful daughter out on the lagoon, now he was having the beautiful mother in a palace . . . could Venice have anything more to offer than this? Ten seconds flat was all it took – Marina shrieked in climactic frenzy and jabbed a finger in between the cheeks of his heaving bottom. Adrian's long back arched and he squealed as he spurted his avid lust into her.

And yes, Venice had more yet to offer him – lovemaking made keener by the edge of true danger. Wearing only a dressing-gown he went with Marina through the dark and silent passages of the Palazzo to her room, next to the Count's, and got into bed with her. Her bed was large and carved and high and canopied, and it stood with its head to a tapestried wall. On the other side of the wall lay Massimo asleep – if he had returned from his nocturnal frolics. The knowledge of her husband's nearness, excited Marina almost to delirium – no sooner was she naked on her back and Adrian's hand roaming over her bountiful breasts, squeezing and kneading them, then she writhed and moaned under his touch in an instant and non-stop climax.

He put his hand between her wide-splayed legs to dabble in her wetness, and her rhythmic moans grew louder. He was sure she could be heard through the wall and pressed his mouth over her mouth to gag her. This muffled her outcry, but seemed to throw her into ever-deeper ecstasy, so that her squirming body was lifting off the bed and falling back, as if by waves of sensation. The strangeness of a continuing climax startled him at first, but then he became fascinated, and wanted to see how long he could make it last.

But he had no way of telling, lying there in the dark with his wet finger-tips playing over her swollen bud and his eager part thrumming against her thigh. He slid on to her quaking belly and plumbed her slippery depths with a long hard push that set her heels drumming on the mattress. His blood was up and he rode her hard and fast, muffling her moaning still with his own mouth. He felt her sharp finger-nails raking down his back and gushed his surging desire into her belly, unable to suppress his own cry. Like an alarm clock running down, his hot throes and hers gradually lessened and slowed, until they were lying in a silent embrace, wet with perspiration and wondering if Massimo had heard them. But when nothing happened, they put their arms round each other and fell asleep.

SIXTEEN

It was the pale light of dawn through the slats of the window-shutters that woke Adrian and the warm softness of woman's body close to him warned him that he was in the wrong bed. He had to get back to his own room before the palace servants were about. Marina lay on her side, her knees drawn up and her bare back to him – he raised himself on an elbow to lean over and whisper, *Arrivederci, Marina* and kiss her cheek. She murmured drowsily as her fleshy bottom wriggled in his lap – he threw caution to the wind and lay down again, his hand between her thighs from the rear, to fondle her.

She lay still, half-asleep but enjoying what he was doing and soon with gentle fingers he probed her petals and touched her rosebud. *This is madness*, he thought, *at any minute now a maid is likely to come through the door and find me here*! The idea of danger excited him so intensely that he lifted Marina's thigh and slid his hard-standing *cazzo* into her. She murmured words that were undistinguishable, and in another second he had his arms round her and her plump breasts in his hands. Half-asleep or half-awake, she pushed her bare bottom against him while he thrust steadily in and out.

He felt her body quivering against his belly and chest to the sensations of pleasure he was inducing, and her long rhythmic sighs aroused him further – as did the knowledge that the Count lay asleep in the next room, with only a wall between. Adrian bounced to and fro against the Contessa's voluptuously padded bottom until he and she reached their climactic moments at the same time and he spurted his morning greeting into her. Marina shook and gave little sighs, but nothing that might be heard outside her room and, as soon as her thrills faded, she went back to sleep again without a word of farewell.

Adrian slid out of the bed and raised the sheet high enough

to plant a last kiss on her warm bottom before putting on his dressing-gown and moving silently to the door. He had no idea of the time and did not want to go exploring Marina's sitting-room for a clock. Not that it mattered anyway – it was daylight and he needed to get back unseen to his own bed. He opened the heavy door of Marina's bedroom an inch or two to peer out with extreme caution. The portrait of a nineteenth century Malvolio with a blue sash glared at him from the opposite wall, but no living persons were about in the long corridor.

He sidled round the door and set off at a brisk walk, wracking his brains for some recollection of last night's route through the darkened palace from his room to Marina's. He had not paid much attention then to the way she took him, being in a state of sexual arousal, his hand inside her negligee to feel her breasts, and her hand clasping his excitable part. But luck was with him that morning – he came across a marble bust of Empress Theodora that he recognised, and from there he knew the way. No one was about, it seemed, and he reached his room unobserved. A glance at his wrist-watch on the night table as he slid into bed showed twenty to six. He yawned twice and fell asleep.

When he woke again it was after nine and his breakfast tray was on the table beside him. The coffee was cold and there was no sign of Teresa. He jerked at the bell-pull and nibbled at a sweet roll while he was waiting, which proved to be some time – and to his amazement, when the door opened at last, it was not Teresa but Luigi the major-domo who came into the room.

'*Buon giorno, Signor Trall,*' he said gravely, bowing towards Adrian, who sat up naked in bed and stared at the silver-haired major-domo in his ancient black swallow-tail coat and striped waistcoat.

'*Buon giorno*, Luigi,' he said, 'my coffee is cold – where is Teresa?'

'It is of Teresa I am here to speak to you, Signor,' answered Luigi. 'May I assume that her services have been satisfactory during your stay here in the Palazzo?'

'Yes,' said Adrian, suddenly thoughtful. 'Why do you ask?'

'A gentleman like you will understand immediately that there is a question of some delicacy,' said Luigi, bowing again in a way that boded no good. 'As Signora Tandy's major-domo I have a responsibility to guard the well-being of the palace servants. This is no small matter, Signor.'

'I think I begin to understand,' said Adrian, frowning. He was at a disadvantage, being naked in bed while a fully dressed and imposing butler lectured him.

'Naturally you understand, a man of the world like yourself,' Luigi said, without the least trace of a smile. 'You have made fuller use of this girl than is usual for visitors, but to that I say nothing, being accustomed for many years to the ways that lively young gentlemen have with female servants. If there is any spiritual or religious consideration involved here, that is for the good Padre Pio, not for me. He will concern himself with Teresa's soul.'

'What precise consideration is troubling you, Luigi?'

'Nothing is *troubling* me, Signor, nothing. But there is an arrangement to be made before you leave to return to England. I thought it best to approach you discreetly – I am certain that you would not wish Signora Tandy or the Contessa Marina to know of your private dispositions. In my experience, Signor, ladies often do not understand the affairs of gentlemen, and can make themselves furious without any purpose.'

I don't believe it, Adrian was thinking, *I'm being blackmailed by the butler!*

'What arrangement have you in mind?' he asked.

'Teresa is a sensible and well-trained girl,' said the major-domo, pursing his lips judiciously. 'She will be a good wife to some man, perhaps one of the other servants, and give him fine children. A girl like that should have the dovry.'

'What's that?'

'Have I said it wrong? I looked at the big dictionary in the Biblioteca to find the English word for *dote di sposa* – the gifts a girl brings to her husband at their marriage.'

'Her dowry,' said Adrian. 'You think that I ought to provide a dowry for Teresa, is that it?'

'*Ecco!*' said Luigi, with an almost imperceptible shrug. 'You have said it, Signor.'

'And how much do you think this dowry should be?'

'She is a poor girl,' said the major-domo, 'she has nothing to bring to a husband. In my judgement, Signor Trall, ten thousand lire is the right amount for her.'

Adrian did some hasty sums in his head and the answer came to about seventy-five pounds, almost two months of his salary at Mallards. It was a lot to pay for a frolic or two with a housemaid but, on the other hand, if Delphine Tandy got to know about his *private dispositions*, in Luigi's tactful phrase, she might withdraw her almost-Cranach paintings from Mallards and leave him with a red face and no profit to bring him back to Venice.

'I defer to your superior knowledge of these matters, Luigi,' he said. 'But I am at the end of my stay here and I do not have that much cash left.'

'I understand, Signor,' said Luigi; bowing his head in a most deferential way, 'but naturally you have it at your disposal in London. If you would not have objections to visiting a cousin of mine there and handing it to him, he will wire it to me, and I will hold it safely for when Teresa marries.'

'Very well,' said Adrian, seeing no point in arguing with the man. 'But when I stay here again as Mrs Tandy's guest, will you expect me to provide a dowry for another chambermaid?'

'That can only be decided if the question arises,' said Luigi with a flicker of amusement on his face. 'I shall do all in my power to make your next stay in the palace comfortable and your arrangements private.'

'I'm glad that we can trust each other,' Adrian said, highly amused by the major-domo's style.

'Si, Signor Trall. We have a very old saying: *fidarsi e bene, non fidarsi e meglio.*'

'And what does it mean in English?'

'To trust is good, not to trust is better. I have written the address of my cousin's restaurant in London, Signor.'

He handed Adrian a folded sheet of paper, bowed and waited. It said in elaborate handwriting, *Trattoria Bella Veneziana* followed by an address in Soho. Adrian assured the major-domo that he would go there with the dowry within a few days of returning to London.

At a little after eleven o'clock, losing himself only once on the way, he presented himself at Delphine Tandy's sitting-room. She was sitting at a little rosewood writing-desk and got up to offer him her hand. He kissed it with all the charm he could muster, feeling suavely Continental. Delphine was very elegant in a loose silk frock of white and golden yellow, tied at the waist with a gold-fringe ended sash. The sleeves were long and broad, the neckline low, supported by narrow golden straps over her well-shaped shoulders. She waved him to a chair and asked him to explain what was involved in asking Mallards to sell her Cranach pictures.

Adrian went through Mallards standard terms of business with her and gave her the papers he had prepared for her signature. She took them over to the writing-desk and put on her tortoise-shell reading-glasses. Before signing, she asked which of them should apply for the necessary licence to export the paintings from Italy. Adrian replied with great tact that in view of the satisfactory agreement they had reached about who had painted the pictures, he thought it better not to trouble an Italian government department with an application requiring an official statement on that very confidential subject.

Delphine half-turned at her desk and looked at him curiously.

'How do you propose to get them to London?' she asked.

'In my luggage, undeclared,' said he softly, going to stand beside her. 'I was very encouraged on the journey here by the laxity of French and Italian Customs officers – I shall have no problems with the *Cranachs* this side of Dover. And later today before I catch the train, I'm going to buy three or four cheap pictures on wood of Saints, to give my friends in London as presents. There's not a Customs man in England who can tell an old master from a trashy souvenir.'

'Someone mentioned that you have been given a genuine antique Saint,' said Delphine. 'Is that Byzantine?'

'Bulgarian,' Adrian told her with a grin, 'though the way in which I got it could certainly be described as Byzantine.'

Delphine signed the papers and gave them to him.

'I'll have the paintings taken to your room so that you can pack them safely,' she said. 'That concludes our business, does it not? Or is there anything else we have to agree?'

'My commission. I'm worth ten per cent to you.'

'You mean in addition to Mallards' ten per cent? But what will be left for me?' Delphine asked, her eyes wide and innocent as she gazed up at him. 'I am a poor woman with heavy debts.'

'With my guidance you will become a rich woman,' said Adrian. 'For instance, there's a bronze in a niche along the corridor where my room is – it's about two feet high and needs dusting.'

'I don't think I remember it,' she said. 'What is it of?'

'A naked man with a curly beard, carrying off a struggling naked woman in his arms. It could be offered in London as the work of a follower of Benvenuto Cellini – perhaps even Cellini himself, and worth a lot of money with the right promotion.'

'And is it by Cellini?' Delphine asked.

'There are areas of uncertainty in art history where judgement is everything,' said Adrian. 'Your bronze *may* be a Cellini, or by a follower of his – or just a nice old knick-knack worth twenty-five pounds as an ornament. You see why I'm worth a commission.'

'How shall I pay it to you – by cheque in London?'

'No, I shall come to Venice to visit you regularly, if we are to be partners in business, and I can collect it in person.'

Delphine held out her hand in token of agreement, and Adrian kissed it and pulled her to her feet. She said nothing when he led her through the double doors into her adjoining dressing-room with the mirrors and golden cherubs, and on through that into her bedroom with the massive velvet-curtained and canopied bed on a dais. He turned to face her and pulled loose the sash round her waist, then lifted her frock over her head and let it fall to the floor. He undid her white satin brassiere, cupped her heavy breasts in his hands and kissed them.

The warm fragrance of her skin and the expensive perfume she applied between her breasts and under her chin made him almost giddy as he touched his tongue to her dark buds. He slid to his knees, trailing his tongue down her soft belly, and pressed his lips hotly to her mound through the fragile silk of her peach-coloured knickers, before slipping them down her legs and off. All this time she had said nothing, and it was only when he stood up again to take her in his arms and press her naked body close that he saw, over her shoulder, something that brought a smile of appreciation to his face.

Over the priceless pictured French tapestry that served her as bed-cover, there was spread out in all its barbarous majesty a large orange and black tiger-skin, the head attached, and the savage jaws open to show long fangs.

'Where did you find that?' he murmured, staring in delight.

'It wasn't easy,' she said, smiling at him, 'do you like it? I got it for you, as a going-away present. Something to remind you of me.'

'I adore it,' he said. 'We must make sure it has memories to haunt me in London and bring me quickly back to you.'

He arranged her on the tiger-skin, naked except for her silk stockings, and threw off his clothes. With a bound he was on the bed and his face between her thighs, his lips nuzzling at the well-trimmed triangle of chestnut-brown hair. Her legs parted wide and she sighed to feel his tongue penetrate her and lap at her hidden bud. His hands found their way into her tender groins, to pull her fleshy petals wide open and expose all. His lips gripped her rosebud and tugged at it, and almost at once she gasped in surprise, *Not yet*! Even as she said it, her loins bucked upwards in abandonment to the ecstacy flooding through her.

Adrian gave her no time to recover – while she still shook in the throes of delight, he was between her trembling legs, his belly on hers and his staunch part thrusting into her wetness. In no time he brought her again to the edge of release, tides of sensation swirling through her from his brisk stabbing. Then at the very instant that she soared into Paradisaical climax, he raised his body on stiff arms and poised motionless above her, their only contact his deep-inserted *cazzo*, as he had come with affectionate amusement to think of it. He looked down at her face, relishing the wild-staring eyes and open gasping mouth. When the critical moments were past and she lay in the little langour that follows, she whispered, *Why*?

'We are going to imprint memories on this beautiful tiger so strong that I shan't be able to stay away,' he said.

He lowered himself on to her belly and resumed his in-and-out strokes, strong and steady, drawing little sighs of pleasure from her. When she was thoroughly aroused again, she tried to outwit him – she hooked her legs over his bottom and met him thrust for thrust with her soft belly. He gripped the cheeks of her bottom and stabbed away with a will, until she reached the point of moaning, her chin up and her head back.

'Yes, now! she gasped, and twitched in climactic spasms. At once Adrian stopped in mid-push and let her pleasure run its course. She stared up incredulously into his face, and gave in to his wishes. Twenty minutes later he had brought her seven times to climax without dismounting or withdrawing his bone-hard part from her.

'You're killing me,' she sighed, her hands on the back of his head to press his mouth to hers.

By now Adrian had held out to the limit of his ability. He

returned her kiss and began to move on her again, and this time there was a different feel to his hard plunging. Delphine felt it and said, *Yes, yes, yes*, exultantly, her knees drawn up and her legs spread to the limit. She did nothing to hurry him, but lay still and let him do it his way – only shrieking when she felt his body tense against her and his hot lust jolt into her slippery depths.

When they were capable of rational speech once more, lying side by side to cool off, Delphine told him that she liked his way of sealing agreements. Then while he was basking in self-satisfaction, she regained the initiative at a stroke.

'I thought you'd be drained dry by your nights of love with my sister,' she said, 'but I underestimated you.'

'You know about that?' he asked foolishly, 'and you said nothing until now?'

'What should I say? Marina jumps into bed with every man who comes to stay with us. Adalbert says she's a nymphomaniac, but I don't believe he knows what he's talking about. She's always liked men, ever since we were girls – she had her first before I did, though she's two years younger. Is she better in bed than I am?'

'An impossible question to answer,' said Adrian, embarrassed by it. 'Why do you ask? You are beautiful and very desirable.'

'I ask because you have been to bed with Marina most nights, but you've made love to me only twice.'

'Not so,' he protested with a grin. 'In that twice I've made love to you more than in all the nights with your sister. And she hardly ever stops talking about the Count. Has he really killed two men out of jealousy?'

'Not jealousy – affronted honour,' said Delphine, stretching her naked limbs lazily. 'Or so rumour has it. But who knows?'

They talked for a while until Adrian felt himself to be well recovered from his endeavours. He asked Delphine to put on her frock – nothing else – and go out on the balcony with him. She humoured him, and they went out on the white stone balcony, to stand with arms round each other's waists, looking down at the Grand Canal and the constant traffic of boats of all sizes and shapes. To their right lay a vista of the golden palaces along the Canal almost to the Rialto Bridge, the shimmer of the sun off the moving waters lighting the elaborate facades. It was as if, thought Adrian, everything lay waiting for a film director to start shooting a Venetian romance.

'If only I had words to tell you how much I love this scene,' he said, reaching behind Delphine to give her generous bottom a good feel through her thin silk frock. 'I want to fix it in my mind forever, so that I never forget what I want.'

His fingers were exploring the cleft between her soft cheeks, and she turned her head to look at him.

'If you had seen it as many thousands of times as I have,' she said, 'you'd know it's just a picture postcard view.'

'For me it represents the enchantment of Venice,' he told her enthusiastically, 'just as you do.'

'Two old whores past their best – Venice and me?' she asked with a chuckle. 'Oh, that wonderful exuberance of youth, when all the world is there for the taking!'

'Then indulge me,' said Adrian, 'let me enjoy my two lovely trollops together.'

Urged by his hands on her hips, she leaned forward to put her folded arms on the stone balcony rail. With his heart beating furiously at the thought of what he was proposing to do, Adrian stood close behind her and raised the back of her frock to her bare bottom. He flicked open his trousers and with a trembling hand guided his upstanding part between her thighs.

'Here?' she exclaimed. 'But everyone can see us!'

'All they can see from passing boats is two people standing close on a balcony,' he countered, with an impudent grin. 'They can't see what we are doing.'

'They can guess!'

'Then let them,' he said, and pushed slowly into her wetness. He felt Delphine tremble against him as she accepted the length of his straining part and, without turning her head to look at him, she sighed voluptuously and said she thought that he would be very good for her, a clever young man on the make like him. He squeezed her hips affectionately and rocked back and forth, his mind ablaze. Once a year in June, on Ascension Day, century after century, each Doge of Venice had gone out in the gilded and scarlet-hung State Barge, to throw a gold wedding-ring into the sea and claim mastery over it. Adrian's interest was not in the sea but in the city, and high on a balcony of the Palazzo Malvolio above the Grand Canal, he united himself to Venice.

Delphine was sighing and jerking her chubby bare cheeks

back at him. Adrian wielded his embedded part with determination and fast-growing delight, his feverish gaze flitting across towers and spires showing behind the water front palaces, as he tried to encompass the whole of the city. This was where he intended to enjoy unbridled pleasure and to make a lot of money.

'Ah, my dear man!' Delphine gasped as spasms of ecstasy took her and drove her shuddering against his loins.

'*Sì*!' Adrian gasped back. '*Sì*!' and delivered his spurting tribute to her mature beauty.

Later on, when Delphine was resting on her Sun-King bed, he dressed and went out. He could have taken one of the gondolas moored at the Grand Canal entrance to the palace, but because of the way the canal curved back on itself, it was quicker to stroll overland through the narrow streets and squares, past the Fenice Opera House and the preposterous church of St Moses, to the Piazza San Marco. He sat at a table outside Florian's cafe, where the band at its most sentimental was playing *Santa Lucia*, and had a cold drink and watched the overfed pigeons begging food from tourists. Then he worked his way along the windows of the shops under the arcades, till he found what he wanted – a seller of pictures of Saints, painted on wood.

As a matter of course he bought one of Venice's patron, San Marco, shown patting the head of a lion as if it were a pet dog – and one of Santa Caterina. According to the shopkeeper, whose English was good, her head was cut off when she would not marry the Emperor because he was no Christian. Santa Ursula appealed to Adrian when he was told that she led 11,000 young virgins from Rome to Germany, where they were all slaughtered by Huns.

'Do you believe there were so many virgins in Rome? When was this?' he asked, and the shopkeeper grinned and shrugged and said that, virgins or not, it was a waste of girls. He accepted with pleasure an extra 1,000 lire to write Adrian a bill of sale for six pictures instead of the three he had bought, which covered Delphine's pictures and the Bulgarian icon if questions were asked going through Customs.

Back at the Palazzo Malvolio he found that the tiger-skin had been neatly folded up and put in his room, with the two 'Cranach' Venuses. He also found Teresa there, clearing up after him. She looked up from her work and said, *Buona sera, Signor Adrian*. The thought came into his head that he had never seen her naked, for all the times she had obliged him, standing or lying down.

'*Buona sera*, Teresa,' he said, giving her his charming smile, and he rubbed his hand up and down the front of his trousers. Her glance dropped to the growing bulge there and Adrian asked her to take off her clothes. That meant nothing to her, but he knew an Italian word for clothes, having heard her use it when she was hanging his in the wardrobe, and he tried it – *Teresa, vestiti* – and he gestured with both hands to signify *take off*.

'*No, no, Signor, non e possible*,' she said, shaking her head as she had done on his first day in the Palazzo, and treating him to a long burst of incomprehensible Italian, she pointed to her ring finger, on which there was no ring, and ran her index finger round it to show where a ring would be, or should be, or might be, or could be, or whichever verb-form was appropriate. *Sono fidanzata*, she said several time, with growing emphasis, so that Adrian came to understand she was telling him that she was engaged to be married.

It seemed remarkably quick, so soon after his forced promise to provide a dowry for her, and he asked suspiciously, *Chi*? – the word for *who*? being one he had learned. In her lengthy answer he caught the name Toto more than once, and understood she was now betrothed to the man who looked after the Malvolio speedboat. Adrian offered his felicitations, but thought it only fair for the provider of her dowry to be allowed to inspect her marriage prospects. After what had passed between them daily for the whole of his stay in the Palazzo, her sudden coyness was little short of ridiculous.

To focus her attention properly, he undid his trouser buttons and tugged up his shirt to let his hard-swollen part stick out. Teresa stared at it as if fascinated, shaking her head all the time, until he sat down on the uncovered mattress, pulled her down alongside him, and put her hand on his cherished part. He felt for her chubby breasts through her white apron and frock, but she pushed him away. All the same, she clasped his hot and hard part in the palm of her hand, jerking it up and down with her usual unsophisticated vigour.

'That's it,' Adrian encouraged her, grinning at her flushed face. He put a hand on her thigh and stroked it firmly through her frock, but she kept her legs clamped together. She smiled to see how his legs trembled and his favoured part twitched to the thrills that the rapid movement of her fingers sent through him, and she murmured a few words in a soothing tone.

'You've turned out to be a tease,' Adrian sighed. 'You used to be more obliging before you got engaged on my money.'

'*Ecco*!' Teresa cried with a grin of triumph as Adrian's legs jerked spasmodically and his essence came gushing out in long jets, to wet her hand.

She had the grace to wipe him with a corner of her apron and kiss his cheek in a farewell gesture he found touching after all her reluctance. He completed his packing, stowing away the collection of pictures in his suitcase, well protected from accidents on the journey by the clothes around them. The tiger-skin was much too large to get in and so it travelled rolled up, the head in the middle. A footman in the purple and yellow livery of the Malvolio arrived to collect the luggage, and at the top of the grand marble staircase Adrian found the dignified major-domo waiting to escort him to the landing-stage.

It was with a curious mixture of feelings Adrian saw that the speed-boat was standing by to take him to the railway station. The footman stowed the luggage, Luigi bowed gracefully, Toto took Adrian's arm to assist him into the boat, and then they were away from the landing-stage and heading at a responsible pace up the Grand Canal. *I say, if Toto knew what his fiance was doing to me an hour ago*, thought Adrian, wondering if the boatman was as touchy about his *honour* as the Count. Clara had been terrified of what her gondolier husband would do when he found Adrian with her – so maybe the urge to violence in these inconvenient circumstances was universal.

The old palaces slid past to left and right – the Grimani, the Volpi, the Bembo – then the boat glided under the Rialto Bridge and followed the Grand Canal hard round to the left. Not many days had passed since Adrian had traced this route in a gondola from the station to the Palazzo Malvolio. He remembered very well what he had been thinking about on that breath-taking entrance to Venice – the escapades of its best-known citizen. Giacomo Casanova, and his exploits in gondolas and bedchambers. Adrian felt that during his short stay in Venice he had made a start towards emulating Casanova's adventures.

That included a naked frolic in a boat out on the lagoon, and a desperate escape through the window into a smelly canal – not to mention the beautiful sisters who rescued him and bathed him – before offering the use of other amenities. A beautiful and lascivious Countess had slipped into his bed when her husband was asleep, Signora Fosca's young *niece* had amused him with her smooth pink split – and Signora Fosca herself, whose black mourning concealed her lack of knickers, had entertained him. Princess Zita had offered pleasures that were thrillingly perverse, but best of all was Delphine naked and sumptuous on a tiger-skin. So much had happened in so short a time!

As for the little disappointment with the chambermaid Teresa, Adrian remembered from the *Memoirs* that in Paris Casanova had made the acquaintance of a beautiful seventeen-year-old girl who was engaged to be married. At a card party given by her ugly aunt, he took Mademoiselle into another room, while the others were engrossed in their game of piquet, and opened his breeches to show her his rampant part. It was the first full-sized one she had seen and her interest was caught. She held it and stroked it and fondled it until the inevitable happened, and proof of Casanova's desire squirted into her hand.

At the railway station a porter took the baggage while Adrian gave Toto 100 lire for his trouble – or perhaps as some sort of token conscience money. The train stood waiting at the platform and he was soon installed in his first-class sleeper, unwilling to believe that his first Venetian adventure was over. He stood at the window while the train crossed the long bridge to the mainland, a grin on his face at the memory of how Gina Luzzi had welcomed him to Venice on the inward journey, sitting astride his lap with her *melons* bared for him to feel.

After a good dinner and a bottle of very acceptable wine in the dining-car, he went back to his compartment to settle down for the night. Ahead lay Milan, and beyond that was the twelve-mile Simplon tunnel under the Alps into Switzerland. Then France, and sometime tomorrow he would be in Paris to catch the boat-train to London. The thought of Paris reminded him that he had never had time to finish reading the book he had bought there in the Place Pigalle – the anonymous *Madame Birchini's Revels*. It had served him well in the taming of Princess Zita: *Raoul's burning eyes stared into the deep cleft between Lavinia's thighs and she sobbed with shame to know a man was looking at her intimate secrets with lust in his heart* . . .

And while on this subject of literature, Adrian told himself, a book he must buy when he reached London was Mrs Elinor Glyn's notorious epic of true lust on a tiger-skin. If Delphine meant to use it as a guide-book for their love-affair, then he ought to see how it turned out. But when he arrived at his sleeping-compartment reading matter of another kind awaited him – a note had been slipped under the door. In flowery handwriting it said simply, *Come to 6*. The invitation must be from Gina, he thought – the friendly rider on trains across Europe, the signorina with the ample *melons*. The idea of riding her into Switzerland was one to bring a smile to his face and a twitch to his ever-eager part.

He made his way along the corridor of the swaying carriage to compartment number 6 and tapped on the door. He heard the bolt pulled back, and then the door swing inwards – and there to his consternation stood Bianca di Torrenegra in pink silk pyjamas! Behind her, on the lower bunk, lay another seventeen-year-old – a slim dark-haired beauty in a cream-coloured nightdress which hardly pretended to cover her pointed breasts, and which ended in a frill of lace halfway down her slender thighs.

'Come in, darling Adrian,' said Bianca, pulling him into the sleeper by the lapel of his jacket. 'This is my friend Maria-Luisa – I've told you about her. We're running away together to London. We want you to make love to both of us tonight.'

Ecstasy Italian Style

'*Leggie e memorie venete* was compiled by Signor Lorenzi, Sub-Librarian of St Mark's, and the cost of printing etc were defrayed by the Earl of Oxford. As the volume was destined for private distribution only it has no fixed price and is so little known, it has not realised its full value ... not only does it afford particulars concerning lewd women and men – and their treatment – but many customs of the Venetians ... and escapades by English visitors are recorded ...'

ONE

When the Contessa took off her frock for him, Roland eased down the scalloped front of her flimsy silk slip so that her plump bare breasts spilled out into his hands. He slid closer to her on the sofa and bent his neck to shower hot kisses on the warm flesh he held, and then to flick at the dark pink buds with the tip of his tongue and make them stand firm. Though he could not see it, a smile of satisfaction lingered on the Contessa's lips and she stroked his hair lightly.

Her hand lay on his thigh, a hand with several rings set with gem-stones and long perfect nails lacquered dark red. Her palm was warm to his skin through the thin material of his trousers, and his thighs moved apart involuntarily when her hand started to move slowly upwards.

'*Carissimo*,' she murmured, 'how very nicely you do that!'

The hand that had been stroking Roland's hair moved down to his cheek, and the stiff six inches in his underwear trembled when her finger began circling gently in his ear.

'Oh Marina,' he sighed eagerly, straightening up to bring his face to hers and kiss her painted mouth. The hand on his thigh reached its goal and her fingers plucked his buttons open and slipped inside. When she clasped him full-handed, the sensation was so intense that he almost spurted his passion into her palm as if he were a schoolboy.

'Come into the bedroom,' she whispered, and together they got up from the sofa and crossed her sitting-room, arms tight about each other, heads turned to gaze deep into each other's eyes, tiny kisses punctuating their slow progress towards the waiting bed.

Roland knew he was wide awake and yet was half afraid it was all an impossibly lush dream. In real life a university teacher did not find himself in a palace on the Grand Canal in Venice making love to a beautiful noblewoman: the Contessa Marina di Torrenegra, dark-haired and cream-complexioned, who had taken off her peach-coloured lace frock and sat beside him on a gilt and ornately carved eighteenth century sofa in her sitting-room to let him feel her breasts.

The sofa might be a little worn and shabby after 200 years of use, as was the rest of the antique furniture in the room, but the Contessa was in the prime of life, strong, lively and ready for anything he had in mind for her – and just what that might be, he was unsure. It was unsettling to think that the sexual experiences of a thirtyish university lecturer – at least a British one – might be somewhat inadequate beside the expectations of this superbly lascivious lady.

A palace bedroom in the afternoon was far from the mundane adventures of his days in London – taking girl students to hear a string quartet playing Mozart at the Wigmore Hall and then back to his small flat for an hour or so of regulation man-over girl-under.

He need not have worried. When they stood beside the bed – a massively carved four-poster with hangings of ivory and yellow – Marina turned to face him and put both hands on his shoulders, kissing him hotly. Roland's arms were around her and his hands rested on her bare back up above her silk slip. Which seemed a very British sort of place for his hands to be at a time like this, he realised. It was not as if he was doing a tango with her at a tea-dance.

That being so, he ran his palms tantalisingly down her back until he was clasping the full cheeks of her bottom through the fine silk of her knickers. Her flesh was so warm, so pliable – he squeezed the full handfuls he held, hard as he could, hoping he could make red imprints with his fingers to look at and kiss better for her. And that led him to insinuating his hands under her slip and down the waist-band of her knickers in the hollow of the back, to grasp her bare bottom and have the feel of her soft flesh directly, without silk between.

The long kiss ended at last, and he expected her to pull free of his hold and get on to the bed. But this was not his flat in Drury Lane and Marina was no twenty-year-old art student. She knelt down gracefully in front of him, staring up at his face, while her skilful fingers completed the undoing of his trousers, which slipped down his legs to his ankles. Before he had time to feel ridiculous, she had his shirt tucked up round his waist and his twitching stiffness in her hand – and then in her mouth.

For Roland this was something very new, something he had only read about and seen in rare erotic drawings. He'd heard it said that when the last King, old Tum-Tum Teddy, got too grossly fat for his lady friends to bear his weight, he sat comfortably in a bedroom chair with his thighs spread apart to be serviced in this way by Court ladies and French actresses. Roland looked down in wonder at Marina's dark-haired head bowed solicitously over his jutting part and his knees trembled weakly beneath him at the wild sensations her lapping tongue was causing.

It was a dream – what else could it be? A voluptuous Arabian Nights dream induced by several days without sexual fulfilment. The intensity of the sensations of delight were proof enough of that. Any moment now he would wake up alone in bed in the dark to find himself spurting his undirected lust into his pyjamas.

But it was not a dream after all, and the Contessa Marina put her hand tightly round his avid part to stop him reaching the end of the road too soon, and removed her mouth from it. While Roland heaved a sigh at the loss of that exquisite pleasure, she stood up with a smile and stripped off her stylish slip and her loose silk knickers. Seen naked, she was gloriously desirable, being full-bodied and ripe, like a sun-matured fruit ready to bite into and suck the sweet juice.

She bent over to remove her stockings, deliberately turning away so that her bare round rump was thrust towards him. Roland at once stepped forward to grasp and fondle the satin-skinned cheeks presented to him. She wriggled her hips luxuriously when his fingers squeezed those plump cheeks and her bottom jibbed back at him when he ran his fingers down the crease between. He would have done more, much more, never before having been in so strenuously arousing a position behind a beautiful naked woman with, it seemed, licence to do whatever he wanted.

And that was a lot – he was going to spread her legs apart a little so that he could put a hand between her thighs and feel her split from behind. And then an arm round her waist and down between her legs so that he could feel her from front and back at the same time – that should be fascinating!

Before he could prolong this exploration of Marina's assets, she stepped away from him to throw back the faded silk coverlet on her four-poster bed and stretch out full length on the ivory sheets. Roland devoured her with hungry eyes while struggling out of his clothes – she lay on her side, facing him, propped on an elbow, her eyes bright with anticipation of pleasure. Her legs were stretched out to their full length and crossed at the ankle, and he saw the colour of the little patch of curls where her sumptuous thighs joined was the same shade of almost-black as the hair of her head.

She was in no mood for long and tender love-making, he found when he threw himself on the bed beside her and reached for her breasts. She was not one of his girl students, to be cajoled by repeated kisses and caresses to a gentle penetration and slow ride to the peak of sensation. She wanted to be devoured whole. At the instant he touched her she rolled over on her back, took a firm grip on his jerking stiffness and pulled him to her – on to her warm belly, her legs open wide to offer herself to him. Roland was so aroused by her enthusiasm that he let her control the proceedings – he had all to gain and nothing to lose.

Her hand groped down between their bellies to guide him into her, and she was as wet and ready for him as if he had played with her for fifteen minutes. He penetrated her with a single hard thrust, bringing a long moan of appreciation from her. His hands kneaded her plump breasts while he slid back and forth, a forceful machine-like rhythm that made her moan again and again in delight and jerk underneath him. Her head was upturned on the satin pillow to thrust her chin towards the ceiling, mouth wide open to show her white teeth.

It was no dream – he was quite sure of that now. It was as if his most luxuriant secret fantasy had been made real. As if he had stepped out of 1927 and into 1527 and into Titian's studio, where the sumptuous Venus of Urbino lay stretched out naked on a bed for him to ravage. And ravage was an appropriate word for what he was doing to Contessa Marina – and she to him. She lay spread-eagled in hot desire on the ivory satin bed-sheet, legs wide open as they would go, her hot belly heaving up under his belly as he plunged and plunged into it.

Her fingers were digging into his neck, threatening to choke him. Perhaps it was a Venetian variant of the age-old folk tale that a hanged man's last moments were consoled by the strongest erection and most profuse ejaculation of his life – so strange were the thoughts whirling in Roland's mind through a delirium of ecstatic sensation.

Marina's head lifted off from the pillows to press her mouth over his and force her wet and flickering tongue right into his mouth. In his feverish excitement Roland had the sensation that her belly had opened wider and he was ramming into her depths – those hot wet depths where pain and pleasure could not be told one from the other, and both were equally welcome. In a rising crescendo of shrill cries, Marina's back arched off the bed, lifting his weight on her.

She collapsed beneath him, her climax finished in seconds it seemed, and Roland drove on furiously, his heart racing at the approach of his own crisis. By then he was too absorbed in his own sensations to pay her any attention, and his forcefulness acted on her as a strong stimulant. She squirmed beneath him, sighing and gasping, then she took his face between her hands and covered his open mouth with her own and sucked as if she would draw the breath of life from his body.

Roland let go his grasp on her breasts to slide his hands flat underneath her shaking body and grip the fleshy cheeks of her rump. She began to swung her hips up to meet his strokes, crying out wordlessly for release from the excruciating delight that was racking her for a second time.

Roland gasped to feel his culminating moment rushing toward him at incredible speed. He slammed fast and deep into Marina's slippery warmth, his belly smacking on hers brutally, unable to hear her ecstatic cries for the deafening roar in his ears of his blood pounding through his veins. He heard himself crying out when he spurted his raging lust into her, and her answering cry, a long descending wail of release.

It took some little time before he came to his senses again. Marina lay limp and still under him, her belly and his sticking together clammily with their mingled sweat. Her eyes were shut and she was breathing slowly, almost as if asleep. He lightly kissed the tip of her nose before easing himself off her body, at which she opened her dark brown eyes and smiled at him.

'That was tremendous,' she said. 'You've utterly devastated me, you darling man – I'm all in shatters!'

In the contentment after the most exciting sexual encounter of his life, bar the first one when he was sixteen, Roland accepted that his world had turned upside down and it could never be the same again. And this amazing change had come about in the most casual way. He had been sitting at a little table under the arcade outside Florian's cafe in the Piazza San Marco, with a cup of coffee before him and a two-day-old copy of *The Times*. He was waiting for his Venetian contact, Signor Carlo Missari, to take him to the Accademia Gallery, otherwise closed to the public. Missari was one of the assistant curators there.

It was eleven in the morning and, in the normal Italian way, Missari was late for the appointment. Not that Roland cared at all – he was enjoying sitting in this most famous square. There were the usual tourists about, taking snaps and buying picture postcards to send to Tunbridge Wells, Munich, Lyon and Oslo, or wherever they came from. The most alluring woman Roland had seen so far in Venice was at the table next but one to his own, and she evidently was no tourist. When he asked himself why he found her so interesting, the answer was not at all simple.

She was not particularly young – in fact she was older than Roland himself, and he was thirty-one. At a guess he put her at about forty, give or take. Her face was a little less oval than classical beauty required, and a little rounder. Her figure was good, as far as he could see while she was sitting – she had a full and well-shaped bosom, at least, and a long neck. She would be quite tall for a woman when she stood up, he judged, by the look of the long thighs under her frock.

The frock itself was stunning.. It was made of peach-coloured lace and not much else, knee-length, with close-fitting sleeves that made her wrists seem very slender. By some minor miracle of the dressmaker's art, the frock gathered into a lace rose in front, about the size of an open hand. The rose lay in her lap while she was seated, and Roland guessed that when she stood up it would rest somewhere between two unseen yet key points – her belly-button and the join of her thighs. Make of that whatever you would, it was a provocative area to call attention to.

Her hat was of white felt, with a tall round crown and a wide brim to keep the sun off her face. There was a single strand of pearls round her long neck that if genuine had cost someone a fortune, and several rings set with gem-stones on each of her hands. Whether that was an Italian custom or a quirk of her own was not clear to Roland, but he noted that she also wore a gold wedding-ring. Her white glacé gloves lay on the table beside a glass frosted from the ice in it, but she had taken only a sip or two in the past five minutes.

She was not alone at the cafe, of course – women blessed with her wealth and looks and charm were never alone. It was some comfort to Roland that her companion was not her husband or any other man, but a woman of her own age, also dressed fashionably if less strikingly. The conversation between the two was very lively, with excessive hand-waving for Roland's British taste, nodding and shaking of the head, shrugging of the shoulders, staccato exclamations. If he'd observed this in London he'd be sure they were quarrelling, but he knew even the most ordinary Italian conversations were highly animated.

It occurred to him that he was staring impolitely, and looked away as nonchalantly as he could and watched tourists feeding flocks of fat and waddling pigeons on the square grey paving of the Piazza. At a guess, he put the size of it at 200 yards the long way and about 60 yards across sideways, between grandiose stone-arcaded buildings. In the middle of each long side was a cafe with tables and chairs spilling out into the arcade, and both cafes had a string orchestra up on a little platform. His own band was playing a Strauss waltz, 'Roses From The South'.

It was a wonderfully hot early summer day, the sky above was a deep clear blue, completely cloudless – a blue hardly ever seen in England. It was Roland's first visit to Venice, and the first day of his stay, and he was enjoying it more than he had expected. Mainly for the first-rate dinner he had on arrival at his hotel the night before, and also for the sheer pleasure of sitting in this marvellous Piazza doing nothing.

Not that his enjoyable idleness would last for long. He was in Venice to work, not on holiday, and boring old duty would shortly call. But just for the moment, *dolce far niente*, in one of the few Italian phrases he knew – *it's nice to do nothing*. Except that it was not easy to do nothing in Venice – even his stroll from his hotel to the Piazza San Marco had turned out to be an involuntary sightseeing tour. There was no way to avoid the art and architecture of Venice – the whole city was seemingly constructed of high culture.

He brought himself back to earthy considerations by looking at the two women again. What had been a lively discussion had now deteriorated to a near-argument. Voices had become raised a little, though the music blanketed the words – not that they would have meant anything to him anyway. To judge by gestures and posture, the charmer in peach lace was being accused or blamed for something by her friend in the blue silk jacket, and was defending herself.

Oh, the dark flash of her eyes, Roland thought, entranced by the scene being played out at the next table but one to him. Oh, the passionate heave of her bosom as she refutes the allegation – and oh, the angry twist of her full red mouth as she counters the accusation with sarcastic words. If that's what it was all about. For all he could tell, it might be a brisk discussion of the weather, or the latest fashion. But he didn't believe so.

Now he came to think of it, this unknown woman in the apricot lace frock reminded him a little of Penelope Burrow, to whom he had made love one memorable afternoon in his flat after a visit to the Royal Academy. She was the wife of a colleague of his at the university, and she had that same enticingly well-fleshed look as the Italian woman in the peach lace frock.

In an age of flappers without breasts or backside to please a a chap, that graceful roundness of belly and thighs, that curve of hips, that fullness of bosom . . . it was like stumbling into a lush green oasis after a long trek through desert sands. In his delight that afternoon with Penny Burrow, he had stripped her naked and kissed her from mouth to toes in a daze of pleasure.

There was so much of her to fondle and kiss! Roland's hands were trembling as they roamed over her satin skin, and over her chubby breasts, across her belly and between her open legs. She sighed in appreciation and lay back to enjoy what he was doing to her. When he lay on top of her, it was as if he was cradled on cushions stuffed with swan's-down, very far removed from the angularities of the girl students he had. With them it was more like wrestling when they wound their bony arms and legs round him and jerked their skin-covered pelvis up at him.

Making love to Penny was as voluptuous to the mind as to the body – Roland's sensations grew to an exquisite intensity, his hands under her plump bottom and his fingers sinking deep into the soft flesh. He jerked his head up to stare blindly into her hot-flushed face, while she rocked him backwards and forwards on her with arms tightly about him – until at last he poured a seemingly endless stream of ecstasy into her.

The woman in the peach lace frock had noticed that

Roland was staring at her and turned on him those expressive eyes of hers in a glare of outraged fury. It seemed to him she was not angry at being stared at – she must be well used to that from men – but as if guessing he was preoccupied with lascivious images from other times. That was the insult, to think of making love to anyone else while looking at her!

But that was ridiculous, he told himself, a wish-fulfilment, his guilty reaction at being caught. She couldn't possibly know what was in his mind, unless he had been leering at her without realising it. He looked away quickly, half-turning in his chair to face the other way, towards the church of San Marco across the end of the Piazza.

After St Peter's in Rome this was the most famous church in Christendom, whatever claim the French made for Notre Dame, but there was nothing he could compare it with. It was the only one of its kind anywhere in the world, and a Doge of Venice started to build this fantasia of gold and marble and lacy stone as the private chapel to his palace at about the same time William the Conqueror was knocking up his first rough stone castle in England. Roland tried to put what he saw into words, to capture it – there were five tall round-top arches, each like a giant niche. The interior of each was a riot of red and blue and gold mosaic on the walls, but the gold was dominant.

Under his breath Roland recited Shelley's lines to see if they stood up to the reality:

> Underneath day's azure eyes,
> Ocean's nursling, Venice lies.
> As within a furnace bright,
> Column, tower, and dome, and spire,
> Shine like obelisks of fire,
> Pointing with inconstant motion
> From the altar of dark ocean
> To the sapphire-tinted skies . . .

Above the arches, a balcony ran the whole width of the church behind a white-stone parapet, and in the middle stood the four life-size bronze horses, beautiful Greek workmanship, looted by the Venetians from Constantinople in the long ago, *ad majorem Dei gloriam*, as the Jesuits said, for the greater glory of God.

Behind and above the horses rose five grey onion-shaped

domes that formed the roof. In thousands of paintings artists tried to capture the exuberance of this church, millions of postcards for visitors to send to their friends at home to show them what they were missing, hundreds of millions of tourist snaps, since the day the portable Kodak camera was first invented – yet for all that, San Marco had to be seen in reality to understand its unique place in Western architecture.

Which was all very true and right, thought Roland, very good and proper, very commendable and high-minded. But however much a man might be devoted and enthusiastic in his appreciation of the arts, it was extremely difficult to keep his eyes fixed on San Marco when this marvellous woman was sitting close at hand on the other side. The truth was that Roland wanted to get her into bed, and the prospects of that were nil, he accepted.

His thoughts were diverted from that melancholy conclusion by the belated arrival of the man he had been waiting for – Carlo Missari. He was in his thirties, a plumpish moon-faced man in a pale grey double-breasted suit and a panama hat, his manner cheerful and effusive. He spoke English reasonably well, though with an accent, and pressed a small book into Roland's hand, saying it was *uno piccolo regalo* – a small present. It was a locally published guide-book to Venice, Roland saw.

He was thanking Missari for this very useful present when the Venetian's roving eye spotted the woman in the peach lace frock two tables away. He excused himself to Roland and darted across to pay his respects and kiss her hand, babbling away nonstop. The chance was too good to miss – Roland strode after him to make it clear he wished to be introduced. At this moment he learned that the woman he lusted for was the Contessa Marina di Torrenegra.

Missari introduced Roland as Professore Thornton of Londra, a title he reluctantly disclaimed, explaining that his academic rank was not as exalted as *professore* but only that of a humble *dottore*. Both ladies seemed glad of the interruption – perhaps they had tired of their quarrel – and invited them to sit down.

'What are you doing in Venice, Doctor Thornton?' asked the Contessa in perfect English without a trace of accent, 'Are you sight-seeing?'

'Only in a manner of speaking,' he said, 'I am here to study some of the paintings in the Accademia Gallery for a book I am writing on the themes of Early Renaissance painting.'

He realised it sounded utterly boring and was very pleased when Carlo Missari leaped in to explain that the Contessa was also English.

'Have you lived in Venice long?' Roland asked her at that.

'Almost twenty years,' she said, smiling at him. 'I married the count in Rome before the War, and we decided to live here.'

Leaving them to converse in English, Missari turned all his attention to the other woman, the one in the elegant jacket of pale blue silk. The arrangement suited Roland very well and he set out to make the very best impression he could on the titled lady he wanted furiously to get into bed. A white-coated waiter came to the table, more cold drinks were ordered, the orchestra changed from Viennese to Neapolitan and time passed pleasantly.

A clangor from across the Piazza broke into the conversation as, up on the flat top of the clock tower, two Moors cast larger than life-size in bronze jerkily swung sledgehammers at a great metal bell to sound the hour.

The lady in blue silk glanced at her tiny gold wristwatch to make sure the clock tower was correct and said she must leave. The two men rose, and Roland followed Carlo Missari's example and kissed her hand by way of *arrivederci*. After she was gone, Carlo looked at Roland enquiringly, as if wanting to know if he still wished to be taken to the Accademia and, taking a chance, Roland asked the Contessa if she had any arrangement for lunch. She told him she would be pleased to accept his invitation, and Carlo understood his presence was no longer needed. He took his leave, promising to telephone to Roland's hotel that evening to make arrangements for tomorrow, and off he went.

'Which hotel is that, Mr Thornton?' the Contessa asked. 'Are you staying at the Danieli or the Gritti Palace?'

Her natural assumption was that he was at one or other of the two most luxurious and expensive hotels in Venice. Roland felt it necessary to inform her that the publisher who was meeting the expenses of his research trip was not that generous. He did not think he need tell her that if he'd been paying all his own bills, he would be sleeping in a room in the least expensive *pensione* he could find. As it was, he was at the Hotel Gallini.

The Contessa said she knew the Gallini because it was not far from where she lived. On the way they could stop at the Taverna La Fenice by the Opera House for lunch. Knowing so little about the geography and facilities of Venice, Roland was happy to go along with her suggestion. She had made a good choice, he found when they reached the Taverna.

He let her persuade him to try *anguilla alla veneziana*, small eels cooked in lemon with tunnyfish, and to his surprise he liked it. For desert they ate dry Asiago cheese with a bowl of fresh figs and grapes, and they drank almost two bottles of white Soave wine from Verona between them.

With the coffee they had a little glass of anisette at her suggestion, a sweet and sticky liquor tasting of aniseed, and by then they were both in an exalted mood, and the Contessa was openly flirting with him.

During the meal he had gathered from her lively conversation that she lived in a palace, which had a grandiose ring to his English ear. When he asked if it was very old, she said it was built in the eighteenth century to replace the previous one, which had burnt down. Roland said he would like very much to see it sometime, but would she at this moment like to show him where the Hotel Gallini was, and perhaps come in for a glass of wine or anisette or anything else?

'Out of the question!' she said. 'You can't begin to imagine how fearfully jealous my husband is. Not that I've ever given him the least reason to be. But if he heard that I'd been seen in the Gallini with another man – *Dio mio*! – he would hunt you down and destroy you!'

'Why should he ever get to know you'd sat for fifteen minutes in the Gallini for a drink and a chat?' asked Roland, who knew what was always said about the Italian temperament.

'My family is of some considerable importance here in Venice and very well known,' said the Countess, bristling with pride, 'I am recognised wherever I go.'

'For your beauty, as much as for your family name,' Roland said, making a stab at Continental-style gallantry. It seemed to go down well, and he burbled on for a while, his imagination fired by the wine he had drunk, about the cultural and social significance of female beauty ever since the Renaissance.

'You mean those fat-bottomed women that Bellini and Raphael and Corregio and the rest of them painted?' she asked, raising her smoothly plucked eyebrows.

Roland said he meant real live women down the centuries, not models chosen by artists to suit their own personal taste in female flesh. The Contessa's ready acquaintance with the names of painters of the fifteenth century was commendable, he added, and showed a true appreciation of art.

She told him she had very little interest in art, but having lived for nearly twenty years in a palace where there were more paintings on the walls than he'd find in the Accademia Gallery, the dominant themes and some of the names had stuck in her mind – it could hardly be otherwise. Roland asked what she believed were the dominant themes of Italian Renaissance art, that being not much removed from the purpose of his visit to Venice.

'Sex and money,' she said at once, 'the same then as now.'

They left the Taverna about two thirty and the Contessa led him through narrow streets and over a bridge or two across back canals to a large square he recognised behind the church of San Stefano.

'Your hotel is over there, Roland,' said the Contessa, first names having taken over during their lunch, 'but if you have time perhaps you would like to see a little Bellini painting I have in my sitting-room.'

Of course he would, and she led on past the vast red-brick church that looked as if it had started to lean preparatory to total collapse, along narrow paved alleys and into a small square. There was a modest restaurant on one side, with tables outside, and a waiter clearing away after the last customer. On the other side of the square, taking up the whole width, stood a large eighteenth-century building in white stone, with three tiers of columns.

'The Palazzo Malvolio,' said Contessa Marina, pointing to the carved stone coat of arms above the huge central door. Roland wondered if she would produce from her tiny white glacé leather handbag a key to open the massive wooden door, but as they got closer he saw that he was being provincial. At the instant they set foot on the bottom of the three broad stone steps up to the palace entrance, the door opened magisterially and there stood a footman bowing to the Contessa. A man in livery, no less.

True, his braided jacket and knee-breeches were almost as old as the footman himself, their yellow and blue faded to almost the same colour, but Roland was impressed. Inside the door lay a stone-flagged entrance hall, the walls decorated with muskets and heavy swords from bygone days. The staircase was of marble and was wide enough to have life-sized statues at every third step – naked Roman gods and goddesses.

From there on, Roland was lost. Marina led him up two flights of stairs, along passages hung with oil paintings and through suites of rooms that led into each other and were furnished in ornate gilt eighteenth century style, and eventually into a room that could have contained his entire London flat and still had space left over to park a fleet of buses. This was her own private sitting-room, Marina explained, pulling off her broad-brimmed white hat.

There were pictures on all the walls, many of them obviously family portraits, but over the marble fireplace was a Bellini – unmistakable to Roland's trained eye. He would have gone to it, but halfway across the room Marina caught his hand to pull him down on to a faded rose-pink striped sofa. She put her arms round his neck and kissed him lusciously.

'*Orlando mio*, I want you so much,' she whispered, her breath hot on his cheek, 'do you want me?'

'Since the first moment I saw you this morning' he answered, his hand cupping a plump breast through the lace of her frock. That proved not very satisfactory, and so he put a hand on her knee and slid it up her thigh, on the bare flesh above her garter.

Marina shivered and drew in her breath – and opened her legs. His fingertips touched thin silk, with springy curls and warm skin under it. She let him feel her for a while, then stood up to take her frock off for him. He showered kisses on her plump bare breasts and very soon she had his stiff six inches out of his trousers and in her hand.

'Come into the bedroom,' she whispered, and together they got up from the sofa and crossed her sitting-room, arms tight about each other, and Roland was lost in amazement that he was going to have this beautiful woman.

TWO

When Roland looked closely at the painting over the Contessa's marble mantelpiece, he decided it was by Giovanni Bellini, not his brother Gentile. It showed a woman sitting with her back to a window, looking at her face in a gold-framed hand-mirror. She was naked, with only a wisp of red material thrown over a thigh in such a way as to just preserve her modesty.

Her breasts were part-hidden by the arm holding up the mirror but enough of them could be seen to appreciate their roundness and fullness. Her hair was brown shading towards auburn, parted in the middle and drawn back over her ears. Through the window behind her lay a typical Venetian scene – a canal of blue-green water between tall houses and a gracefully curving bridge with men in cloaks and women in long dresses crossing it.

Marina stood close to Roland while he studied the picture, an arm round his waist. They had rested a while after their third bout in her four-poster bed before getting up. Roland was fully dressed, ready to take his leave, and Marina had put on a most sumptuous long dressing-gown of midnight blue silk.

'You are the expert, *Orlando mio*,' said she, 'tell me what is the woman doing in this picture? Why is she naked?'

'She is waiting for her lover,' he answered at once, entering into the spirit of her question. 'She has taken off her clothes to delight him when he walks into the room, and she is taking a final quick look at her make-up to make sure it is perfect.'

'Her make-up?' said Marina. 'Did they have that four hundred years ago?'

'I don't know for certain,' he confessed, 'but I think so, to judge by the picture. Look how her eyebrows have been plucked to a fine line. And the colour of her hair, it's attractive but it's not quite natural. She's a light brunette who's rinsed her hair with henna or something similar to give that auburn shade. See the clarity and the delicate pallor of her cheeks – either she spent her entire life out of the sun, which must be nearly impossible in Venice – or she has applied a touch of fine rice powder or something of the sort. She's a beautiful work of art ready to be enjoyed.'

'I think you're wrong,' said Marina, 'she wouldn't wait naked for a lover, she'd be sitting there in her best new frock and underwear, so he could have the pleasure of undressing her. Men get very excited at the sight of a pair of silk knickers.'

'Women didn't wear knickers in her day, that I do know,' said Roland, 'underwear was invented less than a hundred years ago.'

'That's not the point,' Marina countered, 'the men then would be just as excited by helping her take her frock off. If you ask me, her lover has been with her and made her very happy and has just left. She hasn't dressed yet, and she's looking in the mirror for any sign of the ravishing she's just had.'

'Would it be her face she examined for that?' asked Roland, grinning at the Contessa in a suggestive manner.

'Why not? Traces elsewhere are easily washed away, but lines of satisfaction or sadness on the face are there for all to see – there is a slight darkness under her eyes, do you see it? He has driven her to the edge of exhaustion.'

'Then she is pleased he has gone and she can rest?' Roland asked, amused by the story-making.

'No, the contentment on her face masks a certain sadness. She is sad he is gone and would like him to come back very soon and do it to her again. Perhaps that's why she is still naked – she is hoping he'll turn round and come back for another hour. And if he does, she's ready to be thrown down on her back and open her legs for him.'

Marina had one arm round Roland's waist and was pressing her hip hard against him. Her other hand was across her body to lie over the join of his legs and rub him gently through his closed trousers. It was no longer possible to pretend they were making up a story about the woman in the painting.

Roland thought it was unlikely he could rise to the occasion again so soon. Twice was the usual limit of his activity when a girlfriend came to his flat for an evening of gramophone music and wine. Though one rainy Sunday afternoon he had in the space of two hours done it three times, and was in the mood to repeat the pleasure half an hour later, but the girl – a flat-chested and bony-hipped blonde from Dulwich – balked at that and told him he was a sex maniac for suggesting it.

All the same, Marina's tickling through his trousers produced to his delight a stiffening of his part, and he turned to face her and put his arms round her to feel her plump bottom through the sheer silk of her dressing-gown. When she began to undo his buttons he knew it was too late to turn back without mortally offending her and never seeing her again. Not that he had any wish to stop – he was feeling good and wanted to get inside her again. However, it was time to take charge and not let her do everything her way, or she would have no respect for him at all.

The antique marble fireplace, which had never in 400 years had a fire in it, had sides carved as caryatids, a pair of identical naked women, one to each side, their heads holding up the shelf over which hung the Bellini painting. They were less than life-size, their sleek bodies curving back into the marble, though there was nothing undersized about the round breasts that jutted forward.

That at least was Roland's first impression, and to check the accuracy of his eye, he turned Marina and walked her backwards a step or two until her back was to the wall next to the right-hand caryatid. She leaned back easily and smiled at him as he opened her dark blue dressing-gown and let it hang loosely from her shoulders. His first delighted observation was the contrast between the creamy skin of Marina's breasts and belly and the near-black silk.

'What are you doing?' she asked as his glance moved sideways from her breasts to the polished marble ones at her side, then back to hers again, then to the caryatid's.

'Checking,' he said, 'my impression was that the man who made your fireplace put full-sized breasts on a half-size woman, but that's not quite true. They're larger than proportion requires, but smaller than yours.'

Marina looked sideways at the carving in some surprise. She had his stiff length out of his gaping trousers now and stroked it with busy fingers.

'My dear, it's late and I've no time for this nonsense. Why are you so hard – I thought that had been settled in bed.'

'Not quite,' he said, one hand feeling her chubby breasts and the other resting on the marble equivalent beside her, enjoying the comparison of texture, warmth and solidity. 'I want to pay my respects to you once more, Marina.'

'Are you sure?' she asked, a fine-plucked eyebrow arching up her forehead. 'Perhaps you mistake me for the marble woman here on my left, you seem to enjoy feeling her. Though I don't know how you mean to go about it – there's nothing between her legs but smooth stone.'

With a grin, Roland ran his hand down the caryatid's belly as far as he could without stooping, but reached only as far down as her inset belly-button. He rubbed his fingertips lightly on the smooth-polished marble, his other hand repeating the gentle movement on Marina's belly, gliding down until he felt the soft warm flesh between her thighs.

Marina looked at him with her head on one side, amusement on her face. The hand with many jewelled rings slid up and down his six-inch length, which seemed with each pass to grow harder and thicker. Her dark brown eyes were half-closed in pleasure when he switched his hand from the caryatid to her breasts and played with them until their russet tips stood firm.

'I've really no time for all this art appreciation,' she said with her teasing smile, 'but just this once for you, Orlando, I shall let you indulge your curious desire.'

She gave a martyr's sigh, without for a moment stopping her stroking of his upright part.

'I shall be forever grateful,' he whispered, thinking she was about to spread her legs wide and let him have her against the wall – he'd not had a girl like that since he was a student and however awkward a way it was, fond memories came back to stir a fierce lust in him.

Annie Davis was in his mind, a pudgy seventeen-year-old he had persuaded to stand against the wall in a suburban cinema car-park after they'd seen the film through. Even fifteen years later the mere thought of Annie standing with straddled legs and her knickers in his pocket was enough to bring him up hard, at any time of day or night. His climax had been violent and profuse – and so was hers – but she never spoke to him again after that evening, because he had become so carried away he failed to pull out of her.

But his assumption was completely wrong – the Contessa had no such intent. She slipped out from between him and the wall, got behind him and put her arms tightly round his waist, urging him a step sideways until he faced the left-hand caryatid full on.

'Put your hands on the mantelpiece,' Marina murmured, her hot breath in his ear as she rested her chin on his shoulder and pressed her belly against his bottom.

She unbuckled his belt and unfastened his trousers completely and let them slide down his legs until they lay like a hobble around his ankles. Then she took hold of his hard-swollen part again, using both hands to grasp it firmly and jerk it up and down.

'But, but . . .' he said, unable to believe the evidence of his own senses as to Marina's intention.

'*Sta zitto!*' she said. 'Be quiet now – you could have had me on my back or on my knees or across your lap or anyhow at all you wanted. I have given myself to you – and would do so again, as often as you wanted me. But now you insult me by preferring a marble woman. It shall be as you wish, Orlando – you shall make love to her. Now put your hands on the mantelpiece.'

'But this is absurd,' he said, doing as she said. In this odd position he looked down and saw how his eager part was jerking uncontrollably to the thrills that the vigorous manipulation of her hands sent racing through him. He realised just *how* absurd the situation truly was and the perversity of Marina's sense of humour.

'Yes, you made a ridiculous choice,' said she, 'and now you must go through with it. Do you find her beautiful, your marble love? Her breasts are a good shape, but they are cold and hard, not warm and giving to the hands like mine. And between her thighs she has nothing for you! She has only marble there, not a warm and willing *fica* like mine.'

Through his haze of sensation Roland registered the Italian word with relish – there could be no more useful word than *fica* for him to know if Marina was representative of Venetian women in general. Except the word for the part of him she was holding two-handed at that very moment.

Before he had time to ask, she went on with her complaint:

'You are perverse, Orlando, and to you a woman of marble is desirable. *Va bene* – you must have her.'

The conviction that he was asleep and dreaming took shape yet again in Roland's dazed mind. The dream was exceptionally vivid and real-seeming, but it could be nothing else but the erotic fantasy of deep sleep brought on by an involuntary erection. In actuality, it was beyond belief that a beautiful Contessa would stand naked behind him and manipulate him sexually in pretended connection with a fireplace ornament. This was Surrealism gone mad – a picture painted by a drunken artist that would never be exhibited in public.

The idea of being a figure in someone's painting was funny to him, and Roland chuckled, struck by the sheer ridiculousness of it all. His hilarity was cut off sharp five seconds later when his belly quaked in an exquisite spasm and his desire squirted out in sharp little bursts. With bulging eyes he saw the spurts splatter on the tranquil face of the marble nude and slide down over her lips and chin.

'*Ecco*!' said the Contessa in triumph over him, 'now you have what you wanted, *caro mio*, you have made love to her! Although you did not have much to give her – or perhaps she is not quite as exciting as you thought she would be?'

Roland hung by his hands from the marble mantelpiece, panting and weak, his legs rubbery under him, staring at the white trickle of his lust between the caryatid's out-thrust breasts, and at last down into the smooth featureless space between her legs, where her split should have been.

His sated part was softening quickly in the Contessa's hands, and he told himself that if this were a dream, he would have woken up by now, with wetness on his belly. But he was still in Marina's sitting-room, even after his climax, and not in a bed. However preposterous, it was all truly happening to him.

It was after six when Roland left the Palazzo Malvolio, shown through the confusing corridors of paintings and the grandiose suites of rooms by the Contessa's personal maid. The maid was a dark-complexioned middle-aged woman, who evidently found him in some way amusing – she darted surreptitious looks at him on their trek through the palace, grinning secretly and trying to stop herself laughing out loud. Naturally she knew that he had been making love to the Contessa, but why that should be considered funny eluded Roland completely.

From the small square outside the Palazzo he found his way to San Stefano without trouble, and was soon in his room in the Hotel Gallini. He stripped off and took a long hot shower, then stood for ten agonising seconds with the water on cold, towelled himself dry and put on clean clothes. He went down for a drink feeling much refreshed after his very energetic afternoon, and with some astounding things to think about.

Carlo Missari had said he would telephone later in the day to make arrangements for the morning, but probably to find out how Roland had got on with the Contessa Marina. In the event he was better than his word, and turned up at the hotel just as Roland was beginning to feel hungry and had decided to go out to eat. He thought it obligatory for a first-time visitor to Venice to dine in one of the restaurants overlooking the Grand Canal and conducted Roland on foot for ten minutes along narrow streets to the Rialto Bridge.

The restaurant was on the quay beside the world-famous hump-backed stone bridge, and the whole frontage was open for diners to enjoy the slightly cooler evening air after the heat of the day. Carlo chose a table just inside, from which Roland could watch the boats along the Grand Canal, noisy water-taxis that left trails of exhaust smoke behind them, slow water-buses with steam-engines, thrashing along the water from stop to stop, and stately black gondolas dipping and swaying under the bridge, to give tourists a taste of Venice by night.

When a waiter offered Roland the menu, he declined it, asking Carlo to choose. Lunch with the Contessa had shown him that he knew very little about Italian food, for all the many Italian restaurants he had taken girls to in London. Carlo decided upon *fritto misto*, a deep-fried mixture of chopped squid tentacles, scampi and bits of white fish, and a salad of thin-sliced onion and tomato. The wine was good but anonymous, a fresh white in a carafe.

'Did you enjoy your lunch with the Contessa?' Carlo enquired at last, having restrained his curiosity this long. Roland said he had, and volunteered the information that he had escorted the lady to the Palazzo Malvolio afterwards, and had been shown a very fine Bellini painting.

'Ah, I envy you, Signor Tonoton,' said Carlo, rolling his eyes in a comically suggestive way. 'A marvellous experience!'

'You haven't seen the picture?' asked Roland.

'No, the Contessa favours aristocrats among the Venetians and English gentlemen. I don't think anyone else is invited to view her picture. Did it please you?

'Are we talking about the same thing?' Roland enquired,

and couldn't stop himself from grinning when Carlo burst out into laughter, his shoulders shaking and his hands waving.

'Tell me about her,' said Roland, 'and about her palace full of priceless works of art.'

'It is not her palace,' Carlo explained, 'nor her husband's. It belongs to her sister, Mrs Tandy. The Torrenegras are the poor relations who have nowhere else.'

'Then how did Mrs Tandy come to own the Palazzo Malvolio?'

'I am able to tell you that because the Accademia has been for many years interested in the Malvolio collection. Mrs Tandy is a great English lady who was married to a son of one of your Lords before the War. Count Rinaldo Malvolio fell in love with her when he was in London and she ran away with him and came to live here in Venice.'

'Very romantic,' said Roland, 'but what of Marina?'

'She is the younger sister. She came to visit, and met Count Massimo Torrenegra in Rome, and they were married. He believed that she was rich and found out too late that her father hated foreigners and would give her nothing. Except for their title, the Torrenegra family have possessed nothing since the time of Garibaldi, and so Count Malvolio invited the newly-marrieds to be his permanent guests.'

'At least one member of the family was rich enough to keep them all!' said Roland.

'It was not so. The Malvolio were among Venice's richest for hundreds of years, until the time of Count Rinaldo's father – he was a *bon viveur* who spent nearly everything in Paris and London on women and gambling and other amusements. There were great fears at the Accademia that he would be forced to dispose of the Malvolio collection to finance his frolics, and the loss to Venice would have been irreparable. But he died suddenly in Paris before that happened. It is believed that his death took place in an expensive brothel.'

'So Count Rinaldo inherited the palace and the art collection but not much money to maintain either?'

'Exactly. Then when he brought an English lady to live with him, hope revived at the Accademia. Mrs Tandy had a husband in England, and the Count could never marry her, not even if Tandy divorced her. If a son was born, he would be illegitimate and not able to inherit the title. Perhaps the collection would be left one day to the Accademia – some discreet approaches were made, I have been told.'

'With no luck so far?'

'It is too late now for luck, Roland. The Count was killed in the War fighting the Austrians. He was our greatest aviator and he shot down many enemy planes. But he left everything to Mrs Tandy and not even the smallest painting to the Accademia.'

They finished the carafe of wine and sent for another, and by the time that was emptied, they were on first name terms and it seemed to Roland that he could confide in Carlo to some extent.

'There is something in the air of Venice,' he began, 'it is exhilarating in an unusual sort of way, I find. One understands a little of why artists have always been inspired here by that combination of sky and sea and lambent light. This must account for the magnificence of the nudes – so much sumptuous flesh so freely displayed, the luxuriance of the settings, the feel of ripeness almost to satiation.'

Carlo looked at him curiously and shrugged his shoulders.

'Most artists have liked to look at naked women, Roland,' he said, 'and as we know from their lives, many made love to their models when they'd painted long enough for the day. Religious pictures to hang in churches often caused scandals when people recognised the Madonna or the female saint to be the artist's mistress wearing a golden halo.'

'Male sexuality given free expression accounts for some part of it,' Roland agreed, 'but there is more to it than that. This afternoon I surpassed myself, and that can only be an effect of Venice on a stranger.'

'Ah, I understand now,' said Carlo, struggling to suppress an outburst of laughter, 'you made love many times to the Contessa – yes? More times than you did before, in London, no?'

'Speaking in utter confidence, yes,' said Roland, lowering his voice. 'I made love to the Contessa more times than I ever thought possible. That in itself is astonishing, but to add to it is the remarkable fact that I am not even fatigued.'

'I believe you,' said Carlo, his chuckling shaking his plump body. 'How many times?'

'Six,' Roland admitted, saying nothing about the marble nymph that had been the recipient of his fourth outburst of passion.

'Bravo! We have an old saying about how many times a man can make love to his girl-friend:

> *Uno* – a man tired out from his day's work
> *Due* – a husband giving his wife her rights
> *Tre* – a lover with his mistress
> *Quattro* – a priest hearing a nun's confession
> *Cinque* – a monk in a brothel
> *Sei* – a gondolier taking his siesta.

Did you row very much on the river when you were a student at the university, Roland?'

'What's so special about rowing a gondola?' he asked.

'It makes a strong back,' said Carlo with a giggle. 'But tell me, did the Contessa give you anything to drink in the Palazzo Malvolio?'

'No, I wasn't drunk, I assure you.'

'No, no, you would have fallen asleep after the first time if you were drunken, my friend. But did you drink anything in the Palazzo? Wine, coffee, lemonade, water – anything?'

'What are you getting at, Carlo? You can't seriously believe that she drugged me – that's ridiculous. After we made love the first time, I felt thirsty and had a glass of sparkling mineral water, that's all.'

'And the Contessa poured it for you and handed it to you, yes – then that's how she did it.'

'Did what? What are you suggesting?'

'Nothing – only that the Contessa enjoyed your love-making so much that she wanted more of it and put the *afrodisiaco* in the water she gave you to drink. It does no harm, and many people make use of it, if they can afford it.'

Roland was dumbstruck. He sat silent while the waiter cleared away the dishes and brought them a soft *Bel Paese* cheese with a bowl of apricots and peaches to share.

'No,' Roland said eventually, 'I refuse to believe there is any such thing as an aphrodisiac. They thought so in the past, but science has disproved claims made for various substances quacks used to hawk about.'

'Excellent,' said Carlo, munching away with lively appetite, 'you do not believe that aphrodisiacs exist. Even after making love six times in an afternoon. *Va bene*, remain a sceptic.'

'But . . .' said Roland doubtfully, thinking back to his strong performance with Marina. Strong? A better word was superhuman, he thought. They'd arrived at the palace at three o'clock and he'd left sometime after six. Half a dozen times in three hours surely proved that he must have had a stimulant of some sort to sustain him. Common sense might say *no*, but his experience that afternoon said *yes*.

'What is this aphrodisiac?' he asked. 'What does it look like – it certainly has no taste, if I drank it in water.'

'It can be bought wet or dry,' Carlo told him, 'a colourless liquid is most usual, so that a few drops can be put into the wine or the coffee. There is a fine powder like flour, a creamy colour, which can be put into food when it is cooked.'

'I find this extraordinary,' said Roland. 'What is it made from – do you know? Or is that kept a secret by the makers?'

'In general terms, it is known,' Carlo informed him, 'but the ingredients and the amounts change a little according to who is making it – these recipes are traditional, you understand.'

'We are in the realm of folk-lore, I imagine. But go on, what do they mix up in this stimulant for post-coital slackness?'

'I do not know all the things used,' said Carlo, 'and nor do I know the English names. There are extracts of herbs and roots and some spices, most of it brought from the East Mediterranean and Palestine. But as you have said, *afrodisiaco* is folk-lore and has no effect, so it does not matter what it is made of.'

'Is it specifically Venetian?' Roland asked, ignoring with a grin the other's sarcasm. 'Or is it available in other parts of Italy?'

Carlo waved his hands about and shrugged his plump shoulders and disclaimed all knowledge of what was done outside his home town. Venetians, he said, had been using this medicine for many centuries, the rich ones, for it was very expensive to buy. But why did Roland concern himself with *superstition*?

'All right,' said Roland, 'I concede that it has a remarkable effect. Why do you think the Contessa gave it to me secretly?'

Carlo's thick black eyebrows crawled slowly up his forehead at so stupid a question.

'Because she likes you,' he said finally. 'I think you have a saying in English that you can't get too much of a good thing – is that right? Well, you were the good thing, and she had very much of you. Do you object?'

'I would have preferred to be consulted,' said Roland, and

he put his hand to his mouth to cover a sudden yawn. But Carlo saw it and grinned widely as he consulted his wrist watch and asked what was the time when Roland drank the spiked mineral water.

'Let me see,' said Roland, 'we left the Taverna by the Opera at half past two or thereabouts and walked slowly to the palace – then we sat and talked for a little while. Then there was an event of personal interest which took place in the bedroom, more talk, and then I felt thirsty. Say about three o'clock or soon after. Why do you ask?'

'The effect of the *elisir d'amore* is said to last for seven or eight hours. It is now almost ten in the evening – your time is almost finished, Roland, and soon you will be very tired and sleepy. It would be better to return to the hotel now, or maybe soon you will be too tired to walk.'

'No, the effects wore off hours ago and I feel fine,' Roland insisted. 'Since leaving the Contessa, I have not thought about love-making at all.'

'Perhaps not, my sceptical friend, but the *elisir* is still in your blood and your brain – and in your *coglioni*. If you saw a naked woman now, you would make love to her, one or two times until the effect dissipated.'

'Never,' said Roland, hoping he would remember that *coglioni* seemed to be the Italian word for pompoms.

He started to say 'I am totally satisfied – satiated even,' and yawned wide enough to almost crack his jaw.

Carlo flicked his finger at a waiter and got the bill. Roland took it from him and paid, saying that he was in Carlo's debt for introducing him to the Contessa Marina. They strolled back to the Hotel Gallini, enjoying the cool of the evening, though Roland's legs seemed to be getting heavier and he was yawning a great deal now.

At the hotel entrance he shook hands with Carlo and asked him to telephone about nine the next morning to make arrangements for his visit to the Accademia Gallery to begin his research on the paintings. Carlo smiled at that and said he would telephone after lunch, for he was very doubtful if Roland would be awake until then. Roland felt too tired to argue the point, and made his way slowly up to his room.

Taking his clothes off was an effort, and to hang them in the wardrobe was out of the question. He let them fall to the floor as he undressed, couldn't be bothered to look for his pyjamas, and slid naked into bed and turned off the light.

He expected to be fast asleep the moment his head touched the pillow, but it didn't happen like that. Slow waves of tiredness rippled through him, but it seemed that the Venetian *elisir* was not easily cleared from the system. He lay on his side in the darkness, waiting for sleep to overtake him, but he could not stop thinking about Marina.

Try as he might, he could not stop the comic scene they had played out together in her sitting-room running like a cinema film in his head. After the little farce with the marble figure he had swung round to face her, intending to wreak vengeance in some way or other unspecified. But he'd forgotten his trousers lying round his ankles, lost his balance and grabbed at Marina to save himself from falling on his face. The suddenness of his movement upset her balance, and she tipped over backwards, her arms flailing. She half-saved herself, but Roland's impetus was too forceful to resist.

They wound up on the floor together, Marina on her back with splayed legs, and Roland face down with his nose on her belly.

'Orlando, *carissimo*!' said she with a giggle. 'Your marble woman has not satisfied you and you want my *fica* already! But why should I play second fiddle to a carving?'

'Because you are so very beautiful and forgiving,' he said, and hoisted himself up to sit and admire her walnut-brown nest of curls and the soft pink petals between her open thighs. What a superb sight, he said to himself, how freely she lets me look at it – not like your average British girl who wants the lights out before she opens her legs, so that she can be felt but not seen, at least, not her *fica*.

As if she knew what was in his thoughts, Marina parted her legs wider and pulled up her knees until they almost touched her breasts, opening herself completely to him, her head back on the floor. Roland glanced up at her face and saw there a smile of mingled lewdness and pride as she awaited his pleasure.

'My God, Marina, I've never met anyone like you,' he gasped, 'I'm hard as iron again – even after just doing it! You have bewitched my . . . what's the Italian word for it?'

He spoke truer than he knew, but the cause was not important then, only the deed. He leaned over her, supporting himself on one straight arm, took hold of his stiff length and slipped the head between the soft lips of her split.

'Your *cazzo*,' she said, smiling slyly at him. 'Your *cazzo* is standing stiff, Orlando, and I want it inside me.'

'Oh yes!' he said softly, and he brought his belly closer to hers and speared her as deep as he could go.

Her folded legs were under his chest and a delirious pleasure flooded through him while he thrust into her with long sliding strokes. She was holding her breasts, compressing them to make their firm buds stand up towards him, wanting him to lick them perhaps, but her bent legs were in the way and he could not get at her with his tongue.

'Harder, Orlando, harder!' she moaned, rocking herself along her spine to make her loins rise to his push.

'Yes!' he gasped, bucking into her softness at too furious a pace to last long. 'Yes, Marina, yes!'

'I'm going to have everything you've got to give before we're finished with each other,' she said, her voice shaky under the pressure of overpowering physical sensations. 'Promise me!'

'Yes!' he panted.

Her nails bit hard into the flesh of his bottom, a long spasm shook her, and Roland was instantly overwhelmed by the violence of her climax and spurted into her the jet of his release. The hot split between her parted legs felt like a greedy mouth, sucking at him to draw out his vital essence, even when he had no more. Marina shuddered and gasped under him and heaved her belly up to receive his offering. Her open silk dressing-gown was spread under her squirming back or she would have rubbed the skin off her shoulder-blades on the thick carpet. Roland decided he'd died and gone to Paradise.

Lying in the dark in bed in the hotel and trying to sleep, he knew she had truly bewitched him that afternoon, using a drug as well as her voluptuous body. Even now, hours later, he felt his *cazzo* give a feeble twitch, as if trying to stand up hard one more time to oblige the Contessa. But Nature would not be duped forever, and the quiver faded and passed, and he slipped into a deep and dreamless sleep.

THREE

As Carlo Missari predicted, it was after midday before Roland was up and about after his pleasant exertions with the Contessa the day before. He was ravenously hungry and was just finishing a sustaining lunch when Carlo arrived at the hotel to take him to the Accademia Gallery.

Over lunch Roland dipped into the guide-book Carlo had given him, thinking it was high time he got to know the geography of Venice. The fold-out map at the end of the book was a help – it showed him that the city was fish-shaped, with its head to the left and its tail to the right. Through it ran the slow stream of the Grand Canal, curved exactly like a figure 2, starting from where the fish eye would be, and ending down between belly and tail. The little canals stemmed from the big one, branching off right and left.

The railway station, where everyone arrived unless they came over by boat from the mainland, was at the top end of the Grand Canal, and San Marco and the Piazza at the other end. With those points fixed in his mind, Roland was fairly sure he could find his way about without getting lost, making use of the churches as landmarks. Nowhere looked as if it could be more than twenty minutes walk from anywhere else.

An imprint at the beginning of the book gave the publication date as 1902 and described it as *a practical guide containing photographs and coloured pictures, together with true facts of the main churches and a plan of the town*. But when he read a page at random he realised it would be of limited use, for its version of the English language was downright confusing:

Strange and complicated to the tourist is the numbering of the houses; in fact, every district reaches very high numbers among which the only ones who easily find their way are the postmen, instructed by an adequate training in topography, before being enrolled.

The town is divided into six districts called sestiere. They are Castello, so-called after a fort that is said to be there in defence of the zone; Cannaregio, because of the spread of reeds; Dorsoduro, because the ground is harder than elsewhere; San Marco, because of the world-renowned basilica that is found there; San Polo, after the church there; and Santa Croce.

The names of streets are now written in the Venetian dialect which is most typical, but presents some difficulties to the tourist, and not only to the foreign one. Certain names have been so altered as to be incomprehensible to the Italians as well, and sometimes even to those Venetians who are not so well informed about the history of their town.

From the Hotel Gallini it was a pleasant stroll with Carlo to the Accademia, past the unsafe-looking red-brick church of San Stefano and across Morosini Square.

'I can think of five different saints named Stephen,' Roland said, 'is this church dedicated to the first of them?'

'The Stefano mentioned in the New Testament who was stoned to death at Jerusalem for blasphemy,' Carlo confirmed. 'There is a holy relic under the altar – an elbow bone, I believe. But who are the other Stephens?'

'There's King Stephen of Hungary, who tortured and massacred his peasants to force them to become Christians,' said Roland. 'A Pope made him a saint for that. Then there's the celebrated St Stephen the Younger, who lived at Constantinople and came to a very bad end when he disagreed over church discipline with a Christian Emperor.'

'Of course!' said Carlo. 'I knew of that one. Who else?'

'St Stephen of Perm, a Russian monk who converted countless heathens in his own country, though from what I cannot say. And there is a British St Stephen, who was done in at the same time as St Aaron and St Julius, by a Roman governor of Wales, most likely for making a public nuisance of himself.'

'But how do you know about so many saints, Roland?'

'Early European art is almost all pictures of saints, as you know. One learns to distinguish them from each other. There is a Santa Marina, of course, but her inclinations were not at all like those of the Contessa.'

'She lived and died a virgin, no doubt,' said Carlo.

'Who can say? According to legend, her father was a monk, an irregular beginning for a saint. She disguised herself as a

266

man to join a monastery herself, which is even more irregular for a female candidate for sanctity. She was said to have seduced an innkeeper's daughter while hearing her confession, so maybe she was ambidextrous. In some very remarkable way she overcame all these obstacles and was declared a saint. You can make of that what you will.'

Not far past the square they came to the Grand Canal and the footbridge that led across it to the Accademia Gallery on the other bank. Roland was surprised to see it, thinking there was only one bridge over the Grand Canal, the famous Rialto Bridge, but Carlo explained there were three in all, one by the railway station at the beginning of the Grand Canal, the Rialto in the middle, and the Accademia Bridge down near the end, before the Canal opened out into the basin by San Marco.

The breathtaking view from the bridge inspired Roland to halt halfway across and treat his companion to a few lines of verse:

> There is a glorious city in the sea,
> The sea is in the broad and narrow streets
> Ebbing and flowing, and the salt sea-weed
> Clings to the marble of her palaces.

The Accademia Gallery was, Roland observed, a large red-brick building looking exactly like a church. It came as no surprise to be told it had been just that until Napoleon conquered the Serene Republic of Venice and, with typical French conceit, tried to change everything round. But with only limited success, for things have always been notably resistant to change in Italy.

It being afternoon, the Accademia was closed to the public. For the siesta, of course. It did not open to the public on the Feast of San Stefano, Carlo said with a grin, nor on special festival days, such as the Feast of the Assumption, All Saints Day, Corpus Christi, the Immaculate Conception, Holy Christmas Day, New Year Day or the Feast of the Redeemer on the third Saturday in July. Nor on the *Festa della Salute*, which he could not remember in English, but it was in November. Nor the other Festivals, including the day of the Historical Regatta. And it never opened on Mondays.

'I see,' said Roland, returning the grin, 'you make it very complicated in order to keep the public out.'

'No, no,' Carlo assured him, 'the tourists come all the time and breathe all over the magnificent pictures we are trying to preserve and study. The Americans are the worst – they want to take photographs though we have signs to prohibit cameras. What can I say? Tourists are a great trouble.'

The few remaining hours of the working day were passed quite pleasantly in meeting those of Carlo's colleagues who were that day in the building, and a first cursory look round the whole collection. 'We have eight hundred and eighty-nine pictures,' said Carlo with pride, 'maybe even more if we looked into every store-room and cupboard.'

The names he reeled off on their tour through the building formed a catalogue of the golden history of Italian painting – Canaletto, Carracci, Giorgione, Guardi, Mantegna, Tiepolo, Tintoretto, Titian, Veronese. After a while Roland found his mind had switched off under this assault, and he wandered on beside his guide, murmuring complimentary words and taking in no more.

The pictures that interested him for his book were together in one room – a good half a dozen *Madonna and Child* by various artists, four or five *Coronation of the Virgin*, three views of the *Crucifixion*, an *Annunciation* or two. And pictures of saints he recognised – Peter, Catherine, Helena, Theodore and Monica. Except for the *Marriage of Santa Monica*, which seemed sombre to him for so joyful an occasion, all else was gold and blue and scarlet, a riot of colour and swirling draperies, reminiscent of the church of San Marco in the Piazza.

'The book you are writing,' said Carlo curiously, 'what is it about? What can be said about these pictures that has not been said many times before?'

'Not the pictures themselves, but the themes of fourteenth century art interest me,' said Roland. 'Someone suggested recently that the themes of eighteenth century art were love and money, which may be true. If earlier painters had the same preoccupations, they did not parade them so openly in their work.'

'Surely the early pictures are about religion and God,' Carlo suggested, lifting his hands and raising his shoulders. 'it was a time when the people were perhaps more pious than today.'

'I don't think so. My guess would be that there were as many sceptics then as now, but in the fourteenth century they kept quiet to escape being tortured and burned as unbelievers.'

'Then what was the reason for these paintings?'

'I think the pictures of saints are really about power,' said Roland. 'That's the theme I am developing in my book.'

Carlo eyed him sceptically and left him alone to continue his inspection of the pictures. At about six o'clock they left the gallery together and walked over the bridge to Morosini Square and the cafe there, for a glass of iced vermouth. Carlo said he must be on his way soon, his wife was expecting him for dinner. He asked Roland his plans for the evening, and learning he had none beyond a stroll to the Piazza after dinner, he grinned and offered to take him to a place of entertainment off the regular tourist route.

So it came about that he met Roland at his hotel at nine and took him up the Grand Canal by water-bus, past the Rialto Bridge to the stop by the Ca' Doro, a waterside palace in the Gothic style, and then on foot down narrow streets between tall houses and over a back canal or two.

'This district is called Cannaregio,' he informed Roland, 'it means where the reeds grow.'

'But there aren't any,' Roland objected, 'only buildings.'

'The reeds were here before the buildings.'

'But nowadays the numbering of the houses is very strange and complicated to the tourist and reaches very high numbers,' said Roland, quoting from the guide-book.

'That is true,' said Carlo, not recognising the source.

'Then we're done for,' Roland told him, 'the only people who can find their way are postmen instructed in topography before being enrolled.'

Carlo saw the joke and laughed with him. They turned along a narrow canal with a quay running down one side, where a line of work-barges were moored for the night. The three-storey houses tightly packed along the quay had been imposing a long time ago, with stone balconies and tall arched windows. Neglect and dilapidation had scarred the brickwork and plaster, and the woodwork was scorched bare of its paint by the sun.

Carlo pushed open a door and led the way into a stone-flagged passage and up a flight of stairs. There was a distinct pause after he knocked at an apartment door, then it opened and they were invited in cordially by a woman wearing a white blouse and black skirt. She and Carlo shook hands and chattered away for a while in what Roland assumed to be what his guide-book described as the Venetian dialect.

They were standing in a square sitting-room, the floor tiled in dull red, and little in the way of furniture. Apart from the woman who had let them in, no one else was in sight, and as a place of entertainment, Roland considered it lacking. The woman was introduced as Signora Ricci and she fussed about her guests most hospitably, seating them side by side on a wooden settee and bringing them a glass of wine each.

Roland guessed her to be in her late thirties, so very heavy of bosom inside her white blouse as to be almost a caricature. Her hair was fair enough to be yellow, and her complexion was pinker and less olive than he had come to expect in Italians. Perhaps she had a blonde ancestor from the time when the Austrians ruled Venice. There was a thick gold chain round her neck from which a gold cross dangled on her oversized breasts and bounced when she moved.

'Carlo – I can think of only one sort of entertainment here,' said Roland, not overly pleased to be brought to such a place.

'Perhaps,' said the other with a grin, 'but trust me – here you may experience an artistic performance you will not find in London. The cost is six hundred lira only – nothing to an Englishman of your standing in the academic circles.'

'I've never paid a woman in my life,' Roland objected.

'Keep an open mind,' Carlo urged him, 'you are not paying for a woman from the street – the money is the artist's fee.'

'Do you come here often?' Roland asked, grinning at his own words.

'No, I am not paid enough. I have two small children and my wife to feed and clothe. But at times it is good to escape from the family and dream a little.'

Roland did the awkward arithmetic in his head and concluded that 600 lira amounted to between four and five pounds. He had no previous experience of paying women but it seemed a lot. On the other hand, his publisher was meeting most of the cost of his trip to Venice, and he could put it down to research.

He glanced at Signora Ricci. She was standing across the room with her back to a door, watching them with an expression that betrayed her anxiety as she tried to make out the drift of what they were saying. Seeing Roland looking at her, she treated him to a grin of lewd encouragement, so open that he returned it without a thought, and decided to fall in with Carlo's wishes.

'Yesterday a Contessa, today a backstreet trollop,' he said, 'sex is a great leveller.'

The word was lost on Carlo, who raised his eyebrows in query and then forgot about it when Roland produced the cash from his wallet. Signora Ricci bustled across the room at once, her vast breasts rolling in her blouse, to take the bank notes from him and top up the wineglasses, talking incomprehensibly. She went out of the room, leaving them alone for a minute or two, then came back and held the inner door open. Through it came a pair of younger women, naked and barefoot.

They stood facing the two men, an arm round each other, their hips pressed together, while Signora Ricci introduced them and Carlo translated. Not that Roland was paying much attention to his words, staring in fascination at the two naked bodies that were on show.

'This is Sofia, the one on the right,' Carlo was saying, 'she has twenty-two years and was born in Verona. The other is Marcella, who has only twenty years and is a Venetian. Together they will make an exhibition of *amore lesbico* for *divertimento*.'

At the sight of naked female flesh, Carlo was fast losing his grasp of the English language, but neither he nor Roland cared about that. Signora Ricci retreated from the middle of the room and left the girls to get on with it. They remained where they were, smiling and wriggling a little to make their bare breasts quiver.

Sofia was the larger of the two, attractive in a heavy sort of way. Her skin had the delicate olive tint Roland associated with Southern women, and her breasts were the right size to be held in a man's hands. She was round-bellied and from her deep button a line of dark hair ran downwards into the bush between her thighs. She noted Roland's interest in it and smiled at him while she licked a fingertip and ran it down her line as if to show him the way to her *fica*.

Roland watched enthralled, almost holding his breath when Sofia and Marcella turned inwards to face each other, breasts and bellies pressed together. They kissed, holding each other close, Marcella fondling Sofia's bottom lasciviously. She kept at it until Roland was on the edge of the settee, then smiled over her shoulder at him and brought her hand up slowly between her body and Sofia's, to stroke her friend's breasts.

Sofia sank slowly to her knees on the tiled floor, Marcella following her down, still fondling her breasts. Sofia arranged herself half-sitting, half-lying, her naked body propped on an elbow, Marcella on her knees beside her, stroking her belly now with a slow circular motion. After a little while Sofia spread her legs apart on the floor and displayed her *fica*, or at least the thicket of tight curls that covered it.

Marcella put her hand between Sofia's thighs, found the lips of her split with her middle finger and opened them to display the pink interior.

'*Brava*!' said Carlo, grasping Roland's arm. 'Would you like to play with that?'

'Certain possibilities suggest themselves,' Roland breathed, his male part uncomfortably stiff in his trousers.

Marcella was more slender than Sofia, with thinnish arms and thighs and small pointed breasts set high up. Between them on a chain dangled a silver medal with a saint's portrait on it. Her hair was dark brown and hung thickly to below her shoulders, in defiance of the short-cropped fashion of the day. As if in compensation she had only a wispy little patch of hair between her legs.

'If you could have only one of them,' said Carlo, regaining his knowledge of English expression, 'if you were compelled to choose – what a difficult problem! Yet how fascinating! Would it be Sofia, whose big breasts and broad belly give promises of luxurious pleasure? Or would it be perhaps Marcella, who looks to be the most agile and will in the throes of ecstatic delight turn herself into a savage animal for the better satisfaction of her sexual partner?'

'You sound like a guide-book,' Roland commented. 'Given free choice, I would have Sofia on her back and lie on her belly – and then lie on my own back and have Marcella ride on me.'

While they were speaking, Marcella positioned herself on her hands and knees between Sofia's open legs, with her lean bottom waggling jauntily at the two men. She glanced briefly at them and winked, then pressed Sofia's thighs down flat on the tiles and put her mouth to the pink split between them.

Carlo stifled a moan as he watched, and Roland almost sighed aloud to see Marcella's red wet tongue flicker at the open lips of Sofia's *fica*. Sofia was cradling her head on her arms, her eyes gazing up at the ceiling and her red-painted mouth gaping open, in real or pretended pleasure.

'*Santa Madonna*!' murmured Carlo. 'Have you seen the *amore lesbico* before, Roland? Do you have these entertainments when you are in London?'

'I've never come across them,' Roland muttered, and stared at the girls on the floor as if his eyes would pop out.

Under the manipulation of Marcella's tongue, Sofia writhed on the tiles and panted noisily. Marcella's bare bottom wiggled at Roland, her almost hairless slit seeming to wink at him. She squealed when Sofia seized her by the ears and pulled her face harder into her wet split.

But is this real? Roland asked himself. *Is she exciting the other girl sexually? Or is it only an act put on to trick the customer into believing he's seen something that he hasn't?*

Sofia began to utter shrill cries, as if on the very edge of climactic convulsion. She lay with her back arched up clear of the floor, her thighs spread impossibly wide, her hands tugging at the swollen tips of her own breasts.

Marcella's tongue ravaged her friend's sensitive button, now in plain view since the lips had been rolled back much like the petals of a pink tulip. Sofia screamed, her bare heels drummed on the tiles, and Roland knew this was no pretence.

Before the shock of that realisation wore off, he saw Sofia recover quickly from her climax and roll Marcella over on her back, her bony knees forced up and out to expose the thin lips of her sparsely-haired *fica*. Instantly, Sofia pulled them wide open and pushed two fingers in and rubbed vigorously. While she did this, she stared up at Roland with a grin, daring him to do the same to her. He stared back into her shining eyes as if mesmerised. He saw nothing of Marcella's heaves and jerks as she writhed through her climax, but heard the sobbing and gasping that accompanied it.

While the girls were getting their breath back, so to speak, they seated themselves on the men's laps, bare breasts hanging within a handbreadth of their faces. Whether any decision was made or whether it was no more than chance, Roland had thinnish Marcella across his knees and Carlo had Sofia. On the far side of the room Signora Ricci sat with folded arms, awaiting the outcome. Roland heard Sofia whispering into Carlo's ear, then a moment later she stood up to take his hand and lead him away.

Marcella's arm was around Roland's neck and she turned toward him to press her spiky breasts to his face.

'You like me much, *si*?' she asked in the few English words she knew. 'Come with me.'

'I never thought it would come to this,' he said, to himself rather than to the girl.

She did not understand the idiom, nor did it matter one way or the other. Her predatory hand slid down between their bodies to grip his hardness through his clothes.

'You want me,' she announced. 'Come with me – I can do nice things to you. Put your hand between my legs.'

There may be men who can refuse an invitation from a naked young girl to feel them, but Roland was not one. When she slid her slender thighs apart on his lap he stroked between them and sighed to feel the moistness there.

'Put your finger inside,' Marcella murmured in his ear, 'I am wet because Sofia made me do it – you saw her.'

Roland was unable to resist her suggestion. He pressed two of his fingers between her slippery folds of flesh and touched her wet bud. She giggled and pushed her hand down his trousers to get hold of his stiffness. When she repeated her invitation to go with her, he did not hesitate.

Signora Ricci beamed at them in a calculating way. Marcella led him to a small square bedroom at the rear of the apartment, furnished with an old-fashioned double bed and not much else. She flung herself down on it and opened her legs to show what she had to offer.

'Is nice, *si*?' she asked with a sideways smile at Roland. 'You want put your *cazzo* in?'

Roland took off his jacket and sat on the side of the bed to contemplate the possibilities. He would have preferred to have the other girl, Sofia, and he smiled to himself as he recalled Carlo's comic guide-book words about her – *her big breasts and broad belly give promises of luxurious pleasure*. But the cards had been dealt differently and while he stroked Marcella's thin belly he wondered if she would indeed turn herself into a wild animal for the better satisfaction of her sexual partner. Or if she would merely lie there and let him to get it over with.

'Why you wait?' she asked. 'I have nice things to do to you if you undress.'

With long thin thumbs she rolled back the wispy-haired folds of flesh between her legs to show Roland the moist pink inside.

'Put your *cazzo* in me,' she suggested.

'Right,' he said, making up his mind. Off came his clothes in record time, and he lay beside her on the bed and stroked her small breasts. She let him do that for a while, humouring him, then pulled him on top of her, her knees raised and spread. Any remaining qualms evaporated and he wiggled forward to bring the tip of his trembling shaft to her ready *fica*.

She guided him into her and laughed to feel him pushing deep into her belly.

'*Molto bene!*' she said. 'Now I do something nice for you.'

She was as good as her word – without moving any other part of her body, she contracted and relaxed her abdominal muscles in an exciting rhythm. To Roland it felt as if there was a soft hand inside her belly clasping his *cazzo* and massaging it in a way that made him gasp with pleasure.

'Marcella – that's marvellous!' he murmured.

Her knowing brown eyes stared up at his face, assessing his degree of arousal. The silver medal about her neck bounced and slithered between her breasts to the throb of her muscles, and Roland saw it was embossed with the Lion of St Mark. There were words in Latin round the picture, but too small to read from a distance and meaningless to a man with six stiff inches deep in a willing girl.

Marcella smiled at him and speeded up her tempo. Roland gave a hard push or two, trying to match the rhythm of her squeezing, but she shook her head and said something in Italian that must have meant *lie still*. In truth, the sensations rushing through Roland were so delightful that he was content to lie passively on the girl's narrow belly while she pleasured him.

'Is nice, *si?*' she asked, trying out her English again. 'You like your *cazzo* kissed like this? Lift up on your arms and see what I do to you.'

Roland got his hands flat on the bed under his shoulders and heaved himself up until he had a view all the way down her body to where his thick shaft was buried between her splayed thighs. Marcella spread out her arms on the bed to give herself a grip for more vigorous action, and Roland could see her pale-skinned belly clenching and unclenching to the internal movement of her muscles. He heard himself gasping and stared open-mouthed when his embedded *cazzo* jerked in involuntary spasms.

'Yes, oh yes!' he moaned as he felt his vital essence sucked from him in long waves of ecstasy.

This was true artistry, his whirling thoughts insisted, skill of a high order deployed for his delight, not a quick bang with a young tart.

'*Molto bene*,' Marcella pronounced when he could see and hear again. 'Rest a little, then I get Sofia do it to you again.'

He felt very contented and it was in his mind to tell her he didn't want the other girl. Before he could speak, she was off the bed and across the room, leaving him to stare in pleasure at the lean cheeks of her bottom as she went through the door.

He stretched himself and yawned lazily. The assumption that he would make love to both girls was flattering, to be sure, if perhaps a little optimistic. After all, he was in Cannaregio, wherever that was, where the reeds used to grow and none but a postman could find his way. This was not the Palazzo Malvolio, and he was not with the divinely lascivious Contessa who spiked his drink with some strange local *elisir d'amore*.

The door opened and in came olive-skinned Sofia, her breasts bouncing as she walked, her hair slightly ruffled. At the sight of her coming towards the bed, Roland's limp wet *cazzo* gave a sudden twitch and began to stiffen along his thigh. Astonished, he looked down and saw how hard he was growing, then looked at Sofia, standing beside the bed, and saw the grin on her face.

Had Signora Ricci put something in the wine she gave him to drink before the two girls demonstrated their *amore lesbico*? A deep suspicion entered his head and would not be dislodged. How else could this sudden enthusiasm for Sofia be accounted for, so very soon after having Marcella? It couldn't be more than five minutes!

With a smile but without a word Sofia rolled him on his back and got astride, taking hold of his wrists to lift his hands to her good-sized breasts. He grasped them and kneaded them while she held his stiff *cazzo* between finger and thumb and guided it to the slit between her open thighs. Roland watched fascinated, admiring the line of dark hair that ran down from the button of her round belly to her thick brown bush.

He had been told Sofia was twenty-two and he believed it, though her breasts were slackened by usage and hung down a little. He held them with delight, all the same, revelling in their fleshiness and softness, while her *fica* slid up and down his deep-embedded shaft. That wasn't how Marcella had done it to him, and failing words to explain what he meant, he showed her with his hands – clasping a palm round one upraised finger to demonstrate the massaging grip.

Sofia giggled and stopped her up and down sliding. He watched the look of concentration on her pretty face as she gathered up her inner strength, then he gasped loudly as she began a fierce squeezing of her internal muscles. He had guessed that her soft belly would lack some of the vigour of Marcella's leanness, but he was quite wrong. Sofia's wet *fica* gripped him and milked him far more forcefully than her friend had.

He pulled at her breasts, wanting to get his lips to them but she was shorter than he and it was impossible – not that there was time, for her belly muscles manipulated him so strongly that in less than a minute from entering her, he cried out and spurted his frantic lust into her.

'Sofia, *si, si, si*!' he moaned, and she stared impassively at his contorted face as his climactic sensations thrilled him and flung his limbs about as if in convulsions.

Roland found his own way back to the hotel sometime after ten that evening. When he collected his key from the desk the night porter handed him a letter that had been delivered an hour or more ago. The envelope was large and thick, and on the sealed flap Roland recognised the Malvolio coat of arms.

Aha! he exulted, a letter from Contessa Marina – inviting me to pop round to the palace tomorrow and play games with her. If I'm going to live up to her expectations, I shall need a good night's sleep first.

He opened the envelope and took out a sheet of writing paper, thick and expensive, with the Malvolio arms embossed at the top in large size. The handwriting was bold and beautiful, but the letter was not from the Contessa.

Dear Dr Thornton,
My sister has told me of your stay in Venice in connection with a book on artists that you are writing. Here in the Palazzo Malvolio I have a good collection which might interest you and be of some use for your book. Please come to lunch tomorrow at 12.30.

It was signed Delphine Tandy.

FOUR

On Roland's first visit to the Palazzo Malvolio he was a little too engrossed in the Contessa Marina and his chances of getting her clothes off to pay much attention to his surroundings. The main impression that remained with him afterwards was of miles of corridors and high-ceilinged salons, a fading gold and white eighteenth century style everywhere, and old pictures on every wall.

The invitation to lunch by Mrs Tandy gave him the opportunity to look properly at the palace and its contents, and to bring a professional eye to bear on what he saw. The Contessa had shown him one painting of very considerable value – the Bellini nude over her sitting-room mantelpiece – and that raised the strong possibility that there were other works of art equally good. He set off in good time from his hotel, finding his way to the square where the palace stood without difficulty.

The Venetians called a paved square like this a *campo*, Roland had gathered from the curious guide-book he had been given. In the middle stood an old stone well, of the sort to be found all over Venice. There was an open-fronted restaurant in one corner of the square, a waiter bustling about the outside tables where early lunchers were eating, waving their hands, talking busily and drinking, all at the same time.

A stir in Roland's memory brought to the surface the thought that just such a square as this was the setting for a drawing by Thomas Rowlandson – the so-called *Carnival at Venice*. It was no such thing, but a troop of strolling jugglers performing for a small crowd. The piece-de-resistance was a naked girl turning a back-somersault through a hoop and in the process showing off her hairy *fica* to the onlookers. Another naked girl was moving among the crowd collecting money.

Some of the men present were affected by the agility of the girl acrobat so lewdly that they pulled out their stiff shafts and were stroking them while they stared. Through the windows overlooking the square could be seen couples fondling each other's bare parts. Roland populated the little square in his imagination with Rowlandson's mountebanks and chuckled. It seemed improbable that the Venice Carnival of Regency times had ever exhibited so unabashed a spectacle – but then, Rowlandson was a humorist drawing to entertain the Prince of Wales.

Roland wondered if it was completely beyond the bounds of the possible that the divinely lewd Contessa could be persuaded to take part in a minor re-enactment of the scene. Could she get away from her husband in the middle of the night, when the last and latest reveller had gone home to bed, and before the first pale gleam of daybreak brought out the early workers?

In the silent hour between three and four when all was still – would she agree to meet Roland in this very square, this cobblestone *campo*, and strip naked by the well to dance or turn handstands while he emulated Rowlandson's bawdy spectators and played with his *cazzo* while he watched?

Only to envisage the scene was enough to stiffen his pride in his trousers, so that a furtive adjustment of his underwear was needed to let him walk without strain. Marina's acrobatics in the moonlight and his own self-pleasuring would be the prelude to having her naked on top of the covered stone well. A carnal carnival at Venice!

That led on to another thought, why only here in the square? If that were at all possible, then why shouldn't she agree to let him strip her naked and have her in all the main tourist spots of Venice? On the Rialto Bridge, above the quiet night-time Grand Canal. And in the Piazza, of course, with the domes of San Marco in the distance. Up against the front door of the Accademia, between the smooth stone pillars. In a dozen other well-known and much-photographed parts of the city!

Now he came to it, the possibilities were staggering! What a scrapbook of picture postcards he could assemble to take home with Marina and himself sketched in on the very spot where they had done it together!

The Palazzo Malvolio was an impressive building, seen across the square, and it demonstrated beyond dispute that once upon a time the Malvolio were a very wealthy family, to have built and furnished a family home on this scale. Yet according to Carlo Missari the money was all gone, and the last Count Malvolio had only the building and the pictures as his inheritance from his playboy father. The thought occurred to Roland that if Carlo's version was right and the old Count's principal interests were women, dinner parties, fine clothes, roulette and racehorses, then he would have added nothing to the Malvolio art collection in his lifetime. There would be no works of art produced after about 1860, when the last but one Malvolio launched himself on his life of wine, women and song.

The Palazzo formed one whole side of the square, and was made of white stone, somewhat greyish and in need of cleaning. There were three tiers of Corinthian columns, with tall round-topped windows between, and stone balconies across the whole width. A carved stone plaque displayed the Malvolio coat of arms above an ornate central door at the top of three broad flat steps.

There was a large lion-head black metal knocker on the door, but before Roland had time to raise his hand to it, the heavy door was pulled open and there, bowing deeply to him, stood the liveried doorkeeper he had seen when he came here before with the Contessa. Servants in livery seemed old-fashioned, romantic and pretentious to Roland, but he was in another country and he was a guest, and somehow the idea seemed very appropriate to a household of this sort.

The man's livery was threadbare, his cutaway jacket and knee-breeches faded by age and usage from their original deep blue and yellow, which Roland guessed to be the Malvolio colours, to a nondescript near-grey. Evidently Mrs Tandy tried to maintain the old traditions of the family she had not quite become part of, without having the funds. Three walls of the stone-flagged entrance hall into which the bowing doorman ushered him were hung with steel swords, long-bladed spears and muskets in large decorative patterns, the military relics of the Malvolio past.

Except, thought Roland, glancing round the murderous hardware on the walls, the old Venetian ruling class made its money not by conquest but by trade. They sent their ships to Smyrna and Istanbul and Alexandria to buy luxury goods, which they sold at a huge profit to German and French traders who came to Venice with their mule-trains. Naturally, they had to do some fighting from time to time, pirates, bandits and plain thieves being a part of the natural order since history began, but the Malvolio array of weapons seemed a little bit ostentatious.

In the entrance hall stood a formidable figure, who bowed to Roland with the dignity of an emperor acknowledging an equal. He was a silver-haired man, well into his fifties, and he wore an oldish black swallow-tail coat and pin-striped trousers. For a moment Roland mistook this imposing personage for Marina's husband, the Count Massimo Torrenegra. But he was rather more important than a brother-in-law of the head of the household, Roland realised, when he said his name was Luigi and he was the major-domo. Roland took that to mean he was the butler and ran the household.

In very acceptable English Luigi announced that Signora Tandy was waiting for him in the Lepanto Room, to drink an *aperitivo* before lunch. He led the way up one arm of a stone staircase that rose on either side of the hall, turned at right angles to join together, forming a sort of interior balcony. Beyond could be seen tall arches through which entrance was gained to the first and most important floor.

The weapons of war continued up the white-painted wall beside the stairs, and in a niche at the top stood a life-size marble statue of a man in a breast-plate and sword-belt. Roland took him to be a long-gone Malvolio, and saw there was a matching statue in the far corner of the stairs. It seemed to him very convenient to have *two* ancestors worth commemorating for their martial accomplishments – what if there had been three? Where could the other one have stood?

Through the central arch, and they were walking along a high-ceilinged corridor hung with old paintings, Luigi a pace or two in front to show the way, then through suites of rooms opening into each other, with more paintings and some with murals, and some with marble busts on plinths. Roland recognised several of them as Roman Emperors – beaky-nosed Tiberius, a gentleman to his fingertips, who ran non-stop orgies at his villa on Capri, and big-jowled Nero, who built himself a golden palace at Rome but cut his throat when he lost a vote of confidence and faced being deposed. There was ox-faced Titus, who captured Jerusalem and burned down the Temple, and adolescent Elagabalus who was a transvestite and loved rough trade, and was murdered for it.

Roland wondered which past Malvolio had chosen the

busts, and on what basis. Surely the subjects were not intended to be seen as representing his interests? Or perhaps they were. There was so much art to be seen that it was a positive relief to arrive at last at the Lepanto Room, as Luigi had called it. Through a double door, both wings open, he entered a room with a square-tiled floor, on which lay a Persian carpet or two, looking much the worse for the wear of a couple of hundred years.

Contessa Marina in a white summer frock sat between another woman, whom Roland guessed to be Mrs Tandy, and a man wearing a grey linen jacket and a stiff white collar. Over by the windows stood two other men with their backs to the room, one in bright blue and the other in the long black cassock of a priest. All held glasses with various coloured liquids in them, and not one but two footmen in the family livery stood with silver trays in their hands to make sure no one went thirsty.

The Contessa came across the room to greet Roland and Luigi relinquished him to her with a bow. She held out her hand high, and he took this to mean he was expected to kiss it rather than shake it.

'How very kind of you to come,' she said in a most grand-lady way, as if he'd never had her on the floor with her legs in the air, 'my sister will be so pleased to meet you.'

She took him to where Mrs Tandy sat with the man in the stiff collar.

'I am so pleased you could come, Mr Thornton,' said she, in an even grander fashion, 'when I heard of your interest in our pictures I simply had to ask you to come and look at them.'

Roland wondered what had been said between the sisters. There was no question in his mind that the invitation had been extended because the Contessa Marina wanted to repeat their carnal frolics together. She had inveigled her sister into her scheme with some tale or other about his professional interest in art, but when he gazed closely at Mrs Tandy, Roland felt it unlikely that she could be easily fooled.

He knew that she had to be at least forty-five, from the facts Carlo had given him about her, but she looked younger. She was very much the English great lady, magnificent of appearance, elegant of dress. She wore her chestnut-brown hair longer than fashion dictated, and it was dressed up on top of her head, held there by a pair of tortoise-shell combs studded with small glittering stones Roland assumed to be diamonds. Her face was a perfect oval, her eyes green-grey, her lips discreetly tinted.

All this needed no more than a second or two to take in, but even so she knew he was assessing her and a faint smile showed and was gone. This was the woman who left husband and country to run off with Count Rinaldo Malvolio, and for whom the Count had defied convention and the prospect of marriage and an heir. On reflection, Roland decided he might well have done the same himself, for twenty years ago she must have been stunning. If he'd had a palace to take her to, of course, and no necessity to earn a living.

The man in the stand-up collar rose to his feet and held out his hand at the very same moment a footman arrived at Roland's side with a tall glass on his silver tray. He was wearing white gloves, Roland noted – the footman, not the stiff collar man, whose hands were large and knuckly. He didn't look much like a count, he didn't even look Italian, and above all he didn't look like a marriage partner for lascivious Marina.

There was a good reason for all that – he wasn't any of those things. Marina introduced him as Herr Adalbert Gmund, whereupon he clicked his heels, inclined his head, shook Roland's hand in an unnecessarily hearty manner and announced he was Austrian, not German, and a devoted *amateur* of Italian painting, and most eager to have talks with the esteemed Doctor Thornton of London University and compare notes with him on several points, as the English said, *Nein?*

Roland took at last the glass held out by the patient footman and sipped. It was Italian champagne, so-called, well chilled but still sweetish. By then the two men by the windows had come to meet him, and he was introduced to the real Count Torrenegra, a well-preserved and handsome man in his late fifties, dressed as perfectly as a show-window dummy in a nipped-waist suit of pale blue mohair and shoes so brightly shined they almost dazzled. A certain raffish charm hovered about him; it was in his elegant gestures – his brilliantly white teeth when he smiled (as he did constantly), the purple silk handkerchief bursting out from his breast pocket, the massive gold signet-ring, his well-manicured nails. Roland disliked him on sight, and distrusted him.

The priest was addressed as Padre Pio and he was

described in English by Count Massimo as chaplain to the family. That meant very little to Roland, but he guessed it to be a hangover from the distant past, when noble families had a resident priest for their spiritual comfort and advice, much as they kept people to look after the horses and hounds and a librarian to look after the books. Presumably Pio was a left-over from the time of the Malvolio, with nowhere else to go. He spoke English well, with a marked accent, and proved to be very affable.

At Mrs Tandy's request Roland sat down beside her, Gmund on her other side, the Count and his lady chatting to each other politely, Padre Pio left to his own devices.

'You are working at the Accademia, I'm told,' said Mrs Tandy. 'The director is an old acquaintance of mine – a charming man. We have him for dinner twice a year, mainly to tease him – he hopes I shall leave the Malvolio collection to the Accademia in my will.'

'I haven't met him yet,' Roland admitted, 'but I can see one picture here he'll never hang in his gallery.'

'The mural over there,' Mrs Tandy confirmed with a smile.

The painting almost filled one whole wall of the room, and it needed cleaning to bring up the rich colours overlaid with the grime and dust of the years. It showed a man in a golden fore-and-aft helmet posing heroically on a quayside where a scarlet painted ship was tied up. Recalling the name of the room it was in, Roland made a stab at guessing the subject.

'A Malvolio embarking on his fighting-ship for the battle of Lepanto,' he said, trying to sound knowledgeable without being pompous. 'The painter was of the school of Francesco Guardi.'

'The painter *was* Guardi,' Mrs Tandy said quite firmly. 'You are absolutely right about the subject – it's Marco Malvolio on his way to fight the Turks at Lepanto. He was killed or drowned in the battle and never came back.'

'What is interesting to me is that a much later Malvolio had this scene painted, presumably in memory of his ancestor, three hundred years after the event,' said Roland, showing off.

'There was a good reason for that,' said Mrs Tandy, 'you see, this is the second Palazzo Malvolio, built in the eighteenth century after the first was destroyed by fire. There was a large mural of Marco Malvolio going to war in the Great Hall of the palace that was burnt down, and for the family honour it was painted again here. But eighteenth century Venetians were not very warlike in outlook, and so the new mural was painted in a room of lesser importance. If this palace was destroyed and we had the money to start again, the third mural might well be relegated to the servant's hall.'

But the ironic smile on her face told Roland she didn't mean what she said. He guessed that she had taken on the task of preserving the memory of the Malvolio, and if she could afford to start again, the Lepanto scene would be given pride of place in the family legend.

He was well down his second glass of *spumante* when the major-domo announced to Mrs Tandy that lunch was served.

'We are lunching in the Small Dining Room today,' she said to Roland in a vaguely apologetic way, 'I do hope you won't mind, but as there are only six of us . . .'

She let her explanation trail away gently, and took his arm. The footmen opened a pair of tall white-and-gold doors opposite the ones through which Roland had entered the Lepanto Room, and the little procession made its way through in couples, Roland and Mrs Tandy in the lead, followed by the Count and Countess, the oddly-dressed Herr Gmund and black-robed Padre Pio bringing up the rear.

The Small Dining Room was easily big enough for a polished mahogany table that seated eight in comfort. Down one wall were two long matching sideboards, with six antique silver serving dishes on each, and on the facing wall stood a long rosewood cabinet with a glass front, holding three dozen or so priceless hand-painted porcelain plates. In two corners of the room there were waist-high Sevres jardinieres filled with red and white carnations. Over a massive brownish marble fireplace there were five half-size bronze busts of smooth-shaven men, philosophers by the look of them.

In all, there was as much art on show in the dining room as in a London antique shop, when the pictures were included. They hung in groups on the walls and were Malvolio family portraits, mostly nineteenth century, the men in frock coats and cravats, the women in lace and black bonnets.

Roland found himself seated between Mrs Tandy at the head of the table and Contessa Marina to his right. The white frock the Contessa wore was not quite as simple as he had thought – it was cut on the bias to cling to her breasts and was of *crêpe-de-Chine* so thin as to give an impression of near-transparency. Clothes like that were not made by some little seamstress round the corner, and once again the contrasts of wealth and poverty around Roland aroused his speculation.

Marina's husband, Count Massimo Enrico Francesco Vittorio Giambattista Scaloto Lombardini Manzetta di Torrenegra, sat on Mrs Tandy's left, looking like a much older version of Rudolf Valentino, complete with thin black moustache and soulful eyes of deep brown. He was much older than his wife and well into his fifties, but the little lines on his face had been smoothed out by daily massage, and in his fashion-plate suit he seemed ready for an instant walk-on part in a drawing-room comedy.

Beside the Count sat Padre Pio, the fat little priest in his worn black cassock, chatting amiably in Italian or English to anyone who would listen. At the foot of the table was Adalbert Gmund, the mysterious Austrian and self-advertised connoisseur of art. The priest and Gmund ate heartily, the Count sparingly to maintain his figure; Mrs Tandy and the Contessa picked like birds at their plates.

The food was plentiful and good, and Roland had no hesitation in emulating Padre Pio and clearing everything the footmen set before him. They brought him a high-heaped serving of risotto cooked with tiny squares of ham and peas, then a largish steak cut from a white fish he guessed was John Dory, in white wine and garnished with green beans. After that came the main course – veal cut into thin slices and baked in the oven, served with giant grilled mushrooms and polenta, the yellow puree of maize that seemed to accompany every Venetian meal. The wine glass by Roland's plate was never allowed to be empty – every time he drank a liveried footman topped it up again.

To his surprise, the conversation was mainly about pictures. At first he thought the family were being excessively courteous in confining the talk to his own professional field, then after a while he became aware of undercurrents and innuendos, without meaning to him but very pointed to the others. They were polite to each other, but now and then a snarl or a touch of contempt almost surfaced through the smiles and lively gesticulation. At moments such as these the speaker tended to lapse into lively Italian for a sentence or two.

Roland wished that the table were smaller and the chairs were set closer together. He was being left out of the conversation now it had taken this personal slant, and he would have liked to put his hand on Marina's knee under the table. It would have been nice to slip his hand under her white *crêpe-de-Chine* and up her smooth thigh. Her knickers were silk, he was sure enough of that, and if they proved to be loose-legged, his flat hand would have found its way inside for a feel of her *fica*. But the table was too long and the gap between chairs a good yard – all he could do was smile pleasantly at her when the Count was not looking too closely.

Of course, if he had been near enough to feel her under the table, he guessed she would return the compliment. She'd have her hand down in his lap to rub his standing part through his trousers ... which would be delightful, but very dangerous with her husband so close at hand, and in a condition of suppressed annoyance about something or other.

Family feuds, said Roland to himself, utterly boring to those outside, yet the very lifeblood of those involved. Where people live together like this in the same household, even in a palace of this magnificence, there are bound to be changing affinities and alliances, resentments and old grievances. The battle-lines were not easy to distinguish – Mrs Tandy and the Count were the main contenders, but the others seemed to shift allegiance to one or the other for no discernible reason. The Contessa sided with her husband at times, with her sister at others.

Much the same was true of Adalbert Gmund, whose position was so mysterious that Roland began to think he must be Mrs Tandy's ageing boyfriend. But at times he displayed a male solidarity with Count Massimo. The only one trying to remain unaligned was Padre Pio, who was cheerful though evasive when appealed to for support, like Switzerland determined to be neutral between the warring Great Powers.

And in some unexplained way this whole business seemed to be about paintings. That was strange to Roland, for Mrs Tandy was the sole owner of the Malvolio collection, according to Carlo Missari of the Accademia. What Count Massimo's interest could be was difficult to imagine. It was not likely to be aesthetic, as Gmund claimed his own was, for the Count seemed too shallow a man for that. Financial, then, though *how* was inexplicable.

At about three o'clock, when lunch was finished at last, it had been decided that Roland should be shown the early pictures in the palace, though who made the decision was not clear. Not the Count, who said he had a meeting arranged at four and must leave very shortly to be in good time. Padre Pio also withdrew from the tour, claiming that at his advanced age he found the *siesta* necessary.

Adalbert Gmund took Roland's arm and conducted him through more passages and rooms in search of the thirteenth and fourteenth century pictures he said were masterpieces. Perhaps he was the one who had made the decision, though Mrs Tandy and the Contessa Marina trailed along behind, talking busily to each other in Italian. Through grandly furnished rooms and passages they went, past acres of painted canvas and petrified forests of marble statues and bronzes. They came at last to what Gmund said was the Green Salon, so called it seemed because large panels of veined green marble were let into the walls as decoration.

'There,' said the Austrian, pointing as proudly as if he were the owner of all he surveyed, 'that is the earliest painting in the Malvolio collection. It is a Giotto, of course.'

Roland went closer, and saw a painted wooden panel that once had been an altarpiece in a church. The colours were faded and the perspective was slightly wonky, as was to be expected, and the subject traditional, the Blessed Virgin enthroned in glory with a vertical row of four angels on either side of her.

'It looks about right for Giotto,' said he, not committing himself too far, 'but is there any documentation on it?'

'Naturally,' said Gmund, almost sneering, 'you must ask Padre Pio to show you the Malvolio Archive – there is a full history of every work of art in the palace.'

The ladies joined them and they all looked at the picture and talked for a while. Gmund's interest seemed to evaporate now he had shown off the oldest picture in the place, and he excused himself and strode off.

'That odd little picture in the Library,' said the Contessa brightly to her sister, 'the one with the ruined buildings and the horse – that's very old, isn't it?'

'I knew we should have brought Padre Pio along with us,' said Mrs Tandy, frowning slightly, 'without him we're lost. Adalbert pretends to know everything about the collection, but it's only stray items Padre Pio has told him. I think you're right about the picture in the Library, Marina, but Mr Thornton can tell us – he's our expert today.'

The Library, five minutes walk distant, was a large and

very impressive room lined from floor to ceiling with leather-bound books. Or almost entirely, here and there was wall space enough for a small framed drawing or engraving. There was one painting only, perhaps eighteen inches wide and twelve inches high. It depicted a bearded man in a gold robe lying on the grass looking dead, a saddled horse standing beside him, and in the background three broken walls plastered white.

'I like it very much,' said Roland, recognising its quality, 'it's very early, you're right about that, Contessa. First half of the fourteenth century, I'd say, on stylistic grounds. I can't put a name to the artist, and I'd certainly like to consult Padre Pio's archive.'

'The Malvolio Archive,' Mrs Tandy corrected him, 'please feel free to ask Padre Pio about the picture. I've always taken it to be a hunter fallen off his horse after a bad jump, but I'm sure there's more to it than that.'

'Yes, bearing in mind when it was painted,' said Roland, 'it is almost certain to be a scene from the Bible or from the life of a saint, though I can't put a name to this one.'

'That reminds me,' said Mrs Tandy, 'somewhere about the place there's a carved door panel with Noah's Ark on it. It must have come from a church, originally. Do you remember whereabouts it is, Marina? I haven't seen it for years.'

'Noah's Ark – I know where it is,' said the Contessa, 'in the closed-off stone passage beyond the storeroom where the broken furniture is kept.'

'I'm sure Mr Thornton would like to see the panel,' Mrs Tandy said firmly. 'Why don't you take him there, Marina – I must go and rest for an hour, if you will excuse me, Mr Thornton.'

The ploy was so very obvious that Roland found it hard not to grin as he thanked his hostess for lunch and said *arrivederci*. He was to be left alone with Marina for an hour or two, and it needed no great feat of imagination to guess what for. After the excellent food and wine he was pleasantly elated and in the ideal mood to attend to the Contessa's personal needs.

The storeroom where the broken furniture was kept proved to be at the opposite end of the Palazzo, and up another flight of stairs. A long hike through faded eighteenth century magnificence got them there eventually, and out of curiosity Roland asked if he could peep into the storeroom. What he saw astonished him – an acreage like a furniture depository, three-quarters filled with stacks of dusty chairs, tables, rolled-up carpets – every piece an antique of great sale value if expertly restored. It seemed that the Malvolio had been putting damaged furnishings in here ever since the palace was built.

Beyond, as Marina had said, there was a stone-floored passage perhaps fifteen feet long, which ended in a blank wall. A few dusty paintings hung here, and a dark wooden panel inches thick that was carved with a little boat bobbing on heaving waves. It had a pitch-roofed deckhouse with windows, through which peered four bearded heads.

'Noah and his three sons,' said Roland, 'keeping a look-out for the dove to return to the ark. What a charming little work of art, and certainly very early – thirteenth century, I'd say.'

Contessa Marina had lost interest in works of art, early or late, and she turned to face him, slipping her bare arms about his waist.

'Orlando *mio*,' she murmured, 'have you missed me?'

'Of course I have,' said he, and kissed her while he fondled her breasts through the thin *crêpe-de-Chine* of her frock. She sighed happily and he felt the tip of her tongue slide between his lips. He reached under her frock and above her knickers, to stroke her bare belly. Under his hand her warm flesh was smooth as satin.

'I've missed you terribly,' she whispered.

Roland slid his hand down inside her silk knickers until he touched her short and springy curls.

'*Carissimo mio!*' she murmured, her feet moving apart on the stone flagging of the floor to open her thighs. Roland's hand slid deeper into her flimsy underwear to caress the fleshy lips he found. Marina responded by groping for the hard shaft inside his trousers.

'I want you and I mean to have you,' he announced, determined to assert himself forcefully this time and not be her drugged and obedient plaything. This time he intended to have *her*, and on his own terms.

'Darling – not here,' she breathed ardently, as his fingers stroked busily down below. 'If a servant comes past we shall be seen – and my husband will have you assassinated! Come to my room – it's only on the floor below.'

That was the second time the Contessa had warned him

of her husband's jealousy, the first being when they first met and he invited her to his hotel room. Now he had met Count Massimo, it was impossible to take the threat seriously – the man was a fop and a weakling, incapable of any decisive action, even that of making his own living. That at least was Roland's summing-up.

He ignored Marina's suggestion and pressed her back against the passage wall, his mouth over hers in a hard kiss while his fingers teased between her legs. He could feel the soft split there becoming wet to his touch and her thighs were trembling a little already. He knew she wouldn't be able to resist him now, and this was confirmed when she snatched open his trousers and slid her hand in to grasp at his stiffness.

'This is crazy, doing it here,' she gasped, her hand jerking his headstrong *cazzo* up and down avidly.

But crazy or not, she was fast losing herself in a delirium of sensation as he continued to stroke between her parted legs. Her head was lolling back against the wall and she was rubbing her wetness against his fingers and moaning as her crisis began to approach. *She's ready for me* was the triumphant thought in Roland's mind, *and now I shall have her!*

He dragged her knickers down to her knees, bent his legs and dipped, then pushed strongly upwards and he was in her. Marina cried out at the fierce penetration, her hands clutching at his shoulders. She squealed and bumped her belly against him fast, each thrust sending him slithering deeper into her wet warmth, until a shriek of delight announced the onset of her climax.

Roland was very far gone himself – five more fast stabs and his moment had also come – he cried out to feel his torrent of passion spurting inside Marina's soft belly.

'*Bene, bene, bene*,' she murmured in satisfaction, recovering before he did, '*molto bene, Orlando!* Now come to my room so we can do it lying down!'

FIVE

At the time Roland thought it was by chance, meeting Adalbert Gmund on the way back to his hotel at lunchtime, but as things turned out later it was pretty clear in hindsight the Austrian had lurked about deliberately, waiting for him to pass.

All the same, Gmund pretended surprise on catching sight of Roland, called out *buon giorno, Dottore*, and raised his hat, an old-fashioned straw Panama with a brim turned down all round. *Guten Tag* said Roland in reply, utilising about the only words of German he knew in the vain hope of impressing.

They stood for a moment in the narrow entrance of San Angelo square, in the way of passing Venetians, and exchanged further courtesies. Gmund made polite enquiries about the progress of Roland's studies at the Accademia, Roland asked after the well-being of Mrs Tandy and the Contessa and said he had enjoyed his visit to the Palazzo Malvolio greatly, and was highly impressed by what he had seen of the art collection.

When Gmund established that Roland did not intend to return to the Accademia that afternoon, he insisted on taking him to lunch at a *ristorante* he thought well of. That would enable him to benefit, as he put it, from the great advantage of listening to the *Dottore's* opinion about various artistic matters.

The restaurant was not far away, down an alley, over a back canal, past the Fenice Opera into another square with a church, and there it was, a glass-fronted establishment with an expensive look to it. Herr Gmund seemed well known there, he was greeted with bows and expressions of pleasure and conducted to a table placed to maximum advantage. When Roland looked at the menu and saw the prices, he was glad to be the Austrian's guest.

The food was excellent, Gmund assured him, leave it to him – and without further consultation, he instructed the head waiter to bring them whatever was best that day. That guaranteed they would eat the most expensive dishes on the menu, Roland said to himself, surprised that money seemed to be of little importance to his host. Gmund's clothes were well made, but they were not new by any means, if that could be taken as an indication.

A waiter brought plates of mussels in their shells, a local version of *moules marinières* well garlicked, and Gmund launched into a tactful warning against taking too personal an interest in the Contessa. Roland was surprised, but listened closely and enquired how long she and Count Massimo had been married.

'Twenty years,' said Gmund, 'Marina was twenty-two then and beautiful to drive men mad! It was impossible to say whether she or her sister was the most beautiful. Both chose aristocrats for love and prestige mixed together, I think, and neither man had money enough. But life is made of irony, don't you think?'

'No,' said Roland, 'I've never thought that.'

'Because you are still so young,' said Gmund, 'later when you are my age you will understand what I mean. A year after Marina married Massimo, their daughter Bianca was born, here in Venice, in the Palazzo Malvolio. Massimo wanted a son to succeed him, but it was not so. Yet he came to love his daughter, who grew to be even more beautiful than her mother.'

'The daughter wasn't at lunch with us yesterday,' said Roland who was sorry to have missed seeing a nineteen-year-old beauty with a recommendation like that.

Gmund leaned forward across the table to speak confidentially and a faint aroma of garlic accompanied his words.

'This must not be repeated,' he said, his pale blue eyes hard as they glared into Roland's, 'the year before last, Bianca ran away with a young Englishman. It was a terrible scandal for the family. They pretend that she is in Paris at the Sorbonne, but the truth is that she is living in London unmarried with this man. As you can believe, Massimo hates all Englishmen now.'

'Why are you telling me this, Herr Gmund?'

'*Ach*, you must call me Adalbert, for I know we shall be good friends, and I shall call you Roland. I think you know why I am telling you about the Torrenegra scandal. You have ambitions to be the Contessa's lover.'

Roland said nothing, but looked calmly over the empty mussel shells at the Austrian, wondering what his game was.

'Do not mistake me, Roland, I am not a moralist. There was a time twenty years ago when I was myself deep in love with Marina. I was, you understand, a lifelong friend of Rinaldo Malvolio and stayed often with the family before the War. Afterwards Rinaldo was dead, and my income disappeared when the Allies broke up the ancient and glorious Austrian Empire into these backward little Balkan republics. By good fortune, Mrs Tandy invited me to stay in the Palazzo, out of respect for Rinaldo. I have been here in Venice ever since.'

'Very pleasant for you,' said Roland, not impressed to find a hanger-on, 'but what did you mean by saying I have ambition to be the Contessa's lover?'

What he really meant was: *how much do you know, Adalbert?*

'You are putting yourself in danger,' said the Austrian. 'The Count is insanely jealous of everything that touches his honour – if he suspects you of making advances to Marina, he will stop at nothing.'

'That sounds very Grand Opera,' Roland commented, not taking any of it seriously, 'but he didn't seem to me to have backbone enough for a gesture on that scale.'

A relay of waiters brought them, with deferential flourishes, enormous T-bone steaks. Roland stared at his with a lack of enthusiasm, but Adalbert said it was *bistecca alla fiorentine* – beefsteak in the Florentine way and much to be recommended. As he cut into his own, he answered Roland's question indirectly.

'Because Massimo is *finocchio*, you despise him. That is a bad error, believe me. Two men have so far died because they lacked a proper sense of discretion in their approaches to Marina. You will be the third if you do not take care.'

'What does *finocchio* mean?'

'After his daughter was born, Massimo decided his true taste was not for his beautiful wife, but for young and pretty men. I know for a fact that he has not slept in the same room with Marina since that time, and the relations between them are entirely formal and for show. But that has not diminished his pride in his name and title and he will do terrible things to protect both.'

'I'm sure you mean well,' said Roland, 'thank you for that – but it's really nothing to do with me.'

'*Ach, mein Gott*!' Adalbert exclaimed. 'You think that your little affair with Marina is a secret? Three days ago when you met her she took you with her after lunch to the palace and you made love to her for over three hours. Yesterday, when you were looking at old pictures, she showed you the wood panel of Noah and you had her against the wall. If Massimo learned of it, you would be dead before midnight.'

Roland was flabbergasted.

'How do *you* know these things – did she tell you?' he asked.

'Certainly not! Marina is an honourable person who would never speak of her private affairs. But the Palazzo Malvolio is like a village, my friend, where everyone knows everything that goes on. There are more than forty servants, and their duties take them everywhere. You were seen both times, Roland, and gossip did the rest. Everyone in the palace except Massimo knows that you are Marina's lover.'

'Why doesn't he know?'

'He is not greatly liked, as the Contessa is. The servants do not find him *simpatico* and they conceal her little lapses. This should not make you careless, when so much depends on keeping a secret that can so easily be betrayed.'

'Your point is taken,' said Roland thoughtfully. The *bistecca* was more than he could cope with and he put down his knife and fork and emptied his glass.

'The Englishman who ran off with the Count's young daughter,' he said, 'has anything happened to him? Two years, you said?'

'So far he is safe, and for a reason. Bianca knows her father well and wrote to him from London. She said that if the least harm came to her Englishman, even if he were struck by a flash of lightning in the middle of Piccadilly, she would know who to blame and she would never speak to Massimo again in her life.'

'And that was enough?'

'Massimo loves his daughter and would do nothing against her. But if she ever tires of the man and leaves him, then a fatal accident is sure to happen to him.'

'What a threat to have hanging over your head! Who is he?'

'A young man who came to value some pictures. He stayed for a couple of weeks, did his work, and when he went back to London, Bianca went with him without a word to anyone. We all feared Massimo would run mad with the shame of it – his daughter and a nobody! And without the blessing of the Holy Church!'

Roland was more interested in art than a count's hurt pride.

'He came to value pictures, you said. Where was he from, the National Gallery? A private gallery?'

'He was sent by Mallards, the famous art auction house.'

'Then Mrs Tandy was in earnest,' said Roland.

He was thinking that explained quite a lot. The recent wave of spending he had noted in Mrs Tandy's clothes and Marina's, set against the background of aristocratic poverty seen through the palace itself. He tried to recall what important Venetian paintings had been up for sale in the past two years.

He asked Adalbert what had been sold through London, but the talkative Austrian evidently thought he'd said too much on that subject and did not answer him. That confirmed the conviction Roland had formed over lunch the previous day, that there was some sort of funny business going on in the palace to do with the Malvolio art collection. Not that it concerned him – he was in Venice to look at the pictures in the Accademia, and his only interest at the Palazzo Malvolio lay in getting the Contessa's knickers off.

It struck him that Adalbert drank quite a lot – three bottles of wine had been emptied, and Roland's share was no more than half a bottle. The cheese and fruit had been served and eaten, and Adalbert was drinking brandy. Not that he showed any sign of drunkenness, but his affability had increased and he was grinning almost continuously. He was talking about women again, especially his many adventures as a young man in Vienna where, according to him, every female between the ages of sixteen and fifty-six in pre-War days had been desperate to undress and lie down for his attentions.

Roland listened politely, paying little heed to what he took to be the fictional memories of late middle age. Adalbert must surely have had a reasonable number of girls in his youth, but not on the scale he claimed. Nor did Roland believe that he had done quite all the odd things he said he had with girls – some of them sounded uncomfortable, some simply ludicrous, and some downright off-putting.

'I was in London many times before the War,' said Adalbert, 'I had my shoes made in St James and my suits in Savile

Row. In those days I was a man of wealth and I was invited as guest to many country houses. From this I have experience of making love with English women.'

'I'm sure you do,' Roland answered, wondering if he dare slip away from his host on some excuse of having notes to write up or letters to post. It was a pity he'd told Adalbert of taking the afternoon off from work.

'In my opinion,' said the Austrian, his tone implying that no other opinion on the subject was worth a moment's consideration by any sensible person, 'the English women are not good in bed. Once a great lady was staying with me – in confidence I say to you she was an English viscountess and extremely well-known in Society – at your Ritz Hotel in Piccadilly, which I found a poor imitation of the Ritz Hotel in Paris. I set out to enchant and delight the lady, employing all the skills in love-making I had learned over the years from women in every part of Europe.'

'Heavens above!' said Roland, finishing his brandy. 'Was the lady up to this virtuoso performance?'

His irony was wasted on Adalbert, who beckoned the waiter to bring more brandy.

'It was frightful,' he said, shaking his head slowly, 'in two hours of the afternoon between lunch and tea time I did it with the lady four times, to my complete satisfaction. But in spite of that, she had no climax – not even one!'

'Very disappointing,' said Roland, trying to curb his smile.

'*Ach Gott*, you laugh at me,' said Adalbert, not taking the least offence, 'you are saying to yourself that a silly old man is remembering better days. Perhaps it is so. Nowadays I do not pursue women as I used to, for my tastes have changed very much with the years. I have not long ago made the acquaintance of an interesting person, Signorina Caducci, who entertains gentlemen friends in an unusual way.'

'I've been entertained in an unusual way,' Roland said with a grin, 'it was at the house of a Signora Ricci, I think her name was, in the Cannaregio district.'

'Really?' Adalbert breathed, a gleam of interest in his blue eyes as he leaned forward over the table, 'I do not know this Signora Ricci – what did she do for you?'

Roland told him about the two young naked women, Marcella and Sofia, who demonstrated *amore lesbico* together for visitors and then their control of internal muscles to finish the job.

'But how very fascinating!' said Adalbert. 'How did you

find this remarkable display – you, who have been here only a day or two? I might like to go there myself – what is the address?'

'The typical Venetian dialect used for street names is beyond the grasp of a simple tourist like me,' Roland answered, trying to recall the phrasing of Carlo's ridiculous guide-book, 'while the numbering system in the *sestiere* can be understood only by postmen trained in topography.'

'That is true,' said Adalbert, taking him seriously. 'Would you recognise the house again?'

'I might be able to take you there,' said Roland casually, 'but tell me about your Signorina with the unusual ways – what does she do to please you?'

'Have you read a certain notorious book written about forty years ago by a compatriot of mine, Leopold von Sacher-Masoch?' Adalbert asked.

'Oh, I understand,' said Roland, 'the special talent of your Signorina is flagellation.'

'You know the book, I see.'

'It is almost impossible to obtain a copy in England, but as you would expect, there is an English-language edition that can be bought in Paris. It's years since I read it, but I seem to recall the hero has a girlfriend named Wanda who ties him up and whips him while she wears a fur coat. I remember thinking that flagellation seems to have been a very Victorian pleasure. There were scores of English works on it in the 1880s and 1890s – sold clandestinely in shady bookshops, of course. The thought of being flogged by a woman has never interested me much.'

'It is often the case that we dislike or fear whatever we do not understand,' said Adalbert. 'You should keep an open mind, my friend. Come with me and meet Signorina Caducci – she is a very friendly person and you will find her very interesting.'

'Do you visit her regularly?'

'Once or twice a week – I have other places of entertainment here in Venice.'

'I'm sure you do, Adalbert. Is Signorina Caducci pretty? How old is she?

'Ah, you are not as indifferent as you pretend! I cannot say how old she is, for I have never asked her. But not yet thirty is my guess. Her features – well, I would call her striking rather than pretty. She is not ugly and fat.'

He paid the bill and after a little more conversation on the same topic, the two men left the restaurant agreeing to visit Signorina Caducci who lived, said Adalbert, in the district of San Polo. For Roland's benefit he explained that meant the area round the church of San Polo, over on the other side of the Grand Canal.

From the square where the restaurant stood, a narrow passage between high walls led them down to a floating platform on the Grand Canal which served the *vaporetto* as a stopping place for setting down and picking up passengers. Adalbert paid some tiny amount at the ticket booth and they waited a few minutes until the next water-bus came chugging and dipping across the Canal from the stop at the white-domed church of Santa Maria della Salute, and came alongside the platform with a thump.

In seconds it was off again, making for the Accademia Bridge on its long run up the Grand Canal, past a hundred palaces on either bank. The first stop after Roland and Adalbert were on board was right outside the Accademia Gallery. Though his time and decisions were his own, and no one required him to clock on and keep regular hours of work, Roland suffered a small crisis of conscience at the thought of thirteenth century paintings left unconsidered. By rights he should be in there, wracking his wits over the themes of early Venetian art. Sadly, the scourging of St Thaddeus seemed much less entertaining than what lay ahead at the hands of Signorina Caducci.

Three stops later Adalbert led the way off the boat and then through a maze of narrow little streets with shops and bars and doorways to stairs and flats. They came out into a large square at last, which he announced as the Campo San Polo. And indeed, there stood a large church, named for St Paul, Roland assumed, though reduced to Polo in the Venetian dialect. It was not very impressive as a building, and he said so, only to be put in his place by Adalbert's information that inside were paintings by, among others, Tintoretto and Tiepolo.

More immediately interesting to Roland was that in addition to the church, the square consisted of a number of palaces, one of them recognisably eighteenth century and the others much earlier. Adalbert said they were let out in apartments now, and led the way across the square a touch impatiently. As well he might do, thought Roland with a grin, for in his imagination Adalbert now feels the kiss of the lash, and has no time to fritter away on the decline and fall of Venetian prosperity.

The way led between palaces and over a narrow canal into a small square, one side formed by another palace. A narrow alley led out of the top corner of the square, and some way along it Adalbert turned onto a humpbacked foot bridge over a back canal between tall buildings and halted.

'This is called the Ponte delle Tette,' said he, 'it means the bridge of the tits.'

'Surely not,' said Roland, 'town councils don't choose names like that. The translation must be wrong.'

'It is correct,' Adalbert insisted, 'we have the same word in German as you have in English. The bridge was given this name hundreds of years ago for a reason – in this district lived many whores. To get business, these women stood in the doorways of their houses stripped down to the waist.'

'They do that today in Amsterdam,' said Roland, 'I've seen it myself, when I went over to look at the Rembrandts. Only they sit in windows, not doors.'

'And also in Hamburg,' said Adalbert. 'I have been there and talked to the women through their open windows. They can offer most interesting diversions to men who have become bored with ordinary love-making. But I was telling you of Venice and this bridge – it was here the women met to talk to each other when they had a rest and a little stroll to stretch the legs after lying on their backs all day. And because they went about with their breasts uncovered, it got the name Bridge of Tits.'

'Now I come to think of it,' said Roland, 'a colleague at the university who teaches Medieval History told me that in London in the fourteenth century there was a Sluts' Hole Lane. But with the coming of polite manners, it was changed to Sluts' Well Lane to conceal what went on there.'

'I understand hole,' said Adalbert, 'but what is a *slut*?'

'The sort of woman who used to stand here on the bridge with her tits on show.'

The house they were looking for was not much further on over the bridge. A doorway gave on to a stone staircase with broken treads, where the smell of cooking hung about. The apartment of Signorina Caducci was one flight up, and Adalbert drew himself to his full height, chest thrown out and chin back, and knocked briskly on the door.

In the restaurant he had described Renata Caducci to Roland as *not yet thirty, striking rather than pretty, not ugly and fat, a very friendly person you will find interesting*. Some of it was true, Roland decided, studying the woman who let them into her sitting-room. She could be taken for twenty-eight or twenty-nine, and was probably five years younger. She was not ugly or fat, nor was she pretty in any usual meaning of the word. She was tall and thin, sharp-hipped and long-armed, with breasts much too large for her. Her face was long and wedge-shaped, slanting in from the temples to a pointed chin. Her hair was dark brown, with natural frizzy waves, pulled back to clear her ears and tied with a knot at the back of her neck.

Her eyes were large and darkest brown, her mouth was set in a permanent sulky pout. To judge by her expression, *friendly* was not an accurate description. Perhaps Adalbert had meant she was obliging. On the whole, the only part of his characterisation Roland agreed with was that Signorina Caducci was *striking* of appearance. And striking in another sense.

She shook hands with Adalbert, which seemed odd to Roland in view of their more intimate relationship. If she was pleased to see him, she gave no visible sign of it. She shook hands with Roland when he was introduced as *Dottore Tornoton*, and he found she knew very little English.

Piacere said Roland, squeezing her hand, for he had found out what Italians say on being introduced. But the Signorina merely stared at him sulkily and said nothing, only the tiniest nod of her head acknowledging his presence in her home. Roland waited to see if she would offer them a glass of wine, as the madame in Cannaregio had, where the reeds used to grow. She did not – nor did she ask her visitors to sit down. She stood talking to Adalbert in rapid Italian, and she sounded aggrieved.

Whether this was part of her performance or natural rudeness, Roland couldn't guess. He was fascinated by the effect it had on Adalbert – his face was bright red, his legs were trembling under him and he was breathing fast. And this before anything happened other than the exchange of a few words. The Signorina evidently had a secret power over some men. It couldn't be the attraction of her gawky body, wrapped untidily like a parcel in a pink dressing-gown. It was not the appeal of her manners, for they could hardly be called seductive. It must lie in her eyes, the only beautiful part of her.

After a while she turned on her heel – she was in flat-heeled slippers – and left the sitting-room in a hurry, as if anxious to get away from her callers. Adalbert drew in a slow and deep breath as he turned to face Roland, his face pink with emotion.

'She is wonderful, *nicht war*?' he said. 'I told you that you would like her very much. She is getting ready – I go first and you wait here for me. Then she shall do it for you while I wait and then we go to a cafe to drink and talk about her.'

'I see,' said Roland, more amused than interested, and by no means sure that he wanted the Signorina to do *it*, whatever that was, for him. A voice from another room called out and at once Adalbert dropped his Panama hat on a chair and made a dash for the inner door and the waiting woman beyond.

Roland looked out of the window and could see nothing except the windows of the houses across the narrow street, twelve feet away from him and blocked by net curtains. Signorina Caducci did not feel the need for such concealments – at least not in her sitting-room. No doubt it was a different story in the room where she administered her type of entertainment to clients.

Adalbert had closed the door behind him, but even so, Roland heard the sound of a smart crack. He sat down on the nearest chair, intrigued by what might be going on in the next room. He heard another crack, as of something flexible striking on bare flesh, and a muffled groan.

It was true then – grown men really did pay to be thrashed by obliging women! The Austrian writer Leopold von Sacher-Masoch had given his name to a sexual perversion *masochism*, but Roland had believed till now that this existed only in the casebooks of psychologists and other Viennese-inspired quacks.

He tried to remember the big scene in Sacher-Masoch's book – the idiotic hero, whose name didn't matter, is kneeling on the bedroom floor, his head against the beautiful and cruel Wanda's breasts, rubbing his cheek against her fur coat, because that excites him. In come three black girls in red frocks, bringing lengths of rope. They hold him down while they bind his wrists together behind his back, and then his ankles.

Crack, groan. Pause. Crack, groan. Pause. How long did this sort of entertainment go on, Roland wondered – presumably there was a limit to the amount of suffering any man could enjoy.

In the story the three black girls heave the hero to his feet and use the third length of rope to tie him against a post of the four-poster bed. When he is helpless, his shirt raised to expose his back, lovely Wanda in her white frock and fur coat takes a whip to him and gives him the devil of a thrashing. She taunts him, says she despises him, whacks away at his back and bottom until he squirts off in his trousers and collapses half-fainting in his bonds.

Wanda throws the whip down and stretches herself out at full-length on a sofa. The pretty black girls unbind our abused hero and he slides semiconscious to the floor. But at a harsh word or two from His Mistress's Voice, his back bleeding from the lashing, he crawls across the carpet to Wanda and rains kisses on her foot in total subjection.

Which might be all very well in theory, thought Roland, but a far too drastic form of stimulation to be considered by anyone with his wits intact. That was when Adalbert came back, walking a little carefully, his face aglow with satisfaction.

'Well?' Roland asked.

'*Schon, schon!*' mumbled the Austrian, reverting to his own language under the stress of intense emotion. But taking pity on Roland's look of incomprehension, he collected his knowledge of English and tried again.

'That Renata – she is *wunderbar*,' he said. 'She makes me very happy. I worship her – I kiss her feet!'

'That does seem to be the traditional response,' said Roland.

'Go to her,' said Adalbert, 'she waits for you.'

His smile was as beatific as if he were bestowing a blessing. Roland felt very diffident about submitting himself to pain of this sort, but having come this far it seemed impossible now to back out without losing face. With a nervous grin he stood up and made his way into the bedroom with no more enthusiasm than a man on his way to the scaffold to be drawn and quartered.

Signorina Caducci certainly was waiting for him, and not too patiently. *Presto, presto!* she said when Roland was only half through the door, and he took that to be Italian for *get a move on*. He saw that she had stripped down to her working clothes by taking off the pink dressing-gown. She stood waiting for him in a loose-fitting slip, also pink, with ribbon shoulder-straps. The hem was a hand's-breadth above her knees, revealing thinnish legs and bare feet.

The sulky pout was still on her face when she raised a hand, rubbed thumb and forefinger together, and said *Cinque cento*.

Roland did the conversion in his head and made it nearly five pounds. It seemed a lot. In London a fiver would buy him an all-night encounter with the prettiest tart in the West End. An hour with a girl from along Bayswater Road would be only thirty shillings. In Venice the prices had been adjusted for tourists, he concluded. On the other hand, Signorina Caducci was special, according to Adalbert Gmund.

Roland handed her a 500-lire note, wondering where she would put it. Slips had no pockets – perhaps she would stow it into her knickers. She disappointed him by putting it in the drawer of the bedside table. And then she showed her appreciation by slipping her shoulder-straps down to let her loose slip fall to her waist. Her breasts were big and soft, their weight dragging them downwards in a way that positively cried out for a man's hands underneath to support them! Their red-brown florets were distended in proportion, and were two or three inches across. Roland stared at this remarkable pair of *tette* and was struck by a great urge to suck them.

Before he had time even to get his hands on them, she started to issue orders in Italian, and for the foreigner's benefit she supplemented them with gestures. He took off his jacket and tie and looked at the bed, not understanding if she wanted him to strip naked or what. She pushed him towards the bed, and he saw for the first time that she had laid a clean white towel on it, partly hanging over the side, to protect the cover.

Still speaking in an irritable tone, as if sure that no man in the world could be trusted to get even the simplest thing right, she pushed him sharply towards the towel and made *bend over* signs with her hands. Roland was amused by the surliness of her attitude and did what she wanted, lying over the towel, his body on the bed, his legs trailing down the side, feet on the brown-tiled floor.

By now his sexual curiosity was aroused by the ambiguity of his situation, and he felt the first stirrings of pleasure when her hands reached under his waist to unbuckle his belt and pull it right out of the trouser loops. Then her fingers groped for his trouser buttons, and his *cazzo* began to grow long and hard as she opened them from waist to groin.

It was all an elaborate game, he thought then, the objective to excite ageing *roués* like Adalbert, whose energies had become jaded by having too many women too often in too many ways. But could that be bad?

While these thoughts ran through his mind, Signorina Caducci had pulled his trousers down his thighs, and his underwear, to bare his bottom for her attentions. Cruel Wanda had whipped her boyfriend's back, but Signorina Caducci had other ideas about how men should be treated. He imagined she was staring down at his smooth skin, and tremors of anticipation shook him – those enormous breasts would be dangling over his back while she was arranging his shirt up above his waist. He was half-prepared to swivel over onto his back and reach up to grasp those monstrous delights and pull them down to his mouth. But first he wanted to know what she would do to him.

A second later, he knew! He gasped in pain as she used his own leather belt to lay into his bare bottom. She spoke sharply to him, probably telling him to hold still, for he was writhing about under the lashing. He told himself that her breasts were flopping about as she beat him, that to see them in motion must be stupendous. He told himself he was aching to get his hands on them, but it was useless, the fiery pain of the whipping was too much – it drove every other thought right out of his head. How many times she whipped him he did not know, but the time at last came when she said in her sulky voice *Ecco!* and stopped.

Roland rubbed his smarting bottom with both hands, wondering what the fuss was about. There had been nothing at all sexually arousing about the beating, quite the reverse. There had to be something adrift in Adalbert's physical responses if he reached a sexual climax like that.

He stood up, his trousers sliding down from his knees to his ankles. His shirt was tucked up round his waist and his *cazzo* stuck out as stiff as the bowsprit of a sailing-ship. Signorina Caducci glanced at it, then at the unsullied towel on the bed, and her sulky expression turned to annoyance. Roland had failed to respond properly, her strenuous exertions with the belt were wasted! He was in her bad books!

She gave him a quick shove that sent him sprawling backwards on the bed and with an agility that took him by surprise was on it herself and kneeling on his thighs. Roland stared fascinated at the way her big loose breasts flopped to her movements, then gasped to see her thumb and forefinger close round his bulging part. He gasped again, and this time louder, when she started a rough manipulation of it.

He grabbed at her wrist to make her stop before it became too painful to bear, and again she took him by surprise – quick as a cat she twisted her lean body about and jammed the hard heel of a bare foot under his chin, forcing his head back on the bed and immobilising him. She was speaking to him nonstop in her own language, obviously complaining about him, and her hand on his *cazzo* had accelerated to a furious beat.

Her curious position sideways over his body, her legs splayed to control him, raised her slip halfway up her thighs and gave him a view between her legs. She wore white cotton knickers of a design he'd not seen before, with legs ending in a frill well down towards her bare knees. Her mound was very prominent under the thin material, through which he saw the dark shadow of her bush showing.

At that moment he would have given her whatever she asked to stop this ridiculous amateur brutality and drop her knickers so he could climb on top of her. But like an avenging angel she did not turn aside from the solemnly appointed task. Her heel ground into his throat, her bony knee dug uncomfortably hard in the fleshiest part of his thigh, her fingers wrenched away at his *cazzo* as if she meant to tear it from his body.

'Oh, no, no, no!' Roland wailed, his essence spurting high in a racking climax. He was helpless in her hands and she did not wait for him to finish – at the first quick spurt she slithered off him to stand beside the bed. Like a striking snake her hand seized his pompoms, tight up between his legs, and he shrieked faintly and rolled over as she dragged, to avoid the sharp pain – and he was lying face down again.

'No, no!' he cried out, as Signorina Caducci thrashed at his bare backside with the leather belt, pain and pleasure mingled beyond separation as his lust spurted on to the towel.

SIX

Once the thought of the Rowlandson picture had planted itself in Roland's head, he couldn't get rid of it. Carnival at Venice indeed! It seemed very unlikely that it hung framed on a wall at Windsor Castle, for even if the Prince Regent had displayed it openly to amuse his girlfriends and cronies, it was sure to have been tidied away in Queen Victoria's reign. Along with the other souvenirs of Prinny's zest for wine, women and song, such as his glorious Pavilion-Palace at Brighton, flogged off twenty years after his death to the town council.

Which had nothing to do with Roland's Venetian fixation – to have the Contessa Marina by night across the stone well-head in the little square outside the Palazzo Malvolio. The first thing was to get in touch with her, but that proved more complicated than he imagined. His hotel was proud to have a *telefono* in its reception area for the convenience of its clients, but when he asked a desk clerk to look up the number of the Palazzo for him there was a long pause and an animated conversation between the clerk and the telephone exchange.

The upshot was surprising. Roland was informed in indifferent but perfectly understandable English that there was no *telefono* at the Palazzo Malvolio. *La Signora Tandy* had no need of modern devices. If the Signor Tomtom had the wish to communicate with ladies or gentlemen inhabiting the Palazzo Malvolio, it would be convenient for him to write a letter, which a hotel servant would be instructed to make a speedy delivery of. The paper for writing was provided by the Hotel Gallini and found itself in the writing table in the Signor's room.

Roland thought it over. In the past few days he had begun to understand a little of the unhurried tempo of Italian life, and he had no confidence that any letter he handed to a desk clerk would reach its destination in less than half a week.

Not that there was any way of putting down on paper the frolic he wanted to involve Marina in. After what he had been told about gossip among the Palazzo staff, a letter like that would be a ticking time bomb.

He solved his problem by writing a short note to the Contessa to invite her to join him for a drink and a chat about English satirical artists at Florian's cafe at six in the evening. On his way to the Accademia the next morning, he went out of his way a little to pass the Palazzo and deliver the note himself. That proved to be a ceremony in itself – he banged a knocker on the heavy wooden door until a footman with a haughty frown opened it. But when he recognised Roland as a previous guest of Signora Tandy, he bowed and became deferential.

He took the offered envelope carefully in white-gloved hand and read the superscription several times. Roland had written *The Contessa Marina Torrenegra, Palazzo Malvolio, Venice*, which seemed to him sufficient for a hand-delivered missive, but the footman seemed to find it inadequate. He stared at Roland and asked if the letter were for the Contessa. Roland said that it was, whereupon the footman read the words on the envelope again and shook his head doubtfully.

La Contessa Marina? he enquired, as if there might be dozens of similarly named ladies living in the palace. *Si* said Roland, thinking his easy grasp of the word would settle the matter for once and all. It was only when the footman shook his head again in seeming perplexity that Roland understood and fumbled in his pocket for a silver fifty-lira coin. That smoothed the way at once and he was assured that his letter would be placed in the hands of the Contessa before five minutes had passed. The footman backed into the palace, bowing, and as he closed the enormous door, he laid a finger alongside his nose and almost winked.

If Roland had needed any confirmation of what Adalbert Gmund had told him – that his fling with Marina was known to everyone in the palace except her husband, the footman's conspiratorial gesture provided it. He strolled on towards the Accademia with second thoughts about the wisdom of the open-air romp with the Contessa. If Count Massimo ever got to hear about that he would surely come after Roland to avenge the slighted family honour with a knife and sever the offending pompoms from their owner's body!

All the same, he got to the Piazza San Marco that evening

at five minutes to six and found Marina was there and waiting for him at one of the little tables outside Florian's. They shook hands, there being too many eyes about to risk a greeting more affectionate than that. Over glasses of chilled white vermouth they said how pleased they were to see each other, and all the usual things that are said on these occasions.

Eventually, when Marina suggested that he called to visit her at the Palazzo after dinner for an hour, Roland introduced with care the thought that had formed in his mind.

'You mean do it in the *campo*!' she exclaimed, her eyes round with amazement. 'But that's impossible – we'd be seen. There'd be the most fearful row.'

Roland waved to the waiter for more drinks and went about the curious task of persuading her to risk everything for *amore*. It was not easy – Marina had a genuine dread of her little frolics being discovered by her husband. But by nature she was divinely lascivious, and the sheer effrontery of his suggestion appealed to her. She confided that she'd done it more than once out on the lagoon in a covered gondola, but she didn't say with whom and Roland didn't ask.

So it came about that at two in the morning Roland lurked in the thick shadow about the grand door of the Palazzo Malvolio, hoping no late revellers would walk across the square and spot him. In fact, the time was well chosen and the only creatures about were three or four wild cats slinking across the paving stones. He'd come to realise that there were whole packs of them living in the back alleys of Venice, but only at night did they appear in force to forage.

The palace door swung slowly inwards with a long creaking he hadn't noticed in the daytime, and Marina slipped out and stood looking around the square cautiously. To Roland's surprise, the door closed behind her, though she was nowhere near it. It had to be the doorman who let her out, and she must have confidence in him to keep his mouth shut about her nocturnal prowl.

Roland stepped forward from the thick shadow by the building and touched her arm gently. She wheeled round startled, saw who it was and threw herself into his arms, showering kisses on his face. Roland slipped his arms round her to grasp and knead the fleshy cheeks of her bottom through her skirt. She was dressed in the style of Venetian working-class women by way of disguise – wrapped in a long shawl with a fringe over a blouse and black skirt, her hair in a bun on top of her head.

'This is crazy,' she murmured between kisses, 'we're sure to be seen. Come inside with me and you can stay with me all night in my bed – nobody will disturb us.'

'Not tonight,' said Roland, 'I want you out here in the open, Marina, under the sky.'

The well-head in the middle of the little square was a very substantial chunk of carved stone, round at the bottom where it sat on the paving and square at the top, with a broad ledge for buckets to be rested on it. It was boarded over permanently and solidly, with iron clamps to prevent the cover being taken off. The top was about table height, or a little less.

Roland led Marina out of the shadow of the Palazzo and across the open square to the middle. She was reluctant at first, but she sat herself on the coping of the well and waited for Roland to make a start. With pleasure she unwrapped her shawl and found that her blouse could be unbuttoned down to her waist.

He had it open in seconds, and as he guessed, she had no slip underneath. Reluctant or not, she had given some thought to how best to dress to be ravished in a public place! Roland guessed too that she had no knickers on, but first he gave himself the delight of stroking her bare breasts. There was no moon in the sky, yet in the dimness of the square her breasts gleamed white and their tips stood out darkly against them. He caressed them and teased them to make them stand proudly.

Her thighs were already apart when he put a hand up her skirt and confirmed that his guess was correct – she had no knickers on. His fingers played in her curls and over the prominent lips of her *fica*, and Marina was sighing in high arousal even before he pressed his middle finger into her and stroked her slippery nub. He felt her hands scrabbling at his trouser buttons, then his stiff part was out in the open and being massaged briskly.

In the dark and silent little square in front of the Palazzo Malvolio, he pressed Marina backwards until she lay across the boarded-up well, her head hanging down the far side. Her knees came up, her skirt slid back to her groins, and Roland held her ankles and raised her silk-stockinged legs up to his shoulders.

'Marina – that's marvellous,' he breathed.

He was gazing eagerly at the length of her bare thighs above her garters, along the pearly skin to her loins, ravishing her with his eyes. He stared fiercely into the dark and hairy split that was the centre of her delight, observing how it was pulled open by the spreading of her legs, now lying on his shoulders. Nothing was hidden, Marina was offering herself to him to make whatever use of he wanted. He leaned over her to let the tip of his twitching part touch lightly between the open petals of her flower.

'Oh Roland, oh yes!' she whispered eagerly.

He teased her by making the head of his *cazzo* rub on her wet button until he felt her legs beginning to shake in the tremors that warn a climax is approaching, then raised his head to gaze at her bare breasts thrusting up from her unbuttoned blouse, to see how they rose and fell to the fast rhythm of her breathing.

He slid his hands under the cheeks of her bottom to raise it and with a long push sheathed his distended flesh in Marina's belly. *Si*, she moaned, *Si!* and her leather-shod heels drummed on his shoulders. He realised that her moments of sexual crisis had arrived, long before he was ready. To make sure she wasn't disappointed, he slid to and fro in her by way of intensifying her climax.

When she was quiet again she raised her head to stare up at his face, but it was too dark to make out her expression. She sighed contentedly a couple of times, let her head loll down on the well-side and lay limply awaiting his pleasure. He was iron hard inside her, throbbing with lust and eager to show what he could do. He sank his fingers into the soft flesh of her bottom and made her squeal, rammed hard in until his short curls were flat on hers, and he started to plunge and jab in earnest. He went at her hard – so hard he could see her breasts jolting up and down to his deep strokes. His tempestuous attack aroused in her the lust he had just satisfied, and her loins moved with him.

There was a growing awareness in his mind, in so far as there was place for any mental activity in these moments of ecstatic sensation, that Marina had somehow liberated him. In London his love-making had been conducted in complete secrecy, usually with the blinds drawn and the bedroom in half-darkness, with girls who would blush at the thought of flaunting their bodies naked. Marina had changed his attitude completely in a matter of days, and it was he who had suggested this open-air romp in the night to her. And after an initial quavering she had shown that she was willing to hoist her skirt and let him have her anywhere.

This train of thought vanished as Roland's climax arrived and he stabbed passionately into Marina. Her head jerked up to show her eyes as pools of darkness in the white oval of her face and she gave a shriek that drove the watching cats scurrying away. For Roland there was an eternity of overwhelming sensation while his fierce desire emptied itself into her. Her body heaved about on the well-head under the short strokes, her *fica* held him tight and sucked at him greedily.

After a long time their wild spasms slowed and stopped, until they both collapsed, Roland lying over her, his hands upon her shoulders and his face between her bared breasts.

'*Orlando* – what have you done to me!' Marina sighed, 'I died of love with you in me, *carissimo*.'

He kissed her breasts, his pride flattered enormously, and he was about to murmur an appropriate reply when distant footsteps disturbed him. Someone was walking across the square behind him – and instantly he was up on his feet and fastening his trouser buttons. Marina sat up without hurry, smoothed her skirt down over her thighs, threw an end of her shawl over one shoulder to cover her bare breasts, and slipped off the well and on to her feet beside him.

Arm in arm they strolled in the direction of the footsteps, towards the figure approaching through the darkness. It was a man in a slouch hat, they saw, and as they passed, he raised it without a word. Marina nodded without speaking. Roland had been certain that the promenader had seen nothing, but now he began to wonder if he had been standing at the entrance to the square watching them perform. He asked Marina if she knew the man, but she said *No*. She added that she didn't know everyone who knew her. They halted and looked back to see if the man went to the Palazzo, but as far as they could make out in the half-dark he left the square by the narrow alley on the left.

'I don't care if it's all over Venice tomorrow,' said she in a spirit of defiance, 'it was well worth it, my darling.'

Their stroll had brought them to the square where the church of San Stefano reared up to the night sky. So far they had met no one else and they went on to the deserted Opera, where only a handful of thin cats sat curled up on the stone steps. A few minutes further on they turned into a wide short thoroughfare of expensive shops, closed and shuttered, and Marina asked why they were going to the Piazza.

'Because I'm going to have you in the very heart of Venice,' he told her, and she squeezed his arm and chuckled.

But even at two thirty in the morning, the Piazza San Marco was not wholly deserted. The bands had gone home and the cafes were shut, the hanging lamps in the arcades turned off and dark – but an occasional couple sauntered across the patterned stone paving and groups of young people stood conversing noisily in Italian. Roland thought he could find a suitable nook under the arcades, only to discover that here and there were curled up in sleep gypsies and beggars in this handy shelter.

'Oh,' said he, greatly crestfallen to think his scheme was going awry. Marina came to the rescue by taking him to where a passage ran through the topside of the square to a narrow alley beyond.

The passage had shops down both sides and was mercifully free of sleeping vagrants. Roland seized the opportunity at once by choosing the handiest-looking shop entrance and pressing Marina back against the locked metal grill over the door.

'Is this central enough for you?' she asked.

He smiled at her in the gloom and slipped one arm round her waist to hold her while his other hand went up under her shawl to her unbuttoned blouse and warm breasts. These he handled in growing elation, revelling in their fleshy delight and stroking their prominent buds.

'We must be careful,' Marina whispered, her mouth against his ear, 'the *polizia* patrol here through the night.'

'Are we breaking the law?' he asked, and she told him they were committing an act of indecency in public which would cost him a heavy fine if caught.

'It would be well worth it,' he said, repeating her sentiment of earlier in the little square.

To stop any more irrelevant chatter, he closed her mouth with a long kiss and soon he was pressing his tongue in between her lips and she began to tremble against him. While he was kissing her, he felt her hand slide flat over the long bulge inside his trousers, assuring herself that he was indeed stiff – and then her fingers were deftly undoing his buttons. *Ah Marina, my dear* he murmured and her hand slipped into his now gaping trousers, and lightly touched him, as if checking the stiffness and hard strength of the warm shaft of twitching flesh.

Although his natural desire and abilities were not reinforced by a few drops of the *elisir d'amore* she had put in his drink at their first encounter, Roland was reasonably certain that he would do all she expected of him – and all that he expected of himself. When her hand in his trousers took hold of his pride and slid along its solid length to a quick little rhythm, he was sure of it – Marina would prevent any premature flagging.

He reached down between her knees and passed his hand under her skirt. With the hand not engaged in massaging his *cazzo* to a frenzy, Marina caught hold of his wrist and stopped him as he touched the smooth bare flesh above her stocking tops.

'Well then, *Orlando mio*,' she said, 'you have made up your mind to have me in the Piazza San Marco, have you? But what if I say *No* to you? Suppose I have had enough of you for tonight and invite you to come and see me at home tomorrow?'

'Yes, tomorrow by all means,' he said. 'I will be with you at two in the afternoon and you will give me a drop of aphrodisiac in a glass of wine and I will ravish you senseless.'

'You know about that?' Marina asked quickly, though not put out in the least. 'Who told you?'

'Does it matter? The results were astonishing – afterwards I felt like a hero – like Tristan after drinking the love potion with Isolde in Wagner's opera. Next time there will be no need for secrecy – I'll swallow it happily and die in ecstasy lying on your belly.'

While they were talking Roland forced his hand higher between her legs against the downward pressure of her arm. She pressed her thighs together as tightly as possible, but in this sort of contest she was no match for him. His urgent hand moved higher under her skirt until at last his fingertips touched the soft and warm flesh of her *fica*. She gave an excited sigh and let go of his wrist.

'I was only teasing you, Orlando,' she murmured, her clasping hand sliding up and down his swollen pride, 'I didn't mean it – I haven't had nearly enough of you yet tonight!'

Roland's fingertips stroked the moist lips of her split and she let her thighs open for him to press between and reach her slippery button.

'How much of me do you want?' he asked with a chuckle. 'I've six inches – will that do?'

'It will do very well,' she sighed, feeling him stretch open her *fica* with two fingers, 'if I can have it often.'

Roland's mouth found hers again and his tongue fluttered in it, much as between her legs his fingers were fluttering over a wet and engorged bud. Marina sighed hotly into his mouth when he hoisted her skirt to bare her thighs and curls. She guided his throbbing stiffness up between her legs to where she was open and ready for him, and he pressed straight in.

The iron grille behind her rattled when Roland started to jab in and out of her, and he grasped it with a hand on either side of her and pushed it back hard to silence it. Marina moaned and panted into his open mouth in her fast-rising excitement – she had got both hands into his trousers and round him to sink her fingernails into the flesh of his bottom. Roland's thrusting quickened and she shook like a leaf against him, to the instant a long spasm took him and his desire gushed into her.

'*Madonna mia!*' she shrieked in ecstatic release, bumping her belly furiously against him, rattling the grille like squeaking bedsprings. Roland was sure the noise could be heard across the other side of the Piazza and would bring a police patrol to see what was going on. But finally Marina was quiet again, leaning back with sighs of satisfaction. The grille fell silent, and no one bothered to investigate.

When Roland had made himself decent once more, the promenade through the sleeping city was resumed, though at a languid pace now. Marina led the way through the passage with the shops into a narrow alley beyond, and between closed and dark shops, their windows displaying handbags and Venetian glass and other costly items to catch tourists. They passed a tiny square to the right with the inevitable sixteenth century church, which in answer to his question Marina said was called San Zulian.

Roland could think of three saints named Julian and a Saint Juliana. His guess was that the one commemorated here in Venice was the Julian who in a case of mistaken identity murdered his own mother and father and built a poorhouse by way of penance. At least he died of old age, not like the Julian who lived at Antioch and was thrown in the sea sewn up in a sack to drown. A far luckier man was the

Spanish Julian, who became Catholic to escape persecution as a Jew, and did it so thoroughly that they made him Bishop of Toledo.

Further on they came to another church on the left, very much bigger than Julian's, and turned into a square with a bronze statue in the middle. It was a man dressed in eighteenth century clothes, knee-breeches and stockings, long jacket and a three-cornered hat. Marina explained it was Carlo Goldoni, the famous Venetian dramatist who wrote scores of plays for local theatres about everyday life. Roland confessed he'd never heard of him, and Marina laughed and admitted she'd never been to a Goldoni play.

Two minutes later they came to the Grand Canal and the Rialto Bridge across it at its narrowest point. Roland had smiled over the description in the comic guidebook Carlo Missari presented to him:

One of the most precious peculiarities of Venice consists in the Rialto Bridge on the Grand Canal, most typical of the town and unique in the world through the centuries. The construction of this most famous bridge was commenced in 1588, the purpose to replace a wooden bridge from the earlier times. By then this previous structure was in a shaking condition and near to fall down. The Senate determined to build a bridge of stone, and in competition with many of the greatest of architectural experts, chose at last the design of Antonio da Ponte, which crosses the Grand Canal in one high arch, for the better preservation of navigation, and has shops along both the sides.

It seems to be holding out better than London Bridge, thought Roland, for that had been rebuilt three times in 800 years. The first time when a high tide washed the middle away, the second when half of it was burnt down, and the third during the reign of Queen Victoria, when time and tide had reduced it to *a shaking condition*.

The Rialto Bridge was humpbacked high enough to have broad steps all the way over between the facing rows of small shops. There were walkways behind the shops too, on the outside edge of the bridge, giving a fine view up and down the Grand Canal. Roland took Marina's arm and led her up the flat stone steps to the top of the arch, where they stood side by side and looked downstream over the dark water where only starlight glinted. The busy daytime boat traffic was gone, water-buses and barges, launches and gondolas.

Although he had twice made love to Marina in little more than an hour, Roland was obsessed by the thought of having her again here on the Rialto Bridge. Just as, he told himself, the famous James Boswell had a girl on Westminster Bridge on a Tuesday in May of 1763 – about the time Goldoni was scribbling his endless comedies of everyday Venetian life. Boswell put it in his diary – the diary he kept secret from Dr Johnson:

'. . . *at the bottom of the Haymarket I picked up a strong, jolly young damsel, and taking her under the arm I conducted her to Westminster Bridge, and then did I engage her on that noble edifice. The whim of doing it there with the Thames rolling below us amused me much . . .*'

To be honest with himself, Roland recognised that it was not a literary or historical parallel that drove him – the truth of it was that the Contessa Marina produced in him an intensity of physical desire that no other woman had before. After he had done it to her on the well-head he had been pleasantly satisfied – but by the time they reached the Piazza San Marco he was ravenous for her again. That time left him blissfully fatigued – and now he wanted her again on the bridge, and with a lustful ferocity that astonished him.

The stone parapet was rather more than waist-high. Roland put his hands on Marina's hips with gentle confidence and pressed her against the stonework, facing outwards. He moved close up behind her, until his loins were against her bottom.

'I'm sure we're being watched,' Marina said quietly. 'Do you mind if there are people down there in the shadows looking?'

'No one's about that I can see,' Roland assured her, 'and if there is, the most they can see is our heads and shoulders.'

His fingers were under her skirt, to raise it over her bottom so that he could stroke the smooth bare cheeks.

'You took the *elisir* before you came to meet me,' Marina said in a curious voice, 'you must have done, to be so hot for me – how did you manage to get hold of it?'

Roland did not bother to contradict her assumption. He undid his trousers and let his stiff *cazzo* leap out, quivering in joy at its sudden freedom. He laid it upright in the crease between the soft cheeks of Marina's bottom and pressed himself close to her, enjoying the feel of his hot flesh on her cool skin.

'Orlando,' she sighed, '*che bello!*'

The touch of his skin on her skin was so pleasant that Roland slid up and down gently against her rump, his hands underneath her long shawl and inside her undone blouse to stroke her bare breasts. Marina was rubbing her bottom against him, assisting his throbbing part to slide between her cheeks.

'It's so hot!' she whispered. 'Put it in.'

'In a moment, Marina!'

He reached down from her breasts to get his hands inside the waist-band of her skirt to her belly. She breathed in fast when his fingers moved into the join of her thighs – *Ah, Orlando* . . . she sighed, and he pressed himself closer to her round bottom, to let her feel how hard he was.

'Move your feet just a little further apart,' he murmured, his mouth touching her ear and her exotic perfume in his nostrils.

'Anytime!' she said.

Her feet moved far enough apart on the stone step for him to caress the moist split between her bare thighs.

'This is totally unreal!' she exclaimed softly, 'things like this happen in dreams, not in real life!'

Unreal or not, she arranged herself to lean forward over the bridge parapet with her naked bottom thrust out towards Roland. Her forearms lay on the balustrade, her body braced to receive and withstand his onslaught when it came.

'Do you often dream of making love?' Roland enquired, his curiosity aroused.

'Very often,' she said breathlessly.

'Will you tell me of your dreams, Marina?' he asked eagerly, caressing her *fica* with both hands, one from in front and the other from the rear. She was very wet now and her legs trembled a little.

'Yes . . .' she whispered, 'and you must make them become real.'

'Willingly,' he said, and took his throbbing part in his hand and guided it between her open thighs and up towards where they both wanted it to be. A long push took him inside, all the way till his belly was pressed tightly against her bottom.

He heard the fast-rising excitement in Marina's voice as she moaned his name over and over again, her bottom jerking insistently at him to encourage him to begin. His arms were about her, his hands up under her shawl to clasp her bare breasts and play with them while he rocked back and forth against her bare cheeks.

'Oh yes!' she murmured. 'Do it faster!'

She got her wish – third time it might be that night, but the strength of Roland's desire for her was undiminished. He rammed hard and fast, making her squeal in surprise, his hands crushed her breasts cruelly, and he spurted into her quaking belly.

'Yes – that's it!' she cried out. 'Yes, Orlando, more!'

His furious plunging brought on her own climax instantly. She wailed in ecstatic triumph, and shook so frenziedly her senses almost left her. Roland felt her knees beginning to sag and wrapped his arms tightly around her waist to hold her up while their mutual paroxysm of sensation ran on to its own natural and satisfactory ending.

When at last it was all over, Roland heard her draw in a long deep breath. She was still weak on her legs and he held her up.

'Marina, that was fantastic,' he said. 'You're wonderful!'

'And so are you,' she replied softly. 'How could I guess?'

Then he remembered what he had been told by Carlo Missari and chuckled as he recited the words:

Uno – a man tired out from his day's work
Due – a husband giving his wife her rights
Tre – a lover with his mistress.

'It rhymes in Italian,' Marina told him.

When they were ready to move on she said he had exhausted her completely and she couldn't walk back to the Palazzo Malvolio. Roland asked it there was an alternative, and she took him down the bridge the way they had come, on to the embankment that ran here along the Grand Canal. There was a deserted water-bus stop, where the little waves lapped against the wooden platform, and beside it lay several gondolas moored stern-on between poles.

'There's nobody here,' said Roland, 'the gondoliers are home in bed – it's half past three in the morning.'

'Maybe,' said Marina, and called out in Italian. There was

a stirring in one of the gondolas, and slowly a man sat upright and stretched.

'I've heard of an all-night taxi service in London, but this is ridiculous,' said Roland, handing Marina down into the narrow and bobbing boat. He and she settled themselves side by side on the bench, his arm about her waist, her head on his shoulder, and the gondolier pushed out from the side and turned skilfully to row down the Grand Canal, past the dark and silent palaces.

The voyage was not a very long one – by daylight the Palazzo Malvolio could just about be seen from the Rialto Bridge, where the canal began its final turn to the left at the foot of the figure 2 shape it made. Marina was silent all the way, cuddling against Roland contentedly. He too had little to say, delighted by the way his night-frolic had turned out.

'*Ca Malvolio, Signor*,' said the gondolier standing at his oar behind Roland, who didn't understand. Marina roused herself to explain that the Venetians for reasons unknown usually called a Palazzo a *casa* – a house, and shortened that to *Ca*. To Roland it seemed idiotic, but he said nothing, his attention fixed on the building towards which the gondola was turning.

Until now he had thought the landward entrance to the palace in the little square with the well was the main door. Now that he saw the Palazzo Malvolio from the Grand Canal side, he knew he had been wrong. This was the front entrance, and it was here the Malvolios of the great days arrived or left by gondola.

The high and imposing stone facade extended a long way, and in the centre was a tall arched doorway, flanked by Corinthian columns that supported a stone balcony the entire width of the building. Above those columns rose another tier in pairs, and a double tier again above that. Roland counted seven large double windows on each of the two upper floors, and realised that the palace was even larger than he had guessed from his two visits.

Along the front ran a broad stone landing-stage and a row of wooden pillars rose out of the canal, striped like a barber's pole, but half rotted away. Two gondolas and a motorboat were tied to them, the Malvolio family fleet for getting about town, presumably. There were no lights showing at any of the palace windows, nor did the great doors swing open when the gondolier held his dithery craft steady for Roland to hand Marina out of it. The fare he demanded for the late-night trip was exorbitant and after fierce haggling in what Roland took to be the typical Venetian vernacular, Marina got it reduced by a third.

'He thought we were tourists,' she explained as the muttering gondolier swept away from the landing-stage, 'and I had to set him straight.'

Roland was wondering how she planned to slip into the palace without disturbing anyone, but she was in no hurry to leave him and so bring their strange outing to an end. She leaned against the great black door and he stood close to her, holding her by the waist. He was taller than her by half a head and she stood on tiptoe to kiss him.

'*Uno, due, tre*,' she murmured. 'You are an interesting man, Orlando. Do you know what number four is?'

He thought for a moment and said, *Quattro – a priest hearing a nun's confession.*

'I'm no nun,' said Marina, 'but . . .'

There was no need to put the rest into words, for her hand felt his soft bulge through his trousers. Accepting the challenge, Roland glanced left and right and saw nothing but the Grand Canal stretching away empty in both directions. He slipped his hands under her shawl, unbuttoned her blouse and stroked her breasts gently.

'It is only fair to warn you that I am no priest,' he said to her in a rueful voice. 'The spirit is willing, but the flesh is weak after the third time, and I do not wish to disappoint your hopes.'

'There are other ways of giving pleasure,' she retorted.

At that, he lifted her skirt in front and felt between her bare thighs, above her stocking-tops. *Ah carissimo*, she murmured and a moment later the source of her pleasure was clasped in his palm. He pressed her head back against the palace door with his mouth on hers in a long kiss and behind his closed eyes his vivid imagination had full play and excited him with images of Marina naked and turning backward somersaults through a hoop.

The images were so arousing that with the tip of his tongue he licked round her lips – and in his fantasy it was not her mouth that his tongue touched but the soft lips under her dark-brown curls while she doubled over backwards to go through the big hoops. He slipped his tongue inside her hot mouth, and she fluttered her tongue against his.

He was completely engrossed in his erotic reverie while his fingers teased Marina towards a delicious climax, and he hardly noticed when she unbuttoned his trousers and slipped a hand in to take hold of his half-hard part. She handled it tenderly, so that Roland was aware not of what she did to him but of gently increasing waves of delight.

'*Orlando mio*,' she sighed, 'you are a very special person – no one has ever given me half the pleasure you have.'

'And I've never wanted anyone as much as I want you,' said he by way of returning her compliment, and he at least was telling the truth, though whether Marina was he was unable to guess.

'Then I am yours for as long as you will!' she gasped out as her climactic moment arrived and she rubbed herself against his fingers in ecstasy.

'Marina!' he exclaimed feverishly.

She had his *cazzo* out of his trousers now and rubbed briskly to make it grow to its full length and thickness, then put the engorged head to the wet fleshy lips between her thighs. Roland put his hands on her shoulders and stood still, his breathing fast and irregular as her hand slid up and down to rub the head of his eager shaft against her slippery button.

'Does that feel nice?' she asked with a chuckle. 'Answer me a question, Orlando, are you having me or am I having you?'

What she was doing to him raised him to such a high pitch of arousal that he was unable to remain passive. He reached under her skirt with both hands to sink his fingers into the flesh of her hips and hold her fast, and with a tremendous push he drove his stiffness through her clasping hand and deep into her. She laughed and rammed her belly against his in triumph.

Roland's hands moved round to clasp the cheeks of her bottom while he drove in and out of her, and she pushed herself harder still against him. His mind in a delirium of pleasure, Roland parted the bare cheeks under her raised skirt and pressed his middle fingertip into the tight little node between them.

Marina squealed faintly and bumped her belly at him faster – and each time she jerked forward she felt his hardness slither into her in front, and every time she pulled back, she forced his finger in a little deeper behind. These double sensations overwhelmed her quickly, and she shook against him in climactic spasms. Roland cried out to feel her uncontrollable trembling and released his passion into her – a few drops now rather than a flood, but the very intensity of his sensations stunned him into near-unconsciousness.

When they came to themselves again Marina did up his trouser buttons for him and showed him the way round the Palazzo to the little square with the well and kissed him goodnight. Roland thanked her for the *Carnival in Venice*, and when she asked what he meant, he promised to tell her next time they met.

SEVEN

It seemed very odd to Roland to receive yet another letter from Mrs Tandy asking him to call on her at the Palazzo Malvolio yet that is what transpired the next day. He had still to learn that nothing is ever as it seems in Italy. He was weary by the time he reached his hotel after his all-night romp with Marina round the major tourist sights of Venice and collapsed into bed at about four thirty in the morning, with the *Non Disturbare* sign hung out on his door. He slept well into the afternoon and woke ravenously hungry.

It was too late for lunch anywhere, but on his travels he had noticed a sort of snack bar on the way to San Marco. It was not far from the restaurant where Adalbert Gmund took him for lunch before their visit to Signorina Caducci to be thrashed. Going out of the square there was a bridge over a narrow canal and on the corner on the far side stood the snack bar – a tiny place with standing room for six or seven people between the counter and the door. Roland's guess was that tourists found it a handy stop on their endless strolling round the city, and so it would be open during the siesta.

He was right, and soon relieved his pangs of hunger with a foot-long sandwich of hard and crusty bread stuffed with slices of salami, cheese, tomato and onion, helped down by a glass of Italian beer – a drink he never knew existed until this moment. Afterwards he made his way back slowly to his hotel to shower and shave and change his clothes. He was slightly uneasy at the thought that he had lost another day of studying the Accademia paintings. On the other hand, to have a Contessa by night on the Rialto Bridge was a unique event, and not all the pictures in Venice could outweigh it.

At the reception desk of the Hotel Gallini a letter awaited him – a large envelope with the coat of arms he recognised. Why Mrs Tandy wanted him to call on her the next morning, he found hard to guess. It had something to do with Marina, that seemed sure enough, but what? If her all-night absence had been reported to the Count, the result would not be a polite letter from her sister but a nasty confrontation with her husband. If there was a telephone in the Palazzo Roland could have called her to ask what was going on, but as there was no such modern contraption, he had little choice but to wait and see.

A question which insisted on asking itself in his mind was if Mrs Tandy had a regular lover. From his personal experience of Marina's activities he was certain that she formed intense but brief friendships with whoever was available and suitable, and that he himself was only the latest in a long line of young men chosen to assuage her passions. But from talking to Mrs Tandy over lunch when he had been invited to the Palazzo, Roland had come to an altogether different view of the elder sister.

Whereas Marina played at being completely modern in outlook, with short skirts and short hair, Mrs Tandy made no concessions to modernity that Roland had observed. She was every inch the Edwardian Lady, and though the calendar might give the year as 1927, in Mrs Tandy's estimation it seemed to be 1907, and she still a beautiful and rich young married woman.

When Roland first met Adalbert Gmund, the displaced Austrian, he had taken him to be Mrs Tandy's lover, living at the palace and obliging her on request. The subsequent visit with him to Renata Caducci's apartment to be whipped had put paid to that idea. Roland recalled vividly the beatific smile on Adalbert's face when he came out of the bedroom, limping slightly, and his babble that Renata *makes me very happy, I worship her – I kiss her feet!* Adalbert's dream of bliss was to bend over with his trousers pulled down while Renata thrashed his bare backside until she made his lust spurt out into a towel.

That disqualified him as Mrs Tandy's beau. Roland assumed she maintained the attitudes of her youth towards love-making – the attitude that had persuaded her to abscond from her husband and set up home in Venice with the last of the Malvolio. He thought of her as a well-bred mare, wanting to be mastered and ridden. She would not be interested in Adalbert's need to be dominated, and it was utterly impossible to imagine her wielding the whip on his bottom to gratify him. There was a faint possibility she might let someone she respected thrash her bare bottom, Roland thought, but he would have to demonstrate his masterful nature first in more orthodox love-making.

This train of thought led Roland on to a consideration of how it would be to make love to Delphine Tandy – good, indifferent or superb. There was none of the modern thinness about her, the strange urge girls had to flatten their breasts and make their hips and rump disappear. Mrs Tandy was well-fleshed, in the way of Edwardian ladies, with generous size breasts and a delicious plumpness about her rear and her belly.

To get Delphine naked and on her back might be a very worthwhile and rewarding experience, Roland concluded, although the chance of that was minuscule while he was deeply involved with Marina. Nevertheless, it was a pleasant enough thought to doze off with when he decided to rest again for the remainder of the afternoon.

About six that evening Carlo Missari came unexpectedly to the hotel, to enquire if all was well, two days having passed since Roland had put in an appearance at the Accademia Gallery. Were the arrangements to study the pictures not to his satisfaction? Or was Roland not feeling well, perhaps? Or had he completed his work? Over a cool drink Roland gave him an edited version of his recent escapades.

'*Santa Maria!*' said Carlo, his eyebrows high up his forehead in amazement. 'The guide-books say Venice offers a great variety of interests to delight the tourists and it possesses a unique charm that never fails to captivate the hearts of all who come here – but I never believed that until now. You should light a candle for San Marco to thank him for the good fortune he has sent you in this city.'

'A strange thought,' said Roland, 'the familiarity with which you treat your saints would horrify an English parson. But if I have found something new in Venice, I have also lost something I valued.'

'What thing is that? Your innocence, perhaps?' Carlo asked with a grin of disbelief.

'No, something more useful than that. I came to Venice to see the early Renaissance paintings for the book I am writing – and after only a few days here I no longer care whether I write the book or not. I've lost my belief in its relevance.'

'*Diavolo!* That's a serious matter, Roland. It affects your career. A *Professore* must write books to make his reputation grow bigger, so that he is offered more important positions. To write nothing is to remain unknown and of no significance.'

'I am not a *Professore*,' Roland reminded him, 'only a humble lecturer.'

'*Umble?* What does it mean, this umble? I do not understand this word.'

'Modest,' Roland elucidated for him.

'Pfft! Why do you have to be modest?' Carlo demanded, 'you from the University of Londra! Ah, if we could change places with each other – you to stay here in Venice and look after old paintings and *chiavare* as many women as you like, and I to have your salary for teaching about Italian artists and enjoy myself in England!'

'You'd leave Venice? But you'd find London cold and ugly and not at all *simpatico* after Italy, I assure you.'

'This Venice that your writers and critics describe, it is a dream of theirs,' said Carlo, shaking his head. 'They look at the paintings of Canaletto and Guardi – the Grand Canal and San Marco and the Rialto Bridge and San Giorgio by the moonlight, and they say *Che bello* and *How wonderful* and *How picturesque it is! How marvellous it is to live among all this magnificence!* But this is dreaming. The truth of Venice is what you have seen at the Palazzo Malvolio – people living in a big old house that was built long ago. Much pride and little money. Plenty of past and no future.'

'Have another drink,' Roland urged. 'There are compensations, surely, to offset the discontentments?'

'Some, perhaps,' the other conceded with a wry grin, 'the sun shines every day almost and the wine is cheap. What else could we possibly want? If you do not believe any more the theory of Power being the theme of early Renaissance art, then perhaps I shall write the book instead of you, and make myself so famous that I shall be offered a post as *Professore* at the University of Harvard in America for half a million lira a year.'

'That's a very good plan, Carlo. Do it with my blessing.'

'I shall buy a big fast automobile – a Chrysler painted the scarlet of blood – and drive at one hundred kilometres an hour or more from Boston to New York – with a young blonde girl beside me to hold a bottle of whisky while I drink.'

'My word – what unexpected ambitions lurk in the soul of

an assistant curator!' said Roland with a broad smile. 'What else will the young blonde hold during this wild drive?'

'That is an important question,' said Carlo, 'and it raises another question – what are we to do this evening? Or are you too fatigued from your tour of Venice by night to do more than sit in the Piazza and talk?'

'I've been sleeping most of the day and I'm fully recovered. What do you have in mind? A visit to Signora Ricci's house to see Sofia and Marcella again?'

'No, Venice has other entertainments beside girls. There is a concert of Vivaldi's music this evening in his own church. Do you like his music?'

'I've only ever heard the piece everyone knows by him – *The Four Seasons*. Did he have a church of his own then?'

'He was *Direttore* of music at the orphanage for girls at the church of Santa Maria della Pieta. He taught the orphans music and singing. He was a priest there for many years and his music is performed in the church often.'

If the truth were told, Roland was relieved to accept Carlo's invitation to an entertainment less strenuous than Marcella and Sofia provided at Signora Ricci's apartment. The two men ate a light dinner together at a little restaurant near the hotel and strolled to the Grand Canal to catch the *vaporetto*. The evening was warm and light and it was a pleasure to stand on the boat's foredeck and admire the architecture of the palaces that lined the canal on either bank.

Roland recognised the Palazzo Malvolio coming up on the left as the water-bus chugged along and was in no doubt now that this was the main entrance, not the landward side, imposing though that was too. There was a boatman in the Malvolio colours on the stone landing-stage, doing something to a motorlaunch tied up beside a gondola. Two gondolas had been moored there when he took Marina home at four in the morning – evidently some of the family had gone out for the evening.

There were the steps up to the imposing doorway, and that, he told himself as the water-bus went past, that was the very spot where he had stood the Contessa against the palace wall and had her. It was an interesting thought and he decided to look about the next day for an illustrated guide to Venice with pictures of the Grand Canal and palaces, as a remembrance of the night.

The *vaporetto* came alongside the Accademia stop, where

Roland felt very uneasy about his dereliction of duty. He wondered if his interest in his projected book on early Renaissance art was ever going to revive. Then the boat cast off and steamed under the Accademia bridge, making for the white-domed Salute church and then the stop for the Piazza San Marco.

They disembarked at the stop after San Marco and were part of the evening crowd promenading along the broad quay called the Riva – the only long walk possible in Venice – half a mile by the waterside from the Piazza to the Arsenal. Santa Maria della Pieta was not far along, a small white-fronted church in eighteenth century classical style, four columns sustaining the portico, a bas-relief over the door of St Mary herself. A moment's thought made Roland realise that the church must have been newly built when Vivaldi went there to teach the orphans music.

'You say you have heard one concerto by Vivaldi,' said Carlo as they went into the church and found seats in rows of chairs set out for the audience, 'but he wrote more than five hundred concertos like that.'

'I never knew that.'

'Or else,' said Carlo, 'he wrote the same concerto five hundred times. No one can tell you this, because no one has ever heard all of them played.'

'How did he find time to compose so much music and teach as well?' asked Roland. 'Did he get up early in the mornings?'

'In addition to the concertos he also composed forty-six operas and some cantatas,' said Carlo. 'My theory is that he never went to bed at all.'

When Roland arrived at the Palazzo Malvolio the next morning for his meeting with Mrs Tandy, a footman informed him that the Signora Tandy waited for him in the *Biblioteca* and led him up the marble staircase and through the whole length of the palace to the Library. On his previous visit he had been shown the small painting surrounded by floor to ceiling leather-bound books with the Malvolio coat of arms embossed in gold on the spine – the picture of the man with a beard lying on the grass beside a horse, as if he had fallen off dead.

Delphine Tandy, looking cool and self-possessed in ivory silk and pearls, was sitting at an antique desk of dark walnut which obviously dated from the seventeenth century and was therefore older than the Palazzo Malvolio. Perhaps it had been saved when fire destroyed the first palace. She rose to her feet and came round the desk holding out her hand to Roland, who was so impressed by her magnificent appearance that he kissed it theatrically.

Her green-grey eyes regarded him with mild amusement, and she invited him to sit down. Two antique chairs inlaid with mother of pearl stood together, and when Roland seated himself on one, Delphine took the other instead of going back behind the desk – a friendly gesture that put Roland at his ease and fired in him an optimism that even if she had summoned him to berate him for his antics with her married sister, the interview was not going to be too awful. After all, Marina's private amusements could be no secret to Delphine after so many years living under the same roof.

She had hardly time to ask Roland if he was enjoying his stay in Venice before the door opened to admit a whole procession of people – Adalbert Gmund in a green suit in out-of-date pre-War style, Padre Pio in his shabby black cassock, and a footman in faded yellow-and-blue Malvolio livery with a heavy silver tray. He placed it on the desk and poured coffee for all while hands were being shaken and greetings exchanged.

When they were all settled again, Roland and Delphine side by side in the inlaid chairs, Adalbert on the chair behind the big desk and the fat little priest standing, cup in hand, by the long windows to the balcony, there began a curious conversation – the oddest Roland had ever taken part in. Delphine Tandy took the lead by asking him how he was getting on with his research at the Accademia Gallery.

'Very well,' said Roland, not prepared to admit that he had lost interest in the themes of early Renaissance painting.

'I'm so glad,' said Delphine, 'because I have something to talk to you about. When you were here for lunch the other day I mentioned that we had a few very early pictures, and we showed you all we could remember.'

'Two paintings and a carving,' said Roland, feeling a vague need to be specific about the works of art, though not what he had done to Marina alongside the Noah's Ark carving. 'They are very fine, all of them.'

'Yes. Well, since then, I've had a word with Padre Pio about the early works in the Malvolio collection. He tells me we have far more than three – he thinks at least a dozen and perhaps as many as twenty, including at least one Cimbue and a couple by Duccio. Is that right, Padre Pio?'

'*Si, Signora*,' said the priest, 'and do not forget Pisano.'

'Then you've a better collection than the Accademia,' Roland said, feeling impressed. 'It would be a privilege to see them.'

'Exactly my own thought!' said Delphine, smiling graciously at him. 'It would help you with your book, and it would help me too, if you spent some time looking at these early pictures.'

Roland said he'd be delighted to help her in any way he could but he was an academic, not a fine-art dealer, and he could not give any useful assessment of sale-room value.

'You misunderstand me,' said she, gesturing at the footman to refill the coffee cups. 'The position is this – besides being family chaplain, dear Padre Pio is Keeper of the Archive and has been for the last fifty years or so, for which we are much in his debt and enormously grateful to him.'

The tubby priest bowed towards Mrs Tandy on hearing his name spoken, and pushed his gold-rimmed glasses higher on his nose.

'But Padre Pio was never trained in the appreciation of art,' Delphine went on. 'Though he knows exactly where to find every picture in the Palazzo and can check the date on which it was bought and how much was paid for it ...'

'Can he really!' said Roland, highly impressed now.

'... he feels incapable of forming opinions on the merits of the pictures,' Delphine continued, 'so you see my problem.'

Truth to tell, Roland did not see what the problem was, but a strong and curious undercurrent was making itself felt in what Delphine was saying. He remained silent for a moment, trying to make sense of what was going on.

'As you know already,' said Adalbert Gmund in his accented English, 'I am in my way a connoisseur of Italian painting, and by no means to be considered an amateur in these matters. But I am not able in questions of disputed attribution to resolve any doubtfulness beyond question, as I am sure that you would.'

'It would be my pleasure to assist in any way possible,' said Roland, addressing himself to Delphine Tandy and wondering just what she wanted him to do. 'But if you have as many as twenty works of art from this very early period, it would take a long time to give them the attention required.

I am pretty well done at the Accademia, and there are half a dozen other pictures for me to see in various churches about Venice. It was my intention to leave for England in two or three days time.'

'I do hope we can persuade you to extend your stay,' Delphine said in the friendliest possible way. 'Naturally, we don't want you to be out of pocket over this – why don't you move into the Palazzo Malvolio as my guest for a week or two while you have a good look at the collection?'

'*Ja, ja,*' said Adalbert in support of her suggestion, and the priest over by the windows chimed in with a cheerful '*Si, si.*'

'Stay for lunch while you think it over,' Delphine said, her hand resting lightly on his wrist for a moment. 'My sister will be back by then and she can help us persuade you to move in for a while and give us the benefit of your expert knowledge.'

For some time past Roland had been quite aware that they were not talking about art, whatever the words said. It was plain to him now that all this was a scheme by Marina to get him within easy reach, and she had put her sister up to this preposterous plot with the paintings. The night of tourism with him must have had a strong effect on Marina and she would go to extreme lengths to have him available. If her husband was as jealous as she claimed, the idea was ridiculously dangerous.

On the other hand, he had never believed more than a fraction of Marina's blood-curdling tales of husbandly vengeance – they seemed much too much like novelette stories of Corsican bandits and Sicilian assassinations. It was all very well in Mascagni's opera for the baritone to stab Turiddu to death for rollicking with Lola, but it was impossible to cast sauve Count Massimo in the role of avenging Sicilian husband.

And yet . . . could it be that simple? Mrs Tandy must know very well the risks being run. The very least to be expected if the Count became suspicious was a screaming row. Was she so devoted to her sister that she thought the danger of family upset worthwhile? Roland reached the conclusion that there was more going on than met the eye, and that he was being used in a scheme far above his head to understand. It was asking for trouble to let himself be used, but the idea of being a guest in a magnificently shabby old Venetian palace full of priceless paintings, statues and bronzes, beside the Grand Canal, was irresistible.

Contessa Marina was back from wherever she had been in time for lunch, though not her husband. She congratulated Delphine on persuading Roland to stay on in Venice and examine her early Renaissance paintings, and she did it as calmly as if his stay in the palace was nothing at all to do with her. Over the food and wine in the Small Dining Room, Roland promised himself that he would insist on hearing the answers to a number of questions when he got Marina alone.

No sooner had he accepted Delphine Tandy's invitation to move into the Palazzo Malvolio than the arrangements were taken out of his hands. A maidservant and a footman were despatched to the Hotel Gallini, she to pack Roland's belongings and he to carry the bags back to the palace, and all this while lunch was still in progress. By half past two, when the coffee and fruit were finished and the hour for the siesta had arrived, Roland was shown by another liveried footman to a room in the palace, to find his clothes hanging in the superbly carved wardrobe and his razor in the adjoining bathroom.

On the dressing table lay a Hotel Gallini envelope addressed to him in a florid hand, containing an excessively polite note from the management having the honour to enclose their account for his stay in the hotel and expressing a wish that the Signor Thontron would settle it at his convenience. Roland assumed his move into the Palazzo Malvolio had conferred on him prestige so impressive that a hotel was trusting him to pay the bill before he left Venice.

In fairness to his hostess, he felt he ought to make a start on examining the early Renaissance works of art scattered about the salons and corridors of the palace, but the only person who knew where to locate particular items was, it seemed, Padre Pio the Keeper of the Archive. Roland had no idea where to find him and felt sure that the fat little priest was by now asleep and incommunicado for the rest of the afternoon.

Before he had finally decided to start exploring the palace on his own, a different decision was made for him. Without any attempt at a knock, the door of his room was opened and in came Marina. She turned the key twice in the lock behind her before crossing the room to throw herself into Roland's arms and press her belly against his. He kissed her for some time, then pulled back half a step to get his hands between them and unbutton her white silk blouse and feel her breasts down the top of her low-cut slip.

She meanwhile opened the waist of her red and grey striped skirt and let it slide down her legs. Roland saw that what he had taken to be a slip was pale pink camiknickers, cut close to Marina's body, with the letter M embroidered in dark red on her left breast. Not that it was a suitable time to admire Marina's expensive underwear – she had the tiny buttons between her legs undone in a second and Roland gently pulled the stylish garment over her head and felt her bare breasts with both eager hands. She kissed his mouth briefly and stepped away from him to take off her silk stockings.

For this manoeuvre she turned deliberately away from him to reveal her bare bottom. Roland stepped close to her and fondled the satin-skinned cheeks presented to him, and she wiggled her hips provocatively when his fingers touched the fleshy apricot between her thighs and drew his fingers along the split in it. But Marina was too aroused to let him play with her for long – she stepped away from him again to throw back the bedcover and stretch herself out on her back on the sheets.

Roland stared at her with hungry eyes for a moment – taking in her plump breasts, her broad and welcoming belly, the neat triangle of dark-brown curls between her well-rounded thighs – before ripping off all his clothes. Then he was on the bed and she turned on her side to face him as his arms went round her and he kissed her again, his tongue in her mouth to caress her tongue. But Marina was not in the mood that afternoon for long and tender love-making – her hand gripped his iron-hard *cazzo* tightly and massaged it to urge him into immediate action.

From the first time he had set eyes on her, sitting at a cafe in the Piazza San Marco, all Roland's male desires had insisted that Marina was a fully ripe and luscious fruit, bursting with sweetness and ready to be tasted. It was not so much a question of *making love* to Marina as *having* her, devouring her, gulping her down whole. And she was more than ready to give her body to his appetite – she rolled on her back and pulled him strongly towards her by his throbbing stiffness. Her legs were wide open to receive him, and Roland was in a delirium of sensation when he slid over her and felt her warm belly under his own.

Her tightly clasping hand guided him quickly into her, and

she was as slippery and ready to be pierced as if he had been playing with her for ten minutes. His hands kneaded her soft breasts as he thrust deep into her. Marina began to pant with delight and jerk under him, her arms round his neck and her head lifting up off the pillow to slide her tongue into his mouth in imitation of the way his hard flesh was sliding in and out of her *fica*.

'*Orlando, Orlando,*' she moaned, her legs as far apart as they would go, so that she lay spread-eagled beneath him in frantic desire. Her hot belly heaved under Roland's, matching the tempo of his furious plunging. Then her repetition of his name turned into a crescendo of small broken whimpers and she arched her back up off the bed as an intense sexual climax gripped her.

Roland stabbed fiercely into her belly, feeling her squirming beneath him and crying out in her ecstasy. She was too far gone to know what she was doing, but her belly and hips were jerking up to meet his hard strokes and his hands were under her bottom to grasp her fleshy cheeks and assist her upward movements. He could hear his belly smacking on hers, and then his own panting drowned it out.

They had both reached the point where their bodies and minds alike cried out for release from the intolerable intensity of their sensations. When the release came at last, it was as if a giant bomb had detonated under the bed and destroyed them both. Roland shrieked as he spurted his hot lust into her, and Marina echoed his shriek loudly and collapsed semi-conscious under his bucking body.

When after some time they regained the power of speech, they found their bellies stuck clammily together with mingled sweat, and a delicious lassitude in all their limbs. Roland slid off Marina and lay beside her, while she smiled at him contentedly and sad it had been *stupendo* and he had completely destroyed her. They lay resting in each other's arms, half dozing, until something occurred to Roland.

'Marina, you remember when I made love to you on the Rialto Bridge . . .'

'I shall never forget it,' she murmured lazily.

'While we were standing there you told me you often dream of making love – remember that?'

'Of course I do. Mad, wonderful, exciting dreams – that's why I said it to you on the bridge, because we were doing something mad and wonderful then.'

'You promised to tell me your dreams,' Roland reminded her, an arm over her waist to stroke her back and bottom slowly. 'So tell me now – did you dream that night after I left you?'

'Nothing I can remember, but I slept so soundly after being ravished all round Venice that anything could have happened. My dreams repeat themselves quite often, you know, and sometimes I have the same dream twice in one night.'

'That *is* unusual,' said Roland, 'at least, I've never heard of it before. Tell me one of these repeating dreams of yours – an exciting one.'

'They're all exciting,' said Marina, 'or I'd never bother to dream them. I'll tell you one of my favourites if you like, one I've had for years on and off. It must be based on something or other that happened when I was a girl, though to be truthful I can't think what.'

'A very young girl? Or a nearly grown-up girl?'

'Oh, about eighteen, I would think. In the dream I'm on a train, an express train travelling very fast and it's dark outside so I can't see the countryside to tell where I am. The First Class compartment seats are upholstered in leather of some sort which feels hot and uncomfortable under my bottom. I'm wearing a thin summer dress down to my ankles and a straw hat, so it's before the war.'

'Fast trains and pounding pistons,' said Roland. 'Very suitable.'

'I can feel the leather seat through my dress,' Marina went on, 'and so I know I'm not wearing knickers. I try to think why and remember taking them off in the dining-car to hand to the waiter when he put his hand down my dress to find out if I wanted chicken breast or thigh. Anyway, there are three men in the compartment with me, and there's a Reserved sign stuck on the door to the corridor.'

'Young men? Old men?' Roland asked. 'Anyone you know?'

'No, they're all strangers to me. The man sitting opposite is good-looking and fair-haired and I want to ask him if the next stop will be Didcombe Junction, which is where I'm going, so to attract his attention I open my legs and pull my dress right up to my middle. He's too busy talking to the man next to him to look at me until I climb on his lap and sit astride him with my dress up round my waist.'

'A young lady across his lap with no knickers on ought even in a dream to get his attention,' said Roland with a smile, his hand kneading the cheeks of Marina's bottom, 'but does it?'

'Oh yes – he raises his hat and asks my name and tells me his is Maurice. I undo his trousers and pull out his *cazzo* and it's very long but soft as boiled spaghetti. I tell him he's being impolite and rub it up and down to make him take an interest in me, but he doesn't seem very interested, even after I've made him stiff as a poker.'

'This is turning into a dream of disappointment,' Roland said thoughtfully, 'but you said it was one of your favourites. How can that be?'

'There's more to it,' said she, her hand between his legs to play with his own limp part. 'While I'm trying to make Maurice respond, I glance round the compartment at the other men to see if they're interested. They've both pulled out their own bishops and are rubbing them furiously while they stare at me. It gives me a warm feeling between my thighs to know they want me and I tell them they can do me after I'd finished with Maurice.'

'Nothing like this has ever happened to me on a train,' said Roland ruefully, 'not even on the Brighton line. Do they have you, these strange men?'

'They start shouting at me to forget about Maurice and lie on the seat and have them one after the other. I become so excited by their frantic lust for me that I reach my climax – not just once but again and again, with hardly a pause between. It's too much for the men playing with themselves and they both shoot off at the same time and spray my thighs.'

'And you wake up then, I suppose?'

'No, there's still a bit more. When Maurice sees the cream running down my bare thighs he says, *You won't get that from me* but I know he's wrong. I lick my fingertips and put them in his ears and push my tongue into his mouth, and he slides into me and squirts off like a hose pipe inside me. Then I wake up.'

'Wet and excited, no doubt?'

'Wet and satisfied, because I've climaxed eight or nine times in the dream,' said Marina, and her manipulating fingers had by then teased Roland's part to ready stiffness.

'Oh,' said he, surprised, 'I didn't know that women can reach release in dreams.'

'You've a lot to learn about women,' said Marina, 'and I mean to teach you while you're here. You *are* clever, *Orlando mio*, to think of a way of getting Delphine to invite you to stay in the palace. I was absolutely thrilled when she announced it – how did you do it?'

'What?' Roland exclaimed, sitting up on the bed like a released Jack-in-the-Box. 'It was you persuaded her, not me – what are you saying?'

'Me, darling? I had nothing to do with it. I was astounded, besides being delighted, because Delphine knows what Massimo is like when other men are near me. Especially a handsome and virile young man like you.'

'There is more to this than meets the eye,' said Roland. 'If you didn't persuade your sister to invite me to stay, and I had nothing to do with it, obviously she has some reason of her own for wanting me here. And I don't believe this excuse of looking at paintings in the Malvolio collection for her – that's only camouflage. What can her reason be, Marina?'

'Who cares, *carissimo*?' said she, and sat up beside him to put an arm round his shoulders. 'You know what they say about gift horses. Why don't we simply enjoy this marvellous chance of being together? Whatever Delphine has in mind, you'll find out when she wants you to.'

'I don't like to think I'm being used,' said Roland.

'Why not, darling, if it's fun? I'm going to use you now, if you'll let me . . . and I promise you'll love it.'

Marina's hands on his shoulders pressed him backwards until he was stretched out flat on the bed and her busy hand between his thighs restored the full stiffness his surprise had caused him to half lose. When she had him straining hard upwards she threw a leg over him and sat with her knees either side of his waist and her wet split positioned to accept him.

'You used me for your own fun on the well in the square,' she told him, 'and halfway round Venice! Not to mention having me with my back to the palace wall where anyone on the canal could see us. Now it's my turn to use you.'

Roland watched the little smile of concentration on Marina's face while she steered his stiff six inches into herself. When she had him completely embedded, she rode up and down with slow deliberation. The sensation of her wet and tender flesh sliding on him brought his *cazzo* up thicker and harder and sent throbs of pleasure through his belly.

Marina was staring down at him through half-closed eyes, her face a bright pink as she, like Roland, moved irrevocably towards a climactic release of desire. Her movements speeded up until she was bouncing on his belly frantically and the antique bed set up a rhythmic creak beneath them. Roland felt his belly clench tight as a fist and then his lust came spurting from him in hard spasms. Marina's eyes opened wide in a glassy stare of ecstatic sensation. She was moaning and crying in her climactic passion, her sharp fingernails digging fiercely into the flesh of Roland's belly.

Afterwards he lay still beneath her, looking up into Marina's flushed face. She sat slumped forward in satisfaction, her bare breasts hanging heavily, as if they too had been gratified and were resting comfortably. She smiled down at him and promised she'd make him happier than he'd ever been in his life. But in Roland's mind was the nagging conviction that he'd been trapped into a family feud he didn't understand.

EIGHT

Happily there was time for an hour's refreshing sleep after the Contessa Marina left Roland on his bed and before he needed to bath and dress for dinner. The chambermaid assigned to looking after his room and clothes spoke no English and understood very little, but she managed to convey to him by extravagant gesture and pantomime that in his honour dinner that evening would be in the *Grande* dining room, and that everyone would be in the anteroom to drink at seven thirty.

When it came to explaining to him how to get to the anteroom from where he was, even her ingenuity proved inadequate. Roland offered her pencil and paper to draw him a map of the Palazzo, but she was unfamiliar with the concept of maps and what she drew, after much puzzled head-scratching with the blunt end of the pencil, was no more than a box with squiggles inside it. The problem was resolved by taking him there, and he carefully noted the route for his return journey – the stairs and long passages and turns.

The anteroom, when he reached it, was a large square room in which hung twenty or thirty portraits of Malvolios – a sort of family album. Some were life-size oil paintings, some pastels, some watercolours and some, mainly of children, were pencil or pen-and-ink sketches. The variety of clothing showed the spread over four centuries, the earliest being a thin-nosed Malvolio in a white brocade robe and Doge's cap, and the latest being Count Rinaldo Malvolio, the last of the line, in Italian army uniform, festooned with medals, decorations and awards.

The room was large enough for a dozen Empire-style chairs and two settees, each long enough to seat four people, and not be in the least crowded. The furniture had a scuffed and well-used look about it, as well it might after so many generations had sat on it. A footman stood either side of the open double door, doing nothing discernible beyond looking decorative, and they bowed simultaneously to Roland as he passed between them.

Delphine Tandy was in pale lemon chiffon, her shoulders bare and a double strand of pearls round her neck. Marina was beside her, talking away busily, and wearing a shorter and more daring evening frock than her sister's. It reached her knees, but only just, and was almost backless. But the most striking feature – the thing that could not fail to catch the eye and set the mind racing – was the beadwork pattern that swirled round under the bosom and concentrated itself into an upright oval about where Marina's belly-button would be.

Determined to be Continental, suave and gallant, Roland made a point of kissing the hand of both ladies, and was smiled upon graciously in return. Not so by Marina's husband, however, for on Count Massimo's face was a look of haughty distaste when he nodded to Roland and touched fingers in a parody of a handshake. By contrast, Adalbert Gmund in his comically out-dated evening attire was over-hearty and welcoming, as if thoroughly enjoying the Count's ill-humour.

Padre Pio was decked out with a large pectoral cross of solid gold set with blood-red jewels – obviously lent to him for the occasion from the Malvolio treasures. It dangled on a very long chain of gold links, and he being both short and portly was in constant danger of injury to himself or anyone close by when he moved sharply and the heavy cross swung like the clapper of a church bell. He greeted Roland affably and he was the only one present, in Roland's book, without hidden feelings about him.

Like a figure from a forgotten comic opera, the major-domo Luigi exerted his silent authority over the proceedings. He had positioned himself with his back to the least interesting wall, seemingly out of sight and out of mind, but following with his eyes every move made by the liveried footmen serving drinks to the family, missing nothing, and probably hearing four separate conversations at the same time and storing anything of interest for future consideration. Roland glanced at him and nodded, and the major-domo's face remained so totally impassive that Roland was sure he knew that he'd made love to Marina that afternoon – and probably how many times.

That being so, Marina carefully kept away from Roland after the first greeting. She went over by the long windows and stood talking to Adalbert, and then crossed the room to discuss with Padre Pio something of the first importance, judging by the way she concentrated on the fat little priest and kept herself from looking in the direction of Roland, who remained by Delphine's chair and chatted while he observed the domestic comedy being played out over the drinks.

Count Massimo was a veritable fashion-plate of elegance in a tight-waisted dinner jacket that displayed how excellently he'd kept his figure into his fifties – broad in the shoulder, flat of belly, his face massaged smooth and pink, his silver hair waved to perfection, his pencil-line moustache superior to anything Rudolf Valentino or John Gilbert boasted. Not that Massimo had the least desire to tickle a lady's fancy with it, according to what Roland had been told, but perhaps beautiful young men also found it attractive.

The Count clearly did not want to converse with anyone at all just then, though good manners required it of him, and it was very clear indeed that he did not want to talk to his wife. He hurled a few words at Padre Pio, making the priest shake his head and finger his jewel-studded crucifix as if in search of divine protection. When Marina moved away from Adalbert Gmund, the Count strode across the room to exchange words with him. From his agitation of mind Roland concluded that Count Massimo had been told just before coming down to dinner that the young Englishman had been asked to stay in the palace to look at the pictures.

Wherever he was in the room, whoever he was talking to, the Count kept his eyes on Marina, as if he expected her to betray her guilty passion by throwing her arms round Roland's neck and kissing him in front of everyone. Naturally, she kept well away from him, and gave a studied impression of being engrossed in conversation with others and hardly aware that the newcomer was present. Roland glanced from Marina's bare back to Mrs Tandy's face and saw there a smile of sardonic amusement at the antics of her sister and the Count.

'What do you think of Venice, now you've been here a day or two, Dr Thornton?' Mrs Tandy enquired politely, to draw his attention away from the conjugal discord.

'I'm stunned by it,' he said, and he was thinking as much

of the pleasure he'd enjoyed with the Contessa and with the girls at Signora Ricci's as of the intellectual delights of paintings and architecture. And before his hostess could question further to see what lay behind his comment, he began to recite:

> In Venice Tasso's echoes are no more,
> And silent rows the songless gondolier;
> The palaces are crumbling to the shore,
> And music meets not always now the ear;
> Those days are gone – but Beauty still is here.

'Ah yes,' said Mrs Tandy, 'Shelley, I suppose, a melancholy reflection on the decay of Venice. He came here a year or two after the Battle of Waterloo had removed the odious Napoleon at last from European politics and Englishmen could travel freely about the Continent again. Sadly, he didn't stay here long – he took his family to the Tuscany coast and drowned in a boating accident. For so very young a man he seems to have had children by a great many women – perhaps they were terribly careless a hundred years ago.'

'He attracted well-brought-up middle-class girls who had been left in almost total ignorance of sexual matters,' said Roland, 'and he knew no more himself than what to do with a girl in bed – but the lines are not his, they're by his friend Byron, who made love to far, far more women than Shelley ever dreamed of.'

'Oh, Lord Byron – he was a neighbour of the Malvolio when he came to live in Venice. There's a sketch of him somewhere about the place. He rented the Palazzo Mocenigo, and that's next but one to the Palazzo Malvolio, on this side of the Grand Canal. He lived there with women he picked up round the city – like the majority of men, he had low tastes. Do you like his verse?'

'I find it fascinating, as I find the whole Regency period of absorbing interest, the art, the buildings, the poetry and the novels – all of it.'

'My own impression is that it is too *florid*, apart from Jane Austen's novels,' said Mrs Tandy with surprising primness for a woman who lived in a palace of staggering magnificence, even if it was somewhat faded.

'The rest of the stanza would only confirm your view of Byron as a youthful reprobate,' said Roland, 'when he says:

> States fall, arts fade – but Nature does not die,
> Nor yet forget how Venice once was dear,
> The pleasant place of all festivity,
> The revel of the earth, the Masque of Italy!

–he means Masque in the sense of masquerade, a masked ball at which partners could be exchanged and everyone pretended not to recognise each other.'

'The Venice Carnival has always been a by-word for that sort of casual promiscuity,' said Mrs Tandy, 'there was a time when most of the English nobility came here specially for that.'

Before the conversation became bogged down deeper, Luigi came across the room to bow ponderously to Mrs Tandy and inform her that dinner was ready to be served. She took Roland's arm and together they went through another pair of white and gold doors thrown open by the footmen and into what the chambermaid had described to him as the *Grande* dining room. Big it was, with a table down the centre that would seat at least twenty, and enough empty space about it for a procession to march through.

One look at the murals and Roland said *Tiepolo*, to which Mrs Tandy nodded and smiled approvingly, as if he'd passed his test as an art expert. But the paintings were unmistakable in their rococo elegance of composition and colour. The dining-room walls were divided into ten panels, from waist-height up to the over-arch of the ceiling, and each section depicted a scene from Classical mythology, with above life-size figures.

The unifying theme, Roland saw, was food and eating, and for a dining-room nothing could be more appropriate. Here were seen the ancient Roman gods and goddesses, either feasting or making preparations for it. There was blonde Venus stretched out on a couch of ivory, reaching for a bunch of grapes held by a Cupid.

There was Diana hunting in a forest, aiming with silver bow and arrow at a distant stag, her nude body half turned to show her breasts. There was Mars in a golden helmet, seated on a bed of some sort and polishing a sword, with attendant nymphs about him offering food on salvers and a wine-pitcher.

Minerva, Juno, Mercury – they were all shown round the walls, and on the high ceiling overhead was a banquet scene

– all the deities together round a long table under a blue sky. They were not posed motionless but with a swirling movement and life that was entrancing. They were youthful and alive, these Roman gods and goddesses, and they were very beautiful in a frivolous sort of way, thought Roland, staring upwards with a smile of purest pleasure. It seemed very obvious that at the end of the banquet they would pair off and make love – even the virginal Diana was looking with modestly downcast eyes at Mercury's lap, where a thin fold of drapery concealed what lay between his thighs.

On earth below, where frivolity was noticeably missing from the proceedings because of Count Massimo's ill-humour, places had been laid for six in the middle of the long table. Delphine placed Roland to her right and her chaplain, Padre Pio, to her left. Across the table from her sat the glowering Count, on his left and facing Roland was Marina, who was still pretending not to notice either her husband's sulkiness or Roland's existence.

Adalbert was placed on the Count's other side, across from Padre Pio, with whom he entered into ponderous conversation in Italian. With the faintest touch of malice, Roland wondered if Adalbert had become fluent in what his guidebook described as *the Venetian dialect, which is most typical, but is sometimes incomprehensible to the Italians as well, and even to Venetians not well informed.*

There were a dozen footmen in the room in threadbare purple and primrose livery, serving food and wine, bread rolls and *acqua minerale*, moving silently about the table, while Luigi in black stood behind Delphine Tandy's chair like a ballet-master directing a gala performance of some impossibly intricate work. With respectable intervals between, there arrived at the table course after course in antique silver serving dishes, *frutti di mare*, bean soup, risotto with chicken livers, sole in a sweet-and-sour sauce, lamb roasted in herbs and basted with white vermouth, Asiago goat-milk cheese, then pistachio and orange ice-cream, and finally a great silver bowl of fresh fruit, like a centrepiece set on the table.

The wines changed from white to red and back with the courses and they were local growths, Roland noted – a Bardolino and a fresh white Soave from Verona. He chatted about Italian wine to Mrs Tandy, and about her astonishing murals and asked about the Malvolio who had got Tiepolo in to do his dining room. Hearing paintings mentioned, Padre Pio offered the odd information that the artist Giovan-Battista Tiepolo was paid eight hundred *zecchini* for his work. When Roland asked how much that might be, he said it was equivalent to about fifty thousand lira.

'Which is about three hundred and seventy-five pounds at the present exchange rate,' Mrs Tandy added. 'It has always struck me that the Malvolios made a good bargain to get the director of the Accademia Gallery to work at that rate. The paint alone to cover the walls and ceiling must have cost him half of it.'

Throughout the very long meal and whatever the conversation, Roland's abiding interest was Contessa Marina across the table from him, or more precisely, her daring evening frock drew his attention. While she was sitting down, he couldn't see the spot where the coloured beadwork came together in a very suggestive upright oval, but it was quite distinct in his memory. Marina's breasts were only half-covered by the extremely low-cut bodice and it amused Roland to gaze admiringly at them whenever Count Massimo was looking his way. Massimo turned pale and crimson by turns, a scowl deepening on his handsome features.

Marina was at first embarrassed by Roland's game of annoying her husband and tried to ignore both of them. But when she had drunk a few glasses of wine with the early courses of the meal she began to appreciate the joke. Soon she began to join in the fun by leaning forward to address Roland over the broad table, so that her frock hung a little away from her in front to show even more of her plump breasts. Roland found the sight of them most stimulating, and under the table his male part stood stiff in his trousers. He would have liked to get his hands on them.

When after a couple of hours dinner was finished at last, Mrs Tandy led the way to a very fine room with bronze busts in each corner. This was the Yellow Drawing Room, she explained, so-called because the wall-coverings were yellow – though to Roland the colour seemed to have faded into an indistinct grey shade. The bronzes were portraits of the four most important Malvolios – the one who was elected Doge of Venice, the one who financed Marco Polo's journey of exploration to China, the one who built the present Palazzo, and the one who was shot by Napoleon when he got drunk and insulted the French upstart to his face.

A footman brought fresh coffee and a decanter of cognac, and the family settled down to talk until bedtime. Count Massimo made a point of placing his own chair between Roland and Marina and then ignoring both while he discussed something or other in rapid Italian with Padre Pio. At ten thirty the Count consulted his gold wristwatch, looking very unhappy.

'Is it time for you to leave us, Massimo?' Mrs Tandy enquired with a trace of sarcasm in her voice. He replied that he could not possibly leave while they had a guest, or it would be very impolite. Roland was aware of the undercurrent and thought it entertaining that his presence was inconveniencing Massimo.

'Really, Count,' said he, tongue in cheek, 'please do not put yourself out on my account. If you have an appointment, I hope you will keep it, otherwise I shall blame myself.'

'Certainly you must go and meet your friends, *Massimo caro*,' said Marina, a falsely sweet smile on her face. 'Dr Thornton is staying here in the Palazzo for ages – we must think of him as one of the family.'

'That's right,' Mrs Tandy chimed in, 'treat him as one of us and keep to your customary ways, Massimo. You've never yet let anything upset your evening visits to your friends – why should you make an exception now?'

Red-faced and angry, Count Massimo insisted that he had not the least intention of going out, and to end the embarrassing conversation he poured himself two-thirds of a glass of cognac and took a long swig at it.

Presumably, thought Roland, this is the time of day he goes off to meet beautiful young men and do whatever it is they do together. But his jealousy was preventing him from leaving his wife to her own devices, while Roland was there. It would be sad, if it wasn't so comic.

The conversation flagged after that, and not long past eleven o'clock Contessa Marina rose from her chair and kissed Delphine goodnight. In the general leave-taking that followed, she was able to whisper to Roland undetected that she could not come to his room that night since she was quite certain Massimo would have her watched. *Domani*, she whispered, her eyes bright with sexual invitation, *tomorrow*. Roland hoped that *domani* did not have the same significance as the Spanish *manana*, which usually meant something like *this year, next year, sometime, never*.

He made a point of kissing Marina's hand to annoy her husband and the eager way she squeezed his fingers told him that for her at least *domani* meant she intended to have her knickers off for him the very next day. The hand-kissing had its effect on Massimo, who seized his wife by the arm and practically trotted her out of the Yellow Drawing Room.

Before Mrs Tandy said goodnight to Roland she suggested that he should meet Padre Pio the next morning to be briefed fully on where the early Renaissance works of art were to be found in the palace, and the priest smiled his agreement and nodded like a wind-up doll. She summoned a footman to guide Roland to his room, although he insisted he remembered the way. *Better to be safe than sorry*, said she. *It would be dreadful if you tripped or fell or had an accident of some sort.* Afterwards, following the footman, it occurred to Roland that she might have been worried that Massimo could be lurking behind a statue in a long lonely passage, to waylay him.

The thought was ridiculously melodramatic, he decided when he reached his room. Massimo had behaved like a clown at dinner, but he wasn't likely to plunge a knife into his wife's heart in a rage and then cut her lover's throat in best operatic style – though Roland seemed to remember reading in the English papers of similarly fatal marital squabbles taking place frequently in the slummier parts of Naples. But this was Venice, where lovers and married women were an everyday theme that went back a long, long way. Besides, Massimo was Roman, not a Neapolitan.

Roland's thoughts were floating gently into oblivion and he was already half-asleep when he heard the sound of his bedroom door being opened. Instantly he was wide awake, staring through the dark to make out who had come in. If it was Massimo bound on avenging his honour, then Roland would be out of the other side of the bed like a shot, to grab for his empty suitcase on top of the wardrobe and use it as a shield against a knifing. A better plan would be to find something hard and heavy to crown Massimo with, but nothing suitable came to mind. It had to be a question of taking the knife blade in the suitcase, kicking at Massimo's knees in the dark, and running like hell.

He heard his name spoken softly, and his anxiety evaporated – it was a woman's voice. Marina had given her husband the slip after all, and was here to resume their afternoon pleasures. He sat up in bed with his arms round his knees and smiled – and saw that he was wrong again. The woman in a frilly negligee who halted at his bedside was not Marina but Mrs Tandy.

'Do forgive me if I am disturbing you,' she said in a society hostess sort of voice, 'but it suddenly occurred to me when I was getting ready for bed that it's years since I saw this room and I've only the servants' word for it that it's comfortable and decent. It was very remiss of me not to check before they put your luggage in here, and I simply couldn't rest until I'd made sure you're all right.'

'It's very kind of you to take so much trouble,' said Roland, 'the room is very comfortable, I assure you.'

'Good,' said she, glancing around in the half-dark, 'I see you've opened the window shutters. I sleep with mine open too, but I can never get the maids out of the habit of closing them at night. They keep mosquitoes out, of course, if there are any about, but I think they make the room stuffy.'

'And too dark,' said Roland, 'a little light helps me sleep more easily – and the starlight reflected off the water on to the ceiling gives a superb effect.'

'I'm so very glad you've noticed that, Roland – may I call you Roland? Not all our visitors do, and some say they find it distracting.'

There being no chair closer to the bed than six feet, she sat carefully on the side of the bed itself, her back straight and her feet together on the red-tiled floor. Roland took that as a sign of impending friendship, but felt it wiser to let her set the pace. Great ladies who owned palaces might be in other ways out of the ordinary.

'I really must apologise for not getting up and offering you a chair,' he said cheerfully, 'but the fact is that I have been sleeping naked since I arrived in Venice, the nights being very warm.'

'Naked, are you? I didn't realise. I thought you had pyjama trousers on. I never sleep naked myself – do you know why?'

'Why?'

'I associate nakedness in bed with making love, and if I'm on my own I get too restless to sleep if I don't put a nightdress on. Isn't that silly?'

'But,' said Roland delicately, 'you're not wearing one now.'

It had taken him a little time, staring at Delphine through the dimness of his room, to reach that conclusion, but the buds of her breasts were prominent through her flimsy negligee, and the merest hint of pale skin showed where the silk had slipped a fraction on her thigh.

'Am I not?' she said, sounding moderately surprised, 'I must have forgotten to put it on because I was preoccupied thinking whether this room was comfortable. I meant to ask about the bed in particular – sometimes these old mattresses are as hard as planks.'

While she was treating Roland to her solicitous hostess role he busied himself with undoing the bow that held her sash belt together and opening her negligee to bare her entire body from throat to thigh. She seemed hardly aware of what he was doing until he put his hands on her uncovered breasts and felt them, for he was quite certain now that this was what she wanted from him. Secretly he was regretting his enthusiastic afternoon on this selfsame bed with Marina, and he hoped he could find the strength of passion to oblige Delphine.

To his surprise, his *cazzo* was standing hard between his legs and his heart was beating fast. Then he remembered that in the Yellow Drawing Room it was Delphine herself who had poured his second cup of coffee and handed it to him, not a footman. That gave her ample opportunity to lace it with a drop or two of the local *elisir d'amore* and from the present intensity of his lust for her body, he was convinced that she had administered it.

He leaned forward to put his face between her chubby breasts and breathed in the provocative French perfume she had dabbed there. He held them while he kissed their pink points and felt their bud-like firmness with his tongue. Delphine sighed softly and put her open hand on his bare chest, her soft cool touch was very arousing, particularly when her palm slowly slid down to his belly and stayed there.

'Delphine – I am so happy you're here with me,' he murmured, though it seemed a banal sort of thing to say.

'Are you?' she whispered. 'Then you must make me happy too, my dear.'

From his belly her hand moved down between his legs and took hold of his upright part. She rolled it between her fingers as if to determine what prize she had drawn in this lottery, then pressed Roland down on his back, threw aside the sheet covering him and stroked his throbbing stiffness full-handed.

So strong was the effect of the potion on him that, in spite of the pleasant exertions of the afternoon, it took very little coaxing by Delphine before Roland laid her down on her back and knelt between her spread thighs. He touched her chestnut-brown curls and opened her *fica* with eager fingers, and at once she held out her arms to him in invitation. He laid his belly on hers and one long push took him all the way into her slippery softness.

'Ah, ah . . . my dear Roland,' she exclaimed.

Her legs lifted off the bed to wrap themselves tightly round his waist, and already he could feel spasms shaking her belly.

'It's too soon!' she gasped. 'Stop, oh stop!'

But Roland was aroused beyond belief by the awareness of her almost instant arousal to the very brink of sexual crisis – as what man in his fortunate position wouldn't be! He thrust into her with short sharp strokes, her cries, her gasps, her moans working on him so strongly that he could feel himself growing thicker and harder with each stab. Delphine was beyond rational thought and bounced beneath him vigorously until, as her climax began, she cried out his name, her heels drumming convulsively on Roland's bottom and he jolted his frantic lust into her.

In all, it was a pretty satisfactory performance, he said to himself when they were lying side by side getting their breath back. And he knew he could look forward to a repetition of this energetic delight while the potion she had given him remained active in the system – seven or eight hours, according to Carlo Missari, but less than that in his own experience of when he had been given it secretly by Marina.

And the thought of Marina reminded Roland this was as good a time as any to see if Delphine was prepared to tell him why she had invited him to stay in the palace.

'To look at the paintings,' she said when he asked, 'to help you with your book about . . . what is it about, exactly?'

'The themes of early Renaissance painting,' said he, 'but you don't mean that at all, as we are both well aware. Inviting me to stay here was Marina's idea, I'm certain, but in that case I don't see why you're in bed with me now and not her. You're not interchangeable, not by any means, so why?'

'Take my advice,' said Delphine, 'and stay clear of my sister or Massimo will cause a most fearful row. You saw how he was at dinner because you were staring down Marina's frock. He's more jealous than you imagine and he's quite capable of arranging to have something unpleasant happen to you.'

'It wasn't because he caught me looking down Marina's

frock – he was in a furious temper before that. When did you tell him I was about to become your guest?'

'I didn't, Marina did, when he came back after lunch.'

'And that threw him into a boiling rage for some reason – but how do you explain that? Does he suspect everyone who stays in the palace, on principle?'

'Yes, I'm sure he does,' Delphine said, her voice vague, 'so do be careful – it would be very distressing to learn the police had found you floating out to sea with a broken head.'

'Tell me if I've got it right,' said Roland with a chuckle of disbelief, 'you're here to save my life from the mad Count by ravishing me all through the night to keep me away from Marina. It's terribly noble of you to surrender your body to my beastly lust to protect the family name, and all that.'

'Ha!' Delphine exclaimed, grabbing hold of his limp part and tugging at it. 'You find nothing strange about Marina falling on her back for you at the drop of a hat, so why do you find it different when I do? We *are* sisters, after all. Do you think I don't enjoy making love as much as she does?'

Still it didn't ring true, but Roland knew he'd get no nearer the secret that night. Meanwhile, there were other and far more amusing considerations for a young man in bed with a naked and willing woman. A great lady when her stylish clothes were on, and an obliging wanton when they were off, as the poet Robin Herrick almost said.

Roland twisted away from her grip, doubled over to kiss her belly, then deftly turned her on her face and smacked the round soft cheeks of her bottom lightly, making her shriek and laugh at the same time. And even while he used his hands on her, the image that forced its way into his mind was of Renata Caducci in her pink slip, tall and thin with breasts too large to be in proportion to the rest of her. In his mind's eye he could see her wedge-shaped face below her mop of frizzy brown hair, and the sulky pout of her mouth.

He slapped Delphine's soft bare bottom a little harder as he felt in his imagination Signorina Caducci's hand working at his tormented stiffness in a brutal beat – then the sharp agony of a leather belt whipping at his flesh while his lust spurted out to her manipulation.

These memories and the smack of his hand on Delphine's bottom aroused him furiously. To judge by the way her giggles turned to gasping little intakes of breath, the mild pain was exciting her too – and who could say what images the smacking had evoked in her mind? Roland lay on his side close to her, and with a firm hand pushed her legs apart. He stroked up and down the insides of her thighs, then changed position once more so that he could nip at the flesh of her bottom with his teeth.

While he was inflicting his delicate little bites on her rump his fingers found the wet split between her legs and caressed it without probing inside. Soon her bottom was lifting off the bed and her legs opened wider in anticipation. Now that he had brought her to this pitch of arousal, Roland's intention was to tease her to the limit before delivering the *coup de grâce*, and this urge to make her experience the most intense thrills she could stand was only partly male vanity – he also hoped that by it he might establish a kind of useful superiority.

He trailed his wet tongue slowly along the crease between her cheeks, and let his fingers slide perhaps half an inch into her slippery *fica*. Her bottom jerked up quickly, as if to force his finger deeper inside her, but he prevented it and continued the slow teasing until she was gasping continuously and he guessed that she was almost giddy with desire. Her legs were straining as far apart as they could go as she offered her body in total surrender.

Now she's really ready for it, Roland told himself.

He turned her on her back and pushed one of the pillows under her bottom to raise it. His fingers slipped into her wet warmth and she moaned in delight to feel his stiffness jerking against her flesh as it probed for the portal. When she felt him enter, she took hold of Roland's shoulders and pulled him down on her, until his belly was flat on hers.

'Ah, you dear man!' she sighed, squirming beneath him. 'Don't make me wait any longer – I'm almost fainting for it!'

But he did make her wait a while yet, checking his own eager desire and moving slowly and carefully in and out, to keep her hovering on the brink of ecstasy as long as he could, and for as long as she could!

'Faster, faster!' she moaned, her belly bucking up under him to urge him to greater effort.

Roland resisted the temptation to end it fast, and continued to move with deliberation until she began to moan loudly in the extremity of climactic arousal. Her nervous system refused the overload and her back arched up off the bed as her crisis arrived. So intense was it that Roland was overwhelmed at once. He heard himself uttering an incoherent cry, either triumph or surrender, as his hot desire spurted into her.

NINE

Padre Pio took a certain pride in showing Roland the archives of the Malvolio family – or at least, the room where they were stored. It was a large room lined with broad shelves, on which ancient leather boxes were stacked up to the ceiling, a faded gold coat of arms stamped into the side of each box. There were no dates or other references to be seen, and Roland concluded that the filing system existed only in the old priest's memory.

There was an antique and uncomfortable chair for Roland, but Padre Pio allowed himself no such comfort and stood at a wooden desk, elbow high and with a sloping top. He beamed at Roland and pushed his gold-rimmed spectacles up his forehead, choosing his words carefully to explain that there were certain problems to confront them in the commendable project to examine closely the early Renaissance works of art in the extensive Malvolio collection, problems which the Signora Tandy, a great lady with admirable qualities of comprehension and sensitivity, coupled with an intense regard for the treasured heritage of the past of the most noble family with which she had allied herself, could not be entirely aware.

The interminable sentence was not easy to follow, but Roland understood the gist of it well enough.

'What problems?' he asked. 'The pictures are hanging on the walls and somewhere in these boxes you have the catalogue.'

'It is there that the problem lies – you have put your finger exactly on the location,' said Padre Pio with enthusiasm. 'The old Malvolio Palazzo which stood here since 1451 was burned by accident in the year 1736 and this new Palazzo was built in its place. As you can imagine, many things were lost in the fire.'

'But not the pictures,' said Roland. 'I've seen dozens dating back well before the fire. When I was here for lunch a few days ago I was shown a Virgin Enthroned that Mr Gmund believes to be by Giotto, though I haven't yet looked at it closely enough to form a definite opinion. And the Contessa showed me a carved panel of Noah's Ark which is very obviously thirteenth century.'

'Ah, *si*, the panel,' said the priest dryly, 'someone told me that the Contessa had taken you to see it.'

From his attitude it was very clear to Roland that Padre Pio was well aware of palace gossip about what he and Marina got up to against the wall when she took him to view Noah's Ark. And a further thought followed on from that – had the priest seen it as his duty to warn Count Massimo? That would surely account for the hostility towards him at dinner last night. These were dangerous waters to sail in, thought Roland, and perhaps it had been a dreadful mistake to accept Delphine's invitation to stay in the palace.

But that was another matter, and the business of the day was to find out all he could about the early works of art. Jealous husbands and eager wives must wait their turn.

'The paintings were saved, and some of the furniture,' Roland said, to bring Padre Pio back to the matter in hand.

'That is so, *Dottore Tonton*,' he agreed, mangling the name in his own way, 'the fire was not destructive of everything. Water from the Grand Canal put it out and much was saved, as you have observed with your own expert eyes. It would have been possible to restore the palace as it had been, but Jacopo Malvolio was a devoted admirer of the classical style. The facade to the canal and the facade to the square were rebuilt as you see them now – in Palladian style. The interior was made new, even where there was little damage except smoke and soot – you admired the work of Tiepolo in the dining room.'

'Yet there is a problem, you said?'

'*Si* – the servants were so very occupied putting water on the flames and carrying pictures out to the square, and furniture, to save all they could, that no one had time for the Archive. A most unfortunate result of that is that what you see here goes only back to the rebuilding in 1736 and all the earlier records were burnt in the fire.'

'That's a great pity,' said Roland, 'everything I want to see dates from before the fire. But there must be a catalogue of the collection to give me a starting point.'

'Assuredly there is,' Padre Pio agreed with a sunny smile, 'I myself made a catalogue of all the works of art here – pictures and carvings and statues and bronzes and drawings and books and furniture. That was when I first came here in 1879 as chaplain to the old Count and his family. It occupied me for almost two years, but I had plenty of time for it. The Count lived abroad nine or ten months of every year, in Paris and London, and the ladies of the family were pious by upbringing and sinned very little. My main task was to hear the weekly confessions of the servants, which were never interesting – and the compilation of a new catalogue was a work of love for me.'

'You based it on an earlier catalogue, I suppose.'

'It is most gratifying to be able to discuss these important things with a true expert, *Dottore*. The old catalogue I used to make my own was dated 1816 and there were many additions since then, the Malvolio being great patrons of art and collectors to the time of the old Count, who had other interests. Before the 1816 catalogue there was one of 1798, but it is suspicious and not to be taken seriously.'

'What do you mean – it was deliberately faked?'

'Precisely. Napoleon invaded Venice with his soldiers in 1797 and looted much – even the bronze horses which stand before San Marco. The great families who were clever in time sent away the best of their treasures before the French arrived here to steal from them. The 1798 catalogue tells us the Malvolio made almost everything disappear, and this we see by comparing it with the 1816 lists and the 1769 lists.'

'Very interesting,' said Roland, who felt he was getting lost in the good Padre's detail, 'but what is the earliest catalogue you have?'

'The one made in 1736, when the Palazzo was rebuilt. Whatever existed before then was destroyed.'

'But that should give me all I need, for I doubt if much from the earlier centuries was acquired after that date.'

'You speak correctly, but again, I regret I must explain that it will not be so easy as perhaps you believe to examine these early works. Consider this, *Dottore*, that the Palazzo Malvolio is not the Accademia, it is a private residence, not a gallery for the public to visit and stare. The paintings and sculpture were bought by generations of Malvolio to have something to put on the walls and in the corners of rooms. Experts and scholars such as yourself have another view of the importance of these things, but the great families who bought them regarded them as *furniture* almost, as decorations for their rooms and halls.'

'I'd never thought of it quite like that,' said Roland, 'but now you point it out, I see what you mean. But why should this be a problem?'

'Because the catalogues of which we have been speaking should more precisely be called *inventories*, Signor. They list all the contents of the Palazzo, room by room, pictures, busts, murals, tapestries, chairs, other furniture and items. I will show you – this is the catalogue I made for the Count in 1879.'

From his stand-up desk he handed to Roland a very thick stack of hand-written sheets of paper bound together between leather-covered boards stamped with the Malvolio arms. Roland opened it at random and found it was as Padre Pio had told him – it took each room of the palace in turn and briefly listed its contents.

'Well,' he said at last with a sigh of resignation, 'we have the names of the artists listed here, or the attribution of any doubtfuls. If I go through the catalogue and pick out the names of artists known to have been active before the year 1400, that should serve my purpose. Of course, you will have to explain to me where the rooms are where their works are listed as hanging. Does that sound satisfactory?'

'It will serve,' said the priest with a smile indicating that he was not altogether convinced that any system would entirely work. 'Of course, not everything in the Palazzo now is where it was in 1879. When the War began in 1914 it was feared that the Austrians would fly over Venice in aeroplanes and throw bombs on us. Count Rinaldo Malvolio, before he went away to fight, issued instructions for the most precious works of art to be taken to the family villa on the mainland for safety. He did not return from the War himself, as you know, and when Mrs Tandy ordered the pictures to be brought back here in 1919, she had them hung where she thought best, without regard for where they had been before.'

'So we shall have to refer to her memory for anything we do find not where listed,' said Roland, wishing he'd never got himself involved with the Malvolio collection and its amateur catalogue system.

'You can try, Signor Tuntun, but I remember there were thirty or forty paintings and at least twenty statues and bronzes. The Signora will surely not remember where she ordered them all put – but have no fear, we can locate them by walking through the Palazzo and observing closely, given enough time.'

'How much time?'

'Ten days, two weeks perhaps, should be long enough to look everywhere with the catalogue in hand and make a record of what has been moved and where it is now. It is my duty as Keeper of the Archive to do this, but I have become lazy now I am old and I have been postponing the work for fifteen years or more. How very happy it would make me if you undertook this bringing the catalogue up to date.'

'I wasn't planning on staying that long,' said Roland, 'but I will think about it and have a word with Mrs Tandy. Meanwhile, with your permission I will begin by reading through this 1879 inventory and making a list of the artists who interest me.'

'Excellent,' said the priest, his benign smile quite dazzling in its genial intensity, 'I will conduct you to the Biblioteca where you can sit and work undisturbed until lunch.'

'Thank you,' said Roland, who feared he was going to be asked to make use of the Padre's desk and do his reading standing up, 'the Library will suit me well.'

Once settled at the vast antique writing desk in the Library he made a start on the catalogue. It was slow and hard going, a limiting factor being Padre Pio's elaborate nineteenth century style of handwriting, and his own ignorance of the Italian language. But as he worked slowly through the closely written pages, here and there a name stood out – Veneziano, Donato, Giambono – that he copied into his own notebook, with the catalogue reference. A great find was Uccello, and that picture he determined to see first and give his most careful attention.

By lunch time he had achieved less than he expected, and saw clearly that the priest's statement that it would take ten days or two weeks to identify the paintings that interested him and then locate them in the rambling palace, was no exaggeration, which raised in Roland's mind the question of whether he wanted to go on with the task at all. There was a time when he arrived first in Venice that he would have seized this opportunity to extend the scope of his book, but his interest had waned and he no longer believed that the book would ever be completed.

That notwithstanding, there was much to be said for being the guest of Mrs Tandy for a couple of weeks, enjoying the palatial style of living, having her and the Contessa alternate in his bed, and observing the Count's discomfiture. But against that a faint warning sounded in Roland's mind that the Count might not be entirely a comic opera figure. The comedy might turn sour.

Three people had warned him the Count was dangerous in his rage – Marina, Delphine and Adalbert Gmund. Roland discounted what Marina said about her husband, for he thought her prone to dramatising herself. Nor did he place complete faith in what he had been told by Delphine, for it might only be a ruse to keep him away from Marina and available for herself.

But Adalbert had nothing to gain, that Roland could see, and his warning had been very explicit that he was putting himself in danger by threatening Massimo's honour. And danger in this context meant physical danger. Roland was twenty years younger than the Count and reasonably sure of giving a good account of himself if it came to blows, but that seemed too crude a method for a minor Roman aristocrat.

In this uncertain state of mind in due course Roland found his way, after three or four wrong turnings, to the Small Dining Room.

It was an uncomfortable meal, for neither Delphine nor Marina was there, and Count Massimo was still on his high horse. Stony stares were all Roland got from him, not even a polite word in reply to his cheerful greeting. Nor was there a chance to tell Padre Pio of his slow progress with the lists, for Massimo monopolised the priest's attention with an unending monologue in Italian.

That left only Adalbert Gmund to talk to over the excellent and very ample food and wine. Roland asked how anyone ever knew who was in for lunch or dinner, and was given the obvious reply that Luigi the major-domo knew who was expected for every meal and could be asked. Adalbert in turn enquired how the work was proceeding on the pictures, and Roland asked the self-appointed amateur if he knew where the Uccello painting was to be found in the palace. Adalbert shook his head in ponderous doubt and said he'd never come across any any such thing.

'Paolo Uccello,' said Roland, 'came here from Florence to

do some of the mosaics in San Marco. About 1425, give or take a year or two. One of his very best paintings is in London.'

'A Florentine,' said the Austrian, 'we are all Venetians here, even Massimo. But if you find this picture, I shall be grateful for the opportunity to see it. What is the subject of it?'

'That I can't tell you, until I've got Padre Pio to translate the catalogue entry for me.'

At the end of the meal the Count rose and departed swiftly, a nod to the priest and to Adalbert his only acknowledgements. A grin spread over Roland's face at this deliberate rudeness, and Padre Pio shook his head in sorrow, crossed himself elaborately and said that he had need of his siesta.

Roland and Adalbert sat on for a while over the coffee, their talk inconsequential. Roland was in no hurry to get back to the decipherment of the priest's handwriting, and Adalbert clearly was at a loose end.

'Are you paying a call on the delightful Signorina Caducci this afternoon?' he enquired facetiously.

'I was there yesterday,' said Adalbert, satisfaction shining from his broad face. 'She asked if you were still in Venice, or if you had returned to England. Will you go to visit her, or do you find her highly specialised services not to your liking?'

'I may call upon her,' said Roland, 'if the mood takes me.'

'*Ach Gott, ja* – Marina takes your energy and you have no need or desire to visit the charming Signorina. Does Marina give you the *afrodisiaco* to drink when she comes to your room?'

'These are matters gentlemen do not discuss,' said Roland, an attempt at old-school stuffiness seeming the best way to choke Adalbert off. To his surprise it worked.

'You do well to remind me,' said Adalbert with an inclination of his head indicating mild apology. 'Gentlemen do not discuss their ladies and their little ways, only the common women they make use of for their pleasure. Which reminds me that you promised to take me to meet two young women who are followers of divine Sappho and celebrate her rites of love for the edification of gentlemen.'

'I don't remember making any such promise, but I am in your debt for introducing me to Signorina Caducci. And I don't feel like working on Padre Pio's damnable lists of furnishings this afternoon – so why not? We'll go to Signora

Ricci's house and pay our respects to Marcella and Sofia, if I can find the way.'

'I believe you told me it was in the Cannaregio district.'

'Yes, that's right. We take the *vaporetto* up the Grand Canal as far as the *Ca' Doro* palace and from then on I shall trust to luck and instinct to recognise the way.'

There was no need to wait for a water-bus, Adalbert insisted, when Malvolio boats were available. He showed Roland the way through the Palazzo and out onto the stone-paved landing-stage. On the night Roland ravaged the Contessa against the wall there had been two gondolas and a motor launch tied up, but there was now only a single gondola, the rest of the fleet evidently in service.

A gondolier in Malvolio colours helped them aboard the swaying craft, pushed off from the landing-stage and sent it gliding up the Grand Canal with a deceptively casual stroke of his single oar. Roland had no eyes for the architectural splendours along both sides, being deeply engrossed in studying the map in his guide-book. When he was fairly sure he had located their goal he showed it to Adalbert, who shrugged and said he hoped he had it right.

The gondola passed beneath the Rialto Bridge and skimmed hard to the left to avoid being run down by a barge coming the other way. Adalbert read off the street and canal names from the map and relayed them over his shoulder to the gondolier who balanced upright and imperturbable on the narrow decking behind them. He rowed them on past the *Ca' Doro* and turned sharp right to enter a narrow side canal. Some way along it broadened out and Roland recognised a large and ancient building on the left.

Reference to the guide-book produced the ridiculously useless information that *the facade of the School of the Misericordia was one of the most typical of this style, taking some elements from the Romantic style, eg the drooping galleries.*

'If we turn left into the side canal here,' he told Adalbert, 'and go along it slowly, I think I shall recognise the house.'

Adalbert had a different plan in mind. In competent Italian he instructed the gondolier to pull in and let them off by the bridge.

'Why?' Roland enquired, as he stood beside Adalbert on land again and watched the gondola disappearing fast on its way back to the Palazzo Malvolio – or possibly to some handy pull-in for gondoliers which provided alcoholic drinks and chat.

'I have explained this before, I think,' said the Austrian, 'it is as if we lived in a village where the neighbours spy on each other all day. The gondolier will gossip to the doorman at the Palazzo and to the maids. Soon everyone will know where he took us, to see the sculptures in the *Scuolo della Misericordia* – but if he had taken us further to a house known to you, there would be much speculation among the servants on the reason. And because it is natural to assume the worst about each other, the story would be known to all in the Palazzo that we had visited a bordello together. And if the gondolier had waited outside to take us back afterwards, there would be lurid tales made up of how many times we did it to the women each.'

'It would be unpleasant if Mrs Tandy or the Contessa got to know of our visit here,' said Roland thoughtfully. 'Naturally, you take precautions not to be observed when you go to call on the stimulating Signorina Caducci.'

When the gondola was out of sight they thought it reasonable to move away from the *Scuola* with the typical facade, whatever that might mean, and strolled along the stone quay built along one side of a narrow canal between dilapidated houses. Roland wondered whether to treat Adalbert to his joke about impossibly high numbering and postmen trained in topography, but decided against it. The truth was that he couldn't remember the house number and he was looking for a stone balcony with two pots of red flowers.

Some way along the quay he found it, and pointed to the door, its decades-old paint peeling off to show splintered wood.

'This one?' said Adalbert. 'Lead the way then, you are known here, but I am only a stranger.'

Roland pushed the unlocked door open and went through into a narrow passage with stone flags, from which a flight of stairs led upwards. It looked right, but every door along this endless quay led into exactly the same sort of entrance hall. While he hesitated, a man in uniform came down the stairs. He was by no means young, and he was smoking a cigarette, a holstered pistol at his belt and his peaked cap at a jaunty angle. He stared at the two foreigners lurking in the entrance.

Adalbert instantly broke into voluble Italian, sounding very authoritative. The man in uniform grinned and jerked his head to indicate *up the stairs*, then turned sideways and slid past them and out of the door.

'You actually asked a policeman if this was the bordello we were looking for?' said Roland, his eyebrows raised.

'He is not a policeman,' said Adalbert, 'he is a Capitano of the Bersaglieri.'

'The what?'

'It is a regiment of the Italian Army. He is on leave and here to visit his mother's sister, who lives on the top floor.'

'And was he helpful?'

'*Ja, ja!* He said the two girls who demonstrate *amore lesbico* are up one flight on the left. He wished me *Buon' appetito*.'

'His mother's sister – a likely tale!' said Roland. 'If you ask me, he was here on the same errand as us.'

He tapped at the door on the landing and it was opened almost at once by Signora Ricci, in white blouse and black skirt just as before – perhaps that was her uniform. She recognised Roland and shook hands with him cheerfully, chattering in what he took to be Venetian dialect and drawing him into the apartment.

Adalbert was close behind him and doffed his comic Tyrolean hat with the pheasant feather tucked in the band as he entered. With a straight face Roland introduced him to Signora Ricci as Baron von Gmund, the distinguished international expert on art of the Italian Renaissance. Much to his surprise, she seemed to be impressed, and fluttered about offering chairs and drinks. A curious result was that Adalbert was so flattered and pleased by her deference to his bogus barony that he turned magnanimous and handed her a 1,000-lira note with an imperial gesture.

At that she almost kissed his hand, her heavy bosom bouncing inside her blouse, and ran out of the room to get the girls for him.

'My word,' said Roland, 'Signora Ricci's taken an instant and profound liking to you, Adalbert. It's my guess there's nothing she'd refuse you, if your fancy runs in that direction.'

Before Adalbert could reply, the subject of their talk came back, shooing the two naked girls in front of her. They smiled invitingly at the men and stood in the middle of the room for their inspection, an arm round each other's waist.

'*Ach, mein Gott – schon, sehr schon,*' Adalbert said in a very breathy voice, lapsing into his native German under the stress of strong emotion. Roland could envisage him screwing his monocle into his eye, if he'd had such a thing.

'That's Marcella on the right with the San Marco medal

round her neck,' Roland explained, 'a local girl, who says she's twenty, which looks about right. The taller one with the bigger *tette*, as you taught me they are called in Italian, is Sofia and she's a year or so older and from Verona.'

Adalbert broke into a stream of impassioned compliments – at least Roland assumed it to be that, though as the language was Italian he couldn't be sure. The girls giggled and smiled back at him, wiggling their bare breasts, so evidently he was doing something right. Sofia had recognised Roland and she smiled at him too, running a fingertip down the dark line of hair on her belly.

'*Che bello!*' he said, hoping he'd got the Italian words for *that's nice* right.

Signora Ricci had obviously said appropriately encouraging things to the girls about the visitors, and their demonstration of *amore lesbico* was enthusiastic. They turned inwards to face each other, kissing and caressing breasts and bottoms lewdly. When Carlo brought Roland here, the girls' love-making had been staged on the floor, but this time they used a straight-backed wooden chair which Signora Ricci placed in the middle of the room for them.

As before, the smaller of the two, Marcella, took the lead in their performance, and Sofia allowed herself to be manipulated. She lay across the chair in a way that curved her spine in a half-circle, her head touching the floor on one side and her feet resting on it on the other side. Marcella sank down on to her haunches and gave a great show of feeling Sofia's breasts and then lapping their russet tips with her tongue.

'*Wunderschön!*' Adalbert exclaimed, the clumsy German word amusing Roland.

Marcella was on her knees between Sofia's parted legs and stroking her belly, stretched tight by her position over the chair. She was careful not to obstruct the view of the tuft of tight curls growing over her friend's *fica*. She leaned forward and brought her mouth down on it, stuck out her tongue and ran the tip up and down the lips. When she had wet them, she moved back and used her fingers to open them wide and expose the pink little nub within.

Adalbert's face was dark red and Roland feared that he might be on the verge of a stroke. But then he mopped his brow with a coloured silk handkerchief and grinned at Roland.

'*Phantastisch!*' he gasped. 'Do they go all the way?'

'Oh yes,' Roland assured him, 'as you will see.'

Hearing the two men talking, Marcella glanced up at them for a moment and winked, then put two joined fingers into Sofia and rubbed lightly. Sofia's upside-down face was flushed, her eyes closed and her mouth open. Soon she was squirming her bottom on the chair seat and rubbing her thumbs over the tips of her ownbreasts to hurry on her climax.

Before that could happen, Marcella moved from between her friend's legs to over her down-hanging head, kneeling above it with spread thighs. Roland's *cazzo* was fiercely stiff as he saw Marcella lie forward on the other girl, chin on her belly, and push her tongue into the pink split she held open. Sofia gave as good as she got – she raised her head from its lowly position on the floor to ravage her tormentor's dark-haired split with fingers and tongue.

Though Sofia had been passive till now and stimulated longest it was Marcella who was furthest up the slope to sexual release and who first shrieked as spasms shook her belly. She dragged Sofia's *fica* wide open with hooked fingers and forced her mouth against the swollen button, and Sofia squealed and drummed her bare heels on the tiled floor. Adalbert was babbling in German and Roland pressed a hand between his legs to still the jerking of his stiff and enthusiastic part.

While the girls were calming down, sitting side by side on the floor, their knees up to display the wet lips between their thighs still, Roland asked Adalbert if he had a preference.

'The younger one,' he said, wiping drops of sweat from his brow with his coloured handkerchief, 'the smaller one – she is Marcella, *ja?*'

Signora Ricci came forward from the far corner where she had been sitting while the girls entertained the visitors, a bottle of wine in her hand. She refilled their glasses, making a fuss of Adalbert and addressing him as *Barone*. He loved every second of it and adopted an air of gracious condescension. She asked him which of the girls he would honour with his attention first – Roland guessed the question from the answer. Adalbert pointed to Marcella and named her, whereupon Signora Ricci had the girl up on her feet at once to show him the bedroom.

Roland rose from his chair and offered Sofia his hand to pull her up from the floor. She smiled and ran her tongue round her lips by way of encouragement, and he put his hands on her bare breasts and jiggled them up and down for a second or two to let her see he was keen. As indeed he was – the exhibition of *amore lesbico* was as effective on the male organism as the Contessa's *afrodisiaco*, if not so long-lasting, he reflected.

Seemingly Adalbert in his role as Baron von Gmund warranted the best bedroom, for Sofia took Roland into a smaller room at the back of the apartment. The walls were whitewashed, though not recently, the floor was tiled, and there was space for only a single bed and a chair. Sofia helped him out of his clothes, which she draped over the chair, and made him lie on his back on the bed. *Eccola!* she said as she knelt astride him and with the ease of long practice impaled herself on him.

Roland reached up to take hold of her good-sized breasts and roll them while she slid up and down his embedded *cazzo*. What she was doing to him wasn't exactly what he wanted from her, but it would do for now, he decided, as little jerks of pleasure sped through him. She was looking down into his face and saying something or other that he couldn't understand, but it sounded very friendly. He slid his hands down her body to her splayed thighs and with his fingertips stroked the sparse-haired *fica* into which his thick shaft was thrust.

'*E bene così?*' Sofia repeated, and this time Roland got the meaning of her words – she was asking if he liked it like that.

'*Sì*,' he answered, '*molto bene* – very nice indeed.'

There was something decidedly odd about the way he had been behaving ever since he arrived in Venice, Roland thought lazily as he stared up in delight at the naked girl sitting over him. In London he never had more than one girlfriend at a time, and it was only in the vacations that lovemaking achieved greater frequency than twice a week. But in the short time he'd been in Venice he'd made love to the Contessa, her sister Delphine, and two girls for money – Sofia and Marcella. As for twice a week – suddenly twice a night wasn't even enough!

The air, perhaps? The water? The sense of liberation into sunnier and less repressive ambiance? The spirit of the place? Venice had been the playground for European travellers for over three hundred years. Or was it a lingering after-effect of the *elisir d'amore* Marina had given him at their first encounter in the Palazzo Malvolio? Always assuming that there was any such thing as an aphrodisiac that actually worked.

'*Allora!*' said Sofia, starting to bounce up and down faster under the stimulus of his teasing fingers, but before she could bring matters to a conclusion, the bedroom door was flung open and in came Marcella, the saint's medal round her neck swinging to her quick movements.

Sofia stopped her very pleasing treatment and sat still with her mouth hanging open as she stared at Marcella, who burst at once into rapid Italian that left Roland none the wiser. Then ignoring the dumbfounded Sofia spiked on Roland's upright part, Marcella sat on the side of the bed close to him and tried out her rudimentary English.

'Your friend,' said she, glaring down at him, 'the Barone – he no like *fric-fric*. He go.'

'Really?' said Roland, and though he was not pleased at the interruption so close to the great moment, he couldn't help but be amused by the girl's indignation.

'He no like *this*.' Marcella repeated, parting her knees and rubbing at the hairy lips between her legs to show what it was that Adalbert didn't like. 'He want *picchiare* him on the *culo* – how you say it?'

To make her meaning clear, she reached round Sofia and dealt a resounding slap on her bare bottom. *Ahi!* Sofia squealed at the blow, but with shock rather than pain. She retaliated with a back-handed smack across Marcella's small pointed breasts. The aggrieved girl shrieked and hurled herself bodily at Sofia, who was pushed over sideways. Roland's upright part was dragged out of her, making him yelp in dismay, and suddenly he found he was the battle-ground for the two girls' squabble.

They rolled over him and rammed knees and elbows into him as they smacked at each other's breasts and bellies, and though he tried to twist from underneath, their combined weight squirming on him held him pinned down. They screeched and squealed like a couple of cats fighting in an alley, screamed out shrill words that Roland knew must be obscene insults, and ignored his pleas for a moment's respite to get out from under.

Sofia, being the larger and heavier of the two, had the upper hand before long. Her hands were fastened in Marcella's hair and she dragged her down by it until she could get a knee into the small of her back, and with her free hand slap repeatedly at her bottom. Marcella's writhing to get away from the smacks brought her body round on Roland's belly and chest until he was staring at short range at her wispy-haired slit and trying to avoid getting a thick ear from her jerking knee.

He heard the spank of hand on soft flesh and Marcella's cries of outrage, he felt her smooth breasts slithering over him and against his swollen part – and the dull ache where he had been kneed accidentally in the belly was transformed into a familiar feeling of incipient pleasure. *Oh!* he moaned in amazement and his body convulsed to the ecstatic implosion deep within him that sent his desire racing up his throbbing shaft.

Marcella cried words of surprise to feel the warm spurting on her breasts, and Sofia exclaimed *Cosa?* and ended the smacking. She let go of Marcella's hair and nudged her sideways until she could see Roland's jerking *cazzo* and the incontrovertible proof of his sexual release smeared wetly on his belly and Marcella's breasts. The girls stared for a moment and then giggled.

TEN

In the Library of the Palazzo Malvolio sat Roland working away at Padre Pio's long lists of pictures, sculpture and furniture, wishing he'd never agreed to give Delphine Tandy his opinion on the early Renaissance works she owned. About mid-morning a maid came in carrying a heavy silver tray on which stood an antique coffee pot with a long curving spout, and all the requisites. She set her tray down on one end of the long desk at which he was sitting, and poured a cup for him.

The girl hardly had time to hand him his coffee and leave the room before Marina made an unexpected appearance. With a glance over her shoulder to make sure the Library door was closed, she leaned over Roland, an arm around his neck, and kissed him. He returned her kiss and stroked her bottom affectionately. Before these morning salutations could develop into anything further, she freed herself gently and took a seat on the other side of the dark wooden desk.

'I don't want to interrupt your work,' she said, 'I know how important it is, but I thought I'd look in for a minute and see how you are. I missed you last night – it's two nights since we made love and I get most dreadfully lonely on my own in bed. Do you miss me, my darling? If only I dare slip out at night and come to your room, but I know Massimo is having us watched.'

That seemed very improbable to Roland, but he said nothing to spoil Marina's enjoyment of her propensity for the dramatic.

'I *shall* think of a way to outwit him,' said she, smiling at Roland in a conspiratorial manner. She looked very attractive in a sleeveless frock of thin tangerine-coloured silk, held low on her hips by a white leather belt with a square gold buckle.

'You'll see,' she said. 'In the meantime, how are you getting on with Delphine's paintings, are they as genuine and valuable as people say?'

Roland thought the question odd. How could there possibly be any doubts as to the authenticity of the art collection – rich patrons like the Malvolio weren't to be fobbed off with fakes over the centuries. And why should it be Marina who asked him a question so curious – not knowledgeable Adalbert, not Delphine herself, but feather-brained Marina? There was funny business of some sort going on to do with the paintings, he was certain of that, but for the life of him he couldn't imagine what. Some sort of conspiracy was afoot, but it was impossible to know how many were involved, or why.

'It's a slow job,' he said, flicking a finger at the stack of paper on which Padre Pio had recorded the contents of the rooms as they were in 1879, 'and there's so damned much of it. Do you know that the Malvolio collection is almost as extensive as the Accademia collection? It's quite staggering – and completely unknown to scholars and the art world.'

'Well of course,' said Marina, 'you can't have people coming to poke round your house because they want to see the pictures, can you? Have you come across any surprises yet?'

'I'm not sure. There's a picture listed here as by Uccello – a major artist of the early Renaissance. Padre Pio has made out his own handwriting to mean that the subject is Saint Theodore killing a dragon. He thinks he remembers it, but he can't have seen it since about 1914 and it's not in the room listed for it – which means I've got him trotting round the palace trying to locate it.'

'Surely it was St George who killed the dragon,' said Marina, refilling his coffee cup. 'Sugar?'

'Uccello's most famous painting is St George and the dragon, and it's in London,' Roland explained. 'It's almost fairy-tale in concept – he has St George in armour on a milk-white horse, sticking a long spear into the dragon's head. The dragon looks like a gigantic green frog, and it has big beautifully coloured wings like a butterfly – it's a most charming dragon and it's being taken for a walk on a long gold chain by a pretty lady in a pink cloak and a golden crown. That raises the question of whether George has performed a public service by destroying a dangerous monster or made a mistake and killed a lady's pet.'

'It sounds absolutely delicious,' said Marina, 'Uccello must have had a lovely sense of humour. Perhaps the St Theodore is a joke too.'

'No, I don't think so, though it is probably as marvellously unreal as the St George. There are four Theodores I know about – one who was tortured to death for burning down an expensive Greek temple, one who upset the Emperor Constantine by going on about adultery, one who was sent by a Pope to be Archbishop of Canterbury, and one whose mother was a fifteen-year-old prostitute.'

'I've heard of children rebelling against their parents,' said Marina thoughtfully, evidently testing the thought against her own experience of her daughter running away with a strange man, 'but to become a saint seems carrying things too far. Will this be the Theodore in your painting?'

'No, it has to be the arsonist. He was a professional soldier before he took up with the Christian church, and when he was stationed in Egypt he killed a monster that was eating people. Padre Pio informs me that this Theodore was the first patron saint of Venice, before St Mark, and says there is a statue of him down on the waterfront by the Doge's palace.'

'I don't remember seeing it,' Marina said. 'Where exactly?'

'When you disembark for the Piazza San Marco, you come ashore between two tall stone columns. There's a funny-looking beast on top of one – that's the Lion of St Mark. And on top of the other is St Theodore, standing on a dead crocodile.'

'All these years and I've never noticed!' Marina exclaimed.

'It's high up and hard to see,' said Roland, 'but it gives a clue as to what we may expect when Padre Pio finds the picture, if he ever does find it. I'm sure it will be Theodore hacking a crocodile to death – and it will be enormously valuable.'

'Delphine will be pleased,' said Marina lazily, ignoring the doubt expressed that the painting might not be found.

She hadn't gone back to the other side of the desk after she handed Roland his second cup of coffee – she was sitting on an armchair of gilded wood with a tapestried back and seat, seven or eight feet away from him.

As he watched, she leaned back and slid the skirt of her silk frock up above her knees, using both long-fingered hands. He found himself staring in admiration at the smooth bare skin of her thighs above her stocking-tops. He cast a hurried glance at the Library door, to assure himself it was safely closed, then to Marina again. The tip of her tongue was showing pinkly between her lips and her frock's upward glide had been halted halfway between knees and groins.

Roland's heart was bounding in his chest as he stared at the ivory white flesh of Marina's thighs and his eagerness to kiss her there was so strong that his *cazzo* stood full-size. Marina noted the long bulge in his trousers and smiled at the ease of her first success. But when he started to get up from his chair to fling himself on his knees between her legs and feel up her frock, she told him to sit still.

'I've endured agonies of frustration for two nights past,' she said, 'now it's your turn to suffer a little. You may look but not touch – understood?'

'As you wish,' he murmured, quite sure how it would end.

His mouth opened in a sigh of pleasure as, very slowly, she started to raise her frock again, till he glimpsed the lace hem of her underwear. Higher still, but so slowly! And higher yet, and his stiffness was throbbing in his trousers as he obtained at last a full view of Marina's elegant knickers – they were of orchid-pink silk, trimmed with lace, and cut in the open-legged French style.

With her frock held high round her waist, she sat still as an artist's model posing for him. He stared greedily at the curve of her belly filling out the flimsy silk garment, then at the shadow between her thighs where her tuft of dark brown curls showed through the thin silk.

'I'm going to have you, whatever you say,' he murmured.

He was as frantically aroused as if she had stripped naked, though all she had done was let him see her underwear.

'Do you think so?' Marina asked. 'I may have something to say about that. Just stay where you are, Orlando, and enjoy the show while it lasts.'

She stood up slowly, tucked her frock into the white belt to hold it up, and slid her knickers slowly down her belly. First he saw her belly-button – a round and deep dimple that seemed to beg to be invaded by the tip of a wet tongue! Her hands lay in her groins, thumbs hooked into the top of her knickers, fingers with gem-stone rings and nails that were lacquered bright red.

She put her tongue out in friendly mockery at Roland's intent expression and slid her knickers a little further down, till he could see the top edge of her walnut-brown curls. By then his stiff *cazzo* was trembling so swiftly that he pressed a palm down between his legs to hold it still. *Marina*! he breathed in appreciative delight as she slid pale pink underwear right down her thighs to her gartered stocking-tops, letting him see the prominent pink lips within her dark curls.

She slipped her knickers right off and smoothed down the thin silk of her frock to conceal her charms. Roland stared round-eyed at her as she came to him, and held out his arms to take her and pull her down on his lap while he kissed her and put a hand up her frock to stroke what she had shown him. But she did not sink into his embrace as he intended – she told him to put his hands down and sit still.

With a hand on his shoulder she pushed him back in his chair, while she flicked his trousers wide open. He was so certain she would grope inside to get hold of his jerking part that he was astonished when instead she pushed her wadded silk knickers in under his shirt and fastened his trousers over the bulge.

Wordlessly, he stared down at his lap, thrilling to the soft feel of the silk around his throbbing stiffness. Marina smiled slyly and pulled up her frock to her waist again, then sat down bare-bellied astride his thighs.

'Does that excite you, Orlando?' she asked softly.

'Oh yes,' he sighed, his hands down between her parted thighs to feel her, but she prevented that by taking his wrists and lifting his hands to her breasts. Her frock unbuttoned down the back, he found, and could be slipped off her shoulders – so too could the narrow straps of her lace-edged slip – and his hands were fondling her plump bare breasts.

'Two whole nights I lie awake thinking about you!' she said. 'But you never came to me. And now you expect me to strip naked and spread my legs for you to take your pleasure!'

'And for two nights I have been awake thinking about you,' he replied with total disregard for the truth, 'but I daren't take the risk of being found in your room.'

'Then you know a little bit about frustration,' said she, 'is this how it felt to you? Be honest with me now.'

She slid along his thighs until her belly was close up to his and began to bump rhythmically against the long bulge that was his stiffness bundled in her silk knickers. Voluptuous feelings made themselves instantly apparent, and he squeezed her breasts and rolled them in his hands.

'Something feels very hard against me,' Marina murmured,

her open mouth seeking his in a long kiss.

The bumping of her loins against him moved Roland's twitching part in the soft silk, and soon she had him in an erotic daze that bordered on ecstasy. From her breasts his hands slid down to her hips, and underneath her, his fingers clenching hard in the smooth flesh of her bottom. He sighed into her open mouth at the growing sensations in his belly as his shaft was rubbed on the silk of her knickers.

'Now you feel what torment it is to be left alone all night,' Marina murmured. 'You're utterly desperate to put it inside me – but I won't let you. I'm practically naked, Orlando, knickers off and my frock up round my waist! One hard push and you're in – but I'm not going to let you. You're going to make love to my underwear, as your punishment for not coming to my room.'

Roland was dazed by the feelings rippling through his entire body from the rhythmic bumping of her plump mound against him. He stared into her velvet-brown eyes and felt himself drowning in thrilling sensation. Her beautiful face moved back a little from him so that she could observe his expression, and her red-painted mouth opened in a mocking smile.

'*Orlando mio,*' she said, her fingers busy with the buttons of his shirt, 'I've got you where I want you.'

Her words hardly reached his mind, for his excitement was now at the point where it was irreversible. His hands clutched hard at the cheeks of Marina's bare bottom, and he cried out to feel her long scarlet fingernails pinch his exposed nipples now she had his shirt open. His body heaved and jerked in abandon while his furious desire squirted into the silk knickers wrapped over it in soft folds.

'Do it, Orlando!' said Marina fiercely. 'Do it!'

His sensations grew keener to the cruel gouging of her nails and his head jerked against the chair back until he was staring blindly up at the intricate plaster-work of the ceiling. Marina rocked backward and forwards heavily against him all the while he was pouring out his ecstasy in a hot flood.

All too soon the throes faded and Roland's gasping slowed to sighing breaths. He held Marina's hands to end her ravaging of his exposed nipples, he sat still, feeling the slipperiness on his belly and the wet silk clinging to him.

'Why did you do that?' he asked lazily, slumping comfortably back in his chair.

'To get you going, of course,' she said, and slipped from his thighs and was kneeling on the floor before he guessed what she intended. She put her hands on his knees to force them wide apart, then unbuttoned him and retrieved her wet pink knickers from his belly.

'Ruined,' she said in mock severity, holding them up for him to see the result of his climax.

She took his limp part between her red-nailed fingertips and raised it vertically, then leaned over him to suck it into her mouth, making him sigh pleasurably at the sensations that were soon flickering through his belly. Even before she had him up to his full length and thickness, Roland guessed that he'd been given the *elisir d'amore*. Marina must have put it in his coffee secretly, when she refilled his cup.

He sighed again, partly in pleasure and partly exasperation – he felt he should be consulted before so drastic an action was taken – after all, it was *his* body. But then, much of Marina's charm lay in her waywardness and utter irresponsibility. And he owed her at least an afternoon of love-making, after being apart from her for two nights. Very well then, she had started off the process by slipping him the *pozione* all unaware – he would take advantage of her action and reduce her to a whimpering and limp mass of ravaged flesh by the time he was finished with her!

Her tangerine-coloured frock and her slip were still off her shoulders and hanging round her waist, her chubby breasts bare and available close to him. He reached out to feel them, while her diligent attentions caused his *cazzo* to rear up to its full height and more – and still she caressed the unhooded purplish head with her hot tongue.

'Marina, Marina,' he sighed, watching how his shaft trembled between Marina's scarlet-painted lips as it tried to thrust in deeper and swell up to an impossible size! Her dark brown eyes glanced up to meet his, and with a long blissful shudder he saw and recognised in them an unappeasable hunger for sensation and bodily satisfaction.

She was up from the floor and astride his thighs again, close in to his belly, and this time there was no wadded silk between his shaking stiffness and her dark-curled split. She didn't try to stop him touching her now – she pushed her knees outward and let him play with her as much as he liked. The feel of her warm and smooth lips under his fingers was delightful and she gasped *Si, si, si, carissimo* when he parted them and pressed a finger inside to find her secret button.

She leaned forward to rest her hand on his shoulders and let her well-developed breasts dangle freely to encourage his hands to stroke them. Roland smiled at her and felt down between his belly and hers to grip his distended shaft, wet from her mouth, and steer its head into the opening of her soft split. At once she dropped a hand between her legs to help him find the way in and raised herself a little above his thighs for him to push up hard into her.

Roland held her bouncing breasts while she rode him with fast and nervous little jerks of her body, her eyes staring at short range into his, her mouth open in a grin of concentration. Soon his hands were again gripping the cheeks of her bare backside to assist her brisk little up and down jolting. This was only his second time – his previous experience of the *elisir* suggested a half dozen times before he started to slow down, and maybe more if she had increased the dose this time. He dug his nails into Marina's bottom to pull her closer, forcing his hard length yet deeper, and with his mouth touching her ear, he whispered the rhyme Carlo Missari had told him – except that it didn't rhyme in English:

> *Uno* – a man tired out from his day's work
> *Due* – a husband giving his wife her rights
> *Tre* – a lover with his mistress . . .

'Yes, darling Orlando,' Marina sighed, and continued with the lines herself:

> *Quattro* – a priest hearing a nun's confession
> *Cinque* – a monk in a brothel
> *Sei* – a gondolier taking his siesta . . .

'I'm going to have you at least six times before the day is out,' Roland whispered, 'this is only number two.'

'No it's not,' Marina sighed, 'you haven't had me even once yet. First you made love to my knickers, which doesn't count at all, and now it's I who am having you, *carissimo*, which doesn't count either.'

'Then next time I shall force you down on your back and there will be no question about it – and that will count as the first of the six.'

In his condition of exalted sexuality he had total confidence that he could do it six times at least before he collapsed.

'*Si*,' Marina gasped, her bouncing on him speeding up markedly, 'but the rhyme doesn't end at six, you know. You can keep going after you've been a gondolier. The last number is *dieci*.'

'*Ten*? And who does it ten times, darling?'

'A pigeon in the Piazza!'

Marina's body shook against him and her splayed legs in their sheer silk stockings were twitching out of control. Roland gave a grunting gasp of delight to recognise the indications of her approaching sexual crisis and thrust hard and fast upwards into her to reinforce her rhythmic bouncing. Immediately she cried out and shuddered in spasms of ecstasy, her climax pitching him over the edge headlong into his own, his hot passion spurting into her. The pleasure was so acute that he lolled back limply in his chair after he had finished, Marina's head drooping upon his shoulder.

When they recovered a little, Roland wanted to go on playing, but Marina insisted on dressing herself decently and made him tuck away his dangler and do up his trousers. She said it would be lunch time soon and it was silly to take any more risk in the palace.

'But you can't stop now!' said he, 'I want to make love to you all day!'

'And you shall,' she promised, 'but not here.'

'Where then – can we get a room in a hotel?'

'Someone might recognise me. I've got another idea, *carissimo* – come with me to my fortune-teller.'

'Fortune-teller? Whatever for?'

'Last night I had a dream – a very strange one I haven't had before. I want to know what it means, whether it's good luck or bad luck coming.'

'That's ridiculous! Dreams don't mean anything.'

'Mine do,' said Marina firmly, 'and I know a fortune teller – her name's Maddalena – who is very good at divining the meaning of them.

'But we're not living in the sixteenth century – this is 1927! How can you be so superstitious?'

'Why shouldn't I be superstitious, if it gives me pleasure? You needn't believe if you don't want to – come with me to see her, and afterwards we'll make love for as long as you like.'

'But fortune-tellers are all charlatans,' he protested, 'they only do it for the money they get from gullible people.'

'I'm sure you're right, darling,' Marina agreed with a smile, 'but I've never known this one to be wrong about my dreams. And besides, I gave you the last drop or two of the *elisir*, so you won't stay hard for long. I can get some more from Maddalena.'

'Good God – you get it from a fortune-teller?'

'Where do you think I buy it – at a chemist's shop? It's not exactly on doctor's prescriptions, you know.'

'She makes it, this palm-reader of yours?'

'I don't think so, but people like her have it to sell. So do you want to come with me or not?'

'Yes, then. I want a bottle of this remarkable physic to take home with me when I go. How much does she charge?'

'That depends whether she likes you or not. I've never had to give her more than fifteen hundred lira, but she charges a friend of mine two thousand. She has been known to turn people away if she finds them *antipatico*. So you must smile and be pleasant to her.'

Roland guessed that *antipatico* was the opposite of *simpatico* and nodded his understanding. The price sounded steep – it came to over eleven pounds sterling, about a week's wages for a university man like himself, but having experienced its effect, he had to have it, even if it cost twice that. With luck, he thought, grinning to himself, he could charge it to the publisher financing his trip, as academic research of some sort.

Once he had agreed to go with her, Marina decided they must leave right away.

'We can't have lunch here,' she insisted, 'not with Massimo at the table. It would be in my thoughts and in yours that we'd made love this morning and mean to do so again this afternoon – he would be sure to notice something and then the balloon would go up!'

There seemed to be an element of common sense in that, thought Roland, and he shuffled his papers into a tidy stack on the big old desk and went with Marina. She led him through the Malvolio collection that hung in corridors and suites, down the marble staircase and out through the door on to the Grand Canal. There was only one gondola moored at the landing-stage, and the motor-launch.

'We'll take the motorboat,' said Marina, 'it's quite a way.'

The boatman handed her in, Roland scrambled in beside her and with a roar of the engine they were skimming away from the side with the wheel hard over to bring them round to head downstream round the long run that led to the Accademia Bridge.

'We're not going to Cannaregio then – ' Roland asked, trotting out his joke again, 'where the house numbers range so high that only topographically trained postmen can find their way?'

'What *do* you mean?' said Marina. 'We're going to Castello.'

As Roland recalled his guide-book, the Castello district was the most easterly part of Venice, the tail of the fish, an area almost blank on his map except for the church of San Pietro. It was named after *a fort that is said to be there in defence of the district*, was the guide-book's futile explanation. There was a clear need for a postman trained in topography to go and find out if there was a fortified castle or not.

The boatman in his faded Malvolio colours handled the craft with insolent ease between two slow-moving water-buses, under the Accademia Bridge and on towards the white dome and steps of Santa Maria della Salute.

'This dream of yours,' said Roland, guessing that the boatman sitting in front of him and Marina could speak no English, 'why is it so important?'

'I told you – it's a dream I've never had before. At least, I can't ever remember having it. So it must mean something either good or bad, and I want to know what.'

'Will you tell me about it?'

'Yes, though you weren't in it,' said Marina, her hand resting lightly on his thigh, behind the boatman's back, 'maybe you can make something of it. I was being driven in an open car through the countryside, the car was white, with red leather upholstery, if that means anything. There's a chauffeur with a thick black moustache, wearing a dove-grey uniform and polished riding boots.'

'That seems to date it back to before the War,' said Roland.

'Oh yes, because there were two other girls in the back with me and all of us were wearing long summer frocks and big hats. None of us was over eighteen, I think, except the very handsome man with us, who was in his twenties. He was wearing a striped blazer, I seem to recall, and white flannels.'

'But was there room for four people in the back of Edwardian open motorcars?' Roland objected.

'Silly question,' said Marina, digging her fingernails hard

into the back of his hand, 'this was a dream – anything at all can happen in dreams.'

'Yes, sorry. Go on then – you were driving in the country?'

'We were going along a long straight road between fields of yellow wheat, and it looked almost like Sussex. But there were rows of tall poplar trees on either side of the road, so it may have been in France, I suppose. It was a hot day and after we'd driven miles we stopped for a picnic. We sat on a grassy river bank where the water was so clear you could see pebbles on the bottom and little fish swimming by. I remember there were sheep on the opposite bank. We opened the picnic hamper and ate cold pheasant and game pie and drank champagne . . .'

'This is a good-class dream,' Roland commented with a smile, 'Fortnum and Mason hampers only – no ham sandwiches and tea out of a thermos flask for you!'

The motor-launch was passing the landing for San Marco and he pointed to the two tall round granite columns that marked the entrance to the Piazza.

'There you are – on top of the one on the left – that's Saint Theodore standing on a crocodile he's just killed. See? Those columns were put there seven hundred years ago.'

'What curious things you know about Venice,' said Marina with a faint smile, 'but if I asked you to find me a fortune teller or someone to supply an *afrodisiaco* you wouldn't know where to begin. Why do you persist in seeing Venice as an art gallery?'

'That's not entirely true,' Roland retorted.

'Yes, it is. You preferred the Rialto Bridge to make love on instead of a bed. Tell me one thing you've discovered that has nothing to do with art and history, just one!'

'I know where to find a woman who for money will thrash your backside until you reach a climax,' he replied.

'No! But how extraordinary! How did you find her?'

'To be truthful, I didn't – Adalbert did. He likes that sort of thing. I find it a bit of a joke.'

'Live and let live,' said Marina, 'but what I said is true – you've seen nothing yet in Venice but pictures and churches. Paintings excite you more than people. I see I must dress up in costume like the women in old pictures, to make certain your interest in me stays hot.'

'Would you really do that for me?' Roland asked eagerly.

Without bothering to reply, she sank her nails into the

flesh of his thigh through his grey flannel trousers, making him wince a little.

The boatman opened the throttle a notch or two now they were away from the confined waters of the Grand Canal and the boat skimmed alongside the stone-built Riva quay, with the buildings of Venice to the left and open water to the right. The sky was impossibly blue and cloudless, stretching out forever and ever.

'Go on with your dream,' Roland suggested, 'so far all we've had is an expensive picnic.'

'Well, Reggie – that was the name of the very handsome man we had with us – was sitting opposite me on the grass, propped on an arm and with one knee raised. I looked up at him while he was eating and he'd unbuttoned his trousers – I could see dark hair showing and his limp thing was hanging out. Something made me go straight over to sit beside him, and he told me to hold my glass underneath his Wee Willy Winkie and let him dip it in the champagne.'

'I say!' Roland chortled. 'Was it chilled, the champagne?'

'I don't know – don't interrupt me. I did what he asked me to and straightaway it started to go stiff and long. Reggie didn't say anything, but he was smiling at me while I watched his bishop stand up hard. When it was stiff as a poker he took hold of it and rubbed it up and down – and it grew so long and thick I couldn't believe it! Then out poured out long spurts into my glass, all frothy and fizzy, just like champagne. So much came out that it brimmed over the top of the glass and ran down my hand and wrist and dripped down on the grass.'

The Malvolio boat sped past the canal entrance to the Arsenal – the shipyard where in the great days the Venetians built the wooden fighting-galleys that conquered an eastern Mediterranean Empire for them. *A big building where the famous ships of the Republic issued,* said the quaint guide-book, *founded in 1104, it was very well renowned and Dante himself mentions it in the XXI canto of the Hell in the Divine Comedy.* Which was all very well in its way but not worth interrupting Marina's curious dream to tell her of irrelevances like Dante's Inferno.

'The other girls were both watching me,' Marina was saying, 'and they were laughing, but I didn't care. Reggie was gushing warm and tickly on my hand and I felt like licking it off, but didn't know if I should, not till he told me he wanted me to taste it.'

Roland was thinking that the Contessa Marina seemed to have extremely graphic dreams – and remembering what she told him a few days before about her train dream, where she had seduced a man in a hat with other men watching, it was very obvious there was only one thing she dreamed about. In a way that seemed odd, bearing in mind her waking appetite for sexual satisfaction, at least Roland found it odd, having no acquaintance with Professor Freud's academic theorising on the female sex drive.

Meantime, her dream-tale and the warmth of her hand resting on his thigh were starting to arouse him. He hoped the boatman wouldn't glance back over his shoulder, and put a hand on her knee, sliding his fingertips over the sheer silk stocking. She gave him a brief smile and went on with her story.

'I raised the full glass to my lips and drank the contents in one long swallow. The taste was very sweet, like runny sticky honey straight from the honeycomb – I felt thrills of pleasure between my legs as I drank it down. When the glass was empty I held it upside down over my face and stretched my tongue up to lick the last drop – and straightaway I had the most wonderful climax.'

'And woke up feeling wet and sticky and contented?' enquired Roland, who recalled how the train dream had ended.

'You realise I've no knickers on?' she murmured. 'You soaked them right through and I couldn't put them back on.'

Roland slid his hand up her thigh over her frock until it lay in her groin. Between his fingers and her dark-curled *fica* there was only a layer of fine silk. He wondered if he dared caress her with the boatman sitting directly in front of them. By now he had become very excited, the Venetian *elisir* still working potently in him, his male pride standing exceedingly hard along his belly.

Marina settled the matter for him by opening her legs widely. Through her thin frock his fingertip found her split and moved slowly along it.

'The point is, Orlando,' she said softly, 'my dream didn't end there. The other girls were still laughing and then one of them said Reggie had tricked me, because his wine wasn't vintage. I turned to ask him if it was true, but he'd done his trousers up and wouldn't speak to me.'

'How very vexing,' said Roland, keeping a straight face.

'Well obviously I can't leave it like that,' Marina told him,

'I have to find out what it means.'

'In your experience,' Roland said, his fingertip moving with luxurious ease on her, 'what sort of meaning do you find your dreams generally have?'

'This one might be a warning about you,' she told him, 'don't you see that, darling? I mean, I've never had the dream before – only since you started to rape and pillage me. So I'm sure it must be something to do with you, though Reggie doesn't look at all like you.'

'Rape and pillage?' said Roland with a chuckle. 'Was it you gave the *elisir* to me or did I give it to you? If your silly old fortune-teller claims it's a bad luck dream and advises you never to take your knickers down for me again – what then?'

'She's never wrong about dreams,' Marina answered carefully, 'but that would be a bit drastic, my darling. I do hope nothing like that will be said.'

'Because you don't want to give me up?'

'Don't be idiotic – of course I have no intention of giving you up. But I shall worry every time we do it, if I think it's bringing bad luck.'

The motorboat had followed the long curve of the shore, and the eastern tip of Venice was in sight. The boatman throttled the engine right back and turned towards the land and then into a narrow canal that ran between old and dilapidated buildings after a while. Roland took his hand from Marina and she smiled at him while she closed her legs and smoothed down her frock. A word to the boatman and he halted by cracked stone steps in the quay, holding the boat steady while Roland climbed out warily before reaching down to assist Marina.

As he had expected, the boatman had been told not to wait for them, and off he chugged slowly, to find the way out at the far end of the canal.

'I've been warned about the Palazzo Malvolio gossip,' Roland said, 'and I'm slightly surprised you let him bring us this far. Won't he be able to guess now where we're going and spread the word?'

'I trust him,' said Marina carelessly, 'he's brought me here dozens of times. Besides, he doesn't know exactly where I go.'

'I can't imagine what he thinks,' Roland commented, staring about him as they strolled along a narrow street away from the canal. It was clear enough to him now why this area was almost blank on his map – there were no sights here for the tourist to see. It was where the poor of Venice lived, huddled in decrepit old tenement buildings, where plaster had cracked on the dirty walls, where paint peeled in rags from doors, where the paving was broken and dangerous, where lines of washing hung across the streets from side to side.

'Of course,' said Marina, who was totally unaffected by their dismal surroundings and the curious stares of poorly dressed women from open windows and doors, 'I've had a dream something like it before, but it didn't end so unsatisfactorily, that's why this version worries me.'

'What was unsatisfactory about it?' Roland asked. 'You said you had a wonderful climax in your sleep.'

'Yes, but Reggie tricked me somehow, didn't he? Before, you see, when I've had a picnic dream the other girls don't laugh at me – they rush over and want a sip from my glass. And when it's empty the girls hold Reggie down while I open his trousers and play with him till he's stiff again.'

'And then he gives you another glassful of froth, I suppose.'

'Why no, darling, nothing so repetitious. He tells the girls to hold me down and as I try to jump up and run away they knock me over on my back. One girl holds my ankles and the other one has my wrists – they're both terribly strong and they stretch my body, pulling brutally in opposite directions and spreading my legs wide apart . . .'

'Rape and pillage!' said Roland, laughing, then was silent when he saw how flushed Marina was and how she trembled. He put an arm round her waist to support her, and she leaned heavily against him.

'Then Reggie's on his knees between my legs,' she gasped, 'he literally rips off my knickers – I can hear the silk tearing in his hand. His *cazzo* is sticking right out of his trousers and it's grown enormous. I'm terrified and start screaming, but he pushes it into me and it's so big it stretches me wide open!'

She was shaking hard against Roland and he pulled her into an open doorway and set her back against the cracked wall. He felt guilty for playing with her in the motorboat when there was no opportunity to relieve her tension – that and the force of her dream had brought her to the brink of sexual climax.

'The girls twist my arms and legs besides pulling them,' she gasped, her belly pressing up to Roland's, 'I'm crying out at the top of my voice in agony and fear, because I know my bones will break in a minute ... and Reggie's huge *cazzo* is churning my insides to mush and I know it will split me wide open when he reaches his climax and floods me ...'

Surreptitiously, hoping nobody would pass by, Roland put his hand down between Marina's thighs and gently rubbed the back of his hand against her *fica* through the thin silk of her frock.

'I scream and scream,' she panted, 'and somehow I love being raped and abused like this. I love every second of it – and I reach a climax at least ten times ... oh my God ...'

Her words trailed off as her belly thumped against Roland and she shook in the convulsions of sexual release. Her throes were hard and short, and when they ended she laid her cheek against his and whispered:

'Does that makes sense, Orlando?'

ELEVEN

It seemed to Roland that even a specially trained postman would have difficulty in identifying any particular address amid the squalor and dereliction of the street through which Marina was conducting him. Overhead tatty washing was strung from balcony to balcony; at ground level the buildings were a succession of one-room junk shops. Yet Marina had no trouble in locating the doorway where the fortune-teller lived.

The house number had long since faded into indecipherability, but she turned in without hesitating and led the way upwards by crumbling flights of steps to the very top, under the roof. Roland followed up the unlit and gloomy stairs, fascinated and charmed by the way the cheeks of her bottom rolled alternately under her silk frock as she raised each leg in turn.

A cracked and peeling wooden door stood half-open at the top of the stairs, as if in invitation. Marina tapped once and went in, Roland close behind her. They were in a small and half-lit room, the wooden shutters being almost closed over the dormer window to keep out much of the daylight.

'*Buon giorno, Contessa*,' said a woman's voice, '*buon giorno, Signore.*'

The fortune-teller was sitting at a square table set close to the wall, staring at them, her hands folded in her lap. Roland had expected to meet a wrinkled old crone, though he could not explain why, and he was surprised to find that she was no more than thirty or so – his own age. She was dressed with as little style as most of the poor women he had seen about the city, in a short-sleeved floral frock of red and green, with no waist and a hemline down to mid-calf. If any flappers were to be seen in Venice, Roland hadn't come across them, nor did he now expect to.

'*Buon giorno*, Maddalena,' said Marina, 'I've brought a friend to see you – *Professore* Thornton from Inghilterra. He would like to buy some of your *elisir*.'

She had spoken in English for Roland's benefit, but Maddalena seemed to grasp the key words and went into a lengthy tirade in Italian, flashing her dark eyes at Roland, shrugging her meaty shoulders repeatedly, gesticulating with her hands. All this activity caused her breasts to roll about in her frock and show to anyone interested how very large and loose they were.

'She wants us to sit down,' Marina told him when at long last the fortune-teller paused to draw breath.

They sat side by side across the table from her, on a pair of unmatched chairs that looked as if they'd come from one of the junk-shops below. Remembering the price of the *elisir d'amore*, Roland began to wonder if this display of abject poverty could be real, or a cover against prying municipal officials seeking to collect taxes.

'Tell her about your dream,' he said, 'that's the main reason for being here, isn't it?'

The fortune teller listened intently while Marina related her dream at length. Now and then Roland caught a word or two that he recognised – *cazzo . . . champagne . . . erezione . . . orgasmo* . . . but all he concluded was that Italians called champagne the same as the French and the English did. At the end of it Maddalena took Marina's hands in her own across the table and stared intently into her eyes while she asked questions.

When she was satisfied with the answers, or so it seemed, she foraged in an old and battered wooden chest that stood behind her on the floor, and produced a large rolled-up document that Roland thought might be a map. But when she unrolled it on the table top, he saw it was something very different.

'It's her *Libro del Destino*,' Marina explained, 'the Book of Fate. Have you ever seen anything like it before?'

It was a sort of chart, Roland saw, big enough to cover the table top, and it was made of something more durable than paper – vellum, perhaps, or thin calf-skin parchment. Someone had put weeks of work – perhaps even months – using a black ink of some sort to divide the space into small squares, each with a symbol drawn in it. There were a thousand squares at least, but only thirty or so different symbols, repeated in diagonal rows.

Roland had never seen anything like it, and could only

begin to guess at its use. It seemed to him the symbols had meanings that were vaguely occult – he could distinguish a pyramid and a skull, crossed keys, a hand holding a dagger, a sailing ship, a crescent moon, an eye set in a triangle, an anchor. Trying not to grin and offend Maddalena or Marina, he thought it of some significance that these were also symbols used by tattooists to adorn sailors' arms. Although what the actual significance could be was by no means apparent to him.

'How many squares are there?' he asked, wondering what could be the mathematical base of this hocus-pocus.

Marina asked the question for him and translated the answer as *four times four times*, which was beyond his powers of mental arithmetic to calculate.

He watched the reading of the Book of Fate with a scepticism worthy of a university lecturer. Maddalena kept asking stabbing questions, and as the replies came, her fingertips shifted up and down the lines of symbols. She had broad capable hands and short fingers, with silver rings on each finger and both thumbs – flat plain rings.

Eventually she settled for a particular square on the chart and spoke slowly and clearly to Marina, who seemed surprised by what she heard. Roland had been listening closely, out of pure curiosity as he assured himself, but he could make no sense of the fortune-teller's words.

'What did she say?' he asked Marina. 'Tell me.'

'I asked if my dream means good luck or bad luck,' she said, 'and the *Libro del Destino* gave a very strange answer.'

'What?' he demanded, beginning to lose his composure.

'It said my dream indicates an increase in riches.'

'That's ridiculous! It was a dream about sex, not money.'

'But dreams are rarely about what they seem to be about,' she answered firmly, 'I thought everyone knew that.'

Roland could see Maddalena eyeing him suspiciously across the table. Perhaps the Italian word for *ridiculous* was close enough to the English for her to understand what he said – or perhaps she had caught the disbelief in his tone of voice. Either way, if she took against him, he wouldn't get the *elisir*. He smiled pleasantly back at her and in a low voice asked Marina what to do to make a sympathetic impression.

'Ask her for a reading – it's only two hundred lira,' Marina advised.

'But I can't remember any dreams!'

'It doesn't have to be a dream – you can ask questions about anything that is important to you.'

'Like what?'

'Well . . . the book you came here to write – will it make you famous? Would you like to know that?'

'I know the answer to that one already,' said Roland, a touch of regret in his voice. 'Let me think – yes, I've got it. Will you interpret for me?'

Marina explained to Maddalena that her friend wished to ask a question of the *Libro del Destino*, probably adding that he had been very impressed by the answer to her own question, to judge by the length of the speech she made. The fortune-teller seemed placated by whatever was said and reached across the table, her palms turned upwards, for Roland's hands. He put his palms flat on hers and her short fingers gripped tightly.

He stared into her broad face, noting her square jaw-line and high cheekbones. Her unwinking eyes were a very dark brown, as was her hair, drawn back and tied at the nape of her thick neck – and she looked closely into his eyes, as if searching out his sincerity – or lack of it.

'What do you want to ask?' said Marina.

'Ask her if I shall find the lost article I'm looking for.'

Marina translated for him, and the fortune-teller's grasp on his hands grew tighter still and he had the impression that she was pulling him towards her, their eyes getting closer together and hers dark with unfathomable thoughts. He told himself that was romantic story-book nonsense, and that Maddalena was trying to mesmerise him and trick him into believing whatever she said in answer to his cryptic question. To break the spell, if spell it was, he glanced deliberately down at the vast loose breasts inside her cheap frock.

Tette, that was the word Adalbert told him for them when they went to visit Signorina Caducci, and *tette* seemed somehow very appropriate as a description for the fortune-teller's huge soft danglers. Roland decided that it would be very exciting to get his hands on them, and went on to ask himself what it would be like to have her on her back and make love to her.

He thought he detected a trace of amusement in her eyes when he looked into them again, and more than that even, a glint of *I dare you to try*! But her face remained impassive and perhaps he was imagining it. She spoke a few words staccato, and Marina repeated in English:

'Odd or even? Quick – without thinking!'
'Odd.'
'Again – quick!'
'Odd.'
'And again!'
'Even.'
'Again!'

In all, he was asked the question five times, and gave random answers in reply, certain that the whole procedure was nonsense and that nothing whatsoever depended on which he chose. If she had asked him four times, there might have been some connection with the earlier disclosure that the chart had *four times four times* squares.

But to Maddalena the answers had some esoteric meaning, and she let go of his hands to reckon on her fingers – though quite what she was calculating was her secret. From watching her at work earlier on Marina's question, Roland was certain that the Book of Fate was operated by means of a numerical formula but for the life of him he could not see how Maddalena extracted a number from a chance sequence such as odd, odd, even, odd, odd.

Be that as it may, the fortune-teller's stubby fingers were smoothing their way across the chart, making something or other match. Her forefinger stopped at last on a square containing a heart pierced by an arrow. After a pause, she gave her answer – or if we are to be precise, said Roland to himself, the answer of the *Libro del Destino*.

'What did she say?' he enquired of Marina.

'She said it does no harm to sweep the same room twice.'

'Pearls of wisdom!' said he mockingly. 'I could have got an answer like that out of Old Moore's Almanac, for all the use it is. Still, thank her for me, and say I shall sweep diligently. And ask about the *elisir* again.'

There followed a lengthy conversation between Marina and the fortune-teller, with hand-waving and shoulder-shrugging on both sides. Finally, with a sly smile on her broad face, Maddalena rolled up her chart and put it back in the wooden chest.

'She says she hasn't any of the *elisir*,' Marina reported. 'I can't tell if she's telling me the truth or whether she doesn't want to sell it to you. Smile at her and look pleasant while I try again. She's very easily offended, and you're not exactly a believer, are you?'

More conversation in rapid Italian – or the typical Venetian dialect, no doubt, thought Roland, trying not to let the woman notice his wry amusement at the entire rigmarole of persuasion, refusal, flattery, compromise, conciliation. This time Marina had better news.

'She really doesn't have any of the *elisir* here at the moment but she can lay hands on some if we give her a couple of hours. And she's agreed to let us stay here while she goes out for it. Do you want to make love in a fortune-teller's den, Orlando? I said you'd pay two thousand lira altogether for the *elisir* and the room and your reading from the Book of Fate – is that all right?'

'Fine,' said he, reaching for his wallet and careful not to show his dismay at the price.

As soon as Maddalena had the money in her hand she became all smiles. This one room under the tiles contained her facilities for fortune-telling, sleeping, washing, cooking and eating. She took Marina and Roland by the hand and led them to her low bed against the opposite wall, chattering away all the time. At her request they stood side by side, clasped hands stretched over the bed, while she fetched a handful of dried and shredded herb mixture from her wooden box.

'Pot-pourri on the bed?' Roland asked, eyebrows rising.

'Patchouli, I think,' said Marina, 'to bring happiness – hush now, or you'll upset her.'

What came next was the strangest thing Roland had ever seen. Maddalena stood at the foot of the bed and scattered pinches of her dried petals and leaves over it while she recited a poem – it was obviously that because even to Roland it rhymed after a fashion:

> *Questi segreti io sapro,*
> *Lucciola mia libera ti lasciero*
> *Quando i segreti della terra io sapro*
> *Tu sia benedetta ti diro*
>
> *Se questa grazi tu mi farai*
> *Nel tempo che balliamo,*
> *Il lume spengnerai,*
> *Cosi al l'amore*
> *Liberamente la faremo*

That done, the fortune-teller drew Roland to the side to

hand him a small glass bottle stoppered by a waxed cork.

'*Profumo per fare l'amore*,' she said with a cunning grin and to make sure he understood properly, she dabbed her fingertips on her breasts and down her belly to where her heavy thighs met under her drab frock.

'*Afrodisiaco?*' he asked.

She winked at him lewdly and gave him a long explanation that meant nothing to him. But he guessed she was telling him of the marvellous ingredients that went to make this rare and precious perfume, for he thought he recognised a word or two, and surely *rosa muschiata* and *orchidea spagnola* must mean musk-rose and Spanish orchid, though he had not the least idea what flowers they could be – not the sort to be found in an English country garden, he suspected.

He stood with an arm round Marina's waist, watching while the fortune-teller threw a printed kerchief over her dark hair and left the room. She pulled the splintered door firmly shut after her, whereupon the lovers sat down on her bed.

'The verses,' said Roland, 'what did they mean?'

'I can't remember all of it – it was something about knowing secrets and being blessed and putting out the light and making love many times. I suppose it must be some sort of folk charm.'

'She's very versatile, your Maddalena,' Roland said jokingly, 'fortunes told, palms read, charms, spells, talismans supplied to order, potions, lotions, poisons and aphrodisiacs! London was full of people like her in Shakespeare's time, but nowadays the best you can hope for is an old lady reading tea leaves for half-a-crown in the suburbs.'

'You shouldn't mock what you don't understand,' said Marina.

There was no point in carrying the conversation any further – Roland put his hands on her hips and kissed her lightly. At the same time, his fingers were busy with the square gold buckle of her white belt, and when that hung loose, he reached behind her to undo the buttons of her frock. She raised her arms up above her head when he slid it from under her bottom and up her body, revealing smooth bare thighs pressed close together. The frock was off and discarded, and Marina sat in only her stockings and short slip.

Her orchid-pink slip was enticingly short, its lace-edged hem coming down only just low enough to cover her belly-button. The matching knickers which ought to have clothed her below were of course missing – soaked through by Roland's spurting desire and left hidden somewhere in the impressive Library of the Palazzo Malvolio. Marina's soft white belly was bare, and the walnut-brown curls where her thighs were pressed together.

Roland went down on his knees beside the bed and devoted his attention to removing her flesh-covered silk stockings slowly. First he slipped rosebud-embroidered garters over her knees and off, then rolled the first stocking down, letting his sensitive fingers trail lightly over her skin, exciting her and himself.

When he had both stockings off, he stroked up her bare thighs and sighed to feel their satin-smoothness. He pressed her legs gently apart and stared in delight at her dark-brown curls and the fleshy lips of her *fica*. She crossed her arms to take hold of her slip and lifted it over her head and dropped it on the bed beside her, cupped her hands underneath her bare breasts and jiggled them up and down.

Her ploy worked at once – Roland clasped her by the waist and put his mouth to her right breast and flicked his tongue over its bud. She was easily aroused, and soon hitched herself up on her hands to slide her bottom backwards on the bed and lie down at full length. Roland feasted his eyes on the bounties of her body, naked but for the green-stone necklace round her neck.

'It's time to keep your promise, Orlando,' she said, 'and you promised to make love to me all day.'

Roland stripped himself naked in record time, his eyes never leaving her body. He sat on the side of the bed and stroked her thighs – her legs were together modestly when he began, but as his hands moved over her smooth flesh, she moved her knees away from each other slowly, and put her hands underneath her head. He remembered the little bottle of scent the fortune-teller had given him, *profumo per fare l'amore*, she had called it, perfume for love-making.

The waxed stopper had been pushed in so hard that it took him some time and effort to prise it out with his fingernails. He sniffed at it, and was disappointed. It was sweetish, not very strong, a sort of flowery essence that a young girl might wear to her First Communion.

He shook a few drops out on to Marina's breasts and smoothed it on her skin with his fingers. The warmth of her body seemed to release the fragrance hidden in the liquid, and an intenser perfume reached his nostrils – the floweriness turning now to a muskiness that was pleasantly erotic. Much more interested, he dabbed the perfume round Marina's breasts lavishly, and then in the smooth hollows of her exposed armpits.

'Oh, I like that,' she said.

Roland splashed a little onto her belly and smoothed it into her warm flesh with the palm of his hand.

'Yes, oh yes,' she murmured, her loins jinking upwards softly and slowly, 'that's lovely.'

The perfume had increased in strength as Roland spread it on her, to a provocative headiness that made him almost giddy with pleasure. The effect on Marina was much the same, he observed, for she opened her legs in invitation. He sprinkled the perfume into her soft groins and eased it in with gentle fingertips. A little cry escaped her and her legs opened wider.

Roland progressed to her walnut-brown curls, combing a little of the perfume into them with his fingers. She sighed again and again at the touch and her legs jerked nervously. Roland pushed the cork back into the little bottle and set it carefully down on the floor, then leaned over her to caress the fleshy petals of her *fica*. The result was astounding – her back arched up off the bed until she balanced on her heels and shoulders, and she cried out in shrill delight as climactic ecstasy washed through her body in great waves.

As Roland watched her writhing and jerking, there came into his mind a thought that made him gasp. Twice in half an hour he had seen Marina overwhelmed by involuntary orgasms, and it was extremely exciting to observe – and to help bring about. There was some combination of factors, one being the perfume perhaps, that made her more than usually open to suggestion, and highly sensitive. This was an opportunity that might never come about again in his life, and it was not to be missed.

It had been the telling of her dream, or her daydream maybe, that had triggered her first involuntary release, standing in the doorway. In Roland's memory was a clear image of two young girls holding Marina's arms and legs and pulling away from each other ... and a man on his knees between her parted legs, a long hard *cazzo* sticking stiffly out of his unbuttoned trousers. And the words she had gasped out when Roland held her tight to stop her falling: *I know he's going to split me wide open when he reaches his climax and floods me . . . I scream and scream and I love every second of it . . . I reach a climax at least ten times . . .*

Roland was sure he knew what would have an instant effect on her – he reached for his belt from the floor, buckled it tight about her wrists, pulled her arms up above her head and lashed the belt end round the cast-iron rail at the top of the bed.

'What are you doing?' Marina gasped, her body bucking as she tugged against her bonds.

'Ravishing you,' he replied, reaching for her silk stockings. 'Your worst nightmare is about to come true.'

He had one leg stretched out and attached by the ankle to the iron rail at the bottom of the bed before she seemed to grasp completely what was in his mind. Her free leg kicked out at him and her bare foot missed his face by inches as he ducked – then he had her ankle and overcame her struggle by brute force while he finished tying her down.

'You're helpless and at my mercy,' he said, staring down with lustful eyes at her lush spreadeagled body. 'I've decided to be Reggie and split you apart with my giant implement.'

He positioned himself between her parted thighs and saw that she was staring wide-eyed at his stiff part, jutting up as high as his belly-button. It was swollen and hard, and it twitched, though to describe it as *giant* was overstating the facts. But to a woman on her back with her legs fixed apart, it probably looked impressive enough.

'Oh no!' said Marina, proving him right, 'you'll never get that in me – it's far too big!'

Roland ignored her protest, his fingers stroking quickly up and down the wet and prominent lips of her dark-haired *fica*. In three jerks her bottom rose up off the bed and she was making a loud panting sound. Her eyes rolled up in her head to show the whites, her mouth opened wide, her limbs shook in their bonds – and Roland saw that she was teetering on the threshold of release – and he had hardly touched her! He opened her wide and pressed the ball of his thumb to her slippery bud, and at the touch she screamed in climactic ecstasy.

Roland sighed and forced himself to remain still, though his overwhelming desire was to hurl himself on her belly and pierce her with his impatiently throbbing part. But there was more yet – much more he wanted to do to her first, and he waited for her to calm down. When her eyes opened at last and she was looking at him in wonder, he resumed his game with her.

'I've got you tied down and you can't escape,' he told her, taking his stiff length in his hand to jerk it up and down, 'no matter how many times you keep on reaching your climax, there's no getting away – I'm going to ram this into you and split your belly wide open . . .'

Words failed Marina as she stared at his hand moving firmly on his engorged shaft, and she made a gurgling noise.

'Scream,' he said, 'I want to hear you scream when I tear you wide open. Scream, Marina!'

His other hand was down between her legs, and as he finished speaking he slid two joined fingers into her and pushed as far as they would go. The words and penetration pitched her into an instant sexual seizure. Her dark brown eyes were wide open but unfocused and there was a trickle of saliva from a corner of her mouth. She was uttering a continuous high-pitched shriek, rolling from side to side to the extent her bonds allowed.

Roland removed his hand and sat back on his heels, astounded by what he had achieved. He stared fascinated as the squirmings of Marina's perspiration-slippy body gradually subsided, and her shriek fell to a continuous moan. After a long time only a tremor or two shook her belly, and she was silent. Eventually her eyes opened and she looked up at him, slightly dazed by the intensity of her sensations.

'Orlando,' she murmured languidly, '*carissimo* – you will kill me if you make me do it again.'

It was an invitation not to be turned down – Roland laid his belly on hers and slid his distended length right up into her hot wetness. Without a moment's pause, he stabbed frantically, hearing her cry out, *You're splitting me apart!* and crying out himself, *Yes, yes, Marina, I'll burst your belly wide upon!* She went into climactic convulsions at once, so strong that she brought Roland's crisis in seconds, and with savage thrusts he fountained his lust into her belly and screamed himself in his furious release.

When he eventually came to himself again, Marina was silent and limp under him. He eased himself off her and picked at the knots in her stockings to release her legs. The silk stockings were laddered and ruined, but that didn't matter. When he took the leather belt off her wrists she opened her eyes and smiled at him and held her arms out to show him the red marks on her skin. He rubbed her wrists gently to restore the circulation.

'That was *stupendo*,' she said, 'the sensations were fantastic and I thought I'd die of them. Let's do it again when we've had a little rest.'

Roland lay beside her and they talked of Maddalena and if her *Libro del Destino* was of any use – Marina set on its accuracy in interpreting her curious dreams, Roland sceptical of methods of fortune-telling, prediction, dream reading, and other signs and omens.

'You were asking about the Uccello painting you can't find in the palace, weren't you?' Marina asked. 'Why are you concerned about it? There are hundreds of pictures on the walls, not to mention busts and statues by the gross.'

'I'd like to find that particular one,' he said, 'if it's in the palace still. It's an Uccello the art world doesn't know of – and it would be a triumph to announce its existence.'

'Well, you heard what the Book said – you're to look in the same place again. But you haven't looked anywhere yet – you've made Padre Pio go hunting round for you.'

But Marina's heart was not in it – she was hot to continue their sexual games, and all the time they talked she never left off touching Roland and kissing him and stroking him, her hands and lips roaming across his chest and belly.

She had him on his back with his half-hard *cazzo* clasped in her hand, trying to rouse it fully. A thought struck her, and she got the little glass bottle from the floor and started to massage the fortune-teller's *profumo* into his belly and around his pompoms. The heavy and musky fragrance set his blood racing, and Marina's too, though she scarcely needed help in that.

'Tell me about the woman who spanked you,' she said, fingers rubbing the perfume gently into his now upright shaft, 'did you like it? What's her name?'

'Renata,' said Roland, enjoying the little tremor of pleasure Marina's attentions were sending through him, 'I went there to see if it was like Masoch's novel, but it wasn't really.'

'Adalbert's got a copy of that book in German,' said Marina, 'it's got illustrations by somebody he says was quite famous in Vienna, though I forget his name. There's one of a man tied to one of the pillars of a four-poster bed naked and a woman in a long fur coat whipping him. Is that what you went for?'

Roland's pleasant little sensations had developed into a daze of erotic bliss as Marina's experienced fingers touched him and teased him, spread the perfume on him, urging him slowly toward the familiar ecstasy.

'It was all different,' he murmured, 'she had no whip and she pulled my trousers down and used my belt across my backside. It hurt quite a lot – and it certainly didn't excite me. Masoch's hero squirts off on the carpet when Wanda flogs him. Then when he's unbound, he crawls naked across the floor to kiss Wanda's foot – but nothing like that happened to me.'

'Is she pretty, this Renata? Did she strip naked for you, or did she have a fur coat on?'

'No, she's tall and thin and plain and she wore a cheap pink slip while she did it.'

Ordinarily Roland would have been excessively wary of talking about one woman to another. They took things so very personally that even the most casual remark could cause offence so deadly that it might never be forgiven. But now he had been permitted a role in one of Marina's fantastic dreams, he felt it might be safe to share a secret of his own with her – up to a point.

'So what did you do when you found that being beaten was no use?' she asked. 'Did you have her the proper way?'

'No, I don't think she does that. She grabbed hold of me and handled me so furiously that she made me do it – and as soon as she saw it spurting she started to thrash my behind again. She need not have bothered, but I suppose the point was to make me experience the actual sensations of sexual Masochism, in case I came to like it and wanted more.'

His male part was at fullest stretch and jerking of its own volition. Marina let it alone then, not wishing to precipitate an emission before she was ready for it. She asked him to roll over on his face, and rubbed Maddalena's perfume into the cleft between the cheeks of his bottom.

'No marks left on you,' she commented, 'she couldn't have hit you very hard. Wasn't it even a little bit exciting?'

'Not even a little bit,' he assured her, though he spoke with less than the complete truth. Although it had been painful when Renata thrashed him with the belt, his *cazzo* had stood up hard enough, otherwise she wouldn't have been able to manipulate him by hand while holding him down helpless on his back with one of her bare feet under his chin.

'Perhaps she should have spanked you with her hand, *caro* – it might have produced a better result,' said Marina.

Before Roland had time to say it wouldn't, she landed a sharp smack across his bottom, making his body jerk so that his *cazzo* was rubbed against the bedcover he lay on. Marina smacked him again, to see what his reaction would be, and he let her do so half a dozen times, enjoying the rub of the coarse bedcover at each spasm. But he had no intention of wasting his strength on a threadbare cover, as he had on Renata's towel, and he rolled on his side to avoid further blows.

'I'll tell you what would be exciting,' he said, his face now as pink-flushed as his bottom, 'let me spank you, darling.'

'Why not?' she said. 'I've never had my bottom spanked, even though I've often thought about it. Italian men don't seem to be interested.'

With no more ado, she slid her legs over the edge of the bed and arranged herself with her knees on the floor and her torso lying on the rough coverlet. Roland moved round behind her, his stiff part jutting out and nodding to his movements. He was too high up, or she was too low down, for a satisfactory spanking, unless he sat on the bed beside her. But then he would not see the effect of his slaps.

He fetched one of the rickety old chairs from near the table and placed it so that he had a perfect view of Marina's exposed bottom and was in the ideal position to smack it. For a time he contemplated her chubby-cheeked bare bottom, then he remembered the fortune-teller's perfume and smoothed a few drops on to her – first on her white cheeks and then down the deep cleft, his fingertip tickling at the puckered node between them, making her gasp and her body jerk.

The heady fragrance of the perfume made his head spin and his stiff part was throbbing impatiently. He raised his hand and smacked Marina's bottom hard, enjoying the sting of the blow as his palm landed on her wobbly cheek. She let out a shrill yelp of surprise and discomfort, and thus encouraged he spanked her a few more times.

But the *elisir* was still working powerfully on him, coupled with the insidious effect of the *profumo* and he was unable to look away from her plump and dark-haired *fica*, tantalisingly on view from the rear between her parted thighs. He slipped from the chair to kneel close behind Marina and steer his quivering pride to the moist split waiting for his pleasure.

'Orlando!' she sighed. 'Have you spanked me enough?'

He gripped her well-rounded hips to steady himself, drew in a long breath and with a strong push drove his swollen length right up into her. She cried out pleasurably to feel her *fica* so well filled, and Roland initiated rhythmic strokes that delighted them both. Marina was moaning continuously, her body shaking to his determined strokes so much that her soft breasts were flopping under her, until he reached under her and seized them, his feverish hands squeezing and rolling them vigorously.

Through his delirium of pleasure Roland could hear his belly smacking against Marina's bottom, hot flesh on hot flesh, and a long exclamation of joy burst from him as he spurted his desire into her. Her bottom thumped back at his belly to force him in further, and she wailed in her climactic sensations.

They lay on the bed to recover, Roland's head pillowed on her soft belly, the mingled scent of musk rose and female eroticism warm in his nostrils. The premonition he had felt at the start of their sex-play had proved to be absolutely correct – it was a day to be remembered, a chance that might never be repeated in his life, not even with Marina. It must not be wasted.

'Darling Marina,' said he lazily, the feel of her flesh under his face, 'tell me another of your dreams. Are they all set in England twenty years ago, like the train and the picnic?'

'I often have Venetian dreams,' she answered, 'usually about making love in a gondola going up the Grand Canal, or stripping naked on top of the Clock Tower in the Piazza and shouting down to the tourists to look at me ... things like that. But a month or two I had a most curious dream about the Prime Minister.'

'Our Prime Minister?' said Roland in amazement. 'The pipe-smoking Mr Stanley Baldwin? You can't find *him* exciting!'

'No, no, of course not – I mean our Italian Prime Minister, Signor Mussolini. I dreamed I was being received in audience by him in the Quirinale Palace in Rome. He was wearing a grey suit with a carnation in his buttonhole, and he sat in a big chair with his back to the windows. I knew I was there to ask him for something, but I couldn't remember what.'

'Have you ever met him?' asked Roland in surprise.

'No, never – he's an awful brute, huge and strong and formed like a boxer. They say he throws government typists across his desk and rapes them several times a day.'

'And this happened to you?'

'Nothing so common! I'm not a little typist. I was annoyed by his dreadful manners and asked him why he hadn't got up to kiss my hand when I came into his office. He said his feet were tired from standing all day making a speech from the balcony to the huge crowd outside. That seemed to make sense, so I decided to overlook his rudeness. He asked me to take his shoes off and rub his feet, and without a second thought I went down on my knees on the carpet.

'I say – it's not a political dream after all!' said Roland.

'He was wearing English-made black brogues,' Marina went on, ignoring the interruption. 'I pulled the first shoe off and saw he had no socks on. I knelt there holding his bare foot in my hands and he said, *That's better* and wiggled his toes. They were long strong toes, more like fingers – and he pushed his foot up my skirt and started to tickle me between the legs. That's when I realised I hadn't any knickers on.'

'That seems to be often the case in your dreams, my darling,' said Roland with a grin.

'He told me I could call him Benito when we were alone, and I felt his big toe pushing up inside me while he sat calmly there with his arms folded across his chest. It was so exciting that I was giddy from the sensations and I was afraid one of his staff would come into the office before I reached my climax . . .'

Roland turned his head on Marina's soft belly to look between her breasts toward her face. Her eyes were shut in reminiscence and her expression was one of barely contained lust.

'He reached out to hold my hair and pulled my face into his lap,' she whispered, 'his trousers were undone and his enormous bishop was sticking straight up. He pushed me down on it and I opened my mouth and took it right in and sucked it . . . it was so big and strong . . . so marvellously *brutal* . . .'

'Darling Marina,' Roland interrupted her, his male part hard and ready again, 'I love this dream of yours, but it was with the wrong man. Kneel down on the floor and let me put my toes between your legs...'

TWELVE

It took Roland the whole of the next day and night to recover from his games with the Contessa Marina in the fortune-teller's hovel. He slept until midday and woke to find cold coffee and a plate of sweet bread rolls by his bedside, brought hours before by a chambermaid who had given up hope of waking him.

He ate the rolls, being very hungry, while he decided what to do. His conclusion was it would be sensible to vanish from the Palazzo Malvolio for the rest of the day, in case Marina came looking for him. Not that he didn't want to see her again, but not yet – not until his sexual responses were functioning fully and adequately once more.

Lunch with the family was out of the question, for she would be there, he guessed. He washed and dressed and left the palace fast but almost furtively by the landward door into the square with the stone well. An easy ten minute stroll in the sunshine brought him to the Accademia Bridge, and he was in time to find Carlo Missari preparing to leave for lunch and a siesta for the rest of the afternoon. Carlo's moon face beamed in pleasure to see him, and he was even more pleased to be invited to lunch.

'But let's stay on this side of the Grand Canal,' said Roland with a conspiratorial wink, 'I don't want to be seen by anyone from the Palazzo Malvolio.'

'Ah, the Contessa Marina is a lady who makes many demands, I can see,' Carlo commented, 'but you will be safe with me.'

He put on his panama hat and led the way out of the Accademia Gallery and across a narrow side canal into a large square with the inevitable sixteenth century church in one corner. Opposite was a restaurant with five or six tables out on the paving, and the waiter standing by them welcomed Carlo as an old acquaintance.

'The church of San Trovaso,' said Carlo, pointing across the square to the not particularly distinguished building, 'do you know who that was?'

'I've been torturing my memory ever since I saw it marked in the little guide-book you gave me, but no such person comes to mind. He must be a local Venetian saint — what did he do?'

'There is no *he*,' said Carlo with a grin, 'Trovaso is a *they*. The church is dedicated to Saint Gervasio and Saint Protasio.'

'Don't tell me!' Roland exclaimed. 'It's another example of your typical Venetian dialect!'

'Precisely so! No one knows why or how, but in the course of the centuries we Venetians have shortened the names of Gervasio and Protasio into *Trovaso*, so that we have in a way invented a saint who never existed.'

'And highly appropriate too,' said Roland, 'because Gervasio and Protasio never existed in the first place. Fifteen hundred years ago the Bishop of Milan discovered some old buried bones and decided they were the remains of two Christian martyrs. He made up names for them, and they became widely venerated. It's fascinating to know they live on in Venice, so to speak, under another name.'

It occurred to Roland that the human credulity that gave names to anonymous old bones and built churches in their honour was the same that caused Maddalena's clients to pay for their questions to be answered by the Book of Fate. But he thought it better not to involve Carlo in that line of speculation.

The cold drinks they had ordered arrived, and they decided on a light lunch, starting with rice and peas, followed by scampi cooked in wine and a thick sweet tomato sauce, with a salad of fennel, sliced tomato and onion. And naturally a carafe of *vino bianco* from the barrel.

'You may laugh at our San Trovaso if you wish,' said Carlo, 'but in his church you will find a mural of the Last Supper by Tintoretto.'

'Very nice, I'm sure,' said Roland, 'but it's about Uccello I want to talk to you.'

'Paolo Uccello? We have nothing by him in the Accademia. He was not Venetian. But there are mosaics in San Marco thought to be by him.'

'Yes, I've seen them — in the side chapel of the Madonna

dei Mascoli, scenes from the life of the Virgin Mary, beautifully done with a magnificent architectural background. The verger or whoever it was I talked to gave me a garbled tale of Giambono, Castagno and Uccello working together on these mosaics, but it didn't sound all that convincing. I asked what Mascoli meant and he said it was the Venetian word for *masculines*, and wives pray before the Madonna's altar to conceive male children.'

'So they do!' said Carlo with a chuckle. 'That's because the Madonna's children were sons, Jesus, James and the others. It is not the origin of the name – the chapel was called that because it was paid for by a men's religious club.'

'Why did they do that?'

'Who knows? Perhaps to guarantee their sins with women would be absolved without a heavy penance. But what is your interest in Uccello, Roland?'

First swearing him to secrecy, Roland set out the mystery of the missing masterpiece from the Palazzo Malvolio.

'But this is stupid!' Carlo exclaimed. 'A picture disappears and no one knows it's gone, because no one knew it was there in the first place!'

'No one but a fat old priest,' said Roland, 'and he views it as a piece of furniture and thinks he will find it in an attic if he looks long enough.'

'*Dio mio*! This is not the way to organise and preserve an art collection as important as the Malvolio! The Count ought to have given it to the Accademia, not to a foreign mistress.'

'Maybe,' Roland said doubtfully, 'but the collection was his to dispose of as he wished, not some sort of national treasure. A month ago I would have agreed with you completely, but I have come to understand the family point of view since moving into the palace – their home is not a museum for tourists.'

How very pleasant it was, Roland was thinking, to have lunch here in the open air under a striped awning to keep the sun off and surrounded by buildings of interest and note, observing the local Venetians and tourists strolling across the square about their business. He felt he could get used to this sort of life very easily, and to the life of the Malvolio palace, given half a chance. But the voice of Carlo brought him back from a dream of everlasting holiday to the problems of the present.

'You can see the result of this aristocratic arrogance – an

unknown masterpiece stolen and sold, forever lost to the world of culture!'

'Maybe,' said Roland again, 'but there is a faint possibility that it has not yet disappeared off the face of the earth into the secret vault of a megalomaniac American business tycoon.'

'You have evidence of that?'

In truth, he had nothing of the sort, merely a hint from the fortune-teller's Book of Fate that it was still worthwhile to look for the picture. It was out of the question to tell Carlo that – the response would be surely be mockery and scorn.

'Not evidence exactly,' said Roland, wondering why he placed the least credence in Maddalena's words, 'but I came across the merest hint that it might still be recoverable. More than that I cannot reveal.'

'Well, well,' said Carlo, jumping to conclusions, 'then you must know who took the painting. Was it the old priest?'

'No, I don't think so. But this is not a subject to talk about until I am certain who is responsible.'

'And when you are sure – what will you do?'

'That will depend on who took it, don't you agree? I am not a policeman, Carlo. I think I have some sort of responsibility to Mrs Tandy to inform her of the state of her collection, but what happens after that is not my business.'

'As a *professore* and a man of culture and erudition it must be your business what happens to the Malvolio collection after this. It can happen again – the pictures can be disposed of one by one in secret. Only you can prevent this barbarity.'

'One step at a time,' said Roland, impressed by the force of Carlo's words and the passion with which they were spoken, and the vigorous hand-waggling and dramatic facial expressions that went with them. 'Before I leave Venice you may depend on me to give all due consideration to the preservation of the Malvolio collection.'

'Good, good! I rely on your word. Shall we have fresh fruit and cheese now or ice-cream?'

'I shall have that wonderful cassata ice-cream. And perhaps in the meantime, dear friend, you can enlighten me on something I do not understand in the very interesting guide-book you gave me. It is in the section on St Marks church – here it is: *In the front of the central door a square opening called pozzo is covered with mosaics of the sixteenth century. The mosaic St Mark in ecstasies on the door belongs to the same period.*'

At about two-thirty Carlo said he must leave, as his wife

would be wondering by now where he was. Roland decided to stay on for a while and drink another cup of coffee with a little glass of cognac. He wanted to stay clear of the Palazzo Malvolio for the rest of the day, in case Marina was looking for him, but it was difficult to know what to do in a city where the galleries and other places of cultural interest closed for the afternoon. And for safety's sake he thought it better to stay on the opposite side of the Grand Canal to the Palazzo.

After consulting his guide-book he decided to go and look at the church of the Angel Raphael, which according to his map was not very far away. Churches named after angels were rare, in his experience, because of the problem of obtaining a suitable holy relic. Bits of saints could be bought openly on the ecclesiastical market, thumbnails, toe-joints, legbones, and with that sanctifying the new church, you were in business. But a feather from an angel's wing was somewhat harder to get hold of.

On the other hand, where saints were concerned, Venice was a law unto itself. The guide-book was not very forthcoming. All it had to say was: *The Church of the Angelo Raffaele, containing an exquisite work of the eighteenth century Stories of Tobiolo by Guardi on the walls of the organ*. No hint as to which of the Guardi brothers had painted the picture on the organ, which in itself seemed an odd thing to do. But the lives of the brothers were totally obscure, except, Roland remembered, they had a younger sister who married Giambattista Tiepolo, who painted the murals of Roman gods and goddesses in the dining room of the Palazzo Malvolio.

On another subject the guide-book had some curious information to offer – that on the quay alongside the narrow canal on which stood the Angel Raphael's church and the Palazzo Zenobio was to be found the house where Veronica Franca plied her trade three hundred years ago. She charged two *scudi*, it said, and after she retired founded a home for fallen women. That being so, thought Roland, either two scudi was worth a lot more than it sounded, or Veronica worked an eighteen-hour day on her back and saved hard.

He set off from San Trovaso square at last, following a side canal in a westerly direction, unhurried and reasonably content with the world. But as events fell out that afternoon, he was not to see the sites commemorating the Angel Raffaele and the rich whore Veronica Franca.

He thought he had solved the guide-book's mysterious

reference to the Stories of Tobiolo. It had to be Tobias, a pious sort of chap in the Bible. He married a rich girl named Sara, who was a virgin after marrying seven times, because the demon Asmodeus turned up on every one of her wedding-nights and strangled her husband stone dead before he had a chance to get his leg over. But Tobias was in favour with God, and after the wedding feast the Angel Raphael popped into the bedroom and chased the foul fiend Asmodeus off for him.

Roland was aroused from his elucidation of the artistic but not the marital puzzle by the sound of footsteps behind him. No one walked that fast in Venice, not that he had yet seen, and curiosity caused him to turn to see who was in such a hurry. He saw two men, walking very fast side by side, taking up most of the width of the quay between houses on one side and the canal on the other. Both were heavily built men, unshaven and dressed in rough and dirty work-clothes. One held a short cosh down by his thigh, the other held a long thin knife flat against his chest, to make it inconspicuous. They were staring at Roland, and the expression on their ugly faces was unnerving.

Without a second's hesitation he ran like a jack rabbit away from them, utterly convinced that they meant to do him in. With hoarse shouts, they came pounding after him. He dodged round a couple of gossiping women and ran flat out, looking for any way of escape. The narrow streets of Venice and the crisscrossing canals and bridges favoured the hunters, not him – and at the end of the quay he was on there would be a long narrow street between tall buildings, he was sure of that.

These were Count Massimo's hired assassins, he thought, chest constricted and his breath starting to wheeze at the effort of running at top speed with no possible finishing-line in sight. The doors of the little shops he passed were closed and bolted for the siesta and it was pointless to dart into a house entry for refuge – the thugs would follow him in and cut his throat in the privacy of someone's landing.

Nor was there any escape in diving into the canal to swim to the opposite side and bolt that way – there was no quay on the other side, only crumbling brick walls rising out of the murky water. The assassins had chosen their spot well. He could hear their thudding feet not far behind him, and had an unpleasant feeling that they were both strong enough to outrun him. Why is there never a *carabiniere* about when you need one? he thought.

Massimo's men hadn't found him by chance. They'd followed him from the restaurant, looking for a good spot for a murder. And that meant they'd followed him to the restaurant and waited for Carlo to go. From which it followed that they had been lurking outside the Palazzo Malvolio for him to emerge that morning.

An old man with white hair put his head out of a doorway like a shortsighted tortoise peering out of its shell. His toothless mouth opened at the sight of Roland pelting towards him and the two thugs close behind. He pulled his head back in and shut the door quickly.

The end of the quay was in sight. A little bridge crossed the canal where it took a turn to the right, and the street went on between close-packed buildings. In this extremity, Roland heard behind him a new sound – the burble of a boat engine. Over his shoulder, not daring to stop for an instant, he glimpsed a taxi – a motor-launch! He waved his arms and shouted, and the boatman brought it level with him and called out something or other he couldn't understand.

'*Si!*' he shouted back at the man. 'Taxi!'

If he stopped for a second to let the motor-launch pull into the side the assassins would have him, they were so close, and he'd have the knife between his ribs before ever he got aboard.

'Here I come!' he shouted at the top of his voice, mainly to encourage himself, and with his next two running steps he came to the edge of the stone quay and leaped out over the water. An anguished yell went up from the boatman, who probably expected his craft to be capsized or wrecked when this madman landed in it, and roars of baffled rage came from the pursuers.

The launch was a yard and a half out from the quay and a foot or two below it. Roland crashed down into the open cockpit just behind the boatman, twisting his ankle and falling to his knees with a wail of mixed despair and relief.

'*Presto, presto, presto!*' he gasped, thankful he remembered the Italian word for quick. The boatman looked at him as if he were a dangerous lunatic, then glanced up at the two thugs who were standing on the edge of the quay above, the lethal weapons out of sight. Something in their faces perhaps convinced him to open the throttle and carry Roland away from their attentions – or perhaps it was the thousand-lira note Roland was by then waving at him. He skidded his boat in a power turn under the bridge to the right and along the canal at a highly illegal speed.

'*Inglese*, Signor?' he enquired over his shoulder, 'I spicka the Anglish. Why these men they run after you? You *fricafric* their sister, maybe?'

Roland's right ankle was hurting badly and both knees were aching from coming down hard on the planking. He sat with legs drawn up on the faded cushions and rubbed his ankle. The knees were bruised, he guessed, and could be ignored for now, but the ankle was sprained and needed attention before he walked on it again.

He had no idea what the Italian for *murderer* might be, and he had no desire to become involved with the police if the boatman was overcome by civic responsibility – it seemed simpler to go along with his peculiar local assessment of the situation.

'*Si*,' he agreed. '*Fricafric* sister. Beautiful girl.'

The grinning boatman at once launched himself into a lengthy and boastful account of carnal deeds with other men's wives and sisters in English so distorted that Roland gave up even trying to understand. He sat back in the sunshine, pondering what best to do next, until his rescuer suddenly remembered his job and asked where he wanted to go.

'Arsenale,' said Roland.

He congratulated the boatman on his prowess and was given an assurance that Tino Niccolini was at his service day and night for quick getaways from angry relatives of beautiful women – and he could be found by enquiring in any cafe or bar along the Fondamenta Nuove.

Roland had decided to disappear for a few hours. If the thugs reported to Count Massimo right away that they had bungled the mission, he would be thrown into a panic by the prospect of his intended victim making a complaint to the police. If his ugly henchmen slunk away into a backstreet to get drunk in thwarted rage without reporting their failure, Massimo would be gleeful when Roland was missing at dinner – and how much greater would be the impact on him of his victim's resurrection.

As a safe refuge, Roland had settled on Maddalena's hovel – and on her for fast treatment of his damaged ankle. *Fortunes told, palms read, charms, spells, talismans to order, potions, lotions, poisons and aphrodisiacs*, he had joked, and he was sure, *folk cures and remedies, skin whiteners, abortifacients, wart-removers and rat-repellents*. It had to be – she was in the line of descent from the wise women, quacks and wizards of the past.

He didn't know her address, not even the name of the street, but he knew it was near a canal that ran inland from the Riva, in a part of Venice where there were remarkably few canals. She was sure to be well known in her neighbourhood, and if he couldn't find the house on his own, a few lira to anyone he saw standing about would produce the information he wanted.

And so it proved, though he suffered agonies from his ankle climbing up the stairs to her room under the roof. The door was ajar and he went in with the merest tap, to find her asleep on the bed in the same drab reddish and greenish flowered frock he had seen her in before. It was, after all, siesta time, and a glance at his wristwatch confirmed it was not yet four o'clock. Maddalena opened her eyes and sat up quickly when he hobbled into the room. He dropped thankfully on to one of her rickety chairs and stretched out his leg.

'*Buona sera, Signore*,' she said, padding across the floor on big bare feet. She also asked him what he wanted, or at least, that was how he interpreted her words because that was what the expression on her face said.

'I've hurt my ankle,' he said, having not the least idea what the Italian word for ankle could be, and to make up for it he raised his leg and pointed. It was only then starting to occur to him that it was going to be damnably difficult to involve in his scheme a woman who spoke no English, he knowing only two or three words of her language.

Maddalena went down on her knees to undo his lace and remove the shoe. When she eased off his sock he grunted in pain.

'*Si, la caviglia*,' she said thoughtfully as she looked at his badly swollen ankle.

At least he now knew the word for it, Roland reflected, if it was any help.

'And the knees,' he said, touching them gingerly, 'they were bruised when I fell on them, I think.'

She understood his meaning and helped him from the chair and across her room to the bed. He sat down, and somewhat awkwardly she squatted on her haunches and unbuttoned his trousers. Roland let her do as she pleased, the thought of sexual pleasure not then in his mind – or at least, only as the dimmest of possibilities in the background, much the same as if a hospital nurse were to help him out of his clothes before treatment.

He shrugged himself out of his jacket, and by then Maddalena had his trousers right off and was examining his knees. After a doubtful shake or two of her head she fetched from somewhere in the room a thin glass vase – he could think of no other word to describe it – with a glass stopper shaped like a mushroom. The contents were a thick liquid of a pinkish-whitish colour.

It had an almondy sort of smell, he noticed, when she poured out a handful and applied it liberally to his injured ankle. By way of bandage she wrapped a red-and-white checked handkerchief round his ankle and knotted the corners together to hold it. He leaned back on his elbows on the bed, while with a light touch she smeared more of the unguent on his puffy knees. His ankle was not aching quite so badly now his weight was off it, and he thanked her.

'*Grazie*, Maddalena,' he said, pleased he knew the right word. He could hardly help noticing while she was attending to his injuries how her gigantic breasts swung under her frock. And it seemed that she was well aware of his interest, for with a grin and a few words that were meaningless to him she put her hand up under his shirt and felt the limp part in his underwear. She looked at him with a knowing grin on her broad face, her eyes glinting in an open display of amusement.

'*Molto stanco, il cazzo,*' she said, '*completamente esaurito.*'

At least *stanco* was one of the words Roland knew – it meant *tired*, which seemed a reasonable description of his bishop just then. He guessed that *esaurito* meant something like *exhausted*.

'*Si,*' he agreed, returning her grin, '*La Contessa.*'

'*Certo!*' she exclaimed, her fingers kneading his fleshy part expertly. '*La Contessa e moltissima avida!*'

The word sounded near enough to avid for Roland to decide it meant greedy – which was true enough – Marina was *very* greedy for love-making. She couldn't get enough of it, not even after she had reached her ninth or tenth sexual climax, as the frolics of yesterday on this very same bed testified. But there was not the least possibility of having a useful conversation about it while the mighty barrier of language stood between the fortune-teller and himself.

Evidently Maddalena came to a similar conclusion, and without the formality of more words she flipped up Roland's shirt-front and undid the waistband button of his underpants, laying bare his belly and slack male part. He looked down in mild surprise at what she was doing – she dipped a couple of fingers in the glass vase and smeared the same balsam on the shaft and head of his *cazzo* as she had used to treat his ankle and knees.

She clasped him full-handed to rub it in thoroughly. Perhaps the slippy unguent had instant curative powers quite unknown to medical science, or perhaps the friction of a woman's hand upon so sensitive a part was sufficient in itself – but the upshot was that Roland observed his limpness stretch itself and begin to grow longer and harder in Maddalena's grasp.

'You're a bold woman,' said he, not bothering with language, 'I came here to have my ankle seen to, not that.'

With her free hand she brushed back his hair from his brow, it having fallen forward while he was looking down at her short stubby fingers gripping his now respectably hard and long part. She talked to him in a low and crooning voice while she pulled loose his tie and unbuttoned his shirt collar, not for a moment halting the rhythmic play of her other hand.

Roland slid his legs apart on the bed and sat up to pull his shirt over his head and get rid of it. Maddalena smiled and put a hand flat on his chest to press him down to lie on his back.

'Do you know,' he said, talking more to himself than to her, 'I've been wanting to have you since the first instant I laid eyes on your *tette*. Did you guess that?'

Only the one word got through to her, but it was enough. She let go of him for a second or two while she hauled her flowered frock over her head and dropped it on the bed beside him. Under it she wore a loose chemise of pink artificial silk down almost to her knees. That too came off, and her breasts hung naked in all their overdeveloped fullness for him to feast his eyes on.

'They're enormous!' he sighed. 'The biggest I've ever seen.'

'*Si, enorme*,' she agreed proudly, her disengaged hand taking him by the wrist to pull his hand to them. He needed no further encouragement – in fact he needed none at all, his heart set on feeling these huge breasts uncovered for his close inspection and admiration. He used both hands to feel her vast and fleshy pendants, his stiff part jerking to this added stimulus.

The reaction brought a smile of approval to her face. Roland gasped in protest when she again let go of his throbbing *cazzo*, but his sigh became a grin when he saw she was only standing up to slip down her long-legged knickers and take them off. She was close enough to the bed for him to reach over and touch the thick bush of very dark curls between her meaty thighs.

'*Eccola!*' she said, and Roland's fingers were exploring the thick lips under the curls.

She slid her feet well apart on the floor to let him feel her – attending to his tired part had evidently aroused her, for he was able with ease to slip two fingers deep into her. Her broad hips wriggled pleasurably and she cradled her great breasts in her hands, her thumbs rolling over their long reddish tips.

'*Eccola*,' said Roland cheerfully, wondering what it meant. He fingered Maddalena until she was breathing loudly and fast, her loins and plump belly starting to jerk backwards and forwards, and her *fica* so hot and slippery that he thought she was in the throes of a climax. He hooked his fingers inside her and pulled her bodily towards him.

At that, she pushed him down on his back and got astride him on her knees, her huge breasts dangling loosely above him like an avalanche of flesh that threatened to overwhelm him and sweep him away. Her hands were between her thighs, and as he watched she opened herself as neatly as if opening up a fresh oyster. A cunning sort of smile played over her face, to see how excited he was becoming, and she half-closed her eyes while she slipped her fingers into herself and rubbed over the prominent pink nub she was showing him.

But the limit was quickly reached – it required not very much of such direct stimulation to raise Maddalena to a near-crisis of sexual sensation. She took her fingers away from herself in a hurry and seized Roland's twitching length – and in another second she had it inside and was sitting firmly over his loins, completely skewered on him.

'Ah, Maddalena, that's marvellous,' he sighed, 'I feel that I'm being used and abused!'

There was no need for words, even if either had understood

the other, for both were excited almost to the limit. She rode up and down on him very vigorously, her breasts flopping to her movements, the sight driving Roland into a veritable frenzy of lust. She babbled away without a pause, and he guessed she must be telling him how wonderful it felt to be spiked on him.

Not that it mattered whether he understood what she said or not, for her heavy slogging on his belly had brought him to the instant of climax. He stabbed up into her in wild spasms when his essence spurted, and Maddalena gave a hoarse shout at the moment she too was overwhelmed in a maelstrom of sensation. Her head jerked back as if someone had gripped her hair and pulled sharply; straight up at the ceiling she stared with sightless eyes, her belly jerking in and out in billowing waves of flesh, while her *fica* held Roland tight and sucked at him greedily.

When they were calm again she became very attentive. She made him lie still and rest while she wiped the perspiration off his face and chest, using her knickers in lieu of a towel. Roland lay comfortably on his back with his arms folded under his head while he enjoyed her fussing over him. She wiped his belly and then carefully dried his slack male part. She inspected his ankle, to make sure the kerchief was still in place.

She asked him how he had hurt himself. He didn't understand her words, but with a finger resting on his bandaged ankle she addressed him in an unmistakably questioning tone of voice.

'It's a long story,' said Roland, baffled as how to he might try to explain to her the events along the back canal.

'*Si, una lunga storia,*' she said, nodding. '*E poi?*'

She was sitting facing him on the bed, her legs folded under her, her massive *tette* hanging over him while she massaged his thighs expertly, her fingers digging into the muscles to loosen them most pleasurably.

Roland decided to embark on the daunting task of relating his misadventure by means of gesture, hand signs, facial expression and words which he hoped sounded Italian enough to make sense. *Enemy*, he said several times, *due*, holding up two fingers, *kill* and he drew a finger across his throat, *assassinate for money*, and he rubbed thumb and forefinger together, then remembered to say *lira*.

It was a long and exceedingly complex narration, but at

last the essentials seemed to have lodged firmly in Maddalena's mind and she looked at Roland with renewed interest, her massage of his thighs forgotten. She got off the bed and went to her chest on the floor by the table she used for fortune-telling, coming back with the *Libro del Destino*. She unrolled it, indicating to Roland with an imperious flick of her hand that he was to move over and make room for her to spread the chart on the bed.

He wondered how she would overcome the problem of language to ascertain his odd and even choice – he didn't know the words in Italian. She did it very simply, by taking his hand and showing that he was to extend one finger or two fingers without pausing to think when she gave the order to start.

Roland was sitting with crossed legs, Maddalena was lying at full length, propped on her elbows with her head over the chart of squares and symbols, tracing along the rows with her finger. Her giant breasts were like two plump cushions under her chest, supporting her, Roland thought while he patiently awaited the pronouncement of the Book of Fate on his plight. He considered the whole thing ridiculous, but had the good sense to keep his views to himself.

Maddalena had found the appropriate symbol, and Roland choked back a disbelieving laugh to see that it was a hand holding a dagger upright. That was too much of a coincidence – she had to be faking the reading. When she spoke the words of wisdom, they were without significance for him until she acted them out in a pantomime of outlining an upright post or tree with both hands and then chopping at its base with the side of one hand.

'It's like a children's party game,' said Roland, 'you act it and I guess it! I think you're chopping down a tree – but that tells me no more than I've told you – that someone is trying to have me killed. We didn't need a *Libro del Destino* for that.'

She was rolling up her chart, its message delivered, and knew by Roland's disappointed tone that he had misunderstood. When the *Libro* was safely out of the way, she again drew her tree in the air between them, took his wrist and used his hand to make the chopping motions. She tapped him on the chest to make sure the interpretation was clear – he was the axe, someone else was the tree.

'Well, I suppose that's comforting to know,' he said, 'if I had any trust in fortune-telling. But unfortunately for us both you don't know the people involved and the insignificance of my own position in relation to them. One unimportant university teacher against seven hundred years of family history!'

His words meant nothing to Maddalena, but she could hear the doubt in his voice. She drew her imaginary tree in the air once more, making the trunk broader this time and reaching up higher than before. *Grande*, she said, and then flattened her hand into an axe and said, *Piccolo*.

'I think I see what you mean,' said Roland, 'it takes only a small axe to cut down a big tree, or some such gem of folklore your grandpa told you. Well, thank you for your encouragement and support and may the omen prove favourable.'

His fascination with her colossal breasts, half-flattened as they were under her, got the better of him. He reached over to slip his hands beneath them and the bed and curl his fingers up into the wealth of warm flesh. Maddalena smiled slyly up at him and wriggled closer until she could clasp his soft part in her hand and play with it.

It didn't take much handling of her breasts before his bishop was standing upright and ready to conduct services. Maddalena squirmed closer still on her belly, until she could open her mouth wide and close it wetly over his pride. A dozen passes of her tongue and he felt himself at full stretch inside her mouth. She put her head back to grin up at his face, her mouth open to let him see her tongue lapping underneath the uncovered purple head of his shaft.

'Yes, I want to do it again,' Roland sighed.

'*Si, ancora*,' she murmured, pausing in her stimulation, but only for a moment, before she drew at least half of his swollen length into her mouth, her hot breath surging over it. Roland gave himself up to the thrills that rippled through him, gazing down his body to where his stiffness stood sharply upwards from the tuft of hair between his thighs. As Maddalena's head bobbed up and down, he stroked her coarse dark hair, pushing it back from her face.

Into his mind came the memory of beautiful Marina down on her knees performing this same service of loving friendship for him in the Library of the Palazzo Malvolio, after she had taken her soaked silk knickers out of his trousers. She had held his wet part between her scarlet-nailed fingers and caressed it with her hot tongue until it reared itself up to an impossible size. And she had taken him all the way, sucking his essence from him in long throbs of ecstasy.

Maddalena had other intentions. Now she had him almost at the point of no return, she quickly pushed him over backwards. He was sitting close to the edge of the bed and there was no room for him to lie – he yelped in surprise as he felt himself going over. But as his head touched the floor, Maddalena sat herself across his loins, her weight pinning him. He waved his arms to regain his balance and struggled to pull himself up, but there was nothing he could do.

Maddalena was on him, hot to have him, and she had pushed his shuddering length right up her wet split. She rode him hard and fast, ignoring his gasping pleas to be let up. He had joked to her before about feeling used and abused – now he felt that he was being ravished, and it was no joke, she was having him!

Fortunately for him, her crisis was quick in coming and with a shriek of triumph she jerked in ecstatic climax, thumping him hard down on the bed. Roland was overmastered instantly by the pulsing of her throbbing belly – he wailed and spurted his hot lust up into her.

THIRTEEN

It was still very early in the morning when Roland walked along the shabby street where Maddalena lived and down to the stone quay that went curving away beside the glistening bright blue sea to where the pointed top of the San Marco bell-tower could be seen a mile and a half away above the rooftops. His ankle felt very much better – in fact it hardly hurt him at all – but he had no intention of risking it on such a long walk.

He waited by the *vaporetto* stop on the quay, and early as it was, two or three workmen were there beside him. The first boat came very soon, but in the wrong direction – it was from San Marco and on its way to the Lido, the mile-long strip of land he could see on the horizon, where the bathing beaches and holiday hotels were to be found.

It was only a few minutes before a boat came the other way to bump alongside the wooden landing-stage, then with a clatter of its engine it was off again, carrying its passengers towards the distant heart of Venice. Roland decided to disembark at the stop for Piazza San Marco rather than stay on the boat while it chugged round the long bottom bend of the 2-shaped Grand Canal to the stop nearest the Palazzo Malvolio.

He strolled up between the two tall columns, St Theodore to his left and St Mark's winged lion to his right, and along the side of the Doge's Palace into the great square. The sky was palest blue and the air fresh and cool, and already the signs were that it would be a beautiful day. The two cafes that faced each other across the Piazza hadn't opened, customers being in bed and asleep still.

The vagrants had been rousted out of the arcades by a morning police patrol and sent on their way. The swarms of pigeons that lived on the ornate facade of the church were scuffling on the paving, pretending to look for food whilst knowing well enough that they had to wait for the first wave of tourists to be fed. The only human Roland passed as he strolled across the square was an ancient municipal employee with a metal scraper fixed on a long handle, cleaning up the worst of the bird droppings.

He cut through to the lopsided church of San Stefano and in a cafe nearby had a cup of hot black coffee, so strong that it made his head spin for a moment. When he came at last to the Palazzo Malvolio by way of the little square with the stone well, he was quite surprised to see the great doors standing open and a servant sweeping the steps.

'*Buon giorno*,' he said as he went in, and the servant – it was the doorman with his livery jacket off and his shirt sleeves turned up – responded with a deep bow and a leering grin. Roland tried to remember which boring French person it was who stated that no one is a hero to his valet – nor to the doorkeeper, he thought wryly, the man who observes our going out and coming in and knows who stays out on the tiles all night.

In his own room he scrubbed himself thoroughly in a hot bath to get rid of the faintly musky smell that clung about his body from his frolics with Maddalena. During the long hours of the evening and night she had doused his important parts more than once with her special *profumo per fare l'amore*, besides lacing his wine with drops of her fresh supply of *afrodisiaco*.

He put on clean clothes and left his room, making for where he thought Delphine Tandy's quarters would be. He'd never been asked there, but simple logic said her private suite would be on the side of the palace overlooking the Grand Canal.

He knew where to find Marina's bedroom, having been there on his very first visit to the Palazzo Malvolio – and the doorman also knew, the train of thought continued, who went out all night and who brought a friend in for a hour or two of frolic. In fact, the doorman was probably the source and origin of most of the gossip that ran through the palace like the proverbial wildfire, whatever that was.

In the picture-lined passage outside Marina's bedroom Roland stopped to consider. What he was about to do was very chancy – to go uninvited into Delphine Tandy's bedroom might well offend her and get him his marching orders. But the circumstances were desperate enough for him to insist on talking to her before she spoke to any of her family – and if she had him booted out into the street, what of it? At least he would be safer if he left Venice that day.

Roland had a good sense of direction. From Marina's door he walked quietly in the direction he guessed led toward the Grand Canal side of the palace. Round two or three corners and past a priceless marble statue or two of naked goddesses, and there he was, looking at a group of three important-looking double doors of white and gold, ten feet tall and with the elaborate Malvolio coat-of-arms in high-relief over the top.

He chose the centre door, for no particular reason, drew in a deep breath and pressed down a brass curlicue handle. One side of the door opened inwards and in he silently went. He was in a dressing room with a matching pair of vast polished wardrobes, a huge dressing table with an oval Baroque mirror over it, with carved wooden cherubs round the frame, their gold leaf looking tarnished. At each end of the room were more double doors, this being a suite in the typical eighteenth century palace style.

He was sure the Grand Canal lay to the right, and as quietly as he could he opened the doors on that side and eased himself through. He was standing in the biggest and most ornate bedroom he had seen outside the Palais de Versailles. Enormous mirrors in gold frames lined the walls, one side was shuttered windows, from the ceiling hung a vast chandelier of red Venetian glass – and opposite him on raised steps stood a canopied bed as big as an Emperor's campaigning tent.

Roland crossed the floor swiftly and mounted the steps up to the bed. Delphine lay asleep on her side facing away from him, her glossy chestnut-brown hair spread out over the lace-edged pillows. Into Roland's mind came something she had said to him when she visited his room late at night, his first night under the palace roof, in fact. She'd told him she never slept naked because that made her too restless to sleep.

She had a rounded shoulder uncovered, and it was bare, but he could see the narrow strap of a night-dress and he wondered how long it was and if it had ridden up while she slept, to uncover her bottom. In his trousers his well-used part stiffened slowly but inexorably.

He had thought when he woke up at dawn that morning alongside Maddalena that the *elisir* she had dosed his wine with was out of his system – after so much sexual exercise and three or four hours sleep it was reasonable to assume that. Yet reason was proved wrong now as he stood at Delphine's bedside. One cup of coffee and a bath seem to have revived the *afrodisiaco* effect.

Made reckless by his surging desire, he stripped off all his clothes and slipped into the vast bed behind Delphine and moved up close to her. The touch of her warm bottom against his eager part confirmed that her nightdress had ridden up while she was asleep, baring her below the waist. He put an arm gently over her hip and felt upward under the soft silk nightdress until a plump breast lay in his hand.

Delphine half-awoke to find herself being fondled delicately and when Roland whispered his name into her ear and stroked her belly, she sighed in pleasure and drew up her knees. Roland lay close to her with a hand beneath the fleshy cheeks of her rump to probe with careful fingers the soft petals between her legs. He heard her breath drawn quickly in when his exploring fingers entered her and touched her secret bud.

'What a lovely way to be woken up,' she murmured, still half-dreaming, 'why don't you do this every morning?'

'You'd like that, would you?' he asked, as she lifted her thigh to let his fingers play freely in her developing wetness.

Soon she was pushing her bare bottom against his belly to mean she was ready to be penetrated by something thicker and harder and more exciting than his fingers. He moved in closer yet, his hand steering his *cazzo* underneath her and to the moist split that awaited him. Delphine reached down between her parted legs to help him find the angle of approach, and with a strong push he sank half or more of his length into her.

'You dear, dear man,' she sighed voluptuously, and her bottom squirmed against him.

He rocked backwards and forwards slowly, teasing her with his half-thrust until she was sighing continuously in giddy desire. His restless hands were up inside her silk nightgown, fondling her chubby breasts and his own desire was so intense that only by a great effort of will did he prevent himself from stabbing in fast and finishing it.

Step by step he raised her up the long delightful slope from sleepy acquiescence to churning excitement and then to frantic lust. *Ah, ah, ah* she gasped, and her bare bottom bucked at his belly to speed up his movements and push him in deeper. The tip of Roland's wet tongue was licking inside her ear, his deft fingers pulled and stretched the sensitive tips of her breasts.

He slammed his belly fast against her fleshy cheeks, hearing the slap of flesh on flesh – then together he and she reached their climactic moments. He uttered a moan of triumphal delight as his hot desire spurted into her, and she echoed it instantly with her own long wail of ecstatic release.

When it was over at last they lay in a pleasurable afterglow still cuddled closely together, his hands clasping her breasts, until his male part dwindled and softened and slid out of her. Delphine turned on her back and put her hands under her head.

'What brought that on?' she asked curiously. 'Don't tell me you dreamed about me and woke up hard?'

'Well, why not?' said Roland. 'You're a very desirable woman – why shouldn't I dream about you? Amazing things can happen in dreams, you know.'

'So Marina has told me, many a time,' said she dryly, 'but I know you weren't dreaming about me last night because you were out somewhere tom-catting. You disappeared yesterday and nobody has seen you till now.'

'There's something I have to tell you, Delphine,' said Roland determinedly, 'I was not out tom-catting, as you so bluntly put it. I've been hiding in fear of my life, and didn't dare return to the palace before dawn this morning, when I felt reasonably sure no one would be watching for me.'

'What's this?' she demanded. 'Is this a joke?'

Slowly and with the utmost clarity, he related the attempt on his life by the side of the long narrow canal and his escape by water-taxi. He said nothing about Maddalena the fortune-teller, only that he had found a cheap room for the night in an obscure part of Venice and had lain low until first light.

The room had not been cheap – Maddalena asked for two thousand lira when he left, as the price of treating his injuries, reading in the *Libro del Destino* on his behalf, feeding him with chunks of bread and salami and providing a draught of red wine laced with her most potent *afrodisiaco*, letting him make use of her home as a refuge from assassination and allowing him the freedom of her body all night.

But that was nothing to do with Delphine, and it would surely put her in an unsympathetic mood to be told. On the other hand, Roland had no hesitation in disclosing his settled belief that Count Massimo was behind the attempt.

'I did warn you,' said Delphine, 'but you wouldn't listen to my advice to stay away from my sister. Now you begin to realise how jealous he is.'

'Jealous enough to commit murder – or to pay for it!'

'You can't be sure they would have gone that far,' Delphine said thoughtfully, 'perhaps they would only have beaten you and thrown you in the canal. The knife may have been to frighten you, not for use.'

'It succeeded. You agree your brother-in-law paid them?'

'Almost certainly. There are nearly as many pickpockets in St Mark's Square as pigeons, but robbery with violence is not a crime you hear of in Venice. It would be very bad for tourism. For your own sake, you'd better catch the midday train. It's a pity you've put yourself in this impossible position, because I hoped you'd be able to stay long enough to make a proper study of the paintings.'

'The attempt to murder me or intimidate me was nothing to do with Marina,' said Roland, his mind now made up. 'Count Massimo hated me from the first moment he heard you invited me to stay and look at your pictures for the book I came to Venice to research.'

'I remember you made that point before,' said Delphine. 'What are you suggesting?'

'I can tell you from my examination of the Malvolio catalogue that an extremely valuable painting is missing from the palace. If you hadn't invited me to stay, its absence would probably be unnoticed in his lifetime, and any new archivist wouldn't know where to start looking.'

'What painting is missing?'

'A St Theodore by Paolo Uccello. It was one of those taken to the mainland for safe storage during the War, that you brought back afterwards to the palace. You hung them where you thought they looked best, not where the 1879 inventory listed them.'

'I might remember it – what does it look like?'

'I have no certain information of that – it is listed only as by Uccello and of St Theodore. But a reasonable guess is that it shows a man in a helmet and breast-plate fighting against a large and scaly monster of some kind.'

'Do you mean the knight in armour spearing a dragon – the one that hangs on the first landing on the Grand Canal side? I've always assumed it's St George. That's not missing – at least, I saw it yesterday when I came in.'

'It is St George and the dragon, that one,' Roland confirmed, 'it's by Vittorio Carpaccio, who was a generation after Uccello – yours is a version of the one in the church of San Giorgio on its little island out in the lagoon. It would be interesting to find out which he did first – was yours a trial run for the larger one in San Giorgio, or did a Malvolio see the other and so admire it he commissioned a similar picture for himself?'

'Lord knows,' said Delphine, sounding mildly bored. 'Does it matter? That's the only picture I remember with a dragon.'

'The Uccello must have been hung in an out-of-the way corner for its absence not to be noticed,' Roland said, 'I can't find even a faded rectangle on a wall – something else has been used to cover the spot where it was. It will take ages to check what is out of place, working from Padre Pio's inventory.'

Delphine shook her head.

'What makes you think Massimo has taken it away?' she asked.

'The attack happened after he'd overheard me at lunch telling Adalbert about the Uccello I couldn't locate. To me that seems more than coincidence. And there's something else – I was vain enough to think I'd been invited to stay in the palace because Marina had put you up to it, and you'd invented this tale about wanting me to give an opinion on your collection. But it wasn't that at all, was it?'

'What do you mean?'

'That you really did want me to look at the collection, for a very good reason – you suspected Massimo was helping himself to a picture or two and you expected me to turn up the proof.'

'What gave you so very remarkable an idea?' Delphine asked, her eyebrows rising.

'It's the only answer that makes sense. But as until now you didn't know for certain that anything was missing, how did you come to suspect your brother-in-law in the first place?'

'You must understand that Massimo has never had any money in his life, only debts. His family spent themselves into poverty two generations ago, more completely even than the Malvolio – at least Rinaldo left me the Palazzo and a small income to live on. But since the day Marina married

Massimo, they've had to live here with me – all the Torrenegra properties were sold off ages ago in apartments. Their daughter was born here and lived all her life here until she ran off with . . . well, never mind that now.'

'Not an easy situation for a proud man,' said Roland.

'Not for anyone. I've tried hard these past twenty years not to give him or Marina the least impression that I look on them as dependents. I like having them live here – how would I exist alone in this great barracks of a building?'

She had turned on her side to face Roland while she explained the position. Her plump breasts hung a little slackly and her chestnut-brown hair was in need of combing. For the first time Roland was aware that she was a woman in her mid-forties, very well-preserved and capable of voluptuousness of appearance with the aid of elegant clothes and discreet make-up. But her prime had passed.

'Five or six weeks ago,' she said, 'Massimo suddenly began to spend money on new clothes for himself and Marina, and trinkets that are very expensive – a wristwatch and a gold cigarette-case, things like that. He said an old aunt of his had died in Tivoli, which is near Rome, and remembered him in her will, but I didn't believe him. I've met Massimo's family – most of them have been here over the years to stay – and no aunt of his ever had the price of a gold cigarette-case to leave anyone. I knew he'd been up to something then, and it wasn't that difficult to guess where his money came from, though I couldn't prove it.'

'Nor can I, in a legal sense. But I've told you what I guess and what I know. I'm sorry I can't stay, but it's too dangerous and I'm off to pack and catch the next train for England. What you do about your brother-in-law is for you to decide. There is one thing you might care to pass on to him – I've written down a full account of the attack on me and why I believe Massimo is responsible – and I've given it to a blackmailer.'

'A blackmailer? What on earth do you mean?'

'Someone who can't read English but understands the document is valuable and will get it translated and use it to extract a share of Massimo's ill-gotten gains. He must have an awful lot of money hidden away, even though he couldn't get anything like the true market price for the painting.'

'You've involved someone in a confidential family matter, and I want to know who.'

'That's my little secret. Poetic justice, don't you think? I won't be here, and he'll think he's won. But then, when least he expects it, he'll get a nasty shock.'

Roland's acquaintance with Maddalena had been brief, but very intensive. He had every confidence in her cupidity and willingness to further her own interest at Massimo's expense.

'What sort of hair lotion do you use?' Delphine asked, oddly changing the subject. 'Or is it talcum powder? There's a faint and interesting scent about you I can't place.'

Evidently his bath hadn't entirely removed the last traces of Maddalena's *profumo per l'amore* from Roland's skin.

'It must be the bath crystals I use,' he said as casually as he could manage, 'Cedarwood I think it's called.'

Delphine's face was against his chest and she was sniffing at his skin delicately. Her nose moved down to his belly.

'It's not cedar,' she said, 'more like roses, but not quite.'

'Do you like it?' he asked, feeling the tip of her tongue on his belly.

'It's very sensual,' she murmured, and her breath was hot on the skin of his thigh. After that she said nothing for a while, for she had taken his limp part into her mouth and was busily stiffening it for him. That was soon achieved, for the effect of the large amount of *elisir* Maddalena had put in his wine the night before had not yet worn off.

He rolled Delphine over on her back and knelt upright between her splayed legs, to stare down lustfully at her over-ripe body and gloat to see her heavy breasts rise and fall to the ragged rhythm of her breathing. His hard-swollen part was in his hand and he caressed it fondly while he watched the palpitations of Delphine's smooth belly, and grinned to see how she spread her legs wider still for him. The lips of her *fica* pouted wetly and were pulled open, splitting her tuft of chestnut curls neatly.

'Give it to me,' she said softly, dragging her rumpled silk nightdress over her head to be completely naked.

Roland looked up at her face to see her expression – and her eyes were shining – she *knew* she had him where she wanted him. A sigh escaped him as he lay forward with his belly on hers and she grasped his hot and throbbing shaft to bring it up to the entry she blindly sought. With a strong push he sank the length of his stiff flesh into her wetness, and his springy curls were tight on hers. She wound her legs about his waist hotly, and he plunged and gasped in rapture, the force of his thrusts making her breasts wobble and roll under his chest.

He lunged faster and harder into her smooth wetness, making her moan and wriggle her belly against him. Her ankles crossed over his back, her hands pulled his mouth down to hers. Roland was thrusting very quickly, unconscious of everything but his urgent need, but it was Delphine who came first to the instant of crisis. Roland felt her frenzied convulsions under him and the smacking of her belly against his.

Her heels drummed on his back and her tongue was in his mouth and vibrating like a humming-bird sipping nectar. Ecstasy raged through him and he cried out round Delphine's gagging tongue as he emptied his desire into her belly in gushes that racked him from head to foot.

Some time later, when he was lying on his back in languid and delicious content, sorry that his stay in Venice had come to so abrupt an end, Delphine slid out of bed. Lazily he watched her put on a dressing-gown of palest green silk.

'No, stay there,' she said, putting the belt round her waist tightly to make her breasts prominent under the thin silk, 'the safest place for you for the next few hours is here in my bed – if Massimo is after you, he won't think of looking here. I'll tell my maid to see you're not disturbed till I come back.'

'But what about my train?' Roland asked.

'We'll see about that later. Trust me for now and stay here.'

With that she was gone. Roland had no objection to doing what she said. The night had been a strenuous one, with Maddalena on her back – and sometimes on top of him, always hot for more – while the *afrodisiaco* was like fire in his veins. And after his twice-repeated morning song with Delphine, he was beginning at last to feel pleasantly fatigued. Two minutes later he was fast asleep in the magnificence of the great Malvolio canopied bed.

When he awoke he lay thinking about his plans. By now it was too late to catch the midday train but there was another in the early evening he could be on. Nothing had changed his decision to leave Venice that day, for although Delphine might confront Massimo and get some sort of compensation for her painting, the simple fact was that the Count would then have it in for Roland more than ever. Better by far to slip away unscathed and leave the way open for Maddalena to put the squeeze on.

He got out of bed and started to dress. He was hopping on one leg pulling his trousers on when he heard the door behind him open and footsteps across the honey-coloured wooden floor. He turned, doing up his buttons, to tell Delphine of his decision. But it wasn't Delphine – it was the Contessa Marina, and a look of displeasure darkened her beautiful face.

'I guessed this was where Delphine had you hidden,' she said. 'Damn you – do you know what you've done? You've caused a most terrible row!'

Marina was standing at floor level, Roland was three steps up on the platform the bed stood on, and it made him uncomfortable to be looking down at her. He sat on the bed to reduce whatever advantage his position gave him. To smile seemed quite out of place, considering her upset mood, but he tried hard to keep his tone pleasant.

'I know exactly what I've done,' he answered, 'I've told your sister that one of her valuable paintings is missing, and I am leaving Venice this evening.'

'This business about being attacked – did you make that up?' Marina demanded. 'I must know!'

'It's perfectly true, and I've a witness who rescued me with his boat. I could have been killed or seriously injured.'

'A witness – I didn't know that. Did you report the attack to the police?'

'I have no wish to involve you in an enquiry of that sort,' he said with great diplomacy, 'not after the marvellous nights we've had together. The simplest solution is for me to go.'

'Then you're absolutely convinced Massimo sent the men after you because of me?' Marina asked, her expression softening. 'I mean, this silly business about pictures – that's nothing to do with it really, is it? If Massimo has been up to anything with them, that's a side issue altogether. Tell me I'm right.'

She stood with her hands clasped in front of her, her velvety brown eyes raised in hope to Roland. It was impossible for him to disillusion her.

'Of course it was over you, Marina. Your husband is insanely jealous of you, and he suspects that we are lovers.'

In her joy she came bounding up the steps to fling herself on her knees in front of him and pull his head down to kiss him. A moment later she had his trousers open and pulled out his slack part and fondled it affectionately.

'This is hardly the place,' Roland murmured, giving a breast a light squeeze through the silk of her blouse.

'I don't care,' she said, between kisses.

Her cajoling hand had made his *cazzo* grow long and hard and thick. He undid the buttons of her saffron silk blouse and slid a hand down the top of her fragile slip to feel her fleshy warm breasts and run his fingertips over their dark pink buds. Her eyelids closed in languorous pleasure and she sighed lightly – and Roland reversed position with her, so that she sat on the bed and he was on his knees.

He slipped her brown skirt up her legs and pushed her knees apart, so that he could slide a hand into her knickers and feel her warm split. Then in a sudden access of lust, he pulled her knickers off completely to reveal the trim little patch of dark brown curls where her sumptuous thighs met – a brown so dark it was almost black. He bowed his head to press a fond kiss to the *fica* that had given him so much pleasure – in his bed, on the Rialto Bridge, in the Piazza . . .

'Orlando,' she murmured, 'how beautifully you do that!'

Roland stood up and leaned over her, his unbuttoned trousers sliding down his legs to his ankles. He pushed Marina backwards and her dark brown eyes stared at him with hungry passion while she opened herself wide for him with nervous fingers. His shirt was tucked up in front, baring his belly and his quivering six inches of hard flesh which jutted out towards her. Without hesitation it found its haven and a long smooth push took it in.

The instant Marina felt herself impaled, she brought her legs up to grip Roland tightly round the waist and pull him into her hard and close.

'Oh Marina,' he panted, his thrusting urgent, and she babbled incoherent words, her belly jerking to his rhythm, her breasts rolling under the silk of her pale green slip, the sight adding to Roland's intense arousal. Only a heartbeat or two away was the moment of climactic release for them both – when voices at the door froze them in mid-stroke, in mid-throb, in mid-gasp.

The blood was roaring in Roland's ears, yet through that he could distinguish two voices just outside the door, Delphine's and a maid's. They were speaking in rapid Italian that he did not understand, but he was certain they were both about to come into the room and discover him and Marina in the very throes of love-making.

He stared down into Marina's eyes, his mouth hanging open and his body curved over her like a bow, and she stared back into his eyes, a startled expression on her beautiful face, her legs clamped hard round him. Neither moved a muscle nor flickered an eyelid, they were hardly breathing, and that in total silence . . . The conversation outside continued, and Roland could guess at the gist of it – Delphine was asking if he was still in bed and the maid was telling her that he was asleep. And that raised a question or two in Roland's mind – did the maid know Marina was with him, and was she protecting them both?

But though the surprised lovers held very still and hardly breathed for fear of discovery, their minds were not wholly in control of their bodies. Despite his whirling thoughts, Roland was unable to suppress or ignore sensations of intense pleasure caused by the hold of Marina's slippery flesh on his distended *cazzo*. By no effort of will could he prevent it from vibrating rhythmically inside her, adding to the sensations.

Nor was Marina able to bring to a halt the gentle spasms of her internal muscles. She stared up at Roland with bulging eyes and her belly was massaging his embedded hardness as if it were a hand clasping him. She and he alike were teetering giddily on the very edge of ecstatic release, and nothing would save them.

Roland's mouth gaped wide open in a silent scream as the most ravishing sensations burst inside his belly and his lust gushed hotly into Marina. Her eyes rolled up in her head to show the gleaming whites, but she forced herself to be silent while she shook in the throes of wild passion. The nerve-wrenching mental agonies he and she endured of imminent discovery intensified to an excruciating degree the fearful delight they experienced and the effort required not to make a noise or writhe in exquisite release brought them both to the very point of collapse.

Half-fainting from the unbelievable strain, Roland was aware that the voices had gone from outside the door – Delphine must have been persuaded by the maid to let him sleep on for a while longer. The relief was so overwhelming that he fell forward on Marina's belly and rammed into her with convulsive strength and speed to spurt his last few drops.

She too had been listening intently through the throbbing joy that had her in its grip, and released at last from the fear of Delphine coming into the bedroom, she heaved her loins up fast to Roland's flickering thrusts and gave a long moaning wail of utter surrender.

When she recovered, she kissed Roland repeatedly on the mouth and eyes.

'*Orlando,*' she murmured, '*stupendo, stupendo!*'

Still struggling to catch his breath, Roland disengaged from her clinging flesh and pulled up his trousers, anxious to leave Delphine's bed before worse befell. Marina had been so very well pleasured that she went along with anything he said, and in two minutes, their clothing decently adjusted, they were outside in the long passage lined with priceless paintings that led to the marble staircase.

Safe inside Roland's room, Marina sat down on the bed rather than one of the chairs and told him what had happened that morning while he lay asleep. Delphine had sent for Massimo, who had found her in the Library, flanked by Padre Pio and Adalbert Gmund. She had accused him outright of stealing her picture and cited the assault on Roland as proof. Massimo had reacted with his usual conceit, not troubling himself to deny it but simply challenging her to prove his involvement.

At which point, said Marina, Delphine informed him there was no need for her to prove anything at all. Massimo was no longer welcome in her house and would kindly arrange to move out that day, leaving instructions where his belongings were to be sent on when the servants had packed.

'Good God!' Roland exclaimed. 'Has he gone already?'

'The motorboat took him to the station an hour ago to catch a train for Roma,' said Contessa Marina, looking demurely down at her hands clasped in her lap. 'I am to follow in a few days when he has decided where to stay. Or at least that was what he told me when we said goodbye.'

'And will you?'

Marina made no reply – she stared at his face as if making up her mind, then smiled at him briefly and slowly unfastened the buttons of her saffron-yellow blouse and opened it. Under the flimsy silk of her slip her breasts were prominent and very enticing. While Roland watched, she slid a shoulder-strap down to bare her left breast and cupped it loosely in her hand for a moment or two. The fingertips of her other hand played lightly over the dark-pink tip, teasing it to stand firm, and Roland in thrilling expectation found himself eager to find out how nice it would feel to touch her buds with the tip of his tongue.

'It can't be more than ten minutes since you ravished me till I thought I was dying,' she said softly, 'and yet I see a bulge in your trousers that hints at wicked expectations. Did my dear sister put a drop or two of *elisir d'amore* in your coffee this morning? Or don't you know?'

Roland showed his teeth in a wolfish grin and said nothing. A moment later Marina uncrossed her legs and leaned backwards on an elbow on the bed while she pulled her brown skirt slowly up above her knees. Roland sighed as he contemplated lustfully the smooth and gleaming flesh of her thighs through the silk of her stockings, and then the soft bare skin above the gartered tops. Then the lace-trimmed edge of her eau-de-Nil knickers took his attention and the thought of what pleasure awaited him behind a morsel of easily removed silk.

'What do you think I should do?' she asked, her long fingers slipping into the loose leg of her French-cut knickers to touch the dark curls still hidden from Roland. 'Ought I to follow my husband to Roma? Or stay here in Venice with my sister?'

'I don't know, Marina,' he sighed, watching her fingers move slowly and provocatively between her thighs, 'it's not for me to say.'

'But it is, Orlando,' she insisted gently, 'it depends on you completely. If you stay on here to study Delphine's pictures I shall stay here with you.'

'But ... but ...' he stammered, astonished by her offer and not at all averse to the idea. A few months undisturbed work in the Palazzo with Padre Pio's inventories as a starting-point and he could produce a *catalogue raisonné* of the important and unknown Malvolio collection.

Publication would bring him world acclaim among art historians – and a professorial chair for sure! The chance of a lifetime was being offered to him casually, in return for making love to a sex-struck Contessa! And her charming sister too – though it was for the ladies to arrange how his nights and spare time were to be allocated between them.

And with Massimo out of the way it might be possible to trace the stolen Uccello and force its return. There couldn't be many dealers in Venice capable of handling a deal of that importance even if it were legitimate – and for a crooked deal, maybe only one.

'You want to ravish me again,' said Marina, her body starting to tremble lightly to her self-induced sensations of pleasure. 'You know you do – you want to make love to me all the time! And I so much want you to! Come here and lie on the bed with me, Orlando.'

Rapture Italian Style

ONE

'Here, on this very spot, I was most stupendously ravished one wonderful night,' said Contessa Marina, her voice vibrant and her eyes shining. 'It was so romantic, Mr Jervis – one of the most marvellous nights of my life.'

Beside her on the Rialto Bridge in the centre of Venice, Toby Jervis looked at her in polite amusement. The white stone hump of the bridge on which they stood spanned the Grand Canal in a single arch. Down below, the surface of the water glinted in the sun, choppy from the boats that passed.

There were chugging water-buses, waddling like ducks as they moved tourists about on their sight-seeing. There were gondolas with long thin necks like black swans. There were fat and noisy motor barges loaded with crated wine and vegetables, the trucks of Venice, and sharp-nosed launches that are its taxis. As the setting for a romantic interlude, the Rialto Bridge appeared to Toby to be no more convenient than Trafalgar Square, leaning on the plinth of a stone lion. Most especially for a titled lady.

The top of the balustrade was above waist height and Contessa Marina rested a white-gloved hand on the stonework. She was looking earnestly at Toby while she revealed her unlikely secret. Her frock was *haute couture* and costly, anyone could see that, an elegant knee-length sheath of shantung silk in a delicate shade of magnolia. Her hat was wide-brimmed and of white straw, with a scarlet-striped ribbon round the crown.

'Do I shock you?' she enquired, a hopeful gleam in her eyes, 'Englishmen are so conventional in matters of love.'

She was English-born herself and a Contessa by marriage. She had lived long enough in Italy to acquire a manner of speaking which was vaguely foreign. It was not exactly an accent, more a lilt – a rhythm to her sentences that was un-English.

'Why no,' said Toby, playing at man of the world, 'you have enchanted me, with this glimpse of your secret life. Was it a good friend who ravished you or someone you met casually?'

'He was a guest staying with us in the palace, just as you are,' Marina said, her dark brown eyes searching Toby's face to see if he intended any impoliteness by the suggestion that she might have picked up a stranger and let him have her against a wall. He recognised his false step and quickly put it right.

'Naturally he was someone you knew and liked,' he said with a charming smile, 'but it happens sometimes that two people meet and are so strongly attracted to each other that they make love at once. At a dance in London last season I met a very pretty Dutch girl – the daughter of someone at their Embassy – and it was as if a thunder-bolt struck us while we were doing a tango. We couldn't help ourselves – there was nothing for it but to rush outside on the terrace in the moonlight – by good luck the summer-house was empty, and we did it there.'

'Ah, the hot blood of youth!' said Contessa Marina, sighing gently. 'What was her name?'

'Margriet.'

The Contessa smiled and nodded her head in a gracious little gesture of approval.

She had to be over forty, Toby estimated, twenty years older than himself, but she had kept her figure and complexion well. Naturally, her style was that of her Edwardian youth – the round hour-glass figure of full breasts and bottom. In Toby's eye she was top-heavy and over-fleshed, compared with the sleek young ladies he knew well in London – slender 1929 beauties with delicate bodies, thin wrists and ankles. By some miracle of Nature they had elegantly small bottoms that hardly showed beneath their skirts. When you undressed them they had long and slender thighs that twined over your waist and held you tight while you lay on their flat and narrow bellies.

'This bridge is a very busy crossing-place,' he said. 'How on earth did you manage to make love here without being arrested?'

'It was about three in the morning,' said the Contessa, with a smile to reward his interest in her escapade. 'Between party-goers on their way home and the earliest workmen starting their day, an hour of silence and calm descends on Venice.'

'You had been to a party yourself and it happened on the spur of the moment, I suppose?' Toby suggested, letting his careful gaze roam down his companion's body, from her prominent breasts to the rich curve of her belly and thighs under magnolia silk. He wondered what sort of knickers she wore and whether she had slipped them down her thighs or taken them off altogether while her unnamed friend had her here. They would have been standing up, of course, there was no other way.

'No, it was not a sudden whim,' she answered, taking note of the direction of his glance, 'my dear friend had planned it in advance – he is a very idealistic person and he had a longing to make love to me here on the famous Rialto Bridge.'

'Leaning against the parapet?' said Toby with a wry smile on his face and his eyebrows arching upwards to let her see he was asking a question, not making an assumption.

'I stood here, as I am now,' said Contessa Marina, turning to face outwards down the Grand Canal. 'Orlando stood close behind me, so close that his body touched mine. He put his hands under my skirt and lifted it up over my bottom to stroke me. We were here on the bridge purely to make love and I had no underwear on that night. My cheeks were bare for him to touch.'

'Orlando – is that his name?'

'No, that's what I call him. It seems to suit his fiery and poetic nature so well. Only a poet's extravagantly romantic soul could have been inspired to want me here, by night on the Rialto Bridge.'

'Ah, Orlando is a poet,' said Toby, slightly puzzled. He had only ever met one poet, William Yeats. And he was Irish and did not have the look of a man who would ravage a titled lady on a bridge by night. But you never knew with artistic types.

'He is a Professor of Fine Art,' the Contessa replied, just a little sharply, displeased by these constant interruptions to the tale of her night of love under the stars. The hint was not lost on Toby, who at once tuned his voice to sympathy and warm understanding to urge her to continue.

'And there you were in the moonlight,' said he, touching the back of her gloved hand just briefly to suggest a bond between them, 'the fabulous picture-postcard view of the

Grand Canal by night spread before your eyes, your heart ablaze, and Orlando close behind, embracing you.'

'You put it so well, Mr Jervis – I think you too must have a touch of the poet in your soul. Yes, here we stood, he and I on that marvellous night, pressed close together, so close that I could feel how hard he was against me. He undid his trousers to let his *cazzo* stand between the bare cheeks of my bottom.'

My God, why is she telling me all this, Toby wondered, hardly able to believe his ears. Never ever had any woman confided so openly in him. The girls he knew – however intimately – didn't talk about what they did with other men, past or present – that would have been embarrassing all round. For a start, a question of comparison of performance would have arisen – whether it was mentioned or not, it would lurk in the mind.

The fact was that he'd never met a woman like Contessa Marina before. As she was too old to have any sexual interest for him, he found her confidences amusing and slightly indecent – almost as if an aunt began to relate the girlish pranks of long ago.

'So that I wouldn't be recognised if we met anyone who knew me I borrowed some clothes from my maid,' the Contessa went on, 'you must imagine me dressed as an ordinary Venetian working-class woman, in a sleeveless blouse and long black skirt, with a shawl round my shoulders. Oh yes, and my hair pulled up in a bun on the top of my head.'

'How fascinating!' said Toby, humouring her. 'If anyone you knew passed by, they would take you for a gondolier's woman and not the beautiful Contessa Marina di Torrenegra. It seems that disguise was once an integral part of courtship and love-making – at least in operetta. Perhaps it was – I believe that Madame du Barry dressed up as a shepherdess with her hair in a ribbon, and no knickers, when she strolled out into the private garden at Versailles to be ravished by King Louis XV.'

'Yes, yes!' said the Contessa, turning towards him, her hand on his arm, her face aglow. 'I have read that somewhere.'

In truth, Toby was not at all sure whether it had been Madame du Barry and Louis XV or Madame de Montespan and Louis XIV, who played at nymphs and shepherds when they were in the mood for a frolic on the grass. But the thought pleased Contessa Marina that was clear and, since it was important to Toby to be on the best of terms with her and her sister, it could do no harm to indulge a little in historical embroidery.

'The celebrated Lola Montez dressed as a gypsy girl to arouse King Ludwig of Bavaria,' he said, without the faintest idea of whether it was true or not. 'With nothing on under her peasant blouse and skirt she ran with flowing hair, barefoot, through the woods of Neuschwanstein Castle, to lure the handsome young King to chase her. She would let him catch her by the lake, all flushed and panting for breath, and throw her down on the grass on her back to ravage her.'

'But surely she *was* a gypsy?'

'No, she was an Irish cabaret dancer.'

'How interesting that you know all these things,' exclaimed the Contessa, evidently anxious to get back to her own story of passion and fulfilment, 'I shall insist you tell me more, when there is time.'

'Whenever you like,' he said, 'but please go on – you told me that Orlando's hands were on your charming *derrière* . . .'

'No, his *cazzo* was pressed against my bottom,' she corrected him, 'his arms were round my waist and he had both hands under my shawl – I had undone my blouse for him and naturally I wore nothing beneath it . . .'

'I say!' Toby murmured, putting admiration into his tone.

'Yes,' said the Contessa, her dark brown eyes shining and her voice dropping almost to a whisper, 'it was one of the moments in life that you never forget, that tiny interlude of high and breathless anticipation before I felt him slide up into me.'

Toby was wondering when this could have been. Titled middle-aged ladies did not bend over on public bridges to be ravished from the rear – it must be an escapade of her youth, twenty or even twenty-five years ago. It had made a lasting impression on her, that much was clear.

'What more can I say?' she continued, her voice vibrant with emotion. 'Together we made passionate love here under the night sky. Orlando murmured my name over and over again, and told me that he adored me eternally. The stars were in my eyes – I was rapt up to Heaven.'

Toby was trying to picture the scene, the Contessa leaning on the bridge balustrade with her well-fleshed bare bottom stuck out and her boyfriend standing up close with his stiff *cazzo* – useful word to know – pushed into her from behind and his hands gripping her breasts tight while he rammed away. Any night-time passer on the bridge would have stopped dead in his tracks to watch the comic scene – and perhaps even given a brisk round of applause at the end.

To judge by the Contessa's words and manner she had been a real enthusiast in her youth, and the culmination of Orlando's *alfresco* performance would surely have inspired her to loud and ecstatic wails, Toby judged. Not entirely unlike the wild cats of Venice that slept all day and came out at night to pursue to a moaning chorus of desire their amorous affairs in the street.

'I am honoured that you have allowed me to share this truly delightful memory of past bliss with you,' he said, sounding as sincere as he possibly could. 'How vividly you have brought it to mind, as if it were only last night, though I imagine it was some time ago, before the Great War.'

'Why no,' she said, blinking in surprise at him, 'it was only two years ago – no, it was three – how quickly time flies. What made you think it was longer?'

Toby's mind was racing as he sought frantically for a way out of the problem he had created for himself. If the Contessa got the idea he thought she was too old for frolics by night on the Rialto Bridge – or for that matter anywhere else – she would be so insulted that he could probably say *goodbye* to the prospect of profit that had brought him to Venice.

'But how marvellous!' he said, and he took her right hand in its white glacé leather glove and raised it to his lips, bowing in mock homage. 'I am lost in admiration, Contessa! The reason I had the mistaken impression that these wonderful events were not recent is that romance seems to have died out – at least, in England. But with a lady of your exquisite sensitivity and natural charm, a hot-blooded Italian gentleman like Orlando to acompany you, I see that here in Venice romance still lives and thrives. And I am delighted to hear it.'

'Orlando is English,' said the Contessa, staring strangely at him, 'he teaches at London University.'

The information took Toby aback, but he hid his confusion in a pleasant smile and shook his head as if in wonder. In fact he *was* astonished – it had never before occurred to him that such serious-minded bores as university teachers could be persuaded into carnal frolics in public at three in the morning. The more he thought about it the more certain he became that *Orlando* was not the initiator of the comedy, but had been persuaded by Contessa Marina to ravish her on a bridge over the Grand Canal.

It was difficult for Toby, like all visitors, to accept that the Grand Canal is not merely a tourist attraction but the main street of Venice and carries much of its traffic, both human and freight. It winds for more than two miles through the city in the shape of a figure 2, south-east from the railway station to St Mark's Square. Along its banks stand 200 ancient palaces, in one of which lived the Contessa Marina and her sister – the Palazzo Malvolio.

The Rialto Bridge spans the narrowest part of the Canal, halfway along, and from where Toby was standing with the Contessa the Palazzo Malvolio was just discernible, on the furthermost point of the left bank where the Grand Canal starts its final long turn to the east and the open water. At that distance and through the heat haze no details could be made out, but it was a large and handsome eighteenth century edifice in the high Palladian style. Toby had been a guest there for the past two days, since arriving in Venice; the invitation not the Contessa's but her sister's, who owned the palace and with whom she lived.

On that day when they stood on the Rialto Bridge and she told him of her adventure, the Contessa was taking him to lunch with a friend of hers. In the normal course of events she would have gone the short distance in the traditional way, by gondola, two of these wobbly craft being tied up at the landing-stage of the Palazzo Malvolio, with muscular gondoliers waiting dressed in the family colours. But Toby had persuaded her to go on foot so she could point out some of the sights along the way.

Walking, it seemed, was not Contessa Marina's favourite form of physical exercise, but Toby Jervis was tall and good-looking in a typically pink and blonde English way, his manner charming as well as persuasive. She led him at a steady pace through the narrow alleys and across the little squares, pointing out such notable sights as the Church of San Stefano, which looked about to fall over sideways, and the shop where she always bought her gloves, and then further along the Church of San Salvatore with a Queen of Cyprus buried inside, according to the Contessa.

Beyond it lay the Campo San Bartolomeo, an open square lined with cafes and bars where businessmen in dark suits and serious hats argued and haggled with each other, waving their arms and drinking little cups of jet-black coffee. Toby couldn't imagine what sort of business would be transacted in Venice, other than hotel-keeping and pizza parlours. He asked the Contessa, but in vain – she professed a complete ignorance of what she described as *trade* and a total indifference to it.

Her scorn for money-making made Toby worry slightly about his own position in her esteem. On the other hand, she would surely never have told him of her frolic on the bridge if she regarded him as a mere tradesman. Perhaps she saw dealing in antiques as a profession, perhaps even a branch of the fine arts, and not a business. Which was the impression he had been taught to foster in all his dealings with wealthy and self-opinionated owners of desirable items from the past.

In the middle of the square, and of no interest to any but a pigeon or two using it as a temporary perch, there was a statue of a man in eighteenth century clothes – long coat and knee-breeches, a three-cornered hat and buckled shoes.

'Carlo Goldoni,' the Contessa Marina explained, then seeing Toby's blank look, 'Venice's greatest dramatist.'

When that produced no response, she added that he had written well over 100 comedies, some of them still put on. Toby asked if she had seen any of them on the stage and she said *Of course* but she was vague as to whether she found them amusing. From which Toby guessed that her theatre-going was a matter of being seen in the right frock with the right escort by others of her own kind, while what the actors were doing up on the stage was of little importance so long as it was not outright offensive.

Just past the square they turned left and there was the Grand Canal and the steps of the Rialto Bridge with its double row of tiny jewellery and knick-knack shops for tourists. On the very top of the hump Marina had put her arm on Toby's arm and halted to relate how she had been pleasured there by night, as if that made the spot a major tourist attraction! And when they moved again, down the other side of the bridge, her hand was lightly on his arm – nothing so blatant as linking arms – but a gesture from an earlier and more formal age.

It was a gesture that caused Toby to ask himself if Contessa Marina was perhaps making a delicate first overture. Could it be that she expected him to be so inflamed by her tale of love that he would push her into the next convenient doorway to have her standing up against the wall? The thought seemed ludicrous to him. She was quite old enough to be his mother! Yet when he turned his head to smile at her politely, there was a gleam in her eye that sent a strange little shiver down his spine.

When they stepped off the grandiose bridge on the right bank Toby saw with surprise they were in the fruit market – a narrow street with stalls on both sides, leaving little room to pass. The colours and textures of the high-piled fruit were a delight to see – there were yellow-skinned melons, bright red cherries, glistening oranges, green figs and pastel-shaded peaches with a down on them like a young girl's . . . but Toby did not know what the word was in Italian and so he left the thought unfinished.

The Contessa resumed her guided-tour chatter as she steered him left and right through the stone-paved little streets where nothing moved on wheels except an occasional barrow piled with goods and pushed by sweating men. She pointed out the Church of San Aponal, whoever he might have been, as they passed, but her mind seemed engrossed in a theme much less holy. With a throaty little chuckle suggesting delicious depravities, she told Toby that her dear friend Zita, with whom they were to have lunch, had a certain reputation . . . and she pinched his arm to suggest what that might be.

'She is a lady who enjoys the company of men?' Toby asked, a tiny worry in his mind about Contessa Marina's expectations of him. He was starting to feel a little hot under the collar, for the time was after midday and the sun was at its highest in the sky. Toby was dressed for the occasion in a light-weight summer suit of cream-coloured linen bought for his trip, a plain white shirt from Jermyn Street, a striped tie and a jaunty Panama hat – perhaps it was the warmth of the Contessa's conversation that was heating his blood.

'Zita's husbands disappointed her badly, you see,' continued the Contessa, 'the first one was much too old to please a young girl and the second shot himself. Her third was Prince Ivan of Bulgaria. He was young and strong enough, but turned out to be a monster of cruelty who whipped her. He was murdered by a mob of rioting peasants during the War and so she came back to Venice to make up for lost time.'

'Whipped her? Oh, surely not!' said Toby.

'I assure you it was so. Every night of the week he stripped her naked and bound her upright against a bedpost with her arms over her head, and thrashed her with a horse-whip.'

'Good God!'

'Thrashing her aroused him sexually, you see, and by the time she was screaming and sobbing he had excited himself so highly that he threw the whip down and raped her. And in an unnatural way, if you take my meaning.'

'And he was a prince, you said?'

'Of the bluest of blue blood, with ancestry traced right back to Todor the Flayer – the military leader who died fighting the Turks in the thirteenth century. You must have read about him in your history books at school.'

'Not that I can remember, but it sounds to me as if the whole family were unpleasant.'

'I've never been whipped,' said the Contessa in an earnest tone of voice, her hand squeezing Toby's arm, 'Orlando tied me to a bed once and spanked my bottom – I enjoyed that, though it didn't last very long. We both became excited so fast that he couldn't stop himself jumping on me and ravishing me. Have you ever whipped a woman, Mr Jervis – no, I can't keep calling you that while we're exchanging our deepest secrets, can I! May I call you Toby?'

'Of course,' he said at once, pleased at this sign of growing trust, which must surely help his plans along in due course.

'And you must call me Marina,' she said, bestowing a gracious smile on him. 'I was face down on the bed with my ankles pulled apart by the way Orlando tied me – the beast used my stockings as bonds and they were utterly ruined!'

'A fascinating scene, it must have been!' said Toby, amused and appalled at the same time by an inner vision of the plump Contessa spreadeagled on a bed, face down on the pillow and her chubby bottom bare for a brisk spanking.

'A fond memory,' she agreed at once, her voice almost purring with pleasure, 'but you haven't answered my question yet, Toby. Have you ever whipped a naked woman?'

'Why no – I imagine that very few men have, not in civilised countries.'

'It is possible to be *too* civilised, my dear Toby. What might begin as consideration and restraint can become weakness and insipidity. I find this detestable in a man.'

The firmness of her voice left no doubt in Toby's mind that the Contessa Marina entertained hopes, or dreams, even into her forties, of being swept off her feet into the arms of a bold and dashing movie-star type of hero. She longed to be bent over backwards in his strong grasp, her mouth crushed under his in a burning kiss. Then thrown down breathless and helpless onto her back, her knickers ripped away, and ravaged impossibly long and hard.

In all fairness, Toby did not regard himself for a moment as a candidate for this scenario, clear though it was becoming to him that Marina was edging his imagination that way.

To keep in her good books was the most important thing in the world to him. Not that he had ever contemplated the possibility of pleasuring her to ensure her goodwill. But her frank account of how *Orlando* had performed mightily was a hint of what might be required. Toby fervently hoped he would find a way out of an impasse so unappealing. Although she was steering him into it, the truth was that she was not particularly his type of woman.

A touch of wit and humour might save the situation, perhaps – a scandalous tale of the rich and famous to fend off interest in himself – and towards others more adapted to her need?

'According to what I have heard, one who would be in perfect agreement with you is Madame Lupescu,' he said lightly.

'Crown Prince Carol of Rumania's mistress? Why do you say that? I have never heard anything of interest about her. They say her red hair and green eyes make her quite irresistible to men, but all the pictures of her I've seen in newspapers and magazines make her look rather common. Her father was a small shopkeeper, or something of the sort, I believe.'

The haughtiness of good old British snobbery had led Toby into yet another difficult position – Contessa Marina would bitterly resent any implied comparison between herself and the Rumanian woman, even a royal mistress. Invention must come to his aid.

'That's only a facade to hide the real truth,' he said, 'she is illegitimate and was born in a travelling circus. Her mother was the daughter of a knife-thrower who was seduced at the age of fifteen. As to who he was, there can be no certainty, but rumour strongly suggests Madame Lupescu's father was a Rumanian aristo having a fling.'

'Dio mio!' exclaimed the Contessa theatrically, and her grip tightened on Toby's arm. 'And such a one shares the bed of the future King of Rumania!'

'From the age of seven little Magda was trained for the

circus as a bare-back rider,' said Toby, well into his stride now and careless of the reputation of the Crown Prince and his flame-haired girlfriend. 'For her performance she was as near naked as possible without attracting the attention of the authorities and being sent to prison. She wore only a flimsy ballet *tutu* – and pirouetted on one leg on the horse's back while it trotted round the sawdust ring.'

'I begin to understand at last,' Contessa Marina said, almost whispering, 'brought up in such surroundings she would be well used to rough treatment and blows . . .'

'Just so,' said Toby, nodding his head and dropping his voice to suit the mood of confidentiality. 'Prince Carol is obviously a hot-natured Balkan, as your friend's Bulgarian husband was in his prime. Those in a position to know the truth say that Carol and Madame Lupescu go riding together very often, he in proper riding-kit and she in her circus costume.'

'*Madonna santissima!* He ravishes her in the open? But they have been living in Paris for years because of the scandal!'

'Yes,' said Toby, never flinching, 'the French government is very understanding about the *amours* of foreign royalty. Part of the Bois de Boulogne is closed daily to the public on the order of President Briand so that Crown Prince Carol can indulge in his favourite form of sport.'

'How marvellous! But how can you possibly know about this?'

'Because a friend of mine lives in Paris and scribbles a sort of Society gossip-column for the main evening newspaper. When he heard a whisper of what goes on in the Bois he hid up a tree with a photographer. They waited until the gendarmerie cleared the area and went away – and did this for three days in a row before the Prince and his lady friend rode close enough to the tree they were in for clear pictures to be taken.'

'There are photographs? But surely never published!'

'It would be impossible to publish them in a newspaper,' Toby agreed at once.

'But have you seen them yourself, these pictures?'

'Oh yes,' he answered untruthfully. 'Imagine the scene – it is a clear sunny day, and two riders canter side by side under the trees. They are in the very heart of Paris and yet as alone and as free as if they were in the Prince's private estates in Rumania. Madame Lupescu's body is hardly hidden at all by her tiny costume . . . she stands on her horse's back, barefoot, bare-armed, bare-headed, bare-legged – and needless to say – bare-bottomed. She balances perfectly on the well-trained animal and the Prince flicks at the cheeks peeping out under her *tutu* with his riding-crop . . .'

'Oh!' sighed the Contessa.

'Her mouth is wide open. She utters tiny screams – perhaps of fear, of excitement, of anguish, until her lover is so aroused that he seizes the bridle of her horse and brings it to a stop. He embraces her bare legs in his arms and pulls her down until he can rain kisses on her bare belly . . . need I say more?'

'Yes, more,' said the Contessa, 'I want to hear it all! Tell me if your friend took a photograph of the supreme moment when the Crown Prince threw her on her back and ravished her.'

But her eager curiosity was not satisfied, at least not then, for, engrossed in Toby's mendacious tale, she had led him through a warren of narrow streets and old buildings until they reached the little square where her friend's home stood. The imposing door was before them and a young manservant in a black tail-coat and a stand-up stiff collar waited to usher them in.

TWO

The manservant in black swallow-tails at the door bowed deeply to Contessa Marina and Toby realised that they had arrived at her friend Zita's. Nothing she had said to him prepared him for what he saw – the whole side of the square was dominated by a four-storey palace built of brick the centuries had weathered to dusty pink. The windows were tall and narrow, pointed at the tops like an English church, and the balconies were of enlaced stonework. Under a stone-carved coat of arms on the wall stood a vast double door of dark wood, one side open in welcome.

'*Buon giorno*, Tonino,' said the Contessa in acknowledgment as she and Toby swept past the bowing servant into a stone-flagged entrance hall. Another manservant in black tailcoat was waiting to conduct them up a grand marble staircase and into the large airy salon where nine or ten people were chattering at the top of their voices, drinks in hand.

'*Marina, carissima!*' screeched a voice in the throng.

The Contessa cried back, '*Ciao, Zita cara!*' and the hostess detached herself and advanced to bestow her greetings on the newcomers. She and the Contessa kissed each other fulsomely on both cheeks and exchanged appropriate words in Italian, before the Contessa introduced Toby to Princess Zita. He considered it sensible to rise to the occasion by kissing the bejewelled hand she offered. It wasn't every day you ate with a princess, even if she was a harridan.

She was older than Marina – well over fifty, he judged – but well-corseted and made-up against the dilapidation of time. Her bosom was prominent as a balcony under her stylish cerise frock – and her bottom and belly were well contained. Her fingernails and mouth were painted a bright blood red, her eyebrows plucked to so fine a line that they seemed almost to have vanished. But it was her hair that drew the eye – she wore it piled on top of her head and it was dyed a sumptuous Venetian red.

Her English was very passable, Toby found, and she chatted of nothing much very adroitly while yet another manservant brought him a glass of cold sparkling wine. Before long a very handsome young man in a white silk suit and a heavy gold wristwatch came to join them. Princess Zita said in a proprietorial sort of way that his name was Marcello and Toby tried to shake hands, only to receive a brief nod, his outstretched hand ignored. After an awkward pause he dropped it, wondering if Marcello could be of so very elevated a position that it was bad form to touch him.

The truth was though that Marcello was a sulky-looking young fellow a year or two younger than Toby himself, say twenty-one or twenty-two. A certain sensuousness clung to him like a perfume but, in spite of his appearance and presence, he did not have the air of one born to the purple. His dark brown eyes were heavy-lidded – the type that in England were called *bedroom eyes* and his lips were a little too full and a little too red. The thought occurred to Toby that Marcello might be *peculiar*.

If Marcello understood any English he concealed it very well and stood looking bored while Zita talked to Toby. She noticed his mood and responded by pinching his cheek and addressing him in cooing Italian. Marina smiled at the words and Marcello gave her a scowl in return, making Toby think that the Princess was patronising her pretty young friend. Moments later Zita put her arm in Marcello's and led him away into the crowd of guests.

'Her grandson?' Toby asked Marina, who shrieked with instant laughter and explained that Marcello was Zita's *ragazzo*.

'Her what?' he asked, wondering if it meant what he thought it meant.

'You know, her *boyfriend*, as you might say. She keeps him and gives him money and presents and he repays her kindness in bed. He's very good at it, she says. But he's very jealous and wary when he sees someone as good-looking as you talking to Zita. He doesn't want to lose his place in her affections.'

'And if he did, what would he do for a living? What was he when the Princess found him?'

'I think he was a law student who'd been asked to leave.

Some sort of minor scandal hung over him. If Zita ever tells him to pack his bags I don't know what he'll do – he could hang around the Danieli Hotel or the Gritti, I suppose, to pick up wealthy American widows looking for a fling. But there are quite enough good-looking boys doing that already, and the competition would be fierce.'

In the next twenty minutes Marina took Toby round the room to introduce him to the others. There were fourteen for lunch, he noted, and more women than men. With an exception or two they were of Zita's generation, all very stylishly and expensively dressed, clinging to whatever remnants of beauty the years had not yet effaced. The men were much younger, though he saw no other as young as Marcello. Zita's *ragazzo* was evidently a favourite of all the ladies present and he preened himself visibly, like a cockatoo, every time one of them addressed him.

A name that lodged in Toby's mind was of one of the youngish women present, Anna-Louisa Ziani, the Princess Zita's daughter. She was in her early thirties, strikingly dressed in a silk frock with black and white zigzags. She had smooth dark hair, a tribute to regular brushing by her maid, but it had to be said that she was somewhat plain of face, not very tall but sturdy, with a solid-looking bosom and broad hips.

Toby tried to remember which of Zita's husbands had fathered her. Surely not the Bulgar who laid into Zita's backside with his *whip* – it was either the Milan banker who perished through over-exerting himself, or the German landowner who blew his own brains out. But Toby had been paying only casual attention to Marina when she related her friend's sad experience of marriage and he couldn't recall exactly.

The room they were in was decorated in shades of red and gold and brown. With a professionally trained eye Toby noted that it was a treasure-trove of paintings and small sculpture. A shame, he thought, that so much valuable art was exposed to billowing clouds of cigarette smoke by the guests. Princess Zita self-evidently had acquired enough money from her departed husbands to live her life as she pleased, now she was a widow for the third time. The daughter did not look much like her, except for a general similarity of beaky nose and strong jawline.

When they went into the dining-room Toby found he was seated halfway down the table, between Anna-Louisa on his right and a thin woman with blonde-dyed hair on his left. Dieting had made the blonde woman thin almost to the point of emaciation – she had almost no bosom under her frock and Toby didn't remember her name, although she was a Contessa. She was an American from Pittsburgh, Pennsylvania, USA, she told him, and his guess was that her father had bought her a titled and blue-blooded, though poverty-stricken, husband with good old green-back dollars.

Coal mines and iron foundries formed the basis of Pittsburgh wealth, as Toby remembered his school geography lessons, but he also knew that after two generations the new rich were accepted by the old rich, even in England. The English old rich mostly descended from sharp-eyed speculators who made a fortune in the house-building boom of eighteenth century London and bought titles. A few were descendants of sharp-eyed ladies who parted their legs in the seventeenth century for the Merry Monarch or his brother James. Human nature being much the same everywhere, the history of the aristocracy of Italy would be very similar, Toby considered.

The food was delicious and the wines excellent, both served in profusion, and Toby was enjoying himself. Anna-Louisa spoke English reasonably well and when he asked where she learned it she said she'd been to schools in Zurich, London, Paris, Lisbon and Rome, from which he concluded that her father had been the troubled German who shot himself dead.

'Did I hear right – you're staying with Marina at the Palazzo Malvolio?' asked the American-born Contessa on his other side. She had already invited Toby to call her Sally.

'Yes and no,' he said, pondering for the first time the small etiquette of making love to a flat-chested woman. No problem was involved, according to his own experience with the flappers of London, who by a miracle of biological evolution grew up to be entirely without breasts, hips or bottoms, irrespective of how buxom their mothers were.

His own preferred way was to plant a token kiss on each flat nipple while stroking between their legs. A woman of an earlier generation like Sally might perhaps expect more in the way of pretence and be displeased if she didn't get it. After all, she grew up in an era when hour-glass figures were admired – which meant lots of flesh round the chest and bottom.

'What do you mean, yes and no?' she asked, sipping her

glass of chilled white Soave while she prodded her fork at the crabs cracked open for her on her plate. 'Yes or no?'

'*Yes*, I'm staying at the Palazzo Malvolio, but *no*, not as the guest of Contessa Marina. I was invited to stay by Mrs Tandy.'

There was a pause while Contessa Sally appeared to be giving earnest consideration to his words, mulling them over for some hidden meaning or secret cryptogram. Toby wondered if she might be slightly deaf – or even slightly daft.

'Dear Delphine – she's almost my closest friend,' said Sally, sounding not at all sure about it, 'her life was very romantic, just like a Rudolph Valentino movie. But it went wrong.'

'Really?' said Toby politely. 'She has a wonderful home.'

'Falling down round her ears.' Sally declared, 'she'd have to spend a fortune to put it right. And she hasn't got it. I guess the fairy-tale Prince turned out to be just a frog after all.'

'That would be the last of the Malvolio family?' said Toby, who had done some research into Mrs Tandy's background before leaving London.

'That's right – Rinaldo Malvolio. Before the War he was with the Italian Embassy in London for a while and met Delphine. She was married to one of your British honourables and was pretty bored, I guess. She and Rinaldo fell in love like a fairy story and ran away together. They lived here in Venice until he got killed in the War. Rinaldo was a national hero, practically. He left her everything, but that only amounted to the palace and the stuff in it and what there was left of the Malvolio money – which didn't amount to a whole lot because his father lost most of it in the Casino at Monte Carlo, and the rest went on women in Paris.'

'My lifelong ambition is to be a rich playboy spending money like water on frivolities and beautiful women,' said Toby, 'but I have to work for a living.'

'Do you?' said Sally, her thin eyebrows rising in surprise, as if the idea of meeting on a social basis a person who *worked* was new to her and not quite pleasant. 'What is it you do?'

'I'm with Fitzroy Dalrymple, the London antique dealers,' he said, 'my father is one of the directors and he brought me into the company when I left school.'

'I've heard of them,' Sally admitted, after one of her long pauses that seemed as if they should mean something but didn't – at least, nothing Toby could fathom, 'in fact, now I come to think about it, my husband disposed of some ugly-looking stuff to them when I redecorated the palace. So what are you doing in Venice, buying or selling?'

Toby was spared the awkwardness of evading her question by a diversion at the head of the table, where the Titian-haired and bedizened Princess Zita sat, with Marcello at her side. She was half-turned towards him, feeding him morsels from her own plate as if he were a pampered lapdog. Her other hand was well out of sight under the table, but from the angle of her arm it seemed to Toby that she was groping her young friend between the legs while she fed him.

Presumably this was the treatment to which he was accustomed, but something was amiss for, as Zita raised another forkful of creamed crab to his pouting red lips, he smacked her hand away rudely and cried out, '*Basta!*' The guests round the table glanced away as Marcello poured out an accusatory diatribe in furious Italian and Zita soothed him by dropping the fork on his plate and stroking his face with the hand in sight. And perhaps doing the same lower down with her other hand.

The other guests might be looking away politely but not Toby – his curiosity could not resist watching the little display of petulance.

'What was that all about?' he asked Sally, when Marcello was calm again and sipping from a glass of wine that Zita held for him. But the American Contessa pretended not to hear and spoke to the guest on her other side. Toby feared he had made a gaffe in referring to the outburst and, by inference therefore, to the relationship between the Princess and her pet. But his question was answered unexpectedly from his right – by Zita's daughter.

'Marcello was complaining that my mother always tries to make him eat too much,' said Anna-Louisa, her voice implying neither embarrassment, disapproval nor acceptance, 'because if he grows fat from it, he says, she will not want him any more.'

'I suppose he's right,' said Toby thoughtfully, staring along the table to where Marcello sat purring now, rubbing his cheek against the bejewelled hand that stroked it, his lustrous dark eyes half-closed. 'Has he been a friend of the Princess long?'

'It is seven or eight months now. He is not very satisfactory because he has a childish temper but my Mama is fond of him and forgives him. One day he will go too far and she will tell the servants to throw him out.'

'Yes, I can see that he might be a bit embarrassing about the place,' said Toby, who was astonished that anyone in Princess Zita's position would put up with that sort of nonsense from a hired lover.

'And you, Signor Jervis?' said Anna-Louisa with a pleasant smile. 'How long have you been with the Contessa Marina?'

Toby glanced across the table to the right, where Marina was chattering happily away to the man next to her – a slender man with an olive complexion and black hair brilliantined down flat on his head. He was about to say he'd arrived in Venice the day before yesterday when the implication of Anna-Louisa's question struck him. He felt himself blushing crimson at being bracketed with Marcello.

'Look here! There must be some misunderstanding,' he said. 'I am *not* on those terms with the Contessa – nor anyone else, for that matter.'

'Ah, I have annoyed you!' said Anna-Louisa, who seemed to be enjoying his discomfiture, no doubt because he had the temerity to speak of her mother's private arrangements. 'But there is no need to be ashamed – we who are Marina's friends know that she makes a special friend of every handsome young man who stays at the Palazzo Malvolio. Why shouldn't she? Her husband the Count left her some years ago and lives in Roma.'

'I am sorry to hear it,' said Toby, and he meant it. Now the purpose of Marina's confessions on the Rialto Bridge were quite clear – they were overtures, as he had suspected at the time.

His gaze fell by chance on Anna-Louisa's hand, where she wore a broad golden wedding-ring. She saw what he was looking at and answered a question he had no intention of asking.

'No, my husband has not left me, Signor Jervis,' she informed him with another smile, 'he is in India to shoot tigers.'

'Does he shoot many?' Toby enquired.

'Yes, and leopards in the Congo and lions in Kenya – and wild pigs in Poland, and he goes to South America for the . . . what do they call the big cats there?'

'Puma, I believe. He must have many trophies, if he is a keen big-game hunter.'

'Many, many,' said Anna-Louisa, 'an entire room full of them. Do you shoot animals? Foxes, perhaps?'

'In England we shoot only birds – pheasants and grouse.'

'Then you are a hunter too. After lunch you must see the room with the trophies.'

It was three o'clock before lunch finished and even then some of the guests did not leave the table. They sat down again when Zita had gone, taking Marcello with her, rearranging themselves in a small group at one end of the table to gossip on as long as the attentive servants continued to fill their glasses. Some few said their goodbyes and left, others drifted off into other parts of the palace to look at this and that. Contessa Marina was one of those still sitting at the table, her cheeks glowing as she talked with much hand-waving to those about her.

She was speaking in fast and fluent Italian, but even so Toby was able to distinguish the words *Madame Lupescu* and knew that she was passing on to her friends – perhaps even with additions of her own – his wildly fictional account of the *amours* of the Crown Prince of Rumania.

'Come,' said Anna-Louisa, 'I will show you the triumphs of my husband's ability with a rifle. We will return before Marina is ready to leave and I will arrange it that one of our boats takes you back to the Palazzo Malvolio.'

The room with the trophies was down on the ground floor and it was a man's well-furnished study. There was a large desk of dark wood, half a dozen red-padded chairs and a matching sofa, with a terrestrial globe a yard in diameter in a frame standing on the polished parquet floor. Around the walls could be seen the evidence of Marco Ziani's sporting skill – mounted heads of wild animals.

Toby stared in amazement at a profusion of lions, tigers, leopards, cougars, pumas, lynx, panthers, cheetahs and jaguars. Signor Ziani obviously had it in for cats. True, there were two or three spike-nosed rhino on show, a dozen wild boar and long-horned buffalo, but these were hardly more than an afterthought and the ludicrous question formed in Toby's mind if Ziani, when he was not abroad on safari, went stalking the Venetian alley cats by night with a revolver.

'Well, what do you think?' Anna-Louisa asked, and something in her voice caused Toby to abandon his survey of the trophies and turn to look at her. She was standing against the big desk, her bottom half-perched on it, and she was holding up the skirt of her very stylish black-and-white silk frock.

The thighs she had half-uncovered were strong and full, Toby saw, and smoothly bare above stocking-tops held up by red garters.

'Admirable,' said Toby, looking up from her legs to her eyes, his response wary to this sudden and very unexpected unveiling. Anna-Louisa accepted his compliment at face value, or seemed to do so, and raised her skirt higher, to reveal small knickers of white lace, through which he could see the darkness of hair.

'How good are *you* with a rifle?' she asked.

'I'm pretty handy with a shot gun,' he answered, entranced by what she was showing him.

'A shot gun,' she repeated, 'I think I like that – a big blast to knock everything down. Is it a double-barrelled shot gun?'

'Never use any other sort,' he said, grinning at her. Now the shock of her sudden display was wearing off he could feel his *cazzo* growing stiff and long in his trousers. Surely she didn't expect him to make love to her in risky circumstances where the door might be opened any moment by prowling guests!

Anna-Louisa held her skirt up waist high with one hand while with the other she pulled her knickers down her thighs to bare her belly and a thick tuft of dark brown curls.

'I say!' Toby murmured.

And well he might, for the situation was entirely outside his experience. Although his male part was standing stiffly upright there was still something mildly comic about a woman of quality flashing her muff at him. At least it had the merit of avoiding misunderstandings – there was no point in pretending she had brought him here to see hunting trophies.

It was a different sort of sport she had in mind and Toby was astonished by the casual way she took it for granted he would pleasure her at the drop of a hat – or rather, at the drop of her knickers. But then he reminded himself that she was Zita's daughter and perhaps that explained it. To have a mother who played with her *ragazzo* under the table at lunch must make for a lax attitude towards the conventions.

And truth to tell, though Anna-Louisa was ten years and forty pounds avoirdupois above Toby's ideal for sexual enjoyment, he had no intention of letting an opportunity like this slip past. To frolic with the daughter of a princess after lunch, and in a Venetian palace – male conceit demanded that he did it! And he was in an elevated state of mind from the considerable quantity of excellent wine he had drunk at lunch.

He moved towards Anna-Louisa, meaning to take her hand and lead her to the red leather sofa behind him and spread her out on it. But she grasped his hand and tugged before he did, and told him to sit beside her on the desk. While he was doing that she removed her knickers completely and then her shoes.

She stationed herself in front of him, very close between his knees, her feet apart, and at once he put his hand between her open thighs and felt her.

'What do you call this in your language?' he asked her, his fingers exploring the prominent fleshy lips.

'My *fica*,' and her hands were busy undoing the jacket of his cream linen suit and then the trousers. She felt inside to clasp his stiff *cazzo* and pull it out where she could look down at it with an appraising eye.

'Double-barrelled, I like that!' she said, her hand sliding briskly up and down.

'Ah,' he sighed, his fingers teasing inside her warm split.

'It stands long and hard,' she said, resting her chin on his shoulder, '*molto bene*. You show me what you do to Marina with it, yes?'

He was already at full stretch from her massaging and as she continued he began to breathe heavily against her ear.

'You're mistaken,' he murmured, 'I've done nothing to Marina, nothing at all, I assure you.'

'But you will!' she said with a chuckle. 'If you are telling the truth and she has let you sleep alone for two nights as you say, then there is a reason. But you will not be alone in your bed much longer if I know anything about her.'

'You seem to know a lot about her.'

'Everything – we are very good friends. And for once I enjoy the pleasure of having one of her *ragazzi* before she does.'

Toby was trembling with sensation as she plied his stiff part with a firm hand – and he wondered how she intended they should make love in so unpromising a position. The problem was solved easily – Anna-Louisa pushed him over backwards until he lay on the desk with his legs dangling over the side. He stared down his body and saw how his rearing *cazzo* was held and manipulated by a hand on which there gleamed a fortune in precious gems.

At this moment he thought she was going to climb on the desk to kneel over him. *When in Rome . . .* he thought, not knowing that there were many differences in style and scope between Rome and Venice. He meant that allowances had to be made when travelling abroad for the unusual way foreigners went about things.

He'd seen pictures – illustrations mostly of classical works of art – that showed women impaling themselves on men's spikes. Hitherto he had regarded this reversal of traditional roles as an interesting aspect of ancient Roman decadence, a handy sex-technique for men too jaded to do it properly. Towards the end of a long night's orgy, perhaps, when the spirit was still very willing but the flesh had weakened, it would be convenient just to lie passive and let the woman do the work.

Actually, on his way to Venice by train through Paris, he had acquired a packet of postcards from a shifty-looking man in a Basque beret on the Place Pigalle. Two or three were of naked women showing off their bodies – mostly they had big dangling breasts and broad backsides. Some were of women on their backs with their legs apart and men on top of them, the women's faces showing expressions intended to suggest ecstasy but in reality not very far removed from boredom.

One picture showed a fat-bottomed naked female sitting over a man who had a waxed-point moustache and was still wearing his shirt. It was a comical sight and proof that the French were just as decadent as the ancient Romans were.

Maybe the Italians were as decadent as the French – it seemed very likely to Toby. But Anna-Louisa couldn't possibly think he wasn't up to it! Obviously she regarded herself as in complete command of the situation and she viewed him as no more than a useful instrument of her pleasure.

While Toby was coming to terms with this strange thought she did as he expected and got up on the desk on stockinged knees. What happened next astonished him as never before.

She knelt, not over his loins but astride his head, holding her silk frock up round her waist. With a shock of disbelief he stared up at very close range at her hairy split – then, before he understood fully what she was at, she lowered herself slowly until her fleshy *fica* lay on his mouth.

He had never until this day found himself underneath a woman in this way. He had kissed more than one girlfriend between the legs to arouse them, but the girls in question had been lying on their backs at the time, with long slender legs parted for his attentions, awaiting his pleasure. Toby was used to being uppermost and setting the pace. But Anna-Louisa's bare thighs were clasping his head in a grip not easy to break and she was rubbing her split against his mouth.

Well, why not? he thought suddenly. Unfamiliar thoughts were flashing through his mind. *Why not go all the way?* After a moment's hesitation he pushed his tongue in where he was being forced to kiss. He found her nub immediately and lapped at it – and in no time he could hear her gasp while she slid over his mouth with increasing insistence.

A possible explanation occurred to Toby of why he was on his back on a desk underneath an excited woman. It was those damned trophies on the walls – she resented her husband's absences to kill wild animals and his neglect of her. She was compensating herself by collecting her own trophies – here in Ziani's study, on his desk. Which of them had the more, Toby wondered, she or he? Had she had more men on this desk than there were mounted heads on the walls?

Whether he was right or wrong, Anna-Louisa did not let him go *all the way*, as he had put it to himself. All the way she would certainly insist on going, but she wanted something rather more substantial inside herself, something thicker and harder, when the destination was reached. With this in mind she climbed off Toby's face and lay down on her back beside him, gesturing to him to climb on top of her. He scrambled up until he was on his knees between her legs, staring in fascination at her broad belly and wet hairy *fica*.

Her frock was round her waist and her knees were drawn up and splayed outwards – and while Toby stared she put her beringed hands on her bare thighs above her stocking-tops. Casually, she pulled herself open, smiling up at him while she revealed the moist pink inside.

Toby uttered a grunt of approval and threw himself forward to lie on her belly. He felt her grasp his throbbing stiffness and steer it into her. He pushed in deep, sinking with delight into her warm wetness, then slid back and forth strongly.

'*Ah si – bravo!*' said Anna-Louisa is a gasping voice.

She got his trousers halfway down his legs and was clawing at his bottom with her painted fingernails, inflicting deliberate pain to spur him on, as if he were a horse she was riding at a gallop!

I'm not a horse, he thought wildly, I'm a rhinoceros out in the African bush and I'm charging at you with my massive horn, Anna-Louisa! Shall I stab it into you and rip your belly open – or will you drop me first with a bullet and put my head on your wall as another trophy?

The strange idea aroused him to new heights – he jabbed hard and fast into her belly and brought on a rapid response. Anna-Louisa jerked and moaned under him, heaved her belly up to meet his thrusts – and at the instant her climax began, Toby flooded her *fica* with eager passion.

'*Aie!*' she screeched, '*Ancora, Tobiolo, ancora, ancora!*'

THREE

Alone in a hot and stuffy room up under the roof of the Palazzo Malvolio, Toby sat on a gilt-wood *chaise-longue* with embroidered upholstery that was badly torn and contemplated the fascinating subject of female bums.

There were two basic shapes, he reflected – but no, that was not quite so: there were three *fundamental* shapes. According to the woman's general body shape and size, her bottom could be as round as two melons – or two pumpkins if heavily built. But it might also be pear-shaped, which was elegant in young women but droopy in older ones. A third possibility, though rare, even in young girls, was a bum formed like a furled tulip.

What had set this train of thought going in his mind were the stacks of old furniture that surrounded him. He was on the top floor of the Palazzo in a storeroom where broken furniture was kept, an attic reached through endless corridors of faded eighteenth century magnificence and up flights of stairs that became less impressive as he mounted. First there was the white marble of the grand staircase which rose from the entrance hall to the *piano nobile*, the floor where the drawing room was placed. Then came a wide and beautiful wooden staircase with marquetry work that led upwards again to the floor where the bedrooms and private rooms were.

From there a staircase not easy to find climbed to the servants' quarters. This was tiled in red, many of the tiles cracked by the tread of millions of footsteps over the course of 200 years. A part of this extensive acreage under the roof was enclosed as a single large room, and here the Malvolios had been putting broken furniture since the palace was built. Why they had never bothered to have it mended astonished Toby, but there was no accounting for the habits of the very rich. It was said about that very superior person the late

Marquess Curzon that he never wore the same pair of socks twice. And the Czarina Catherine of Russia ordered a different guardsman to be sent up to her bedchamber each night.

The storeroom was about three-quarters filled with stacks of dusty chairs, rolled-up carpets, tables, a bed or two, commodes and cupboards, cabinets and bookcases. Every piece in sight was an antique of great value if properly restored, which was what had brought Toby to Venice. Word had reached his father through trade gossip that a family of impoverished Venetian aristos had an incredible store of cast-off furniture which might be for sale. After getting in touch with the owner, who proved not to be Venetian at all but an English lady of middle years who had inherited the palace and contents, Jervis Senior had despatched Toby to inspect the goods and make Mrs Tandy a moderate offer.

The two first days of his stay as a guest in the Palazzo were a time of waiting while a team of servants did what they could to disperse the dust of centuries and stack the furniture more conveniently for Toby to get in and make a list. After that he could form a conclusion about the amount of restoration work required. Before making any offer to Mrs Tandy he had orders to telephone London to give his father his assessment and have it agreed.

In half a day he had listed thirty-seven assorted chairs, eleven tables of various sizes, from a broken-legged dining-table for twelve down to a round occasional table finely inlaid with mother-of-pearl and what looked like a sword slash across the top. He looked round at the size of the room and at the amount still to catalogue – cracked cabinets, broken-backed writing tables, collapsed footstools, rickety credenzas, inlaid secretaires with doors hanging off – so much, so much! It was all too obvious it was going to take him days to complete the inventory. And longer still to survey individual damage and form a sensible estimate of the cost of a repair job in London. That being so, he decided to sit down for a rest on the dust-faded *chaise-longue*.

How on earth did all this furniture come to be broken in the first place? he wondered as he stared about. Were the Malvolio family in their great days more than usually aggressive at home? Did the men draw swords and fight duels to the death in the drawing room? What furious Malvolio had nailed shut a Baroque rosewood writing table? The elegant rococo prayer stool with a painted porcelain plaque let into the elbow-rest – a picture of the Madonna to assist the devotee's concentration – why was the plaque smashed and half of it missing and irreplaceable? A sudden rage by a Malvolio at a prayer unanswered? And how could some long-forgotten lady damage so badly the petit-point upholstery of her *chaise-longue* – it would have required more than a rake by her fingernails in a transport of passion!

From staring at chairs and other items Toby's thoughts turned to the ladies who had sat on them, and it was only a small step from that to female bottoms. And the clothes that covered them. The earliest furniture he had so far come across was older than the palace itself. The original Palazzo Malvolio had been built on the site in 1451 and destroyed by fire in the eighteenth century. The new Palazzo was built on the same foundations in 1736, in what was then the height of architectural good taste, a version of Palladianism. Self-evidently, a lot had been saved from the fire, not only the paintings but some furniture too.

From the paintings he had seen Toby tried to recall what fine ladies wore in 1451 when they lived in the first palace. Silk robes pulled in tight below the breasts, he thought, cut low to display lots of cleavage, close-fitted long sleeves and ground-sweeping skirts with trains. And under that, what? – a thin underskirt and nothing else, so the curve of the bottom was displayed to best advantage. Seated in thin clothes on one of the unpadded wooden chairs of the day, there would be precious little between a lady and the seat. A well-fleshed bum would be an advantage.

When the Malvolios moved into the rebuilt palace in the eighteenth century, the ladies of the family would be wearing skirts with hip-panniers, he thought. Still plenty of bosom displayed and more arm, with half-sleeves. When they sat down they arranged skirts and panniers so that not too much leg was seen – legs in white silk stockings tied just above the knee. Knickers had not been invented, of course – an enterprising gentleman sitting at a lady's side could slip a hand under her voluminous skirts and feel what she had between her bare thighs.

The rips in the embroidery Toby was sitting on now – had some act of passionate and violent rejection caused them? And what about the four-poster bed in a far corner? Naked ladies lay in it once, with their legs apart to be pleasured. Perhaps a long-gone Malvolio romped in it with several females at the same time, it was big enough! That would set it creaking mightily – although it was hard to see how it could have broken off about a yard of the elaborate baroque wood carving round the top of the frame, ten feet above the floor. Unless he had made a swing out of the sheets and swung a naked girl back and forth in it.

On further reflection, it was easy to visualise the Contessa Marina in a four-poster of that sort. Not in a swing, but lying at ease half-sunk into a soft feather mattress, her knees apart and raised, her arms outstretched in a gesture of welcome. Easy as well to visualise her sitting on one of the wide comfortable armchairs stacked up here in the depository. She had the sort of lush figure that went with this type of overblown furniture.

Her bottom was of the round shape and, though overplump for Toby's taste, it would surely have made a fine sight when she leaned over the parapet of the Rialto Bridge and let her friend Orlando lift her skirt. A soft, white, round bottom shining in the moonlight, thighs parted to allow a glimpse of curly dark hair where the mound was revealed – a subject for a painting by Tiepolo, a life-size mural for a bedroom, perhaps – a vision of pearly flesh and luscious curves!

Anna-Louisa's bottom he hadn't seen, though he got very close to it when she sat on his face! But from what he recalled of her clothed, it was round and prominent in an old-fashioned way that was no longer thought modish. There was only one woman at Princess Zita's lunch with the style of bottom to interest him – the American, and she was much too old. She wore clothes that fitted tightly to show off her lean and flat bottom – and Toby knew it would be firm to the touch, resistant to the pressure of fingertips sinking into the cheeks. Her figure was right for the ideal model he admired – small breasts showing only as the gentlest of swellings under her frock, narrow hips, no belly to speak of and long thin thighs. What a shame she wasn't twenty years younger!

The thin and bosomless American-born Contessa Flagranti had insisted that the Palazzo Malvolio was falling down round its owner's ears, but Toby knew this was an exaggeration. Neglected and dilapidated it undoubtedly was, however, otherwise he would not have been sent to Venice by Fitzroy Dalrymple, purveyors of antiques to the nobility and gentry.

His first sight of the Palazzo was days before the odd events at Princess Zita's lunch party. He had arrived in Venice by express train from Paris and came out of the railway station on to the broad quay where water-buses and gondolas pick up passengers. A porter trotted behind with his luggage and a thickset middle-aged man in old-world purple and yellow livery, much faded and worn, came up to Toby and bowed. At first Toby thought the unusual clothing was for the benefit of tourists, much like the beefeaters at the Tower of London, but the man soon explained in fractured but intelligible English that he had been sent by Signora Tandy to take Signor *Giovise*, that being his tortured version of Jervis, to the Palazzo Malvolio.

He had an open motorlaunch tied up next to the gondola rank, into which he settled Toby and the suitcases, and sped out into the continuous traffic of the Grand Canal. He weaved his craft round and past the chugging *vaporetti* whose decks swarmed with sight-seers and the gliding gondolas bearing honeymoon couples taking a breather between bouts in hotel beds. The buildings on either side of the Canal slid past and Toby was stunned by the visual grandeur of Venice.

His field of interest was furniture, not architecture, but it was not necessary to be an expert to appreciate the splendour in stone that centuries of persistent human effort had built up and left as its memorial. Past white domes of churches built to honour saints unheard-of, and past palaces of marble and mosaic erected by wealthy businessmen when the English nobility lived in draughty fortified castles, past warehouses more handsome of design than King Henry VIII's palace in London, and so to the white Rialto Bridge arching over the canal. Then again more palaces, some in stone, some in brick weathered pink, some in terracotta plaster, with awnings and blinds and private moorings and striped poles that stuck up out of the water.

The boatman pointed up ahead and announced, '*Eccolo, Signor, il Palazzo Malvolio,*' and Toby sat up straighter to see where he had been invited to stay for a few days by Mrs Tandy. It was on the left bank, where the Grand Canal curved to the left. The style of it was recognisably eighteenth century, which made it almost new for Venice. At that time Toby had not seen Princess Zita's palace – 300 years older than the Malvolio but by no means the oldest inhabited house in Venice.

The Palazzo Malvolio was faced in white stone that the years had turned greyish and was in need of expert restoration. There were Corinthian columns spaced along the frontage supporting a line of stone balconies the width of the building, above them rose another tier of columns and above them a double tier of smaller columns. Thick wooden pillars rose up from the water in front of a broad stone landing-stage that ran the width of the building, pillars striped like a barber's pole, but cracked and split and half-rotted through by water and sun.

They were used for tying up boats and were painted in the colours of the family who owned the palace – which Toby already knew from his boatman's faded clothes to be yellow and purple. A footman came out as the launch stopped alongside and he too was in livery – long jacket, knee-breeches and white stockings, as threadbare as the boatman's attire. It was all too apparent that Mrs Tandy had fallen on hard times. Regrettable though it was, this state of affairs worked in Toby's favour, he thought. Beggars can't be choosers, as they say, though people too often had grandiose ideas of what their possessions were worth. They became disillusioned and bitter when presented with a hard cash offer below their expectations.

He followed the footman through an imposing doorway into an entrance hall dominated by an elaborate marble staircase. Here an imposing figure stood waiting for him – a silver-haired man wearing a black swallow-tail coat. He bowed ponderously to the visitor and announced that he was the major-domo and that his name was Luigi. Toby guessed that in England he would have been the butler. He conducted Toby up the broad staircase, on either side of which life-size statues stood in niches in the walls.

They were figures from Classical mythology, of course – with this style of architecture nothing else was possible. There was a naked Venus holding out an apple and a Hercules wrapped in a lion-skin, the marble of both looking dirty and in urgent need of attention. They would look good in someone's garden, as long as it was big enough and if Mrs Tandy was minded to sell them, which seemed unlikely.

In the days since his arrival by launch Toby had come to know the Palazzo Malvolio a little better, though he knew there must be acres of mirrored salons and tapestried rooms he hadn't seen yet. But here he was on the topmost floor, trying to produce an inventory of several centuries of discarded furniture. His long digression into reflections on women's bottoms and the pleasure they afforded was having an insidious effect on him. There was a slow stiffening inside his trousers, a feeling of bulging, a new strength making itself apparent.

He laid his palm over the swelling part as if to comfort it a little and grinned to feel it jerk against his hand. He was in need of a friendly woman but there seemed to be none available to him. If Anna-Louisa Ziani could be believed, Contessa Marina indulged herself with every good-looking young man who stayed in the Palazzo Malvolio. But apart from her confidences to him on the Rialto Bridge, she had given no sign of wanting any closer acquaintance.

His conclusion was that Anna-Louisa's characterisation of the Contessa was an exaggeration inspired by the natural cattiness of women. It was impossible to take it as solemn truth when it was all too apparent that Anna-Louisa was seizing the chance to score over her absent husband, and over a friend, at the same time.

And score she had. She'd rubbed Toby's face in it, literally, and though he grinned at the memory, it was in his mind to get his own back if an opportunity served. How that could be done he had only the vaguest of thoughts, but it seemed to him that honour would be satisfied if he could get his *cazzo* inside her mouth and spurt his lust down her throat.

While he pondered the satisfaction that would bring, in his mind was a vision of Anna-Louisa Ziani kneeling in front of him, his throbbing part in her mouth. His fingers rubbed slowly over the thin material of his trousers, giving him pleasantly exciting sensations. He was so engrossed in his thoughts of how he would be revenged that he failed to hear a distant door open and close. He came out of his reverie with a start when a voice behind him spoke his name – and he whirled about on the *chaise-longue* to see Marina standing only a few steps away.

The Contessa was dressed very smartly in a blouse and pleated skirt. The blouse was of turquoise blue silk and long, down to her hips and worn outside her cherry-red skirt. It had a small scalloped collar and a frill that continued the scalloping all the way down the front to the hem. The sleeves belled out below the elbow to very wide cuffs, which were scalloped to match the collar. Toby rose to his feet rather awkwardly, being conscious of the long bulge in the front of his trousers.

'Have you finished your inventory already?' she asked with a smile of encouragement as she came round the gilt-wood *chaise-longue*.

Toby explained that he'd hardly made a dent in the work yet and had sat down to evaluate what he'd seen so far and how best to tackle the rest. Marina nodded, gazing down at the long rips in the embroidered upholstery, and sat carefully, indicating he should do the same. Toby sat down beside her, the two of them divided by a jagged gash.

'I've been thinking about what you told me,' she began, 'when we went to Zita's. About Prince Carol and Magda Lupescu, I mean – and how he whips her bare bottom with a riding-crop. Have you ever whipped a woman, Toby?'

'You asked me that before and I said no. As I recall it, you have more experience in this direction than I have.'

'No, no, it was poor dear Zita who was tied up and flogged by her husband night after night,' said Marina, resting her hand lightly on Toby's arm, 'you weren't listening properly, you bad boy!'

'But I listened with bated breath, I assure you! You took me into your confidence enough to tell me that your friend Orlando tied you down on a bed with your silk stockings, remember? And smacked your bare bottom.'

'So he did,' she said, with a faint smile of contentment. She slid cautiously along the torn upholstery towards Toby and the bottom in question was poised half over the rip to allow her to sit close to him. Toby smiled at her somewhat warily, uncertain if more confidences were on the way about her past frolics with Orlando and other friends, or whether she had in mind something more substantial than memories.

Her plump breasts hung heavily inside her turquoise blouse – Toby could see how they showed faintly pink through the flimsy silk – a fair warning she was wearing nothing else beneath. Her belly curved out gracefully under her bright red skirt which, in sitting, had pulled up to display round knees. She could hardly be said to be wildly attractive to an admirer of lean *Vogue* type women, thought Toby, wondering why he *did*, after all, find her attractive. Her haunches in the close-fitting skirt were broad to his way of thinking, her silk-stockinged legs somewhat too fully fleshed.

But for all that, style and taste apart, no healthy young man could possibly ignore the Contessa Marina's bodily charms. Toby found himself staring at her prominent breasts and wanting to fondle them. Would she be outraged if he raised a hand to touch her?

'Really, Toby!' she exlaimed. 'The way you're staring at my bosom with a grin on your face is simply indecent.'

For a second or two he thought of apologising but there was no need. Her words were intended as a come-on, not a put-off, and he watched in delight as she slowly undid the pearl buttons concealed by the frill down the front of her blouse and opened it wide. Her breasts hung soft and heavy, like ripe fruit to be plucked, the skin an opalescent white and the prominent buds were a rich red.

'Look all you want,' she said, holding the blouse apart with both hands, 'I know how devastating an effect my breasts have on men. It's been like that since I was a girl. I've been painted in the nude by artists many times, you know. The first ever was Augustus John when I was a debutante in London. When I married the Count and came here, every young Venetian artist wanted me to sit nude. I never refused, because I think one has a responsibility to art and culture, don't you?'

While she spoke she was cupping her breasts in her hands and seemingly admiring their weightiness and texture, bouncing them up and down just enough to keep Toby's attention riveted while she chattered on without waiting for an answer to her question.

'Rodolfo Angelotti – you must have heard of him?' she said. 'A most talented young sculptor. He did a torso of me – just from the waist to the neck, to immortalise my breasts. It was a very exciting venture. I had to strip off completely and get down on my hands and knees over a wooden box. Rodolfo filled it slowly with liquid plaster of Paris and made me stay still like that, while it set.'

'I say – that does sound exciting!' said Toby, visualising the scene in the artist's studio. 'Did it take long to set?'

'The thing was, we had to throw it away and start again twice over. You see, no man can ever resist me naked, and certainly not Rodolfo – he insisted on making love to me from behind and that made me jerk about and spoil the plaster cast while it was still wet. It took all afternoon to get a perfect cast. Then he used it to make a clay model, which looked absolutely stunning. He was going to have it cast in bronze – he'd got no money so I said I'd pay for it. What a masterpiece it would have been!'

'Something prevented him?' asked Toby, staring at her fleshy breasts in wonder. They represented a sort of challenge – they demanded to be handled. Which seemed odd, somehow – love-making was so much more straightforward with a slender woman offering no such diversions from the smoothness of her belly and thighs.

'My husband Massimo found out that I'd been sitting nude for Rodolfo and went into a fearful rage. He stormed into the poor man's studio – I don't know how he found the place because it's in a miserable old tenement building near the Fondamenta Nuove. He shouted at Rodolfo and threatened him! He smashed the clay model with his ebony walking stick and ground the pieces under his foot on the floor!'

'Good God – jealousy on that scale is terrifying,' said Toby, easing himself away from the bare-breasted Contessa.

'It's all right,' she assured him, 'Massimo lives in Rome now – I haven't seen him in years. I do as I like. Don't you think my breasts are superb, Toby?'

'Superb,' he agreed at once, smiling at her to impress the sincerity of his pronouncement.

If the truth were told, Marina would have been more pleasing aesthetically to him if she were flat-chested. Or had only tiny and inconspicuous swellings. The fact that Toby's male part was standing stiff and hard was merely an animal reaction and of no significance.

'Of course, artists are not what they were,' said Marina with a touch of sadness, 'not even the Italians. Ever since the War they've lost interest in painting beautiful women. Nowadays it's all pictures of giant cog-wheels and airplanes and silly racing-cars and machines of various sorts. I can't make sense of it any more.'

She sighed and reached out to take hold of Toby's wrists and put his hands on her bare breasts. The skin was satin smooth to his touch, the flesh warm and soft.

'There's something very odd about young men, artists or not,' she said, 'who prefer oily and dangerous machinery to the feel of a woman's breasts. Do you like modern paintings, Toby?'

'I prefer the feel of soft breasts to spanners,' he said with a thoughtful smile, handling her boldly now, the balls of his thumbs flicking over her outstanding buds.

Marina's hand was on his nearer thigh, a dreamy expression in her dark brown eyes. She undid his trouser buttons and took out his fleshy stiffness.

'Yes, I can see that,' she said, 'they say *this* never lies – but sometimes I'm not so sure. Once upon a time, if a man was interested, then it stood hard. If it stayed small and soft, he was a waste of time.'

'I can't believe that's ever happened to you, Marina.'

She said nothing, but he heard a sigh, as if of annoyance at some memory. Her hand clasped his pride firmly and slid up and down in a pleasant rhythm. He pressed her warm breasts in his palms and rolled them.

'It was standing up in your trousers before I arrived,' she said. 'When you got up I could see the bulge – what were you thinking about? A girlfriend in London?'

'Why no – to be honest, I was thinking about you standing bare bottomed by night on the Rialto Bridge,' he said boldly.

It was partly true – he had thought fleetingly of her frolic with Orlando, though if he were to be as open as he claimed, he would have to admit that what had stiffened him to full stretch was his fantasy of revenge on her friend Anna-Louisa.

'Really?' said Marina, raising her finely plucked eyebrows. 'Was the thought of my little adventure so very exciting?'

'Oh yes,' Toby sighed, 'very exciting indeed, Marina.'

'Are you married?' she asked.

'Lord no! Whatever gave you an idea like that?'

'Because you seemed so very reluctant to touch me, although I was sitting here with my breasts hanging out for ten minutes at least. That made me think you are in love with someone in London – your wife or a girlfriend, or someone else's wife. Are you?'

'There's no one,' he said, his voice a little unsteady as the sensations of approaching release spread through his belly from his throbbing *cazzo*. 'I want to make love to you, Marina – stop before it's too late!'

'It's *never* too late,' she said, her hand moving faster and harder on him. He felt his leaping male part becoming thicker and harder by the moment in her grasp. In another moment it was going to happen – his belly would clench and spout his frantic desire into her hand.

It was a moment for action, for self-assertion, and Toby rose to it by seizing Marina by the wrist and standing up, dragging her to her feet. Ten quick steps through the stacked furniture brought them to the rococo *prie-dieu* with the broken porcelain plaque and he pushed Marina down on to her knees on its dusty and faded mauve cushion.

The Contessa Marina's waking and sleeping thoughts were so attuned to possibilities for pleasure that she understood at once what Toby wanted to do, and she began to ease her pleated red skirt up her thighs. Toby got down on his knees behind her on the hard floor and put his hand under her skirt, between her legs. He gave a sigh of pleasure to feel the bare flesh of her thighs above her stocking-tops, so very soft and exciting to the touch.

'Then it's true,' she murmured, still occupied in getting her close-fitting skirt up to her hips, 'my adventure on the Rialto really did arouse you! You want to do just the same to me as Orlando did!'

'I mean to outdo him,' said Toby somewhat boastfully, unaware of what he was committing himself to.

But there was no place then for caution or reservations – his exploring hand had found lace and then the smooth silk of her knickers. She sighed this time, perhaps because of his light caress, perhaps because of what he had just promised. Her knees slid apart on the worn cushion of the prayer stool and his fingers gently insinuated themselves through the open leg of her knickers. Her mound was prominent and thickly curled, and with an excitement that shook his whole body he fingered the warm lips.

By now her skirt was well up over her bottom, bunched around her waist. Marina was trembling with anticipation – she put her arms flat on the ledge with the painted plaque of the Blessed Virgin and leaned forward in a gesture of total surrender. Toby eased her ivory-silk knickers down her thighs and fondled the plump round cheeks he had uncovered.

All this flesh! he was thinking. *Far, far too much! It's so frightfully old-fashioned, a bottom like a pair of down-stuffed pillows and big balloons of breasts to match. It's worse than old-fashioned – it's in poor taste – positively déclassé!*

Yet, in spite of his strictures, there was no denying that his *cazzo* was throbbing and rearing out of his gaping trousers, and what Toby wanted most in the world was to thrust it deep inside the dark-haired split he was feeling. Marina turned her head to the side to catch sight of him out of the corner of an eye, her mouth open in a fixed grin of delirious anticipation. Toby set the head of his leaping part to the awaiting slit and pushed in strongly.

She uttered a shrill little cry of delight to feel the deep

penetration and jerked her loins backwards at him to push him still further in, if that was possible. Toby put his arms round her and cupped her big soft breasts in his hands. *Too big, much much too big for elegance* he was thinking even while he gripped them tight to hold her while he rode on her back in a briskly staccato rhythm. Golden sensations in his belly warned him that his moment of crisis was here – with a loud gasp of triumph he thrust hard into her slippery *fica* and spurted passionately.

Her head jerked back sharply and her climactic shriek sounded through the low-ceilinged room, across an acre of dusty and broken furniture. Her pleasure was short of duration and when it was over she straightened her back slowly, sliding Toby off, until she could half-turn on her silk-stockinged knees to kiss his mouth lightly and run her fingertips down his cheek.

'You did that well, *carissimo*,' she said, smiling graciously at him.

'Better than Orlando?' he asked with a slow grin, expecting the answer *yes*.

'That still remains to be seen,' said Marina, her hand down between their bodies to clasp his wet and softening *cazzo* in an experienced and skilful grip. 'Orlando ravished me more than once that night. The Rialto Bridge was what the Italians call a *momento culminante* – it was the second or third time, I forget which. But the finishing touch was when he brought me home in a gondola and had me with my back against the palace wall, facing the Grand Canal.'

Toby said nothing, wondering why he'd been so thoughtless as to brag about outdoing Orlando. Suddenly his pride was at stake – not to mention his honour, if that meant anything. He put his hand between Marina's legs and fingered the wet and loose lips there, feeling inside to touch her secret nub, and observed how she gasped and closed her eyes and trembled when touched there.

'The bed over there,' she murmured, nodding to the vast four-poster with the broken top, 'can we get to it?'

'We can try,' said Toby, his fingertip fluttering lightly on her hidden bud to take her to orgasm quickly again and slow her down to his own pace, 'I shall strip you naked on it and throw you down on your back with your legs wide open . . .'

'*Si, si!*' Marina gasped. 'Oh yes!'

477

FOUR

Besides Mrs Tandy and her sister, the Contessa, there were two other members of the household Toby had become acquainted with at dinner on his first night at the Palazzo Malvolio. One was a small fat priest in a threadbare black cassock – Padre Pio, who must have been seventy. He wore round gold-rimmed glasses and smiled much and, luckily, he spoke reasonably good English. He was, he told Toby proudly, Confessor to the Malvolio, and had the honour to hold that appointment since the year 1879.

It occurred to Toby that there were no more Malvolio, but it would have been impertinent to say so. Count Rinaldo had crashed in his fighter plane during the War without marrying the woman he carried off from England. But perhaps – who could explain these curious feudal religious customs – perhaps the Confessor to an aristocratic family was appointed for life in return for his food and a garret under the roof. It seemed unlikely that the regal Mrs Tandy had much to confess by way of sin – and as for the Contessa Marina, she was much too pleased by her antics to entertain any feelings of guilt.

The other permanent resident in the Palazzo was Herr Adalbert Gmund. Toby took him to be German until it was explained he was an Austrian. Gmund was a man of about sixty, stocky, with the remains of sandy hair clinging to his round head like moss to a boulder. His mode of dress was curiously old-fashioned, just as if he had bought no new clothes in the twenty years that had passed since 1909. He wore stand-up hard collars and heavily starched cuffs, very narrow trousers and a waistcoat, even in the heat of Venice, with a gold watch-chain on display.

Gmund, too, spoke reasonably good English but, apart from some general conversation at meal times, Toby had no dealings with the mysterious Austrian. Not until the morning after Contessa Marina visited the old furniture storeroom, and learned what other use a prayer stool could be put to. Toby was hard at work with his notebook, writing down descriptions of the pieces of furniture and his assessment of their sale value if restored. He was feeling hot, dusty and dishevelled, and was by no means unhappy at being interrupted when Adalbert Gmund appeared.

'*Ach du lieber Gott!*' the Austrian exclaimed, looking round at the stacked furniture. 'What a mountain of old rubbish! You will be with us for years, my dear chap.'

'Well, for another week or more, at least,' said Toby.

'If one week, why not two?' asked Gmund, smiling ferociously as he stared at broken-backed chairs and commodes. 'I've come to invite you to take a drink with me before lunch. You must be ready for a break from your labours.'

Toby accepted at once, put away his notebook and followed Gmund out of the repository and down the servants' stairs. Apart from the obvious pleasure of taking a rest from a tiresome job, he was hoping that he could tap Gmund for information about the household which might be useful in formulating an offer for the damaged antique furniture.

Distances in the vast and run-down Palazzo were impressive. From the attics to Adalbert Gmund's quarters was a considerable march along wide and high-ceilinged corridors hung with priceless oil paintings and through suites of reception rooms that opened into each other and through sitting rooms and music rooms with long-disused pianos, harpsichords, spinets and gilt harps with slack strings, and through tall and faded rooms with no obvious purpose at all except to house marble statues of naked gods and goddesses, busts of stern-faced and bearded Greek philosophers and smooth-shaven Roman emperors.

By the time they reached their destination Toby acknowledged that he was lost. Gmund's private sitting room was comfortably furnished, though everything looked worn and in need of some attention. With a proud flourish Gmund produced from an ornate cupboard a bottle of Scotch whisky.

'Glenfiddich,' he said, wrinkling up his face in a gesture of appreciation as he showed Toby the label, 'a good make, *nein?*'

'Excellent,' Toby agreed, watching in astonishment as his host poured two large glasses full.

'Chin chin,' said Gmund, and they drank to each other,

Toby wondering why foreigners thought English people said that when they drank.

It was early in the day for so large a quantity of whisky and he confined himself to a moderate swallow. Not so Gmund who, to Toby's amazement, drained his glass in three rapid goes and then poured himself another equally large.

'Sit down, sit down, Mr Jervis,' said he jovially, waving at chairs with the hand that held the bottle. When they were seated he offered to top up Toby's glass but was not put out when his offer was politely, declined.

'Sit down, sit down, Mr Jervis,' he said. 'Often I was invited to shoot the grouse before the War. In those days I was rich and travelled much.'

'Have you lived here in Venice long, Herr Gmund?' Toby asked in a bland attempt to move the conversation in the direction he wanted it to go.

'Please, call me Adalbert,' said Gmund, his geniality greatly enhanced by his generous intake of Glenfiddich. 'I am the guest here of Mrs Tandy since the War ended. You must understand that Count Malvolio was my friend before and I stayed often with him and became acquainted with his gracious lady, Mrs Tandy. Since the break-up of the Austrian Empire my estates are no more and I am very kindly invited to live here.'

'I say, what rotten luck!' said Toby. 'About your estate, I mean, not about living in Venice. I suppose Mrs Tandy invited the Contessa Marina to live here when her husband left her.'

'No, Marina and Count Massimo came to live here from the day they were married. That was more than twenty years ago. He was here until two or three years ago and then returned to Rome and the rest of the Torrenegra family.'

'I see. I took him to be Venetian,' said Toby.

'*Nein, nein, nein* – his family is from Rome. Marina made his acquaintance when she went with Delphine and Rinaldo Malvolio to see the sights of Rome. Like many other of the aristocratic families of old Europe the Torrenegra have been paupers for as long as anyone can remember.'

By now it had become obvious to Toby that Adalbert Gmund had no liking for the departed Count and, inspired by the second glass of Glenfiddich he had consumed, was quite happy to reveal any dark secrets he might know.

'When Massimo met Marina he owned nothing,' Gmund

continued, 'nothing at all but his good looks and his fine clothes, which he never paid for. He married Marina because he knew Rinaldo would ask them to come here to live permanently in the palace. Marina told me that she paid their fare on the train to Venice from Rome.'

'Was she very distressed when he deserted her?' asked Toby, savouring another sip of his whisky.

'*Mein Gott* – she was pleased to be rid of him. The marriage to Massimo was a disaster! She was twenty-two and so very beautiful that everyone fell in love with her. Her daughter, Bianca, was born a year later – a most beautiful child who is now grown up and is a greater beauty than even her mother was. But Bianca ran away with a young man and Marina blamed Massimo for that.'

'Why?' asked Toby, fascinated by these revelations.

'Well, Massimo had married Marina to assure a roof over his head and food in his mouth. As soon as Marina told him that she was pregnant, his duty to continue the Torrenegra line was done and he felt free to pursue his true preference.'

'He'd met another woman so soon after his marriage? My word, that's a bit thick!' said Toby.

'You misunderstand, my young friend. Massimo's interest lay with pretty young men, not with his beautiful wife. Only family duty forced him into bed with her – as soon as there was a child the relations between them ended and he amused himself with young Venetian lads.'

'Oh Lord, he's one of those, is he?'

Toby thought he now could see why Marina displayed so bold an interest in other men, and it seemed a good moment to ask about the mysterious Orlando who had performed so memorably by night on the Rialto Bridge. Adalbert would surely know all about him.

'*Ach ja*,' said the Austrian, shaking his round head gloomily, 'his name is Roland and he is a countryman of yours. He came to look at the paintings a year or two ago, that being his *métier*, fine art. Mrs Tandy asked him to stay here and make a catalogue of the Malvolio picture collection. He and Marina became close friends.'

'So I believe,' said Toby with a grin.

'Most unfortunately Count Massimo became aware of his wife's interest in the young professor and tried to chase him away. In the end it was Massimo who was sent away.'

'He was cataloguing the paintings, was he?' said Toby with

a thoughtful glance at the walls of Adalbert's sitting room. 'Was it with the possibility of a sale in mind? There have been no major sales of Venetian School collections in London recently.'

'The catalogue was never finished,' Adalbert explained with a heavy frown. 'Marina and Roland became so infatuated with each other that she strengthened his passion by giving him to drink a certain *elisir d'amore* that can be obtained here if you have enough money. With this he was making love to her a dozen times a day.'

'Oh what rot!' said Toby. 'You're pulling my leg. Everybody knows there's no such drug. This business of aphrodisiacs is no more than tales from the days of Casanova when chaps were more gullible.'

'*Jawohl!* The Chevalier Casanova, the most famous citizen of the Republic of Venice after Marco Polo,' said Adalbert with a chuckle. 'He certainly knew about the *elisir*, which may be seen from the feats recorded in his *Memoirs*. But though you may find it impossible to believe what I tell you, the word you used is correct – it is a *drug* and a very dangerous one. Roland became addicted to it, or perhaps to the constant pleasure that he got from its effect on him. In less than three months he collapsed and it was thought he would die of exhaustion of the nerves.'

'Good God!' said Toby, taking a large swig of whisky to calm himself. 'That puts things in a different light. Did he die?'

'Good doctors and careful nursing helped him to survive, but his constitution was too enfeebled to complete his work with the pictures. He returned to London, a sadder and weaker man. Poor Marina was heart-broken.'

'So the catalogue was abandoned? But is Mrs Tandy interested in selling pictures?'

'You must ask her that yourself. But let me, dear Toby, offer in friendship a word of advice about Marina. You have been here several days now so without question she has arranged to make love to you. Twenty years ago I was a lover of hers, so I know how wonderful it is to ride her belly.'

'Look here – this is no way to speak about a lady!'

'Some things need to be said,' Adalbert replied, 'there is no reason to become angry. I liked Roland Thornton and we enjoyed some amusing adventures together with a local *puttana* or two. I was sorry when he became unwell and it would be a pity if that happened to you also.'

'Quite so,' Toby agreed fervently.

'You do not have to be afraid of the murderous jealousy of the Count, now he has gone away,' Adalbert continued, 'but you must be on your guard if Marina offers you a drink when you are alone with her.'

'You think she might put some of the fabulous *elisir* in it?'

'Yes,' said Adalbert, 'Marina is a glutton for love and never has enough. No man can satisfy her. So be careful, if you wish to avoid the fate of Roland Thornton, a healthy young man who became a physical wreck in a few weeks.'

In the broken furniture room Toby had made love to Marina on her knees on the *prie-dieu* and on her back on the four-poster bed and open-legged across his knees while he sat in a carved and gilt armchair with one arm cracked through. Three times – which he considered a splendid effort, though Marina had not said whether he had outdone Orlando. Nor had he asked, in case she expected more.

To do it a dozen times sounded like an episode from a French novel – or even from Casanova's account of his youth. It would certainly bring on a rapid decline in health, assuming it was mortally possible, even if spurred on to frantic excess by the local Venetian aphrodisiac – always assuming that there was such a thing. Adalbert was right – he would be careful about taking anything at all to drink from Marina's hand, just in case.

'But while we speak of love,' said the Austrian, filling his own glass again and replenishing Toby's half-drunk glass from a bottle that was now nearly empty, 'I have something interesting to show you – very scandalous and extremely entertaining.'

He got up and went ponderously into the next room, which Toby took to be the bedroom of the suite. To judge by what remained in the Glenfiddich bottle, Gmund had absorbed enough whisky to keep him genial for hours – it was a good time to press on with questions about Mrs Tandy and her background.

But when he came back the conversation was destined to fly off in a totally different direction. He carried under his arm a large flattish leather-bound book which Toby guessed to be a photograph album. He sat down opposite Toby and held it up for him to see all of the front cover. It was of dark red morocco leather, somewhat faded, and in the bottom right-hand corner there was an entwined ER monogram in gold, with a crown above.

'Can you guess who this book belonged to?' he asked, smiling broadly.

'The coronet suggests an owner with a title,' said Toby, 'but beyond that I have no thoughts before seeing the contents.'

'Ha! The coronet, as you call it, is a royal crown,' Adalbert corrected him. 'The R stands, as you must know, for *Rex* – king. This album belonged to the father of your King George.'

'Old King Teddy? But how on earth did you acquire it?'

'Aha, I see I have your interest now,' said Adalbert, laying a thick finger alongside his prominent and red-veined nose in a gesture that meant nothing to Toby. 'I am on good terms with an international dealer in exotica and curiosa. Are you ready now to see what photographs His Majesty collected?'

Without waiting for an answer he opened the book and held it up, the covers against his barrel chest, displaying to Toby a large sepia photograph of a naked woman.

'I say!' Toby exclaimed, leaning forward to look closely.

The picture showed her lying full-length on a low divan with needlework cushions. She lay with an arm hanging over the side, her hand almost touching the carpet, the other arm bent up and resting under her head. The knee nearest the camera was raised to hide what lay between her thighs. Toby stared at the plump breasts on show, at the meaty thighs, at the woman's long nose and dimpled chin, then down at the name scrawled in ink in the bottom corner of the photograph. It said *Lillie*.

'You recognise who it is, naturally,' said Adalbert.

'Mrs Langtry, I suppose.'

'She died three months ago in Monte Carlo, an old lady of seventy-five or more,' said Adalbert, who seemed well-informed.

'I read that in the newspaper at the time,' said Toby. 'May I see the book?'

It was handed to him and he flicked through the pages quickly without looking very closely. Altogether there were over twenty women photographed naked, some showing more of themselves than others. He paused to examine one who evidently had no misplaced modesty before the photographer. She half-sat, half-lay back in a big velvet-upholstered armchair, wearing black stockings with frilly garters and shiny leather shoes. She was smiling full at the camera, both hands behind her head to push her breasts out. Her long and surprisingly slender legs were crossed, but a neat patch of hair was visible below her round belly.

The name written in the corner was *Hortense*, which conveyed nothing at all to Toby. He turned a page or two, reading names rather than looking at the women. So much flesh, he thought, so much thigh and belly, so many balloons of breasts – they really did wallow in it in those days!

He stopped at the page where he saw *Skittles* written. She was standing in front of a large gilt-framed cheval-glass, a sort of striped turban wrapped round her head, concealing her hair. Her fine-featured face was sideways to the camera, as she looked at her reflection, but her naked body was fully displayed to the viewer. Her thighs were loosely together as she stood, inviting the beholder to step up close and put his hand between them.

'Skittles was the nickname of a famous Victorian courtesan,' said Toby. 'Her real name was Catherine Walters. This picture must have been taken in Paris, where Edward went often when he was Prince of Wales.'

Adalbert had come round to stand behind Toby's chair and look down over his shoulder at the photographs.

'That is correct,' he said in his accented English. 'It may surprise you to learn that I myself saw her once. I was a young man then and she had become plumper than in this picture.'

Over the page Toby found a photograph of a very darkhaired woman kneeling on an ornate chair, her back towards the camera. Her body was half-turned as she looked back over her shoulder, one full breast revealed in profile. She had arranged herself to show off her round smooth bottom to best advantage.

The name written in the corner was *Alice*.

'Do you know who this is?' Adalbert enquired.

'I take it to be Mrs Keppel,' said Toby.

'That is so. An aristocrat who was King Edward's mistress for many years. What a beautiful *Arsch* she has! What a joy to kiss it! She is the one I like best of all. Ah, if only I had met her when I was young and rich!'

'Do you know that she is still alive?' Toby asked, 'although she must be over sixty. She and her husband came to live in Italy. They have a villa near Florence, I believe.'

'*Ach so?*' Adalbert exclaimed. 'Then I will not go there,

for it would be too painful to see her old, after this wonderful photograph.'

'Yes, we are all happier with our illusions,' said Toby, who had reached the conclusion that King Edward's photograph album was a fake. Why he thought that he was not sure – there were no obvious clues in the photographs. The women were attractive and the backgrounds were sufficiently luxurious to support a claim that these were a King's girlfriends. And yet . . . perhaps years of training to recognise genuine antique furniture from clever copies had given him a feeling for what was real and what was faked.

The question in his mind was – did Adalbert know the album was not genuine? Or did he believe he had acquired a fragment of Edwardian social history?

'Can you identify all the pictures, Adalbert?'

'Not every one of them, no. There is Alice Keppel and Lillie Langtry and the Countess of Warwick – see, the one marked Daisy who lies naked on a tiger-skin rug. Let me show you – there she is, holding a spray of white flowers across her belly to cover her chief attraction. But what superb breasts she has – and how lovely her smile!'

Toby stared at the photograph. The woman's long dark hair was arranged loosely around her head on the striped skin she lay on and she was smiling into the camera, which had photographed her from ground level, looking along her naked body from over her shoulder. Her left hand held the strategically placed spray of camellias and she wore no rings. Would the real Countess have removed her wedding-ring to be photographed nude for a lover? On the assumption that she would have posed naked at all before a photographer, even if requested by a royal lover.

'Others I can put names to,' said Adalbert, 'are Miss Walters, here named as Skittles as you said before. Hortense Schneider was a famous French lady of pleasure and Sarah Bernhardt was a celebrated actress I am sure you have heard of. But who these others may be – Nancy and Louise and Maxine and Elise and Marie and the rest of them – I cannot say. Only the King himself knew all his ladies.'

'Your dealer friend must have excellent connections to obtain an object like this,' said Toby, closing the album. 'I would be very pleased to meet him, if that is possible.'

'It can be arranged,' said Adalbert, 'though he does not deal in furniture. Now, it is time we went to lunch. One more drink first, yes?'

Toby was glad to have a guide for the journey from Adalbert's quarters to the Small Dining Room, so-called. The large one was used only for grand occasions. The table in the Small Dining Room sat eight and was made of beautifully polished mahogany. In spite of its name, the room itself was big enough to hold a small dance with, say, not more than two dozen people. Against one of the walls stood two long matching sideboards, on each of which stood five or six heavy silver serving dishes. Over by the opposite wall stood a glass-fronted rosewood cabinet which displayed thirty large porcelain plates with painted landscapes – of superb quality and marvellously profitable to sell, thought Toby, the first time he saw them.

On each side of the door there was a Sèvres *jardinière* three feet tall and, facing that, a marble fireplace of mottled yellow with half a dozen bronze busts standing on it. What was visible of the walls between family portrait paintings was a pleasant pinkish ochre.

Lunch at the Palazzo Malvolio was a fairly casual meal, Toby had been given to understand when he first arrived. On this particular day neither Mrs Tandy nor the Contessa Marina put in an appearance. Padre Pio was pleased to have Toby's company, for Adalbert Gmund had gone silent as his Glenfiddich caught up with him. He ate little, but drank a lot of wine and would very obviously sleep away the afternoon. Toby ate well but drank no more than a glass or two after his larger than usual intake of whisky.

Padre Pio enquired how the furniture listing was getting on. Besides being Confessor to the Malvolio, he was also Keeper of the Archive, which included maintaining the record of pictures, other works of art, furniture and furnishings. But, he pointed out with a shrug and a smile, when something became damaged and was carried up to the attics, it was struck off his lists and for all practical purposes ceased to exist.

'These lists of yours sound very useful,' said Toby. 'May I see them sometime?'

The fat little priest agreed at once, astonished that anyone except himself could be interested in old lists. He chattered on in a friendly manner, while Adalbert seemed to retreat into himself. When the main course of white fish cooked in wine and herbs was finished and the servants brought fresh fruit to the table, Padre Pio summoned to his side the immensely dignified major-domo, who had been standing silent between the sideboards watching the liveried servants with his eagle eye.

He bent down to put his ear close to the priest's mouth. Toby heard a murmur of almost apologetic Italian, at which the major-domo nodded his silver-white head, his lips pursed. He flicked a finger at two of the footmen. Not a word was said but they understood his instructions and between them eased Adalbert out of his chair, their hands under his arms, and more or less carried him from the room.

Toby felt it would be bad form to say anything about it but Padre Pio was not so abashed. Perhaps he saw an opportunity to deliver an object lesson.

'I hope you can forgive this little scene,' he said, his head on one side in an attitude of confiding. 'Herr Gmund sometimes drinks more than is good for him. When he comes to the dining room in this condition, it is necessary before the end of the meal for him to be carried to his bed. Otherwise he slides down under the table.'

'He seemed perfectly all right when we were talking before we came in to lunch,' said Toby, standing up against the clergy on behalf of his new acquaintance. 'Perhaps he is not very well.'

'He is not at peace with himself,' said Padre Pio sadly.

'Really?' Toby said, and his disbelief must have been clear in his voice for the priest looked at him thoughtfully.

'Signor *Giovise*,' he said, mangling the name, 'Herr Gmund and I have been friends for many years. In addition, he comes to me twice a week to make confession. Do you think I am mistaken on what troubles him?'

'No, no,' said Toby hastily, adding his appologies. After that he thought it better to beat a retreat and not wait for coffee to be served. The day was hot, though it was only June, and he decided to go to his room for a quick shower to refresh himself before going back to the attics to resume work.

He took a certain pride in finding his way back unguided to the room allotted to him. From the Small Dining Room it was a fair hike, up a secondary marble staircase and then along two corridors hung with large oil paintings of battles fought long ago with pike and musket, through a gallery hung with an array of landscape paintings that would make the owner rich for life if they went to auction.

His room was large and square, the high ceiling of close-set dark wooden beams in the early Venetian style. The shutters had been closed against the midday heat and Toby stripped naked and threw his clothes untidily on the bed. It was a bed of some style, placed with its head up against a wall and with crimson curtains that swagged out round the head and were held up by a golden cherub affixed to the wall. Toby considered it would be a very good bed to romp on with a woman, the Contessa perhaps, if she could be persuaded to join him on it. Evidently Venetian ardour was not dampened by the sight of the two-foot tarnished silver crucifix on the wall facing the bed, though Toby found it a bit much for his bedtime taste.

The bathroom next door was vast – obviously it had once been a bedroom and was converted to its new purpose sometime after the idea of hot and cold running water had replaced a line of footmen and chambermaids with buckets. The bath was an enormous tub on lion's-paw feet that had once been gilded. Over it hung a copper shower-head quite the size of a large dinner-plate and it was under this that Toby stood and turned on the tap marked *Freddo*. As he had earlier discovered, the so-called cold water was never really so, from which he deduced that the tanks were up under the palace roof and kept warm by the summer sun.

But the tepid water was refreshing and he stood beneath the slow spray for a long time. He was hoping it would cool down a particular part of him that insisted on raising its head firmly towards the ceiling. He told himself that he had drunk too much wine at lunch, being reluctant to admit that perhaps Adalbert's photos of naked women had affected him. They were fakes, after all. But, said a whisper in a corner of his mind, though they may not have been a King's mistresses they were real women showing off their bare bodies.

The stiffness did not go away and eventually Toby got out of the bath and patted himself dry with large but worn towels that had the letter M embroidered in the corner. He strode into his bedroom stark naked and was brought up short by the sight of a chambermaid hanging up the clothes he'd thrown on the bed. With not even a towel about his waist, he had no secrets from her at all. She was a woman of about thirty, dark-haired and round-faced, small of stature and plumpish, dressed in black frock and white apron. She glanced at his upstanding part and smiled faintly, as if she found the sight comical.

Hardly knowing what to do for best, Toby sat down on

the foot of the bed and crossed his legs, though that hid nothing in the state he was in. The maid assumed correctly that he intended to get dressed and brought him his shirt and underpants. The wine was in his head, or maybe Adalbert's pictures were, for instead of taking the clothes she held out, he put a hand up her skirt.

'*Ah, no no!*' she exclaimed, grabbing at his wrist to stop him. Unabashed, Toby pulled her down on to his knees and thrust his hand further up between her thighs. His fingers found the short leg of her knickers and slid inside, and an instant later he could feel curly hair and warm flesh.

'*Basta, signor!*' she said, trying to catch his wrist.

'Look at the state I'm in,' said Toby, his face close to hers and all his charm at work. 'Oh, if only you could understand me – although there's not much I could say to add to what you have already seen. Surely you could feel a little pity for me in my extremity. Let me be happy – it will only take a minute.'

The maid listened to him with a quizzical look on her round face, not understanding a word, but knowing exactly what he was saying to her. She shook her head, more in sorrow than in anger it seemed to him, and squeezed her legs tight together, which only served to encourage him. With the tip of his middle finger he tickled the warm lips she was trying to protect.

'*Ebbene*,' she said with a shrug of the shoulders.

Her hand slid down his bare belly and took hold of his stiff part. That was very promising, thought Toby – though she still kept her legs close together. Her fingers slid up and down, the ball of her thumb on the sensitive head.

'*Va bene cosi*,' she said, speeding up her movement when she realised how very aroused he was already. Toby gasped loudly as he forced his hand hard up between her hot thighs and into her loose knickers to feel her properly. She stared into his face and grinned at him and, knowing it was too late for him, parted her legs suddenly. His essence came spurting out, splashing up his bare belly and he babbled and sighed while she drained him in wet throbs.

When he was finished she got up from his lap and he lay back on the bed to get his breath and rest for a minute. From chest to groin trickles ran down his skin and his stiff part was at last softening and diminishing in size. His eye lit on the big silver cross on the wall opposite and he looked away, feeling uncomfortable to be reminded of religion at a moment like this. It was only as the chambermaid was at the bedroom door to leave that he thought to ask her name.

'Maria, signor,' she said with a smile.

FIVE

On Saturday evening Mrs Tandy gave a dinner party for some of her friends and Toby was invited. This would be his first meal in the fading splendour of the Grand Dining Room and he looked forward to it immensely. He worked in the attics all morning and took a stroll alone about midday towards the Rialto Bridge, pleased to be out of the palace and among crowds for a while.

The tourist season had begun, packing the narrow streets with visitors from half of Europe – Germans with guide-books open in their hands and serious expressions, French couples looking for cheap places to eat, English people in search of culture and a nice cup of tea – and, of course, Americans, intent on enjoying themselves in spite of foreigners and their inferior ways. Toby stood on the centre of the bridge, staring down the Grand Canal to the just-visible Palladian frontage of the Palazzo Malvolio near the bend. He was standing with his arms on the balustrade, in the exact location where, if the Contessa Marina's account was to be believed, she had been ravished by night.

The question in Toby's mind was why she had made no effort to repeat their pleasures of two days ago in the furniture store. The encounter had demonstrated to him the considerable pleasure of rattling her from rearwards – and from forwards, too, and the other way – and had certainly demonstrated to her that he was a worthy performer. That being so, he had fully expected her to want to repeat the experience at regular intervals. But he had hardly seen her since then.

According to Adalbert Gmund, Marina could never have enough love-making, and the Princess Zita's daughter had said much the same on the occasion she had made a trophy of Toby. But somehow Marina did not seem to be living up to her reputation with him, and though he reminded himself that he really didn't much enjoy making love to plump women with big fat breasts and wide hips, he would nevertheless make her very welcome if she turned up in his room at night.

If he had known where her private suite was in the palace he would long since have paid her a social visit – at mid-morning, or during the afternoon siesta-time, or an hour before dinner when the chances were that she would be dressing. But to ask where she was to be found would give the game away instantly, and the palace was too large and rambling for him to go wandering about on the off-chance of finding her rooms.

From his vantage-point on the bridge Toby spotted a couple of restaurants down on the quay below, overlooking the Canal. They were busy but a table was found for him and he chose a modest sort of meal, certain that dinner that evening would be lavish. Afterwards he strolled as far as St Mark's Square, guided by a tourist map he bought at a booth near the bridge. In the Square he lazed away an hour at a cafe table with pistachio ice cream in a silver cup and coffee with froth on top. And so back to the palace for an hour's doze on his canopied bed, before it was time to bath and dress.

Naturally, he had brought his dinner jacket. The chambermaid had pressed it lightly to remove any suitcase creases and hung it in the elaborately carved wardrobe along with his dress shirt, also pristine from her hand. Speaking of which, he said to himself with a grin, she had used that hand to good effect when he was in a state. Why she refused to lie down properly on the bed for him was a bit of a mystery. All the same, she had helped him out and he must remember to tip her generously when he left.

It was while he was getting dressed that he made a discovery that was interesting in more ways than one. He was standing in only his shirt by one open door of the wardrobe holding his highly polished evening shoes awkwardly in one hand and a pair of black silk socks in the other. One of the shoes slipped from his hand and landed in the bottom of the wardrobe with a thunk that reverberated with an unexpected hollowness.

He dropped the other shoe to hear it again then stood back a pace or two and looked at the wardrobe carefully. He put it at very early eighteenth century, thirty or forty years older than the Palazzo Malvolio itself. It was made of solid dark walnut with three thick columns on the front framing two doors the size of ordinary house doors, their panels elaborately carved. The base it stood on was about a foot high and naturally was hollow, but even that much space underneath didn't entirely account for the sound he had heard. It was as if there was a sounding-box.

A thought occurred to him and he squatted bare-bottomed to feel slowly round the carving of the base. A rosette in a swag halfway along the side seemed to give a little under his touch and he pressed hard. He heard a muffled click as if a catch was released, and inside the wardrobe the front edge of the bottom rose a little – just enough to reveal two recesses into which finger-tips could be inserted to pull the whole bottom upwards.

It swivelled easily enough on its concealed hinges to reveal a secret compartment in the base of the wardrobe not more than six inches high but six feet wide and three feet or more from front to back. There was nothing in it. Toby sat back on his heels and thought for a moment.

Before safes and strong-boxes were invented, the well-to-do needed somewhere to put jewellery and other valuables. He had seen small secret drawers before, mostly in old writing-desks, but never anything as capacious as this. Finding it caused him to realise it was possible that the damaged wardrobes up in the furniture store had secret compartments, all of them. When he went up there again he would make a careful inspection – and a lucky find of a purse of gold coins or a legal document or two would be interesting, though unlikely.

But that could wait for Monday. First there was the pleasure of attending Mrs Tandy's grand dinner party, and he intended to have a whole day off on Sunday and go sightseeing. He resumed his interrupted dressing, clicking the secret panel closed.

When he saw the Dining Room he was suitably impressed. There were twenty-four for dinner altogether and the long table down the room seated them easily. Table and chairs were eighteenth century and very fine but the murals dominated the room, as they were meant to.

Tiepolo, said Toby to himself, glancing round in fascination, *the Malvolio of the day actually paid Giovanni Battista Tiepolo to come and paint his dining-room walls for him.*

Round the walls there were ten scenes with life-size figures of ancient Roman gods and goddesses. They were shown naked, or as near to it as was convenient in a dining room. Blonde Venus lay on an ivory couch and reached out for a grape from a bunch held by a winged Cupid – her body artfully twisted to make her breasts prominent. Her belly was bare right down to the tops of her thighs, where a wisp of almost transparent drapery saved her modesty.

Elsewhere on the walls was Juno wearing a silver crown with stars, dark-haired, dark-eyed, sitting on the bank of a stream. The disposition of her legs concealed what was between, though her very full breasts were well displayed. Minerva wore a brass helmet and leaned on a spear, her round shield conserving her propriety, though letting her bosom be seen. The goddess Toby found most interesting was Diana, shown hunting in a wood. She was seen almost sideways, a drawn bow in her hands, aiming an arrow at a distant stag. She wore nothing but a quiver down her back and was slender and long-thighed.

The male gods were all athletes with Mars even more muscular than the others. Like Roman statues, their athleticism did not extend to all parts of the body – the parts which would have been of most use in encounters with the charming goddesses were definitively undersized. Graceful, one might say, rather than useful. Since human anatomy has not undergone any particular change in historical times, Toby knew that Tiepolo was merely following a convention that the Romans had copied from the Greeks. By the same token, a deity not included in the murals of the Malvolio dining room was the Garden God, who was usually shown over-endowed, with a shaft a foot long and as thick as a wrist.

On the high ceiling overhead the gods and goddesses were all assembled for a banquet. In the antique Roman style they had no chairs but reclined on one elbow on divans arranged like spokes about a long table laden with food on golden plates and wine in long-necked golden pitchers. By contrast the banquet below was staid, the plates being only of fine china and the diners fully dressed – though some of the ladies were in low-cut frocks that displayed a good area of bosom.

Toby found himself placed about two-thirds of the way along the table, Mrs Tandy at the top, up to his left, and Marina at the other end. Adalbert Gmund was seated on the other side of the table, though too far away to talk to. Next to Adalbert on his right sat the Contessa Flagranti, the American woman Toby had met at Princess Zita's lunch who had told him to call her Sally after less than five minutes' acquaintance.

The Princess and her sulky *ragazzo* were not present but her daughter was. Toby had kissed Anna-Louisa's hand and took care to be thoroughly charming to her during drinks before dinner – not that he felt terribly well-disposed to her after all, but if there was to be any chance of paying her back for making use of him he had to present an appearance of amiability. She smiled coolly at his attempt at ingratiation, but when they parted she gave him a little pout which he considered promising.

He found himself seated between two ladies of style, in their different ways, but unfortunately neither understood more than a few words of English. To his right was Signora Tornante, a fine-looking woman in her late thirties. She wore a lot of jewellery round her neck, at her ears and on her hands, mostly diamonds. Her short evening frock was in orchid pink, a wrap-over design with a bow on her right hip. Toby was pleased to see her bosom was of modest proportions and her bare arms long and thin.

On his other side sat Signorina Renata Mascoli, her jet-black hair cut in a short bob and arranged in a deep wave over an eye – a fashion much in evidence that year. She was small and spare of figure, her chin pointed and her expression dissatisfied. In shiny green satin evening frock with a deep and tight sash, her lean body was shown to good advantage, or so Toby considered.

Both ladies were eager to converse at some length with the handsome young Englishman but the language difficulties made it hard work. Toby gathered that Signora Tornante's husband – a shifty-looking fellow placed up near Mrs Tandy's head of the table – was a politician and held office of some sort in Prime Minister Mussolini's newly elected Fascist government. Not that Fascism was a subject Toby knew much about, except that it was being promoted in London by Lord Curzon's son-in-law, a Member of Parliament called Oswald Mosley.

Signorina Mascoli conveyed that she was an artist, though it was too wearisome to go into what sort of artist she considered herself to be. Her *haute couture* frock and the hint of costly perfume she exuded showed very clearly that she was the child of a rich family. Perhaps she wrote poetry, thought Toby as he smiled his most charming smile at her. It might be very nice to get her into bed – with her lithe build and look of sulkiness she could well turn into a leopardess when her knickers were off and her belly kissed.

At the far end of the table, on Contessa Marina's right, sat a dark-haired Italian in his forties, as good-looking as a film star and radiating waves of self-confidence and superiority. He and the Contessa were on the best of terms, chatting like close friends, exchanging secret smiles and fleeting touches of the hand. And that, said Toby to himself, is why she hasn't dropped into my room at bed-time. Even though it was his firm opinion that Marina was too big-breasted and round-bottomed to please him, a faint jealousy stirred in him at the thought of someone else enjoying her favours instead of himself.

The food and wine were delicious – and almost overwhelming in quantity. The liveried footmen skipped silently about the table with their silver serving-dishes, bringing course after course of thick fish soup with golden croutons, risotto with chicken livers tinged with garlic, grilled fillets of John Dory, veal cutlets with thick sauce of wild mushroom and vermouth . . . on and on, with white Soave and red Bardolino wines changing with each course.

Throughout the lengthy meal Luigi, the major-domo, stood like a statue behind Mrs Tandy's chair, directing operations without a word. He wore a better black swallow-tail coat than his day-time one, and round his neck hung a chain of heavy silver links carrying an elaborate plaque engraved with the Malvolio arms.

When, after six kinds of cheese and five kinds of fresh fruit with aromatic black coffee, Mrs Tandy rose gracefully from her chair to indicate that dinner had ended, the company followed her into the Lepanto Room. The route lay through a high-ceilinged corridor hung with old paintings to a double door where footmen in Malvolio livery bowed the procession into a large room which was dominated by a mural filling one entire wall. It seemed to have been recently cleaned to rescue the rich colours from the dust and grime of years.

It was a quay-side Venetian scene, with just a glimpse of the Doge's palace in the background. A scarlet ship with half-set sails was making ready to cast off, the deck swarming with men holding pikes and swords. But all this was only the setting for a man in the foreground, most sumptuously dressed and wearing a golden fore-and-aft helmet. He was posing heroically and there was no doubt at all in Toby's mind that here was a superb example of family propaganda.

'Marco Malvolio boarding his ship to take part in the Battle of Lepanto against the Turks,' said Adalbert Gmund, who was now at his elbow. 'It was painted by Francesco Guardi, but only two hundred years after the event it depicts.'

'Excellent piece of work,' said Toby, whose interest in murals was very small, for the obvious reason they could not be bought and sold at a profit. 'Did he come back?'

'*Nein*, his ship went down and him and his crew with it during the fighting. You can read in the Malvolio Archive of how much he spent on himself and his ship, if you ask Padre Pio to show you the accounts. The Malvolio were very rich in those days.'

'Who is that man Contessa Marina is talking to?' asked Toby.

Adalbert turned to look. By the French windows to the balcony Marina was in intimate conversation with the man who sat next to her at dinner. Seen standing up, he was not tall, but his shoulders were wide and his hips narrow, and his stylish dinner jacket nipped in sharply at the waist to flatter his figure.

'*Ach ja*, the *Dottore* – his name is Ottorino Pavese.'

'He's a doctor?' asked Toby.

'Not a medical doctor. Marina is in love with him insanely.'

'Since when?'

Two days ago on her knees on the *prie-dieu* she had given not the least sign that she was in love with anyone at all and the assertion by Gmund astonished Toby.

'Since perhaps three months now. They fell in love I think at the Carnival this year. You look surprised, my young friend. Do you think she should make love with no one else but Ottorino? He has business interests in Bologna and is not always here to be with her.'

Around the Lepanto Room stood typically long Venetian sofas, upholstered in tired-looking gold damask, and a dozen matching chairs. The well-dined and wined company sat or stood as they thought best, chattering busily, while more liveried servants glided soundlessly about the room carrying more coffee, liqueurs and brandy. Adalbert bowed to the thin American woman when she approached and was about to effect introductions when Toby said he had already met the Contessa Flagranti.

She was in a shiny black satin tube of a frock that served to emphasise the leanness of her figure. It was cut in a deep V in front, and that revealed how little bosom she had. The hem was cut on the slant sideways, being a mite above her left knee and halfway down her right calf. Her long thin arms were naked and perfect, in Toby's estimation, and adorned with broad jewelled bracelets on each wrist.

As they talked about nothing much, the pitch of her voice and the slightly feverish glow of her cheeks suggested to Toby that she had not stinted herself on the wines during dinner. A glass of pale golden cognac in her hand, which she waved about while she talked, confirmed him in his view that she was in a genial frame of mind – one might almost say *elevated*.

The French windows stood open but the air was still and warm – and when Marina and her lover, Pavese, slipped out, it was for a breath of cool air, surely. Or so Toby tried to tell himself. But there was a very different theory in his mind that he could not ignore and a stirring of an unpleasant emotion he refused to accept as jealousy.

He suggested to Sally Flagranti that the room was warm and a moment on the balcony would be pleasant. She was too occupied with talking and smiling to listen to what he said, but he took her thin arm and she accompanied him without demur. Perhaps she was unaware that they were changing position, so involved was she in a confused account of her last shopping trip to Paris.

The balcony outside the Lepanto Room looked over the Grand Canal below, and was so long that Marina and Pavese at the far end were only shadows.

'I can just see the lights of the Rialto Bridge,' said Toby.

The Contessa Flagranti stared into the dim distance, but she continued talking. Her English had by stages acquired a faint Transatlantic twang, and presumably her Italian was similarly affected at this stage of the evening.

'Where do you live, Sally?' Toby asked, to stem the seeming endless flow of words.

'What? she said, her brain registering after a second or two that she had been asked a question. Toby repeated it.

'Over there,' she said vaguely, waving the hand holding the nearly empty glass. What was left in it flew out over the stone balustrade and fell to the quay below where the visitors' boats were tied up alongside the Malvolio boats. Toby guessed that the boatmen were all inside, in the Italian equivalent of the servant's hall, getting mildly drunk, playing cards or chasing the maidservants. He gently removed the glass from Sally's hand and set it on the stone coping.

'Over there? On the other side of the Grand Canal?'

'Right on the waterfront, just round the corner. You can't see it from here.'

'Can I come and visit you there?'

'Sure,' she said, her tone extremely vague, as if the thought of callers was unfamiliar to her, 'what was your name again – Toby something?'

'Jervis,' he said. He held her wrist to steady her arm while taking the glass from her and he was still holding it, though Sally seemed not to notice. It was so fine-boned that his thumb and middle finger met round it. The feel of her skin was making him aroused – his *cazzo* was standing upright in his trousers – or was that because at the far end of the balcony he could see a dark shadow moving against another dark shadow. No more than a trick of the star-light reflected up from the Grand Canal, perhaps, but Toby was convinced that Marina had her back to the wall between French windows and Pavese was ravishing her.

He dropped the hand that was not holding Sally's wrist until it was between them and he gently stroked up along her thigh, delighting in the feel of the smooth satin of her frock under his fingertips.

'That's right,' she said, 'Toby Jervis. You're English. I met you at Zita's. Do you live in Venice?'

Wondering just how drunk she was, Toby reached down to get a hand under her frock and slid it up to feel her bottom through her silk knickers. The cheeks were small and taut – the perfect shape, by his standard. Then why not give her a little thrill, he asked himself, though it was not really of her pleasure that he was thinking.

'Not on a Saturday or a Sunday,' she said, her mind grappling still with the business of visiting. Toby's fingers were in the cleft between the cheeks of her bottom and he paid no attention to her words. His hand slid round her bony hip to her belly and down to the join of her thin thighs, feeling warm soft flesh through thin silk.

'Who's that along there on the balcony?' she asked, looking over his shoulder to where Marina and her lover were locked in a passionate but silent embrace. By now Toby's upstanding part was throbbing so vigorously that something had to be done about it. He got his fingers under the lace round the leg of Sally's knickers and touched soft wispy hair and warm flat lips. With his other hand he opened his jacket and trousers and pulled out his hard-straining part.

Contessa Flagranti, née Sally Mawby, was not very bright, as Toby had registered when he met her first at Princess Zita's lunch. He had found that there was usually a short delay before she answered a question, while she ruminated on the meaning of the speaker's words. It was now apparent to him that the wine she had freely indulged in at dinner had increased the time-lag – indeed, so lengthy was the delay in her thought processes now, that matters had reached the stage of a man's hand in her knickers before she grasped the situation. Her response, at last, was also muted.

'Hey, what's going on?' she said, sounding puzzled. 'Are you trying to get fresh with me, Tommy?'

'It's Toby,' he answered as he wrapped her thin-fingered hand round his stiffness.

'Call it what you like,' she said, 'where I come from that's a pecker. What in the hell are you doing? Oh!'

Her absurd question was answered by Toby pushing the tip of his longest finger inside her to touch her sensitive button. No further explanation was required and she grasped his hardness while considering her reaction to this unexpected approach by a comparative stranger. Her hand was cool, while Toby's *cazzo* was hot with excitement. The contrast produced in him sensations so delightful that his knees trembled and he felt he was right on the verge of discharging his rapture.

'You're about to be Tobied,' he murmured urgently, thrusting his hips forward and brushing her hand away from his throbbing part. A stab of purest delight through his belly made him gasp and he felt the first spurt racing up his hard length.

He stabbed it up into the loose leg of Sally's underwear, to probe the flat lips of her *fica*, but it was already too late to penetrate her. He clutched her round her narrow waist as his legs shook and his hot essence squirted into her knickers.

'Goddam it!' she exclaimed, trying to push him away from her as she felt the wet surge on her skin, but he held her tightly through his jolting gushes until he was done. Then he released her and pushed the silk handkerchief from his breast pocket into her hand.

'Goddam you!' she said furiously and threw the handkerchief in his face, turned on her high heels and stalked away into the palace. Toby leaned against the stone balcony balustrade while he did up his trousers, the faint after-throb of delight still in his belly. He stared at the passing boats below in the Grand Canal until his wet part slackened and went small, before going back into the Lepanto Room to find the footman serving cognac.

Marina and her friend had left the balcony before he did and inside she was nowhere to be seen, though Ottorino Pavese stood in an admiring group of ladies, looking more like a film star than ever. Presumably Marina, like Sally, had gone to rearrange her underwear after the ravishing. Though Toby thought it most likely that Sally's knickers were too soaked to keep on and she would have to pass the rest of the evening and go home without them.

He had taken no more than the first sip of his cognac when a spiteful laugh at his elbow caused him to turn, and there stood Anna-Louisa Ziani and Adalbert Gmund, both staring at him with the oddest expression. The Austrian's broad face was flushed an unhealthy-looking colour and it was obvious that he had drunk too much again.

'We were having a wager, Anna-Louisa and I,' he said to Toby, 'on how long you would be out on the balcony with Contessa Sally – longer than Marina and her friend, or not.'

'Really?' said Toby in an as disinterested a way as he could manage. 'Why?'

'Because Anna-Louisa thinks Ottorino does it faster than you, though I do not understand how she could form this idea,' said Adalbert, with a leer to indicate that he knew very well why Signora Ziani was qualified to pronounce on the comparative speed of sexual performance of the two of them.

'How amusing,' said Toby coldly, 'a small bet, was it?'

'Yes, quite small,' said Anna-Louisa, 'ten thousand lira.'

Toby did the sum in his head – at 134 lira to the pound that was about £75. To Anna-Louisa that might be a small bet, but it represented almost a month's salary to him. Nor from what he'd seen did he think Adalbert could afford to lose that much on a bet.

'I take it that Signora Ziani won,' said Toby, giving her a mocking little bow.

'*Nein, nein* – she bet on you and I bet on Ottorino,' Adalbert replied with a grin.

'I don't follow the reasoning,' Toby said, 'a moment ago you said Signora Ziani favoured Pavese – so why bet against him?'

He addressed the question to her directly, but she deigned to make no reply. With another leering grin Adalbert explained that Anna-Louisa had been sure that Marina was never contented with once and would detain Ottorino on the balcony for a second and perhaps even a third go. To her surprise and chagrin that did not happen and they were first back. Whereupon Adalbert excused himself and strode unsteadily across the salon to where a footman was dispensing cognac.

'I'm sorry to have cost you money,' Toby said to Anna-Louisa, grinning at her in amusement.

'It is of no consequence.'

'But the thought makes me uncomfortable. I shall call on you to apologise in more fitting circumstances?'

'But why should you call on me?' said Anna-Louisa distantly. 'I have had you once already.'

Before he could think of a suitable answer he saw Mrs Tandy beckoning to him from where she sat on one of the long damask sofas with the dark-haired Signorina Mascoli beside her. Before he could make his excuses to leave Anna-Louisa, she had herself swept away from him.

Mrs Delphine Tandy was a woman of stately appearance, oval of face and strikingly good-looking. Her chestnut-brown hair was not bobbed or cropped in that year's fashion but long and piled up on top of her head. Her eyes were green-grey and her skin a fine ivory. She was in a midnight-blue velvet, deeply *décolleté* to show nicely shaped shoulders and an expanse of bosom. About her long neck was a diamond choker, her only jewellery except for a ring or two.

Very Edwardian and very regal, thought Toby, sitting down on the sofa in the space she made for him between herself and the pretty Signorina Mascoli. But, like her sister Marina, there was too much of her for his taste, too much bountiful flesh giving an impression of weightiness and ponderousness of movement.

'You've met Renata,' she said, favouring him with so gracious a smile that made him wonder if he was really a guest or merely a tradesman being flattered, 'she was fascinated to hear of your interest in my old furniture.'

She broke into mellifluous Italian for the girl's benefit and Toby smiled at them both in turn, especially at Renata Mascoli, whose lean body was much to his liking. He imagined slim strong thighs under her green frock, thighs to clamp round your waist when you lay on top of her. Her bobbed hair was so shiny black that he knew she sported the same hue between the legs. Though she was not as slender as Sally, she had the advantage of being twenty years younger and he wanted her.

To this end he set himself out to be particularly charming to her, though ignorance of each other's language was a limitation of some severity. Mrs Tandy was helpful with words and phrases and seemed delighted to see them getting on well together. Not match-making surely, thought Toby with a secret smile, that was not what he had in mind at all. He enquired about the artistic interests Renata had mentioned at dinner and was told that she knew a great deal about textile design and would like to pursue it as a career, except that young ladies in Venice did not have careers, they got married to suitable young gentlemen.

By eleven thirty the guests were beginning to say their *good nights* to Mrs Tandy and drift away. That gave Toby a chance to take Renata aside and ask where she lived and if he might see her again. She pouted and said it was *molto difficile* and then smiled and indicated that she would try to arrange something.

By midnight the last guest was out of the Lepanto Room, the motorboats below were unmoored and skimming away along the Grand Canal. Toby found his way to his room with the assistance of a footman to guide him and went to bed feeling pleasantly tired. The room was very dark – the chambermaid had closed the shutters against the night air, as they always did, and Toby hadn't bothered to open them. It was too much trouble to get out of bed again and he lay in the dark thinking about the evening.

The event with the thin American woman out on the balcony had been unexpected. In retrospect it was highly comical, shooting his hot sap into her knickers while she was woozily asking what he was doing. It wasn't the real thing but it was better than nothing. The real thing – the thing he most wanted after dinner – would have been to ravish Marina on the balcony. But she had opened her legs for her regular boyfriend, and Contessa Sally had borne the brunt of Toby being thwarted.

Just as well Padre Pio hadn't chosen that moment to go out on the balcony – the sight of couples at each end busily engaged in what his Church regarded as a sin would surely have spoiled his evening for him. Except, now Toby thought about it, the fat little priest hadn't been there all evening – neither at dinner nor afterwards. Evidently he wasn't asked on social occasions. It was not easy to pinpoint Padre Pio's status in the Malvolio household . . . but there weren't any Malvolios any more, and with that vague thought Toby drifted into sleep.

What woke him from a dream in which he was trying to persuade Renata to let him put his hand up her jade-green frock but did not know the right words in Italian – what woke him up half an hour after nodding off was the extremely pleasant sensation of a hand holding his stiff part and sliding up and down. He gave a sigh and reached out to feel big soft naked breasts. She came a little closer, her lips touching his cheek, the fragrance of expensive French perfume highly arousing.

So Marina had come to his bedroom after all! Once out on the balcony with her boyfriend hadn't been enough, and he obviously hadn't stayed the night. Probably had a wife and family to go home to somewhere. So Toby was used as a make-shift, a second-best. The idea annoyed him and he gripped her breasts hard and was about to push her out of bed and tell her to go . . . except the touch of her hand on his taut *cazzo* was far too delightful to refuse.

He felt down her warm belly to put his hand between her plump thighs and ravage her split with his fingers. It was moist and loose, ready for him – and why not? He could hardly expect her to turn her back on the regular boyfriend at a moment's notice. She was murmuring *ah ah ah* as his fingers sent thrills through her and her hand on his hardness was responsible for so intense a throbbing that he could delay no longer.

He rolled her on her back, his hands on her hips and his lips pressed to hers in a long hot kiss. He felt her fleshy thighs moving apart as he slid onto her broad belly, feeling as if he was lying on a feather-bed. She had untied his pyjama bottoms while he was asleep and they were halfway down his legs. Her hand was between their bodies to guide him neatly inside – he pushed in deep and began a quick stabbing movement, feeling himself grow harder and thicker all the time.

Underneath him Marina was bouncing furiously on her back, gasping incoherently. It seemed only seconds since he slid deep into her slippery wetness – but already she was starting a wail of climactic release, jerking her belly up at him. He cried out and spurted his frantic desire into her, savaging her body with his piercing part, pouring out his soul in long gushes.

When it was over he rolled off her and they lay side by side in the dark.

'Oh my dear man, that was marvellous,' she said, speaking for the first time.

'Good God!' Toby exclaimed, sitting upright with a sudden start. 'You're not Marina!'

He fumbled for the light switch of the bedside lamp. Beside him, her monumental naked body shining in the yellow lamplight lay Mrs Delphine Tandy, looking very pleased with herself.

'Of course I'm not.' she said with a smile, 'Marina is in bed with Ottorino. How very ungallant of you to make it so obvious that you'd rather have her than me.'

'No, not a bit of it,' he said, lying down close to her, 'but you took me by surprise.'

'And you took me by storm,' she replied, reaching out to take his now limp *cazzo* in her hand. 'It was absolutely delightful and I'm glad I popped in to see you.'

'I think it was I who popped in,' said Toby, 'and I'm glad.'

He turned off the light and her abundant body was only a pale gleam in the dark. Feeling her breasts and belly was very nice, he found. As long as he didn't have to look at her, the weight of so much warm flesh was surprisingly pleasant. This seemed to him somewhat confusing, in view of his firmly held opinion that only lean women with hardly any bottom and even less bosom were the ideal of female beauty. But with his fingers at the little patch of curls she was offering him, it was pointless to worry about either modern fashion or theories of aesthetics.

'Ah, Toby, Toby!' she sighed.

SIX

On Sunday morning Toby woke late and alone, with only the trace of Delphine's perfume on his pillow to show that she had been with him. He stretched and yawned and looked at his wristwatch on the bedside table – and was very surprised to see that it was after ten o'clock. On previous days the maid had woken him with *caffe-latte* and soft rolls at eight thirty.

He was about to get up and make for the bathroom when a light step outside and a tap at his door informed him that he had not been forgotten. There was no need to call out *come in*, whatever that was in Italian. It wasn't included in the list of useful phrases he'd found on the back of his street map and guide to Venice, along with addresses of ristorantes, trattorias, bars, pizzarias, hotels, pensions and the water-bus routes.

On the other hand, whoever compiled the list of phrases had a curious idea of the habits, wishes, needs or necessities of the average tourist. *C'e qualcuno qui che parla inglese? – Is there anyone here who can speak English?* – that wouldn't get you far if the answer was a plain *No*. As for *Non capisco – I don't understand* – that was equally useless because any Italian who was not simple-minded would have guessed it already. And as for *Lo scriva, per favore – please write it down* – what earthly use was there in having anything in writing which you couldn't understand spoken?

This was to be a morning of surprises. In came not Maria but a footman balancing a tray with a small silver coffee-pot and a plate of sweet rolls. Toby had seen him about the palace before – he served in the Small Dining Room – but didn't know his name. Like most of the Malvolio menservants he was at least fifty, from which Toby deduced that employment was hard to find in Venice and when you had a job you stuck with it, whether you liked it or not. Heaven knows what pittance the palace servants got, but at least they had regular meals and a roof over their head.

The footman set down the tray on the bedside table and went to the windows to throw open the shutters. In streamed glorious sunlight, making even the tarnished silver crucifix on the wall gleam and revealing the worn patches on the purple and primrose livery the man wore. Mrs Tandy really ought to have new outfits made for her staff when she was paid for the damaged furniture, Toby reflected, and perhaps she might, but most likely she had other priorities.

He sat up in bed as the footman poured *caffe-latte* for him.

'Thank you,' he said, taking the cup. The coffee had cooled considerably on its long journey from the kitchens, but if you lived in a ramshackle eighteenth century palace you couldn't really expect hot food or hot drinks. 'But why so late? And where is Maria?'

He didn't expect to be understood or to receive a reply that made sense. But this footman had acquired a reasonable working knowledge of English.

'I am Emilio, sir,' he said, 'today it is *domenica* – Sunday, you say.'

'And everyone stays in bed till ten on Sunday?'

'No, sir,' said Emilio, shaking his head and smiling at the same time, 'on Sunday everyone gets up early.'

'Except me, it seems. Why is that?'

Emilio's grasp of English was far from perfect, but it served well enough to explain the regular Sunday arrangements in the Palazzo Malvolio. At eight thirty the family went fasting to Confession with Padre Pio, and at nine they heard him say Mass in the private chapel. Then at nine thirty they took *colazione* – breakfast – together in the Small Dining Room. A big breakfast, said Emilio, after the *tensione* of the confessing and *la Santa Communione*, not the rolls with conserve only but ham and eggs cooked in the English way and bread-toast.

There was an uncomfortable feeling down in the pit of Toby's stomach. Surely Delphine wouldn't get straight out of bed after what they'd done together and tell about it to the plump little priest in the shabby cassock and gold-rimmed glasses? She was English-born and English people didn't do that, only Italians and other foreigners with incomprehensible customs.

'The *family* goes to confession and Mass, you said,' he began with caution. 'Do you mean the Contessa?'

It was a fair bet that Marina had been required to become

a Catholic when she married Massimo Torrenegra. Even so, it was a bit much if she had to tell the owlish Padre Pio she'd been out on the balcony last evening with her boyfriend and he'd had her knickers down.

'Si, Signor,' said Emilio, 'la Contessa Marina.'

'And Mr Gmund?'

It seemed a racing certainty Austrian Adalbert was Catholic, though he might well have given up practising it.

'*Certamente* Signor Gmund goes to the confession and the Mass. And also Signora Tandy, of course.'

'Thank you, Emilio, you may run my bath,' said Toby, somewhat staggered by the implications. How embarrassing – he'd never be able to look Padre Pio in the face again! He certainly wasn't going to face him across the lunch table that day – it was too soon after the event for there not to be a look of reproach in the priest's eyes, assuming Delphine had told all. For Marina too, maybe, but she sinned so constantly that the Padre must by now have given up on her. No, the newcomer would be the object of ecclesiastical disapproval.

By eleven Toby was bathed and dressed and out of the Palazzo, leaving word that he had gone sight-seeing and would not return before evening. With only one wrong turn along the way he found the corridor where marble busts of ancient Greek philosophers seemed to sneer at the passer-by. This took him to the top of the broad stone staircase that led downwards to the entrance hall on the landward side of the palace. Two life-size marble statues stood at the top of the stairs – bearded men wearing breast-plates and swords. Toby assumed they were Malvolios of centuries ago. In keeping with the military theme, the walls on either side of the stairs were decorated with steel swords, long dangerous-looking pikes, muzzle-loading muskets and flint-lock pistols.

In the stone-flagged hall sat a door-keeper in faded livery, half-dozing. He rose to his feet while Toby was descending the long flight of stairs, to open one leaf of the massive wooden door and bow him through. Outside in the bright sunshine, Toby stood for a moment on the broad and shallow stone steps, behind him the massive Corinthian columns of the palace facade. Before him lay the pleasant little square of which the Palazzo formed one whole side. It wasn't really square at all, more oblong but with one side longer than the opposite side, and in the middle there was an old stone well, once the only source of water.

In the far corner there was an open-fronted restaurant with

a dozen tables outside and a single waiter in evidence, it being too early for even the earliest of lunchers. Toby walked across the square and out by a narrow passage-way that turned into a hump-backed bridge over a small back-canal where an abandoned and derelict barge was moored, half-filled with greenish water. Another narrow street between tall buildings brought him into a square with a newspaper kiosk and, at the far end, a handsome classical building which proved, when he reached it, to be the Fenice opera house.

According to his street-guide a right turn at the next church and then a left along a street of expensive shops and past yet another church and he'd reach the Piazza San Marco, which was a good place to aim for. When he emerged into the huge arcaded square with the Byzantine domes and arches of St Mark's church across the far end, he found it full of Sunday strollers, local and foreign. The two cafes that faced each other from opposite sides of the Piazza were doing excellent business, the waiters ferrying trays of ice-cream, coffee and drinks to the rows of outside tables, and the band of each cafe in full flight, each striving to outdo the other.

Toby found a vacant table outside Quadri's cafe and ordered coffee and cognac. On a Sunday morning in London it would never have occurred to him, but here under a bright blue sky amongst strolling crowds it seemed to him a suitably daring thing to do – civilised, sybaritic, raffish almost, just a touch decadent – in short, very Continental. There were thousands of pigeons in the Piazza, waiting for passing tourists to feed them, waddling about between the cafe tables and people's feet without a trace of fear.

After half an hour of watching passing girls and wives, Toby was trying to make up his mind which direction to take next and with the aid of his map had more or less decided to walk along the broad quay from the Doge's palace past the Bridge of Sighs towards the Danieli Hotel, when he saw Adalbert Gmund come into the Piazza and walk towards the cafe. When he came nearer Toby stood up and waved. Adalbert was dressed in a Tyrolean hat with a long feather in the side and an impressively out-dated suit of grey flannel with a belted jacket.

'*Buon giorno*, Toby,' he said, taking a seat at the table, but only after shaking hands. 'I have come to meet a friend, and it is fortunate you are here. He is the person you wished to meet, the one from whom I obtained the King's photograph album.'

Toby had no particular wish to meet the man, whatever he had said at the time. The album was a fake, though Adalbert didn't know it. But the dealer must have known it and perhaps it would be interesting to meet a purveyor of manufactured *memorabilia*. It was a trade that had flourished since the Middle Ages and would continue to flourish for as long as human gullibility persisted – which probably meant until the crack of doom.

Once it had been religious relics – every Catholic church in the world was stuffed with bits of Saints' leg-bone, toenails, mummified fingers, skulls, all produced and sold at high prices to the Faithful by the fakers of the past. In St Mark's across from where Toby sat was a dried-up body which Venetians knew to be St Mark the Apostle. It was only because Cromwell's troopers had cleaned them out that English churches no longer showed bits of hair, skin and other portions of allegedly holy anatomies.

When religion began to recede the conmen turned their hand to producing Classical relics – ancient Greek vases, Roman silverware, Egyptian scarabs and mummy-cases. An uncomfortably large proportion of what was on show in museums across Europe had been made in tiny backstreet workshops in Italy or Alexandria – and authenticated by great experts in London and Paris.

Paintings too, naturally, as there simply were not enough Old Masters to go round. Anyone who'd made his pile from boots and blankets for soldiers in the War, or canned plum and apple jam for the trenches, wanted a Constable or a Gainsborough for his sitting room to enhance his slightly shady background, or a Matisse or a Renoir if he had pretensions to sophistication. It was a law of Nature that demand created supply – as long as the cash was available. Hence the acres of oil paintings with famous names at the bottom that were the handiwork of highly talented but anonymous daubers.

Fine furniture, of course – Toby's own interest – the market for English and French eighteenth century furniture had proved to be utterly insatiable, price no object. Brilliant fakers were hard at work everywhere, knocking out gilt armchairs by J-B-C Sene, cabinets by Gilles Joubert, rosewood dressing-tables by Thomas Chippendale, carved tables by

William Kent, anything you liked by Robert Adam. A firm like Fitzroy Dalrymple which guaranteed the authenticity of every piece it sold, or your money back with an apology, needed to keep its eyes very wide open.

The contents of Mrs Tandy's attics, damaged though they were, were a treasure-trove. With a little remedial carpentry, waxing and polishing, regilding and tactful touching up, the profit to Fitzroy Dalrymple would be breathtaking. A coup on this scale would be the foundation of Toby's career – or so he intended.

'Let me order a drink for you, Adalbert,' said Toby, nodding to the busy waiter.

'Thank you. Only coffee, please, black,' said the other, and Toby's face must have registered surprise, for Adalbert went on, 'I have been confessed and absolved early this morning and I feel myself to be in a state of benediction.'

'Yes,' said Toby, keeping his tone as neutral as possible 'I have something I'd like to ask about that, if questions are not offensive.'

'About confession or about absolution?'

'To be frank with you, Adalbert, I have been privileged to be granted the favours of certain ladies since I came here, and I am slightly disturbed by my own position in regard to a priest who has been informed of this.'

'Pooh!' said Adalbert, unimpressed by the roundabout way of putting it. '*Ladies*, is it? You have had Delphine as well as Marina. And why not? Why should you be disturbed? Neither of them will mention your name when they confess their sins, only that they have been with a man.'

'That's all right then,' said Toby, sighing with relief.

'Of course, Padre Pio knows it must be you,' Adalbert said with a malicious grin, 'especially when Marina confessed she'd done it with two men. But what of it?'

'It's damned embarrassing, having your personal and private affairs recited to a parson. He'll take a pretty low view of me after hearing that.'

'What else has he heard about you, I wonder?' said Adalbert with his superior grin. 'All the servants go to confession too, you know. Have you interfered with any of the maids yet?'

'Good God!' Toby exclaimed in dismay. 'My name will be mud.'

'Not a bit of it,' Adalbert assured him, 'Padre Pio has

heard everything in a life time of service to the Malvolio. He knows we're not saints, and he expects us to sin all day, everyday – otherwise he wouldn't have a job, isn't that so?'

It seemed to Toby that there was a serious flaw in Adalbert's reasoning, but he couldn't quite put his finger on it. Not that it mattered, one way or the other – he was only a visitor and would be gone in another week or two.

Before there was time to take the religious question further the friend Adalbert was in the Piazza to meet arrived, not very late. Signor Corradini was a thin man in his fifties, with what might be described as a scholarly stoop. He was wearing a white linen jacket and black trousers, a made-up collar and a purple cravat. Altogether, thought Toby, a rum-looking chap. Rummest of all was his hair – it was thin and receding, and it had been dyed a glossy black.

He shook hands courteously and sat down, Adalbert signalling to the waiter. When informed that this was Toby's first visit to Venice, he asked what were his impressions of the city, and obviously expected an enthusiastic answer.

'To be candid,' said Toby, 'what I have seen of it so far is discouraging. I can't see a city at all – only a big open-air museum falling down round your ears. You have grossly neglected your heritage, Signor Corradini, and when it finally collapses into the sea, nothing much will be lost.'

The Venetian's mouth opened and closed soundlessly, much like a goldfish in a glass bowl. Adalbert, too, stared at Toby as if he had taken leave of his senses.

'But visitors come from every part of the world to see Venice – they come by the million, year after year,' he exclaimed in defence of his adopted city, while Corradini still gaped.

'So they do,' Tony agreed, 'look at them, walking about here in the Piazza. They buy a trashy coloured glass gondola for the mantelpiece and a silly straw hat – and that's what Venice has become – a cheapjack bazaar.'

'Nonsense – they come to see the wonderful paintings and the architecture,' Adalbert insisted.

'The buildings are crumbling away,' said Toby, 'and you can't really see the paintings because they're in dark corners of old churches, black with candle-smoke and rotten from damp.'

'We are poor people,' said Corradini, recovering his power of speech at last. 'Once Venice was very rich, but in the past two hundred years the story has been of decline.'

'Who's to blame for that?' demanded Toby. 'The money didn't simply evaporate – it moved on.'

'You have some interesting ideas, signor,' the Venetian said, eyeing Toby with a new respect.

To change the subject to less controversial matters Adalbert said he'd shown the photograph album to Toby, who had made some extremely interesting comments on it. Toby racked his brains to think of anything at all he'd said about the fake album to its proud owner, and could remember nothing.

'*Benissimo!*' said Corradini. 'King Eduardo's pictures are very . . . *stimolante*. Are you a collector Signor *Gierovesi*?'

Toby smiled to hear another version of his surname and said he didn't collect anything, but he found such unexpected little revelations of human nature in its private pursuits interesting and worthy of close attention. And if Signor Corradini happened to possess any other items of this nature, he would be pleased to examine them.

'You must show him your superb portfolio of Rops engravings, Niccolo,' said Adalbert, 'perhaps he will buy it, if the price is reasonable.'

'Rops?' said Toby, trying to place the name.

'Felicien Rops, the Belgian artist who worked in Paris,' said Adalbert, 'a connoisseur of the female body – and its pleasures and perversions.'

He made it sound as if Rops were as well-known as Daumier but the name still meant nothing to Toby.

'If you have a moment, Signor, come with me to my *bottega*. It is only five minutes away,' said Corradini, his eyes alert with the prospect of making a sale, 'and at the same time you shall see the prints I promised, Signor Gmund.'

'Good,' Adalbert agreed, 'come along, Toby.'

They left the Piazza at the end opposite to San Marco and by the route Toby had come, into the wider street with shops, then to an alley. The window of Corradini's shop displayed a row of oldish books bound in musty leather and a few lithographs in faded colours, showing military uniforms of long ago. Toby was amused and baffled to see that though the street was not at all long, the number of Corradini's premises was 2187. Apparently the Venetians had a sense of humour about numbering.

'During the summer season I am open for business on Sunday,' Corradini announced, unlocking the door.

He ushered them through the shop, which was no more than a counter and a few shelves on which stood more old books, dusty wooden boxes and a few framed prints, into a small room at the back. It was extraordinarily untidy, littered with yellowed and dog-eared printed papers, broken-backed books, cardboard boxes filled with fading prints and similar antiquarian debris.

Toby accepted the chair offered, certain that Corradini could never make a living out of the rubbish on show. All this was a front to hide his real business. The nature of that soon became apparent, when from a locked cupboard he produced a large and not-very-new-looking portfolio of the sort artists use to carry sketches and watercolours about in.

'These etchings are by the great Felicien Rops,' Corradini announced. 'I met him once in Paris when I was a very young man – that would be in 1895 or 1896. He was a very humorous artist, in the tradition of Marcantonio Raimondi.'

When he saw the names meant nothing to Toby he shrugged till his shoulders were up to his ears and handed him the portfolio. Toby undid the bow with which it was tied and opened it across his knees. Inside were a dozen or so black and white pictures printed on thick paper. The top one made him smile – it showed a man in a tail-coat, his trousers open and his stiff *cazzo* in his hand. He stood with bent knees beside a bed, on which lay a woman with her clothes up round her waist. Her heels were up on the man's shoulders and he was at the point of penetration, but into the lower of the two apertures offered to him. Down on the floor stood his top hat, and in it a rolled document tied with a ribbon. Presumably he was a lawyer dealing with a client.

Toby went through the portfolio slowly, smiling at a picture of a plump naked woman mounted on a large wooden rocking-horse. Her thighs were straining wide apart and her long hair flew out behind her head with the speed and violence of her rocking – in another moment she would take the jump . . . Another showed a girl with a fringe sitting naked on the side of her bed, one foot up on a nearby chair, pleasuring herself with a candle in a long brass candlestick. There was a particularly amusing picture of two women sitting tightly together on a padded chair. One wore only stockings and chemise, and that was pulled up to show her plump thighs and belly. The other woman, a friend making a call perhaps, was fully dressed and wore a hat, her curving fingers feeling between her friend's thighs in an affectionate manner.

'Eleven masterpieces by Felicien Rops,' Adalbert said with a smile on his face, 'you can see his initials on every one – in the corner there – the letters FR run together. I would like to buy this portfolio, but my friend Niccolo demands too much.'

'If the gentleman is interested . . .?' said Corradini, head on one side and eyes alert as he looked at Toby.

'Thank you, but Signor Gmund has first claim,' Toby countered politely, 'and after winning money yesterday he may be able to afford the portfolio now.'

'*Davvero?*' said Corradini, raising his bushy eyebrows in the direction of the Austrian.

'Not enough to pay your price, Niccolo,' he said regretfully, 'but I can now talk seriously to you about the lithographs by Peter Fendi.'

Toby guessed that the conversation was being conducted not in Italian but in English for his benefit. He asked who Fendi was.

'A great Viennese artist of the early nineteenth century,' Adalbert explained, 'he was appointed Court painter to the Emperor Franz Josef the First. He painted many portraits of the Emperor and the Imperial Family. But in secret he also painted watercolours of the favourite Viennese pastime. Nothing was known of these until 1910 when they fell into the hands of a publisher brave enough to bring out a selection of them in a limited edition of six hundred copies.'

'Almost unobtainable now,' said Niccolo Corradini, 'and very, very expensive. But I have been able to obtain six pages of a copy that has been damaged and fallen to pieces.'

From his locked cupboard he produced a large red folder and opened it to show the loose pages within. Toby knew by now what to expect and was not disappointed – they were of gentlemen and ladies disporting together in athletic postures, on chairs, on beds, in wooden bath-tubs. The gentlemen were extraordinarily well endowed, the ladies were neatly trimmed between the legs and had backsides like beer barrels.

Toby was not greatly impressed – the figure-drawing seemed hardly good enough to be the work of a Court painter, and the poses were lifeless. Although unnaturally thick and long shafts were being introduced into well-sized slits, the owners didn't look as if they were very interested.

But Adalbert was of a different opinion – he took the folder and carefully studied the lithographs while Corradini and Toby watched him.

'Will you take them with you?' the dealer asked, sure that he'd made a sale.

'No, I am taking Signor Jervis to meet another friend. Please have them delivered to the Palazzo Malvolio.'

When the business was concluded hands were shaken all round and Adalbert led Toby in an unexpected direction – down a dark and very narrow alley that led to the Grand Canal and a waterbus stop.

'Where are we going?' Toby asked. 'What's this about meeting another friend, Adalbert?'

'Be patient and you will see.'

The *vaporetto*, when it came chugging up to the landing-stage had less than a dozen people on board. The two men found a seat up forward and watched the grandiose buildings along the banks slide past, Adalbert putting names to them. Toby considered the feat meaningless, except for postmen, and stared in silence. As the boat rounded the long curve the white facade of the Palazzo Malvolio came into view and the long straight reach up towards the Rialto Bridge.

'From here it is a pleasant walk to where we are going,' said Adalbert, preparing to disembark as the propeller went astern and the boat nudged into the wooden landing-stage short of the bridge. Side by side they strolled to the square where stood the statue Contessa Marina had pointed out – the very prolific playwright whose name he had already forgotten. They left the square by a street with shops on both sides, but not the sort of shops that interested tourists. Here was where the locals bought cheap clothes and shoes.

'The quarter is a poor one,' said Adalbert, which made Toby wonder how the Austrian living in a palace on the Grand Canal came to have a poor friend. The little streets turned left and right till he felt quite lost.

'The prettiest church in Venice,' said Adalbert, pointing to the white, grey and yellow marbled little building ahead across a narrow back canal, 'Santa Maria dei Miracoli. It has an image of the Blessed Virgin which performs miracles of healing.'

'Very useful,' Toby commented.

'But unhappily, it does nothing for the difficulties of age,' the Austrian continued. 'All my life I have needed women every day, but I found myself slowing down some years ago. For a time I found it stimulated me to go with very young girls but that wore off in time. Then by good chance I discovered that a good whipping restored my powers but that ceased to have the proper effect eventually. But last winter I became acquainted through a Venetian friend with Signorina Benedetti, who has other means of stirring the blood.'

Away from the Church of the Miracles they were in a maze of narrow little backstreets between old and decrepit tenements. Ancient ochre plaster had peeled off in great patches to expose crumbling brick-work. Overhead, washing-lines stretched across the street, bearing worn and faded shirts, thin towels, slips, underwear and garments not easy to put a name to. Warped wooden doors from which any paint had long ago peeled off stood open to give views of dark stone flags and worn-down staircases. All up three storeys of dilapidation the windows stood open to let the inhabitants lean elbows on the sills and gaze out vacantly at nothing much.

It was not the sort of area Toby wanted to be in, or even to pass through. The dwellings of the poor could be seen in every city in Europe by those who took an interest in that sort of thing. For himself, he would rather have been on the terrace of the Gritti Palace Hotel with a cool drink. But he had come this far and might as well go the rest of the way, although by now he was pretty sure why Adalbert wanted to visit Miss Whatever.

'Look here,' he said, 'it's nearly time for lunch. Are there any good restaurants around here? You can put the visit off to this afternoon.'

'*Nein, nein,*' Adalbert retorted, 'the appetite for food will be greater afterwards.'

'But damn it all – it's only a couple of hours since you were confessing your sins and all the rest of it. Oughtn't you to give it a bit longer before starting to collect black marks?'

'On Sunday mornings after Mass I feel so clean that I have to visit a friend. It is not natural to remain in a state of grace for more than ten or twenty minutes. The slate has been wiped clean, as you say, and I have to write something on it before I can feel comfortable again.'

Toby abandoned the argument. They rounded a corner into yet another little street of depressing slums and Adalbert turned into a door. Toby followed him up a dark staircase to the top floor, where two doors faced each other across a tiny landing. Before Adalbert had time to knock, the right-hand door opened – obviously the occupant had been leaning out of the window and seen them below.

The woman who opened the door and invited them into her small sitting-room was less than thirty, Toby guessed, and not plain exactly but her appearance had an uncared-for look that aged her. Her hair was a frizzy brown mop, her eyebrows untidy, her face devoid of any trace of make-up. She wore a loose blouse of white and a black skirt, and not much underneath, to judge by the way her breasts hung slackly down inside the blouse. They were far too big, of course, thought Toby, wondering what extra special techniques of love she possessed to inflame poor old Adalbert's waning desire.

Adalbert presented him to Signorina Rosa Benedetti and they shook hands before she went off into high-speed Italian. Polite though it was, of course, to shake hands on being introduced, to Toby it seemed strange and amusing in view of what they were here for. Adalbert replied in what sounded like fluent Italian, his tone courteous.

'She is very pleased to make your acquaintance, Toby. Go with her and I will wait here.'

'Are you sure? I mean, You're her regular friend and I'm the new boy here.'

'I insist. Off you go! By the way, I gave all the cash I had with me to Niccolo – you don't mind taking care of things here, do you? Give Rosa a thousand lira.'

Toby brought out his wallet, calculating in his head. It was well over £7, which seemed to him a lot, even for two of them. Tourists had to accept being fleeced anywhere but Adalbert was a resident here and ought to get local rates. Nevertheless, he handed Rosa a banknote with a flourish, and she showed signs of being pleased with it. Toby guessed advantage was being taken by the Austrian to reward the woman with a bonus for services past and to come.

The finances being arranged to her satisfaction, Rosa smiled at Toby and led him into the adjoining bedroom. It was another small square room, with a window onto an alley at the back. She pulled a threadbare curtain across to block the view from over the way and indicated to Toby that he should remove his jacket and shoes and lie on the bed. It was a rickety-looking piece of furniture with a dark wooden head-board that had cracked right across.

While he was preparing himself for whatever curious event she had in mind, she undid the buttons down her blouse and took it off. Under it was an artificial silk slip of nondescript colour which did little to hide her sagging bosom. Before Toby could ask her to keep it on – though she wouldn't have understood him anyway, she had pulled it out of the waistband of her skirt and over her head.

She made it clear she was proud of her overdeveloped breasts by bouncing them up and down on her palms, saying a few words in Italian which could only mean *do you like them?*

'Spectacular,' said Toby, concealing his aversion to dangling breasts the size of water melons. The word pleased her.

'*Si, spettacolare,*' she agreed with a grin.

Off came the black skirt to reveal pink knickers with loose legs to halfway down her thighs, a shadowy bush showing through the flimsy material. Nothing so far had put Toby in the mood to frolic with her, and he was wishing himself out of it and over on the other side of Venice when she got onto the bed on her knees and flipped open his trousers. She tugged them well down his legs, turned up his shirt, opened his shorts and took hold of his limp part. She said a word or two which meant nothing to Toby but made him fear she believed he suffered from the same difficulties as Adalbert – a highly displeasing notion!

She pushed his knees up and apart, kneeling between his feet, and stroked the inside of his thighs before running her fingers down between the cheeks of his bottom. Toby closed his eyes and squirmed to feel her press a fingertip into him, not knowing if he liked the sensation or not. Then in another instant her head was down between his thighs and she had his still soft part in her mouth and was sucking strongly, her cheeks drawn in. Little enough of this was needed to bring him up to full stretch – at which she gave a muffled grunt of triumph.

What the devil am I doing here in this awful place with this unattractive woman? was the question running through his mind. Unable to produce a sensible answer, he stared down in mingled dismay and fascination at Rosa's face hovering above his belly – she held his stiff-straining *cazzo* straight up vertically with short thick fingers, her mouth lips closed tight on the purple head. She sucked rhythmically up and down, pausing for a moment at the top of each stroke while her tongue lapped over the crown. Down below her other hand held his pompoms, tugging gently at them as if to stretch them longer.

So this was Adalbert's latest way to get his drooping part to stand up straight and do its duty! A woman with a mouth like a housemaid wielding a Hoover vacuum-cleaner! It was simply too banal for words, was Toby's disapproving verdict ... and it had to be admitted that she'd got him enormously excited in next to no time ... his upright part was throbbing between her fingers. And, feeling his high arousal, she sucked in a frenzy, until his belly began to contract and his knees spread wide apart.

He gasped and jerked and it felt to him as if his whole body was somehow pulling itself up toward his chin. The contractions in his belly grew stronger and longer – this was it, this was it! He gave a brief cry as Rosa pushed her forefinger into him up to the second knuckle, every muscle tensed, and sort sharp spasms racked him as he spurted his hot essence into her mouth.

Afterwards he lay with closed eyes, recovering and assembling his thoughts. It was the first time he'd been pleasured like that by a woman and it had been very exciting. So much so that, he found to his amusement, he wanted it again – his *cazzo* still stood long and stiff, with scarcely a hint of the normal droop and dwindle that followed the sexual climax. Rosa was standing beside the bed in her cheap pink knickers, her breasts flopping loosely as she moved – she was urging him to get up and go into the sitting room so that Adalbert could have his turn.

'*Ancora*,' said Toby, smiling at her and holding his stiffness in his hand to draw her attention to its condition. She grinned and shook her head and said something in which he distinguished the words *Signor Gmund*.

'Let him wait five minutes,' Toby retorted, but Rosa turned away from him and took a step towards the door. For a thousand lira Toby felt he was entitled to more consideration. He came off the bed like a shot, his trousers sliding down his legs, to grab her about the waist and swing her round. She had no time to cry out in alarm before with a push he sent her sprawling on to the bed face down and, despite the trousers hobbling him round his ankles, he had moved in to snatch her knickers over her bottom and halfway down.

The cheeks he had uncovered were white and soft-looking, much too meaty for elegance, of course, he registered with a mental tut-tut. But there below the crease between them, lay a pair of plump lips. The brief struggle had roused Toby and he had lost sight of what he had originally wanted from her. A sight of the real thing had turned his mind in that direction and he fully intended to jab his twitching *cazzo* into it to unburden himself of his burning lust.

'*Aspetta! Aspetta!*' Rosa was groaning awkwardly, her face pressed against the coverlet, but Toby was in no mood to listen to anything she might say, even if he could have understood it. He pressed his finger deep into her dark-haired split to open it and she squirmed on her belly, still protesting. He shuffled in close between her splayed legs and when she felt the head of his throbbing part touch her, she reached round behind herself with both hands to grasp the cheeks of her bottom and pull them apart.

'*Qui*,' she said, no longer complaining but telling him what to do. More than that, she took his hot-headed part between thumb and forefinger to position it up between the soft white cheeks. At last Toby realised that he was being offered an alternative to the ordinary route to pleasure and the idea staggered him. It was abnormal and perverse, Continental and decadent... quite deplorable... yet the shock of the unfamiliar and forbidden had an instant effect on him, and with a long gasp of astonishment at himself he pushed against her puckered knot of muscle until he sank into her.

He advanced into this unknown territory cautiously, thrusting slowly and carefully as he stared down at his slippery length vanishing down in the crease of her bottom. He used both hands to hold the soft cheeks apart and gripped so fiercely that his fingers sank deep into the flesh. Then it was as if a sudden fever seized him and he was ramming frantically, making Rosa groan as her body jerked on the bed to the brutal rhythm of his assault. It was over in seconds – with a gasp of total disbelief Toby gushed his fiery passion into her.

SEVEN

On Monday morning Toby made his way with pleasant anticipation up into the dusty attics of the Palazzo Malvolio to search for secret compartments before getting on with his valuation of the discarded furniture. The huge wardrobe in his bedroom yielded nothing except the notion that hiding places existed and, to be honest, it was not likely that there would be anything of value left in anything moved up to the attic in the dim distant past. But there was a sort of mild treasure-hunt eagerness about the search itself.

From where he stood not very far from the door, surrounded by writing tables, *chaise-longues*, tables of different styles and ages and the rest of the clutter, he could see three wardrobes. Strictly speaking, *wardrobe* was not the right description for all of them, since its usage to mean a cupboard to keep clothes in dated only from about the beginning of the nineteenth century. In the Middle Ages the most usual piece of furniture anyone had to keep spare clothes in was a chest – plain, carved, painted or otherwise decorated according to social status and available wealth.

Over by the wall he could see an excellent example of a chest for clothes – a *cassone* as they were called in Italian, a long wooden box on carved feet, the top domed and the whole painted in red and gold – though the colours had faded badly, as might be expected in 500 years. He could just make out the Malvolio coat of arms on the front, and another coat of arms, which he was sure indicated that it had been a dowry chest, brought by the daughter of someone rich marrying into the Malvolio clan. One foot was gone, making it sag at one end, and from where he stood it looked to have a serious woodworm problem. But all the same, repaired and cleaned up it was worth a lot, not as usable furniture but as a rare antique.

There would be no secret compartments in that. Standing

alone in a sort of clearing was a tall walnut *armoire*, as it might be called instead of wardrobe, with carved panels on the front and sides. Middle 1600s, Toby decided, and it looked promising. By the far wall, a devil of a job to get to, stood an astounding baroque cupboard, eight feet tall, with curlicues, swags and a plethora of carved dusty gilt decoration. It was long and wide enough to take a girl in and lie down with her. The left-hand door of four was off its hinges and propped against the side of the massive piece.

Finally, half-hidden behind the parts of a dismantled tester-bed, he could see an outrageous little rococo confection, its sides bowed gracefully outwards, with flower designs painted on it. That looked promising, since he was sure it had originally stood in a lady's room. From where he stood it wasn't possible to see how it was damaged or how badly.

Where to start? With the easiest one first, he decided, and took off his jacket and tie and rolled up his sleeves. He moved with care between the stacks, threading his way as if through a maze towards the *armoire* that stood alone. It was a very fine piece of furniture, he saw when he reached it, superbly made and even under a coating of dust the carving was clearly the work of a master hand. Each panel had a different rural scene and there was no damage at all. Toby opened the two doors toward himself and was amazed to see that the entire bottom was smashed right through. That disposed of any secret compartment, but why would anyone have done that to so handsome a piece?

Perhaps someone else was looking for a secret compartment in the past, but what a way to go about it! Or could someone have been locked in and broken his way out? But it would have been easier to force the doors open than smash the solid planking of the bottom. It was a problem without a solution, and Toby left it alone and set course for the distant tester-bed behind which he had caught a glimpse of a charmingly painted rococo wardrobe.

It proved quite difficult to get to it, mainly because of the bed in between. To save space it had been dismantled and stored on edge, the massive wood-frame bed, the ten-foot tall carved head-board, and the solid wooden tester or roof. It was out of the question to get round it, and to climb over might bring the whole lot crashing down. Toby made a wide detour round stacked writing desks and chairs, and came at the wardrobe another way.

To see it was a delight – he almost drooled when he at last got within touching distance and flicked over the panels with a handkerchief to see the painted flower displays under the dust. On display in the Bond Street windows of Fitzroy Dalrymple it would cause a sensation – and a rush to acquire it. They could set their own price on so superb an example of mid-eighteenth century Venetian craftsmanship. Toby couldn't remember the names of any Italian furniture-makers of the period except Pietro Piffetti, and he had worked in Turin, not Venice. Not that it mattered – a browse through reference books would produce a suitable name to put on it when it was offered for sale.

But it had nothing in the way of secret compartments – he saw that straight off. It stood well clear of the ground on carved gilt feet, and there was no unaccounted-for space at the bottom or at the top or anywhere else. That left the baroque monster, and in the twists and turns to get to the rococo treasure Toby had lost sight of where the big one was. Eventually he stood on a rickety chair – plain oak with a triangular seat and probably dating from the 1500s, to get a better view round the dimly lit attic. The back was broken and its top half missing.

He was nearer his goal than he thought – he spotted the elaborate carving straight ahead and set off towards it. He slid sideways between a lacquered writing cabinet with gilt-work and mother-of-pearl inlays and a rosewood dressing table that looked French, and there it stood. *Stupendous* was the word that formed in his mind as he stared at the largest piece of furniture he'd ever seen. You could take more than one girl inside – there was room enough for a romp with two or three of them. It had four doors, one hanging off where the topmost hinge had broken away from the wood, and only a very large dressing room could ever have accommodated it. Still, if you lived in a palace you had rooms as large as you liked.

The wardrobe stood on a solid base over a foot high, adorned with carved borders. Toby opened the three doors still on their hinges and stepped up into the capacious interior – he could stand upright in it with no problem. Except for an ancient and drooping cobweb across one back corner it was empty. He stamped his foot experimentally, listening hard for a sound that would indicate a secret place below, but that told him nothing. He climbed out and knelt to tap across the whole internal floor, then gave that up and started to feel round the base carving.

There was a lot of it and it all seemed solid, there was no discernible give, however hard he pressed. So perhaps there was nothing to be found. But, to make sure, he got up and stood back a pace or two to examine the front – was there perhaps a secret compartment in the top rather than the bottom? No, he decided, the reason being that Italians of the eighteenth century were not tall. To get at a hiding place eight feet above the floor would be far too inconvenient for them. Any secret compartment had to be in the base.

He sat down on the floor and considered the possibilities. In his bedroom the wardrobe-floor had hinged upwards, but that was not the only way – not even the best way, because if shoes were kept there, or in those days maybe a gentleman's dress sword or whatever, all that had to be cleared out before the compartment could be opened. With that thought in his mind, he felt again along the front of the ornamental base for any item of carving that could be gripped and pulled. And found it straight away – he pulled at two matched rosettes a yard apart and a section of the base fell open towards him on hinges.

He let it down to the floor and peered into the space he had revealed – and there was something in there! In mounting glee he reached in and took hold of whatever it was, and drew it out carefully. It was a flat square bundle, about two feet each way and wrapped in dusty green cloth. He laid it on the floor and unwrapped it with caution, his heart pounding.

It was a triptych, three wooden panels hinged together that could be opened out and stood up. And on it, as he had guessed, was an oil painting on a religious theme. What he had found was a small portable altar-piece once used for private prayers and devotion. The centre panel had the Madonna enthroned in glory with her baby, and each side panel had two Saints. St Mary was in blue and the child was naked. Under the throne lay a scarlet cloth which hung down in great folds over the steps. It was not hard to recognise St Francis on the right-hand panel – he was the bare-foot one in the monk's brown robe. And St Sebastian – the arrows sticking out of his body identified him. There was a Saint in armour on the left panel, holding a long lance – there was no telling who he might be – and a grey-bearded old Saint in only a loin-cloth and a look of extreme misery.

The colours were bright and beautiful but Toby knew his find was very old and very valuable. He was interested in paintings not for their artistic worth but as furnishings. A well-chosen and well-placed picture on a wall could do wonders for a room. The better the name, the better the effect, so to speak. What he had here was unsuitable as decor – religious pictures had no great attraction these days. But he was quite certain that he'd found a small masterpiece by an early Venetian painter, one of the pre–1500 artists. There were experts easily found in Venice – and in London, of course – who could study the technique and put a name to the painter.

Naturally, the triptych belonged to Delphine Tandy, who had inherited the palace and contents from the last Malvolio, as Toby understood the circumstances. But even the last Malvolio hadn't known he owned this work of art, because he'd never seen it and evidently it was not listed in Padre Pio's archives. How many generations it had been hidden in this superlative ancient wardrobe was as impossible to say as who had concealed it there and why.

On the other hand . . . suppose Toby had not found it . . . suppose he had made Mrs Tandy an offer for the contents of the attic, she had accepted, and the damaged furniture had been shipped to London for restoration. And suppose the painting had then come to light . . . whose property would it then be? Strictly speaking Mrs Tandy's, perhaps, but could she have inherited an item that the testator didn't know existed anyway? Bearing in mind what the cash value of the item probably was, ownership would become a question for lawyers to argue out before a judge.

A legal contest with the client did the reputation of a firm like Fitzroy Dalrymple no good at all. Thinking it through to a logical conclusion, Toby formed the view that it was better for both sides to remain in complete ignorance of the existence of the triptych. Then neither would lose anything nor gain anything and good relations between company and client would continue in the hope that at some time in the future Mrs Tandy should decide to sell some of her other possessions.

All that was needed to preserve this happy state of affairs was for Toby to dispose of the work of art privately and pocket the proceeds. A very reasonable solution to an otherwise tricky little problem. There was time to think out the details later – for now it was a question of putting the painting back into the safe place where it had lain for so long, and fetching it again when his work in the palazzo was finished and he was ready to leave for London.

He closed the three wooden panels and wrapped the triptych in the length of old green damask he had found it in, restored it to the secret compartment and closed the false front. The catch mechanism held it shut as well as the day it left the maker's workshop, and there was no visible sign that anything out of the ordinary existed in the base of the great wardrobe – except for where Toby's exploring fingers had made tracks in the dust. Not that anyone else was likely to come up to the attics to inspect the broken furniture – all the same, he went over the base with his handkerchief, eliminating any traces.

After a find like that there was no question of carrying on with the inventory for the rest of the day. Very considerable wealth was within his grasp and he was too elated to make lists of tables and chairs. He went down to his bedroom to wash away the dust and change clothes to go out – where, he had no idea at all, but out into the sunshine of Venice.

Half an hour later he was at the great door on the landward side of the palace, about to leave, when the liveried doorman bowed and handed him an envelope. There was no stamp on it and it obviously had not come through the mail, and nor did he know the flowing handwriting in which his name was inscribed – quite correctly, for once – *Mr T Jervis*. He tore the envelope open disgorging a sudden waft of lavender perfume and unfolded a thick sheet of handmade paper.

There was an elaborate coat of arms embossed at the top, two lines of writing, and a large and indecipherable signature. The message was a terse but polite request to call at the Palazzo Flagranti between two and four that afternoon. Remembering the displeasure with which the American Contessa had left him after the incident on the balcony on Saturday evening, Toby found it surprising to receive the invitation. But on second thoughts . . . perhaps Sally had decided she could do a lot worse than ask him round for an encore in more comfortable surroundings.

Naturally, he wasn't going to let her decide on the terms, or she might get the idea he was another *ragazzo* like the Princess Zita's Marcello, to be had if and when it suited her. He'd go there now and, if she was out, leave his name and let her start the process all over again. With this in mind he followed the by now familiar route from the Palazzo Malvolio to the church of San Stefano and through a square where weary tourists sat at an open air cafe to rest their feet and on to the Accademia Bridge. Sally had told him on the balcony that she lived on the other side of the Grand Canal 'on the waterfront'.

Over the bridge there were a few people standing about before the Accademia Gallery – visitors by the look of them. If he had time, Toby meant to visit the famous collection of Venetian art before he left Venice. His interest in it was slightly higher now than before he found the triptych, as he thought there was a good chance of seeing something in there to match the style of his find, which would be a useful pointer to identification. It was a wicked shame that all those early artists hadn't put a set of initials in a corner of the canvas, as modern painters always did, so there was no doubt whose work it was.

Away from the Accademia he found himself in a very quiet part of Venice, a middle-class residential sort of quarter, with few people about in the narrow streets. To get across a narrow side canal that barred the way, he had to make a long detour to find a bridge – and came out into a large square with an ordinary-looking church and a cafe which had no customers. He sat at one of the outside tables and ordered coffee and cognac while he studied his street-guide. It was not very helpful, since it did not put names to the streets or canals. But on the back, as if to make up for its general uselessness, it gave a list of *Tombs and Residences of Illustrious Men*, as it put it, this being the English language version.

The Illustrious Men were a mixed bunch and it needed a little thought to recognise some of them under the English *alias* they had been given: Francesco Petrarca had to be the Italian poet who fell for a twelve-year-old girl and invented the sonnet. George Byron could only be Lord Byron, who frolicked his way round the Mediterranean and wrote racy verses. Richard Wagner, Wolfgang Goethe – the boring old Germans were easily placed. But what about Michael Angel? It had to be Michelangelo, although Toby had the impression he spent most of his life at Rome painting churches for various Popes. But on the back of the street-guide it claimed he lived *at the Giudecca*, which the map identified as the large island at the bottom end of the city.

John Ruskin lived at the Pensione Calcina at the Zattere, it said, which was the name of a canal-side walk not very far from where Toby was sitting. Except that he didn't really live there – he stayed there on his honeymoon and wrote an unreadable book about the beauties of Venetian architecture. More interesting was the information that the French lady novelist George Sand, her *ragazzo* the poet Alfred de Musset, and Charles Dickens lived at the Danieli Hotel. But surely not all at the same time, Toby thought, raising his eyebrows in amusement. *George*, whose real name was Aurore Dupin, was renowned for screeching rows with de Musset. Dickens would have been piously shocked.

The waiter brought the coffee and cognac – Toby had ordered a large one, to get him into the right mood of don't-give-a-damn before meeting Sally. *Si, si, signor, Palazzo Flagranti*, he said when asked and nodded his head vigorously. He pored doubtfully over the street-guide until he located San Trovaso Square, where the cafe stood, and pointed to a line of palaces on the bank of the Grand Canal just north of where they were. When Toby set off again, he knew no more than when he started, but he crossed a deserted side-canal or two and eventually emerged into a tiny square with a large palace type of building across one end. At a ramshackle newspaper kiosk he enquired if it was the Palazzo Flagranti and was pleased to be told it was.

The building was much older than the Palazzo Malvolio, a good deal smaller than that rambling barracks, and in an altogether different style. *Venetian-Gothic* was the term Toby had picked up to describe this fairy-tale collection of tall and narrow windows, little balconies with stone fretwork and pointed-arch doorways. He hammered on the black-painted cast-iron knocker in the shape of a lion's head and waited. It was very much better maintained than the Palazzo Malvolio, as was to be expected if Sally had brought a slice of her Pittsburgh father's fortune to the marriage with Count Flagranti.

The door was opened by a manservant in a neat black suit, who stared impassively at Toby and answered in near-perfect English that the Contessa was expecting no one. Even when Toby showed the letter with a crest on it, he remained unimpressed. When at last Toby produced a 100-lira note, the imperturbable servant said he would enquire if the Contessa was at home. At least he allowed Toby into the hall to wait.

The hall was an eye-opener. The Palazzo Flagranti might

be 1350 Venetian outside, but the interior was pure 1925 Paris. The original stone flagging had vanished under highly polished black and white squares, and in the centre stood a table with a rectangular glass top and wrought-iron legs. The Contessa most definitely had redecorated her husband's old family palace!

The neat manservant returned after five minutes to announce that the Contessa would see him and led him up an open staircase – whatever it had been in 1350, nowadays it had a curving thin gilt handrail and sharp-angled treads – to the main floor and into what Toby took to be the Contessa's own sitting room. She went to the *Exposition Internationale des Arts Decoratifs*, said Toby to himself in wonder as he looked round, *and came away converted to the French Art Deco style*. The low armchairs and a *chaise-longue* of a shape that was more or less oval were of ash and sycamore blended, with pale green silk upholstery.

The wall-coverings were beige and silver, and the Gothic shape of the windows lost behind semi-transparent curtains of heavy beige silk with shell motifs. The overall effect was stunning, and made Toby revise upwards his estimate of Sally's dowry from Pittsburgh PA.

Although the Contessa was not expecting anyone that morning her face was expertly, though lightly, made-up and hair brushed glossy and beautifully parted. She was all in white – a simple little frock that had cost as much as Toby earned in a quarter. It was sleeveless and came only to her knees, her thin elegant legs and arms delighting Toby. The bodice was cut in a long V that showed she had no bosom worth mentioning, and exaggerated the length of her slender neck. She got up from a chic writing desk made to match the other furniture and stared at Toby. 'What are you doing here?' she asked in a doubtful tone, 'I said this afternoon.'

'*Buon giorno*, Contessa,' Toby answered very politely, to put her in the wrong.

She did not offer him her hand to kiss and she did not invite him to sit down. She stared warily at him, as if he were a very dangerous creature she could not understand. In the forthright American way she came straight to the point.

'So why did you do it? I've got to know.'

Toby smiled as charmingly as he knew how and shrugged enough to impress her with his assumed Devil-may-care attitude.

'Fate decreed it,' he said. 'You are so slender and elegant

– I was lost the moment I saw you. The ladies I have met here are so . . . how can I put it? So . . . overblown. I am a passionate man, but so much flesh repels me.'

For a man declaring himself opposed to plump-figured women he had a lot to keep silent about. In the space of a day or two he had sampled the charms of Contessa Marina, Delphine Tandy and Anna-Louisa Ziani. Not to mention Rosa Benedetti, who had the biggest breasts he'd ever laid hands on. Well, so he had allowed himself to be sidetracked a little, but the reality was that he adored elegance and style and thin women.

'When I saw your superbly slender figure,' he went on, 'there was no possibility of restraining myself. Do not for an instant think that I mean to apologise for that wonderful act of passion and I would do the same again, given the circumstances.

'You must be out of your mind,' said Sally, trying to grapple with his bold assertion.

'I assure you I am a very rational person,' he answered, sure that the battle was won already, 'it is generally agreed there are two types of desirable women, one desirable to look at and the other desirable in bed. Most men believe a woman desirable to the eye is not necessarily desirable in bed.'

'What?' Sally asked, struggling to follow.

'It is quite simple, to be desirable to look at, a woman must be slender, not plump, delicate of bones and features, prettily dressed. To be desirable in bed a woman should be buxom, with a large bosom and broad hips, robust enough to take a man's weight on her. And, of course, she should be perfectly naked.'

'What are you talking about?'

'I maintain that this preference for over-fleshed women is a peasant taste,' said Toby, 'and as little worthy of attention as peasant art. Or in countries like yours and mine where there are no peasants, it is a proletarian taste – a yearning by the underfed and miserably housed for comfort and luxury of a sort, represented in their eyes by abundance of female flesh.'

'I think you're crazy,' Sally murmured, still standing a few feet away from him, her arms by her sides, staring at him.

'We of the cultured classes have a truer appreciation of what is desirable in a woman,' said he, smiling so that he shouldn't sound too serious, 'and for me you typify the ideal,

Sally. For instance, your long slender arms...'

Suiting the deed to the word, he stepped forward and took her right arm in his hands, one circling her wrist and the other clasped just above the elbow. Her head turned and her pale eyes continued to stare at him, her red-painted mouth slightly open, but no words emerged. Toby stroked her arm lightly a few times, praising the shape and elegance. She wore a broad gold bracelet on her wrist, studded with precious stones. He suggested it was a perfect complement to her slenderness and lightness, and said nothing about its obvious value.

'As for your legs,' he continued, advancing his cause, 'they are as near perfection as one could hope to see.'

He went down on one knee swiftly while he was still speaking and raised her white silk frock on one side to reveal her right thigh down to her knee. He ran his fingertips down bare flesh above her gartered silk stocking and held forth in a flattering manner on the slenderness and shapeliness of her legs. When he first touched her skin she jumped a little, like a horse shying nervously, but then stood still again.

'Perfection, perfection,' said Toby, 'I can think of no other word to describe legs like these. Your hips are of course quite divine in their space elegance – would you mind taking off your frock for a moment to let me see how very narrow they are?'

There was a short delay while the Contessa's mind registered his words and examined them for a meaning. Toby had expected it and took full advantage of it by rising to his feet and easing the frock up her body. Whether Sally in her slowness of uptake was confusing him to some extent with her dressmaker – or even perhaps with her doctor – she took hold of the hem herself when it reached waist level and finished pulling it up over her head and off.

'Delightful, utterly delightful,' Toby pronounced, standing a pace or two back for a better view. The Contessa was revealed wearing an ivory-white silk slip that ended at mid-thigh, sewn round the yoke with tiny blue forget-me-nots. He advanced again and put his hands on her hips, a judicious look on his face as he squeezed his hands inwards.

'Gracefully narrow,' he said, 'how very seldom does one see a woman so truly desirable. If you'll take the slip off, I'll see how close I can get to circling your waist with my hands.'

'You're leading me on,' she said, the message getting through to her mind at last.

'I'm admiring you, Sally, as an elegant and desirable woman ought to be admired – otherwise what is the point of elegance and desirability? Unless men catch their breath when they look at you, you might as well let yourself get fat and wear frumpy clothes.'

That seemed to reach her quicker than his earlier remarks – a moment or two of hesitation, and she pulled her slip up and off altogether. She was wearing open-legged knickers of palest blue.

'The hips,' said Toby, bold now that he was getting his way, 'I must see your hips.'

Without a word she bent forward and slipped off her knickers, then stood with her head tilted to one side and her thin arms hanging loosely while he looked at her body. By what means she achieved this degree of emaciation he couldn't tell, but it seemed to him that she was the ideal model as seen in Vogue and other high-toned fashion magazines. Her breasts were virtually non-existent – slight swellings with large pink buds. Bony hips poked prominently through her skin like small handles, her flat belly had the merest dimple in the middle, and the hair between her slender parted legs was no more than a light brown fledging that exposed the narrow split completely.

She represented Toby's ideal of female shapeliness – if only she had been twenty-five years younger he would have insisted that she ran away with him. As it was, his eager part stood stiff in his trousers and twitched in anticipation. He moved near to her and put his hands on her waist, trying unsuccessfully to force his thumbs and forefingers to meet round her.

'Have you seen all you want?' Sally asked him, and her gaze was still blank, though their faces were close together.

He transferred his grasp to her prominent hips and used them to draw her nearer still, until her bare belly was against his trousers and his hardness pressed against her. The touch goaded her into action – she slipped a hand between their bodies and flicked open his trousers.

'You tried to rape me at Delphine's,' she said, with her hand clasping his upright part and massaging it vigorously. Toby was not sure if it was a statement or a question, a complaint or an accusation. He eased back a little to get his own hand between her thighs and feel her.

'You damn well nearly succeeded,' she sighed, moving her feet a little further apart. 'Where did you get that idea from? Do I look like a cheap pick-up, goddam you?'

'You looked like an elegant and very desirable lady then, and you do now,' he murmured, his fingers prising her gently open. He heard her moan lightly as his finger found the way inside and played over her tiny bud. He put his other arm round her and felt between the taut little cheeks of her bottom, just as Signorina Benedetti had done to him, and pressed a fingertip to the little knot of muscle there.

'You're a pervert!' she exclaimed in a shrill voice, and her emaciated body shook as if she had a high fever. Toby utilised both fingers to good advantage and her climax came very quickly – she squirmed in his grasp, her thin belly bulging to the push of her narrow loins against his hand. Her throes continued for longer than he expected, the intensity decreasing only slowly, till with a final sighing gasp she subsided.

She lifted her chin from his shoulder and eased back to stare into Toby's eyes at short range.

'Why'd you do that to me?' she asked.

'Didn't you like it?'

'I thought you were going to try raping me again.'

'I mean to,' he said, 'but I felt that I owed you something – you had no pleasure on Delphine's balcony. Now we're level.'

'You've got the craziest ideas!' said Sally.

'And you've got the most exciting body I've seen in Venice,' he told her. While she was putting that remark through the slow processes of her thinking, he stooped and picked her up bodily – she weighed almost nothing – an arm under her thighs and one round her back. He carried her across her marvellous Art Deco sitting room and sat her on the edge of the oval *chaise-longue*.

He knelt between her feet, pressed her knees apart and kissed the rose-pink buds that stood out from her flat chest in a sort of brief homage. The fragrance of the perfume she spread lavishly over her warm skin, even so early in the day, made Toby sigh in delight and become almost giddy.

She stared into his eyes with the merest hint of expectation while his hands slid up her lean thighs – and as if the touch set off an automatic reaction, her legs spread wider to present her sparsely haired and long-lipped mound. Toby put his palms flat on the thin flesh of the insides of her thighs, well above her stockings, and she leaned back on stiff arms with her head thrown back on her long neck. His finger pressed into her split and within seconds he was able to throw her into a delirium of sensation, her long flat belly throbbing in and out.

All this time his *cazzo* stuck out from his wide open trousers and trembled. He slid closer in to her on his knees and put his hands palm-up under her bare bottom to lift her a little while he steered his length to the lips between her legs. She gasped to feel the blunt head nuzzling her, then with a sharp jerk he pushed right up inside her. They were belly to belly, her head lolling back loosely, her eyes staring at nothing, her painted mouth slackly open. Toby grasped her protruding hips to steady her while he thrust quickly in and out.

'Oh my Gahd . . .' she moaned, 'oh Gahd . . .'

To the rhythm of his thrusting her thin arms and legs jerked loosely, almost as if she were a rag doll shaken by a careless child. A feeling of power gripped Toby to see the effect he was having on her and he stabbed faster, his hands clenched tightly on her bony hips. A sensation so very intense that he cried out in surprise started somewhere deep in his belly and in a blaze of delight he fountained his hot excitement into Sally. She responded with a shrill climactic wail and slapped her belly against him in fierce spasms, until her arms gave way and she collapsed on her back. He fell forward on her, the last few twitches of his climax making his swollen length jerk in her slippery *fica*.

It took some time before Sally's thoughts were sufficiently collected for her to formulate a comment on what had happened. She lay quietly on her back, naked but for silk stockings, with Toby fully dressed on top of her. Eventually she spoke to him.

'Of all the nerve!' she said, sounding surprised. 'You think you can push your way into my sitting room and do what you like to me? I'm going to ring for the servants and have you thrown out on your ear, you British gigolo!'

'No, you're not,' said Toby, keeping his weight on her belly to pin her to the *chaise-longue*, 'you loved every second of it – you haven't been done like that for years.'

'So what makes you think I want to be now?' she asked, thin lines of concentration on her peach-powdered forehead. 'What in Hell will my husband say if he ever finds out!'

'He won't,' said Toby, 'it will be our secret.'

The Contessa Flagranti took her time thinking that over.

'Did you mean any of that stuff about being slim and elegant, or was that only a come-on?' she asked.

'I meant every word of it,' he answered, 'I would rather have you anytime than Marina Torrenegra.'

In a way that was true, or an approximation of the truth. His mind assured him that the bony Contessa was his *Vogue* magazine ideal and therefore to be preferred. Just as he chose spindly legged Chippendale chairs over heavy Victorian armchairs in red plush. Or Sally's own *Art Deco* style over Edwardian mahogany. The fact that his part stood up just as hard for plump-fleshed women as for thin ones was a meaningless physical reaction that proved nothing at all.

He quoted the comparison of Chippendale and Victorian styles to Sally, not sure if she would get the point. He watched her eyes lose their focus while she slowly turned his words over in her mind for a meaning. He let her ponder for a minute and then introduced a new thought into the proceedings, so as to confuse the one she was grappling with.

'This is what we are going to do, Sally. I'm going to take my clothes off and be stark naked. You are going to put on your pale blue knickers and that pretty slip with the forget-me-not embroidery.'

'Why am I going to do that if you're in the buff?' she asked and frowned slightly in her effort to discover a reason for the proposed behaviour.

'I explained to you the importance of slenderness, elegance, style and texture,' he said. 'Bare skin on bare skin is a banal dream of the uncultured plebeian. Persons like ourselves have a more advanced feel for delicate pleasures and we know there is a great deal to be said for the kiss of silk or fur against the body. So, when I am naked and you in your silk underwear, I intend to sit you across my lap while I sit bare-bottomed on one of your green silk armchairs and have you again.'

'Oh!' she said thoughtfully.

And when you are in a receptive mood, I mean to ask you about Delphine Tandy and her circumstances, he added to himself, and about Marina and her boyfriend with the ridiculous matinee-idol looks.

Aloud he said:

'Then I'm going to stand with you against the wall with

your long white curtains draped round us and do it to you again in your knickers.'

'I was right the first time,' she said, gazing into his eyes with interest, 'you're a pervert. So take your clothes off and get started.'

EIGHT

By the middle of his second week in Venice Toby was nearly two-thirds of the way across the damaged furniture attic and he had made useful notes on individual pieces and what restoration was needed to make them saleable. In the cryptic notation used by sellers of antique items to conceal their profit from buyers he noted down his estimate of the lowest sale figure for each. He could already see that the final total was going to be very impressive and it was vital to keep this confidential in view of the fact he proposed to offer Mrs Tandy a fifth of it.

Even that would still be a great deal of money – especially in so poor a country as Italy. If she bargained hard, though he doubted that, he would let himself be pushed up to a quarter of his estimate, but not above. If she held out for more, then he would offer his regrets and prepare to leave for London right away. This would be a chancy game of bluff, in which he banked on the probability that she had already spent the money in her mind and wouldn't want the delay of getting someone else to come in and start cataloguing again to make a new offer.

Rather than that, Toby would expect her to give in and call him back and accept his figure. But there was still a lot to do before he was ready to finalise his figures and speak to London by telephone to get his proposals authorised by his father at Fitzroy Dalrymple. Ahead of him there still loomed half an acre of dusty cupboards, dressing-tables, chairs of all sorts, footstools, cabinets, sofas and all the rest of it, stacked any old how and not easy to examine properly.

He was trying to make up his mind about an upright chair of painted beechwood with a tapestry seat and back. The shape said it was late eighteenth century and highly desirable but the tapestry pattern, though superb in its way, seemed to be at least half a century later. A possibility was that the chair was a fake, but Toby could think of no reason why the then-rich Malvolios would acquire anything not authentic.

A more obvious explanation was that the original tapestry had been damaged and replaced in mid-nineteenth century – then damaged again later, for the chair was wobbly from a cracked front leg. But why repair it at all, when the good old Malvolio way was to shove things up in the attic and forget them?

Questions like that were beyond answering. He was resigning himself to never knowing why or how these byplays of history came about when he heard voices behind him and turned. Over by the door, almost lost behind the stacks of furniture between, stood Contessa Marina and her slick-looking Italian boyfriend. She waved at Toby and he put away his notebook carefully in his hip-pocket before tackling the maze-like route between the stacks to reach his unexpected visitors.

Ottorino Pavese was in a pearl-grey double-breasted suit that fitted him like a glove and looked expensive. A handkerchief of purple silk cascaded from his breast pocket, matching a foulard silk tie of the same colour with lemon-yellow jags woven into it. His almost black hair was beautifully arranged in glossy waves, his shoes, when Toby got close enough to see, were black-and-white patent leather. In short, he looked like a film star making a personal appearance for his devoted fans.

By contrast Toby felt hot, sweaty and dishevelled. He was in rolled-up shirt-sleeves, his jacket lying on the *chaise-longue* with the ripped upholstery on which Marina had seduced him days ago. He knew his hair was untidy, a lock falling raggedly over one eye, his trousers creased and his shoes dusty. Pavese took all this in with one glance and his chest seemed to puff out an inch or two extra at this confirmation of his own superiority.

'You don't mind being interrupted for a minute, Toby?' asked Marina, not expecting any answer to her question. 'You've met Ottorino, of course.'

The two men shook hands politely. At Delphine Tandy's dinner party they had been introduced but had not conversed, and only now did Toby come to learn that the *Dottore* spoke no English at all beyond *yes* and *no*. This caused him to wonder why Marina had brought Pavese to the attics.

Could it be Pavese's interest was not in meeting him again but in having a look at the furniture? Adalbert Gmund had told him Pavese had business interests in . . . Bologna, was it? Could these interests include fine antiques? Though if that were true, wouldn't Delphine give first option on the damaged furniture to her sister's chum. Another damned mystery but one that might not be impossible to solve.

Marina looked marvellously desirable that afternoon in a sort of sleeveless costume of pale cream with a large coral design of flowers. The upper part was a long blouse, buttoned down the back and worn outside the skirt, which was of the same material and had a scalloped hemline. She had several gold bracelets on each wrist and a heavy gold chain with an ivory crucifix around her neck. Toby looked at her quizzically, wondering if she and her boyfriend had been at it. He decided it was too soon after lunch and they were probably going to Marina's room when they left the attics.

'I'd offer you a seat,' said Toby, sounding hospitable, 'but, as you see, everything's a bit dusty up here. The *chaise-longue* isn't bad if you're careful not to sit on the torn bits.'

Marina looked at the giltwood *chaise-longue* without even the faintest of blushes – looked at it as if she'd never seen it before, not as if she'd sat there while unbuttoning her blouse to show off her plump breasts before she was dragged to the prayer-stool to be thoroughly ravished. It made Toby smile to see her sit down where she'd sat that memorable afternoon with him and tell Pavese in Italian to sit beside her.

The *Dottore* pulled a white lawn handkerchief from his sleeve and flicked at the embroidered upholstery before sitting on it. He arranged himself in a careful pose, his chin up and his back straight, one elegantly trousered leg stretched out forward and the other drawn gracefully back.

'Ottorino so very much wanted to have a look at the furniture you've come from London to take away,' said Marina, 'so when he brought me back to the palace after lunch I thought we'd nip up for a second.'

'The *Dottore* is interested in antique furniture?' Toby asked with a friendly smile at the man.

'Only as a collector,' said Marina, guessing the drift of the question, 'he doesn't buy to sell again. Some of the old things up here are very nice. Can you really repair them?'

'There are restorers in London who can,' he answered, 'though it's very skilled work and very expensive. I'm not certain that a lot of these pieces can be brought up to sale-room state.'

He wasn't telling the truth – so far he'd seen only one item he thought beyond restoration – a curious little dressing-table on bronze legs with a top of fine-grained green marble and an oval mirror held up by a gold *putti* with little wings extended. At least, that's how it had looked originally, but an insanely hot-tempered Malvolio in times past had evidently taken a heavy hammer to it. This rare and unusual gem lay in battered pieces.

Marina and her boyfriend exchanged lengthy comments in rapid Italian, with much hand-waving, eye-flashing, lip-curling and similar accompaniments. She turned back to Toby.

'Ottorino would like to know – if you decide to buy it all – how will you transport it to London? I mean, there seems to be so awfully much of it.'

The question had been in Toby's mind since he first laid eyes on the attic and its contents – there was far more than he had ever expected and far more than Jervis Senior imagined when he sent him to Venice. This was no question of a dozen or so items in crates to be loaded on a freight train to clatter across Europe to the Channel. The only practical way he could see of transporting all this furniture was by sea. That would involve getting it boxed up by local carpenters, loaded on barges for the journey down the Grand Canal and along the Giudecca channel to the Venice docks.

It might be weeks before a coaster out of there was bound for an English port but it was the only way. In his figuring he needed to allow for timber and labour for the crating, and for barges and freight by sea – not to mention insurance, which would be arranged in London.

He outlined this to Marina in reply to her question, not sure why Ottorino wanted to know about the mechanics of transfer but certain now that he had a reason of his own for this interest in the furniture. As nonchalantly as he could, Toby enquired of Marina what this might be. She obviously didn't know and took a minute to confer with him. Instead of translating what Ottorino replied, she paraphrased it, as far as Toby could make out.

'Ottorino is immensely interested in Classical antiquities of all kinds and he sometimes has a similar problem – moving them from where he buys them. For his own collection, of course. But as he says, he only acquires small things, never anything that can't be lifted in one hand – Roman silverware and cameo rings, small Greek painted vases and weapons – that sort of thing.'

Toby's field of professional expertise was furniture but he knew a little about other antiques, particularly those that could be used to decorate a room. He looked at Marina's boyfriend and asked himself if he was the sort to be a genuine collector – or a dealer in fake antiques at high prices.

'I'd love to see his collection,' said Toby, sure there was no such thing. 'You've seen it, of course.'

'Well, no,' Marina said, 'he keeps it in his house at Bologna. He has only a four-room apartment here with just a few bits and pieces. Naturally, I can't go to Bologna because his wife and family live there.'

'What a pity,' said Toby, becoming ever more thoughtful about the flashy-looking *Dottore* Ottorino Pavese in his smart suit.

'So you see, he's absolutely fascinated to know how you mean to move this vast bulk of heavy stuff. You're going to need an awful lot of papers for Customs at both ends.'

'Nothing I haven't arranged before,' Toby said, noticing that Ottorino was glancing round the attic carefully, as if looking for specific items. In the mighty jumble here, he couldn't fail to find many examples of whatever pleased him – chairs, tables, desks, wardrobes. He rose to his feet, brushing fastidiously at his elegant grey suit, and spoke in a friendly manner to Toby.

'We must leave you,' Marina interpreted, 'Ottorino thanks you for allowing him to see the historical treasure of the Malvolio past and wishes you well with your work.'

'Thank you,' Toby responded, shaking Pavese's extended hand again. '*Grazie, Dottore.*'

He saw them to the attic door, which stood open while he was working in the futile hope that a breath of air would somehow penetrate the stuffy expanse below the roof. He watched them go along the narrow passage towards the servants' stairs, noting that Ottorino's arm was round Marina's waist even before they turned the corner out of sight. He could guess easily what the boyfriend had said to Marina when he got up from the tattered *chaise-longue* – he'd seen and learned all he wanted up there in the attic and he was in a mood to take her to bed. They were on their way to her room.

Seeing Marina sitting on the tattered *chaise-longue* had set

Toby's fancies running. His male part was halfway between soft and stiff, in limbo between limp and hard, and hung heavily in his trouser-leg. He had to admit that he wanted it to be him on the way to her room with Marina for an afternoon of frolics and not her ridiculously self-pleased boyfriend. Not that she came anywhere near his ideal of the desirable female form – she was much too heavy-bosomed, broad-hipped and plump-bellied. Not a patch on Contessa Flagranti, with her thin limbs, flat smooth chest and almost hairless slit. Sally had proved, in fact, to be such an inspiration to him when he paid his respects to her at home that he'd ravaged her three times before departing. And she'd begged him to come back again soon.

All the same, he couldn't deny that he was hot for Marina at that moment, over-fleshed or not. It irritated him that he was left alone in the stuffy attic while she romped with someone else. She had led him on, there was no other way of putting it, making use of him when it suited her and dropping him instantly when her regular chum came back to Venice from wherever his nefarious business took him for a few days. *It's damn well unfair*, said Toby to himself, *and it won't do!* He decided to confront her later in the day, when *Dottore* Flash Harry was well off the premises. Late that night, when everyone was in bed. He'd go to her room and give her a piece of his mind. And a stiff piece of something else if he got the chance.

He still didn't know where to find her rooms in the rambling labyrinth of the Palazzo Malvolio. *That's easy enough!* he said out loud in his annoyance. All he had to do was follow her now. He was out of the attic at once and darted along the passage to the stairs, between rows of ancient oil-paintings badly in need of cleaning, halting at the top of the servants' stairs. No one was in sight and he hurried down the red-tiled steps making as little noise as possible. At the bottom he looked to right and left cautiously, keeping himself hid in the closed staircase, and caught a glimpse of them a hundred yards away, turning the corner where a half-size bronze of Hermes stood in the angle.

He gave them a few seconds to get away from the turn before he flitted smartly along the passage after them. The paintings here were mainly of religious subjects, suitable for an Italian palace, perhaps, but inappropriate as decor for a smart London residence. He pressed himself close to the wall across from the naked Hermes with winged helmet and tiny *cazzo* between bronze thighs, while he put half his face and an eye round the corner. He recognised where he was – ahead, hardly more than fifty yards away, he saw the top of the polished wooden staircase with the beautiful marquetry work. Still in view, retreating, he saw the backs of Marina's and Ottorino's heads as they descended.

It was important to note which way they turned at the bottom, as he knew that floor to have a particularly complicated layout of rooms and suites, passages and landings. He skated on hands and knees to the top of the stairs and concealed himself as best he could behind an ornately carved newel-post. When Marina and Ottorino reached the bottom they turned neither right nor left – they stopped. Toby ceased breathing, afraid that they'd heard him behind them and stopped to check.

But he was safe and undetected – they'd only stopped to kiss. He observed Ottorino with his hand in Marina's floral-pattern costume to stroke her breasts. The kiss lasted for a long time before Marina pulled away with a chuckle and said something in Italian that got her boyfriend moving again.

They turned to the right. Toby went swiftly and silently down the stairs on tiptoe and headed after them. Some distance away, halfway along a broad and handsome passage lined with life-size marble statues of men in togas, Ottorino opened a tall door for Marina to go through. He followed her without even a glance in either direction and didn't bother to shut the door behind him.

Toby followed quickly, sneering at the serious-faced marble Romans – poets to a man by the look of them. He angled his head cautiously round the half-open door and drew back in panic, his heart skipping a beat. Marina and Ottorino stood not ten feet away, in the first of a long suite of rooms. Tall white-painted double doors repeated at intervals gave a long vista of a row of windows with worn sun-blinds pulled down, walls covered with faded damask, enough gold-framed oil paintings to fill an art gallery, endless statues, tapestry and gilt furniture the worse for wear, areas of waxed flooring large enough for a London *palais de danse*.

The Contessa and the *Dottore* stood locked in a passionate hug beneath a painting of a crafty-looking man with a goatee beard and a red Cardinal's hat. Presumably it was a portrait of some long-gone Malvolio who had chosen the Church as his career but hadn't made it as far as Pope. Ottorino's hand was up Marina's skirt and her sumptuous loins were visibly twitching at his touch. Her own right hand and much of her arm were thrust down the front of Ottorino's trousers. Toby pressed himself closer to the wall and shut his eyes, not daring to breath.

The murmur of the lovers reached his ears and his unruly part was at full stretch by this time, hard upright in his underwear and throbbing. He began to regret embarking on the pursuit so thoughtlessly – there must be other ways of finding out where Marina's bedroom was – perhaps as simple as bribing a servant – the maid Maria, for instance.

After a while, he heard Marina giggle and then footsteps going away. He waited until he was sure they had crossed the first of the rooms, took his shoes off and went after them. He winked at the Cardinal as he passed and kept to the side of the vast room until he reached the next, and waited there behind one wing of the door for Marina and her beau to reach the end of the suite.

There was another corridor of paintings beyond, with gold and white doors set in the walls between them. Toby peeped with one eye from his hiding-place and watched his quarry go into a door no more than thirty yards along. It clicked solidly shut behind them and this, he guessed, might at last be Marina's quarters.

He looked round for landmarks to help him find his way back to it later. A monumental sculpture in dusty marble stood at the far end of the passage – the Three Graces by the look of it – a naked trio of young women staring blankly at each other. He had seen the group before and was fairly sure he knew how to reach it from the other side.

All the same, he felt he'd better make certain before giving up the chase – the door they'd gone through might only be the way into yet another suite of empty rooms that led on to more corridors of pictures. He flitted to the closed door, went down on one knee and put his eye to the keyhole. There was no key in it – he'd noticed before that not a key was to be seen in a door anywhere throughout the entire Palazzo Malvolio, not even in the rooms converted into bathrooms. Except, that is, in the huge locks of the door that opened on to the Grand Canal quay where the Malvolio family gondolas and speedboats were tied up, and also the door that led out to the small square on the landward side of the palace.

He was spying into a large square sitting-room and there was no one in it. Not on the long green and gold sofa, not in any of the matching armchairs, not by the marble fireplace, not by the priceless eighteenth-century rococo rosewood and mother-of-pearl sideboard on which were ranged bottles of gin, sherry, cognac, and Italian coloured liqueurs he didn't recognise. Cautiously, still carrying his shoes in his hand, he stood up to open the door and slide into the empty room. At once his nostrils caught a trace of Marina's perfume and he saw another door, just like the one he had come through, set in the far wall.

He crossed the sitting room noiselessly and knelt to put his eye to the keyhole again. He'd found what he was looking for – he'd know where to come late at night to confront the Contessa – he was looking into her bedroom. The bed was a very large and impressive four-poster hung in green and gold drapery of damask or something like it, adorned with a positive wealth of looped thick cords terminating in huge gold tassels. It was the sort of bed in which princes and cardinals played games with their girlfriends – or their boyfriends if it so happened they were that way inclined. At present the useful-looking luxurious bed was not in use for any purpose.

Over by the tall windows stood a pair of gilt armchairs that brought a small sigh of admiration to Toby's lips. They were of yew, with delicate spiral fluting on the legs, half-padded arms and more elaborate hand-carving along the back and arms. Green-and-gold upholstery matched the colours and pattern of the bed.

At present one of these highly desirable antique chairs was occupied by Ottorino Pavese, who lolled casually in it with his wavy dark-haired head on the superb carving of the back. Out in front of him sprawled his elegantly trousered legs, carelessly parted. He had taken off the jacket of his pearl-grey suit and it lay neatly folded on the other chair. His flashy purple tie was fully exposed, a sight unpleasing to a discerning eye. And something else was exposed too, his trousers being open wide to let his *cazzo* stick up stiff as a brass poker.

Marina was on her knees in front of him, licking the unhooded head of it – the colour very nearly matched his silk tie. She had taken off her two-piece costume to reveal a *crêpe-de-Chine* slip of palest lemon, shaped to fit her heavy breasts and round hips. The initiative was entirely hers it seemed – Ottorino lay with an expectant look on his film-star profile, his eyes half-shut, while Marina's wet tongue licked along the length of his stiff part from base to tip.

'*Carissima* . . .' Ottorino sighed, just loud enough to reach the ear of Toby beyond the door. Marina stroked his upright part between fingertip and thumb while she leaned closely over him to breathe hotly on his bared belly, her tongue wandering slowly downward to his groin.

Toby's face was burning with desire and envy while he watched Marina nuzzling at the almost black curls from which Ottorino's shaft sprang. His own was throbbing menacingly in his trousers, and it leaped furiously when Marina raised her face a little to take the head of Ottorino's – dark and swollen with passion – into her mouth. Her boyfriend jerked in the elegant armchair, tremors of delight shaking his body. For an instant she slipped the whole head into her mouth and her cheeks hollowed with the strength of her sucking. She pushed it out again, wet and shiny from her tongue, and Ottorino's heels in their black-and-white shoes drummed briefly on the polished wooden floor.

Toby thought at first that she'd pushed Ottorino to a climax, but though his *cazzo* was leaping in her hand there was no spurt of essence. Marina opened her mouth again and she swallowed the trembling part she held, sucking it in to the limit. Ottorino in a delirium of sensation writhed on the chair, hands clenched on the carving. This passivity was a surprise to Toby. By now he expected the Italian to have jumped up and swept Marina across the room to the four-poster bed and pushed her down onto her back. If it had been himself enjoying her teasing, he would certainly have flung her down and ravaged her before now – or exploded into her mouth.

The *Dottore* was a good few years older than Toby but what of it? He was still in his prime – at a guess in his forties, but athletic-looking and vigorous. Why was it taking him so long to respond properly to Marina's stimulation? He was keen enough on her – he'd stopped twice on the way through the palace from the attics to fondle her. And he showed no sign of wanting to stop what was being done to him. On the contrary, he seemed to be enjoying it very fully. But as Marina continued her labour of love, although Ottorino squirmed and moaned and trembled, he seemed to get no nearer to the grand moment.

It was then that Toby remembered the curious warning Adalbert Gmund had given him – be careful of accepting anything to drink from Marina if he was alone with her. There was supposed to be an *elisir* that aroused and strengthened the sexual passions but was dangerous in excess. Marina had been infatuated with the man she called Orlando – a university teacher from London named Roland Something-or-other – and she had doped him with the secret potion till he was making love to her a dozen times a day. If Adalbert's tale could be believed, that is.

Except that, according to the Austrian, the continuing effort of satisfying himself on Marina had weakened Roland until his constitution was undermined and he collapsed of total nervous exhaustion. They'd managed in time to nurse him back to health, or enough to get him back to London, but his physique was shattered for the rest of his life. Or something like that, though it sounded too much like a sermon to be taken at face value. Toby decided it would be interesting when he got home to go looking for this Roland chap at London University and see if he'd made a full recovery in the couple of years that had passed since.

Meanwhile, what if Marina had been slipping a spoonful or two of the *elisir* into drinks for Ottorino, to keep him right up to scratch? According to Adalbert she'd taken up with him at the Carnival that year, which would be over three months ago. So if Ottorino had been on the stuff without knowing since then, and performing to the satisfaction of Contessa Marina, by this time he should be considerably weakened.

But he wasn't in Venice all the time. His wife and family at Bologna would expect to see him reasonably regularly. And there was his business, whatever that might be – it took him away for several days at a time. This might explain why he had lasted so long. Not being permanently in Venice meant he had these breaks from continued dosage and daily endeavour.

But it was taking its toll, to judge by what was happening on the armchair. Ottorino's classic features were distorted and scarlet, his mouth hung open and his limbs were shaking. It was evidently the moment when something had to happen – either he would go into a sexual climax or a stroke, one or the other. A long wailing cry penetrated the door to reach Toby's ears and Ottorino's loins bucked upwards as he fountained his suddenly released emotion into Marina's sucking mouth.

The sight of Ottorino's deliverance reminded Toby of how very fraught he was himself – his *cazzo* had been so desperately hard for so long that it was becoming painful. He pressed a hand to the front of his trousers to stop the throbbing and was amazed to feel how thick and long his surly part had grown. But there was nothing to be done about it – he wanted to stay at the keyhole to see how the comedy was resolved.

If Marina was hot to have her Romeo *dottore* make love to her she had done the wrong thing, in Toby's judgement. After so very protracted a climb to the peak of sensation, it was pretty sure Ottorino wouldn't be able to do much for her for hours. But she must have known that before she began.

Toby had his answer soon enough. Marina got up and went to a superb breakfront dressing-table veneered in symmetric contrast patterns and came back to Ottorino with a large bottle of 4711 Eau de Cologne. She soaked his white linen handkerchief with it and wiped it over his sweating belly and in his groins and down the insides of his thighs inside his trouser-legs. She lifted his limp and shrunken part and gently wiped that, then flicked his purple tie over his shoulder and raised his shirt-front to get at his black-haired chest. That revived him enough to open his eyes and smile at her while he murmured words that Toby did not catch.

What followed interested him particularly as it answered his mental query about Marina's intentions. She held out a hand to Ottorino and together they moved across to the four-poster. She didn't bother to turn the cover down, she got straight on to it and lay on her back. Before he joined her there, Ottorino took off his vivid tie and his impossible black-and-white shoes. His trousers he kept on, which indicated to Toby that his guess was correct – Ottorino was in no condition to climb on to Marina's belly and rampage her.

But he pulled her pretty *crêpe-de-Chine* slip up to her waist and took her knickers off. She smiled at him and said something which brought a pleased grin to his over-handsome face. Then he arranged himself face down between her parted legs and showered kisses by the dozen – by the gross almost – on her bare belly. He worked his way with calculated slowness to her bush of brown curls and the thick pouting lips there to be found. Toby's view of the action was very restricted now they had moved from chair to bed. The four-poster was set sideways to the door, not end-on, so that Marina's raised thigh blocked most of the view but for Ottorino's matinee-idol profile.

For a man who'd experienced unbelievably intense emotions not five minutes before, Ottorino's assault was ardent to say the least of it. Limp and useless though his male part had become, his tongue was evidently strong and tireless – and he was using it in the right place. Marina's head rolled from side to side on the pillows and she panted like a steam-engine rolling up an incline at full throttle. *Si, si, si, tesoro mio!* she was gasping out as Ottorino plied his wily tongue and hit the right spot. Before another minute had passed her silk-stockinged feet jerked up off the bed and her legs kicked out in the air in an uncontrollable flurry.

There's no doubt about that, thought Toby, his emotions high and pent, *he's hit the bullseye!* The very violence of Marina's release had its effect on Ottorino, who seemed to burrow deeper down still between her thrashing thighs and staunchly redoubled his efforts. Marina's climax turned into the longest Toby had ever in his life witnessed or even believed humanly possible. She kicked and screamed, squirmed and squealed, and thumped at Ottorino's sleek head with her fists, until Toby became anxious that they were doing each other a dire mischief.

Not a bit of it – after an astounding five or six minutes of sustained shrieking and fierce spasms, Marina collapsed limply and lay still with her eyes closed and her jaw hanging slackly.

Ottorino levered himself up until he was kneeling between her splayed legs and looked down at her with an odd expression on his face. At least, Toby thought it an odd look, but he might have been mistaken, only seeing him sideways and not full face. But he thought there was more desperation than admiration in it – which made a sort of sense. On the other hand, the look might have been one of calculation, as if the man was telling himself he still had Marina under control. In which case he was fooling himself, in Toby's estimation.

Staring fixedly for so long through the keyhole was starting to make Toby's sight swim. He straightened his aching back and sat back on his heels – and pressed both hands over the jerking hardness inside his clothes. What to do? He could find his way back to his own room and try his luck with Maria the maid. She might not agree to lie down for him but she'd demonstrated her willingness to oblige by hand – which would at least bring him blessed relief from his high-tension frustration. Not that she would be easy to get hold of, it being still siesta-time. Worth a try, though.

He took a last look through the keyhole before he departed to trace the labyrinthine passages and suites. Ottorino was on his side, an arm curled under his head and his rumpled silver-grey trousers halfway down his legs. He appeared to be deeply asleep with his back to Marina. She was sitting on the side of the bed in her slip and silk stockings, and her expression was one that might be interpreted as apprehension. Or maybe not – perhaps it was only annoyance that Ottorino was so obviously coming to the end of his useful service.

Toby took a chance – he tapped with one finger on the bedroom door. There was a long pause – he looked through the keyhole to see Marina on her feet by the bed and staring at the door. She glanced down at the sleeping man and then back at the door. She probably thought it was her maid tapping discreetly. Toby stood up and tapped again. After a delay of ten or fifteen seconds he heard a low voice close to the other side of the door.

'*Si?*' it said. He tapped again very lightly and waited. The handle turned and the door was opened a little. Marina's face showed astonishment when she saw who was there. She looked back over her bare shoulder at the bed, anxious that Ottorino should not be disturbed.

'I must talk to you,' Toby said softly, and he reached in to clasp her bare upper arm and pull her into the sitting room – a smooth and fast action which took her by surprise. All the same she closed the door quietly behind her and nodded her head to indicate he should follow her away from the bedroom. Across the room she sat down on the long Venetian green-and-gold sofa and smoothed her pale lemon silk slip down her thighs, although it wouldn't reach as far as her knees.

'I was taking my afternoon nap,' she said, with total lack of truth. 'What do you want, Toby?'

What he did *not* want just then was conversation. His need was too urgent for the niceties of social convention. Nor when she looked closely at him could she imagine that was why he was in her quarters – there was a tousled and fraught look about him, standing there in his shirt-sleeves, with his light yellow hair untidy and his cheeks flushed pink from his inner stress.

Without a word he ripped open his trousers and let his stiff *cazzo* flip out, swollen and flushed with passion. He didn't for an instant wait for Marina's reaction – he flung himself on his knees at her unshod feet and took hold of her ankles.

'What are you doing . . .?' she began to say, and by the third word he'd bent her knees upward and set her feet up on the sofa she sat on, the ungainly position completely exposing her dark-brown tuft and the shiny-wet lips of her split to him.

'Oh you beast!' she exclaimed, no longer in any doubt what he wanted, and there was a note of admiration in her voice besides the routine reproach. For all her forwardness and initiative in sexual encounters, Marina secretly harboured romantic thoughts of being dominated and brutally used by a strong man – a trait Toby had noticed in her when they talked on the Rialto Bridge.

'Take your slip off,' he said, his fingers teasing her *fica* – wet from Ottorino's tongue and from the arousal it had caused. She obeyed him at once, shrugged the flimsy garment up over her head and dropped it beside her on the worn damask upholstery of the sofa. She tucked her heels back under her ample bottom and splayed her knees wide to give Toby an unobstructed view of her belly and plump breasts.

But he was too furiously aroused and desperate to waste time handling her. He held his stiff length in his hand and guided the big purple head into her wetness, pushed strongly and slid right in. She gasped and parted her knees wider, pulling them back until they were touching her breasts, opening herself to the utmost for him.

A fierce pleasure gripped him hard while he stabbed into her hot belly with short fast strokes.

'Faster, faster!' she moaned, catching his frenzied mood.

'Yes!' he panted, his voice harsh and shaky at the stress of the tremendous physical sensations that were overpowering him.

His fingernails dug hard into the soft flesh of her bottom and with a groan he released his pent-up lust into her in great gushes. Marina shuddered and gasped at his ferocity and rolled her eyes upwards as the climax took her. From inches away Toby stared into her upraised and dark-flushed face with a fixed and glassy glare, while his belly clenched in ecstatic throes.

For seconds that felt like minutes, like hours, like timeless Eternity, they heaved and jerked and moaned together in unison, the many bracelets on Marina's wrists jangling together to the spasms of her body. Neither she nor Toby noticed the door to the bedroom open slowly, or knew Ottorino was peering at them in their cataclysmic joy. He stared with dull eyes, holding his unbuttoned trousers up round his middle with one hand. For ten seconds he stared at the scene on Marina's sofa, then with a shrug he closed the door and went wearily back to bed.

When their delirium had run its course and they became aware of their surroundings once more, Marina stroked Toby's face and smiled at him in a calculating sort of way, as if weighing up his potential as a replacement. He returned her smile, just as calculating, though for another reason. He was still pleasantly embedded in her clasping slipperiness and it was in his mind to seize the initiative and establish a moral hold on her.

'That was stupendous,' he said, fondling her heavy breasts, 'let's move into the bedroom and do it again lying down. I want to get on top of you and ravish you into the mattress.'

'Toby . . .' she breathed, her dark brown eyes blinking for just a second. It was impossible to take him into the bedroom while Ottorino was fast asleep on the four-poster with his trousers down. And it was equally impossible to explain why she couldn't take Toby into the bedroom. In silent amusement he watched her face and the curious emotions that flickered across it – like at cinema screen – while she beat her brains furiously for what to say.

'There isn't time now,' she said, looking truly disappointed, 'I've got to go out to meet someone. If I don't get dressed now I shall be late.'

'Man or woman?' he asked, dragging out the agony for her.

'A woman friend,' she said at once, 'you've met her – Flavia Tornante.'

'The politician's wife,' said Toby, recalling the slim woman in pink who had sat next to him at Delphine's dinner party. The woman with all the modern jewellery round her neck and wrists – politics seemed to be a profitable business in

Italy. 'Let her wait – she'll understand when you explain what detained you.'

'I can't do that,' Marina said, her hands on his shoulders to push him away from her, so that his dwindling part slipped out of her warmth. 'It's not just social with Flavia. But I'll make it up to you, darling. I'll come to your room tonight and we'll make love till dawn.'

With that he let her go, satisfied with his success in giving her a difficult few minutes over the boyfriend in the bedroom in best French-farce style. And pleased that she had promised a frolic that night. He bobbed his head to plant a kiss on each breast and stood up to leave.

NINE

In the Contessa Marina's sitting room, alongside the bottles on the highly desirable rococo sideboard, there stood a large and elaborate silver frame and in it a photograph. It showed Marina with a man of fifty or thereabouts, in a well-cut English-style blazer and a striped cravat, and between them with an arm about each was the most beautiful girl Toby had ever seen. She had an oval face and long, straight black hair down to her shoulders.

He guessed it was Marina's missing daughter, the one who had run off with a young chap, according to Adalbert Gmund – Bianca was her name. And the man in the photograph had to be Marina's missing husband, Massimo, who had taken himself permanently off to Rome to chase pretty young men – again according to Adalbert – who might be slandering the absent Count.

It was very obvious Marina was attracted to men with dark and smouldering film-star profiles and soulful eyes. Assuming that the photo was a true likeness, Count di Torrenegra could have understudied Rudolf Valentino or Ramon Novarro in any movie and melted the heart of every female in the cinema. Not to mention the effect on other sensitive parts of their anatomy. And now she had Ottorino Pavese – a man cast in the same mould. If ever his so-called business interests let him down he could begin a new career as an international gigolo.

Such were Toby's unkind thoughts on seeing the photograph in the heavy silver frame. He noticed it as he left Marina's room, as he was almost pushed out, in fact, she being anxious to get rid of him in case Ottorino woke up. Not that it meant anything much to Toby now that he had slaked his urgent passion – he had guessed from the start that Marina was the sort who always took up with men who used her for their own private ends. Her nature guaranteed disaster every time.

Toby had more sense than to let himself be drawn into her web of fantasy emotion, of that he was certain. He intended to enjoy everything she offered while he was in Venice – and then slide away with a fond but quick goodbye as soon as his business with Mrs Tandy was completed. But that was still some way off and a more immediate consideration was what to do for the rest of the day? After his hard thrash between Marina's legs he was in no mood to climb back up into the dusty attic and carry on looking at old furniture. Nor, when he reached his own room, was he in the mood to lie down and doze.

He took a shower and dressed in clean clothes, deciding to go out. Where, he didn't know, but there was so much he hadn't yet seen in Venice. The siesta hour was coming to an end and there were people beginning to move in the streets as he ambled along towards the church of San Stefano and its square. An idea came into his head and he went straight past the cafe where he meant to sit and order a cooling drink. Adalbert's friend – purveyor of royal photo-albums with doubtful origins – might prove to be a useful source of information if tackled alone.

His shop was not far from the Fenice Theatre, which sounded simple enough, except that there were canals round three sides of the theatre and a complicated system of little bridges to get where you wanted to go. After a try or two, Toby found the right alley and there was Corradini's shop-window with its tatty old books and dog-eared lithographs you wouldn't wrap a pound of sausages in.

The shop door was unlocked and a cracked bell sounded when he pushed it open and went in and tapped on the counter. There was a pause before the proprietor appeared from the back room, his spectacles pulled down his nose. He was wearing a sort of loose grey dust-jacket over dark trousers and a white shirt, a tie of horizontal red-and-blue stripes the only colourful item on him. Even his black-dyed hair had a faded look – perhaps he was due for a visit to his barber for a quick rinse in whatever inky stuff was used to ward off the encroachments of late middle age.

'Signor *Giovese*!' said Niccolo Corradini, nearly remembering his visitor's name. 'It is good of you to visit me. Please come into my private room and take a seat. I've had an offer for the very rare Rops portfolio but I haven't sold it yet, if you are interested.'

He ushered Toby into his musty den behind the shop and to a chair. To judge by the bits and pieces littering a table behind Corradini's own chair, he had been working on something using a magnifying glass and artist's brushes of various sizes, all of them very small. He had put away whatever it was he was turning into a valuable antique before coming into the shop, perhaps in the long drawer under the table.

'Thank you, but drawings of big Belgian ladies in the throes of lust are not my cup of tea,' said Toby politely. 'I was more interested in the photograph album Herr Gmund showed me.'

'Yes, a very rare collection,' said Corradini, whose English was better than Toby remembered. 'In fact, a unique collection, as there is only one.'

'I wonder if that's true,' said Toby, remaining very polite. 'When someone goes to the expense of finding suitable women and paying them to pose naked, and the trouble of making a leather album look thirty years old, and researching the names to write on the pictures – maybe he can recover his investment and make a good profit by selling just one album. But surely it would be very tempting to make several and offer them in different parts of Europe to collectors of Edwardian erotica. Don't you agree, Signor Corradini?'

'You are suggesting that the album of King Eduardo's pictures is not genuine?' said Corradini, sounding angry, not dismayed.

'I do not suggest,' Toby countered, 'I state categorically – the album you sold Herr Gmund is a fake.'

Corradini was up on his feet, waving his arms like a windmill in his anger, hissing at Toby to leave his shop at once.

'Be calm,' said Toby, not budging, 'I know the album is faked because I saw one exactly like it in London not six months ago. It belongs to a rich old Baronet who met the British ladies of King Teddy's harem. His eyes were as dim as his memory, because he was convinced the photographs he had were real. And so was I – till Adalbert showed me his identical album.'

There was not a word of truth in Toby's story but he thought it sounded convincing enough to change Niccolo Corradini's tune and in this he was correct.

'*Dio!*' exclaimed the dealer, smacking his own forehead in a gesture of deepest dismay, 'then I have been cheated by the man from whom I bought it! I have been deceived by a man I trusted and have known for years! He showed me a letter written by an English milord to prove the album was genuine. I bought it from him in good faith, Signor *Giovannesi*, and I sold it to Signor Gmund, a collector who is also a friend, also in good faith.'

Toby grinned at him, impressed by the display of emotion in so futile a cause. Corradini misunderstood the grin.

'I must go to the Palazzo Malvolio to inform Signor Gmund of this terrible discovery and give him back the money,' said he, pathos in his voice, his arms no longer waving about. 'He will be most upset – or have you spoken to him already, Signor?'

'He's very happy with his photographs of naked ladies,' Toby said, 'why should I shatter his illusions?'

'But he must be told the truth,' said Corradini, although his statement sounded rather more like a question.

Toby shrugged.

'Look here,' he said, 'you can't expect me to believe that as wily a dealer in exotica as you was taken in by a fake album of naughty photos. You knew when you acquired it that it was dud. In fact, speaking very frankly, Niccolo old chum, I think it's highly possible you had a hand in putting it together. It could have been your swindle from the beginning. How many King Edward photo-albums have you sold to rich idiots so far?'

Corradini sat down again looking thoughtful. He didn't answer the question, but he became slightly more open.

'No, Signor *Giovo*,' he said, mutilating Toby's name even more curiously under the stress of his emotions, 'it was not my idea – the honour goes to a young colleague. But I too must speak as frankly as you have. You have no means of disproving the authenticity of Signor Gmund's album. You *say* you have seen one like it but words are easy. You cannot show this so-called album as proof because you do not have it. But I can show the letter signed by Milord Buckingham in support of my claim.'

'You misunderstand. I don't want to prove or disprove anything at all. I want you to know that I'm not taken in. And if ever a suspicion arose in Adalbert Gmund's head whether the stuff that you've sold him might not be genuine – not just the album alone but the rest of his collection – you'd lose more than just one customer. He'd be sure to spread the word round Venice amongst the other collectors, which would be bad for your business.'

'What is it you want to keep silent?' Corradini asked, his colourless eyebrows creeping up towards his dingily black hair. 'Money, I suppose. I have very little. My colleague takes the profit and leaves me only a small commission on the sale.'

Toby leaned back in his uncomfortable chair and laughed.

'You're a natural actor, Niccolo,' he said, 'you should be on the stage in one of that chap Goldoni's Venetian comedies.'

His use of the other's first name brought a different note to the proceedings. Niccolo Corradini looked at him thoughtfully.

'*Ebbene*,' he said with a lopsided smile, 'well then? What do you want?'

'It's not so much what I want as what I can offer,' said Toby carefully. 'I shall be here in Venice for another two weeks or so, if all goes according to plan. Between then and now there's a proposition I am turning over in my mind – with considerable possibilities for making money.'

'Ah, that can be very interesting, Signor Toby,' Niccolo said as he pulled at his lower lip, 'what sort of proposition?'

'I'm not ready yet to lay it out – I need another day or two. First I must know whether I can trust you as a partner. Second, do you know Ottorino Pavese?'

'You must decide for yourself if you can trust me,' Niccolo said, 'as for *Dottore* Pavese, I am acquainted with him.'

'Done business with him?'

'Perhaps. Why do you want to know?'

'That's something else I shall explain later, when I tell you what I have in mind. What did you trade together – terracotta plaques from the brothels of Pompeii – something like that?'

'We are not partners yet, you and I,' Niccolo said mildly.

'True enough. Let's go and have a drink together. Is there a bar or a cafe round here? Or do we walk to the Piazza and join the tourists?'

'There's a cafe beside the Fenice.'

He locked up the shop carefully and they set out together up the narrow alley.

'There's something you can do for me,' said Toby, 'a token of goodwill, if you like.'

'What is it?'

'I found one of the girls in the photograph album attractive, in an amusing sort of way, you understand. If it's possible to arrange, I'd like to meet her.'

'Meet her?' Niccolo repeated, raising his scraggy eyebrows again.

'Meet her as she is in the photo.' said Toby.

'Naturally,' Niccolo said with a casual shrug, 'there's only one reason to meet any of the women who posed for the pictures. Perhaps it can be arranged – I shall make enquiries. Which one interests you?'

Toby did not reply until they were seated at a table outside a cafe corner-on to the Fenice Theatre and a waiter had brought the drinks they ordered. Niccolo had Scotch whisky, while Toby had dry vermouth with ice and soda-water.

'The name at the bottom of the photograph, supposedly in the handwriting of His late Majesty, is Hortense,' he said, raising his glass in salute to his companion. Niccolo nodded back as he listened. 'She is wearing black stockings and nothing else, and she is sprawled across an armchair, with her legs crossed.'

'I know the one you mean,' said Niccolo. 'I don't know what her real name is, but I can find out. She lives in Padova – you English call it Padua. The photographs were taken there.'

'Padua – yes, the train came through it on the way to Venice, and it's not far inland from here,' said Toby.

'About forty kilometres,' Niccolo confirmed. 'Livy, the historian of Rome, was born there in 59 BC. It will be a short journey by train for the Signorina. Why have you chosen to meet that one? Do you find her very attractive – more than the others?'

It was a difficult question to answer. By accepting money to be photographed naked for the bogus album she had demonstrated that she was not a woman of good family or a respectable way of life. In fact, there could be no doubt what she was. She earned the same living as Adalbert's plump friend, Rosa Benedetti. But there was something about her – probably the reason why she was selected for the album – a look of *don't-give-a-damn* which had amused Toby and held his attention.

Why he should bother with the elaborate affair of getting her to Venice, he wasn't sure. It was perhaps useful as a trial of Niccolo Corradini's willingness to be helpful, though that was only an excuse. More honestly, it was about the satisfaction of a passing whim and might turn out to be a big disappointment.

'She has a nice smile,' he answered, evading the question.

Niccolo flapped his hands and shrugged his shoulders almost up to his shoulders.

'There will be some expenses,' he said, 'the train ticket – a gentleman like you will naturally wish the Signorina to travel in the First Class. You cannot take her to the Palazzo Malvolio and you will require a room in a discreet hotel. Do you want me to arrange that for you?'

'I don't want to meet her in a hotel,' said Toby. 'I want to take her out into the lagoon in a gondola. Can you arrange that for me – a discreet gondolier?'

'I have several friends who are gondoliers. There will be no problem. It will be necessary to have a covered gondola, so you and the Signorina are not observed while you are together.'

'Yes,' Toby agreed, 'the sort of gondola with a roof that you see in old pictures of Venice, where a gent in knee breeches and lace cuffs is giving a hand down into the boat to a young lady in a black mask and a crinoline.'

'You wish to dress for the Carnival, Signor Toby?'

'No, that was just by way of example. The young lady may wear whatever she pleases, as I intend to take her clothes off while we are gliding across the water. All except her stockings, that is. I should like her to wear black silk stockings, so that she will look as she did in the photograph.'

'*Molto bene,*' said Niccolo, sounding faintly amused, 'leave all to me. I will inform you when the arrangements are made and when the Signorina arrives at the railway station. It will take a day or perhaps two days.'

With that they parted, Toby paying for the drinks. He drifted through the early evening strollers, pausing to look into shops as the fancy took him, back towards the Palazzo Malvolio. He was wondering if he'd made a dreadful mistake asking Corradini to find the woman in the photograph for him. And as for having her in a gondola – he must have lost his senses to even suggest it. Even in a closed craft, the awareness that a gondolier in a striped shirt and straw boater was never more than three paces away the whole time was practically guaranteed to keep him limp and useless. The whole episode would turn into a fiasco, with a strange woman curling her lip at his feebleness.

It would be better to go back right away to Corradini's shop and tell him to call it off. For long minutes Toby stood dithering in front of a tiny food shop with a vast array of massive types of sausage dangling in rows. *Salami, mortadella* ... he knew only those two names. Long, livid, gnarled lengths of choice meat ... he turned away from the display and continued his walk with his mind made up – he would go through with the rendezvous afloat. This might be the only time in his life when he had the chance of a frolic in a gondola. Marina might do it, if he asked, but then it would be on her terms, not his.

When he reached the Palazzo the liveried doorman bowed deeply and in broken English gave him to understand that Signora Tandy had expressed a wish to see him on his return.

'Thank you,' said Toby, 'where?'

The doorman said La Signora was in the Biblioteca, which Toby guessed was the Italian word for Library ... wherever that was in the rambling old Palladian structure. The difficulty was quite simply resolved – a footman was summoned to conduct him to it. Short of asking, there seemed no easy way to determine just how many of these footmen in yellow and blue there were on the pay roll, though that seemed a vulgar way of expressing it. It was unsettling that Toby couldn't remember seeing the same footman twice, with the exception of the man who guarded the entrance to the square on the landward side of the palace and the one on the door of the Grand Canal entrance.

The one guiding him now led him up the marble staircase with the weapons and through interminable picture-hung corridors and rooms, past rows of marble busts of Emperors, Senators, Generals and assorted heroes, past the Renaissance bronzes of mythical personages displaying themselves in the nude, and past endless arrays of artistic bric-à-brac acquired by twenty generations of Malvolios. Though Toby had never yet been inside Buckingham Palace, he thought it must be rather like this, with so much magnificence on display everywhere that no one noticed the art treasures any longer.

The footman ushered him with a bow into a large room that had floor-to-ceiling bookshelves round three sides, the other side being windows overlooking the Grand Canal. The shelves were all packed tight with old-looking volumes bound in leather, with a Malvolio coat of arms embossed on the spine in tarnished gold. Delphine Tandy was sitting at a large writing desk of very dark walnut, with legs carved as semi-naked women – their breasts on show but floating drapery below the waist. Toby put it at about 1650, which made it older than the palace itself, saved maybe when the first Malvolio palace burnt down.

She glanced up from a daunting array of what looked very much like bills strewn over the desk top and asked him to sit down, not sounding very friendly.

He sat and gazed at her in what he hoped was an encouraging sort of way. By the look of her she had been in the palace all day working on the accounts, for she was dressed informally in an outfit of hip-length tobacco-brown blouse over a pleated skirt a shade of two darker. The clothes were from a good house but not very new. Nevertheless, her chestnut hair was skilfully pinned up on her head and she had an air of grandeur about her which was independent of what she wore. Even in a coal sack she would still keep that regal look, Toby thought, wondering how.

Unwelcome though the thought might be, it could be something to do with her physical stature and presence. For instance, Sally the bone-thin Contessa across the other side of the Grand Canal never managed that regal look – at most she could assume an air of authority clearly based on having more money than you did. A substitute that worked on the lower orders, maybe. Delphine did not have any money – at least, not a fraction of what Sally had, unless she sold everything in the Palazzo Malvolio. But she had the look of being born to command others.

'Mr Jervis,' she began very formally, taking Toby by surprise after their romp together in bed on Saturday night, 'extremely disturbing stories have reached me about you. I'm sorry to have to speak to you on a matter which is not my business, but while you are a guest here your doings reflect on me to some extent.'

Oh Lord, said Toby silently, *what's she heard about? Nothing to do with Marina – everybody has her, that's old news. Out on the balcony with Sally the night of the dinner party? Could we have been seen by somebody? She can't possibly know about the visit with Adalbert to his friend in the Castello district and that's not the sort of thing to bother her. Edwardian gents of her youth popped out to pick up a tart without any fuss. There's been some sort of breach of good manners, though I'm damned if I know what. It can't be the after-lunch scene at Princess Zita's with Anna-Louisa – that was expected of me – in fact, I was pretty much taken advantage of.*

'You met Contessa Flagranti in my house,' said Delphine, 'and you went to call upon her.'

'I first met her at Princess Zita's when Contessa Marina took me there for lunch,' said Toby, baffled and worried what this might lead to and very anxious to retain Delphine's goodwill.

'That's neither here nor there,' Delphine retorted, 'I cannot have you insulting my friends while you are under my roof.'

'Insult? Does she say that I've insulted her?' Toby asked, astonished by the accusation after the rampaging session he and Sally had enjoyed together.

'Not the Contessa,' said Delphine in a tight-lipped sort of way. 'Franco Flagranti is one of my oldest friends in Venice, and you have behaved abominably to him.'

'Count Flagranti, you mean? But I've never even met him!'

'He opened the door when you went there.'

'No, the major-domo opened the door,' said Toby. 'An elderly man with thin white hair and a black suit . . .'

The glare on Delphine's face said it all.

'Oh my God!' Toby exclaimed, trying very hard not to smile. 'Don't tell me I tipped the Count himself!'

'You know very well who it was – he was here at dinner with Sally last Saturday.'

'If he was, he made no impression at all on me,' Toby said in considerable surprise. 'I took him for a butler when he opened the door at the Palazzo Flagranti.'

What a gaffe! he was thinking, tipping a chap to let you in for a frolic with his wife. And an aristocrat! It must rate as the worst breach of manners in the whole of recorded Venetian history! But the thought was so comic that he had to laugh – and he thought he'd have a stroke suppressing it. Even then, he couldn't entirely keep his face straight and in a while, after secretly working out the implications herself, Delphine smiled briefly.

'Seriously – you didn't realise it was the Count?' she said. 'You gave him money to let you in to see his wife? He'll never live that down if it gets out. Poor Franco – you must promise not to tell a soul.'

'No one would believe me,' said Toby, and he wondered where the Count had got to while his wife was being ravaged in her elegant Art Deco drawing room. Surely some idea of what was going on must have crossed his mind? Or did he think they were discussing fashion and style for hours on end?

'Then we'll let the matter drop,' Delphine said.

The brief smile had gone from her face and her mood

seemed to Toby needlessly severe.

'How are you getting on up in the attics?' she asked, in the same sort of way she might ask an incompetent plumber when he'd be finished unblocking the drains. He saw that although she'd accepted his explanation of the misunderstanding with Flagranti she wanted him out of the Palazzo Malvolio as soon as possible. No doubt she thought him a liability about the place.

'The inventory is coming on nicely,' he said with a winning smile, 'another week should see it finished. Then I'll be in a position to make you a firm offer.'

It would be finished long before that but Toby had decided to spin it out. Why hurry because the owner wanted to get rid of him, when he was enjoying his stay in Venice?

'Good,' said Delphine, looking fairly pleased to hear that he would be soon gone.

She stood up and came round the massive desk as if to go to the door. Toby rose from his chair, but he decided he would not be dismissed like that – he wasn't one of the palace staff. Instead of opening the library door for Delphine to leave, he sauntered to the wall of books opposite the windows and looked at titles.

'Books of this quality in leather make wonderful furnishings for a room,' he said. 'Whose collection was it?'

'No one particular person,' Delphine said, 'the Malvolio were always patrons of the arts, including literature. The works of Goldoni are here somewhere, in several dozen volumes. And all of the Italian poets back to Dante and Petrarch.'

'He lived in a house facing the lagoon, on the quay not far from the Danieli Hotel,' said Toby, recalling this perfectly useless information from the *List of Illustrious* on the back of his map of Venice.

'Who did?' Delphine enquired, looking puzzled.

'Francesco Petrarcha, the poet. Dante came here on a visit too but I don't think they know where he stayed. An inn, maybe.'

'My word, you have been taking an interest in Venice!' said Delphine. 'The poets are over there on the other side of the room. These books are mostly on architecture,' and she took one from the shelf and opened it to show engravings in the text of buildings in the grand Palladian style.

Her tone had changed only slightly though, Toby noted –

she still had him listed as a nuisance about the place. He waited until she replaced the book on the shelf and turned to go, then with a quick stride forward he had her trapped against the bookshelves, his belly pushing against hers.

'Stop that!' she said.

Goodwill be buggered, he was thinking, *I won't be treated like an underling. She'll either sell the damaged furniture or not – and now I've found the triptych I don't really care one way or the other. So let's have less of the great lady and minion and rather more of the man and woman thing.* He smiled insolently at her and slid an arm round her waist to hold her still while he put his other hand up under her loose tobacco-brown blouse and felt her breasts through her thin chemise.

'Let go,' she said furiously. 'Who do you think you are!'

'I'm the man whose bed you crept into on Saturday night,' he retorted as he handled her fleshy delights vigorously. Far too large, he thought, *melons* where apples would be better. Through the thin silk that covered them he plucked at their soft buds.

'That was a mistake,' she said instantly, trying to wriggle free, 'I had a little too much to drink, but that doesn't mean you can do what you like because of a silly slip on my part.'

'You didn't think it silly at the time,' he pointed out, 'you told me it was marvellous. And I was absolutely wrung-out when you left. So don't try that *I was drunk* stuff – it won't wash.'

To save her the trouble of thinking up a reply, he closed her mouth with a long kiss, forcing his tongue between her lips. At the beginning she resisted, endeavouring to push him away from her, but soon he felt her begin to shiver against him.

'But why now?' she asked him curiously when the kiss at last ended. 'If you're so keen on me, how is it you never come to my bedroom?'

It sounded too silly to say he didn't know where her room was and didn't like to ask the servants in case it started gossip – besides, he had been well enough taken care of in the daytime. To avoid answering he reached down between her knees to slip a hand under her pleated skirt. She caught his wrist and stopped him at the moment he touched smooth bare flesh above the tops of her silk stockings.

'No, not here, Toby. Come to my room tonight.'

'Yes, tonight,' he agreed, forgetting he was expecting

Marina in his own room that night, 'but I want you now as well.'

He was forcing his hand higher and higher between her thighs, against the downward drag of her hand. She clenched her teeth and squeezed her legs together tight but he was winning. When his fingers slipped past the lace and into the open leg of her knickers, she sighed in resignation and let go of his wrist.

'Suppose someone comes in,' she said, trying to sound logical and sensible. 'It would be very embarrassing.'

'Stop fussing,' he said, running his fingertips through the thick curls of her fleece. When she felt him stroking the lips of her *fica* she let her muscles relax and her thighs move apart into a more comfortable position. An instant later he eased his middle finger into her.

'Have you done it in the Biblioteca before?' Toby asked with a grin on his handsome face.

'No, of course not,' she gasped, her belly squirming slowly to the jolts of pleasure caused by a finger playing delicately over her bud. He caressed her deftly with one hand while he was unbuttoning his trousers all the way down, then took her hand and pushed it through the slit of his underwear. The stiffness and strength of what throbbed against her palm quickly overcame any initial reluctance she may have had.

'This is highly indecent,' she said, 'at least we could go to my room if you insist on making love in broad daylight.'

'Here and now,' said he, 'not somewhere else later.'

She sighed and shrugged her shoulders in acquiescence, taking hold of his hardness. Her remark about daylight made him wonder what Count Rinaldo Malvolio's preference could had been. Surely the afternoon siesta hour was when Italians enjoyed a frolic? The thought vanished from his mind as Delphine slid her hand up and down his solid length, sending rapid thrills through him. A gasp escaped him as his mouth found hers again and his tongue fluttered on her tongue in much the same way that his fingers were fluttering between her legs.

He raised her thin pleated skirt up to her waist and felt her trembling against him. His fingers hooked over the top of her silk and lace knickers and eased them almost down to her knees.

'Come on, then!' she murmured, suddenly impatient, and both hands went into his open trousers. She took out his *cazzo* and steered it up between her meaty thighs – and at the first moist touch he knew she was open and ready. He pressed straight in.

At least she had stopped bothering whether anyone might come into the Biblioteca or not. Toby slid in and out strongly, both hands clasping the cheeks of her bare bottom. They were large and soft, not at all the sort of thing he admired, but he found the weight and texture strangely exciting, as was the roundness and warmth of her bare belly against him. For a moment or two he felt real anxiety that he might succumb to the cheap lure of lower-class taste for plump women – how truly awful it would be to spend the rest of his life lying on top of fat round bellies and *tette*, as the Italians called them, like fleshy balloons!

The anxiety was overwhelmed and carried away by sensations of delight flooding through him. Delphine was pushing her loins at him in time with his thrusts and there was no opportunity then for doubts or reservations about elegance, style, aesthetics or any other abstracts – only the huge and swelling desire to gush his desire into her wet and welcoming *fica*.

'Rotten beast, making me do it here!' she gasped faintly as she bumped her belly against him harder and faster. Each time she jerked forward he felt his hardness slither deeper into her until their bellies smacked together. It was not him doing it to her any more – she had taken over and was doing it to him! And making him experience fierce palpitations of pleasure.

He pressed her harder back against the tiers of leather-bound books and tried to snatch back the initiative, ramming into her as strongly as he could. *Let me, let me!* he was gasping as he dug his fingernails fiercely into the flesh of her soft bottom. But the rhythmic contractions of the velvety channel that held him prisoner was driving him into a delirium of ecstasy, beside which nothing mattered at all. Delphine was moaning and shaking against him, out of control and running away with him.

There was nothing Toby could do, even if he had wanted. With a wolfish howl he drove faster and harder until he fountained his lust into her in long spasms. She squealed and squeezed him so tightly to her heaving bosom that it felt as if all his ribs were cracking. He didn't care – in the ferocious ecstasy that had seized them both he wanted to destroy her and be destroyed by her at the same time. He rammed and gasped, gushed and shook on wobbly legs, moaned and sighed, convulsed and cried, hanging on to her by his embedded fingernails, while she shrieked and squirmed against him like a wild beast caught in a steel trap.

When at long last the tremendous sensations faded and slowly they became calmer, Delphine sagged back against the books, her head hanging forward, her arms falling away from Toby to dangle loosely at her sides. Gradually he unclenched his fingers from her bottom and leaned against her to support himself, his knees being shaky still.

'What a rotter you are, making me do that here,' she said with a note of wonder in her voice.

TEN

There were four at dinner that evening in the Small Dining Room – Delphine Tandy in dashing black and white, Contessa Marina in off-the-shoulder flame revealing about two thirds of her bosom, Adalbert Gmund looking vaguely old-fashioned, and Toby casually elegant. Padre Pio had gone to Chioggia, Adalbert said.

Seeing Toby's blank look, he explained Chioggia was an island at the southern end of the Venetian lagoon, twenty-five kilometres away. The Malvolio had been connected with the cathedral there ever since it was rebuilt in the seventeenth century – something to do with the choir, Toby gathered, though the explanation was not all that clear – and the family Confessor was there as representative of Malvolio interests. How a defunct family could in any sensible manner have interests to represent was beyond Toby to figure. A polite smile and nod seemed the appropriate response.

They were well into the meal, beyond the grilled giant *funghi* and the deep-fried calamari with lemon slices, the white bean and pasta soup, the risotto with tiny clams, and were enjoying thin-sliced veal served cold in tuna sauce with capers, when it struck Toby that he had by sheer carelessness put himself into a highly fraught position. Earlier that day, after his bizarre encounter with Marina in her sitting room, she had promised him to come to his room that night. And later that day, when he had been on the verge of ravishing Delphine in the Library, she had asked him to go to her room that night.

Two women, one night. Two *ficas*, one *cazzo*. It wasn't going to work. And whichever one he chose, he would offend the other. If Marina came to his room and found he wasn't there, she would guess immediately where he had gone and why – nothing seemed to be secret between the two sisters. If he didn't show up on time in Delphine's room, she would instantly guess why.

This is preposterous, he said to himself, in deep chagrin. And it wasn't a question of choosing between two lithe young women. Not a bit of it! He felt trapped between two aunt figures, two overfleshed middle-aged women eager to clamp him to their plump bellies with their meaty thighs. It seemed to him that Venice wasn't living up to his expectations – where were the slender and darkly beautiful Signorinas? He was being fobbed off – and made to feel guilty about it! Well, Delphine and Marina would wait in vain that night for him to jump on either of their fat bellies and ravage them. They could get as angry as they liked – he simply didn't care.

Apart from a certain amount of embarrassment, did it matter? As the Chinese saying went: *shame fades at nightfall, but debt endures from day to day*. So if he was booted out of the Palazzo Malvolio by Delphine Tandy because she felt scorned, he had the triptych to take with him, and his instinct told him that was valuable enough to make a great difference to his life. On the other hand, he would like to complete the deal and acquire the furniture, partly for the sake of his own future reputation and also to show Fitzroy Dalrymple and his father that he was a man to be trusted.

'Are you feeling quite well, Toby?' Marina asked, seeing how flushed his face was. Delphine looked across the table at him with a slightly perturbed expression and enquired if the veal wasn't to his liking. Adalbert reached over to pat him on the back and push a glass of chilled San Pellegrino mineral water into his hand.

He refused the water and downed almost a full glass of Soave, beautifully cold, whereupon the footman stationed behind him refilled the glass. When he felt a little better, he reassured the company that nothing was amiss, and the meal and chatter, resumed. But something was very badly amiss and he racked his brain for a way of setting it right. If there was one. If not, then a way out that wouldn't disgrace him beyond redemption in the eyes of the ladies.

Nothing occurred to him as plates were changed deftly by the attentive footmen and the veal was followed by peach ice-cream, local cheeses and fresh fruit. Even when the four of them rose from the table and moved into the Yellow Drawing Room to drink coffee and sticky Italian liqueurs, he could think of no way out. Then, while Delphine was in discussion with the major-domo over some household arrangement or other and Marina was out of the room briefly – to powder her nose, as she put it – the gleam of an idea struck Toby. It was a long shot but better than nothing. He turned to Adalbert Gmund and, in a rapid mutter, explained his awkward predicament. The Austrian gazed at him pop-eyed for a moment or two and laughed.

'If you can get me out of this, Adalbert, when I get back to London I'll send you something special for your collection.'

'*Ja?* What will you give me?'

Toby weighed up his man and thought he had the ideal bait for him. Lewd and snobbish all in one, that would get him.

'You know of Magda Lupescu, of course,' he said, 'mistress of Crown Prince Carol of Rumania.'

'Everyone knows of her,' said Adalbert, his face displaying intense interest, 'there are many stories told in Society about her and the Prince.'

'How would you like a large photograph of her, taken recently in the Bois de Boulogne? Stark naked on horse-back.'

'*Ach*, I have heard from Marina this pastime of naked riding in the Bois,' said Adalbert with a grin. 'She told me you have a friend in Paris who took the photographs – is this true?'

'On my word of honour,' said Toby, lying without a flicker of embarrassment.

'There is more than one photograph, I have heard,' Adalbert said, his pale blue eyes gleaming with greed and lust, 'perhaps even of Madame being whipped on her bare bottom, yes?'

'Perhaps,' Toby agreed, sure now that the bait was taken and the hook ready to stick fast if he reeled in carefully.

'Tell me about it, please. What does it show, this picture?' Adalbert asked.

Toby thought quickly, inventing the details as he talked.

'It shows the lady naked, standing bare-foot in short grass and leaning against a horse's side, with her arms hanging over its back,' he said, 'her bare bottom is very well displayed. To the left stands the Prince in hacking jacket and jodhpurs, with a riding crop in his hand, slashing at her fleshy cheeks. It is a superlative photograph, an authentic eye-witness record of a fragment of European history in the making.'

'*Phantastich!*' Adalbert murmured. 'Does she stand with her legs apart or together?'

'Slightly apart,' said Toby, fairly sure it would be no great problem to get a photographer he knew well in London to set up the scene with a suitable girl, very early one morning in Bushy Park or somewhere out of the way. He'd need a male with a thick black moustache and a receding chin to impersonate the Prince.

'For the whipping photograph, perhaps I will rescue you from your difficult position,' said Adalbert.

'But I can't get any more copies,' Toby said in bogus dismay to get the hook in deeper. 'The French Secret Service found out that the pictures had been taken and confiscated the negatives. I'm sure President Briand has a set of prints.'

Marina was coming across the worn yellow and red carpet which gave this Drawing Room its name. She was smiling at Toby and evidently in a mood to resume their earlier encounter, just as soon as could be decently arranged.

'Good,' said Adalbert, 'that will make the photograph rarer and more valuable. Promise me the whipping picture and I will do everything to help you. Yes or no?'

'Payment by results,' said Toby quickly, 'get me out of this mess and the photo is yours.'

Then Marina was beside them and a footman brought round cups of coffee on a heavy silver tray and Delphine had finished her instructions to the major domo.

'Shall we play a rubber or two of bridge?' Delphine asked.

'Not tonight,' said Marina, sipping at her coffee, 'I'm sure I don't know why, but I'm quite exhausted. I'm going to have an early night for once.'

To make her point further, she yawned delicately, the back of a hand to her mouth. By rights she should be tired, Toby said to himself, she has had an exciting half hour with Ottorino in her bedroom and an even more exciting quarter of an hour with me in her sitting room afterwards. But her eyes are sparkling and she doesn't look tired – her plan for an early night has nothing to do with sleeping and everything to do with me.

'Do you know, I've been feeling slightly tired myself,' said Delphine, 'has it been exceptionally hot today? I was too busy with the household accounts to get out, even for an hour.'

'It has been a beautiful day,' said Adalbert, understanding what was going on and grinning.

'Really?' said Delphine dismissively. 'An early night will do us all good – Marina's quite right.'

574

'Then, while you ladies repair your beauty in sleep, I shall look after our young guest,' said Adalbert. 'Finish the coffee, Toby, and we will stroll to the Piazza and hear the band for an hour and drink a glass of cognac, *ja*?'

'That's dashed kind of you,' said Toby with a polite smile. He avoided the eyes of Delphine and Marina, certain that both of them were looking daggers at Adalbert for making this stupid suggestion. The two men rose together to bow politely and wish the sisters *buona notte* before leaving the Yellow Drawing Room. Adalbert led the complex way to the main staircase down to the Grand Canal frontage of the palace which surprised Toby who distinctly remembered Adalbert saying they'd stroll. But he was not going to argue with his rescuer, though so far it was only a temporary reprieve. The ladies would be waiting for him to return to the palace, Delphine in her own bed and Marina naked in his.

'Are we going to the Piazza?' he asked Adalbert.

They were sitting side by side in the gondola, sliding down the black waters of the Grand Canal, where tourists and honeymooners were ferried about by moonlight in true romantic style. Adalbert nodded briskly and in a low voice not to be overheard by the gondolier behind them explained that the palace servants gossiped tirelessly about their betters, with the result that everything was quickly known. Their destination would within an hour reach Delphine and Marina via their maids, who would hear it from a footman, who would be informed by the doorman, who in turn would have been told by the gondolier when he got back.

'I see,' said Toby, very thoughtful at the implications of so effective a chain of communication, 'so he drops us off and we carry on from there?'

'Correct.'

'Then where do we go?'

'You must wait and see. You have put yourself in my hands.'

'Is it really true that the servants spy on us in the palace – I mean, some chaps might find that embarrassing.'

Adalbert grinned at him slyly.

'It makes no difference whether you and I are embarrassed or not,' he said, 'we are watched. Who we talk to, which rooms we go into, when we go out and when we return. Those who live in a palace must tolerate their life being lived in public. There is no need to be alarmed. It was known when you made love to Marina and where, and with Delphine

– it was in the Library, I think, which is exceptional for her. Her custom is to take men friends to her own rooms and do it only in bed. It seems you have made a distinct impression to persuade her to break with the custom of many years.'

'Good God!' Toby exclaimed, appalled to learn that so much was known.

'Marina – now there is a cat of another colour, as we say,' Adalbert continued, enjoying Toby's obvious discomposure, 'with a man she finds *simpatico* she will do it anywhere, standing up or sitting down, on her back or on her knees. But this you have discovered already, according to what I have heard.'

'But I shall never be able to look either of them in the face again!' said Toby.

'There has been some gossip that you did things to one of the maids that a gentleman never does with servants,' Adalbert went on remorselessly. 'Delphine asked if I believed it, but I said that in my opinion you are an English gentleman and above such lapses from correct conduct. Some misunderstanding took place – the maid knowing no English and you having no Italian. Was this how it happened?'

'Absolutely,' said Toby, almost blushing at the memory of how he had pulled the chambermaid down on to his lap in an attempt to get a hand up her clothes. 'It was damned decent of you to stand up for me, Aldabert, and I am truly grateful.'

The gondola moved on steadily down the Grand Canal, past the lighted windows of the Palazzo Flagranti on the right bank and under the Accademia Bridge, the busy waterway broadening out as it approached its end. Toby stared carelessly at the soaring white colunms and domes of Santa Maria della Salute as they rowed past, and then the long low brick and stone buildings of the Customs House. It was surmounted by a gold ball, on which a life-size figure of Fortune stood and turned to show which way the wind was blowing.

That was the end of the Grand Canal, on the right now lay the wide Giudecca Channel, down which a cargo ship was making its way from the docks to wherever its destination lay. The gondola moved in to the left past the Gritti Palace Hotel and drew into the quay at the broad entrance to the Piazza San Marco, by the Doge's Palace. Toby climbed very carefully out of the swaying craft, by no means impressed by

Venice's characteristic mode of transport. He wondered yet again if the rendezvous he'd asked Niccolo Corradini to arrange with Signorina Blackstockings in a gondola was going to turn into a farce. Gondolas were damnably wobbly things – if you climbed aboard a girl spread out on her back and banged away too hard, you might turn the boat over and find yourself in deep water with your trousers down.

On the other hand, Venice's best-known adventurer, Casanova, claimed in his Memoirs that he'd rummaged Signorinas galore in gondolas so maybe they were more stable than they seemed. Toby stood on the grey-stone slabbed waterside between two tall and slender columns while Adalbert got himself cumbersomely ashore, thanked the gondolier and said various things to him in Italian which no doubt included the information that his services were no longer required that evening.

They walked side by side up past the eighteen pointed arches along the side of the Doge's Palace and stood for a moment looking at the strolling crowds in the Piazza. Both cafes were doing good business, their bands playing competitively across the Square at each other, and waiters busily at work between the long rows of outdoors tables, bringing coloured ice-creams, *cappucino* in small cups, and expensive drinks.

'Are we staying here for a drink?' asked Toby.

'No, I have many friends,' said Adalbert. 'We shall meet some of them and get drunk. But not here. Here it is not amusing.'

'How long can we keep going?'

'*Chi sa?* Who knows? When we become bored with the first lot of friends we shall meet some others and get drunker.'

'This is your plan, is it?'

Adalbert smiled at him seraphically and nodded.

'At dawn someone will take us to the Palazzo Malvolio,' said he, 'helpless as babes, as I think you say in English. Tomorrow morning we shall sleep until we recover. Then I shall apologise very humbly to Delphine and Marina for dragging you round town drinking all night. I take the blame for everything. I shall be in disgrace for a day or two and you will be the innocent,'

'Right – where do we start?'

'This way,' said Adalbert, leading off at a brisk pace past the Bell Tower and the golden Byzantine facade of St Mark's in the direction of the ornate Clock Tower, where a large group of sight-seers were waiting for the life-size bronze Moors on top to swing their hammers at the huge hanging bell and sound the hour of nine o'clock.

'I hope you have brought money with you,' he added by way of afterthought. 'It is not cheap to drink with my friends.'

'Some,' said Toby, and left it at that.

They passed under the colonnade and through a passageway and into a narrow street of shops. Evening strollers in pairs moved leisurely along, stopping to look into windows. Toby remembered going this way before – they were heading north and would reach the Rialto Bridge eventually. That being so, it would have been easier to have the gondolier take them there directly from the Palazzo Malvolio, instead of this elaborate roundabout route to cover their trail. Did it, after all, matter what the gondolier told the doorman? When he'd dropped them off, wherever it was, he couldn't know where they went after that.

But Adalbert was not making for the Rialto. He turned off the known street and less than five minutes later Toby was lost in a labyrinth of alleys, passages and footbridges over narrow back canals. It was not at all well lit now they'd left the main routes, and no one could be thought fanciful for wondering if it was entirely safe to venture, looking well-to-do, into these secluded parts.

'Where are we, Adalbert?'

'Castello,' said the Austrian, which was unhelpful, for Toby knew from his street map that the Castello district included at least a quarter of all Venice.

They turned a corner and found themselves at the beginning of a long street, long for Venice, that is, with very few lamps to illuminate it. The buildings on either side looked unnaturally tall, but that was surely a trick of the light – or of the lack of light. There was a neglected look about the whole street, an atmosphere of decay. They passed along between the houses, the stone slabbing broken underfoot, and Toby's heart was sinking at the sight of shutters barred across windows, not a chink of light escaping from within, and heavy closed doors which were sure to be bolted.

'Here we are,' said Adalbert, stopping by a more than averagely wretched paint-peeling and splintered door. The number beside it was 4463, which was absurd. The Venetian system of numbering houses was beyond him. Toby accepted.

'It is better if you give me your money,' Adalbert remarked, 'you are a stranger here and do not know the way of the house.'

'What is it – a *bordello*?' Toby asked, none too pleased.

'Of course not! It is the house of a good friend.'

'Then why do we need money? Does your friend charge for the drinks he serves his guests?'

'Certainly not!' said Adalbert, sounding indignant. 'There will be other guests and we do not know who. On some evenings one meets strange people here.'

It all sounded odd and slightly menacing, and Toby thought it only sensible to hand over all the paper money he had with him, which was a little over 3,000 lira, the equivalent of about £25 in sterling. He had left behind in the Palazzo Malvolio, locked in the rosewood bureau in his room, traveller's cheques drawn on the Westminster Bank amounting to another £80.

Adalbert hammered on the door with his fist until it opened a crack and yellow light flooded out. A woman Toby guessed to be a servant stood there, wearing black. She evidently recognised Adalbert, and stood aside to let him and Toby enter. They went up a flight of creaking wooden stairs behind her without a word said, hearing the sound of several voices ahead. They came to a large square room that was poorly lit and stuffy where, round a long table, sat six or seven men and women. The evidence of the littered table was that they had recently finished their dinner and were talking over more wine.

The host got up when Adalbert and Toby came into the room. He was a man in his forties, heavy-jowled and paunched from years of over-eating, his dark hair thin and streaked with grey, two gold teeth plainly visible when he spoke. He wore a dark suit that might have been expensive but now looked baggy and in need of pressing, and a plain green-and-blue silk tie down which he had spilled something during the meal. He greeted Adalbert with effusive hand-shaking and shoulder-patting, and bowed slightly when Toby was introduced, but that might have been mocking.

To judge by what Toby saw about him, Signor Lorenzo Bissa had seen better days. He had obviously been born and brought up in better circumstances and was now down on his luck, surrounding himself not with the sort of people invited to dinner by Mrs Tandy, but by the shifty pack sitting round the table eyeing the newcomers. The women were cheaply but flashily dressed, with bare arms and much cleavage on show, the men with an overbold yet furtive look. All were on the make, in Toby's book, and he saw the sense in Adalbert taking care of the money.

Signor Bissa made the guests sitting next to him change seats so he could have Adalbert on one side and Toby on the other. It was no doubt intended as a sort of honour, but for Toby it was an empty one, the host speaking practically no English beyond *chin chin* and *bottoms up* – two curious phrases he made much use of after he had filled large glasses with red wine for Toby and Adalbert from the impressive array of opened bottles stretching down the middle of the table. There must be an English phrase-book for foreigners, thought Toby, trying to empty his glass in long continuous swallows, and in this book are printed such odd and unlikely bits of pseudo-English as *bottoms up* and *bless my soul* and *will you take tea, Madam*?

The woman on Toby's left knew no more English than he Italian but her lively temperament more than made up for it. She was no great beauty but she made the most of what she had. Her frock was of some shiny black material, totally backless, and cut low enough in front to show off most of her chest. She had a string of artificial pearls round her throat, tied in a choker with an end hanging down in the broad space between her half-exposed breasts. They were modest in size, he noted, which may have been a minus factor in Italian eyes but drew his personal approval.

She had pushed her chair back a little from the table and her knees were on show, in shiny stockings. There was a long fringe to the bottom of her frock and, to Toby's eyes, it was a year or two out of date. It had probably been shortened, he thought, as hemlines crept up year after year. Her eyebrows had been shaved off completely and replaced with thin dark arches drawn in some cosmetic or other. Her lips were rouged to a dark red and her face was heavily powdered, perhaps to make less obvious the mole on her right cheek.

Her name was Fioretta, she said. She held him fascinated by the vivacity with which she carried him along in conversation, neither understanding the other's language, her hands never at rest but forever gesturing, touching, tracing concepts in the air. Her fingertips flitted over the back of his hand at one moment, tapped his wrist at another, touched his shoulder, his tie – a virtuoso performance that drew him closer towards her, until her perfume tickled his nostrils and engaged his senses. It was not an expensive French perfume but it was sensuous in its way, heady rather than subtle.

His glass was filled and refilled, by Lorenzo at first, then by Fioretta. The wine was drinkable but that was as much as he could say for it. All the same, the effect of more glasses than he counted while he and Fioretta were engrossed in each other's semi-intelligible conversation had its effect on him. He began to think he understood what she was chattering on about, a sure sign that drunkenness was approaching, and he began to believe that the few words of Italian he could manage were coherent and meaningful to his smiling companion.

Time passed and the company round the table drank and smoked cigarettes and talked and changed places to converse with other people. Some left, and newcomers arrived to greet Lorenzo and take a seat at his table and a glass or two of wine with him. A quarrel broke out between two women who shrieked at each other until their host silenced them with a roar. Of all this by-play Toby took no heed, he was happily drunk and content to exchange endless inanities with half-drunk Fioretta on whose stockinged knee his hand now rested, in the long fringe of her frock.

Next morning it was hard to remember anything much except the fringe of Fioretta's shiny black frock and the warmth of her thigh felt through her stocking. He woke up slowly to a headache that was devastating in its malignancy and a sick sensation down in his stomach that sent him staggering and groaning to the bathroom. When the worst had happened and his stomach felt slightly less queasy, he washed out his mouth with cold water, swallowed four aspirins and fell back into bed.

At least he was in his own bed – that is, the bed in the room assigned to him in the Palazzo Malvolio, the oversized bed with its head against the wall and crimson curtains hanging from the fist of a gold cherub up near the high ceiling. How he had got into it was another matter.

In the feverish half-sleep of a hangover he tried to remember if he'd made love to Fioretta. He knew he'd had his hand in the side of her backless frock to feel her breasts, though that was later on, after they'd left Lorenzo's, he thought. Adalbert had taken him to several places during the night – he could recall dark deserted streets, flights of dark stairs he'd stumbled up and down, a moonlight gondola ride from somewhere to somewhere else with five in the boat. Five? Fioretta had gone with them when they left Lorenzo's, and another woman as well – a woman with the reddish-gingery hair you could see in any painting by Titian. She kept sliding her hand in his trouser pocket. So who could the fifth person have been?

They'd been in someone's apartment and Adalbert and the other woman had played cards with the owner and two or three visitors while he went into the bedroom with Fioretta. But it was pretty vague in his recollection, except for feeling her breasts when she took the black shiny frock off. Her breasts were pleasingly modest in size, widely separated, their tips pointing away from each other as if they'd quarrelled. He could distinctly recall trying to explain that to her and, even though he didn't know the Italian words, she'd laughed as if she understood him.

He couldn't remember taking her knickers off or having her on the bed. Nor if she and the other woman had stayed with them to Adalbert's next port of call. Was it at the card-playing place or after they moved on that he got into a fight? He'd punched a man in a light brown suit, though the reasons for it did not come to mind. That raised the further question – had the man in brown punched him back? Presumably Adalbert, when he surfaced, would be able to provide an answer or two. At one of the places they were in there had been a demonstration of lesbian love by two naked women – Toby had a feeling it might have been during their last visit of the night. He was pretty sure that Fioretta and her friend had gone by then.

The love-scene was jolly interesting – one woman sat with her legs wide apart on a chair and the other got down on her knees and used her tongue. The one being pleasured looked as if she was enjoying it, but you never knew – it might be put on. Maybe they'd changed places for round two, but in Toby's memory there was only thick blackness and he guessed he'd fallen asleep in the middle of the act. In fact the only thing he could remember after the two naked women playing together, was being dropped on the marble stairs by two footmen in dressing-gowns carrying him up to bed. Adalbert was nowhere around but someone had got him back to the Palazzo Malvolio.

When he woke up again he felt hot and sweaty and guessed

that it must be afternoon. The shutters were closed over the windows to keep out the sun and the excruciating headache had gone, at least. Marina was sitting on the side of his bed and wiping his brow with a handkerchief dipped in cold water. That was what had woken him.

'*Caro*,' she said softly when she saw his eyes open, 'do you feel a little better for your sleep? It's almost three o'clock – I'm very cross with Adalbert for dragging you round all his disreputable friends. I've already given him a piece of my mind and he's gone off in a huff.'

The poor bastard, thought Toby, but better him than me. I'd rather be dead than wake up hung over and find Marina screaming at me. He's earned his fake photo of bum-whipping and I'll make arrangements to have it taken as soon as I'm back in London.

'But you're so hot, my poor Toby,' said Marina, and she flung aside the thin sheet that covered him and unbuttoned his pyjama jacket and laid him bare from throat to belly button. She went into the bathroom and came back with a thin hand-towel soaked in cold water and wrung out, and perched on the side of the bed to wipe his chest and cool it a little. Naturally, Marina being Marina, she continued her ministrations of mercy by untying the cord of his pyjama trousers and slipping them down to his knees so that she could wipe his sweaty belly.

'Is that better?' she asked. 'Open your legs, Toby.'

He felt a trickling of wet coolness in his heated groins as she squeezed the towel against his skin and under his sweaty pompoms. He sighed in expectation fulfilled when she took hold of his fast-stiffening *cazzo* and wrapped the wet towel round it for a moment or two . . .

'It's standing up, *carrisimo*, she said, 'but I doubt if it's good for much, the state you're in. You look quite shattered – pale and weak. Oh, I hate that Adalbert!'

The truth was that Toby was suffused with a hot itchy feeling of arousal and badly needed to plunge his hangover stiffness up her and be done with it. And, for all her care and sympathy and commiseration for his weakened condition, Marina was not one to let a hard-standing *cazzo* go to waste. She dropped the towel on the floor and pulled her expensively thin pullover with the red and grey zigzag stripes up to her armpits to show her breasts – he had long ago guessed from the way her nipples were prominently visible through the stylish merino wool that she had nothing on under it.

He stared blankly at Marina's heavy breasts, which she had uncovered to excite him, not knowing his lack of enthusiasm for the fuller figure. They hung a little low and slack, but were commendably well preserved for a woman of her age, he conceded grudgingly. He stuck out his tongue and waggled it at them, as if conveying that he would like to lick their russet tips, but hadn't the energy to rise from his bed of suffering. Marina arched her back and jiggled them. She put her palms under them and bounced them up and down. Toby replied with little kissing movements of his lips.

Marina stood up and stripped off her skirt – a high fashion garment in the most delicate shade of grey – to reveal knickers of palest green silk so fine that the neatly trimmed dark-brown bush between her thighs showed through. Off came the knickers in a moment, as did the pullover, and in only her stockings she leaped onto the bed and knelt beside Toby. With a flush on her face and her eyes shining, she had his pyjama trousers off in no time and was astride his thighs, her eager hand gliding up and down his hard-swollen part.

Over her bare shoulder Toby could see the two-foot long cross of tarnished silver on the wall facing him and closed his eyes to be rid of the sight.

'*Carrisimo* – are you up to it?' Marina asked with a note of urgency in her voice, misunderstanding his eye-closing.

'Oh yes,' he answered with determination, and looked at her just as she raised herself up a little to position his hardness to her liking. Still holding it between firm fingers, she sank down slowly, driving it into her.

'Oh, yes!' he said again, thrilled by the warm fleshy clasp and the promise of relief. He jerked his hips up a few times to let her see he was ready and she responded instantly. She rode him with zestful energy, an expression of set concentration on her face and her hands squeezing her full breasts.

'*Dio, Dio!*' she was gasping '*ah si, si, si!*'

Toby closed his eyes again and gave himself up body and soul to being ravished by her, his heels thumping on the mattress as tremors of pleasure flicked through him. Lost in a delirium of sensation a memory crept into his mind from the previous night – Fioretta leaning over an iron balcony-rail above a deserted street with her frock up round her waist and her knickers down her legs while he did it to her from behind. And somewhere else on a dingy staircase with the ginger-haired woman, whoever she was, when he couldn't stop giggling because her hand was in his trouser pocket rousing him again. Had that come to anything?

Marina bounced faster and his passions spurted from him, huge sensations of delight wiping out all conscious memory. He beat at her thighs with clenched fists, writhed between her legs and rolled his head from side to side on the hot pillows, all the discomfort of his hangover wiped away by the ecstacy that shook him.

Marina's own crisis came quickly and she cried out, *Madonna santissimia!* in her spasms. Then she sat trembling astride him, head hanging forward and her hands still clutching her breasts. Toby turned his sweating face to look at her, grateful for her assistance and wishing she'd go away now and let him sleep.

He awoke again much later, to find Marina gone and Delphine standing at his bedside, staring at him. He was stark naked and uncovered, his *cazzo* small and limp.

'You look hot and smell sweaty,' she said. 'It's almost five o'clock. You've been sleeping all day. Have you got over your night out with Adalbert?'

Toby sat up cautiously and put his feet on the floor, sitting on the side of the bed until he was certain he could stand up without falling over. His stomach felt better and his head. He smelled his own sweat and wrinkled his nose.

'I'm beginning to feel hungry,' he said, 'that's a good sign. And you're right – I reek. Hang on while I take a shower.'

He headed for the adjacent bathroom, not much caring whether she waited or not. The shower-head was as big as a dinner plate but even full on produced only a slow drizzle of tepid water. It was better than nothing and he stood beneath it to let the water flow down his body, enjoying the cool. He opened his eyes and saw that Delphine had followed him into the bathroom – and was peeling off her emerald and beige silk frock. Her knickers, brassiere and stockings followed, till she was as naked as he.

'You're pale and still shattered – you need a hand,' said she by way of explanation – or self-justification – or whatever her motive was for her comment. Toby didn't mind which it was – he was content to lean his bare back against the tiled wall behind him while Delphine soaped his body. She washed the sweat from his hair, then under his arms and over his chest, in his groins and down his belly. Eventually her hand clasped his soft and dangling part and washed it attentively, trying to stiffen it.

Her chubby belly was close to him – he laid a palm on it and stroked, telling himself that so much flesh was far from *chic* – although in all honesty he had to admit that he quite liked the feel of it. And of her bush of dark curls, when his hand moved down lower. A soaking had darkened the natural chestnut, but it was still a shade or two lighter than Marina's walnut. In the matter of breasts there was nothing much to choose between them – both were over-endowed, by Toby's standards. Though it would be nice to duck his head down and suck one of the reddish tips pointing firmly at him.

He was given no opportunity to carry the thought into action just then. Delphine moved in close, her belly touching his, her fingers grasping his now stiff part and guiding it between her parted thighs. She rose on tiptoes for a moment, then lowered herself slowly to push his hard length slowly up into her.

'Silly boy,' she said, 'getting drunk all night in low haunts with Adalbert – he'll hear from me when he turns up! You could have been in my bed – I'd have given you a marvellous night.'

Toby smiled to realise he was being rummaged by both sisters on the same day. Any why not? He felt he owed it to them, for disappointing them the night before. Marina had already had her compensation – he hoped he would be able to oblige Delphine. It seemed sensible to lean against the cool tiles while she rocked back and forth in a gentle motion that produced very pleasant sensations and conserved his remaining energy. The tepid water sprinkled down between them, washing over her plump breasts and down between their bellies.

Even moving as steadily as she did, Toby felt his *cazzo* swell to its biggest and jerk stiffly inside her. She sighed to feel the movement in her belly.

'You're done for, Toby,' she said, 'I won't stop until you've made your apology properly!'

Her fingernails sank sharply into his bottom, as his had in hers the time he had her up against the books in the Library – and he cried out in sudden surprise. Delphine thrust her belly against him in a relentlessly steady rhythm. Toby stared down round-eyed at her breasts heaving and falling against his chest to her ragged breathing, and knew she had aroused herself up to the point of climax. *Oh, oh!* she panted, then her eyes closed and her mouth fell open as she went into convulsions of ecstacy and rammed her plump belly at him furiously.

Her climax and the feeling that he'd been semi-raped affected Toby at once – with a long wail he stabbed into her hot and slippery *fica* in short quick strokes that brought on his crisis at once.

When they were calm, they stayed where they were, letting the water slide down over them, till Toby's *cazzo* softened and slid out of its warm haven and hung between his legs. Delphine took the soap again and carefully washed it for him, then went down on her knees to plant a kiss on the shrunken head. She said she expected him in her room that night without fail.

ELEVEN

By lunchtime on Thursday Toby had almost finished his work in the attics. The inventory and notes he was making had filled an entire notebook and over half of a second one. He was seated on a curious folding stool with cast-iron legs not far away from the wall furthest from the door, with ten or a dozen items left to inspect. The stool was unlike anything he'd seen before – it was obviously very old, most probably dating from the 1500s and not very comfortable. The armrails had been gilded, a pattern of foliage where it could still be seen, though most of it had rubbed off. The cushion was missing, but it would be no great problem to replace; he thought a flattish pad in red and gold tapestry would look most authentic.

He had been surprised to learn that there was no telephone in the Palazzo Malvolio. Mrs Tandy, he had been told by Adalbert, regarded the invention of the telephone as a backward step in a civilised society. She said it would kill off the art of letter writing, if anyone could pick up a gadget and talk to anyone in any part of the country. Perhaps there was some sort of use for it, but not one she could possibly approve of – lazy servants could order supplies for the household from shopkeepers without going to inspect the quality. She wanted nothing to do with it.

Twice so far Toby had been forced to walk to the Venice Post Office to telephone London and report on his progress. This was an unsatisfactory way of conducting business, in his view, but he had no choice. His next call to Fitzroy Dalrymple was going to be the most important one – he would give Jervis Senior his estimate of the cost of restoration and the possible sale price of the goods, and ask approval of the offer he intended to make to Delphine Tandy.

He looked at the remaining pieces of furniture to be assessed and noted down in his book. From where he sat it was difficult to see the full extent of the damage and the undisturbed dust of decades, even centuries, might be hiding a lot of breaks and scars. If he finished today, he could talk to London tomorrow. On the other hand, why hurry? Fascinating things had happened to him in Venice and it was a pity to rush away without giving the city in the sea time to produce a few more surprises. If he called it a day now and finished the work sometime tomorrow, he could postpone calling London until Monday, no one expecting to hear from him during the weekend.

He went down to his room to shower before lunch, meaning to take the afternoon off and go sight-seeing. When he approached the Small Dining Room he found there were guests for lunch – an informal arrangement, or everyone would have been notified in advance. But Ottorino Pavese had dropped in during the morning to see Marina and had been asked to stay, and Delphine had been out shopping with Anna-Louisa Ziani and brought her back. Padre Pio was in deep conversation with her, his gold-rimmed glasses twinkling in the sunlight through the tall windows. Toby kissed her hand and she spoke politely, though slightly distantly, to him. Which was a cheek, he thought with a grin, in view of what they'd done to each other.

Dottore Pavese also seemed somewhat distant when he and Toby shook hands. In fact, he appeared to experience some difficulty in recalling who Toby was, until Marina reminded him. Whereupon he nodded and enquired if he was making good progress with the *catalogo*. He nodded again when Toby said it might be completed this week and offered his sincere congratulations. Fortunately for Toby's peace of mind, and maybe also for Marina's, neither of them knew the *Dottore* had seen them doing it together in her sitting room.

That apart, there was a certain uneasiness in Toby's mind. He sensed an interest by Pavese in the damaged furniture that was keener than mere politeness required. He couldn't possibly know about the painting in the secret compartment – the only one who knew of its existence was Toby himself. All the same, in view of Pavese's oddness it would be sensible to find somewhere else for it. It surely wasn't beyond the unreliable and mysterious *Dottore* to talk Marina into letting him ferret round up there.

Adalbert was slightly subdued still. He had been in disgrace for a day or so, as he predicted, but all was well again now, on the clear understanding that he didn't take Toby out and get him drunk. The unspoken addition was – *at least not when either of the ladies of the palace expected personal attentions of an intimate kind.* Not that Marina would need him, Toby judged, not now Ottorino was back on the scene. And Delphine was very much a bedtime person – she regarded daytime frolics as vaguely bad form, it seemed, from what Toby could make out. The frolic in the Biblioteca against the bookshelves was an exception. That still left him wondering what she and the late Rinaldo Malvolio did about the siesta hour before the War.

Much of the conversation over lunch was gossip about friends in Venice – what they were doing and with whom, where they had gone to and where they had just come back from. And large parts of it were in rapid Italian. Toby felt excluded on both counts and eventually worked out that Ottorino Pavese was responsible. He was the one steering the chat and he kept the Italian going whenever Marina or Delphine lapsed into English – evidence that he had a grudge against Toby, whatever his reason, and was not to be trusted.

The sooner the valuable triptych was moved to a safer place, the better. Though where? If he brought it down and put it in his suitcase, the maid might find it in her endless tidying-up and start to make guesses – perhaps report the find to someone. An answer occurred to him – put it into the secret compartment in the base of the wardrobe in his room, the one that had set him off on the search for others. There he could keep an eye on it without arousing suspicion.

Delphine had seated Pavese on her right, obliquely across the table from Toby. Padre Pio sat on her other side and even his clerical presence did not deter Pavese from saying things which were evidently scandalous for, though Toby couldn't understand, Delphine, Marina and Anna-Louisa Ziani were in fits of laughter and the Padre's expression became glazed. He disapproved, that was pretty obvious, but he knew his place and kept quiet.

After a while he turned slightly in his chair towards Toby to acquaint him with the discoveries he had made about the damaged and discarded pieces of furniture up in the attics by comparing successive palace inventories. Toby was glad of the opportunity to talk to him – for one thing, it went some way towards making him feel not so left out. And he understood what the priest was telling him – if they could identify the items upstairs that had been taken off the inventories it would be possible to say who had made individual pieces and the year in which they were bought. Provenance of that sort would add to the sales value in London.

Across the table from Toby, Anna-Louisa was nibbling her food and talking and gesturing with her perfectly manicured hands in expert manner – you could never learn the skill, Toby decided, you had to be born Italian. She was in a very pretty white-and-pink flowered silk frock with a sash of the same material tied low on her hips and her very dark hair newly cut in a sort of short Eton crop with a parting on one side and one curl shaped like a comma on her forehead. Though she was laughing at the *Dottore's* remarks and adding comments of her own, very much at her ease, Toby was made aware by something hard to define in her manner that she was still a Princess's daughter. If Pavese went too far, she would turn him to stone where he sat with one look of those dark brown eyes!

Let Pavese make a comment, for instance, about Princess Zita and her sulky *ragazzo* and he would be gorgonised before he had time to draw another breath.

Toby was listening with one ear to Padre Pio's enthusiasm for antique furniture, and with the other ear to Marina translating for his benefit Ottorino's wickedly comic comments on Contessa Flagranti and her futile endeavour to acquire good taste by the expenditure of large sums of American dollars. He was paying no real attention just then to either, because he was trying hard to attract Anna-Louisa's favourable attention by staring across the table into her eyes.

Yes, dear Signora Ziani – or whatever is the correct title to address you by, he thought to himself with a surge of goodwill – for surely the daughter of a Princess must be more than just a Mrs – I had my face between your thighs last week. I am certain you remember it as well as I do, Anna-Louisa, how you sat over my face and pressed your hairy *fica* against my mouth.

She stopped speaking just then and returned Toby's look, a brief smile on her pleasantly plain face. Was it imagination or did he see a flicker in her eyes to suggest she had remembered their *tête-à-tête* in Signor Ziani's study, with stuffed tiger and lions heads as witnesses? Of course, *tête-à-tête* was quite wrong as a way of describing their little interlude. It wasn't head-to-head at all – more like head-to-groin.

Seeing that she was looking fully at him now, he pouted his lips at her and let his tongue dart out between them for half a second, fast as an adder striking. Perhaps she understood – she half-closed her eyes for a moment. Perhaps she didn't – because she turned to Adalbert on her right and held forth at length in Italian. But Toby guessed the chances were that she understood perfectly well – women usually knew what was going on in men's minds.

When lunch ended at about two-thirty everyone seemed to be in a hurry to leave the table and there was no long chatter over the coffee and liqueurs. Ottorino and Marina were first away – heading for her room, Toby thought, with a grin he didn't bother to conceal as he said, *Arrivederci, Dottore Pavese* and received a nod in return. It was impossible to tell whether Ottorino or Marina was keenest – both showed every sign of being in a hurry to reach a private place to strip their clothes off and roll on each other belly-to-belly. If Marina was slipping him sly drops of the mythical *elisir d'amore*, as Adalbert maintained, she had obviously spiked his wine over lunch. He was practically oozing lust from every pore.

Anna-Louisa said she needed to get home by three o'clock when she expected a telephone call from her husband. He had become bored with the ease of shooting tigers in India and had sailed to Port Soudan, she said, where the telephone system worked for only two hours a day, if that. He was hiring camels and native guides to go into the Nubian Desert to hunt the wild *bedawaluf*. Toby asked what they might be, at which she shrugged casually and said she supposed it was some type of dangerous creature.

Toby was anxious to get up into the attics while Marina and Ottorino were frolicking each other to a standstill. He wanted the triptych out of there and down in his own room, for safety sake. Padre Pio was muttering he must go to the Chapel before his siesta. His usual way was to go straight up to his own room from the lunch table and Toby concluded that the *Dottore*'s malicious gossip had unsettled the fat little priest.

It wasn't at all clear who or what he meant to go down on his knees and pray for. Heavenly forgiveness for the evil-tongued *Dottore*, perhaps? Or a better appreciation of the Venetian style of interior decor for Sally Flagranti? Or absolution for the priest himself for listening and letting himself be amused, however furtively, at some of the jokes?

Toby had looked at the Chapel on his vague wanderings through the palace. It was a magnificently ornate example of a private *capella*, a place of worship for a great family, emblazoned with a riot of gold and gilt, statues of Saints with wire halos over their heads, tall-backed chairs for worshippers and superbly embroidered cushions to kneel on – and all as faded and worn as the rest of the palace. This was the setting for the Malvolio's private devotions over the centuries, where they had explained to their Confessors what sins of anger, pride, lust or whatever had caused them to break up so much expensive furniture.

It was a great pity that such things were never written down by Confessors, for juicy details would have added thousands to the price Fitzroy Dalrymple would get when the pieces from the attics went on sale in London. *Flat-topped writing table, late seventeenth century Venetian, veneered in tortoise-shell and inlaid with brass marquetry, square-tapered legs, fluted, round brass feet. Slightly restored to remove sword slash aimed by Bernardo Malvolio at his unmarried sister, Francesca, in October 1792, on finding her in a compromising situation with a Doge's grandson.*

Or: *Four-poster bed in walnut, made circa 1615 for the Malvolio family, whose arms are carved on each side. The top frame (now restored) was accidentally damaged in March 1902 when Count Paolo Malvolio entertained two members of a French ballet company then visiting Venice to dance Lac des Cygnes at the Fenice Theatre.*

And best of all would be something like this: *prie-dieu with inlaid flower patterns, 1755, made for the chapel of the second Palazzo Malvolio, built after fire destroyed the first. Broken in half when Jacopo Malvolio bludgeoned his Confessor to death with it for refusing him absolution after a notorious liaison. Expertly restored.*

Adalbert had imbibed a lot of wine with his lunch and was red in the face and a trifle glassy-eyed. He announced that it was siesta time to anyone who happened to be listening to him. Then he winked slowly and lewdly at Toby and indicated by pushing a thumb into his own mouth that he was going to call on Signorina Rosa, up in the back streets beyond the Church of the Miracles, and avail himself of her expert oral services.

'Toby,' said Delphine, putting her hand on his arm as he

was getting ready to leave the dining room, 'do you mind awfully if Signora Ziani has a look at the old furniture up in the attic? She'd like some idea of what interests you, in case she decides to sell off some surplus pieces she has in storage.'

'Of course,' said Toby, smiling very politely at Anna-Louisa, who seemed to have forgotten about the telephone call from Port Soudan. 'It's dusty up there, I should warn you, but there's a lot of interesting things to see.'

'I won't come with you, if you don't mind,' Delphine said, 'I have a mountain of papers to go through before the bookkeeper comes in tomorrow to tell me how badly off I am.'

Toby took that as a hint to himself that she would like him to finish his work soon and make her a cash offer. He nodded and said he would take every care of the Signora Ziani. The two women kissed each other's cheeks effusively, chattering of when they would meet again. Delphine went off in the direction of the Biblioteca, which she evidently used as an office, and Toby led Anna-Louisa Ziani by way of the picture-hung gallery beyond the Small Dining Room towards the Music Room, thinking it was a short cut to where they wanted to go.

In the event he was mistaken. He and Anna-Louisa crossed the Music Room, which was large and light, containing a spinet with inlaid case, a harpsichord with brass fittings, a grand piano, a harp with a gilt frame and many strings missing, and chairs to seat eighteen people. In the four corners of the room were plinths of pink marble five feet high on which stood life-size bronze busts. Toby recognised the youthful features of Mozart in one and assumed that he and his sister had been paid to play in the Palazzo Malvolio on their Italian tour. And a long-nosed fellow with the warts in the opposite corner must surely be Liszt, who stayed in Italy for years and could easily have been invited to Venice to play. As Toby recalled, the old keyboard thumper had lived openly with a princess in Rome.

The busts at the other end of the long room were not so easy to identify. The chap with the hayrick hair and floppy bow-tie was probably Felix Mendelssohn, Toby thought – he toured Italy in his twenties. Anna-Louisa said perhaps it was, but it might be Niccolo Paganini. She was certain the fourth bust, a round-faced man wearing a long curly wig, was one of the Scarlattis, most likely Domenico, the son, who gave harpsichord recitals for a living before he emigrated to Spain.

'Spain? What an extraordinary thing to do,' said Toby, whose impression was that Spanish music consisted entirely of guitar strumming and foot-stamping, 'when did he do that?'

'I'm not an historian,' said Anna-Louisa, uninterested in what musicians and other hired hands got up to, 'in the early years of the *Settecento* – the eighteenth century, you call it.'

'Then he couldn't have played in this Music Room,' said Toby, 'this palace wasn't built until the 1750s, after the fire. But if his bust is here, there's a connection with the Malvolio. He no doubt played for them in the first palace on this site.'

'For a Neapolitan player he was quite good,' said Anna-Louisa with a shrug that asserted the superiority of musicians born in Venice. The shrug also made clear her view that musicians were paid to entertain guests while they chatted over a glass or two of wine, and it was of no particular importance which strummer, scraper or tinkler was brought in to do it.

The tall white double doors at the far end of the Music Room did not open on to the landing of the marquetry staircase up to the next floor, as Toby had thought. They found themselves in another room, much like the Music Room but empty of furniture of any kind. A row of large oval medallions hung along one wall, moulded dusty portraits of Heaven knew who. Musicians, Malvolios, mendicants, mathematicians, monomaniacs, musketeers, mountebanks – all gone and forgotten, whoever they were. Beyond it lay another long passage lined with large paintings of Saints and other notable persons of the past. Toby sighed almost in despair until, half way along it, fifty yards away, he spotted a white marble group of three naked young women. It was the Three Graces, a landmark for him in his pursuit of Marina.

'This way,' he said with a sudden rush of confidence, taking Anna-Louisa's arm. From this point he knew the way – along the passage off which Marina's private quarters opened, to the foot of the broad marquetry staircase up to the next floor. Behind one of these doors, at this very moment, Toby reflected, Marina and Ottorino Pavese were in the last gasps of passion. Or maybe not. He led Anna-Louisa along without even a sideways glance, without even an eyelid flicker.

And while he thought it possible she had been to Marina's sitting room in the past and knew where it lay, she passed the door without comment. But evidently something of the sort was in her mind and she came to it indirectly after they reached the end of the passage.

'You deceived me,' she said, as they were climbing slowly up the stairs, his hand under her elbow as support, 'when we first met, you asked me your English questions about my Mama and her little friend Marcello, you remember? You told me you were not Marina's *ragazzo*.'

'I was telling the truth,' Toby answered.

'I know that now I have seen how she is with Ottorino but at the time I thought you were lying, which was the natural thing to do.'

Toby found this female logic somewhat confusing and tried to counter it.

'You were trying to embarrass me by suggesting that Marina paid me to make love to her,' he said.

'*Che assurdita!*' she exclaimed, flashing a look at him with dark brown eyes sparkling with amusement that was malicious to the point of making him uneasy. 'How can a man be embarrassed to admit he is the companion of a lady?'

'It may not embarrass Marcello to be paraded by the Princess but I am not in his position,' said Toby.

'You deliberately told the truth to deceive me,' Anna-Louisa insisted. 'Why did you do that?'

They were at the top of the beautiful staircase. Toby paused for a moment to recall the way from here through the maze of rooms filled with faded eighteenth century magnificence to the final stairs – the servant's staircase up into the attics.

'You have nothing to say?' Anna-Louisa demanded.

'This way, I think,' said Toby, making up his mind to humour her in her twisted reasoning, it being too complicated to argue against it. 'Please don't take my little deception too badly. I was very greatly attracted to you and in my ignorance of polite manners here I thought you might be inclined to disregard me completely if you believed I was attached to a friend of yours. Therefore, in the hope of finding you more favourably disposed towards me, I said what I said – only to advance myself in your eyes, you must understand, not realising it might well have the opposite result, but in the event all turned out for the best.'

He was talking absolute nonsense but, by speaking quickly and confidently, he was hoping to bamboozle Anna-Louisa. In this he was reasonably successful – she was silent for some time while she mulled over his words, probably translating them inside her head into Italian, to see if they made better sense. While she was thus occupied, Toby guided her past rows of old Roman gents in long togas, paintings of battles, portraits of members of the expired Malvolio dynasty, some of whom were impressive, though others looked as if they were certifiable.

'So you find me attractive?' she said at last, giving up her struggle to turn his words into something comprehendible. 'But I suppose you say that to all the women you meet.'

'Only the attractive ones,' said Toby, straight-faced.

They came at last to the cracked red-tiled stairs that led up to the top floor and then to the long attic stacked high with furniture.

'*Gesumaria!*' cried Anna-Louisa in astonishment. 'So much! I expected to see two or three chairs and an old table – will you really buy all this from Delphine and take it to London?'

'Yes, if we can agree on a price,' said Toby. 'Delphine said you had some pieces in storage you might decide to dispose of, but not on this scale, I imagine.'

Anna-Louisa paid no attention to him. She wandered over from the attic door to where the stacks began on the dusty floor and looked at the nearby items closely.

'There are some fine things here,' she said, 'see that chair, it must be made by Andrea Brustolon. Mama has a pair of them.'

Toby sidled in between other pieces to get to the half hidden item she was pointing at. It had caught his attention from his first day in the attics, being extremely unusual. It was more a stool than a chair, the seat supported by carved wooden figures of black slave boys in turbans. He had seen plenty of Venetian candle-holders before, shaped as negro slaves, but nothing like this.

'It was a speciality of Brustolon,' said Anna-Louisa when he mentioned this, 'furniture with black slaves. He came to Venice from up in the Alps where they learn wood carving in the winter because the snow keeps them in their houses. What is wrong with the chair that it has been thrown out and is up here in the *soffitta*?'

'Let me see,' said Toby, sinking down on his haunches to look more closely at it. The handsomely carved figures were dressed in eighteenth century style – long coats and knee breeches. The paint had faded, dulling the original green, crimson and gold.

'This boy is split from the shoulder down,' he said, touching the crack with his finger and wondering how it had happened. It would be no great problem to restore, he was thinking, and as a rare item the piece would be very valuable. Now he had the name of the maker from Anna-Louisa he could ask Padre Pio to look up the date of purchase in his archives. Perhaps the original price would be noted – that would be interesting.

Anna-Louisa had joined him in the furniture jungle. Without a word she sat down on the faded cushion of the unusual piece. It creaked, but gave no sign of collapsing, which encouraged Toby to think the split was not as deep or extensive as it seemed at first sight. Then she got up and dusted off the back of her pink-and-white flowered dress.

'Sit down,' she said, 'I have something to say to you.'

Toby unbuttoned the blazer he had put on for lunch and sat on the antique seat cautiously. Anna-Louisa, standing in front of him, reached under her frock and slipped her knickers off. They were of white silk, Toby saw, small and prettily embroidered. A moment later they were draped over a small circular table from which a large part of the veneer was peeling away. Early nineteenth century, Toby's mind registered automatically – not later than 1820, but what a state it was in!

'Which part of me do you find attractive?' Anna-Louisa asked him as she held her frock up round her waist.

Toby's gaze switched from the table to the sensuous curve of her belly and the fleece of dark brown curls below. Her thighs were strong, not at all the sort of slender white limbs that he liked to stroke and kiss, nor was her belly narrow and flat as he preferred in women. Yet undeniably his male part was growing stiff very quickly in his trousers – he had noticed before that it paid very little heed to his aesthetic standards, but simply reacted more or less indiscriminately to female nakedness.

Anna-Louisa's painted red mouth curved in a smile as she saw the curious expression that flickered across Toby's face while he debated how to answer her question. To be ruthlessly honest with himself, it was her ankles that came closest to the ideal. They were remarkably slim for the roundness of her calves and the fullness of her thighs, as prettily turned as the legs of a Chippendale chair, for example. But honesty of that sort was sure to give deadly offence. Half-truths and outright lies were far more acceptable, in the circumstances.

'Impossible to say,' he told her, 'I find you attractive in your entirety, as a person, not as a compilation of parts.'

'Bravo – a very discreet answer!' she said mockingly. 'And a very polite one! I can even say a very *English* answer – or is it only a timid answer? Do you not agree that some parts of me can give you more pleasure than others, and for that reason must be more attractive to you?'

'Every part of you is a pleasure to look at,' Toby insisted, 'and therefore attractive.'

'Really? Are you saying you want to make love to every part of me? Do you wish to put your *cazzo* in my armpit or between my breasts? Do you want to rub it on my thighs? In my mouth, perhaps, or in my ear? Shall I hold it between the soles of my bare feet, or bend over for you to use my bottom? Is this what you mean?'

While she was posing her elaborate question, she hitched her skirt round her middle and sank to her knees before him, gazing fixedly into his eyes while she unbuttoned his trousers from waist to groin. He felt her pulling his shirt up out of the way and then her hand clasped his stiffness.

'Yes,' he said, staring back into her eyes.

'What does it mean, this *yes*?'

'It means I'd like to do all of those things to you,' he said in a jerky voice, wildly excited by what she had said and what she was doing to him.

'Toby, Toby,' she said, sighing, 'you think that I came here to your attic to make love with you? The vanity of men!'

'There's a four-poster bed over there,' Toby murmured, his eyes still staring into hers, 'you could lie on your back with your legs apart while I make love to every part of your body.'

'What presumption!' she said softly, her hand sliding up and down with skill. 'Be silent before you annoy me – and don't you dare look away – look at me!'

He stared unblinking at her face, at her brown eyes fixed on him, her pleasantly plain face so very well made-up, the comma of a curl on her broad forehead, and he felt tremors of delight through his belly from her touch on his upright part – which in grateful response to Anna-Louisa's handling was jumping in her clasped palm. She straightened her legs and stood up quickly to straddle his lap with her bare thighs.

'Look into my eyes!' she reminded him sharply as his glance wavered briefly towards where she gripped his bounding flesh between forefinger and thumb to keep it straight up

'I've been told he has a wife and children at Bologna,' Toby said, 'and has business interests in other places. What is his business, do you know?'

'Something to do with old Roman and Greek artefacts, I think. He tried to sell me a set of silver spoons once, very nice ones which he said were of the first century anno domini. He told me they came from a villa found in diggings near Paestum, which is to the south of Naples. Of course, I didn't believe him.'

'Why not? Didn't they look genuine Roman?'

'They looked entirely genuine, and worn and marked exactly as anyone would expect them to be from being used for years to eat with and then buried for centuries and then found and cleaned. But it is Ottorino himself who does not seem genuine and so it is good to be suspicious of what he says.'

'You think his business is selling fake antiques, then?'

She shrugged again, disclaiming all knowledge of trickery by her ex-conquest, for to call him an ex-lover, Toby considered, was to overstate the case – Signora Ziani didn't have lovers in the ordinary sense of the phrase. She had a series of admirers, whose faces she sat on. At least she had gone a long way toward confirming Toby's guess about Pavese's source of income. Or one of them.

'Why should Ottorino be interested in the broken furniture in this attic?' he asked.

'You must be mistaken about that,' said Anna-Louisa, her hand sliding down into Toby's open trousers to ascertain if his limp part was ready to be stiffened. 'He is not interested in little amounts, only the things he can sell for hundreds of thousands of lira.'

'We're talking millions of lira here,' said Toby, waving his free hand to take in the contents of the attic. 'That may make a difference.'

Anna-Louisa looked at him closely to see if he was serious.

'You can repair these furnitures and sell them in London for millions of lira? If Ottorino knows that, he will be trying to think of a way of getting the money for himself. Perhaps he has a friend in Bologna or elsewhere who knows about furniture and would be his partner.'

'A friend here in Venice, even?' suggested Toby.

'Perhaps. There are many dealers in antiques in Venice and a few makers of fine furniture, even now. But if Ottorino intends to buy the furniture and sell it himself, why does he wait?'

'The very question I've been asking myself. I don't know. But I'm certain he's plotting something as soon as I've finished my valuation.'

Anna-Louisa's interest in Toby's problems was only slight, at best, and disappeared altogether the moment she managed to make his male part grow stiff and hard again. Her hand slid up and down it, she pressed her mouth to his and thrust her tongue in, the tip vibrating against his tongue. He felt her thighs, which some men would have called magnificent but which for his taste were overdeveloped, move apart. His middle finger found its way into her wet *fica* and she gave a long moan of delight into his mouth.

'*Mettimelo dentro, Toby!*' she sighed and, though the Italian words meant nothing to him, he guessed she wanted him inside.

'Let's go to the bed over there,' he murmured, his fingertip busy at her slippery button.

He had still to learn that she totally ignored suggestions of this sort from men, in order to show who was in charge. Without even the courtesy of a reply, she got up from his lap and waved him to his feet. He thought she'd agreed about the four-poster and in consequence was amazed to see her go down on her knees. She lay forward over the black-boy seat, her elegant silk frock pulled up and her belly resting on the faded cushion.

'*Adesso – prendimi!*' she said quickly when he hesitated from sheer surprise. Whatever the literal translation of the words, it was very evident that she wanted him to stop dithering about and get on with it. Nothing loth, he shed his jacket and knelt behind her to run his hands over the voluptuous cheeks of her bare behind. They were too big, of course, too round and soft, too much flesh – yet they were delightfully arousing to touch and squeeze, to stroke and palpate. His furiously stiff *cazzo*, sticking out of his undone trousers, nodded up and down rapidly in total agreement with the sentiment.

'*Ah si, caro!*' Anna-Louisa moaned in delight when he probed between her open thighs to caress the long lips here, '*di piu,*' she said, which he knew meant *more*. He slid two fingers inside her, skimming lightly over her wet bud, his other hand gliding over the roundness of her smooth cheeks, enjoying the feel of her warm flesh. A very *low* and *common* taste, he said to himself in reproof – it would be far more enjoyable if her bum was lean and sylph-like, a *Vogue* model shape, sleek, sophisticated! On the other hand, maybe not – the truth was that her exposed rear had aroused him enormously and he was going to revel in fleshy delight to his heart's content, common or not!

'*Si, si, carissimo, ancora,*' she murmured to the touch of his fingers in the open furrow of her curly-haired mound.

Toby inched forward on his knees to bring the purple head of his wildly throbbing part to her entry. He pushed hard to force it in deep and she squirmed about joyfully on the antique seat, making it creak.

Toby was highly aroused. He lay on her back, slamming in and out with hard thrusts that made his belly smack on the softness of Anna-Louisa's bottom.

'*Piu forte!*' she gasped, enjoying the brutality. It required no knowledge of the Italian language to understand that she was urging him on harder.

Toby panted and shook as his ravening desire swelled towards bursting-point.

'*Sto venendo! Sto venendo!*' Anna-Louisa wailed blissfully.

The frantic note in her voice warned Toby she was announcing the start of her climax. He rode her faster and harder, ramming with all his might, feeling the crisis rushing unstoppably on at him. She screamed and writhed under him in furious ecstacy, and with a sharp crack the damaged slave-boy split into two and the stool collapsed sideways. They were tipped off without even knowing what was happening, rolling over together on the dusty floorboards. A spasmodic clenching of Anna-Louisa's muscles when she struck the floor expelled Toby's *cazzo* from her palpitating slit and, gasping in shock, he spurted his lust over her stylish pink-and-white silk frock.

TWELVE

The name of the woman in Adalbert's fake photograph album, the one in black stockings with a string of pearls around her neck – the one who lay back in an armchair with her legs crossed and her arms behind her head to push her breasts out, the one who had caught Toby's interest – was Gilda Borlano and she was twenty-six.

He learned this from her when he met her outside the railway station at the top end of the Grand Canal, where she arrived on the train from Padua. It was just after eleven on a fine bright morning, the sky an almost cloudless blue; it was already hot and with the promise of getting hotter. Toby recognised her immediately, though she was shorter than he expected – but, after all, photos taken sitting down give no true impression of height.

Her naked thighs had looked long in the picture but that was only because of the contrast of the flesh tones with the black of her stockings. The main thing, he told himself with relief, was that she wasn't dumpy. She was two inches or so over five feet and in proportion, neither breasts nor bottom oversized.

She wore a navy-blue cotton jacket and skirt over a pale blue blouse with a scooped-out neckline and no buttons. And, as asked for, fine black stockings. *And frilly garters*, I hope, Toby said to himself. She came straight toward him through the jostling crowd that had got off the train – evidently she had been given a description of the man in Venice who wanted to meet her. Toby was wearing his light tan gaberdine suit with his straw boater. And to give just a raffish touch, a pink bow-tie he had bought since arriving in Venice.

'Signor *Gerovese*?' she asked with a smile, mangling his name ruthlessly, and when he nodded and smiled back she told him her name and said she was very much pleased to see him. They shook hands while he responded with *Piacere*, which Adalbert had said was the proper thing to say on meeting someone. Then, to control the proceedings and get the adventure started, he took her arm and steered her across the broad quay that ran the width of the station, to where his special gondola waited.

Why the Venetians had chosen to name their railway station or the quay outside after Santa Lucia was unclear to Toby. She was a Sicilian virgin, according to Padre Pio, who was denounced as a secret Christian by a pagan suitor she spurned, was arrested and sentenced to service in a local brothel but miraculously saved from the Fate Worst Than Death by angelic intervention – though not from martyrdom, for the annoyed authorities simply had her throat cut.

The connection with railways was not easy to discern – but on the other hand, Toby reflected, one of the important stations in London was named after St Pancras. And information about him provided by Padre Pio was equally baffling. Pancras, it seemed, was executed in the year 304 in Rome at the age of fourteen – which was fifteen hundred years before George Stephenson managed to get the world's first railway service running.

The gondola arranged by Niccolo Corradini was tied up at the Fondamente Santa Lucia, the quay where public gondoliers waited in the faint hope that some unwary traveller off a train would hand them a suitcase and ask to be taken to the Gritti Palace Hotel at the far end of the Grand Canal. Or even across to the Grand Hotel on the Lido, for which the fare would be distinctly outrageous.

Watching them, Toby had formed the impression that gondoliers sat smoking cigarettes and gossiping to each other all day long and were ignored by every sensible traveller. It was better to ride round Venice on the *vaporetto*, at five times the speed and a fiftieth of the cost of a gondola.

How in the circumstances they managed to exist was a mystery. A form of outdoor relief seemed highly unlikely in a poor country like Italy. Perhaps, thought Toby, the gondoliers are secretly bookie's runners, ferrying cash and slips between punter and an undercover Honest Guiseppi sitting in a cafe all day and raking it in. What Venetians could actually bet on was beyond guessing – the lack of large open spaces ruled out horse-racing. Or even dog-racing.

All this he chattered away to Gilda while they made their way to the waiting gondola. She understood perhaps one word in each ten and a puzzled frown appeared on her face.

'*Gondolieri*? Dogs? *Giocare? Ma che cosa vuol dire?*' she asked, her thick eyebrows rising up towards her fringe of brown hair in puzzlement. Toby was rather taken by the fringe, which did not lie flat on her forehead but had a little kink to the left. Her eyes were very clear under it and a beautiful shade of golden brown. She was not a great beauty, as Marina had been – according to Adalbert – at the same age, but there was about her a very seductive air.

Happily for Toby he was excused answering her question about dogs and gondoliers by their arrival at the gondola rank. The craft assigned to him lay prow-on to the quay, moored to stakes rising out of the opaque water alongside a narrow wooden jetty.

As arranged by Corradini, Toby had met Mario, the gondolier, earlier that morning by the Rialto Bridge, safely away from the Palazzo Malvolio and curious eyes. Mario was a burly man of forty or so, wearing the usual gondolier rig of dark trousers and a white shirt with rolled-up sleeves. A day or two had passed since last he shaved and when he spoke he exuded the aroma of garlic. But he had a smattering of English, as of French and German, good enough to cope with a foreign tourist in his boat, and he had been briefed carefully by Corradini.

The only covered-in gondolas Toby had seen were in paintings. Turner's pictures of Venice in the Tate Gallery showed them and he was British and reliable. And they were shown in a Canaletto painting he'd seen in the National Gallery. But they were not in evidence on the Grand Canal. Either they'd gone out of style or they were only for winter use, he reasoned. Whereupon he had spotted one the very next day – though obviously designed for a particular purpose. It's deck-house, so to call it, had glassed sides and contained a black coffin heaped with flowers. It was on its way across to San Michele, the cemetery island where all good Venetians were buried, Adalbert explained on being asked.

Nevertheless, the fact that Niccolo Corradini had through his contacts produced a covered-in gondola showed that there still were such things. The cabin, if it could be so described, was a box with a curved roof set amidships, open forward for the view and closed at the back, giving some privacy from the gondolier standing there to row with his long thin oar. The sides opened, having louvred panels set in them, Toby discovered. They stood open at present, but he meant to close them in due course.

When he and Gilda were settled on the cushioned seats in the low-roofed cabin, Mario pushed off from the rickety jetty into the main-stream traffic of the Grand Canal, turned the gondola in its own length and set off at a leisurely pace. Palaces and churches slid by on each bank, the Scalzi church looking like a two-tiered white-iced wedding-cake, then over on the right bank green-domed San Simeone Piccolo.

Red-roofed Palazzo Labia went past on the left, leaning as if for support against the red brick bell-tower of San Geremia, a church built sideways on to the Grand Canal. Further on, across on the other bank, there was an astonishing pink building like a fairy-tale fortress, seemingly standing on thin stone pillars rising out of the choppy water – the Fondaco dei Turchi, not a fortification at all, but a warehouse built 800 years earlier for ships to unload foreign imports.

A little way on stood a squat building of dilapidated brick, with a few small and square windows set high in the blank walls as if to withstand a siege but this was no fortification – it was only the grain store the Venetian government ran up in 1300 or thereabouts.

Opposite the granary stood the mighty Palazzo Vendramin – but this was not a sight-seeing trip – at least, nor architectural sights. Mario rowed the gondola level with the columned facade of the Palazzo Pesaro, moving in to the left, then turned up a narrow side canal. He was taking a short cut to the open lagoon from the top of the figure 2-shaped Grand Canal. Tall buildings rose on either hand, shuttered windows and high balconies with flowerpots. Footbridges arched over to connect alleys on left and right. A barge heavily loaded with goods came pushing past the gondola, making it pitch and roll.

Meanwhile Toby and Gilda were conversing as best they could, a mixture of words and gestures. Did she often come to Venice? No, there was nothing much to do there, but sometimes she came with friends on a Sunday outing. Didn't she think the buildings were impressive? Anywhere in Italy you could see old buildings – Padua had old buildings of its own, the church of San Antonio and the Palazzo della Ragione. Why did Signor Toby want to meet her in particular?

Which photograph of her posing naked did he mean –

there were so many? It was possible that in one of them she wore black stockings and sat on a striped velvet chair as he said, but she did not remember that one in particular. No, she didn't know of any special collection of pictures of herself and other naked women. She was never told who or what the photographs were for, and never troubled to ask, if the money was good. Signor Toby had requested her to wear black stockings today because of the photograph he had seen, yes? Did he like her then – and did he truly think she was *bella*?

Toby had his arm round her, of course, and she was leaning a little against him, but the open sides of the gondola prevented any further acquaintance developing, and there was little point in closing them while they were still among water traffic and visible through the open front of the cabin. In the side canal, after the barge had gone past, he became slightly bolder with her, hugging her more closely to him and kissing her cheek. She responded at once by turning her face to him, to be kissed on the lips. It was on her part a kiss expertly judged to signal complete acceptance without any kind of demand on him. Even her hand resting on his out-stretched thigh was a sign that she was at his disposal and waiting for him to decide what he wanted.

For some reason he did not understand, Toby found the thought extremely arousing. He was not required to impress her, seduce her, persuade her, cajole her – a simple payment via Corradini had taken care of all that. She had come to Venice entirely for his pleasure. He found that thought liberating and knew it was going to be a day to remember. He slipped a hand under her thin jacket to cup her left breast. Without a let-up in the kiss she moved her hand up his thigh to stroke between his legs.

'I say! Damned foreigners with their rotten habits – it's a confounded disgrace! Don't look at them, Mavis!' exclaimed an indignant British voice nearby.

Toby broke off the kiss and looked up, to see another gondola sliding towards them between the high and crumbling brick sides of the narrow waterway. The man airing his views loudly was not middle-aged, as Toby had imagined, but under thirty and had a short moustache of the type associated with the Army. He was wearing a red-and-yellow striped blazer with an elaborate crest on the breast pocket. The woman whose susceptibility he was shielding from a display of public immorality was young, fair-haired and pretty. She was wearing a broad-brimmed hat suitable for Ascot, with white gloves, but she sat on the low gondola seat in a way that revealed her knees under a short white frock.

When the two gondolas passed closely enough to reach over and shake hands – if their occupants had been on good terms – Toby raised his boater and said, *Buon giorno, Signor* in what he hoped was a passable facsimile of a native Italian accent. The irate stranger glared at him and said, *Filthy foreigners!* loudly and clearly. His pretty companion averted her shocked eyes from the corrupting spectacle of Gilda's hand between Toby's legs. Then the boats were past each other and Gilda was asking him why the other Signor was *furioso*.

'They're honeymooners, I imagine,' said Toby, grinning. That was a word Gilda had heard before and understood.

'*Viaggo di nozze?*' she said, her thick eyebrows rising in an expression of puzzlement, 'but then he must be very happy – why is he *furioso* because he sees you kiss me?'

Toby gave her breast a gentle squeeze and tried to explain it was seeing him do that which caused the annoyance. Or maybe the sight of her hand stroking between his thighs. It made no sense to Gilda, who looked even more puzzled. Toby decided it was far too complicated, even without the language limitation, to come up with a sensible reason for red-and-yellow blazer's reaction, so he attributed it to jealousy.

'*Gelosia?*' she said, only slightly less puzzled.

'That's right – you are prettier than his wife and that makes him envy me.'

She partly believed it, at least enough to shrug and drop the subject. The waterway they were following opened out widely and they came level with a stretch of elaborate baroque edifices on the left. One looked like a church, though its blank walls were plastered in grey, the neighbouring building had a white marble facade with columns and statues, the rest of it being red brick and terracotta-tiled roof. Then the canal debouched into a wide square inlet resembling a harbour, built up all round, and with barges and work-boats of every description tied up. There ahead at last lay the open lagoon, smooth blue water stretching to an invisible low horizon. Toby smiled at Gilda while he closed the louvred shutters on the sides of the cabin.

'*Ecco!*' said she, a useful word Toby had learned could mean *Now!* or *Well!* or *There!* or *Here we are!* or *Look at that!* Or it could be used just to show you were taking an interest in whatever was going on. He turned towards Gilda to unbutton her loose navy-blue jacket and tug her blouse out of her skirt. He slipped a hand under it, finding a slip that felt like silk but which he assumed was artificial. He fondled her breasts for a while through it, unwilling to hurry through any part of his adventure afloat.

Eventually he discovered the top of the slip was loose enough for him to put his hand down and stroke her bare breasts. They were modestly sized but their fleshy softness in his palm was highly exciting.

She let him continue in this pleasant way for some time while the gondola made its slow and dipping way out into the open and calm lagoon, where there was no one to peer in at them or make idiot remarks about foreigners and their habits. It was warm in the cabin with the sun beating down on the roof and Toby's hard part was throbbing joyfully. Gilda flipped his trousers open and slipped a hand inside. She knew a great deal about stroking a man's upright part, Toby acknowledged, as pleasant sensations began to ripple through him.

Playing with her breasts had made the buds firm and prominent under his fingers and he was pleased to think he could make her excited too. Inside his open trousers her fingertips slid with delicate deliberation along his hard *cazzo*, then over its sensitive tip. Her head was on his shoulder and her face had a dreamy look, her eyes half-closed and her lips parted a little. Toby reached down to slide his hand under her thin skirt and up in a slow caress between her legs. He ran his fingers over her stockings and her knees moved apart for his hand to go higher, above her stocking-tops, and along her smooth-skinned thighs to her underwear.

Her knickers had short wide legs that allowed his hand to slide in easily and move upwards to feel delicately between her thighs – to a patch of curls smaller than he expected. He pictured in his mind's eye the photograph of her in 'King Edward's' album of girlfriends. It had struck him even then that so little was on show between her crossed thighs that she must surely clip her thatch regularly, rather like tending a garden by mowing the lawn and trimming up the edges. He stroked warm soft petals of flesh under the curls and drew his middle finger upwards between to find her nub. She murmured softly as he caressed it, her body trembling against him.

The gondola dipped to the oar as it moved slowly out into the lagoon, away from prying eyes. Toby wanted Gilda to be naked as in the photograph – he had meant to look up in the Biblioteca dictionary, if there was one, the Italian word for *undress* but in his excitement after he got Corradini's instructions to meet her he forgot. He moved his hand from between her thighs and plucked at her jacket and skirt while he asked her to *take them off – everything except your stockings*.

She got the meaning and sat up to shrug off her summer jacket and pull her blouse out of her waist-band and up over her head. Her slip was of ivory-coloured rayon, as he'd guessed when he touched it, with a thin band of machine-made lace round the top hem.

She unfastened her navy-blue skirt at the hip and raised her bottom from the gondola seat while she pushed it down her legs. Toby slipped forward from the seat to kneel facing her and help her take the skirt off. She touched his eager face lightly with her fingertips and smiled at him, before wriggling the slip up her body and over her head. *Bellisima*, said Toby at this baring of her breasts, mainly because he imagined she expected him to say something in praise of her. She smilingly said something in Italian, which he interpreted as an invitation to take down her knickers.

He obliged by hooking his fingers in the top and easing them down, under her bottom and along her thighs, his eyes gleaming with desire for what he was uncovering. Her belly was a delight – smooth and clear, broad and gently curved, with a perfectly round button sunk deep in the middle. Her legs were together as closely as was possible without hampering her unveiling, hiding all that lay between, except for just a hint of curls.

Toby finished taking off her knickers and leaned over to kiss her warm belly, then pushed the top of his tongue into its sunken button. She giggled a little, which he found delightful.

The boatyards of Venice have built gondolas to the same plan, more or less, since the year 1500 or thereabouts – long and narrow and curving high up out of the water at each end, like a thin slice of melon. At the prow the first few feet are covered in and at the stern four feet are decked for the gondolier to stand on to row. Between lies about eight feet of open boat, or whatever the boatyards reckon in centimetres. At each end is a bench facing inboard and wide enough for two people to sit side by side. Halfway along the open part, and set not centrally but to one side, stands a spare chair with only one arm. This odd-looking item is meant for a fifth passenger.

Experts on the history of Venice maintain there are excellent reasons for all this but, as these reasons appear to be lost in the mists of the past beyond all recovery, there is no point in asking.

The chair had been removed from Mario's gondola for this very special occasion, allowing more room for what was to happen. On his knees under the low cabin roof, Toby reached for the faded red cushion from the forward bench and placed it on the boards that gave a useful flatness within the curving hull. He slipped the other cushion from under Gilda and put it beside the first to provide a comfortable place for her to lie, with him beside. Leaning over her, propped on an elbow, he paused in admiration, his hand motionless on her thigh. He had been absolutely right about the fine black stockings – the contrast with Gilda's body tones was superb. And she was wearing the frilly garters of the photograph, or a similar pair. Perhaps she remembered more than she had admitted. After all, she wasn't on oath and there was no need to tell the truth if she preferred not to.

Not that it mattered. Her beautiful brown eyes looked up at him, her face was in repose as she awaited his pleasure. There was so much he wanted to do to her that it was a puzzle knowing where to start. Her breasts perhaps – they had his wholehearted approval, being handsomely proportioned to his way of thinking, not insignificantly tiny, like Contessa Sally's, nor oversized and too fleshy, like Contessa Marina's. He leaned down to kiss their dark pink buds and flick the tip of his tongue over them.

He smoothed his hand down her belly and her legs moved slowly apart on the boat cushions. As he had guessed when his hand was in her knickers, her patch of dark brown curls had been trimmed from a probably luxuriant natural spread to a narrow triangle poised above a strip between her thighs to enclose her *fica*. It was a very stylish arrangement, thought Toby while caressing it – aesthetically pleasing and sexually arousing. What more could anyone possibly want?

Her mound was understated, not full and bold as Marina's

was, but a gentle fleshy rise. Then as if in compensation, the lips that split it were prominent, pushing forward in an excitingly sulky pout. They parted so easily to Toby's slowly up-drawn finger that a more-than-ordinary frequency of usage suggested itself – a thought that did nothing to deter him. Far from it – it made him even more aroused, and with two splayed fingers he opened the lips wider to see her bud. It stood pinkly wet, ready to be touched, ready to send shudders of pleasure through her belly. She had made it apparent that she was his to do what he liked with and neither of them was in any hurry, with the whole day paid for.

Toby's fingers continued their slow ravishing and very soon her bare back was writhing on the thin boat cushions, while her stretched-out legs in their fine black stockings trembled. *Ah si* she murmured, *si, si, cosi!* Her hand groped in his unbuttoned trousers to find his throbbing length and have it out. She was massaging it deftly, but before she had been at it long enough to make him lose control her body began to twitch convulsively and her back arched up in a climax of pleasure that delighted Toby. He pressed his mouth over hers and licked her tongue as she gasped, her belly shaking beneath his hand in her throes.

When she was calm again she sat up and rolled him on his back beside her. He had removed his jacket when they lay down on the boat bottom and she tugged at the ends of his pink bow-tie to undo it and unbutton his shirt.

One hand was inside, flicking at his flat nipples, her other hand in his trousers and on his belly. Her fingernails combed through his curls before they nipped at the fleshy base of his quivering shaft. Then her hand was round it, gripping it tight, pointing it straight up, her mouth coming down to meet it. Toby gasped loudly when her lips closed over it, enclosing the head in her wet mouth. He felt her tongue lap over the swollen head and knew he was only seconds away from spurting out his intense desire.

'*Carissima!*' he gasped, bringing into play one useful word he had learned in Venice, and he put his hands on her shoulders to roll her over on her back quickly. He slid on top of her at once in a paroxysm of desire, his belly on hers. He sensed her legs parting for him and with a single hard push he drove deep into her wet warmth.

She was babbling excitedly as he thrust in and out with short stabs, but whether she was saying the same things

Anna-Louisa had said when he ravaged her on a broken stool in the attic, he was in no condition to decide, even if he had understood. Gilda pushed his trousers down his thighs and sank her short fingernails into the cheeks of his bottom. He moaned in pleasure and slid in and out of her slippery-wet *fica* with long fast pushes. In some remote part of his mind it seemed that the gondola was rocking, as if in choppy water, but what did it matter?

Gilda was uttering little squeals of ecstasy and clawing his bottom like a wild-cat, her knees drawn up high and her thighs holding his hips tightly. He rode her faster and harder – his belly imploded and he gushed his essence into her.

She squirmed frantically beneath him, shrieking loud and long – so that not only the gondolier heard her but probably all the passengers on a ferryboat steaming past 500 yards to starboard. Long after Toby's tremors of delight had ended, hers ran on, her belly bumping up at him, her legs kicking.

He lay quietly on her, his deeply inserted *cazzo* still giving an occasional reflex jerk and staying hard for a while yet. Not until her after-glow had faded like a golden sunset declining below a distant horizon did he ease out of her – and before he could dismount she reached up to fling her arms about his neck and kiss him passionately. She assured him he was *molto gentile* to make love to her as if he loved her and not the way the men she knew usually did. The Italian words were lost on Toby, even though she repeated them several times. At least he understood that she was very well-disposed to him.

But the gondolier standing on the stern called out words that he did understand, a warning that they would reach the island of Murano in ten minutes. Toby rolled on to his back to pull up his trousers and button them, then sat up to wrestle with his bow-tie. Gilda dressed herself, her slip first, sitting up on the cushions, before she raised her knees to put on her ivory-coloured knickers.

This mildly acrobatic process was interrupted and spun out to five minutes when Toby decided to push her down flat again and kiss her belly as a mark of . . . respect? Devotion? Gratitude? The actual emotion was confused, but the kissing seemed a good idea and he continued downwards to kiss her *fica*. The feel of its soft loose lips under his mouth set off pleasant flickers of lust in his loins – altogether a much more enjoyable set of sensations than when Anna-Louisa sat on his face and rubbed her split on his mouth.

Eventually the kissing had to stop and the dressing completed decently. The cushions were replaced on their benches and Toby and Gilda were sitting side by side, holding hands, the louvred shutters open, when the gondola made its landfall at the island of Murano, or rather the cluster of little islands that made up Murano, and rowed up the main canal.

Here on this island the glass blowers had their little family factories, Toby had read, being kicked out of Venice itself in 1290-something for burning down entire districts of alleys and tenements full of people by careless use of their furnaces. This was where their descendants lived and worked ever since to make the superb Venetian mirrors that once upon a time graced the bedchambers of the nobility of Europe. Nowadays the glass-blowers had sunk to twisting molten glass, soft as toffee, into garish red-and-blue miniature gondolas to sell to tourists from Guildford as souvenirs.

While Mario rowed them up the main canal. Toby looked at the buildings lining either side. They were typical two-storey red-tiled squarish buildings, plastered in pink and ochre, in need of repair and maintenance. Mostly the ground floors were little shops selling salami and mortadella, big round cheeses and wine in big flagons. Along both sides of the quay lay work barges of battered wood, most painted blue, but in need of a new coat of paint. A few men sat about smoking and staring – the arrival of a covered gondola with a well-dressed foreigner and an Italian woman inspired a virtual buzz of conversation.

Here and there the ground floor of a house had been made into a tiny family restaurant with a table or two out on the quay. There was nothing to choose between them and so Toby pointed at the next one ahead and called out to Mario to stop there. The gondola glided in to the broken stone quay and a waiter with an apron down to his ankles sprang forward to grasp the top of the cabin and steady the craft while Toby disembarked. He held out his hand to help Gilda ashore, her hair combed, her clothes in perfect array, her expression happy.

Toby gave Mario a 100-lira note to find himself something to eat – far too much money, being nearly a pound. But he felt he owed the man something for the agonies of frustration and jealousy he must have suffered on the trip out from Venice while hanky-panky was in full progress in the cabin.

Mario took the money with a grin and promised to return in two hours. He vanished in the direction of a fisherman's bar he'd spotted back along the quay.

The waiter couldn't have been older than sixteen and had to be the son of the proprietor. He seated Gilda and Toby with a flourish and spread a checked tablecloth for them. He brought bread and a bottle of red wine to keep them going while he explained what was available for lunch and took their order.

Toby was feeling very pleased with himself. At long last, he reflected, Venice had come up to scratch. He'd had a break from big-breasted middle-aged aunties demanding to be ravished, and not even Italian, either of them. As for Anna-Louisa Ziani, she might be half-Venetian by descent and daughter of a princess, but her ruthless exploitation of the male sex was not Toby's taste. Up in the attic, after the black-boy chair had dropped them on the dusty floor, she became so ferociously aroused that he was half-afraid she was going to bite his *cazzo* off. It was not to be wondered at that her husband preferred the East and shooting at man-eating tigers with a rifle – no doubt he felt it safer.

Although Toby had entertained some misgivings before meeting Gilda – misgivings which Corradini's unspoken but unmistakable scepticism did nothing to soothe – the idyll in the gondola on the peaceful lagoon had turned out very well indeed. It was not too much to say that it fulfilled a dream of what Venice *ought* to be about. The century and a half that had rolled under the Rialto Bridge since Casanova lived and frolicked his merry way around Venice had been abolished for a day while Toby pursued the same pleasures afloat. A pity Gilda was not Venetian but it didn't affect things. No one got everything he asked for because life was never that well organised.

'Drink and eat, Gilda,' he said with affection, stroking her hand on the table, 'then after a stroll to stretch our legs, we shall go back to Venice in the gondola and make love again all the way.'

She couldn't possibly have understood his words, but she gave him an enthusiastic smile and said, *Si, Signor Toby!*

THIRTEEN

Toby was in his third week at the Palazzo Malvolio by the time he completed his inventory of the furniture up in the attic and worked out an estimate of the cost of restoration in London, to which had to be added the cost of crating and shipping – but they were relatively minor. With enormous difficulty and vexation he got through on the telephone to Fitzroy Dalrymple at about eleven in the morning, generally a good time to catch his father. They discussed his figures over the crackle and hissing of the long-distance wire, Toby standing up in the noisy Venice Post Office while Jervis Senior, he guessed, was sitting comfortably in his office, with a mid-morning glass of fine sherry to hand.

When it was all agreed, Toby walked back to the palace to find Mrs Tandy and make his official offer. But the telephone call had taken so long that it was well after midday when he climbed the grand marble staircase on the landward side of the palace. He decided to postpone the business chat until after lunch and tackled the seeming endless journey up to his room through a kilometre or two of faded eighteenth century splendour, to wash his hands and comb his hair. It occurred to him to wonder whether the Malvolios of the grand old days went out much or came home often. Perhaps they avoided the long trek by staying in their rooms for months on end, having servants bring food and drink on a tray.

At twelve thirty he went down to the ante-room where members of the household who were in for lunch assembled for a drink. A name for the ante-room there must be, he guessed, as virtually every room in the palace had a name – the Music Room, the Small Dining room, the Lepanto Room, the Banqueting Room, the Yellow Drawing Room, and so on and so on – but if he'd heard the name for what he called the ante-room he'd forgotten it. One of the footmen he recognised stood at the open double doors to bow him in, another he did not recognise served drinks from a heavy silver tray. Padre Pio was there, sipping a small glass of white wine and, to Toby's annoyance, Ottorino Pavese, who was being chatted to by Marina. She was wearing a yellow silk frock that made her look like a very well-fed and chirpy canary.

Business aside, the courtesies had to be observed. Toby was unsure of precedence, but it couldn't be too terribly wrong to put the Church first. He nodded his head in a friendly sort of way to Padre Pio, feeling it right to draw the line at bowing to a clergyman, especially a foreign one and a Roman Catholic. He made a great play of kissing Marina's hand, hoping to upset her Italian boyfriend, who paid no attention. Finally he shook hands with Ottorino, noting the limp grip and the pallor of his film-star face.

Marina must have picked up a hint of Toby's dislike, for she said that Ottorino wasn't staying for lunch – he'd popped in to see her that morning and wanted to pay his respects to Delphine before he went. It seemed far more likely to Toby that Ottorino had been in Marina's room frolicking all night and was only now strong enough after a morning's sleep to take his leave. There were creases in his shirt-collar to show that it wasn't a clean one that morning, and there was a red spot of dried blood on it from where he'd nicked himself shaving – most likely with a toy razor used by Marina under her arms.

Delphine and Adalbert came into the ante-room chuckling over something or other that had amused them. Ottorino made a great performance of kissing her hand before pushing off. An idea of considerable usefulness appeared in Toby's mind as he stared at the handsome Italian's retreating back.

'I have something of the greatest importance to say to you – but in private,' he said to Marina, forcefully to impress her, but not loud enough for anyone else in the room to hear. 'After lunch – come to my room at three.'

He left her slightly open-mouthed, while he went to Delphine to convey his polite greetings, this being his first sighting of her that day. He said nothing about being ready to discuss business with her, as he had planned to on his walk back from the Post Office – that was now postponed for twenty-four hours. She did ask him, though, having been made aware by means of the palace servant's gossip-service that he had gone out that morning on foot – to the Post Office it was believed.

'Yes, I spoke to London this morning,' he said, 'I thought it best to check insurance rates. Quite soon now I shall be able to convey what Fitzroy Dalrymple are in a position to offer.'

He thought that sounded suitably businesslike to satisfy her for the time being. She nodded and said *good*, from which he had to conclude that she wanted him out of the Palazzo Malvolio as soon as possible. A damned shame, he thought, it would be nice to hang on here for another week or two but obviously I shall never live down the mistake I made with her dear old chum Count Flagranti. She's more peeved about it than he is. After all, he did take the tip I offered!

When they sat down in the Small Dining Room Toby waited until Marina had chosen a chair – leaving one vacant between herself and Delphine for him – and then seated himself on the far side of the table, opposite her. He was trying to create an air of mystery to capture her imagination – he did not mean to let it be compromised by her hand on his thigh under the tablecloth.

She treated him to lingering and smouldering looks while they progressed through the meal, from the marinated sardines with onion rings, the creamy tripe soup, the risotto with spinach and peas, the lagoon eels lightly done in lemon juice and olive oil, the thinly-sliced pork fillets in breadcrumbs, the sharp-flavoured and blue-veined Gorgonzola cheese, the fresh apple tart with lemon ice-cream, the succulent purple figs in antique silver bowls.

Toby enjoyed some of every course, although he ate and drank sparsely, not wishing to be sleepy that afternoon. He wanted to stay alert and active – his plan entailed giving Marina the shock of her life. The idea that had come to him when they were in the ante-room before lunch sprang from a recollection of the day she walked with him to Princess Zita's palazzo. Something she said then had convinced him that for all her sophistication and readiness to indulge her sensual appetites, she was really an old-fashioned romantic. In secret she wanted to be snatched up by a handsome sheikh in a burnous, galloping past on a white stallion – scooped up and thrown over the steed's withers – and carried off to his tent in the desert to be stripped naked and chained hand and foot.

And, of course, to be ravished impossibly often by her brutal and swarthy Bedouin abductor – he naturally being endowed with a *cazzo* standing at least a foot long and thick as his wrist. When she told Toby of Zita's misadventures with her third or fourth husband, Prince Ivan, there was a tinge of regret in her voice that she hadn't been the one tied naked to a bed-post and daily flogged and ravished unnaturally by a deranged Bulgarian. Well, some small part of her secret dream was to become reality that very afternoon.

Back in his room Toby changed into light grey flannels and an open-necked sports shirt. One of the items that formed part of his professional kit was a thirty-foot length of waxed string with a knot at each foot. He found it useful for measuring the size of a piece of furniture for record, and it could be rolled up in a conveniently small ball to go into a pocket. He was proposing to turn this humble bit of equipment into a fearsome instrument of torture for Contessa Marina's benefit.

He sat out on the balcony of his room in the sunlight and cut the length of cord into three-foot pieces with a pocket knife that also formed part of his travelling kit. It had a thin and very sharp blade that was useful to probe joints looking as if they had come apart and been reglued, for checking under loose bits of veneer – and it had a tiny square-ended and blunt blade for taking screws out, to see if they were antique hand-cut or just modern machine-turned replacements.

He took the ends of his nine pieces of waxed string, each a yard long, and bound them tightly together with a tenth piece. His make-shift whip looked reasonably genuine but looks alone were not enough, it had to be effective up to a point. To try it, he went into his room, raised the cat-o'-nine-tails over his shoulder and slashed at the bed fiercely. The knotted cords struck the threadbare nineteenth century crimson damask bedcover with a thwacking sound. This seemed to him reasonably intimidating. Whether it would actually hurt was another matter – authentic cats were made of heavier and stronger stuff than waxed string.

But, to be sure, he slipped off his white shirt, held the whip in front of him, the knotted ends trailing on the floor, took a deep breath and flicked it upward and over his left shoulder as hard as he could. He had seen old engravings of Roman Catholic penitents flogging themselves like this on

Holy Days, trying to convince God they were sorry for whatever they'd got up to and wouldn't do it again if He let them off this time. Usually sins of the flesh, so-called, required the flesh to be chastised in this grotesque and very uncomfortable way.

The knotted ends stung Toby's bare back but it wasn't really painful. And he needn't hit quite that hard, anyway. He put his shirt on, rolled up the cords round his hand into a bundle and slipped it into his trouser pocket. Nothing much showed when he stood in front of the long cheval-glass. And if Marina noticed a bulge there, she would very naturally decide she was causing it and she expected no less.

She was due in fifteen minutes – if she came! He was fairly sure that she would – he had said he had something important to tell her and female curiosity alone would bring her to hear what it was – even if she guessed it was only an excuse to get her into his room for a frolic. But the prospect of that was even more sure to bring her – from the look of Ottorino Pavese he hadn't been up to much that morning! He'd most likely slept heavily till midday after the *elisir*-induced excesses of last night. Leaving the Contessa to stew!

Presumably in the Catholic faith there was a section of Hell reserved for lechers. And if the priests wanted the punishment to fit the crime, it would be an Eternity of sexual arousal and frustration.

Come to think of it, amongst Toby's father's books there was an illustrated Dante which Toby remembered seeing years before, published in the 1860s, he thought, and the engraving might be by Gustave Dore. The Second Circle of Hell was where Catholics ended up if they dabbled outside lawful matrimony. There was a picture of a good-looking woman, Francesca da Rimini, with long hair and a straight-nosed Pre-Raphaelite look about her. Toby racked his brain until he remembered that Francesca was married to an important chap in the 1200s who wasn't up to much in bed – so that she fell into the habit of afternoon frolics with her brother-in-law Paolo.

Her husband came home unexpectedly one day and found them at it – and being a hot-tempered Italian he reached for his trusty stiletto and stabbed them both to death on the spot, so sending their sinful souls to Hell.

As far as Toby could recall from the book, the sinners sent to the Second Circle were harried everlastingly about the sky, or what passes for sky in Hell, by a tornado – or the sort of twisting wind-spout that seemed to be a feature of the American Midwest. Francesca and Paolo, stark naked and itching to get at each other, were whirled round and round endlessly like paper kites in a gale, never able to grab hold of each other as they passed.

On reflection, poor Marina's torment last night was not being unable to get a grip on her lover's *cazzo* – that would have been simple enough while he lay snoring. Her torture was that she couldn't make it stand up for her!

That, of course, was not the problem of the chaps who whipped themselves in penitence on Holy Days. Presumably theirs stood up stiff too often and led them into temptation. A good lashing was meant to quell the urges, as well a reminding God that the self-flogger felt sorry for what he had done – or was thinking of doing.

It was all pretty rum, really, Toby considered. If instead of whipping their shoulder-blades they'd given their stand-up part a good lashing with the scourge, its sinful pride would surely have vanished quicker and it would have gone limp. Maybe even forever, if they lashed hard enough!

There was a quick tap at the bedroom door – it opened before he had time to rise from the chair, let alone cross the room to answer – and in came Marina. She was ten minutes ahead of time, Toby noted with a grin. She came a step or two towards him and stopped. She didn't take the chair he offered, she simply stood looking at him.

'What is so important, that you are rude enough to tell me to come here? Don't you realise the risk of being seen and talked about by the servants?' she demanded.

She was trying for the upper hand, but Toby had no intention of letting her achieve that. He stood with a straight back and shoulders, head held high, feet firmly planted, and stared into her eyes forcefully.

'You'll find out soon enough,' he said, not at all polite. 'I know you'll be astounded when you do. Take your dress off.'

'What!' Marina exclaimed, trying for outrage but not getting at all close to it.

'I want to see your breasts,' he said, 'take your dress off.'

'I didn't come her to be treated like a street-walker,' she snapped at him. 'What on earth do you think you're up to?'

'Bare your breasts,' he said again, not being drawn into any sort of discussion. 'Get them out – I want to see them.'

He squared his shoulders and glared, radiating aggression and self-confidence. In his imagination he was Signor Ziani beating through the steamy fever-ridden jungle of Franjipani, face to face with a snarling yellow-and-black tiger, his trusty Mannlicher rifle aimed for the heart. Though in point of fact his trusty weapon was not aimed at anything – it dangled loosely in his trousers. And when it was cocked and raised, it wouldn't be at the heart he aimed it.

His insistence and assurance were making Marina irresolute. A moment or two passed in silence, then she dropped her eyes from his fixed stare. She shrugged her shoulders as if to say *I may as well humour the lunatic for the time being – but if he thinks he can browbeat me, he's sadly mistaken*. With no more ado she unfastened her canary yellow frock, bringing a hard smile flickering over Toby's face while he watched her pull the frock over her head. Under it, she had on a creamy-white petticoat with an embroidered yoke.

'Your breasts,' he repeated, 'I still can't see them.'

Marina took her slip off too, still not meeting his eyes, and stood round-shouldered for his inspection. *Too heavy and fleshy* he said to himself, staring at her uncovered breasts, *not chic*. But pleasantly exciting to handle, he knew from past frolicking with her. Bountifully oversized for the hands, soft and bouncy to grip and roll – and if the truth were to be told, the sight of Contessa Marina's out-moded, non-chic, too-fat, but for all that *interesting* bouncers was making his limp part grow longer and thicker.

'You've seen them – now are you satisfied?' Marina demanded in a late gesture of opposition.

'Take your knickers off,' he said, ignoring her question, 'and your stockings. Strip naked.'

This was not at all what she had anticipated when she came to Toby's room. No doubt she had expected him to embrace her and kiss her, undress her slowly and lead her to the canopied bed, stroke her breasts and belly – and eventually spread her on her back and mount her – all very traditional. But none of that was happening. She was not being wooed, not even perfunctorily. Her consent was not being sought, her pleasure was not considered. She was being brutalised, abused, treated like a paid creature, or a servant – almost like a slave! And yet there was a sort of shameful excitement in being made to strip naked, a curiously arousing humiliation in being stared at so arrogantly.

She bent forward to take down the creamy-white knickers that matched her discarded slip, even down to the embroidery. She balanced on each leg in turn while she took off her garters and silk stockings. And when at last she was completely naked, she straightened her shoulders and faced Toby, her uncertainty all gone. She understood the power her bare breasts and belly – and the patch of walnut-brown curls between her well-shaped thighs – had on men. Seeing her nakedness turned them into *her* slaves.

From now on she had the upper hand – all her life men drooled over her body and begged on their knees to be allowed to stroke her breasts and kiss her between the legs. Many a time she had made Ottorino crawl to her on his belly and beg her to lie down for him.

Toby had written the scene differently. Her newfound boldness was not part of his plan at all and he had to demolish it.

'You've deceived me,' he said coldly, eyeing her body up and down with what he hoped was a scornful expression on his face.

'What do you mean?' she asked, frowning slightly when he did not try to put his arms round her and run his hands over her.

'You deliberately led me to believe you enjoyed my company in bed,' said Toby, trying to sound very annoyed, 'but where were you last night when I wanted you?'

'I made no promises,' Marina retorted.

'Promises are for engaged couples and newly-weds,' said Toby dismissively. 'I want no promise from you except the promise of pleasure your body offers. This you deny me.'

'No, don't be angry, Toby. I'm here with you now – take me,' she said quickly.

'Your behaviour has been completely unacceptable,' said he, a black scowl on his face. 'If you think you can excuse yourself by opening your legs for five minutes, you are mistaken!'

His pretended anger was having an effect. Marina's expression of eagerness faded slowly as he stood silent, and glared at her.

'What do you want me to do?' she asked tremulously.

Without answering, Toby approached her, his steps deliberate, and put his hands on her bare shoulders. She reached out to put her arms round him and clasp him to her bare bosom, certain his obstinacy had collapsed under the irresistable attraction of her nakedness. But Toby pressed down hard on her shoulders and made her sink to her knees on the tiled floor. She stared up at him with a look of incredulity, then her expression cleared as she guessed what he wanted.

She unbuttoned his trousers to pull out his upright part, and sighed pleasurably to see what she held. In some unexplained way, playing the domineering role had aroused Toby intensely – Marina's eyes fairly bulged at the close-up view of his *cazzo* bobbing in front of her face, thick, hard and strong . . .

'You've been very rude to me, you know,' she said with a pout as she took him in hand. 'I pride myself on being a sport and a broad-minded person but there are limits.'

'Be silent,' said Toby, as forcefully as he could manage, and from his pocket he drew out the make-shift scourge. 'You know what is expected of you.'

Before she could give voice to the outrage and horror dawning in her eyes at the sight of his light-weight cat-o'-nine-tails, Toby brought his arm down strongly over her shoulder, aiming to lash her plump bottom. He scored a hit and she squealed. With his left hand he clasped the back of her head to pull her face toward his belly. She squealed again when her bottom was lashed a second time – though the amateur instrument was of the wrong material to cut into flesh and cause real pain.

Toby was so close to her that his stiff shaft was rubbing on her face, but Marina shut her mouth and stopped her squealing – silently defying him to do his worst.

'I'm going to thrash you unconscious,' he said coldly, trying to make his voice sound like a sadistic sex-maniac on a spree – however that might sound. 'First I shall whip your behind to a mass of scarlet weals so that you won't be able to sit down for a week – then I'm going to throw you down on your back and flog your breasts until you're screaming in agony . . .'

While he was threatening her with his programme of horrors he continued to lash at her bottom, spacing out the blows.

'Mmm, mmm!' Marina begged, her mouth still tight closed in a show of resistance – *Death Before Dishonour* – but she was still clinging hard to his thighs with hot hands, no doubt to prevent herself collapsing to the floor. Or perhaps for another reason.

'And when I've got you lingering on the edge of consciousness and praying for the flogging to stop,' said Toby, sounding grim as he could, 'I'm going to force your legs wide apart and stand between them to thrash your belly and your *fica* until you slide into a dead faint.'

'No!' Marina gasped, her mouth open at last. 'That hurt!'

By chance one of the strings had caught her between the plump cheeks and the knot on the tip of it had flicked a tender part.

'Hurt?' he exclaimed, 'it's meant to hurt – you'll writhe in agony before long! And when you faint and lie senseless on the floor with your belly criss-crossed with red marks, I'll fling myself on you and jam my shaft up you – I'm so hard and swollen I'll split you open! And I'll ravish you as you've never been done before, Marina! I'm going to fill your belly full till it overflows – and the pleasure will be all mine! You'll be out like a light and won't even know you're being violated!'

'Oh my god,' she murmured, her fingers gripping the flesh of his thighs through his trouser-legs, 'this is a nightmare!'

'Nightmare? It's your dream come true,' he retorted harshly. 'You need blame no one but yourself for what I'm going to do to you – you ask me if I'd ever whipped a woman and I lied.'

To prevent the exchange of threat and protestation becoming a conversation, Toby plied his string-whip faster, wondering all the time if it was doing more than tickle, and rubbed his stiff part against her cheek. Marina gasped and gave in – she steered the unhooded purple head to her mouth.

'Yes!' Toby cried out in exultation to feel the edges of her teeth grip the shaft lightly to steady it for her wet tongue to lap over the head. 'Yes – you know what you have to do!'

He stopped flailing her bottom, both hands on her shoulders to support himself, the home-made whip hanging loose down her bare back to keep her aware of its proximity and readiness to strike again if he so chose. Marina's hands were on his bottom now, fondling the lean cheeks through his trousers and pressing herself against his thighs. Her eyes were closed – she sucked at the *cazzo* that filled her mouth, the wet little sounds much intensifying his pleasure.

She knew very well what pleasure she was giving him – and, if proof were needed, in her mouth his already fully hard part was becoming thicker and stronger yet under her ardent attentions. For a moment she came up for air, clasping his wet *cazzo* in her palm and rubbing quickly up and down to prevent his excitement from subsiding for even an instant. Her face was flushed as she looked up into his eyes. She wiggled her bare bottom and gasped, *Whip me, Toby!*

The moment he laid into her behind again she slid his shaft back into her hot mouth and used her tongue furiously. His legs wobbled under him as the familiar sensations ripped through his belly – he stopped whipping and grabbed at her shoulders again for support as the muscles of his belly and thighs went into spasms. His lust fountained into Marina's busy mouth in violent spurts, his head went back and he cried, *Aaah*, loins bucking and knees shaking.

She sucked him dry, her naked body shaking against his legs, then her head too lolled back on her neck and she stared up at Toby with unseeing eyes, her red-painted mouth wide open in a long wailing cry. He realised then that she had reached her own crisis and, to intensify and prolong her throes, he raised the cat-o'-nine-tails and, with shaky arm, laid into her bottom with whatever remnant of strength he could muster.

She jerked and twitched to the cuts, screeched and yowled in ecstasy, then slowly subsided at his feet, her clutching hands sliding inch by inch down his trousered legs, his shaft plucked from her mouth. Toby stared down as she folded up on herself in utter relaxation, her head between his parted ankles, the pale and smooth expanse of her back revealed to him, and the round cheeks of her bottom, faintly pink from his thrashing. In a way he found most remarkable, she seemed to be abasing herself as if by instinct before him, acknowledging him Lord and Master! My word, he thought, is this how it was for Rudolf Valentino in his Sheikh get-up?

In a while Marina shivered and raised her head. She sat back on her haunches and looked up at Toby with calm eyes. He shook his cat-o'-nine-tails loosely between them, making the knotted ends flick over her full breasts and their prominent buds. From a corner of her mouth a little trickle ran down her chin. Toby held his hand out to her and when she took it pulled her to her feet and led her across to the canopied bed by the wall. He was not about to let her off the hook – the scene ran on for a long time yet in his mental script.

He ordered her to undress him and stood by the bed while she stripped him of shirt and trousers, underwear and socks. And as she disrobed him, she touched her mouth to the parts she bared – his chest, belly, his limp and sticky part, thighs and feet.

He sat upright on the bed with his legs crossed and his back straight and, to keep Marina in mind of her subordinate status, he motioned for her to lie face down on the bed in front of him – a suitably symbolic arrangement for *Sultan and Slave-Girl* he considered, delighted at how he was getting away with it. It would make a nice painting to hang on the wall, he thought with a grin, if a handy artist happened to be passing with brushes and canvas. Something along the lines of Jean-Auguste-Dominique Ingres, the French johnny who made a fortune painting imaginary pictures of naked slave-girls in Sultan's harems – plump women with wide hips and swagged bellies and breasts on them like balloons. A lot like Marina, in fact; overfleshed and overblown, the way Turkish Sultans preferred their playmates. That was in the great days of the Ottoman Empire, which had now thoroughly collapsed as a result of the desert exploits of Col. Lawrence during the Great War. Lawrence of Arabia, a man never interested in naked harem-girls.

To Toby's way of thinking the end of the Ottomans was a pity, as the handful of poor republics, tin-pot kingdoms and desert sheikhdoms it had been shattered into were not likely to match it for cruel splendour. In a republic you couldn't hope to have a decent harem stocked with beautiful women sprawled out naked on silk cushions round a fountain, and guarded by black eunuchs in turbans with long curving scimitars. All you'd find would be a dismal political assembly of garlic-scented lawyers endlessly wrangling about tax-allocation.

Not of course that he personally was in favour of plump women with breasts like balloons. It was terribly old hat these days. The ideal *Vogue* young lady had no breasts to speak of, and her bottom was flat and trim, her hips narrow . . . and yet it had to be said that, from where he sat, the view down Marina's back to the cushiony cheeks of her backside was pleasing. And more than just pleasing, if a chap was honest with himself – the sight of Marina's bare bottom was definitely stimulating. My trouble, he admitted to himself, is that I have low tastes. And as long as they stay secret, I'm in favour of indulging them.

But not at this moment, of course. The show he had put on for Marina had a particular purpose.

'Marina,' he said, 'why have you been letting Ottorino ferret about in the attics? Why is he interested in what I am doing – what does he hope to achieve?'

'Don't know,' she murmured, her chin on her hands as she lay looking up at him with clear eyes.

'But you do,' he insisted. 'You'd ask him out of curiosity. I want to know, Marina. Is he waiting to see what I offer, so he can outbid me?'

'Ottorino doesn't want to buy any old furniture,' she said in a fairly assured sort of way that Toby half-believed. 'It's not his pidgin – he doesn't know anything about furniture.'

'Then is there some specific piece he's after?'

'I don't think so, really not. He seemed more interested in wardrobes than anything else, but he was not very forthcoming.'

At least it was a starting-point. Toby knew for a fact there were three wardrobes in the attic, each one a damaged masterpiece. There was a mid–1600 walnut one with doors and side panels carved with country scenes of harvesting and hunting. There was a charming rococo one with doors painted in flower designs – a superb piece of work! And the four-door baroque monster, eight feet tall and long enough to sleep four with room to spare. He had found the triptych in the big one. The bottom of the walnut one had been broken through by a mad Malvolio a very long time ago, while the rococo piece had no secret compartment.

'Interested in wardrobes, was he?' said Toby thoughtfully to Marina. 'There's an extremely nice eighteenth century one up there – one of the best I've seen. Does he collect rococo furniture?'

'No, he seemed more interested in a huge thing that he could never get inside his apartment. He spent ages fiddling at it.'

'Why? What was he looking for?'

Marina shrugged, in so far as that was possible while she lay face down, and she slid forward on her belly a little until she could kiss Toby's bare foot.

'He said something about wardrobes having secrets,' she said, 'but I wasn't paying much attention. It's very hot and stuffy up there under the roof and I was bored. Does it matter?'

'What matters to me is why he is poking about up there while I'm out,' Toby answered. 'I've taken a lot of time and trouble making a proper inventory. The company who sent me here expect me to purchase the furniture at a fair price so it can be taken to England and restored. And now I've done all the work and can make Delphine an offer, what do I find? Someone skulking about in my footsteps.'

'Yes, I can see how that must make you terribly suspicious,' Marina said carelessly, her hand resting lightly on the inside of Toby's thigh. 'Look – next time I see Ottorino I'll ask him straight out what his interest is.'

'How many times has he been in the attic, apart from that one time you brought him up when I was working there?'

'Oh, two or three. I haven't bothered to keep count.'

It was obvious to Toby that *Dottore* Pavese knew about secret compartments in antique furniture. He couldn't have known there was a valuable painting concealed in a wardrobe – he must have been searching on the off-chance.

It really didn't make sense. Suppose he'd found something of value – if Marina was with him at the time he'd have to give it to Delphine. Not for a moment did Toby believe Marina could be persuaded to stay silent and let Ottorino take it himself. Nor did he believe she would accept a share. So what was the point of looking for secret hiding-places?

There was another possibility – that Ottorino was not looking for something valuable to take out, but looking for a place to hide something valuable of his own. He knew that the furniture would shortly be on its way to London. Could it be that he was planning to smuggle something into England? And if so, what?

Toby's knowledge of smuggling was limited. He had sometimes sneaked banned books through British Customs on his way back from trips to Paris – English-language publications London bookshops would be prosecuted for stocking. Aubrey Beardsley's romantic novel *Venus and Tannhauser*, and Leopold von Masoch's even more romantic novel *Venus in Furs*. And of course Captain Charles Devereaux' exotically romantic *Venus in India*.

The name Venus in the title was a sure sign of what the book was about! Except for the first and most famous of them all – John Cleland's *Memoirs of a Woman of Pleasure* – of which Toby had smuggled several copies, as presents for friends.

But it was ridiculous to suppose Ottorino wanted to pack the bottom of a wardrobe with naughty books. He would be interested in something that could be sold for a very high price in London, not for a few pounds. Toby racked his brains.

There were rich young idiots, male and female, who dabbled a bit with opium compounds like heroin, but they all had West End doctors who'd write a prescription for them. There was no point in smuggling it. For poor people without sensible doctors maybe – but poor people couldn't afford to buy it if it was smuggled. And as for precious stones and metals, diamonds, gold, platinum and so on – they were imported legally with no fuss.

'When are you seeing Ottorino next?' he asked Marina.

'Nothing is arranged. In a day or two, I suppose,' she said, kissing the inside of Toby's thigh. Her breath was hot and very exciting on his skin, her hand up in his groin, her fingertips tickling the head of his limp part.

'Why not this evening?' he said. 'He'd take you to dinner if you asked him to. A good nourishing meal and a bottle or two of Chianti would do wonders for him. Buck him up. Then afterwards you can ask tactfully about wardrobes and why he is interested in them.'

'Tonight? That's very soon,' she said. 'I mean, he was very tired after last night. Quite exhausted, in fact.'

'What of it? A dash of your famous *elisir d'amore* in his gin and he'll be as frisky as a two-year-old – isn't that so?'

'It's not good to overdo things,' said she doubtfully, though never before in her life had she shied away from excess, if you asked Toby. 'Certainly not with Italian gin. He might collapse altogether.'

'He's about done for, anyway,' said Toby authoritatively. 'No point in shilly-shallying now. The two of you have been going the pace – another time or two at most in bed with you will see him flat on his back. So you may as well make him happy tonight and find out what I want to know.'

Toby's limp part was beginning to stiffen. Marina took it in her hand and massaged it slowly to help on the process.

'It's a terrible responsibility,' she said. 'I don't think I can bring myself to do it to him. We've been very close friends for ages.'

'Only since the Carnival this year, from what I've been told. That's hardly a lifelong friendship. I want to know by midday tomorrow what he's up to with the furniture, so you'll have to get it out of him tonight.'

'Will you whip me if I disobey you?' she whispered.

'I'm going to whip you to make sure you *do* obey,' he answered as he switched back into his domination role, 'you got off much too lightly before – there's hardly a scratch on your backside. This time you're really in for it!'

'Oh, Toby...' she murmured.

'Get up on your knees,' he said, stern and curt, and when she did so, he made her bow down till she could take his now fully stiff *cazzo* in her mouth. The bottoms-up posture put the cheeks of her round pale bum within easy reach of the lash.

'I'm going to thrash you so hard you'll shriek in agony!' he said in as cruel a tone as he could manage, and he swished his home-made scourge at her upraised bottom, scoring an easy hit. A stifled moan escaped her, her strong sucking sent tremors of pleasure rippling through his belly.

'In a while I'll have you lying on your back,' he told her in a grating voice, 'with your head locked between my thighs, while I lash your belly... I'll tie your ankles together and hang your head down from the canopy fixture up there on the wall and flog you senseless before I do you upside down...'

'Yes, Toby, yes...' she gasped, freeing her mouth for a moment while her clasped hand slid up and down his wet shaft, 'whip me and ravage me, please, please!'

FOURTEEN

After Toby had despatched a suitably willing Marina to extract Ottorino Pavese's secret by the use of her bodily charms and an extra-large dose of the aphrodisiac potion she favoured, he had second thoughts. He didn't like Pavese in the least. In fact it would be truer to say that he detested the man but he didn't want to be responsible for his death – by sexual exhaustion or any other way. And, according to Adalbert Gmund, the injudicious use of the potion had damn nearly done for a chum of Marina's a year or two before – the one she called Orlando who'd rampaged her on the Rialto Bridge.

But it was too late by then to have qualms. They'd played the *Marquis de Sade wreaking his depraved and cruel lust on a poor defenceless virgin* to the entire satisfaction of both of them. Then Marina dressed and went and Toby slept until six o'clock. He woke feeling uneasy that he might have let *Dottore* Pavese in for more than he could survive, but when he enquired for the Contessa a footman went in search of her and came back with a message from her maid. The Contessa Marina was out and wouldn't be in for dinner – and was not expected back until very late.

Presumably, thought Toby with a grin, the message came to him from the same maid who applied cold cream to Marina's bottom to soothe it and reduce the redness before helping her to dress to vamp Ottorino. The plan wasn't going to work anyway, Toby could see that now. Marina was not capable of subtlety and, when she started to show an interest in wardrobes, Ottorino would guess she'd been put up to it and why. He'd drop his scheme and that would be the end of it.

Or supposing Marina got him to tell her everything during a night of raging non-stop passion – the chances were that in his already weakened condition a marathon performance would put him into hospital for a long stay. In which case he wouldn't be out and about in time to conceal anything in the wardrobe's secret compartment before it was crated up and shipped off. And if he was reduced to a state of total physical collapse, Toby said to comfort his conscience, no one was to blame but Pavese himself. Nobody forced him to frolic with Marina all night – he did it because he wanted to. What happened was his own responsibility.

The sky through the open shutters was white with early dawn when Toby woke up next morning. Someone was lying close behind him with a hand over his waist to grasp his stiff part and play with it. He lay still for a while, collecting his thoughts and enjoying the sensation of his unseen companion's hand moving up and down delicately. It was, he decided, a very pleasant way to be woken up, and when his *cazzo* began to jerk strongly he gave a sigh and rolled over to face his benefactor. He already knew it was Marina, from her perfume.

'*Buon giorno*, Toby,' she said, and moved her head forward on the pillow to kiss him.

'*Buon giorno*, Contessa,' he said, reaching up to fondle her breasts. Over her bare shoulder he caught a glimpse of a bright scarlet evening frock and a pair of dark silk stockings, thrown carelessly over a chair. Evidently she had come straight to his room from her night of love with Ottorino.

A pretty long night it had been too, Toby thought, the time now being after five in the morning, to judge by the light through the open windows. It was to be hoped she had not wrung out poor Ottorino entirely beyond the prospect of recovery!

He ran his palm down her soft belly to slide his hand between her thighs and found she had her knickers on. Without waiting for her to take them off he flattened his hand against her warm flesh and slid it down the top of the flimsy silk garment. Her curls were under his fingertips and her *fica* was moist to the touch. The lips felt loose and ready and his shaft throbbed and jerked sharply at the imminent prospect of pushing between them into her belly.

As his fingers tickled inside over her wet bud, Toby wondered whether the *Dottore* had succeeded in penetrating that welcoming slit even once during the night, drugged to the eyebrows with stand-up potion though he might be. From what Toby had observed when he trailed the pair of them down through the palace from the attics to Marina's bedroom, Ottorino was far gone even then – and that was more than a week ago.

When he was spying through the keyhole Toby had seen clearly that Ottorino was not in command of the situation – he'd simply sprawled out on a brocade armchair, the wood a yellow-gold yew, one of a matched pair. Marina had been on her knees to open his trouser-front and stiffen his lazy part in her mouth. Even that took longer than anyone might expect. And afterwards he looked done for, until she rubbed his body with 4711 Eau de Cologne to revive him.

It hadn't revived him enough to get his *cazzo* up her, all the same. He'd done the next best thing – he ravished her with his handsome film-star face, she on her back on her four-poster bed and Ottorino lying between her splayed legs to use his tongue. It was Toby's guess that something like that had happened last night in Ottorino's apartment, wherever that was in Venice, not once but as many times as Marina could raise his interest.

She confirmed Toby's unspoken speculations to some extent by tugging at his quivering six inches and murmuring, *Put it in – I want to feel it inside me!* And why not? he thought, the early morning is a pleasant enough time to lie on a woman's belly. He rolled her on her back and threw aside the light bedcover while he crouched beside her to slip off her knickers – magnolia silk with her initial M embroidered in pink on the left hip! Taking off a woman's knickers was a deliciously exciting act for Toby – almost as intimate in an odd sort of way as having his *cazzo* in her. The symbolic value appealed to him – a final unveiling, a revealing of basic femaleness. It was not only the surrender to his eyes of her sexuality but an act of consent to all that came next, an act of submission to his pleasure, a yielding to be infiltrated, penetrated, enfiladed, perpetrated, desecrated, sequestrated, deprivated, immolated, annihilated!

He kissed Marina's belly and wiggled his middle-finger inside her, until her legs were twitching and she begged him to *put it in!* He slid over her and between her legs, bare belly on hers, his pyjama bottoms somewhere round his ankles, but there was no time to bother with them now. Marina's fleshy thighs opened to welcome him and a long push sank his stiffness into her.

'*Bene, bene, bene!*' she gasped. '*Benissimo!*'

Her climax came very quickly after he started long deliberate strokes – well before he was ready she cried out and jerked her belly up at him in quick spasms of release. Toby maintained his steady rhythm, sliding in and out of her wetness without regard for her ecstasy or the lassitude that followed it, and soon she was sighing and shuddering again as he aroused her to a second crisis of sensation that had her heels drumming on the mattress on either side of him.

For Toby her intense response was not only very exciting – it was also amusing. He'd been right about last night – Ottorino's intimate attentions had not been able to satisfy her avid lusts and she had come back to the Palazzo Malvolio in a condition of hot arousal. He slowed his stroke to give her time to recover a little from her second climax, then he stabbed rhythmically when her mouth opened again in eager gasps and her fingernails clawed down his bare bottom.

The unasked question of how many times he could make her do it was left unanswered – the hot wet cling of her flesh about his wildly leaping *cazzo* and the bounce of her broad soft belly under his were so insidiously exciting that he couldn't control himself any longer. His frantic desire spurted into her, to his wailing cry of delight.

A little later, when they lay side by side in the coolness of very early morning, she surprised him by telling him Ottorino's secret plans.

'He has a very valuable painting he wants to sell in London,' she said, stroking Toby's chest in a contented way, much like a cat rubbing itself against its owner. 'There's a problem about getting a proper licence to export it, apparently, because it's a national cultural treasure, whatever they mean by that.'

'I thought a little tactful bribery solved problems like that in Italy,' said Toby nonchalantly. 'Perhaps he hasn't found the most sympathetic official to stamp his licence yet.'

'He's tried everyone but they don't want to let the picture out of the country. It's too important.'

'That does surprise me,' said Toby, 'not that I know anything about paintings, but galleries round Europe have their Titians and Tintorettos and Guardis and Veroneses and Canalettos and Raphaels and Bellinis – what difference will it make to let one more picture leave Italy?'

'None, I'm sure,' Marina murmured, 'but that's the way of it. Nobody understands how official decisions are made, that's why people look for ways round them. Did you know there's a secret compartment in one of the wardrobes you want to take away?'

'Really? It doesn't surprise me a bit, though,' said Toby, a decision to be wary causing him to dissemble until he knew more of the story. 'There are often secret drawers and hiding-places in old desks – sometimes very ingenious – and less often in old cupboards.'

'There's one in the sideboard in my sitting room,' she said, 'I keep some photos of me I don't want my maid to see in it.'

'Who took them?' Toby asked, letting himself be diverted by visions of Marina in nude poses.

'Oh, nobody you know – his name is Antonio Pontecello and he used to have a photographic studio here. Most of his work was wedding photos outside churches. But he did some portraits of me years ago and then asked me to pose for artistic studies.'

'Nude, of course,' said Toby, stroking her belly gently.

'Well, of course nude – otherwise they wouldn't be artistic.'

Toby thought it sensible to get back to Ottorino's plans for the wardrobe, otherwise the digression into Marina's naked body might turn out to be a major diversion.

'So putting two and two together,' said he, 'what we have now is that Ottorino wants to make me an unwitting accomplice in an illegal scheme. He conceals his picture in my wardrobe so as to get it through Italian Customs and British Customs, then sneaks round to collect it in London.'

'It's clever, isn't it?' Marina murmured, her hand on Toby's thigh in a hopeful sort of way.

'It's fiendish,' said Toby. 'If the Customs find his damned picture, I'm the one who's fined and sent to jail. Thousands of pounds worth of furniture belonging to Fitzroy Dalrymple gets impounded by Customs, and then smashed to pieces in search of more contraband. It would be a catastrophe! All for Ottorino's benefit!'

'I never thought of that!' Marina exclaimed. 'I'll tell him it's simply not on. He'll have to find another way to get his picture out of the country, when he feels up to it again. I'll give it back to him when I go round to see him tomorrow or the next day.'

'He handed it over to you?' asked Toby in astonishment.

'He's a bit shaky on his legs,' Marina replied, her hand at rest on Toby's thigh. 'He'll be staying in bed for a day or two to get his strength back. He gave me the picture in strictest confidence and told me how to find a secret compartment in the big wardrobe.'

'The very big one?' Toby asked, knowing very well it was.

'Yes, it's got a hiding-place down in the base – I'll show it to you. Ottorino says you twiddle a couple of rosettes in the carving and a door pops open. He told me to put his picture in there at the right moment.'

'And when's the right moment?'

'After Delphine has sold the furniture to you.'

'I'd like to see this famous picture that can't be exported,' said Toby, thinking hard. 'Where is it?'

Marina got up and went to the chair where her scarlet evening frock lay. Underneath it, on the chair seat, was a flat package wrapped in strong bleached calico, tied each way with thin red cords, blobs of sealing-wax on the knots. She brought it back to the bed and showed it to Toby doubtfully.

'It's awfully well done up,' she said, 'if we open it to look at what's inside, Ottorino will know we've been prying.'

'Self-protection isn't prying,' said Toby firmly, 'I think I have every right to know what's in that parcel. My whole future life and liberty could be at stake. Not very big, is it?'

The package measured about two feet one way and a foot and a half the other, and was perhaps two inches thick.

'It must be a small painting,' said Marina, 'and it's not in a frame – you can feel that through the wrapping.'

She handed it over and sat naked on the bedside to watch when Toby fetched his penknife from the dressing-table and used the thin sharp blade to pick off the sealing-wax carefully before he untied the knots. The calico had also been sewn as a further precaution. He slit one stitch with care, to unthread the rest, keeping the thread. He laid the package flat on the floor and sat on his haunches, his nakedness forgotten, to unwrap it.

Inside were protective layers of chamois leather, bleached linen, thick grey paper, soft tissue paper, and an innermost wrapping of pink artificial silk. This last undid to reveal a worn portfolio of the type used by artists and collectors to keep their unmounted prints in. Inside that were five pen-and-ink drawings on paper going brown with age.

'Is that all?' Marina asked. 'Where's the painting?'

She came to kneel beside Toby, heavy breasts dangling as she bent down to pick up the top drawing and stare closely.

It was a naked young woman with plump round breasts and her hair done in round plaits over her ears. She was standing by a brook with a view of hills and a town in the far distance. She had an arm round the long curving neck of a huge swan standing beside her and rubbing itself against her thigh.

'A working sketch for a painting of Leda and the Swan,' Toby said, wondering what he'd found. 'It was a fairly popular theme with Renaissance artists. Though not exactly like this.'

The woman's free hand lay between her thighs in a way showing that she was pleasuring herself. Toby shuffled through the rest of the drawings. They were all of naked women, posed slightly differently with long hair done in various styles of the early 1500s but with a similar lack of individual character in their faces.

They were all in erotic play of some sort – with Zeus himself in various mythical disguises. To accommodate personal taste he had turned himself into a snorting stallion, a shower of gold, a long-horned bull, a thick black cloud.

'What are they?' Marina asked, sounding puzzled. 'Why do you think Ottorino lied to me?'

'They must be old and valuable, to go to this trouble,' Toby said thoughtfully. 'If they're not fakes, of course. That seems to be a bit of a ticklish question with your chum Ottorino. If I had to guess, I'd assign these simpering virgins to Leonardo da Vinci. Or someone who can copy him very well.'

'How can you tell?' Marina asked.

'I don't think Leonardo liked girls and he usually made them look complete ninnies. You've seen that ridiculous portrait of Mona-Lisa Somebody-Or-Other in the Louvre.'

'No,' said Marina. 'There are far more interesting things to do in Paris than traipse round art galleries.'

'What we have here may be preliminary studies for pictures he never painted. For obvious reasons. Or they might be jottings for his own amusement – leaves from his notebook, sort of thing. Or perhaps they were trial studies for a rich collector of naughty pictures – a Cardinal, or some such.'

'Leonardo da Vinci – but he's tremendously important,' Marina said, though a note of vague disappointment in her voice showed she was not much impressed by the drawings. 'People will pay incredible amounts of money for his work.'

'There's hardly any of his work available,' Toby replied.

'he was too busy designing war machines that didn't work for the Duke of Milan, to get round to painting all that often. Some of his pictures are murals on church walls and rotting away.'

'So what is available must be very valuable?' she insisted.

'I imagine his drawings fetch a good price.'

'That would explain why Ottorino can't get a licence to sell them abroad,' Marina suggested.

'Yes,' said Toby, noncommittal. He'd come to the conclusion that Ottorino's reason for smuggling them out was not inability to obtain official sanction but because they were not his. That situation called for some careful thinking.

'We'll wrap them up again,' said he, patting Marina's bottom in a friendly way, 'and I'll keep them for now. Say nothing to Ottorino when he asks, except that they're in a safe place. Not a word about me, understand? And before I leave Venice we'll decide on the best thing to do with them.'

He was not being entirely candid with Marina – he had already decided what to do about the drawings. After she'd gone to her own quarters, he concealed them with the triptych in the secret compartment of the wardrobe in his room and got back into bed to sleep for two hours until the maid woke him with coffee and soft rolls.

He had made no approach to Maria the maid since the afternoon at the beginning of his stay in the palace – the occasion when she had deflected him from his purpose and calmed him down by hand. Truth to tell, he had been so involved with other women that he had neither energy nor desire to try his luck with Maria again. Whenever she was in his room, bringing his breakfast or tidying his clothes, he and she smiled pleasantly – and the merest bit knowingly – at each other, and left it at that.

Later on that morning he headed for Niccolo Corradini's musty little shop by the Fenice Theatre. The sky was clear and a very light blue, the day was nicely hot, the tourists were strolling through street and square, guide-book in hand, off in pursuit of culture or mid-morning coffee.

Corradini's bell gave out its cracked rattle when Toby pushed the door open and the proprietor looked up from behind the undusted counter, his spectacles halfway down his nose. He wore the loose grey linen jacket that seemed to be the mark of his profession – if indeed his curious dealings in fake antiquarian curiosities could be called a profession.

Clearly he had paid a visit to his barber since Toby last saw him – his thin hair was jet black today.

'Signor Toby, *buon giorno*,' said Corradini, 'I hope that your trip in the gondola was enjoyable.'

'It was marvellous,' Toby answered, 'I've come to thank you and to ask your expert opinion on a confidential matter that could be profitable to us both.'

'Ah, then come into my private room,' and he ushered Toby to the cluttered room behind the shop and cleared a chair of books for him to sit on. Then hastily he threw a thin and worn cloth of green baize over an object he had just noticed uncovered on his work-table. Toby grinned but made no comment, though to him it seemed very similar to the album of naked royal girlfriends that Adalbert Gmund had bought. The leather cover was a lighter shade of burgundy but the gold-blocking in the corner looked a lot like a monogram and crown.

Niccolo produced from one of the battered cupboards standing about the walls a bottle and two small glasses.

'A little glass of *grappa*,' he suggested, filling them full, 'I find it goes well at this time of the morning.'

Grappa, as Toby had found after meals at the Palazzo Malvolio, was a rough and strong spirit distilled from the dregs of wine-pressing. He wished the dealer *salute* and sipped with caution, not swallowing it all down in one go, as Niccolo did.

'Are there many collections of Leonardo da Vinci drawings you know of?' he enquired.

'Do you mean genuine drawings, by Leonardo himself, or do you mean later work in the manner of Leonardo?' Niccolo asked, not able to bring himself to use the word *fake* in connection with works of art.

'Both, I suppose.'

'There are believed to be many collections of drawings which their owners are certain are by Leonardo but which in truth are by later artists inspired by the great Leonardo,' Niccolo said, speaking slowly and with care. 'No one can say how many, as the rich men who buy these works are told they are buying drawings taken from the official State collections in Florence or Milan. Therefore they remain silent.'

'It's a first-class wheeze, telling an unscrupulous collector he's got stolen goods,' said Toby. 'The most amazing forgeries have been foisted on to trusting American millionaires that way – rumour has it there are dozens of Titians and Raphaels in the United States that no art historian has ever seen or heard of.'

Niccolo shook his head sadly, as if dismayed to hear of such crimes inflicted on innocent bystanders.

'There are said to be three Mona Lisas in private collections in the state of Pennsylvania alone,' Toby continued. 'Not that I know anything about pictures, of course, but I have seen what goes on with antique furniture.'

Niccolo pursed his lips in a melancholy way and shrugged his shoulders lightly to deplore the deceit and wickedness of this sinful world.

'Genuine drawings from the hand of Leonardo himself, properly authenticated and above suspicion, are very rare,' he said, 'and they are in great collections here and abroad, well-known to those who study art. I believe there is one such collection in Windsor Castle, that one of your kings bought in the past.'

'But not the king who liked photos of naked women,' said Toby with a broad smile. 'But who knows? – maybe it was. I am talking about erotic drawings in the style of Leonardo.'

'There are none,' said Niccolo. 'Unless you mean anatomical drawings from his notebooks. But they are too scientific to be in the least erotic. You must be mistaken.'

Toby described in some detail the five drawings in Ottorino's package. Niccolo's thick eyebrows crawled up his forehead.

'You have these drawings?' he asked eagerly.

'I know where they can be acquired. They look like Leonardos, but I can't tell if they are real or not. From what you've said it doesn't seem to make a great deal of difference either way. In fact, if a rich tomfool can be found, fakes can fetch more than genuine.'

'That is true,' Niccolo agreed, 'and if they are genuine then they are stolen. There are penalties for that which at my age I do not want to risk.'

'Nor I,' said Toby, 'which is why I am asking your opinion as an expert. If the drawings are stolen, it can't be hard to find out from whom. Most collectors would be so grateful to whoever could return their precious pictures that they would be willing to pay a reward. Or if not, then their insurance company would. And if the drawings are not from a known collection, then they are up for sale and I am open to offers from wealthy amateurs. All of which requires skilful negotiating. I thought of you at once, Niccolo.'

They talked through the possibilities for an hour or more and reached an agreement to share the proceeds, whatever they were, half and half. It was arranged that Niccolo should come to the Palazzo Malvolio the next day to collect the drawings. From his stock Toby chose five elderly and undistinguished engravings of the right size, all nineteenth century views of the Doge's Palace, by various hands. These he intended to substitute for Ottorino's drawings and reseal the package perfectly. Without knowing what it was for, Niccolo was able to provide a used end of red sealing-wax for the knots.

Not that Toby was going to hide the package in the wardrobe's secret compartment – he was determined there should be nothing for even the sharpest Customs officer to find. But he wanted to leave a package with Marina, to convince her she was playing an important part in thwarting Ottorino's selfish plan. She could put it in the secret drawer of her sideboard, where it might be forgotten for generations to come, until the piece wound up in the attic.

Before leaving Niccolo, Toby had him write him a bill of sale on his shop stationery, which was elaborately impressive to the point of absurdity for so very shady and marginal an enterprise – *Religious picture on wood, hinged in three parts, 900 lira*. An anguished look appeared on Niccolo's face as he wrote it, caused no doubt by whatever conjectures were in his mind. Toby gave him a 1000 lira note and held out his hand for the change.

'Please do not tell me where you got this religious picture,' said Niccolo, fumbling in his pockets, 'but do not forget what I said about problems with the authorities over stolen pictures – I have no wish to find myself in prison.'

'Not a chance,' Toby assured him blithely, 'I picked nine hundred lira as the right sort of sum to satisfy Customs when I declare the picture and show the bill. It's nearly £12, and that's a lot of money to pay for a religious souvenir of Venice. I shall buy a couple of those miniature glass gondolas to declare as well and say they're presents for relatives.'

They shook hands on parting, and Niccolo expressed in flowery terms his sincere respect for Toby in demonstrating so complete trust in him over the arrangements for the profitable disposal of the *Leonardo* sketches.

'But of course I trust you, Niccolo,' said Toby, 'just as you trust me not to let the person whose sketches I am handing over to you find out you have disposed of them.'

'*Dio!* Then they are stolen!'

'Not in any legal sense, I can assure you. There are reasons why the person concerned will not complain to the authorities.'

With that Niccolo had to be content. His calculation of what could be made from the drawings was pleasing enough to silence his fears and prompt him to accept a degree of risk.

At lunch in the Small Dining Room Toby informed Delphine that he was ready to discuss figures, at which she hurried everyone through the meal – to the annoyance of Adalbert, who appeared particularly fond of the Adriatic sole in sour and sweet sauce the chef had sent up that day. An expression of martyrdom on Padre Pio's plump round face suggested he too was displeased by the Signora's disrespect for food, but it was not the place of a servant of God to say so.

They were hardly through the calves liver in cream and onions before the footmen, urged on by the major-domo, who had taken a hint from Delphine, snatched away the plates and served cheese.

'We won't bother with fruit or ice-cream,' said Delphine, her wish to get down to business taking precedence over courtesy to the others at her table. 'Luigi – Mr Jervis and I will have our coffee in the Biblioteca.'

Toby snatched a last morsel of soft *dolcelatte* cheese as she rose from her chair and swept him along in her slipstream in the direction of the Library, a footman following in their wake with a heavy antique tray loaded with a silver coffee pot and cups. All this haste, comically inconvenient though it was, put Toby in an optimistic frame of mind. It looked as if Delphine's need for funds was even more urgent than usual – a circumstance which could only help him in his negotiation.

In the Library the footman set the tray on the vast dark desk with carvings of semi-naked women, served the coffee and went. Toby stood, waiting politely for Delphine to sit, and she seemed in two minds whether to put the desk between them or not. When she looked at Toby and caught the grin on his face, she blushed faintly to realise her thought-process was apparent to him and settled for his side of the desk.

'I know we're talking business,' said she, 'but I feel I have come to know you as a friend and it would be wrong to treat you like a tradesman.'

'Thank you,' said Toby, grinning again, 'I too feel we have come to know each other a little more closely while I have been your guest here.'

Delphine was wearing a short-sleeved frock of magenta silk, with a geometric pattern of intersecting thin white lines which had the effect of drawing attention to her full bosom. If Toby had been a breast-fetishist, he told himself, he would even now be plotting to get his hands on her to fondle her fleshy melons – and much more beside. But that was not his taste, he insisted – he was only aroused by lean and lanky women with smooth flat chests and long thin legs. He absolutely did not want to frolic with Delphine this afternoon, not when there was business to be negotiated with large sums of money involved.

'Then we shall settle this matter as friends,' she said, and he nodded and smiled.

After all, he was thinking, if having you slip into my bed by night for a frolic and ravaging you up against the bookshelves over there doesn't create a bond of sorts, I'm damned if I know what does. His eyes flickered automatically to the bookshelves in question while the thought was in his head – the shelves on the left of the door where the architectural books were packed tight from floor to ceiling. Delphine blushed bright red to see the direction of his glance, but she said nothing.

Toby turned his attention to business and explained to her at some length that while the Malvolio furniture up in the attics had a certain intrinsic antique value, some items were damaged practically beyond repair – for example, a blackboy chair that might be the work of Andrea Brustolon which was split in two. Some items would require extensive restoration work by expert craftsmen who had to be paid high wages – for example, a carved wardrobe of about 1650 which had the bottom completely smashed through and some damage to the carvings on one side. Some items were in a not-too-bad condition – for example, a four-poster bed with a length of the carved top frame broken away, which could be replaced, and some scratching on the posts; and an enormous baroque wardrobe with several lead pistol-balls embedded in one side.

He further explained for Delphine's benefit how the furniture would be shipped to England by sea, for which purpose it would need to be crated. That required large quantities of timber and the cost of local skilled labour. Then there was the shipping cost itself to consider and, not least, insurance on the cargo. By the time he had been through this rigmarole he hoped she had revised downward her guess as to what she stood to get. At last he mentioned a figure in pounds sterling, not wanting to become involved in the uncertainties of Italian lira.

On the telephone with Jervis Senior they had agreed his first offer would be a fifth of the estimated sale price when fully restored. But Toby was feeling generous after his meeting with Niccolo Corradini and he offered her rather more – a quarter of the estimated sales price. Not that Fitzroy Dalrymple stood to benefit from the share of whatever Corradini managed to get for the *maybe-Leonardo* drawings. Nor would they get anything out of the sale of the altar-painting hidden away for so many years in a thrown-out wardrobe. But as the saying almost has it – what the eye doesn't see is no skin off the nose.

'Done!' said Delphine, holding out her hand to shake on the deal. 'When can I have it in writing?'

'Now,' said Toby, surprised she had made up her mind so fast.

From the thin black leather document case he had with him he produced sheets of Fitzroy Dalrymple headed paper and moved to the huge walnut desk to write a binding offer on behalf of the company for 127 pieces of furniture, list attached. He made a copy, signed both on behalf of Fitzroy Dalrymple and then asked Delphine to sign in token of her acceptance of the sum named.

'What about the list attached?' she asked, taking the gold-nibbed fountain-pen he offered.

'The details are in my note-book,' said Toby. 'What I'll do is write out a list for each of us. Not describing each piece separately – that would take me a week – but on the lines of *63 chairs, 19 tables, 3 wardrobes, 8 sofas*, and so on. It comes to 127 items in all – believe me, I've examined every last one.'

Delphine nodded, satisfied with the arrangement. Out of sheer curiosity Toby enquired if she had the least idea why so much furniture had been damaged over the years – and why it had been stored under the roof instead of being mended.

'Reckoning from the rebuilding of the Palazzo after the fire gives 127 pieces of furniture smashed in 175 years – almost one major item a year,' he said.

Delphine shook her head.

'The Malvolio always had a reputation for being hot-blooded, for as far back as records run,' she told him. 'My dear Rinaldo died a hero's death in his fighter plane at Caporetto in 1917 flying against the Austrians. You have seen the Lepanto Room, honouring Marco, who died at sea defending Christendom against the Turks off Corinth. Ermengildo Malvolio lost his life in the Venetian wars against the Genoese centuries ago, and Sebastiano Malvolio was killed in the Venetian attack on Constantinople in the Fourth Crusade. Quite apart from wars, many other Malvolios came to violent ends in quarrels and duels.'

'And when they were at home, men like that took it out on the furniture?' said Toby, raising his eyebrows.

'On their family and friends,' Delphine corrected him with a placid smile, 'if a Malvolio fired his pistols at a wardrobe it must have been because someone had irritated him and was hiding from him inside it. A wife, perhaps, or a lady-friend. As for a broken bed – well, I hardly need to tell *you* what goes on in beds that may sometimes damage them.'

'Well, I shall go and start on the list for you,' said Toby, 'and when the Post Office opens after the siesta I'll telephone London to tell them we have reached an agreement. I'll ask for the workshop foreman to be put on the night train to Paris this evening so he gets here tomorrow. Then he can start right away on seeing to the crating up.'

He rose to go, pleased with the way things had gone. Delphine too looked pleased – evidently she had not expected to get that much for the broken furniture. At the door he paused and looked back, and thought she was staring at the shelves near him where the architectural books were, with a wistful look in her eyes.

But after his early morning turn with Marina he was not much in the mood for further frolics at that moment. To be sure, his unruly part was quivering but it was not standing upright. He smiled at Delphine and said he would bring the furniture list to her room if he finished it before dinner. She smiled back at him and said she hoped it would not take him too long.

FIFTEEN

The next morning brought a surprise – a hand-written invitation from Contessa Flagranti to lunch. Toby put on his white linen suit for the occasion and the pink bow-tie bought for his rendezvous with Gilda Borlano in a gondola. In view of what he had been told about servants' gossip in the Palazzo Malvolio he thought it best to walk round by San Stefano and back to the Grand Canal to take a water-taxi to the Palazzo Flagranti.

The invitation said twelve fifteen for one o'clock, which sounded formal enough, although a discreet enquiry of the Malvolio major-domo had informed Toby that Contessa Marina and Mrs Tandy were both lunching at home that day. In other words, neither of them had been invited. The massive door to the Palazzo Flagranti on the stone landing-stage was opened by a manservant wearing a green striped waistcoat under his dark suit. At least, Toby hoped he was a servant, after the unlucky mistake with the Count on his last visit.

He was expected this time – the manservant bowed him into an entrance hall much like the one he'd seen on the landward side of the palace. It had the same black-and-white-squared floor and a glass-topped table, though this one was larger and more massive – the glass sheet that formed the top was three or four inches thick. They went up a rebuilt staircase of wrought-iron in gilt and black, and by a passage lined in beige silk to the Art Deco drawing-room in which he had taken advantage of the Contessa on his last visit. He had timed his journey to arrive at twelve thirty, to let others get there before him and set the chatter going.

Damnation, I'm the first, he thought, seeing the only person in the room was the Contessa herself, *I should have known that Italians arrive half an hour after the stated time!*

Contessa Sally was sitting on one of the impossibly stylish

long sofas, looking very chic in an elegantly simple frock of shantung, a rich snuff colour, with smocking on the shoulders. Her dyed blonde hair lay sleek to her head and she held a long-stemmed glass in her hand. Toby kissed her other hand and murmured politenesses.

She smiled her blank smile, giving the impression that she was trying to remember who on earth he was, then she patted the silk cushions beside her for him to sit down. A different manservant in a black suit poured him a glass of champagne and was given instructions in Italian. Toby did not understand a word, but he noted that the man brought the bottle and stood it on an octagonal satin-wood occasional table that stood near the sofa before leaving the drawing room. He closed the double-door very quietly but firmly behind him.

'I'm glad you came, Toby,' said Sally, evidently remembering his name at last. 'What have you been up to since I saw you?'

Offhand he could think of no part of his activities since the curious ravaging he had given her that he would want to relate. Frolics with Marina and with Delphine, fantastic frolics with the girl from Padua in a gondola, sly deals with Corradini . . . a busy enough few days, but not for idle conversation. He smiled and talked about the delights of Venice, the buildings, canals, churches, and whatever else he could recall of what it said on the back of his street map.

Sally seemed to be listening to his nonsensical chatter with attention, but it was difficult to know if her brain had become switched off. She leaned back and crossed her knees, her short frock riding up to give a glimpse of a long lean thigh swathed in fine silk.

If she had been anyone else, Toby would have jumped instantly to the conclusion that she was out to vamp him. But not Sally, he thought, she has no observable will of her own and responded only after a delay to outside stimulus. And with other guests expected, it was even less likely that she had any particular purpose in mind by revealing a long stretch of thigh. In fact, at that very moment she raised her arm to look at a tiny wristwatch encrusted with diamonds.

'Is it true you're leaving Venice?' she asked him, cutting into his flow of words. 'Why? Are you in trouble?'

'No, of course not! But now my work here is finished I have to go back to London.'

'Work – what do you mean?'

'I came to Venice to value antique furniture for Mrs Tandy. I told you about it when we met at Princess Zita's.'

'I guess I forgot,' said Sally, holding out her empty glass for him to refill from the handy bottle. 'So you don't live in Venice at all, you're only visiting?'

'Right!' he said, laughing at the extraordinary convolutions of her mind. She joined in the laughter, though neither of them could have said why.

'I'd like it if you stayed on,' she said. 'How about it?'

'Marvellous thought,' Toby said, raising his glass lightly to her, 'to live in a palace and have no cares or problems beyond the next dinner-party or ball . . . but I'm one of the unfortunate many who have to earn a living.'

'No you don't,' said Sally, glancing at her diamond-studded wristwatch again, 'you can move right in here and stay with me for just as long as you want. My palace may be not as big as Delphine's rambling old ruin, but it's a whole lot nicer.'

'That's very kind of you, Sally. But I really do have to get back to London – I'm in the middle of a very important deal and I must see it through. I could come back for a week or two in September, if you'd have me as a guest then.'

There was a pause while Sally's mind worked carefully through this information. Toby waited patiently and was surprised when she spoke again.

'I'm not talking about being a guest,' she said. 'I'm talking about something more regular than that.'

'What *are* you suggesting?'

'I've often envied Zita the way she moves young boyfriends in and out of her place,' Sally explained. 'After the way you came rampaging in here last week and did all sorts of things to me, I got to thinking *why not?*'

'You're asking me to move in as your *ragazzo*?' said Toby, an astonished grin on his face at the suggestion.

'Call it what you like. I'll pay all your bills – clothes and stuff like that, and I'll give you presents and an allowance of your own. I'll take you with me everywhere, and that's a pretty full social life. And in the winter when it's cold and raining here I like to travel to Paris and London.'

It was, Toby considered, an interesting career offer, but not one to take too seriously. He could not see himself as another Marcello being groped under the table.

'But,' he said, trying not to grin too much in case she took offence, 'what about Count Flagranti?'

Sally shrugged in the way she had learned over the years from her Italian friends.

'What about him?' she asked.

'He would surely be mortally offended if I moved in with his wife. Or haven't you thought about that aspect of it?'

'What's there to think about?' she countered. 'He does what I want him to. I'd never insult him in front of his friends by getting in a young Italian to play around with – he'd lose face over that. But a Britisher with nice manners is OK.'

'We can't talk about this now,' said Toby, trying to avoid an outright refusal, 'your other guests will be here in a minute.'

'What other guests? There's only me and you, so we can talk this thing over and settle it.'

'Then perhaps we should go in for lunch,' Toby suggested, 'it must be after one o'clock by now and chefs get fidgety.'

Sally's dining room was very different from the comfortably shabby Small Dining Room at the Palazzo Malvolio, and even more different from the Grand Dining Room with the Tiepolo paintings on walls and ceiling. Her walls were decorated in lapis-lazuli stucco between tall narrow mirrors, and the floor was laid with panels of pale waxed oak and black-stained ash in odd geometric patterns. The long table was of sized glass with flower designs in it and rested on a chromium-steel cradle. A dozen armchairs round it were elegantly bucket-shaped and covered in grey silk. Toby stood staring in wonder for a moment or two before taking the chair held out for him by a manservant, next to the taller-backed chair held by another black-suited flunkey for Sally.

'It really is mind-boggling,' said he, 'how you have ridden over the Venetian Gothic style of the palace and created your own modern interior.'

'Why not?' she said. 'I like it.'

If the decor was unlike that of the Palazzo Malvolio, so was the cuisine. Instead of the six or seven courses of an ordinary lunch there, with at least three different wines, lunch in the beautiful dining room of the Palazzo Flagranti was a moderately sized salad of shredded lettuce and diced chicory for the first course, followed by two thin slices of lightly boiled chicken breast with a trace of raisin sauce as the main course.

With both courses the drink was Vichy water. Toby' expression grew so pained that Sally told a manservant to bring a glass of Soave *secco* for him. It was wretchedly apparent now how she had retained her lean figure into her late forties.

The third course consisted of a large Lalique crystal bowl of fresh green figs placed on the table between the two of them. A growing displeasure made itself felt in Toby's inner self. This meagre fare after two and a half weeks of Malvolio hospitality was intolerable. He stared thoughtfully at the servant standing behind Sally's chair, and at the other one, positioned by the door from the kitchens.

'Sally,' he said in an undertone, 'send the servants away.'

'What?' she asked vaguely, chewing on a fig.

He put his hand on her knee under the table and felt up along the inside of her thigh. It was lucky the glass top was opaque from the flower design in it.

'Send the servants away – I'm going to ravage you.'

'Not in the dining room, you pervert!'

'Quickly, or I'll do it to you in front of them,' he said and squeezed the lean flesh of her thigh up above her stocking-top.

There was a wait of several seconds during which she thought over his threat, then she spoke to the servants. They bowed and went out, closing the doors silently behind them.

Toby slipped his hand higher up Sally's skirt, stroking bare flesh, until he touched the lace and silk of her underwear. Her frock rode up as she parted her knees widely and stared at him, a slightly bemused expression on her face.

'Does this mean you take the job?' she asked.

'Nothing to do with the job,' said Toby, 'it's still lunch – and as your cook is so niggardly with food, I'm helping myself to the fourth course.'

While he was speaking his fingers found the way into her loose knickers, to touch the sparse curls and soft folds between her thighs. She stared at him blankly, her mouth hanging open just a little, her pale eyes giving nothing away. Toby almost smiled as through his mind flickered the thought *the light's on in the attic but there's nobody there*. But the *fica* he was feeling was certainly connected to something – when he'd ravaged her before her body had responded strongly, while the fact that she wanted him to move into the palace and do it to her on a regular basis proved that the pleasure eventually percolated through to her mind.

'Up you come!' he said, standing up to haul her to her

feet. In another moment he had his hands on her hips and lifted her off the floor. He kicked her chair over and out of the way and in three strides carried her further down the long table, where it was unset and clear. He sat her on the thick glass top, and pushed her down on her back, her legs hanging over the edge. He flipped her brown shantung frock up over her narrow belly – and revealed a rose-pink *crêpe-de-Chine* slip so thin as to be very nearly transparent.

She lay quite still, staring up at the ceiling, a masterpiece of the decorator's art, domed and with an abstract pattern of curving lines in gold and silver, while Toby was doing what he liked to her. He bared her from groins to throat by pulling up the beautiful and fragile slip, and laid his palms on the pale warm skin of her belly to feel its smoothness. By now his *cazzo* had grown hard and long, and to encourage it to extend itself even further he ripped open his trousers and brought it out. He clasped it firmly and massaged it, while his free hand roamed over Sally's belly, then upward to the hardly visible swellings that were her breasts, to tease the prominent pink buds there.

He could hear her muttering to herself but made no effort to hear what it was. Heaven alone knew what went on in her strange mind at a moment like this! In an access of lust he moved in closer between her knees until he could rub his jumping part on her pretty knickers. They were of the same fine *crêpe-de-Chine* as her slip, a delicate shade of pink, with lace insets and any amount of hand embroidery. He rubbed his hard length slowly and lazily on the silky material, sighing at the sensation of pure delight that rippled through him.

But it was dangerously exciting to do that – it wouldn't take much more to make him gush his pent-up desire on to her silk knickers. He stood back from her to hook his fingers into the waist-band and pull them down her long lean thighs and off. Now she had no secrets from him, he stood between her legs with his stiffness jutting out of his trousers and stared at her body in a spasm of aesthetic admiration, or something similar. Ah those sharp hips, their outline unblurred by fleshy covering! Ah the almost bare lips of her split, where light-brown wisps of hair failed to conceal the shape. He cupped his hand over it to hold it for a moment or two, then pressed his thumb into her.

She muttered, *Oh my Gahd* to herself, her eyes wide open and her face without expression. So lean and lithe, so very

Vogue, Toby thought, so completely unlike the fleshy aunties on whose plump bellies he lay yesterday to pleasure them! Marina in the early morning, naked in his bed, her melons of breasts flopping under him when he lay on her. Delphine in the afternoon, when he took her the list of furniture and was invited into her monumental four-poster bed, her hot round belly quaking under him when she came to a climax. And Marina again at bedtime. She overcame his lethargy by rolling her fleshy body naked on him until his part jerked upright and was ready for her.

Toby stared down in pleasure at Sally's lean body and wished she were twenty years younger. He watched how her flat smooth chest rose and fell to the calm rhythm of her breathing and wondered if she was aroused by what he was doing to her. Yet she must be – tiny palpitations ran across her belly and her legs strained wide apart. He looked up at her face and changed his mind again – she was still staring wide-eyed at the ceiling, not a flicker of emotion on her face. Yet his fingers told him that her *fica* was wet and loose.

So what did it matter? he asked himself and lay forward over her. He aligned his throbbing stiffness with her wet-lipped split and held her by the hips as if they were handles – then a long hard push sank his distended flesh into her. To his utter amazement Sally raised her long thin legs and hooked them over his shoulders, her posture forcing him in deeper. This unusual sign of participation from her excited him, and immediately he began to plunge and rummage. The force of his rhythm set Sally sliding up and down on her backside on the glass table-top.

'I never eat dessert,' she said in a conversational voice, as if nothing out of the ordinary was taking place.

Toby paid no heed. His moment had arrived and he emptied his passion into her with short fast jabs that made her body bounce on the table under him. *My Gahd* was Sally's comment, in a tone that suggested a mild admiration of his prowess rather than any hectic enjoyment. But whatever her thoughts on the subject, her lean belly gripped his spouting part tight and pulled at it in rhythmic contractions.

When calm was restored he helped her off the table and did up his trousers, while she patted her over-blonde hair into normal sleekness, hitched up her silk stockings and smoothed down her frock. He picked up her rose-pink knickers from the floor where he had dropped them in his earlier eagerness to get at her, but she shook her head and did not put them on again.

'Coffee in the drawing room?' he asked with a smile.

'I haven't shown you my bedroom yet,' she said.

The hike was not, he admitted, as long as it would have been in the Palazzo Malvolio from dining room to bedroom but it was still a fair way. However, the bedroom was a masterpiece of Art Deco design and well worth the walk. It was a large room overlooking the Grand Canal, light and airy, the walls hung in rough beige silk, the floor close-carpeted in silver-grey. The furniture – bed, dressing-table, *chaise-longue*, armchairs – were built of ash and sycamore in a clever contrasting design and upholstered in silk to match the walls.

The bed was wide and low, and an odd shape, curving outwards at head and foot, and panelled all the way round in polished sycamore. The specially shaped coverlet had a geometric woven pattern of interlaced circles and squares. Toby did not have to touch it to know it was made of heavy silk.

'It's superb,' he said to Sally, gazing round. 'Have you done the whole palace in this style?'

'All except my husband's den and his bedroom,' she answered, 'he wanted to keep them the old Venetian style. So I agreed to leave them alone. He's got a four-poster bed with the family crest on it, that sort of old-fashioned stuff – and a desk big as an automobile. Not that anybody in this town knows what an automobile looks like.'

'And if I were your *ragazzo* what sort of room would I have?'

'You sleep right here with me,' said Sally, looking surprised by the question, 'and in the daytime we're in the drawing-room together or we're out visiting. I've got two speedboats moored right outside for driving out, with the best boatmen in Venice. And a goddam gondola for fancy occasions.'

While she was telling him all this she was undressing herself rapidly. Off came the beautiful brown frock, the *crêpe-de-Chine* slip, the silk stockings, casually dropped on the silver-grey carpet for someone else to pick up later. And when her lean and pale body was naked, she undressed Toby where he stood – white linen suit, the pink bow-tie that had slipped sideways during the fourth course, his shirt and shorts, his black silk socks. He was entertained by this sudden display of interest by Sally, unlike her normal passive acceptance of sexual approaches. Then it occurred to him that her interest had a business origin, so to speak – she wanted to be sure he was value for money before clinching the offer to employ him in a specialised capacity.

The thought made him grin while she ran her eyes and then her hands closely over his naked body, presumably making sure that everything was there that should be there, and in good working order. Two of everything, a left one and a right one, with the exception of the important part she now held firmly in her hand and jerked at to bring it upright from its deflated condition.

'You smell of lavender-water,' she remarked, glancing up from her main interest. 'That what you use after you shave?'

Toby said that he splashed himself with Yardley's Old English pretty freely after shaving and showering.

'I like that,' she said, although it was not clear to him if she meant the lavender scent or the part now at full stretch in her grasp.

Her hand on his shoulder pushed at him and he understood what she wanted. He backed slowly towards the low bed and stretched himself out on it, his knees bent and his calves close to the polished wood panelling, his bare feet still on the thick grey carpet. Sally looked him over carefully before kneeling on the bed astride his hips. Her open thighs offered him an unimpeded view of her sparsely haired *fica*.

He found the sight pleasing but not, to his astonishment, as arousing as Marina's curly brown-haired mound, in recollection. And Sally's smooth flat chest – could he honestly hand-on-heart claim he would rather stroke it than fondle Delphine's soft and heavy breasts?

He sighed in aggravation at these perplexing questions, only becoming cheerful again when Sally held the swollen head of his shaft to her slit and sank down on him to drive it up into her.

'I don't usually do this for any man,' she said, not sounding in the least excited, in spite of having six solid inches of throbbing flesh in her belly.

'I don't usually do auditions,' Toby retorted with a grin.

A comparison between physical types of women was interesting only as a discussion of fashion styles, he'd decided. Plump or thin, no breasts or full ones, broad bum or flat, hairy between the legs or smooth as a baby – when the blood started to race and the *cazzo* was inside, who cared?

He looked up from Sally's splayed thighs to her face and saw she was staring at him with a curious expression – that is, an expression of intense curiosity. She leaned forward, her hands flat on his chest, while she started a steady rocking movement that sent shivers of pleasure through him.

'It's no audition,' she said, 'it's a dress rehearsal before this show goes on the road.'

Her rhythmic rocking changed to a fast and furious lunging on him that made him buck and squirm between her splayed thighs in mounting delight.

'Oh my Gahd,' said Sally, her voice level, 'don't do it yet.'

She had pushed him too near to the edge to hold him back now. His hands closed on her thin thighs and gripped so hard that he made red fingerprints in her pale cream flesh. Then awareness of where he was slid away as waves of sensation washed over him and drowned him in pulsating ecstasy that went on and on. Sally fell forward to lie on his belly and chest, close joined to him by the leaping *cazzo* she was spiked on.

All through the tremendous climax she had brought on she gave not a cry, not a whimper – and when Toby could take an interest in his surroundings once more, her breathing was as steady and calm as if nothing had happened. Something had, though, and she proved that there was a direct connection between her *fica* and her brain by renewing her offer.

'Fifteen thousand a month to spend, all your clothes and your own room,' she said, 'how about moving in tomorrow?'

'Fifteen thousand what? Dollars?'

'Lira,' she said, 'solid gold wristwatch, cigarette-case – all that sort of stuff. Use one of the speedboats whenever you like. What do you say?'

Toby smiled, hardly knowing whether to be flattered or not by her suggestion. The money was more than £100 a month, and £1200 a year was a pretty good income in London. And nothing to pay for – free living in a palace thrown in. It was not going to be easy to convince Contessa Flagranti that he couldn't accept. In fact, bearing in mind the usual delay that occurred between the time something was said to her and the moment when she grasped the full meaning, it might be damnably difficult.

In the event, it proved to be exasperatingly hard. Toby kept at it, not wanting to offend or annoy her, and though she upped the cash offer a couple of times, he finally persuaded her that he was not for hire. When they parted it was after six o'clock, and she insisted on giving him a pair of heavy gold cuff-links, each set with a glinting diamond. She explained that this was going to be her *hello* present for him, but now he'd turned her down it had to be a leaving present instead.

After dinner at the Palazzo Malvolio he went in one of their motorlaunches to the railway station to meet Mr Briggs off the train from Paris. Briggs was foreman of the Fitzroy Dalrymple work force, a short man with a fierce black moustache, a former infantry sergeant who had survived the Great War, a martinet to those under him, a man to be relied on by those above. Now that the agreement with Delphine was made, Toby was no longer needed in Venice – Briggs was the best man to organise local labour to crate the furniture and ship it to England.

As the motorlaunch sped along the Grand Canal, the lights of buildings either side reflected on the dark water, other craft weaving in and out, Mr Briggs stared about in silent wonder and disapproval of foreigners and their ways – especially a damn fool arrangement of having rivers instead of streets. Toby outlined what he thought Mr Briggs needed to know for now, presented him with the street-map that had been of so little use, and saw him installed in a modest but clean Pensione in a respectable alley off San Stefano square, within easy walking distance of the Palazzo Malvolio.

By three the next afternoon Toby was ready to leave, even if it was the middle of the siesta. He had introduced Mr Briggs to Delphine and showed him the way up to the attics and given him the list of 127 pieces of furniture. A telegraph message from Fitzroy Dalrymple had arrived for Delphine confirming that the agreed sum of money had been paid into her London bank account. Toby had said goodbyes of varying degrees of friendship to her and to Marina, to Adalbert and Padre Pio, to Niccolo Corradini and to Anna-Louisa Ziani, who had dropped in to see Marina.

Most unexpectedly, Delphine gave him a leaving present as a token of her gratitude – for what was not very clear but maybe for his part in refloating her sunken finances. Or maybe it was for something else. It was a portrait cameo set in a black oval mount for hanging on a wall. The subject was a lady with high-piled hair and a pert expression, a nineteenth century Malvolio, said Delphine, but no one knew exactly who.

Marina also gave him a present, a large framed photograph of herself, signed with a flourish across the bottom. On the back was a rubber stamped legend to the effect that it was the work of Studio Pontecello. It was a portrait, not an artistic nude, but that was in the sealed envelope she gave him with orders not to open it until he had left Venice. Toby had no doubt what Marina was grateful for and when she announced her intention of visiting London soon, he gave a fair imitation of being pleased by the prospect.

Adalbert too gave him a leaving present, a single page from a seventeenth century book long since fallen to pieces. The printed text was in French and at the head of the page was a little picture, an engraving of a couple amusing themselves out-of-doors under a tree. The man was very dashing in a curled-up moustache and a ruff. He was sitting on a large boulder with his baggy breeches undone and his stiff part sticking out. A woman wearing a tight bodiced frock and a kerchief round her neck stood with her back to him. She had hitched up her skirts and was lowering herself, bare-bottomed, on to his advantage. Neither looked in the least thrilled by what they were doing, but Toby put that down to the artist not being up to his work.

At first he couldn't think why Adalbert was grateful to him, then he recalled the £25 handed over for safe-keeping when they got drunk together. The whole sum had been spent, Adalbert said next day, on *douceurs* for the women and bribes to keep Toby out of trouble after he'd punched an important official's face. It might even be true, or nearly true. As the money was not Toby's own but belonged to Fitzroy Dalrymple, he didn't care.

Anna-Louise Ziani did not bring him a present, not even the smallest tiger head from her husband's study, but she gave him her hand to kiss. Niccolo Corradini did give him a parting gift – a little leather-bound book with the text in Latin of Ovid's *Art of Love*. It was printed in the year 1463 Niccolo claimed, by the great Aldus who, as Signor Toby surely knew, had set up as a publisher in Venice years before Caxton began his work as a printer in London.

'Thank you, Niccolo,' said Toby, shaking his hand, quite sure that the ancient-looking little volume with cracked covers and yellowed pages was of very recent manufacture

But it was the thought that counted.

So many presents, he reflected, so much gratitude. His stay in Venice had very obviously brought joy and happiness, not to mention profit, into all these lives. It was quite touching, in a ridiculous sort of way.

His bags were packed and in one of them, carefully wrapped, was the marvellous three-panelled painting of the Madonna and Saints he had found by chance and appropriated as ownerless and therefore treasure trove. And with it two small glass gondolas, one bright red, the other bright blue, as part of his Customs deception plan. A boatman had been instructed to deliver him to the railway station and was below on the landing-stage, waiting and grumbling about being made to work in the afternoon.

Toby went up to his room to collect his hat and Burberry – a very English garment there had been no call for in Venice. His luggage was gone, taken down to the launch by an under-footman, but the maid was there, pretending to tidy up. Tipping servants was important to get right and, not knowing the local custom in this he had asked Adalbert, who said 500 lira was enough for a chambermaid. To Toby that sounded mean, and he gave her a 1000-lira note. That was something over £7, but the fiver he thought correct worked out too awkwardly in Italian lira.

Maria was so pleased when he handed her the banknote that he thought he might have overdone the generosity. She was probably paid about a pound a week and her keep, he thought, and in the state of Delphine Tandy's finances, the servants might not have been paid their wages at all lately.

In fact she was so pleased that she gave him a sly smile and moved her fist up and down at waist height in a suggestive way.

'Well, well,' said Toby, highly amused as he smiled back, 'am I to understand this is another leaving present?'

She did not understand the English words but she understood their meaning well enough. She folded the banknote in four, put it in a pocket hidden under her white apron and took three steps forward. While Toby was still grinning, she had his trousers open, his limp part out, and was pulling at it vigorously to make it stiffen up. With Toby that never took much doing – she very soon had her hand clasped round it and was rubbing up and down.

'Lie on the bed with me,' said Toby, thinking she was going

to let him do it to her at last. His hands on her waist urged her toward the canopied bed.

'*No, Signor – solamente cosi*,' she said, grasping his meaning as firmly as she was grasping his upright part. She went down on her knees and used both hands on him, palms and fingertips, long strokes, short strokes, little jerks, flutters, pinches, flicks, fingernails down the length of the throbbing shaft, butterfly touches on the sensitive head. Toby stood with eyes half closed, lost in a delirium of sensation. It was as if his will had been totally suspended, he could only stand trembling and sighing while he waited for the inevitable.

The muscles of his thighs were tense, his knees were locked to hold him steady.

'Yes, yes,' he was whimpering, 'oh yes, yes.'

Maria had him full-handed now, her strokes long and fast as he reached the crisis.

'*Ecco!*' she cried out cheerfully.

His sap spurted violently on her cheek. She swayed back away from him a little, continuing her rhythmic handling, and the rest fell on to her white apron.

Twenty minutes later he was in the Malvolio motorboat on his way up the Grand Canal to the railway station. The afternoon sun was pleasantly hot, the water sparkled with reflected light and the palaces on either bank looked at their decrepit best. A sense of well-being pervaded Toby as he lolled on the cushions, hardly aware of the displeased boatman at the steering-wheel. A couple of hundred lira would put the fellow into a better mood.

The news of Ottorino Pavese he had heard from Marina the day before at dinner was good and bad. Good for the plan to dispose of his naughty maybe-Leonardo drawings but bad for Ottorino. It seemed his doctor insisted he needed a long and complete rest. To get him away from Marina the wily medico had despatched him by boat, train and ambulance to a private clinic he knew about in Switzerland.

According to Marina, the quacks at this clinic understood how to nurse the near-collapsed back to rude health, by many months of injections of unborn lamb's liver, essence of chimpanzee testicles and other arcane treatments. Naturally, it cost a lot of money but what was money where health was concerned?

By the time Ottorino was on his feet again, thought Toby with a grin when he heard this idiocy, the wardrobe with the secret compartment would have been sold. Not that Ottorino would know the cupboard was bare – he'd run round trying to trace the new owner. Even if he found him, it wouldn't help – the lid to the secret compartment would be glued and screwed permanently shut on Toby's say-so when the wardrobe was restored.

The motorboat passed under the Rialto Bridge and turned left round the sharp bend of the Grand Canal. Up there was the spot where poor dear Marina had been rampaged at night by a lecturer chap from London University, Toby recalled with a grin. It was a curious memory for anyone to have of Venice. If he came back in September to stay a month with the Contessa Flagranti, as he had half-promised at her insistence, perhaps he would take time off one night and walk Marina to the Bridge, to try the frolic.

Meanwhile, ahead lay more certain pleasure. He did not intend to catch the overnight train to Paris, as they all thought back at the Palazzo Malvolio. He was going by local train to Padua, twenty miles down the line. Gilda Borlano was waiting for him. Toby felt that Fitzroy Dalrymple owed him a holiday for all his skilful and successful labours on their behalf in Venice.

And a bonus too. Tonight he planned to collect his bonus from the sceptical and pretty nymph he had taken to Murano for lunch in a gondola. She would be waiting for him at the best hotel in Padua, in black silk stockings and frilly garters. And tomorrow he would take her to Paris for a week of fun and frolics.

Headline Delta Erotic Survey

In order to provide the kind of books you like to read - and to qualify for a free erotic novel of the Editor's choice - we would appreciate it if you would complete the following survey and send your answers, together with any further comments, to:

>Headline Book Publishing
>FREEPOST 9 (WD 4984)
>London
>W1E 7BE

1. Are you male or female?
2. Age? Under 20 / 20 to 30 / 30 to 40 / 40 to 50 / 50 to 60 / 60 to 70 / over
3. At what age did you leave full-time education?
4. Where do you live? (Main geographical area)
5. Are you a regular erotic book buyer / a regular book buyer in general / both?
6. How much approximately do you spend a year on erotic books / on books in general?
7. How did you come by this book?
7a. If you bought it, did you purchase from:
a national bookchain / a high street store / a newsagent / a motorway station / an airport / a railway station / other........
8. Do you find erotic books easy / hard to come by?
8a. Do you find Headline Delta erotic books easy / hard to come by?
9. Which are the best / worst erotic books you have ever read?
9a. Which are the best / worst Headline Delta erotic books you have ever read?
10. Within the erotic genre there are many periods, subjects and literary styles. Which of the following do you prefer:
10a. (period) historical / Victorian / C20th / contemporary / future?
10b. (subject) nuns / whores & whorehouses / Continental frolics / s&m / vampires / modern realism / escapist fantasy / science fiction?

10c. (styles) hardboiled / humorous / hardcore / ironic / romantic / realistic?

10d. Are there any other ingredients that particularly appeal to you?

11. We try to create a cover appearance that is suitable for each title. Do you consider them to be successful?

12. Would you prefer them to be less explicit / more explicit?

13. We would be interested to hear of your other reading habits. What other types of books do you read?

14. Who are your favourite authors?

15. Which newspapers do you read?

16. Which magazines?

17. Do you have any other comments or suggestions to make?

If you would like to receive a free erotic novel of the Editor's choice (available only to UK residents), together with an up-to-date listing of Headline Delta titles, please supply your name and address:

Name..

Address...

....

....

A selection of Erotica from Headline

FONDLE ON TOP	Nadia Adamant	£4.99 ☐
EROS AT PLAY	Anonymous	£4.99 ☐
THE GIRLS' BOARDING SCHOOL	Anonymous	£4.99 ☐
HOTEL D'AMOUR	Anonymous	£4.99 ☐
A MAN WITH THREE MAIDS	Anonymous	£4.99 ☐
RELUCTANT LUST	Lesley Asquith	£4.50 ☐
SEX AND MRS SAXON	Lesley Asquith	£4.50 ☐
THE BLUE LANTERN	Nick Bancroft	£4.99 ☐
AMATEUR NIGHTS	Becky Bell	£4.99 ☐
BIANCA	Maria Caprio	£4.50 ☐
THE GIRLS OF LAZY DAISY'S	Faye Rossignol	£4.50 ☐

All Headline books are available at your local bookshop or newsagent, or can be ordered direct from the publisher. Just tick the titles you want and fill in the form below. Prices and availability subject to change without notice.

Headline Book Publishing PLC, Cash Sales Department, Bookpoint, 39 Milton Park, Abingdon, OXON, OX14 4TD, UK. If you have a credit card you may order by telephone — 0235 831700.

Please enclose a cheque or postal order made payable to Bookpoint Ltd to the value of the cover price and allow the following for postage and packing:
UK & BFPO: £1.00 for the first book, 50p for the second book and 30p for each additional book ordered up to a maximum charge of £3.00.
OVERSEAS & EIRE: £2.00 for the first book, £1.00 for the second book and 50p for each additional book.

Name ....

Address ....

....

....

If you would prefer to pay by credit card, please complete:
Please debit my Visa/Access/Diner's Card/American Express (delete as applicable) card no:

Signature ....Expiry Date ....